Unwrapping Love

A Writing Wenches Anthology

Unwrapping Love

Copyright © PageCurl Publishing

Published December 2014

Editing: Patricia D. Eddy
Cover Design: Melody Barber

Introduction

*U*nwrapping Love takes you on a journey through sweet Christmas miracles and steamy holiday hookups. On the holiday wish list this year are twenty-one stories guaranteed to bring you favored holiday traditions, the joy of family, and the gift of love. Whether you've bought this bundle for yourself, or have been gifted a copy, we are happy to invite you into our pages, and we can't wait to spend the holidays with you.

Before you begin, we want to tell you about our snowflake rating scale. This collection of stories varies from sweet to steamy. If you have a preference, scroll through and find the snowflake related to your preference.

❄ The sweetest of sweet stories, these offerings have no sex scenes, though sex may be implied.

❄ ❄ A little steamier, two snowflake stories have light sex scenes and should bring a bit of color to your cheeks.

❄ ❄ ❄ Three snowflake offerings have steamy sex and will leave you a bit hot under the collar (or in other areas).

❄ ❄ ❄ ❄ The steamiest of the steamy, our four snowflake romances have toe-curling sex and may leave you in need of an icy beverage and cold shower.

Shut Up and Kiss Me

by Grace Ravel

To my Writing Wenches, thank you for all the virtual hugs, the happy screams, and the pictures, yes, definitely the pictures. ;)

Chapter One

Christine Emerson wrapped her coat tighter around her, cursing the cold East Coast winter. For the love of all that was holy, she did not understand how her parents put up with such miserable weather. She was very close to going back inside the warm airport terminal and flying back to her apartment in sunny LA when she saw a familiar car stop by the curb a few feet from her.

Seeing her ride did not make her any happier to be back in New York. Which was fine, because he did not look happy to see her either. Christine didn't wait for him to get out of the car. She grabbed her small suitcase and threw it in the back seat of his pristine sedan. She slammed the door with the grace of a sullen child. He stood by the driver's side door, lips compressed, probably angry at the way she manhandled his vehicle but he didn't say anything. Christine had a sudden urge to kick his stupid, old man car to get a rise out of him. But it would be useless. She would get zero reaction, and end up with a sore foot. Nothing riled Hunter Rhodes. The quintessential quiet type, people often mistook his silence for arrogance.

She plunked herself, with the refinement of a tuna can, inside the dim interior of the Lexus. Even its warmth did little to lift her spirits. "Got the short end of the stick, eh?"

He waited for her to put on her seatbelt before he started the car. He was such a rule stickler, never a wrong move in his life, which irritated Christine more. Her sisters didn't call him Hunter the Rock for nothing. Although they found Hunter positively boring with his three-piece suits that never got wrinkled, Christine, God help her, found everything about Hunter sexy as hell, even down to his wing-tip shoes. "No stick. Nancy asked me to pick you up."

"And as the dutiful boy that you are, you happily obliged my mother." She was so morose, at the rate she was going, she was going to need a stiff drink to keep a happy face for her parents.

"Yes," he said, refusing to be baited. So this was how he was going to play it—ignore her sullen behavior until she went away. Well, she wasn't going anywhere. At least not for an entire week.

"Yeah, no need to stroke my ego and flatter this girl into thinking you couldn't wait to see her."

"Is this how this whole week is going to be?"

"Not happy to see me? Don't worry, I can read the big neon sign tattooed on your forehead." Christine wrapped her arms around her. The car was warm, but a chill came from somewhere deep within her.

"There's no sign."

"Please. I could practically see the 'Back off Emerson' sign from the plane."

"I hope we can still be friends," he said with a tone that was meant to placate, but somehow achieved the exact opposite.

"Keep telling yourself that," she said, almost to herself. Friends. That hurt. It really did. She thought she was done being hurt. Apparently not.

"I'm not sure how to talk to you when you're in this mood." He didn't bother looking at her. His attention was on the busy airport traffic.

"You expected me to be happy to see you after the last time?"

"I apologized for that."

"That was precisely the problem, you uptight, self-righteous ass." Her palms itched. She wanted to throw something at him. Anything to get a reaction. Anything to perversely share some of the pain she was feeling.

"Sometimes, Christine, the things that come out of your mouth." He shook his head, reprimanding her as if she was a child.

"I remember you quite liked what I did with my mouth," she sneered.

"Goddammit! Are you ever going to let me forget that?"

Well, there was a reaction. Not quite what she wanted, but she would take it. It was better than the cool politeness they had descended into since 'that night', as if what happened was so awful neither one of them could articulate it.

"Why? Do I get you all hot and bothered?" This time she lowered her voice to a whisper, leaning closer to him. It was meant to push his buttons, rather than to entice him. She knew she held no allure for him. It was a bitter realization, one of the many she had in the last year.

"No." There he went again—his beautiful lips compressed, but he said nothing more.

"Liar. You liked me well enough before. Admit it, I made you feel alive. Perhaps for the first time since Melanie died." *Shut up, Christine, shut up.* But she couldn't stop herself even as she knew she was crossing a line.

"I know what you're doing. You're not going to get a reaction from me by bringing Melanie into this conversation."

She must be pettier than she ever thought, more certifiable than anyone could have guessed. How else could she feel this much jealousy and resentment toward a dead woman? Like the child she felt she was, all she could say was, "I hate you."

He shook his head at her hostile behavior. "You're not one of my favorite people right now either."

Christine had loved Hunter Rhodes from the first time she laid eyes on him. It didn't matter that she was eleven, in braces and braids, and that he was a lanky seventeen-year-old with glasses, or that she only saw him during holidays. She was going to love him until the day she died, and she was going to marry him. But Hunter had a whole different idea. Rather than waiting for Christine to grow up, he fell in love with the first girl he met in college. Worse, he actually married her.

When Hunter wed Melanie, Christine hated her with the intensity of a sixteen-year-old in love. But it was easy to see what the quiet, serious Hunter saw in her. Melanie was beautiful, vibrant, and kind. Like Hunter, Melanie blended seamlessly into the family. So, although in her heart, Melanie was the woman who stole the love of her life, Christine grieved her sudden death, too. But even in her death, she cast a shadow on Christine's life. It hurt her to see Hunter unhappy, drowning in his grief. From the outside, he was doing fine, but Christine could tell there were days when he was barely holding it together.

Chapter Two

Silence filled the car the entire twenty-minute drive to the Emerson home in Brooklyn Heights. Christine did not want to look at him but it was hard. He cut a magnificent profile. He wasn't classically handsome, far from it. Hunter's face was all angles and planes. There was a hardness to him, brought by the tragedies of his life, but his cornflower blue eyes tempered that hardness. Beneath that exterior, Christine knew a different man, a man who was worth loving. Every time she and Hunter were in the same room, he filled it. In the darkness of the small confines of the car she felt him—every molecule, every particle—it all centered on him. No matter how Christine tried to forget him, and she had tried everything—the other men, the dangerous assignments, the thrill-seeking hobbies— she couldn't eradicate him from her heart. It sucked. It hurt. She felt like a total loser.

By the time they arrived at her parents' home, Christine would have given anything for a stiff drink. What was she thinking agreeing to stay an entire week? She was going to go crazy between her parents' well-intentioned but often suffocating concern, her sisters' snark, and Hunter and his perennial air of distance.

"Darling." Her sweet, loving mother wrapped her arms around her as soon as she walked into their home. When her mother held her longer than necessary, she felt guilty for thinking of bailing out on them before the week was out. She was missed. She missed them too, but coming home the last couple of years had become too painful. So, she made the obligatory holiday visits, but none of them lasted more than a couple of days. Until now. "Dad and Holly will be here soon. Jess is in the kitchen."

Great. Her sisters were both going to be here. Individually, she could handle her family, but together, Christine didn't stand a chance. They meant well, but they could be a little intense, especially since her younger sister, Jessica, had gotten engaged. Pasting a smile on her face, she walked into the kitchen, followed by Hunter and her mother. Christine grabbed the glass of wine in front of Jessica.

"Long flight?" Jessica watched her with amusement as Christine gulped down the cabernet. She shrugged as she poured more wine in the now empty glass. It was more like "a long drive," but she didn't say anything. She was mad at Hunter, but saying anything would only lead to persistent questions from Jessica.

"You can always move back," her mother said from across the kitchen. "You don't need to live in LA for work." Christine almost rolled her eyes. Within five minutes of arriving, her mother was already urging her to move back to New York.

"I like LA."

"LA is so blah. No culture. Boring weather. Bad food. What do you like so much about it?"

Christine took another sip of the wine, and looked at her younger sister. Jessica never hid her disdain for anything that was *not* New York. "For one, you're not there."

"That, right there, is the reason why you aren't going to be my maid of honor," Jessica responded with a little more glee than necessary.

"Thank God. I'm not exactly looking forward to wearing puke green taffeta." Another sip of wine. She really should slow down, but she needed it. She could feel Hunter watching her as he leaned against the kitchen counter. This was going to be a long evening.

"It's sage green." Jessica sounded disgusted at Christine's absolute lack of interest in her wedding, or anything girly, for that matter. How many times had her sisters told her she could be beautiful if she tried? But Christine had no patience for all of that stuff.

"Same difference."

"At least I'm getting married," came the not so subtle dig.

"Because that should be every woman's main goal in life." Heaven help her. Between her mother and her sisters trying to nag her into matrimony, she would need an entire barrel of alcohol before this week was out.

"I didn't say that, but being a perennial dater shouldn't

be either."

"I am not a perennial dater."

"Please. You don't last longer than three months, except for Paul back in college."

"Whatever happened to Paul? I liked Paul." Yes, her mother made no secret she liked Paul. He was nice and steady like Hunter. But he was *not* Hunter. Not by a long shot.

"*She* happened," Jessica cut in.

"What's that supposed to mean?" Christine looked at the glass of wine she was holding, calculating if she could kick Jessica from across the kitchen table without spilling it.

"Have you *ever* been in a relationship longer than three months?" Jessica was on a roll tonight. Christine wanted to gag her to stop her from opening her mouth.

"It's not my fault the world is full of assholes."

"Christine!" her mother reprimanded.

Without missing a beat, Jessica continued, "Ever thought it could be you?"

"What's this? 'Badger Christine' night? Or is this your new version of welcoming people? Don't you have problems of your own?"

"Honestly, I don't give a flying you-know-what who you're dating. But Mom and Dad do, so you need to get your act together."

Unable to stay, choking with resentment toward her sister, Christine pushed off her chair. "I'm going for a walk."

"It's dark outside and it's going to start snowing soon," her mother called out to her.

"I won't melt," Christine mumbled as she turned to leave.

Hunter watched the scene unfold before him. The Emersons were a loving family, but in the last few years they had become concerned about Christine. Her visits home became less frequent and shorter. Her parents' worry was a constant source of frustration to her sisters who had tried to convince her to change jobs, or move back to New York, or both. Christine was the most boisterous of the three sisters—always up for an adventure. When they were younger, she often instigated whatever trouble the three of them got into. While Holly and Jessica settled into stable careers and relationships, Christine kept forging ahead on her own. When she graduated with a degree in Marine Biology, her parents thought she would live the safe life of a scientist, locked inside a research facility. They should have known better.

If there was one thing Christine was good at, it was not meeting anyone's expectations. Instead of a lab coat, she traveled around the world documenting exotic marine life, which unfortunately included deep sea diving. Last year was the tipping point with her family when she became disoriented while diving off some underwater caves in Mexico. They wouldn't have known about the incident if it hadn't landed her in the hospital. Since then, a palpable tension within the family had forced them to use any tactic to convince Christine to leave her dangerous job or move closer to home. Silence followed her departure—with a mixture of concern, exasperation and love hanging in the air. Hunter pushed off the kitchen counter, saying to no one in particular, "I'll follow her."

Chapter Three

*H*unter caught up with her a block from their house. The cold had long ago driven people inside their homes. The happy twinkling of Christmas lights hanging on eaves was so incongruent to the silent, deserted streets. "Christine."

She turned back to his voice but kept walking. "Oh, for fuck's sake, can't I have a moment's peace?"

"You don't have to talk. We can just walk," he said as he caught up to her, slowing his long strides.

Christine suddenly stopped, turning to him. "Stop it. Okay? Just stop it."

"Stop what?"

"This! This act of goodness, and politeness. These stilted conversations. Meaningless. Empty conversations about nothing so you can pretend that you and I are okay. That you're a normal functioning human being."

"This is not about me."

"No, it's not about you. It's about me watching you waste your life away, while you grieve for a woman who's been dead for five years. I can't stand it."

"You don't know what you're talking about. I don't know what just happened in there—"

"Are you really that clueless, Hunter? Do you think that was about my dating life?"

"No, they're worried about you. They think you're always off running towards danger. But I know better. You're running away from something. I don't know what it is that you're running from but you need to stop."

"Like you."

"I've never ran away."

"No, but you've retreated. Hiding behind this impenetrable wall." She rested her palm against his chest. It was strong and hard like him. She knew she would never penetrate that wall. Never belong inside it. It was full of Melanie. She dropped her hand, feeling colder.

"You flit around the world—going from one godforsaken place to another, while your parents sit on edge wondering if you're safe, yet you lecture me on the way I'm living my life?"

"At least I'm living."

"Is that what you call it? Living? You're fooling yourself. You're running away—from whatever demons that make you go from one relationship to another, from place to place, doing stupid, dangerous stuff. You know how you can easily tell I'm only functioning at the most basic level? Because you're the same. You're keeping everyone at arms' length."

"Do you know what my demons are, Hunter?" There was a challenge in her eyes that made his heart skip a beat. Dread clutched at him, fearing her answer.

"Don't say it," he warned.

"You." Silence greeted her revelation. It was like an undetonated bomb thrown between them—heavy and dangerous. Hunter took a step back. She expelled a heavy breath, shaking her head at his involuntary reaction. It was official.

Hunter Rhodes was a complete ass.

"You couldn't have known." He tried to deny what she was going to say, afraid things might change between them. But it was pointless. Things *had* already changed between them.

"Of course. Hide what I've known since I was eleven." She turned away, her voice flat. She started to walk, while he stayed rooted on his spot. After a few steps, she turned back toward him. This time there was no flatness to her demeanor. She was angry. It was written all over her. Christine was never good at hiding her emotions. It was one of the things he admired about her—her ability to be always in touch with what she was feeling. "No, I could not have known that an innocent crush would turn into this thing that weighs me down because it grew into this stupid, unrequited love. It would be funny if it wasn't so hysterically tragic and disgustingly dramatic and corny. So I guess, we're the same—me loving you while you love a dead woman. We're both stupid fools. In a sick, twisted way, we both created and deserve our miseries." She turned away from him, gazing at the endless empty streets. "Go away. Tell my mom you did your duty. You made sure I was safe, but please just go away."

Hunter watched her stride amidst the fog that settled into the city, a solitary figure walking down the rows of neatly kept brownstones. He wanted to go after her, but she needed to be alone. Of course, he had known. She wasn't exactly subtle about her crush on him. But that was all he assumed it was—a young girl's fleeting crush on the older orphaned boy whom her family had taken under their wing. He was only a few months away from turning eighteen when his parents died in a car accident. Lost and alone, Christine's father, Robert Emerson, made good on his promise to his college best friend to take care of his only son. The Emersons were his anchor during those dark days when he felt lost, until he went to college months later. There he met Melanie and fell hard and fast for her. Within months of graduating, they were married. By the time he finished law school, Melanie was dead from an aneurysm. There were days when he was flat-out exhausted. He had lived through enough grief in his life to last a lifetime. Christine accused him of being closed off. It was a matter of survival for him. After Melanie, he figured he was meant to be alone.

It was probably why he was always drawn to Christine. Of all the Emerson women, Christine was the easiest to get along with. She was uncomplicated, at least until now. She wasn't demanding, but she took life by the horns and lived it. She filled his silence with happy chatter. They were the exact opposite of each other—he was quiet and logical, she was bubbly and passionate, but together they fit well. For two years after Melanie died, Christine was his rock. She was there for him when no one could stand the gravitas of his grief. Whatever he needed, she was always present—even if all he needed was the company of her silence. Then her phone calls and her visits, which he had taken for granted, became fewer and fewer. Until he was forced to visit her last summer under the pretext of a business trip. He wanted to see her, to make sure she was okay, to make sure *they* were okay. But rather than being okay, things got worse between them and it was all his fault.

"Hunter! What are you doing here?" Within a span of a moment, her look of surprise changed to pleasure then to a something more guarded. She used to welcome him with an exuberance that always made Hunter smile. He had taken for granted that she used to look at him like it was Christmas morning. But something had changed. He needed to know what that was because he wanted his old Christine back. *His Christine.* Had he always thought of her that way? The thought surprised him, but it felt natural.

"I was in town for business. I thought I'd surprise you." He stepped into her apartment without waiting for an invitation. It was a lie. He was here solely to see her. He missed her. Of course, he would never tell her that. Christine would most likely tease him to no end if he did.

"I have plans tonight."

He looked at her, trying to fight through the sudden surge of anger. He flew over two thousand miles to see her and she was dismissing him for some random guy? Of course, she didn't know he flew specifically for her, but it galled that while he lost sleep worrying about her, her life was moving forward.

"Cancel them." He took off his suit jacket, flexing his stiff shoulders from the five-hour flight. He came straight from the airport, not wanting to waste time.

"You can't just come here and expect me to drop everything else."

"I'm only here for one night. Cancel your plans." He spoke to her slowly, as if she was eleven again. She pouted, her typical response when he was about to get his way. She would make a really bad poker player. She had the most expressive face, eyes that often twinkled with whatever mischief she was planning. But those years were gone. Her mischief had turned into a high-risk job. Her eyes, along with the rest of her, had blossomed into womanhood. How had he failed to see that before? Her once unremarkable brown eyes had a glint to them he couldn't quite place. Had she always had green flecks in them? And her face, he always thought she had clear skin, but now he could see the light dusting of freckles across her nose. He had a sudden urge to touch those freckles.

"Did my parents send you?"

"No. Now, are you going to cancel your date or should I cancel it for you?"

"I hate it when you're bossy," she complained, yet she grabbed her cell phone to make the call. While Hunter waited for her to finish, he looked around her apartment. It was a studio, right on Santa Monica beach. Like Christine, it wasn't fussy. He suspected it was just a place for her to sleep, a pit stop until the next assignment took her to whatever part of the world she was headed to next.

"All right, now that I've cancelled my plans for you, mind telling me why you're here?"

He could have lied, but that wouldn't have accomplished anything, so he told her why, exactly, he found himself this morning cancelling his appointments, flying across the country on a whim. "I want to know why you're not returning my calls."

"Missed me?" She smiled at him, but there was a shadow in her eyes. She always had such an easy disposition, but not today.

"Yes." He meant it. Without her calls, without her visits, there was a palpable gaping hole in his life. He hated that feeling. But his answer wiped the smile off her face. She frowned. That surprised him. He didn't know what he expected from his admission, but definitely not a frown. He wanted to make that frown disappear. He only wanted to see her smile—those smiles that made him feel they were only meant for him. "We're friends," he reminded her, desperate to bring the old easiness between them.

She shook her head, almost as if she was trying to shake something off. She turned away from him, opening the sliding doors to her patio. He followed, confused. "What?" But she didn't answer. When had things between them become so muddled? He had a feeling he did something wrong, but he didn't know what it was; worse, he didn't know how to make it right.

She sighed. It was heavy and ponderous. It said everything, yet nothing at all. She looked toward the dark horizon. It was a moonless night. Neither one of them could see the ocean, but they could hear the waves crashing, and smell the sweet, salty air. "Nothing."

He pulled her away from the darkness of the balcony. He wanted, no, he needed to see her face. He didn't know what to expect. Certainly not tears. Christine never cried. Well, except for those silly baby commercials which for some reason always reduced her to tears. "You're crying. Why?" Was it over a man? Was that why she had retreated from him? From her family? That wasn't the Christine he knew, but maybe. How well did he really know her? She had thrown him off balance in the last few months, not knowing what to expect from her.

"Nothing," she said again. It was beginning to sound like a mantra, and he wanted to shake her to get a different answer.

"'Nothing' is not going to make me go away. I flew across the country to see you."

"You said you were here for business." She shook her head and wiped her tears with her hands in the most ungracious, yet adorable way Hunter had ever seen. She had no artifice at all. She was pretty in a conventional way. Men were attracted to her confidence, her candid, sometimes shocking ways, and she was intriguingly, and ridiculously smart.

"You," he said, wiping her tears with his fingers. Her skin was soft, tinged with color. She looked vulnerable, beautiful, and so young. "You're the business. Personal business." He leaned in to kiss her forehead. It was a gentle kiss, the kind that offered reassurance to her but more importantly to him. When he was about to move away, she lifted her head. He wasn't sure who moved. Probably him. Maybe her. But there was a strong pull he hadn't felt in years. For the first time in a long time, he was compelled to touch another person, no, not just another person, but her, Christine. The moment his lips touched hers, everything else disappeared. There was no sound, no air, no smell, just the feel of Christine's lips on his. There was no hesitation in that kiss. It was zero to sixty within a breath. He pulled her into his arms, crushing her against him. Her arms went around his neck. He tasted the salty tears that fell silently on her lips. He wanted to make the tears disappear almost as much as he wanted to keep kissing her. When his tongue touched hers, everything exploded around him, within him. Feelings that had been alien to him for the last five years came running to the fore with a force that surprised him. He felt her push him into the couch. He fell, willingly, taking him with her. Her hands found their way under his shirt. Everywhere she touched him, his muscles contracted. Her hands felt unfamiliar, yet strangely enough, he knew the feel of her. It was like coming home. That single thought was all it took. Good God, what was he doing? This was Christine, his best friend. Quicker than a bucket of ice, his ardor cooled. She sensed the change in him even before he stopped kissing her.

She straddled him, but he could have been on the other side of the world as that deep, yawning distance between them widened by the second. Her eyes, still luminous with her tears, had taken on a glint of anger. She moved off of him, and sat on the other side of the couch, straightening her shirt. She didn't say anything. She didn't look at him. He might as well have been invisible.

"I'm sorry," he said, because he didn't know what else to say. She flinched. *Shit.* He wanted to kick himself, but his verbal diarrhea continued, "That shouldn't have happened. It was all my fault. I was—"

"Leave. Please."

He stopped mid-stream and looked at her as if she had sprung an extra head. Her voice was so quiet, her body still and rigid as a pole, he wasn't even sure if she had spoken at all. Christine was never quiet. She had two volumes—loud and louder. The only time Christine was quiet was when she was very angry or very hurt. He had a feeling she was both. He'd really fucked up this time.

Chapter Four

In spite of the cold, Hunter didn't go back inside. He sat on the steps of the house, waiting for Christine. An hour later, she came back, her steps slowing when she saw him. Hunter sensed, rather than saw her straighten her back as if she was preparing for battle. That small, imperceptible movement bothered him. Stubborn as a mule, he had seen her do that a thousand times but it was never directed toward him.

"What are you still doing here?" Her voice was full of resentment.

He stood up, brushing off the light dusting of mist on his cashmere coat. "We need to talk."

"About what?" She kicked the steps, looking everywhere but at him. When he didn't answer, she regarded him.

Hunter lifted his eyebrow, telling her with that one gesture not to play games. She wasn't good at it, and he could see through her. He knew her too well. She released a breath that sounded tired and leaden. "Fine. Is everyone here?" She nodded toward her parents' house.

Hunter assessed her before he answered. He knew what she was thinking—not another third degree from her family. "Yes."

"Not here. I can't deal with them and you in the same night." She meant it as an insult, and it landed with precision. It stung. But he would deal with her anger. At least she was talking to him.

"They miss you."

"They have a funny way of showing it." She walked away from the house. "Give me your keys."

Hunter shook his head, walking toward his car parked a few feet away. "I've seen you drive. I'm not suicidal, at least not tonight. Hop in. We'll go to my apartment."

"I don't want to go to your apartment."

"It's either my apartment or we go back inside." In response, she yanked the passenger door, and Hunter was sure she said something about hating douchebags. He didn't have to guess which particular douchebag she hated.

In spite of the holiday traffic, they made it to Hunter's Tribeca apartment in under twenty minutes. Christine loved New York, except its winter. In this, Jessica was right—there was no place on earth that could compare to New York. Christine especially loved this particular neighborhood. The cobblestone streets reminded her of Prague, the mixture of the old with the young and hip brought memories of Paris, and so many other smells and sights that reminded her of the best part of living in New York.

Hunter lived in a quintessential New York apartment— an old pre-war building filled with character and charm. Unfortunately, it was also full of Melanie's memories—from the passé shabby chic decor to the pictures hanging on the wall, Hunter hadn't changed anything since her death. So every time Christine walked into his apartment she would cringe at the memories of the dead woman that seemed to fill every corner. However, instead of his apartment on Greenwich Street, he parked underground a block away on Washington Street.

"You moved?" Christine asked as he punched the number five on the elevator.

"You told me my old apartment was depressing."

"It was depressing because it was stuck firmly ten years ago. Can't you do anything halfway? Instead of moving, most normal people would have redecorated."

"Am I actually getting in trouble for listening to you?"

"You always have to do things on the extreme side of the spectrum."

"This coming from you?"

Instead of answering, Christine shook her head. He was right, of course. She had no answer to that. Her life, like his, was measured in extremes—the dangers, the emotions, her runaway mouth, she never quite learned how to walk in the middle of normal. Apparently, neither had Hunter, whether it was his grief or his love for Melanie, he too, had no middle. But the new apartment was a good start. Perhaps he was slowly shedding his past with Melanie. By the time they entered his new home,

Christine was happy for Hunter. If this was his way of moving on, then she was on board.

Whereas his old place was quaint and charming, this one was all modern and sleek. No traces of Melanie here. Except for the pictures. What did she expect? That he would wipe his life clean of her? A wedding picture on the wall, a picture of a smiling Melanie at the beach on the console table, Melanie was still in this place. Christine tried to breathe through the pain when she realized one of the pictures was from their honeymoon in Hawaii. Jealousy tore at her like a shot through her bones. She shouldn't have come. She should have crawled into bed and wished everyone away, including Hunter. Especially Hunter. There was nothing to talk about, nothing that could make things better, at least not for her.

"I'm not sure I can handle any kind of postmortem on our friendship, Hunter." She wanted to turn around and walk out the door. But she didn't. Instead, she walked toward the large windows that overlooked the neighboring buildings. They were so close together, it made Christine feel almost claustrophobic. Or perhaps it was what was inside her that made her feel closed off, small. She needed some air.

"So, we're no longer friends?"

"Were we ever friends?" It was unfair of her to say that, because they were friends. The best kind, yet her pain made her doubt her place in his life, even as his friend.

"I thought we were. You're my best friend. You've always stuck by me." Hunter stood beside her, his hands in his pockets. He looked straight ahead, his gaze unseeing.

"Oh, you mean the whole holding your hand thing after Melanie died." Christine tried to make her tone light. God help her, if Hunter started thanking her, she would break. She didn't want his gratitude. She wanted his love—the only thing he couldn't give her.

"You held my hand for years. When everyone else had moved on and given up on me, you were there."

"Yes, well, it's not like I had hobbies to keep me busy." She moved away from him, but he wouldn't let her, pulling her around to look at him. He studied her for a second as if he was trying to figure her out. But there was very little to figure out about her. Christine was no mystery, she had no secrets.

"Why do you do that?"

"Do what?"

"Minimize things you've done for people. Dismiss yourself and all the wonderful things about you."

"Middle child syndrome." She waved his compliments away.

"You're not a child anymore, are you?" He lifted her face, forcing her to look at him.

Christine frowned. She wasn't sure what he meant by that. "No. But you've never noticed."

"I've noticed." The edge to his voice, spoken no more above a whisper, tugged at her. What was he doing? Hope unfurled inside her, but she quashed it away. Hope was the worst. It made her blind, a slave to what could be, unable to move on.

"Yes, you noticed last summer. And look how that ended."

"I'm sorry—"

"You apologize one more time for what happened, I'm going to punch you in the face. Remember, I know Krav Maga."

"I wasn't going to apologize for what happened. I am apologizing for the way I handled it. I was an ass." He grimaced at the last part, which made Christine smile. Admitting he was wrong was, probably, physically painful for Hunter.

"Wow. Can I record that?"

"No. And if you tell anyone, I'll deny it."

"Well, a lot of people know you're an ass anyway."

He smiled but it had no real humor behind it. "Why do you put up with me, Chris?" He placed his hand on her cheek. He had done this a million times—whether to get her attention, to scold her, or to say something nice, he often touched her in ways that made her feel loved, though no more than a friend. But right now, in the stillness of his home, his touch was different. Christine gave in to the urge, unlike the thousand times before. For a space of a second, she turned her head, her lips touched the warmth of his palm. But that was all she could handle. She moved away, creating space for her to breathe, to think.

"It's all part of that 'me loving you' thing. It's very inconvenient." The lightness of her words belied the heavy feeling behind them.

"Love is like that."

"Yes, it sucks. I'm sure you know all about that."

"You mean loving Melanie?"

"Yes."

"I will love Melanie for the rest of my life."

"I know." Hearing him say the words, even when she already knew the truth, made her want to throw up. "But you need to make room for other people. I don't mean me, before you get ideas that I'm going to start stalking you. You're only thirty. You need to start living."

Like her, he tried to make light of things, but it wasn't quite working. "Like 'diving in underwater caves' kind of living?"

"Not quite. You need to start slowly."

"How slow?"

"Start with getting rid of that old man car."

"Hey! Don't hate on the car."

"You drive the same car as my dad."

"We're both sensible men."

"Sensible is a euphemism for boring."

"Boring is predictable. I don't mind predictable. I like predictable."

After all the things that had gone wrong in his life, of course Hunter would prefer the predictable. This was hardly news. That was why they were a bad fit—Christine thrived on the unpredictability of her life. It was the only way she could function as an adult.

"I guess this is the universe's way of balancing things. You're super smart, incredibly good looking, but you're as boring as toast." That wasn't precisely true. He had a dry wit that always made Christine laugh. He had flashes of spontaneity that sometimes surprised her. But to others who did not know him Hunter was dull. If she were truly honest she liked that few knew the real him, and that she was one of those people.

"I would bore you to tears within a week. Then I'd be just

another Paul."

"Is that what you think?" She stiffened at his words.

"Admit it, you're an adrenaline junkie."

"It's the only way I can forget the suckiness of my love life—or lack thereof."

"I'm not worth it, Chris. You should find someone who matches you."

"You don't think I've tried? What do you think I've been doing hopping from one assignment to another that no one, in her right mind, would ever take? Going on dates like it was going out of style? Bungee jumping in Brazil. Racing in Africa, and all that crazy stuff." She hated this. She hated the assumption that she was pining for him. Well, maybe she was. But she had tried to forget him. Those men who were perfect on paper but never quite made it past first base, the hyper active job, the physical limits she placed on her body—they were all aimed at making her forget. She was not sitting around waiting for Hunter to swoop her up in his arms. She was living her life, as best as she could. She may be in love with him, but she wasn't the helpless, clingy kind of girl.

"Your version of adventure."

"It's Project: Forget Hunter, asshat."

"Did it work?"

"Does it look like it's working? Am I the picture of happiness and contentment?" The bitterness coursing through her was almost physical.

Hunter shook his head. "I don't know. But there are plenty of men out there."

"The heart wants what the heart wants."

"And your heart wants me. For now."

"You can be so insulting, you know that?"

"What did I say?"

"Don't worry, Hunter. I'm not out to jump your bones at the first opportunity, so you don't need to remind me of the millions of eligible men out there. But please, don't tell me what I feel, including thinking that whatever this bullshit love crap I feel for you is temporary. It insults both of us." She moved farther away from him, and from anything she could potentially throw at him.

"I've hurt you again. I keep doing that. I don't even know how."

For such a smart man, he was hopelessly clueless. "That's all right. You've been doing it for years, without knowing it."

"Don't say that." He actually looked hurt and confused which neutralized some of Christine's anger. Somewhat. This wasn't Hunter's fault. None of this was his fault. Her pain, her confusion, her life—none of it was his responsibility or his doing. She was being unfair to him.

"Did you keep my stuff from your old place?"

"Your stuff?" He looked surprised. She shifted topic so quickly, it was probably giving him emotional whiplash. She'd had all she could handle tonight. She was never good at the "heavy" stuff. She was, even at her worst, capable of a certain level of pragmatism that allowed her to go on with her life, even as she wanted to crumble in misery.

"Yes, my stuff. I left my bag at my parents'. I have no clothes." She had spent so many nights and weekends with Hunter, at one point half of everything she owned was at his apartment.

"To your left. Two doors down the right. It's your bed-room." Her bedroom—her own personal space in his home. But that was all it was—a space, maybe a space in his life but nothing more. Not the kind of all-encompassing space she wished she occupied in his life, the way he occupied hers.

Chapter Five

Washing away the grime of cross-country travel, and everything that had happened since, Christine felt much better in an old pair of yoga pants and a sweatshirt that was two sizes too big. She found Hunter sitting on the couch. He too had taken a shower. Even in his old sweats, he looked yummy. Too bad she made that speech about not jumping his bones. Standing in the hallway, Christine was about to leave him alone when he turned to her.

"Come on, I put on your favorite movie, and I made popcorn."

"Your peace offering?" She walked barefoot across the cold, wood floors.

"Did it work?"

"Hmmm, I should make you work harder."

"No you won't. You're too nice not to forgive me."

"Shut up. Someone might hear you. I don't want to ruin my reputation. Just hand me the popcorn." She sat on the other side of the couch, stretching her legs between them. He placed a blanket over them. It was like old times, the countless movies she watched in his apartment, sometimes alone, sometimes with him. The first year after Melanie died, Christine tried to infuse some normalcy in his life. She spent half her time shuttling between New York and college, despite her parents' objections. A few months later she graduated, and instead of going straight to the master's program she deferred her enrollment to be with Hunter. Her world had always revolved around him. Even when she tried to move on with her life by moving to LA, she was always within his orbit. No matter how many times she told herself enough, she always came back. She was, as much as she hated to admit it, terminally stupid when it came to Hunter.

As the black and white movie flickered before them, Christine looked around the dark apartment. The shadows from the streetlights and the TV danced eerily around the room. This place needed some serious decorating. It was so cold, as if no one lived here.

"You need a Christmas tree," she muttered.

"I don't need a tree."

"You're such a Grinch. No one *needs* a tree, but you have to have a tree."

"All right, I'll have one delivered tomorrow."

"Delivered?" She sat up. She considered having a Christmas tree delivered a cardinal sin, given that she grew up in a family who actually cut their own tree. "You're slowly crushing my soul, Hunter. Next thing you'll tell me, you'll have it decorated too."

"There's a company our office uses—"

"Stop right there!" She tossed the blanket and grabbed her boots. "We're buying one right now."

"Right now?" He looked at her as if she was crazy.

"Yes," she answered impatiently, making it sound like *he* was the crazy one for refusing to get off the couch to buy a Christmas tree in the middle of the night.

"It's past midnight."

"It's New York."

"Precisely why any self-respecting person would order one and have it delivered."

"Fine. If buying a tree is beneath you, I'll get it myself." She grabbed his car keys from the console table.

"No way, in hell, are you driving my car." What is it with men and their cars that turned them into possessive little boys? He looked at her sweats and her wet hair. "Are you going dressed like that?"

"Don't worry, I have a coat, and if someone you know sees us you can pretend you don't know me. Better yet, you can tell them I'm the help."

Hours later, and knowing that he was not likely going to make it to work at a decent hour, Hunter gave in to Christine's whimsy. They ended up with a tree that occupied most his living room, and glitter that was half on the tree, half on him. When they were done decorating, rather when Christine was done telling him what to do, they sat across from the Christmas tree, with cooling hot chocolate in their hands. Christine sighed as she placed her head on his shoulder. That little sigh, and her warm body near his, made all of it worthwhile. It took very little to make Christine happy. He had done his fair share of crazy whenever he was with her because he liked making her happy.

They sat in silence watching the Christmas lights. Hunter moved his arm around her. With the familiarity between two people who cared for each other, Christine leaned into his arm, resting her head on his chest. She mumbled something about Christmas, but Hunter couldn't quite catch what she said, because within a few seconds she was fast asleep. He dozed off, too, comforted by her nearness.

Soon enough, the early morning light seeped through the wide windows of the apartment, waking him. He looked down at Christine, still asleep. She had slept on his couch countless times before. He had always taken her presence for granted, knowing she was going to be there for him no matter what. But the last year had shown him what his life was like without her in it. It was bleak. He never wanted to be without her. He should tell her that. But he didn't know quite how to say it. He, who made a living drafting precise contract language, using and manipulating words to suit his purposes, did not know what to say to her.

She stirred. Hunter watched her wake up. He realized he liked watching her. He should feel like a creeper, but it was good to have her in his arms. Hunter waited for that choking feeling to take ahold of him, the one that made him run like a jackass from her last summer, but it didn't come. There was only peace. She looked up at him and smiled. It was so natural, he didn't know what he was doing until he felt her sigh against his lips. His touch was tentative, waiting for her to respond — whether to push him away or to pull him closer. When she shifted to open her arms to him, he knew this was all he wanted and needed. For months he had lived in this empty space, wondering what was missing. It was Christine. She was the one missing, the only thing that mattered.

He kissed her, charged with the intimacy and newness of having his dear friend in his arms. She felt right. For the first time in years, *he* felt right. When she moaned, the last of Hunter's reserve shattered. He grabbed her leg, pulled it over his thigh. Who knew yoga pants and a sweatshirt could be so sexy—they made everything accessible. She pushed him on the couch, moving over him. She was so beautiful, her skin tinged with pink, her eyes bright. She lifted his shirt over his head. Her touch was tentative at first, then she became bolder. Unable to stand the sweet torture of her touch, Hunter demanded, "Your turn."

When her sweatshirt joined his on the floor, he gaped. Dear lord, she was more exquisite than he could have imagined. He moved his arms around her, teasing her neck, then lower. She made impatient demands, but Hunter wasn't rushing this. It had been far too long and he wanted to enjoy every moment of it.

"Slow down," he whispered against her neck, gently nipping her.

"I can't wait. I've been waiting for you forever," she said with a sob. He knew how she felt because it had been forever since he had touched another human being this way, but he had no regrets. Christine was worth those years of loneliness. He couldn't imagine ending his self-imposed celibacy with anyone but her. Without knowing it, this was what he had been waiting for, searching for all these years. This wasn't sex, this was him making love to the person that meant more to him than any-thing, anyone in the world. Finally, everything in his life had fallen into place. Soon the sun rose above the horizon, the bright morning light streamed into the living room, and two new lov-ers welcomed the day with deep sighs and sounds of love and pleasure.

Chapter Six

Christine lay on her stomach, too lazy and satisfied to move. Plus she had the most magnificent view in the world so why should she get up? For the last five days, she had enjoyed this view—Hunter's spectacular ass as he got dressed. She smiled. Those pants and shirt would be gone within the hour but she allowed him to do his morning rituals. He was nothing if not fastidious about his routine. Plus, it was much more fun undressing him anyway.

He turned to look at her. Her hair tousled and her skin still warm from their last round of amazing sex, he smiled. Her heart skipped a beat. *Emerson, you got it bad.*

"It's Christmas Eve. We need to make an appearance to your family."

Ugh. Yes, her family. She had made pathetic excuses for why she had only seen them a couple of times so far. She was sure they didn't believe her. And she was even more sure they wouldn't believe her if she told them that Hunter had taken an entire week off from work to spend time with her, on her, in her, under her, around her. They were used to her staying with Hunter, so at least that part they did not question. God knows what they thought she had been doing. But, at least for now, they were satisfied that she was in the same time zone as them, and not in some dark underwater cave.

When she didn't move, Hunter sat on the bed, his hand skimmed her back. She shivered at his touch. Oh, the things he did with his hands. He should have been a scientist. When they made love he studied and explored her body so minutely with his hands, mouth, and lips. Every single time she felt like a newly discovered cave that welcomed his exploration.

He leaned in to kiss her shoulder. "Come on. I want you to open your gifts before we leave." That was all the incentive she needed. Who didn't love presents?

Christine lifted herself out of bed. Her gaze strayed to the nightstand next to her. It was what was missing on the table that drew her attention—Melanie's picture. He removed it after the first time they were together. At least Hunter was considerate enough to remove the picture of his dead wife while he made love to another woman. But the rest of the house still had traces of Melanie. It was a constant reminder that nothing had changed. Tomorrow, she'd fly back to LA. Both of them would continue existing without living, or at least, Christine would. Depressed at the direction of her thoughts, Christine grabbed the presents she bought Hunter.

When Hunter walked back in, Christine was sitting on the bed against the morning light. Her long hair cast a halo around her in different shades of brown and red. She was so beautiful she glowed from within. Hunter was going to remember what she looked like this morning for the rest of his life.

He had two small boxes wrapped in festive, red paper. "Open this first. This is actually a gift for both of us."

It was a small box, perfect for lingerie. Christine lifted her eyebrow at him, her smile knowing. "Get your mind out of the gutter," he scolded her, choking back laughter.

She smiled. "I think it's been permanently stuck there since last week. And it's all your fault."

"Well, I aim to please." He gave her another quick kiss. Christine learned that staid Hunter was actually very tactile. He touched her at every opportunity, kissed her at every turn. Of course, she melted at every single, spontaneous touch. "Open it."

Shaking the box didn't give her any clues to what was inside so she eagerly tugged the silver ribbon. "Tickets to Indonesia?"

"I was told Bunaken Island has the best underwater diving."

"You were told?"

"Well, more like I did some research." When he saw the

look on her face, he frowned. "You don't want to go?"

"You and me, together?" She probably sounded like an idiot, but never in a million years did she think Hunter would give her this gift. Not the tickets, precisely, but the gift of being with him longer than she anticipated.

"Ideally, yes." He laughed at her silly question.

"For how long?"

"Two weeks. Or more if you want. Apparently, I've incurred a ridiculous amount of vacation days."

"I thought...I mean...I..." She took a deep breath, hoping to gather her thoughts into discernible speech. She tried to talk again but she couldn't form the words. Fear. It was fear that had paralyzed her into silence, and hope. Stupid, persistent hope.

"If I knew plane tickets to some remote island would render you speechless, I would have done this a long time ago."

"I mean us, together. This," she spread her hand between them. "How long?"

"As a couple?" He scowled.

"Yes." Her voice sounded hoarse. Can shock make one lose her voice?

"You want me to put a time limit on our relationship?" If it was possible, his frown deepened.

"We have a relationship?" If she could, Christine would have backed away from Hunter. His face actually darkened. He looked more than pissed.

"What do you think this entire week has been?" he asked in an angry whisper.

"I don't know? Fuck buddy?" Christine realized her mistake as soon as she said the words. She really needed to develop a filter.

"Jesus Christ, Christine. This was all that was to you?"

"I thought to you, maybe. To me, no. Of course not." She tried to touch him, but he moved away from her. He stood in the middle of the room, his hands on his hips.

"So what were you thinking? You were going to get on that plane to LA tomorrow and that's the end of that?"

"I thought that was all it was to you. You told me you'll

always love Melanie. I don't know what place I'm supposed to take in your life when you say things like that." Her voice and eyes pleaded for him to understand.

That seemed to cool his anger. He pulled a chair and sat across from her. "Of course, I'll always love Melanie. She was my wife, but she's gone."

"I don't know if I can replace her."

"I don't want you to replace her." Hunter took her cold hands into his, rubbing warmth into them. He took a deep breath, the kind that meant he was digging for something deep somewhere within him. "When I met Melanie, it was this thunderbolt. I was walking around minding my own business, then boom, it was this quick, instinctive thing. I was instantly connected to her."

Christine was horrified at what he was saying. Not because he loved another woman, but because the thought that he would never feel that way about her was too painful. She tried to pull her hands away from his, but Hunter would not let her go. "No, don't. Let me finish. When she died, I felt like a part of me died. I've never loved someone as much as her."

"If this is your way of asking me to stay longer, you're doing it the wrong way." She tried not to cry. She didn't want Hunter to see how much this was hurting her. She could still walk away from this with some of her dignity intact.

"Just listen, okay?" He paused, looking down at their hands together, seemingly fascinated. Christine wondered what he saw. There was nothing remarkable about her hands. "I thought, well, what are the chances of that happening again? Most people go through their lives looking for their one true love. I found mine. I lost her too soon but I had seven happy years with her. But at the back of my mind, there was still some hope that someday, maybe, if I was really lucky, lightning could strike twice. So I went through life, expecting that if I were to fall in love again, that same thunderbolt would strike again. Then there was you." He paused. Neither one of them said anything for a long time.

With a patience she didn't know she had, Christine waited for him to finish. She took it on faith that he wasn't intentionally hurting her. It wasn't his fault that he couldn't love her the way he loved Melanie. But deep inside, Christine was dying a slow death. "You're my best friend, my savior. You were there, the one constant thing in my life. Through my haze of pain and loneliness, you eased it all just by being you. You've been so much a part of my life that I took you for granted. I'll regret that for the rest of my life. I promise I'll never take you for granted again. I was stupid enough to think you would always be there. Available, dependable Christine."

"You make me sound so boring."

He laughed. "You're anything but. When you stopped returning my calls, when your texts became rarer and rarer, and your visits non-existent, it drove me crazy wondering what I did wrong. Wondering how I could fix it so we could go back to normal. But you cutting me out was the best thing that could have happened to me. My visit to LA...you scared me. I scared myself because I felt," he swallowed, searching for the right words but he couldn't quite find them. "I felt more than I've felt in a long time. Then this whole week, I realized there wasn't going to be a thunderbolt, no sudden connection. You came into my life, and slowly, surely...I can't imagine my life without you. Melanie is in my past. I'm grateful I had her to love. But you, I love. You're my present, my future. I hope, if you let me, you'll be my destiny."

She gaped at him. That long, winding speech was to tell her he loved her? He loved her. Her. When she realized exactly what he was saying, she hurled herself against him. "Oh my God, Hunter," she sobbed in his arms. "That was the cheesiest, sappiest, most beautiful thing I've ever heard." Joy exploded within her in a mixture of laughter and tears.

"Hey. That was *not* easy to say, so give me a break."

"Did you practice?" she asked as he wiped her tears away.

"Will you be less impressed if I did?"

"No, no. I love you more for it." Christine was sure her heart was going to explode. Could one die of happiness? Because there was so much of it, she could barely contain it. Hunter kissed her. She gave everything she had in that kiss. Knowing he loved her made her fearless, more open to him. It was freeing to be told that the man you loved, loved you too.

Hunter pulled away from her, placing the other gift on her lap. Still dazed from that earth-shattering kiss (it really was), it took Christine a few moments before she could focus on the other gift.

"What's this?" She asked as she stared at the antique opal ring, surrounded with diamonds sitting in a beautiful box.

"A ring."

"I know it's a ring. So it's *just* a ring?" Her tone was searching, tentative. Christine, who dove fearlessly into the Amazon River and under icy water, actually looked afraid.

"I didn't think you'd appreciate a traditional engagement ring so..."

"Are you asking?"

"No. Asking would require giving you a choice. I don't want you to have a choice. I'm telling you instead."

She laughed, half-horrified and half-enthralled at what he was saying. "Are you kidding?"

"Actually, yes." He stood from his chair, and knelt beside her instead. "Christine Emerson, would you do me the honor of being my wife?"

"Hunter, get up. I think you're in a sexual haze. You don't propose marriage after a one-week relationship," she scolded him, even though she would marry him in a heartbeat.

"We've known each other longer than most people. Do you think I'm going to let you get on that plane without having a guarantee you'll come back?"

She put the ring on the bedside table, pulling him to her. "I'm yours. Whether you marry me or not, I'm yours."

"Then say yes."

"I am going to be a horrible wife, especially for a big shot corporate lawyer. I'm loud. I've no filter. I'm easily distracted. I'm messy and I can't cook! I'll drive you nuts within—"

"Say yes," Hunter interrupted, ignoring everything she had said.

"Hunter—"

"Say yes, Christine." He held her face in his hands, forcing her to stay still and look at him.

"Yes, Hunter but—"

"Yes?"

"Yes, but—"

"Shut up. Jesus, you don't stop, do you? I love that you're loud. I love that you're easily bored because you'll make my life more interesting. I like that you don't hide anything and you mean what say. I can afford a housekeeper and a cook. If you drive me nuts, which I'm sure will be often, I'll drag you in the bedroom where you can be as loud as you want."

"Yes but—"

"Woman, shut up and let me kiss you."

Second Chance Girl

by C.S. Kendall

Chapter One

*H*er text message said she'd be here in five minutes, to meet her outside so we could walk in together, just like the good ol' days. Had she forgotten that it was the beginning of December and thirty-some degrees?

Apparently.

I rubbed my arms, bouncing in the chill as a winter breeze kicked up. It carried the smell of cigarette smoke to my nose. It's funny how smell triggers memory. All I could think of was Garrett and how the same smell used to live on him. It was always stale, though, like it was days old or acquired second-hand. I shivered, not from the chill, but from the memory, and shook my head, as if that motion could dislodge those skeletons from the closet of my brain.

Bling! I pulled my phone out of my pocket. *So sorry! Thought I was out the door, but fudge making went awry. Be there in 3.*

I rolled my eyes, shoving my phone back into my pocket. For the love of everything holy, I hadn't seen my best friend in two months and she's late to this, our annual tradition. A puff of smoke billowed into my face, inducing a coughing fit.

Without looking at the man smoking beside me, I said, "Could you maybe not blow that in my face?"

"Oh, uh, sorry," he said, turning away from me just as I looked in his direction. I stared at his back, taking in the ripped jeans which hung on his hips with just the right fit. His worn leather jacket somehow both contrasted and complimented the vintage Converse on his feet. He took a puff of his cigarette and then raked the hand holding it through his dark brown hair. Though cut short in back, the front looked like it was long enough to hang into his eyes. Something about him made me curious, and I wanted him to turn around so I could see his face.

Alex's car screeched up to the curb and she hopped out. An apology fell from her lips before the car door even opened.

"Whatever, just hug me!" I pulled her into an embrace,

the tightness of her squeeze expelling all the air in my lungs. I didn't care. "I missed you so much, but I'm freezing now since I've been waiting for you out here for a full eight minutes."

"Shut up, I'm sorry," she said, pouting. "Maybe this'll make up for it?" She thrust a foil-wrapped plate forward.

"Is this what I think it is?"

"Look for yourself and find out."

I lifted the corner of the foil to find several squares of fresh-made fudge on the plate. Without hesitation, I popped one into my mouth, my eyes fluttering under its intoxicating spell as the creamy chocolate spread across my tongue. "Okay, so worth the wait," I said when the piece was savored to the fullest. "Now, let's get inside. Our tree awaits."

Alex linked arms with me, and we walked into the church, the same way we had since I'd met her at this very spot just before Christmas when we were six. The warmth of the building and the smell of being home competed with each other to darn near bring me to tears. People bustled about at the annual Deck the Church Halls event, erecting trees and stringing lights and garland in various corners of the church. I stopped inside, closed my eyes again and breathed it in.

"It's good to be home."

"Well, we've all missed you! This small town is even smaller when you're not in it." Alex squeezed my arm.

"One more semester and then I'll move back this way. C'mon, there it is."

The tree stood in the middle of the foyer, her fake evergreen branches reaching almost to the twelve-foot ceiling. She was bare, awaiting our arrival, and more importantly, our touch. Boxes of decorations were stacked in front of this, the most important tree to be decked in these halls.

Alex ran up to it, giving one of the branches a hug. "Remember the first time we decorated this tree? Your dad was just starting out as pastor here, and you were so shy."

"Yes, and you weren't."

"Nope. As soon as we met right out there," she pointed to the chilly front of the church, where we just had been, "it was friendship at the first word."

I nodded, the memory sweeping over me as a laugh rose. "That tree looked atrocious that year, completely disproportioned."

"No one cared though because we were the cutest. Still are!" Alex put her hands around her face in movie-star fashion, batting her eyelashes at me.

We started rummaging through the boxes one by one, untangling lights, chatting about how we'd organize the ornaments on the tree, sorting tinsel. We were wrapping garland around the tree like Christmas-decorating ninja masters when Alex froze, her gaze locked on the front door of the church building, a hybrid of curiosity and confusion on her face.

"Huh, I didn't think he would actually come inside." I followed her gaze, which hadn't pulled away from the door. It was as if a halo of light surrounded his face and Heaven itself opened to simultaneously rain down its angelic music and stop Earth's time. He swaggered into the church, looking to the right and the left like he owned the place. Dark locks of unruly hair fell into his eyes. He was due for a shave, the scruff on his face only accentuating his ridiculously chiseled chin. His jaw tensed in slow motion, freezing it in its perfection, and the beauty of that act was enough to make my entire body go limp. I recognized his distressed jeans, that jacket, the—cigarette? In one deft move, he pulled it from behind his ear and flipped it through his fingers, landing it in his mouth, his lighter doing somersaults through the fingers of his other hand.

Oh no, he wasn't. The heavens slammed their doors shut, time regained its footing, and the light disappeared altogether. "Excuse me!"

He looked in my direction and then bee-lined for me.

I met him half-way. "What do you think you're doing?" The cigarette hanging from his lips distracted me from his beauty.

He pulled it out of his mouth, holding it between the first two fingers of his right hand. "Uh, looking for my uncle."

"I mean with the cigarette."

"Oh, this?" He held it up, and I was able to get a good look at it.

It wasn't lit.

"Oh," I said.

One side of his mouth turned up. "Bet you feel like a jackass."

"Language, sir!" I hissed in my best church whisper-yell. "You are in the Lord's house, near his birthday, no less."

"Something tells me he'll forgive me, on account of he already knows you're a jackass." He put the unlit cigarette back in his mouth, tipped an invisible hat at me, and turned the corner, heading toward the fellowship hall.

My mouth fell open, any witty or intelligent response eluding me, as I turned to my best friend. My laughing best friend.

"You should have heard yourself. 'Language, sir!' What are you, British?" She held her stomach, almost falling to her knees, unable to catch her breath. A tear fell down her cheek. She wiped it, examined the droplet, and then found that hysterical as well.

"Are you done?" I said.

Alex put her finger up, bending at the waist and doing her best to catch her breath.

"Sorry," she said, once she stood upright again. "One hot guy and you're up here, almighty preacher's daughter about to lay down the law." She pumped her arms like a soldier on command, because that's apparently what a high and mighty preacher's daughter does.

"I thought he lit it up. You can't do that in a church."

"He hadn't."

"I know that now." We dug through the nearby box, selecting ornaments to place at perfect intervals on the tree. "Who is he, anyway?"

"Pastor Mark's nephew. His name is Sawyer. He was standing right outside when I got here."

My brain caught up, reminding me of my curiosity outside, connecting the dots between the back I stared at in the cold and the scene that had just unfolded. "Wait, the new youth pastor, Pastor Mark?"

"Yup." Alex hung an ornament and then stood back,

examining it with a meticulous eye.

"Why is he here?" I froze, tree decoration long gone from my mind.

"He lives with him and his wife. Has since he was a baby, so the story goes. Though he almost never darkens the doorway of this building."

"Well, how old is he?"

"Don't do this." She put her ornament down and turned toward me, squaring my shoulders in her grip.

"Do what?" I frowned, uncertain, but also marginally aware of what she was getting at.

"This thing you do. You think he's troubled—the jacket, the cigarette, the language. So, you automatically want to rescue him."

"No, I don't." I shrugged out of her grip, distracting myself with an ornament.

Alex tilted her head and raised her eyebrows.

"I don't do that anymore." I hung the ornament, paying little attention to its placement.

Alex picked it off the tree, moving it up and to the left. "Sweetie, it's in your DNA. I don't have to remind you how much Garrett hurt you. Don't go near this one. He has a record or something. And take that as a warning, not an invitation. He's trouble."

"He's ballsy, walking into the church with a cigarette like that." I thought about the confidence with which he came through those doors, the air he held. And yet, something else lived in his eyes. What color were they again? I strained my memory to recall, but the encounter was too brief, too focused on other things. Still, I was drawn, and I wondered about his story.

Alex was talking. I snapped my brain back to her words. "He doesn't seem to care what anyone thinks. Says whatever he wants to. He hasn't made too many friends, if you can imagine."

She continued talking, but her voice fell to the periphery again because all I could think about were halos and heaven opening up to usher Sawyer through the door in slow motion.

Chapter Two

That night, the carolers filed into the fellowship hall one by one, with cheeks pinked from the night's chill, but smiles on their faces. Alex and I stood arm in arm, having returned already, sipping our steaming cups of cocoa.

"Gonna have some chili?" she asked.

"Of course. I'm starved," I said. "Besides what's the annual caroling and chili supper without the chili supper part?"

"Let's get in that line then!"

She pulled my arm and rushed us into the line, just before another wave of happy carolers came through the door. Among them was my father. He saw me in line and put up his hand in a half-wave, half-signal. He walked straight toward us, out of breath as he arrived. He stroked the fibers of his graying beard and then unzipped his jacket.

"Hey there, sweetie. We could really use your help serving in the kitchen. Mrs. Liebowitz called and she's ill. We're down a chili scooper. Mom's still out with a group caroling at the nursing home and your sister is with her. I have to give the grace up front or I would do it. What do you say?"

"Of course I'll help, Dad. Can Alex come too?"

"You betcha. Thank you girls. You'll be at the window over there." He pointed toward a closed kitchen window as the line continued to grow behind the only open one. He hollered another thank you over his shoulder as he made his way through the thickening crowd. I pulled Alex this time, as she fake whined about how hungry she was.

"Hush your mouth. Dad's the pastor. I can't exactly balk at serving chili to everyone else because I'm hungry. Besides, we can sneak some of the cornbread in the kitchen while we do it."

"But I'm huuuungry."

"You're a baby. Oh—" I stopped short as we walked into the kitchen. It seemed the only other chili server was the apparently convicted, Heaven-endorsed rebel, Sawyer. Something strange happened inside my chest when I saw him. It resembled what I faintly remembered of my own flip-floppy heart full of anticipation, the kind I got whenever I saw Garrett, but that couldn't be it. I reminded myself that earlier in the day, he was about to light up a cigarette inside the church. Clearing my throat, I took my place next to him.

He surprised me by flashing me a giant smile, which did nothing to quiet whatever was quaking in the vicinity of my heart. "Well hey, if it isn't the Marlboro police. How did I get the pleasure of serving chili with you?"

I stared at him like an idiot, so Alex came to the rescue. "Better believe it's your pleasure. We are going to serve your socks off."

"Are we making this a competition?" he asked me, despite the fact that he was answering Alex.

"Um, sure," I said, my stunned brain waking. I cleared my throat, willing confidence into my tone. "That is, if you're prepared to lose to a jackass such as myself." I repeated his earlier insult and watched as a smile bloomed on his lips. It felt like a kick to the chest, and in response, my heart thundered with even greater emphasis.

"Ooo, she has bite. I like that. Sawyer." He extended his hand.

"Rebekah." I eased my hand into his, a chill crawling up my arm from his warm touch.

His face blanked, his grin falling away. "Smithon?"

"Yes," I said.

He dropped my hand, straightening his shirt. "As in Pastor Smithon's daughter, Rebekah?"

"Yeah, so?" I crossed my arms, defensiveness rising to the surface.

"Oh." He turned back to his window, giving his full attention to the chili.

"I'm sorry, do you have a problem with me?" He wasn't getting off the hook that easily.

"Not so much a problem with you, though your family affiliation does make sense of your need to police the entryway of the church."

"You had a cig-a-rette." I slowed my speech like he was

an idiot. I didn't care how condescending it came across.

He turned and looked me square in the eyes, his face inches from my own. "It-was-n't lii-iit." He stretched out the words, matching my treatment of him. I couldn't help but notice the crystal blue of his eyes now that they stared at mine, only inches away. Or the smoothness of his olive skin, or the height of his cheekbones. Cologne masked the faint smoky scent of his cigarettes, and despite my abhorrence for them, something about the mixture enticed me. He winked at me then, and it snapped me back to the reality of our conversation.

"What is your deal? I guess Alex was right. You don't care what anyone thinks of you or how you come across."

"So, you've been talking about me."

"No, I—well, yes, but don't flatter yourself. Because we certainly didn't." I could feel the heat on my cheeks and my heart was drumming in my ears.

"Well, you're right. I don't care." He looked straight ahead again, busying himself with the chili.

"Know what, dude? Game off. Just serve your chili from that window and we'll do ours from this one." Alex leaned over me, always at my defense.

"Sounds great to me." Sawyer ladled chili into an eager caroler's bowl.

The instantaneous change in his demeanor stunned me silent, and I made a decision then and there. I did not like Sawyer whatever-his-name-was. No matter how crystal blue his eyes were.

A half-hour into window duty, Alex's phone, which sat charging next to our serving window, chirped. She almost dropped the ladle in her haste to remove her plastic serving gloves. Pulling it off the charger she began jumping up and down, screaming.

"What?" I asked.

"Derek's here! He got done early and surprised me. He's at my place, I gotta go!" She took off her apron and her plastic hair cap, shoving them at me. "Oh," she said, remembering who was serving next to us and dropping her voice to a whisper. "Are you going to be okay if I go?" She waggled her eyebrows in Sawyer's direction.

"Yeah, of course. Go!"

"Thank-you-I-love-you!" She kissed my cheek and dashed out the door. Sawyer's gaze shifted in my direction, and then irritation filled it. I wasn't sure if he was irritated over Alex's display or by the fact that we were now alone in the kitchen. The lines were slowing, so we were pretty much just serving second helpings at this point.

After a considerable lull at my window, I turned my back to it, leaning against the countertop. I stretched and watched Sawyer out of the corner of my eye. That's when I noticed his tattoos. He wore a t-shirt under his apron and ink extended from the edge of his sleeve all the way down his forearm where it stopped suddenly, a defined line separating the ink and the rest of his bare skin. I couldn't make out all the designs, but it was beautiful and mystifying how it stopped abruptly. I turned my head to the side, studying it, trying to make sense of it, when I felt Sawyer's gaze on me. I looked up and my cheeks filled with fire.

"Sorry, I was just admiring your tattoo. It's beautiful."

"Thanks," he said, watching me.

"What is it?"

He looked down at his arm. "It's my life story."

"Oh." I didn't feel like prying, and he didn't seem inclined to give more information, so I took to busying myself wiping the counters.

Not long after, we were released from duty. I ducked into the ladies' room to empty my bladder. In the mirror, I found my winter hat had interfered with my ponytail, rendering it lopsided and lumpy. I pulled out the elastic, rustled my raven hair and tried to smooth it into a neater pile on my head. I shrugged at my reflection, reminding myself that there was no one here to impress anyway.

On my way out of the building, I got a text from Alex.

Thx for letting me off the hook! Hope felon boy didn't give you too much trouble!

I laughed, pushed the door open to the outside. Cold air blasted my face as I tapped out a response, and then ran into something solid.

"Ouch!" I said, rubbing my shoulder, and looked up to see the obstacle I'd hit looking back at me with frosted crystal blue eyes. "Sorry," I said. I turned to go and when I looked behind me, Sawyer was frozen in place, watching me. That lit a spark in me, and I decided I'd had enough of his steely treatment. I spun on my heel and marched back in his direction.

"What is your problem, dude? I don't know you, you don't know me. Yet you seem to have made some snap judgment of me as soon as you found out who my dad was. What's up with that?"

"Didn't you do the same to me?"

"What?"

"Make a snap judgment."

"I most certainly did not."

"Oh, but ya did. The whole cigarette thing."

"I simply didn't think it was appropriate for you to smoke inside a church building. What is so hard for you to understand about that? Plus, I misunderstood the situation, so cut me some slack. You're deflecting anyway, so I'll ask again. *What is your problem?*"

He pulled a cigarette from behind his ear and lit it, exaggerating his puff of smoke in my direction. I chose to ignore him. After a long drag he said, "Seems to me pastoral folk are a bunch of liars. At least in my experience. I don't care to align myself with an untruthful lot."

"Do you even know my dad, like really know him?"

"I know enough."

"Wow." I shook my head. "You are a piece of work."

"As are you. I've never seen you inside the walls of this building before and you walk around here like you own the place just cuz your dad's the pastor. Some kind of holy royalty. Well, you don't, and I don't bow to anyone anyway."

"I didn't ask you to. You know what? Whatever." I waved my hand in his direction as I began to storm off.

"Whatever? Really? That's how you're going to end this exchange? I would have expected more from you." He held his hands open, like an invitation.

I turned around, headed toward him again. "Now you know me?"

"No, but I suspect I know your type." His shoulders lifted in a shrug, his eyes searched the air rather than my face.

"And so I'm a liar, too?" I couldn't help how rigid my whole body went, the flair with which I threw my hands up. He was under my skin, in more ways than one.

"Jury's out on that one." His blew a perfectly circular puff of smoke into the air.

I stood back, shook my head, and wrapped my coat tighter around myself. Lowering my voice, I said, "What's your story? Who screwed you up this bad?"

"No one screwed me up. We all make choices and those responsible for me chose wrong. I have my opinions based on that, and for me, nothing makes sense other than saying it like it is."

I wasn't sure what he meant, but his words diffused my anger a little, pulling me in. "So, how is it?"

"Come again?" He cocked one eyebrow and my heart did that flip-floppy thing in response.

"I mean, how is it? If you say it like it is, then how is it?"

"Oh. Well, for instance, life is short. Too short to lie to people, so I tell it like it is, or at least, like I see it. For instance, if you're wondering what my opinion is on your appearance, I think you're a beautiful girl. Normally I tend to be attracted to girls who are little taller and less girl-next-doorsy, but there's something about you that catches my eye. I also think you're a bit self-righteous, but there's that snap judgment you love to accuse me of."

My chest started screaming after he told me I was beautiful, but it quieted enough to absorb the jab that came on the heels of his compliment. "Self-righteous?" I stepped closer to him. "I think you mistake your own judgmentalism for honesty."

"And you don't judge my hair or my attire or my smoking habit?"

"No."

"Bullshit. Everyone judges everyone else on what they see. But that's not even my issue. I bet you would judge the fact that I have a criminal record, that I was a bastard child no one wanted, and that I sometimes, on occasion, tend toward a drinking problem." His face held a challenge, daring me to oppose him.

I frowned, but not because I was angry or irritated or confused. It was a curious frown. I didn't get this guy. Gorgeous, my insides kept reminding me, but offensive. Honest, but obviously so terribly injured. It was the injured part of him that tugged at me, and I wanted to know more.

"I just feel bad for you," I said.

"Hell, pity. I think that's worse than judgment." He released an amused huff and walked past me.

"I think you misunderstand me," I called.

He turned, lifting his arms in the air, inviting me to go on.

"You were friendly until you found out I was a preacher's daughter. Then you cooled. That was after, I might remind you, you called me a jackass."

"In that moment that's how you struck me. But I wanted to start over on account of your undeniable beauty."

"But I'm not beautiful enough to forgive my unfortunate bestowal of parental units."

At this, he chuckled. "Okay, I'll give you that. I suppose it's not fair to judge you only by your family, but I have reasons for my mistrust of men of the cloth."

"You don't talk like a criminal," I said.

"Ha, well, you know...I'm like an onion, layers and all." He watched me, searched my eyes with a kind of intensity that almost made me feel like he could see through me. See into my own injuries.

"So, lay it on me, then."

"What's that?"

"Your reasons for mistrust of pastoral folk."

"Sometime." His gaze held, a whisper of a smile playing at his lips. They caught my attention, his lips. I couldn't help but notice how the top one was slightly fuller than the bottom, how his tongue slid across them as he readied to speak again. "For now, tell me how I've misunderstood you."

"Hmm?" I forced my gaze upward, away from his beautiful lips, begging the stars that he didn't see me staring at them. "Oh, yeah. Well, you assume because you think you know where I came from, that you know me. Preacher's daughter, holier than thou, no tolerance for the likes of you. That's not me. Not at all. You think you scare me off with mention of a record. I'm majoring in criminal justice, to be a parole officer. I believe in second chances."

Sawyer nodded along with my words, as if he agreed, and then he spoke. "And that's just it. I'm not the one in need of a second chance. That's your mistake, the very thing that makes you not unlike anyone else."

My eyebrows pulled together as I watched him walk away. He'd insulted me more times than I could keep up with in the three encounters I'd had with him, and I was left with the strange sense that I should apologize. One thing was for sure, Alex was right about this guy being dangerous for me. I needed to stay away. But I wasn't sure I wanted to.

Chapter Three

"Honey, wake up. We have to get ready for the staff Christmas party." My mom shook my shoulder as I pulled the covers over my face.

"What time is it?"

"It's 12:30."

"And what time is the party?"

"It starts at five this evening."

I pulled the covers down to my chin. "I mean, I know it's lunchtime, but I have four and a half hours. Besides, are you sure I should go? It was fun growing up, but I'm out of the house now. Well, technically. When I'm off at school."

She ruffled my hair, like she used to when I was a kid. "Yes, of course! It's one of our traditions. The staff will expect you." She went to my window, pulling up the blinds and letting the sun into the room.

"Mom!" I shielded my eyes as dots swam in front of them. "I'll be up in a few minutes."

She sat back down on the edge of the bed, worry creasing across her forehead. "You're not depressed, are you?"

"Mom! Of course I'm not depressed." *At least not so much anymore.*

"Well, it's the afternoon, and you're still sleeping. Don't depressed people sleep a lot?"

"I guess some do, but so do tired people, when they have the chance." I pulled the covers back over my head.

"I just worry about you, honey, that's all. You know, since Garrett."

"It's been over a year, Mom."

"I know, and you've barely spoken about it. Or been on any dates since."

I sat up in bed, looking her in the eyes, in an effort to prove my lack of depressed state. "What would you like me to say?"

"First of all, of course, I want to know you're okay." She

rubbed my arm.

"I'm okay."

"And second, I want you to know it's not your fault."

"I know it's not my fault."

"You sound like a puppet, telling me what I want to hear."

I cocked my head and suspended my arm at a ninety-degree angle in the air, all robotic-like. "I am not a puppet, nor am I a robot," I said in my most monotone voice.

"Very funny. Listen, when a man cheats on a woman, it's easy for her to feel like something is wrong with her."

If only all he did was cheat. "Mom, I know all this already. Can we just not? I appreciate your concern, but trust me, I'm okay."

"Okay, sweetie." She stood, kissing me on the forehead. "I know how long you shower, so you might want to hop in."

Several cups of coffee, a thirty-minute hot shower and some food later, I was ready for the staff Christmas party. Fifteen years ago, when my father had taken over as pastor, he also instituted this tradition. In some ways I'd outgrown it, but I knew that if I didn't go it would feel like something was missing from the season. I fluffed my curled hair and added the finishing touch of crimson lipstick, to match my red A-line skirt. Ready or not.

Once I was seated in the passenger seat of my Mom's car, I noticed we were alone. "Where's Dad?"

"He likes to be early and wanted to do some preparations ahead of time, so he went about two hours ago."

"Oh." I laid my head back against the seat, watching our neighborhood pass by through the window, and last night's heated encounter played through my mind like a slideshow. Him walking into the building, him scooping chili, him raking a hand through his hair, holding a challenge in his eyes, daring me to care, to understand. I shook my head, emptying it of his image. "Can I ask you a question?" I asked my Mom.

"Of course, anything."

"What do you know about that Sawyer kid?"

She knit her eyebrows together and didn't answer for a

minute. Clearing her throat first she said, "Sawyer Matthews?"

"Sure, I guess. Is there more than one?"

"Not that I'm aware of. I don't know much about him. Lives with his aunt and uncle. They adopted him when he was little, but I think he only recently found that out. He's had some trouble, that one. We don't see him around much, so it's nice he's been frequenting the Christmas festivities. In fact, I think he'll be there tonight."

Tonight? Like, tonight, tonight? That quickening thing happened to my insides again, and my hand shot up to clutch my chest.

"Are you okay?"

Crap, she saw me. "I'm fine," I said, regaining composure. "He's coming tonight?"

"I believe so. How do you even know him?"

"I don't. I mean, not really. We talked a little last night. He's...interesting."

"I suppose he is. And cute." She smiled, keeping her gaze trained on the road. I didn't need her to remind me about that. I was already doing my best to forget. I don't know why, but I hadn't expected that I'd see him here tonight. Here, among the staff where I was safe. Only his family was staff now. I'd forgotten that fact. I barely knew Pastor Mark. But if Sawyer was his family, it made sense.

We pulled up to the banquet hall, and nerves coursed through my stomach. I swallowed them down, tilting my head toward the sky. This was my family. I wasn't going to let one questionable encounter ruin the night. Still, walking into the party, I felt like a teenage girl going solo to prom. Oh, this was silly. Of course the guy was attractive and I was intrigued by his story, but he was bad news. Not to mention, I wasn't entirely sure he even liked me. I took my seat next to my parents and my sister, and who was across from me?

Sawyer.

He had upgraded his leather jacket to a vest over a button down shirt. His hair was combed and out of his eyes, and though the scruff remained, it was trimmed. I told my heart to shut up as his blue-eyed gaze bored into mine. I tried to look away from him, but he refused to divert his gaze, and it was beginning to unnerve me.

"Hello again," he said.

I looked around, as if he could be talking to someone else, anyone else. He hadn't stopped looking at me since I noticed he was there. "Hey."

Chatter filled the air, the familiar comfort shared by the staff apparent. It swirled around us, the conversation, the laughter, in a blur, like Sawyer and I were the two centerpieces of the scene, the rest falling into the hazy background. We stared at each other, the intensity both terrifying and intriguing. What was going on behind the depths of those blue eyes? They mesmerized me, and I couldn't look away. My heart thrashed violently, and my breath hitched.

I jumped up from the table, squeezing my mother's shoulder to let her know I was excusing myself. I needed fresh air, away from him. He was a mystery. Just last night he told me I didn't understand him, I was self-righteous and potentially a liar, therefore, not to be trusted. Tonight he was practically eye-sexing me across the table, and I wasn't sure what to do with it. Outside on the balcony, I leaned over the railing, wishing I had thought to bring my coat, when I heard the door open behind me.

"Hey," Sawyer said as he stepped through the door.

"Hey yourself." So much for getting away from him, and now I'd traded the room full of familiar faces for one-on-one time with him. I worried he could hear the hammering of my heart, or worse, see it in my neck. It was screaming, his proximity doing nothing to silence it.

He matched his posture to mine over the railing. Side by side, we resided in a bloated silence that threatened to undo me all together.

"I don't get you," I told him, my voice betraying me when it cracked.

He turned his body toward me. If he heard the waver, he wasn't giving that away. "What would you like to know?"

"Last night you were full of contempt for me, and today you're—"

"Yes?"

"I don't know, you keep looking at me."

"I can't help it. Not only are you beautiful to begin with, but tonight you look magnificent. The whole thing, your hair, that outfit. I can't help it."

The heat that rose to the surface of my skin chased away the chill. "Like that," I said.

"What?"

"Those kinds of things you say. I'm pretty, so what? You told me last night that you're not the one in need of a second chance, that I basically don't get you or what you're about at all. And here you are, all cozying up to me because you like my hair."

"I'm not hitting on you."

"Okay, what are you doing?"

"Just talking to you."

"Okay, then. Last night you said you weren't the one in need of a second chance. So, who is?"

"What?" My abrupt change of topic caught him off guard, and he pulled his body away from me, retreating some.

But I wasn't letting up. "You want to talk, so talk."

He threw his head back. "You really want to do backstory stuff right now?"

"More than I want to hear how much you like my hair." I forced my eyes steady, fixing my glare on his face.

"Okay. You asked for it." He exhaled a long breath, removing the cigarette that had been tucked behind his ear and twirling it between his fingers. "I was raised by my aunt and uncle, Mark and Judy in there. It's still weird to call them by their first names, but it seems only appropriate. No idea who my dad is, and my real mom was a junkie, I guess, so she gave me to them. That was all fine and dandy except they told me all along I was theirs. It wasn't until I had to have a major surgery that it all came out. That was three years ago."

"I see. And he's a 'man of the cloth' as you like to say, and that's why you don't trust them."

"Precisely. I mean, aren't they supposed to be the most honest? And here I've been lied to my whole life. And that's why I don't lie. Being lied to sucks balls."

"I'm sorry. But hey, at least you were raised in a good home."

He frowned, the desire lost from his eyes, replaced by last night's contempt. "You still don't get it."

"I'm sorry? Is there something else I should say?"

"My 'good home' is all a lie. One big fabrication. My mom, Judy, had a freaking birth story for me. A birth story! I was seventeen months when they took custody of me." He spit over the railing. "A life constructed of lies can't possibly be considered 'good'."

"What about your mom?"

"Last I heard she was in and out of rehab." His icy stare broke from my eyes, and I felt a pang for him. Without thinking, I reached my hand over and covered his. He looked down at our hands and then at me. "I really don't need your pity. I've done okay by myself until now."

"Yeah, you're so well adjusted. What was it you said about a criminal record?"

He pulled his hand out from under mine, and the rejection inherent in that action stung. "After I found out my entire life was a lie, I needed answers. I got drunk one night and broke into a hospital to try to find medical records about my birth mom. I got caught."

My eyes widened as a giggle rose up in my throat. *"That* is what your charge is from?"

"What? Yes! It's serious. HIPAA and what-not. Plus, I drove there drunk. They take that shit seriously."

"Watch your mouth. There's a room full of preachers in there."

"Do you think I care?"

"I think you do on some level."

He looked hard at me and then turned away.

"So why are you still there?" I asked.

"Hmm?"

"At your aunt and uncle's house. Why do you live there?"

"I have nowhere else to go. Left for a while, but had no choice and had to come back. It was that or the streets."

"Well, what do you want to do with your life?"

"Not sure. I thought I might follow in my dad's-uncle's-footsteps until I found out he was a fraud. Now I don't know anything."

"How old are you?" I narrowed my eyes, studying him, trying to guess before he told me.

"Twenty-two. You?"

"Twenty-one."

"Why do you want to be a parole officer? I mean, what's all that crap about second chances?"

"I don't know. I just feel like so many of those with records never have a chance once they're out. I figure becoming a PO is a good starting place for helping to turn that around, and then I'll see from there."

"I'll admit. I was wrong before. I think you have a good heart."

"Thanks. Seems to get me into trouble, though."

"Ahh, I see. Got burned by it?"

I huffed. "You could say that."

"What was his name?"

"I said I was interested in your backstory, not that I wanted to share my own."

"It's only fair." Amusement danced in his eyes as his gaze searched my face.

I looked around, watching my breath fog the air, considering if I wanted to share that deeply wounded part of myself with an almost perfect stranger, when I had hardly spoken of it with anyone but Alex. I made up my mind. "Garrett," I said.

"He sounds like a tool."

His comment helped relieve the heaviness around that memory and I started to laugh. A smile broke out on Sawyer's face, and he joined in, the two of us laughing like perfect imbeciles in the frosty night. "Thanks for that," I said.

"I do what I can. You should laugh more. I like the way it makes your eyes crinkle." He looked at me with that intensity again, rendering me immobile, unable to look away. No matter, I didn't want to.

"I'm going to do something now," he said. He turned,

taking my face in his hands, and before I had a chance to register what was happening, he planted his lips on mine. They were surprisingly soft, and though tentative at first, they enveloped my own with a commanding presence, like he really knew what he was doing. I wanted to analyze exactly why they seemed so experienced, how many other lips they'd done this with. But as soon as they surrounded mine, I melted into a pool of goo and rational thought was hard to come by. My heart quickened its pace, my stomach dropped out and then filled up with a tingling sensation that extended from my core to every other part of my body, infusing itself within the fibers of my very being until I was a limp noodle in his arms. He pulled me into him, deepening the kiss, and I relished the closeness, the intimacy in the way he held me. My wobbly arms reached up around his neck, and my hands played in the strands of his hair as we opened our mouths in unison, his tongue slipping inside, gliding around, exploring like a pioneer in a new land, engaging mine in a beautifully choreographed waltz.

He pulled away, and my knees literally buckled and my body started to fall. He caught me in his arms half-way to the ground and penetrated my gaze with his own blue pools. Both out of air, we said nothing, only looked at each other, mutually paralyzed by what had just passed between us.

The door squeaked open, and Sawyer shot upright, stabilizing me and then jumping to the railing, casually folding his hands and leaning over it as he had before.

Before *that*.

I cleared my throat and straightened my dress as my mother came outside. "There you are," she said. "What are you doing out here?"

"I needed some fresh air." My voice came out faint and breathy, as most of my oxygen had been stolen.

"Okay, well, the main course is served and most everyone is finished eating. Thought you might like a bite before it gets cleared away."

"Thanks, Mom. I'll be there in a sec."

She closed the door behind her and I turned to look at Sawyer, but he only stared blankly ahead, into the night. I waited as he ignored me. Growing impatient, I said, "Is that it, then?"

"What?"

"You're going to kiss me like that and then get all cagey again."

"I'm not being cagey. I wanted to see what it was like to kiss you, so I did."

"And?" I stomped one foot as I asked.

"And what?" Sawyer refused to look my way.

"What results did your experiment yield?"

"I liked it. Probably too much. And because of that, you should know, it won't happen again."

The heat I felt from that kiss was replaced by an angry fire. "You are impossible! You think because you've been hurt that you can run around and do whatever you like, say whatever you want to say and eff everyone else because, who cares, right? Well, guess what? You can't play with people. They— we—are impacted by how you act. Even the ones you're so injured over, they care about you. They lied to you for a reason. I'm not saying it was right, but they obviously thought it was better than the alternative. Maybe you should cut them some slack. Because until you do, you're going to run through life detached and miserable. And that's exactly what you are, miserable. And best kiss of my life or not, you're not taking me down with you!"

I stormed off the balcony, slamming the door behind me. My appetite was gone, so I told my mom I wasn't feeling well, asked for her car keys, and left. Instead of going home, I drove straight to Alex's apartment. Derek's car was there, but I pounded on the door until Alex pulled it open, rubbing her arms as the cold outside air hit them. "Bekah, what are you doing here?" She looked behind her and then back at me. I was clearly interrupting her ongoing reunion with Derek, but I didn't care. Not this time.

"I need to come in." I pushed past her to find Derek on her couch, lounging in sweats with the TV on. "Hi Derek."

"Hey there Bek. How are ya?" He hopped up and pulled me into a ginormous bear hug, squeezing the air from my lungs.

"Good, I'm good. Can't. Breathe," I said on a gasp.

"Sorry, it's been too long, and I haven't been able to hug you since that dillhole broke your heart."

"Yes, well, I'm here to talk about another dillhole."

Alex gave me a stern look, like I was her child. "Tell me you didn't."

"What?"

"Don't 'what' me. You totally made out with Sawyer, didn't you?"

"No! Okay, kind of." I dropped my head so I didn't have to look at her rebuking expression.

"Rebekah Jean!"

"Want me to say it? I'll say it. You were right. He acts all injured like a little lamb, and, in his defense I guess he is, but he uses it as an excuse to do whatever he wants, taking everyone out in the wake of his own pain."

"I told you. I told you to stay away from him."

"I know. It's just—he pulled me in with his pledge to honesty and his stupid life story."

"Sweetie, I know you love the idea of rescuing all those injured souls out there, but at some point you have to start donning some protective gear. Guys like him, like Garrett, they are a dime a dozen and they will hurt you over and over."

"Garrett is in a league of his own."

"Maybe, but I don't think so. He's not the first guy who cheated with multiple women at the same time while picking out an engagement ring. He's not the only unfaithful jerk out there."

"At least Sawyer says it like it is. I think."

"But you don't know, and you're better off sticking to your studies and then looking for love, just like you planned."

I gave her a hug. I didn't want to cry but somehow the coolness with which Sawyer treated me after kissing me like it was his job brought back all the pain of finding out Garrett's true colors, and those colors ran so deep that not even Alex had the whole story. Tears fell, and my best friend held me until they stopped.

"Okay, we're going to forget about the men in your life

who have hurt you and watch funny movies now. I'll start the popcorn!" She pushed me down onto the couch and ran off to her kitchen to make good on snack prep.

Two movies and three bowls of popcorn later, I felt much better. I thanked Derek and Alex for letting me interrupt their reunion and went home, exhausted and a little less injured, but that kiss lingered still in my mind, refusing to be forgotten.

Chapter Four

When I pulled into my parents' driveway, a dark figure stood on the porch. As I climbed out of my car, he approached me. Sawyer had traded his short sleeves and vest for a hoodie underneath his leather jacket. A cigarette was perched in the usual spot behind his ear.

"What are you doing here?" I asked, the cold in my voice impossible to conceal.

"I came to apologize."

More thunder in my chest. Was he sorry he kissed me? That would explain his strange turnaround earlier. "Oh, is this a first time thing for you?"

"When I apologize I really mean it."

I stepped onto the porch. "Let me have it."

"I'm sorry I kissed you."

His apology sent my heart into my stomach, forcing me to acknowledge how much I didn't want him to be sorry about that at all. But it was anger that bubbled over. "Whatever, I can tell you're out of practice. You suck at apologies." I shook my head and dug around inside my purse for the house key.

Sawyer grabbed my arm. "I don't regret kissing you. After all, it was the best kiss of your life."

"You are something else. Get your hands off me."

"I'm doing this wrong." He forked a hand through his hair and then crossed his arms, leaning back against the house. "Look, that kiss was amazing. Best of my life too, but I shouldn't have done that. I felt it in the moment so I did it, knowing full well it would lead nowhere. You're right—that wasn't fair to you. You've obviously been injured before. It's just..."

"Just what?" I forced my gaze to meet his and regretted it immediately. His eyes were too beautiful, too difficult to stare into. Too...sincere? No, it had to be something else I saw swirling there. I connected with it before, but sincerity in a man was difficult, if not impossible to come by. Garrett taught me that.

"Well, we're both adults. I thought we could handle a

kiss."

"It's handled. Are you done?"

He shifted his weight. "Thing is, it wasn't just a kiss, and I can't stop thinking about it."

"Well, try, because like you said, it's going nowhere." My hand emerged from the bowels of my purse, its fishing expedition done, and I plunged the retrieved key into the keyhole and turned the lock. Aloof, unaffected, that's what I had to be.

"You're right about something else, too."

"What?" I turned back toward him, my hand poised on the doorknob.

"I don't apologize often. I try really hard not to do things I'll end up needing to apologize for, and I didn't expect this to be one of them. I didn't expect that from a kiss."

"Expect what?"

"The intensity, the fire, the butterflies. They were all there. It was magical, really, and it caught me off guard. I'm sorry for how I acted, but I didn't know what to do with it because even though I kissed you, it surprised me."

My insides squirmed, my heartbeat quickened. "It surprised me too, but I don't accept your apology. Not for kissing me. I do, however, forgive you for handling it totally wrong. Now, goodnight." I pushed the door open and went inside, leaning against it as I closed it. I squeezed my eyes shut and put my palm to the door, as if I could feel Sawyer through it. I wanted to feel him, experience his kiss again, especially now that I knew it struck him with lightning, just as it had me. But I couldn't. I was glad he cleared the air, but that was not a road I could travel. It was unpaved and dangerous, and my heart wouldn't be able to withstand the bumps it promised.

After a couple of minutes of standing there, I chanced a look through the peephole. Sawyer remained, leaning up against the house. With one final long look at the door, he kicked off the side of the house and began walking down the driveway.

I don't know what it was—whether it was the Christmas spirit, the way the moonlight made his unruly hair look extra shiny, or my inevitable gluttony for punishment, but I pulled the door open, and called after him. "Want some coffee?"

We sat in the kitchen, two cups of coffee and silence between us, while my parents lay in bed upstairs, long asleep by now. Sawyer tapped the side of his mug with rhythmic movements. I watched his fingers, and all I could think about was how they felt on my face. They were long and slender, and I wondered how it would feel to interlock my own fingers with them. Or better yet, to have those hands on me. I shook my head, trying to empty it of those thoughts.

"What's wrong?" he asked.

"Nothing. Tell me more about this." I grazed my finger along his arm. He'd removed both his jacket and sweatshirt leaving only a t-shirt and exposing his tattooed arm.

He rolled his sleeve up to his shoulder, the definition of his arm in clear view, and my stupid heart seemed to feel the need to tell me how much I liked the look of it. He started at the top, where a Celtic cross spread over his shoulder. At the foot of it, there was a baby. "This," he said, "is me."

"You're Jesus?"

He elbowed me. "No, I liked the cross, and I had it first. It was a reminder of all I thought my life stood for. But this," he pointed to the next tattoo. It looked like some kind of syringe or needle and what appeared to be blood squirted from it, landing in a pool of someone's tears. "This represents my true beginning. Really, there should be lots wrong with me. As the story goes, my mom did a lot of drugs while she was pregnant with me, and for the first year of my life."

I traced the cross, the baby, and the needle with my finger and then looked up into Sawyer's eyes. His gaze darted to my lips and back up again, and then he broke eye contact as he cleared his throat. "This represents what I thought my life was built on." A church building served as the backdrop for the next tattoo. In front of it was a heart with two hands around it, interlocking fingers. Next was a caduceus, the medical symbol, and next to it, a smashed up motorcycle.

"Is that when you were studying to become a doctor?" I teased.

But Sawyer didn't share my jest. Instead, his eyebrows drew together. "No, that represents my accident. When everything changed."

I traced the bike with my finger, my heart reacting in a completely different way. "What happened?"

"Motorcycle versus SUV. The SUV won. It's a wonder I pulled through at all, but I did. I needed extensive surgeries and blood transfusions. Can't do all that without a family medical history."

"Wow." I shook my head. "That had to be horrifying."

"Not the best time of my life." He watched his own thumbs twiddle.

The last picture was the same as the one above, the heart with interlocking fingers. Only now the fingers pulled apart, the heart broken in half. I didn't have to ask. But it was below that one where his arm was completely blank. "What's this about? Why does it stop short here?" My fingers on his arm again sent chills through me, and goose bumps sprang up on his skin.

"The rest is unwritten. A blank slate."

"Hmm. I like that." I traced the dividing line between the unmarked skin and the tattoos. Sawyer sat up, and I drew my hand back, embarrassed by how freely I was touching him.

"Your turn. Tell me about that tool, Garrett."

I wasn't prepared for this sudden switch of topics. "He was just some jerk."

"So, tell me about him. I showed you mine, now you show me yours."

That loosened me up again, and a laugh escaped. "Okay, I guess that's only fair, though I don't have any cool artwork to go along with my story. I met Garrett my freshman year of college. He was in his final semester, working as a TA. He had this great story—a victim of so much hardship. It was as if he saw my do-gooding nature, and fashioned a story to speak to it. It was instant chemistry between us, and as soon as we started talking we started dating. That lasted until last fall."

"And what happened last fall?"

"At that point we were talking about marriage, looking at rings even. And then one night, when he left me at my dorm, I had this unsettled feeling. So, I followed him. You have to know, that's so unlike me, but he was acting strange. I followed him to his apartment, and when I got there, I saw him making out with someone at the door. Right after he left me."

"That's terrible."

"Yeah, well that's the tip of the iceberg, my friend. The apartment was just a front."

"What?"

"I found out that Garrett was married. He had been for two years of our relationship, which means he got married after we'd been together for a year. I remember it well. He had to go away for two weeks on a trip for his new job. Some training thingy. Turns out in the end, I was one of two girlfriends. The other, the one he was making out with, had only been around for a few months. She came along about the time we started talking about rings. His whole life story was completely false, made up. Like, none of it was true, other than his first name."

"He even gave you a fake last name?"

"Yep. I was humiliated. In fact, you are the only one who knows the whole story. To everyone else, he cheated with more than one woman while choosing an engagement ring for me. The end."

"Not even your loud friend knows?"

"Not even Alex."

"Guess I should feel honored."

"It's your reward for giving me the best kiss of my life." I raised my eyebrows.

"Aaaand, the only one since Garrett."

"What?" Sawyer's face broke into a giant grin. "You haven't kissed anyone in over a year?"

"Not a single one."

His smile transitioned into gritted teeth, guilt reaching his eyes. "I'm really sorry. Had I known, I would have held on to my curiosity and left you alone. I just—you looked so beautiful and I made you laugh—it was a moment."

"I told you outside, and I meant it. I'm not sorry." I forced my gaze to hold his, and this time I didn't regret it.

"And hey, it's not your fault, you know. You were an eighteen-year-old girl. He took advantage. The guy's a predator."

"I would have never been with a married man. I feel terrible about this—like I don't know what to do with the guilt. But as much as that, I feel so stupid. I was such an idiot to not see through him." A tear fell, and that served only to fuel my anger. I swiped it, and Sawyer caught my hand.

"No. Don't let yourself feel that for a minute more. You're not stupid; you're a victim. You did nothing wrong."

I shrugged in response as I fought for composure and watched Sawyer's fingers caress mine.

"Tell me something," he said. "You mentioned second chances and believing in them. How can you still, with what you went through with him?"

"I don't know. That's a fair question. I just do. I guess some people aren't deserving of them. But others, like your parents, might be. Consider what a miracle you are—the odds that you're even alive. You're a walking second chance."

He drew his hand back. "I'm not ready for that."

"That's okay. If you're going to forgive them, it has to be something you're really ready for. Otherwise, nothing will change."

"And have you forgiven him?" The question held a challenge.

"I'm working on it."

Sawyer stretched, and I couldn't help but notice how his shirt clung to his muscles. That revelation did nothing to stave off my attraction, but I shoved it down. He stood and said, "It's four a.m. I really should be going now."

"Wow, time got away. I'll walk you to the door."

I made good on my promise, and when we reached the front door, Sawyer stopped, opening his mouth and then promptly closing it, his gaze searching the air. I waited, begging inside my head for him to say something that would extend our time together or promise there would be more in the future. But I knew that wasn't what was going to leave his lips by the way he looked at me. His gaze lingered on face. My own pleaded for an invitation, but that plea went unanswered.

"Well," he said, searching my eyes, studying my lips. The word hung in the air.

Do it. Please kiss me again.

Nothing.

"I accept your apology, for all of it," I conceded. "Thanks for the talk."

"You're welcome. You know, you're really the only one to ask for my story. Everyone else around here just assumes I'm a bad person, so thanks for that. Have a Merry Christmas." With that, he turned to go, walking away from me down the snow-bordered path and into the night.

A strange sadness came over me, like I was losing something. But he wasn't mine to lose, nor was I in any condition to have him, or anyone else for that matter. Besides the fact that it would never work, even with the physical chemistry, I didn't know if my heart was ready yet. I'd known him for two days. Two days filled with a host of insults, a fiery kiss, and a genuine conversation. At the end of it, I was left feeling stripped and vulnerable before him. The short time I'd known him spun me like a dangerous whirlwind, but somehow even in its perilous path, it felt safe to me.

He felt safe.

Chapter Five

"Dude, get up!" Alex shook me violently, and I pulled the covers further over my head. "It's 1:30 in the afternoon. Christmas Eve. You're not allowed to sleep this late on such a day!"

I groaned, peeking out from under the blanket.

"I'm worried about you. Your mom is too. We've been talking about it downstairs."

"Great," I said, pushing myself into a seated position.

"She thinks you're depressed. Says you've been sleeping a lot. And I've barely seen you the last three weeks. What gives?"

I stretched, hazy-minded and unsure if I wanted to talk about this now. If my mom was wrong before, she wasn't far off the mark this time. "I don't know," I said, dropping my arms like they were lead.

"Tell me," Alex whined, and then she rolled her eyes. "This is all my fault. I have been so wrapped up in Derek, I haven't checked on you much."

"Nothing's your fault. Truth is, I don't know what I'm thinking or feeling, but I can't shake the blues. Ever since Sawyer came over after the Christmas party that night and we talked for most of it, I can't stop thinking about him. I don't think he's the bad guy he pretends to be."

"Have you seen him at all?"

"Not once. And we never exchanged numbers, though neither of us would be too hard to track down, but that's looking like a bleak possibility considering it's been three weeks. I have to face the fact that my infatuation isn't mutual. That kiss was truly a one-time thing. But somehow the realization of my rejection has brought back all those feelings of stupidity and loss and guilt from my relationship with Garrett."

"What do you have to feel guilty about?"

I looked at my best friend and was reminded that Sawyer was the only one to whom I had told the whole truth. And I didn't have another confession in me, even for my best friend.

"Maybe that's why it feels so raw. I told him everything, and I haven't spoken about it since it happened."

"Yeah, you probably just reopened the wound is all. What is it about him? Why does Sawyer get under your skin?"

"I don't know, exactly. Part of it was the kiss. It was..." I searched the air, as if somehow the right word would materialize. "...magical. Unlike anything I've ever experienced, even with Garrett. But besides that, there's a candor about him, something so real. And he's probably the first person I've ever met who is as wounded as I am. It's like...it's like we have this kinship over that, somehow."

"You've got it bad."

"Yep, unrequited affection is awesome."

"Once you get back into your routine, it'll all be okay."

"Just have to power through another week, and then it's back to school, and I can put this all behind me. I can't believe I'm looking forward to going back. Every inch of that place holds reminders of Garrett, and I was so eager to get home. Now, I just want to run away again."

"Come on, let's get you up, coffeed and showered, and you'll feel better. We have the Christmas Eve service to get ready for. Don't forget to bring your gift for our annual exchange!"

"I would never forget such a thing."

"Okay, I've got the coffee brewing for you downstairs. Go get yourself a cup and I'll see you tonight. Love you!" She was out the door before I could respond. For the first time in forever I wasn't feeling the Christmas Eve service. I had always loved the yearly tradition and was excited to exchange gifts with Alex, but I could take or leave the rest of it.

Nevertheless, at my best friend's coaxing I got myself around, but my glum mood persisted. The past few weeks had gone by in a blur, and I was half-mad at myself for allowing it to happen. The other half of me was numb. All this time I'd worked so hard to get over Garrett and now, two days was all it took to get hung up on another man. Here I was, three weeks later and still unable to shake him, even if I wanted to.

The church was abuzz with merry Christmas church-go-ers. I did my best to smile and exchange pleasantries with everyone there, but I was distracted, looking for Sawyer. I didn't see him, despite my constant crowd-scanning. I gave up, my disappointment souring my mood further, as I prepared to take my seat. The usher handed me one of those little candles on cardboard for the end of the service a capella rendering of "Silent Night" and candle lighting ceremony. I had long kept to myself how unsafe I thought the whole ordeal was, in favor of its beauty and serenity. Pushing my skirt beneath me as I took my seat, I looked up just in time to see Alex and Derek run-ning down the aisle to me, my best friend holding a beautifully wrapped box.

"Here!" She thrust it at me, her cheeks pink, her eyes bright with mischief and joy, her blond hair a little frazzled. She sat down in the pew next to me, out of breath.

"Have you two been—" I pointed my finger between her and Derek suspiciously.

"No, no. I almost forgot your gift and had to run and get it. Open it."

"That's sweet, Al, but we can wait until after the service."

"No. You have to open it now. And scoot, we're sitting with you."

The music began to play, the lone piano drumming out the melody of "Joy To The World." Alex motioned for me to open the gift with a silent gesture while Derek beamed. I pulled the ribbon and unwrapped the paper with careful attention to keeping it quiet. Within the illustrious wrapping I found a box of tissue. Unopened. I held it forward, my face contorted into a confused frown, my shoulders lifting in a shrug.

Alex nodded, a grin spreading until it consumed her face, and then she gave her attention to my dad, who now took his place at the front to read a scripture. Her gift was odd, but then Alex was known for giving me things that seemed meaningless but harbored a great deal of thought and sentiment. I would have to wait until after the service to ask her what it meant. I tucked the box next to my purse on the floor.

The service passed, like every other before it, its predictability in part filling me with reminiscence and warm fuzzies, the distraction from my longing heart welcome. As the service drew to a close, Alex tipped her candle into mine giving it light and raised her eyebrows at me. The light of our candles cast shadows on her face, but I could see her smile anyway. She was such a weirdo. We sang "Silent Night," blew out our candles, and I reached for my purse in preparation to leave.

"This year," said my father, "we're going to end our Christmas Eve service differently. Please have a seat. I have asked two people to speak about how they've personally experienced hope and restoration leading up to this holiday season. First, Susan, please come tell us about how your heart has filled with hope."

Susan McCleary approached the platform, taking the microphone from my dad and launching into a five-minute exposition of her hope while battling breast cancer. Hers was a happy ending—an all clear, just a week before Christmas. I applauded with the rest of them and, touched by her story though I was, I was also eager to get home and sip some cocoa by the fire in my PJs.

"And to end our service tonight, I've asked Sawyer Matthews to talk with us about restoration. Son."

My breathing and heart stopped in unison as Sawyer approached the front. He was here, and three weeks had done nothing to dull my attraction. He was stunning tonight. His scruff was a full-fledged but very neat beard, his hair combed out of his face. He still wore his leather jacket, atop a button-down shirt and his dark, crisp jeans were absent of their usual wear and tear. I wasn't aware I had taken Alex's hand until she squeezed mine.

Sawyer cleared his throat. "Evening. Not many of you know me very well, but I grew up with Pastor Mark and Judy. I knew them as my parents until about three years ago. That's when I found out they had adopted me from pretty horrible circumstances." He paused, clearing his throat again. "Well, when I found this out, I was angry with them. Livid. I was so overcome by my own rage, I didn't stop to consider the choices they had to make, the sacrifices taking me on as their own required. This went on until almost a month ago. For me there was no other option than to distance myself from them, to do everything they wouldn't want me to."

His gaze found mine across the sanctuary. "But then I met someone. This person had had her teeth kicked in too, but in a different way. Except she, unlike me, had hope for people. Hope they could change, faith in second chances. Despite how life had chewed her up and spit her out, she hung on."

Mist formed in my eyes, and Alex was already on point, placing the gifted box of tissue in my lap.

"And I got to thinking," he said, his gaze fixed on me. "It's funny how differently people respond to hurt. My hurt shut me down, caused me to give up on people. Hers fortified her belief in changing them, even if she couldn't change the one who hurt her. And if she could do it, if she could get beyond her pain and move on, still believing, why couldn't I? I was inspired. It took me some time, but I worked up the courage to approach my aunt and uncle—my parents—and have an honest conversation with them, something I avoided for three years. And though we have a long way to go, we're on our way to being restored. So, this Christmas, I am thankful. Because without that chance encounter with the second chance girl, I never would have stepped foot on this road."

The congregation clapped and there was a collective gathering of belongings, but I froze in my seat. As I sat there clutching the lone tissue I'd dabbed my eyes with, the Christmas Eve crowd filed out. Sawyer's gaze was never far from mine as he made his way to me, stopping every few steps for a handshake and words of affirmation. When he reached me, we were alone except for a few stragglers. I stood as he approached the aisle, and he didn't slow his pace until his arms were wrapped around me and he was tipping me back. His lips found mine and this time there was nothing tentative about the way he kissed me. It was hungry, the kiss of a man who knows what he wants. I kissed him back with the realization that it was me. He wanted me, and heartbreak and all, I wanted him back. He stood me up and pulled back, both of us holding on to the other for balance, both of us out of breath.

"Full disclosure," he said. "I was a good kid, like really good. Straight A-'s, focused on school, one girlfriend in high school. Since then I've dated around but nothing stuck. I did a year of college, to get my feet wet, and that's when the accident occurred. After that, I didn't know what I wanted.

"When I found out I was adopted, I did the most rebellious thing I could think of and went out and bought a pack of cigarettes. I gasped through the first few but stuck with it until I could smoke them with ease. Next was alcohol. It was easier to drink than think about how confusing everything was. I was drunk the night I broke into the hospital—I think I told you that."

I nodded, my eyes filling with more tears.

"I tried my hand at stealing, but I didn't develop a taste for it. I did some pretty heavy partying but didn't get into drugs too much, though I did experiment some. They're not for me. And now I'm ready to get back on track. Some of those habits are going to stick, they just are. What you see is what you get with me. I can't promise I won't hurt you, but I do promise to never lie to you. I'm sorry I haven't spoken to you since that night. I couldn't. I knew if I saw you again, I wouldn't be able to stop myself from kissing you, and I had to figure this all out first. And I know we just met, but I also know that since that night I can't stop thinking about you, and I don't want to.

"Rebekah," Sawyer held my hands and pulled me close, steadily watching me. "I know you're going back to finish up school, but I want to make a go of this. I want to be the one to help you move beyond your pain, just like you've helped me get started moving beyond mine. So, I ask you, will you fulfill my one Christmas wish? Will you allow me to be your second chance?"

I searched his eyes, my heart pounding like I'd just run a marathon. All I found in them was what had been there all along: sincerity.

Tipping my face to his, I laid a soft kiss on his lips. "Yes."

Could it really be that two wayward, injured souls found each other in the mire of pain and mistrust? There was no way I wasn't going to find out.

Stay with Me

by Allison Winfield

This book is dedicated to my husband. Love you.

Chapter One

What an asshole.

First, he showed up fifteen minutes late to pick me up for dinner, and then, I had to pay for our meal. I'm sure he forgot his wallet on purpose. Why do I always go out with jerks like him?

As I stormed out of the restaurant, I realized that I was stuck downtown, in the middle of December, without a ride. Shit! Luckily my cell phone went off. It was a text from Ryan from work.

Are you really not coming to the Christmas party, Scrooge? It's fun!

Well, The Crazy Coffee Bean was just down the street from the restaurant and Ryan or somebody would probably give me a ride home. What the hell. I could pretend to like Christmas and other people for twenty minutes.

As I walked in the door, I swear every head turned to me in shock. What? Just because I never went to work functions didn't mean they had to look so surprised. Hmm. Or maybe it was because my dress was a little on the revealing side. Dammit. Ryan walked up and handed me a plastic glass of wine.

"I didn't think you'd show up. It was my witty text, huh, Quinn?"

"No. I was in the neighborhood."

"Right," he said with a laugh. "Come on. I staked out the couch by the fireplace and I know you won't want to talk to anybody else, so we can be anti-social together."

"I'm not anti-social." But as I said it, I thought about it. In the two years I had worked at The Crazy Coffee Bean, this was my first time at a work party. I didn't go out after work with anyone, and besides Ryan, I didn't really know much about my coworkers. And I only knew Ryan because he wouldn't leave me alone. He was like a puppy that wouldn't stop following me around. And truth be told, he was a very cute puppy.

Tonight, he was dressed in a hunter green Henley shirt

that made his eyes sparkle and a pair of sexy, faded jeans. He was one of the lucky guys that never had to worry about styling his hair. It always looked great; the kind of hair that causes every woman over eighteen to want to run her fingers through it.

"So why did you come? You obviously weren't coming here in that dress. And I text you and invite you places at least once a week and you never show up," Ryan said, bringing me back to reality.

"What's wrong with my dress?"

"Nothing. You look amazing in it. But it isn't a Christmas-party-at-work dress. It's an I'm-looking-for-a-man dress. Were you on a date?"

So I told him all about my shitty date and the fact that I only came so I could find a ride home.

"First off, you know you could have called me and I would've picked you up, right? And second, the reason all your dates end up shitty, is because you date shitty guys. You pick guys who don't want a relationship and only want a friend with benefits. You need to set your standards a lot higher."

"Fuck you. It's not like that at all. Although I don't want a relationship, my standards are high enough. Besides, I thought you were in school to be a medical doctor, not a shrink."

"Touché."

Three glasses of wine later, I was pretty drunk. I stumbled off to the bathroom and locked myself in a stall. A minute later, I heard someone walk in. Actually, two someones.

"Why does he hang out with her? He's gorgeous and smart. She's a slut who won't give him the time of day no matter how much he begs."

"I know. He has no taste in women. Or maybe he just needs to get laid. I mean look at her dress. She obviously puts out." They giggled as they left the bathroom a short time later.

I managed not to cry as I listened to them. Why *did* Ryan like me? Did he want to sleep with me? For the first time in years, Eric popped into my head. He was my first actual boyfriend in high school. He was sweet and caring. Telling me he loved me, I fell for every lie: hook, line, and sinker. After taking my virginity, he took off.

I staggered out of the bathroom and back into the front room. Ryan walked over to steady me with a hand on my arm.

"What's wrong? Are you ready to go?"

"Yeah. I'm a little tipsy and tired."

He led me outside and guided me into his Toyota Prius. We were quiet on the way to my apartment; both of us lost in our own thoughts. I wouldn't let another guy take advantage of me. If he wanted to have sex, that was fine but there wasn't any need to act like a nice guy. I'd come on to him and then maybe he'd leave me alone.

After he parked in front of my building, he rushed around to open my door.

"I'll make sure you get in safely."

"Okay. Thanks."

He even waited while I dug my keys out of my bag and unlocked my apartment. Turning back to him I said, "Thanks for driving me home."

"You're welcome. I told you, you can call me whenever you need—" His sentence was interrupted when I kissed him. Shock had him frozen for a moment, but he recovered and started kissing me back.

Grabbing the front of his shirt, I pushed the door open and pulled him in after me. We continued kissing as we bumped our way down the hall and into my bedroom. I pushed him onto my bed and shut and locked the door. Twirling around, I untied the neck of my halter dress, letting it fall to the floor. All I wore underneath was a pair of black, lacy panties. Walking towards the bed where Ryan now sat on the edge, I reached out to take off his shirt. He caught both of my hands in his.

"Q, I like you. But I don't want to have sex with you when I know you're definitely drunk."

"So you don't hang out with me just to hook up?"

"What? Why would you think that? I hang out with you because I like you. I like, like you. Why do you think I invite you out all the time? I want to show you that if you date a good guy, your dates will be much better than if you stay with the shitty ones."

"I heard some girls talking about us in the bathroom. They said you need to get laid."

He eyes twinkled. "I like you. You know that. If I was just after sex, would I have waited two years? Go out with me Friday. Please?"

He looked so sweet and earnest that even in my drunken state, I couldn't find the words to turn him down.

"Okay. I'll go out with you on Friday just to get you to stop asking me. But I want you to know that I'm not looking for Prince Charming."

"That's fine with me since I'm not royalty."

I pulled on a pair of yoga pants and an old t-shirt. I walked him to the door where he kissed me on my forehead and left.

I woke up with the worst headache in the history of hangovers. I groped on the end table hoping to find a stale glass of water. Instead I found a bottle of Tylenol, a bottle of water that was still cool, and a note.

Hope you don't feel too terrible. See you Friday. Ryan

Aww. I guess there was an advantage to dating a nice guy. I swallowed two Tylenol and drank the bottle of water. Twenty minutes later, I felt good enough to stumble to the kitchen and chat with my roommate, Samantha, before she headed to work. Thank God I was off today.

"What time is it, Sam?" I asked as I dropped into a chair at the kitchen table.

"It's 9:15. You're up early, especially since you came in pretty late last night."

"I couldn't sleep. Did we wake you?"

"No, but I went to bed around midnight and you weren't home yet. Who's the other half of that we?"

"Well my date was the worst and I ended up without a ride. So I headed to the work Christmas party and Ryan drove me home."

"You could have called me to come get you. What are roommates for? So you hooked up with Ryan? He's gorgeous."

"No. That's the weird thing. I started kissing him and dragged him into my room and he told me that he didn't want to hookup while I was drunk. He asked me out on a date."

"Oh my God! That's great. He's sweet and smart and way better than most of the guys you date."

"Who cares what kind of guys I date? I don't plan on marrying any of them. I'm only looking for a good time."

"Well if you do decide to settle down, Ryan would be a good place to start. I have to get to work. See you later."

Since I was home alone and had no plans, I decided to climb back into bed. I grabbed my phone out of my purse and saw that Ryan had texted me.

Good Morning Beautiful.

God, this guy won't give up, will he?

I texted him back.

I'm not beautiful. You don't have to leave me notes and texts. I didn't change my mind about going out with you on Friday since last night.

His response was almost immediate.

You ARE beautiful. I wasn't worried you had changed your mind. I was checking in to be nice. Get used to it.

Thanks. Shouldn't you be working?

I'm @ work.

Well as your boss, I have to tell you that you're not supposed to be on your phone.

Sorry Boss. I can't help it. Besides you're only the assistant manager.

I'm serious. Get back to work. Bye.

Bye.

Chapter Two

The week passed in a blur of work and boredom. Friday, I worked eight to four, but at noon I went to hide in the office, using the excuse of placing the order for supplies we needed. I had been dropping stuff all day and was totally distracted. I knew exactly who to blame: Ryan.

He had been sweet all week: texting me once or twice a day, leaving a latte ready for me to drink when I showed up at work. And now, all I could think about was our date tonight. He refused to tell me where we were going, insisting it was a surprise. I wanted to look great, but at the same time I worried about dressing inappropriately for whatever he intended for us to do. Ryan deserved a good girl, not someone like me, but I could pretend for his sake for one night.

After I got home from work, I decided to take a bubble bath. It helped me relax and I lay in the hot water thinking about where Ryan might be taking me. When I finally emerged from the steamy bathroom, it was 5:30 and Ryan was supposed to pick me up at 6:30.

After wasting twenty minutes searching my own closet, I decided that the perfect outfit was hiding in Samantha's closet. After a quick perusal, I decided on a wrap dress with a cute sweater and heels. Thank God we lived in San Diego and didn't have to deal with real winters.

I left my brunette hair down since I liked the way it was slightly wavy. I was finishing up my makeup when the doorbell rang. As I put my heels on, I looked at the clock. It was only 6:20. Was Ryan early?

I opened the door to find Ryan and a bouquet of the most beautiful flowers I had ever seen. They were bright and colorful and looked more like a wildflower bouquet than one he would have purchased at a flower shop.

"Thanks. These flowers are beautiful."

"You're welcome. Every beautiful woman deserves beautiful flowers."

I gave him a smile as I went to find a vase to put the flowers in. Once we were in the car I asked him again where we were going.

"Dinner and a concert. Sound good?"

"Sure. What concert is it? Am I dressed okay?"

"You're dressed perfectly. It's at a small bar downtown, The Spot? The performer's name is Jameson Brax. Have you heard of him?"

"I love The Spot. I watched Alicia Keys perform there a few years ago. I haven't heard of him. Is he a singer? What genre of music is it?"

"He sings and writes his own songs. I guess it's a combination of pop, R&B, and a little soul. His first album is called Without You. The album is kind of sad and about longing and unrequited love."

"That sounds interesting. Where are we going to dinner?"

"I was thinking that tapas restaurant that just opened? Or we could do Italian?"

"Tapas sound great."

Once we were seated, we decided on some tapas to share. Over our sangria, I tried to get to know Ryan a little better.

"So you're in med school? Should I start calling you Dr. Collins?" I asked.

"I'm not in med school yet. I've sent in applications for early admission to a couple of schools. If I get in, I'll start in June."

"What schools?"

"Well, I love San Diego, so I applied to UCSD and then as a huge long shot, I applied to Johns Hopkins."

"Hope you like snow. You'll freeze to death if you have to move to Baltimore."

"You've never even seen snow so how would you have any idea what winter would be like?" he said and then stuck out his tongue.

"How do you know that?" I asked.

"You told us when Zach went on vacation, what? Two winters ago? To Colorado?"

"That's right. I would love to see snow but I don't think I could ever move out of California."

"You've always lived here?"

I nodded.

"Do your parents still live here?" he asked.

"I never met my Dad. Mom couldn't exactly narrow it down. I don't even know where she is now. She left with her then boyfriend when I was seventeen," I said.

"And you haven't heard from her in what? Almost five years?"

"Yeah. Her boyfriends were more important to her than me, so fuck her."

"I'm sorry. That's shitty."

"What about you? Your parents still live here?"

"Yep. My parents still own the house I grew up in. My brother and sister are both older. They're married with kids," he said.

"Everything you want one day, huh?"

"Of course. How could you not?"

"Well I've never had a loving family to inspire me. I got nothing but abuse."

"Abuse?"

"Yeah, a couple of mom's boyfriends used to like to hit me with a belt. And one of Mom's boyfriends came in my room when I was almost fifteen. He tried to put his hand down my pants and I started screaming. I told my mom what he was doing, but she believed him when he told her he had come in my room because he heard me having a nightmare. The next night when he came in my room, I had a knife. I told him I would stab him if he ever came in my room again. Evidently, I convinced him 'cause he never tried anything again. Granted, he did dump my mom a few months later."

"Jesus. I don't know what to say," he said, running his hand through his hair.

"You don't have to say anything. It is what it is. Some of us don't deserve happy endings."

"Or maybe you deserve one even more because of all that crap."

I cocked my eyebrow.

"I think you deserve the happiest of endings. You're smart, fun, and beautiful. Sometimes the hardest thing to see is what's right in front of you."

I blushed but was saved from answering when the waitress brought us our food. The rest of dinner was full of wine, great food, and interesting conversation.

Ryan grabbed my hand as we walked into The Spot. It looked like a typical dive bar, but they managed to entice lots of up and coming acts to play there.

I picked out a table while Ryan went up to the bar to get us a couple of drinks. He found me sitting at the table, to the right of the stage, as the lights began to dim.

As he handed me my beer, he commented, "This looks nice and cozy,"

"I figured this was as private as it gets."

The next couple of hours flew by. Once Jameson Brax sat down at the piano, everyone went silent as he drew us in with his melancholy melodies and haunting lyrics. His emotions and wanting were so strong that I found myself tearing up during two different songs. It was as if he knew me and the way I viewed life. One song was about Jameson needing someone to stay with him, so that, even for one night, he wouldn't have to be alone. He played some of the songs on his album, some covers of some famous songs, and even a few Christmas carols. But no matter what the song was, you could hear his pain and longing just below the surface. His songs made me think that while Ryan and I would never work in the long run, maybe I should try for a little while.

When the show was over, we decided to head back to my apartment to hang out and watch a movie.

"What did you think of the show?" Ryan asked as we drove back to my place.

"I loved it. He's an amazing singer."

"I'm glad you liked it. I was worried that it might be a little depressing, especially for a first date. But I also wanted to take you to see him. I knew you'd like it."

"Actually, instead of being depressed, I feel a little hopeful. Who knows what the future holds?"

"That's the theme of his album. That even though right now may suck, and he's lonely, he knows that someday everything will work out."

After debating the merits of my DVD collection, we decided on *Anchorman* as our movie of choice. Before we started the movie I ran to my bedroom and ditched the wrap dress and push up bra, in favor of a t-shirt and pajama pants. I pulled my long hair up in a messy bun. Movie nights go hand in hand with comfy clothes. When I walked back into the living room, Ryan was sprawled on the couch with his shoes kicked off and a goofy little smile on his face.

"What?"

"Nothing. I love the Hello Kitty pants."

"They were a gag Christmas gift from my roommate last year."

"I think they're cute."

"I think it's cute that you know who Hello Kitty is," I said with a smirk.

I curled up on the couch and Ryan sat next to me, with his arm casually draped over my shoulder. We had watched about half the movie when I felt his gaze on me. I met his eyes.

"What?" I asked.

"I had a really great time tonight."

"Me too. I'm glad that I gave in to your dating demands."

He leaned down and kissed me softly on the lips. Then he went back to watching the movie, but all I could think about was that kiss. How could one little kiss have sparked my desire so much? And how could he calmly continue watching the movie?

I leaned over and laid my head on his chest. I wrapped my arm around his waist and gave him a small squeeze. His chin moved as he bent down to kiss the top of my head. I thought I was going to have to make the first move but his hand moved from my arm, down to the edge of my shirt, and underneath. He left it resting on my ribs for a minute before his hand rose higher and came up to cup my breast. He rubbed his thumb back and forth over my nipple, all the while pretending to be watching the movie.

Fine, if that's how he wanted it. Two could play that game. I lightly ran my nails up and down his thighs through his jeans. After a minute, I trailed them further up and crossed from one hip to the other and down the other leg. I was careful to avoid the growing bulge in his pants. This time when I made my circle, I let my knuckles brush against him as they went up and around. His heart started to race under my cheek. Neither of us was pretending to watch the movie anymore.

His hand snaked out from under my shirt, grabbed my bun, and tugged gently. My face turned up to his, accepting the kiss he brushed against my lips. Then he mashed his lips to mine and took my breath away. I opened my lips to try and catch my breath, but he took that as an invitation and slipped his tongue in my mouth. We kissed for a minute until he pulled back and started trailing kisses over my jaw and down my neck. Ryan reached down and pulled my shirt over my head and tossed it on the floor. Kissing, licking, and nibbling his way up my torso, I ran my fingers through his hair. As his mouth found my nipple, I gave his hair a gentle tug and ran my hands down his chest. I could feel the hard muscles of his chest and abs through his shirt. Continuing south, my hands found and worked to unbuckle his belt. I finally got it undone and freed from his jeans, when he suddenly stood up.

"Come on. Let's go into your room," he said, reaching out to help me off the couch. I turned off the movie and then we left the room. He followed me down the hall, tracing his finger over the tattoo on my shoulder blade.

"Do you have any other tattoos besides these butterflies?" he asked.

"I have a tattoo of my astrological sign on my ankle."

"Butterflies and your sign? Typical girl tattoos," he said with a snort.

"Do you have any tattoos?" I asked even though I already knew the answer. Good boys don't get tattoos. I pulled him into my room and closed the door.

"Nope. I'm saving my first one for someone or something extra special."

"I got the tattoo of the butterflies because I've always liked them since I was little. I liked how they changed from something small and ugly into beautiful creatures that could fly away from here. They were free."

He kissed my tattoo and wrapped his arms around me from behind. I leaned back and was thankful that he was here with me. His arms slid down and with them went my pajama pants.

"Okay. I think we need to even out the nakedness. I'm down to my thong and you only have your pants unbuttoned," I said as I started undoing the buttons on his shirt.

"I can see your point." Unzipping his pants, he kicked them off his ankles. I undid the last button and slid the shirt over his shoulders and down his arms. Flying through the air, his shirt crash landed onto my desk chair and I reached down to slide his underwear off. He picked me up and we both tumbled onto the bed.

"Slow down," he whispered against my neck. "I want to ravish you." He caressed my face and smoothed my hair back.

He took both my arms and pinned them above my head with his hand. He then went back to kissing my neck as his other hand drifted down my ribs and hips and lightly rubbed me through my panties. I wiggled my hips and tried to push against his hand, but it was already moving back up to my chest. He pinched and tugged on my nipples until I thought I would lose it.

"Ryan, I want you so bad. Please," I begged.

He leaned down and kissed me deeply, and then slid down my body and pulled my undies off. He grasped one of my legs and kissed a line from my ankle to my knee and from my knee to my thigh and higher to between my legs. When I was on the edge and couldn't tell his lips from his tongue from his fingers, I reached down and rubbed his head.

"I'm so ready. Please come here. I want you in me."

Sitting up, he looked down at me with his adorable smile. He pulled his underwear off while I handed him a condom I'd pulled out of the side table. After rolling it on, he returned to his spot on the bed.

He kissed me sweetly so I reached down and grabbed him. I ran my hand up and down his length and then around to cradle his balls. He groaned and spread my legs to enter me. I felt him hard and wanting as he slid into me. Ever the gentleman, he tried to take it slow and sensually but I couldn't stand the suspense. I reached around him and grabbed his ass. I wrapped my legs around his waist and moaned in his ear. His inhibitions finally overcome; he quickened the pace and pounded me with each thrust. I lifted my hips to meet him stroke for stroke.

I could tell he was close so I bit his earlobe and as he found his release, I followed a couple seconds later. Once he caught his breath, he rolled onto his side and slid his arms around me. As I lay cocooned in his embrace, I realized that for once, I did like cuddling. Or at least I did with Ryan.

Just as I was falling asleep, I felt Ryan get up from the bed. I rolled over and watched him pull on his shirt and look under the bed for his pants.

"What are you doing?" I asked.

"I'm going to head home. I doubt you're the kind of girl who wants to cuddle, and I don't want to press my luck," he said as he picked up his jeans.

"Umm." My voice was so shaky I could barely get the words out. "Will you stay with me?"

"You want me to stay?" He dropped his pants back on the floor.

"Yeah," I said as a stray tear fell from my eye. He was

sweet, kind, and gentle. Ryan was truly one of the nice guys and I wanted to stay with him and sleep next to him even if only for tonight. He pulled off his shirt and climbed back into bed.

He wrapped his arms around me and whispered, "Sweet dreams."

Chapter Three

I woke up early Saturday morning, bright sun streaming in through my window. I rolled over and untangled my limbs from Ryan's. Well, this relationship, or whatever you want to call it, was full of firsts. First time I enjoyed cuddling after sex, first time waking up next to a guy I'd had sex with. Hmm. Should I make him breakfast? He was such a sweet and caring guy that I wanted to do something nice for him. I grabbed my robe and threw it on as I tiptoed out of the room.

After I did a quick inventory of the pantry, I determined that the only breakfast foods I had were bagels and fruit. I sliced two bagels and put them in the toaster. While they browned, I made quick work of slicing some fruit: apples, a banana, pears, and a few strawberries. Arranging everything on a tray, I decided that it would have to do.

As I walked into my room, I noticed that Ryan was in the bathroom. I made my bed and set the tray on it. I was pulling on jeans and a t-shirt as Ryan came back.

"What's all this?"

"I hope you like bagels and fruit. I don't cook much. It was this or cereal."

"I think it's perfect. I love bagels."

After we ate, Ryan went home to get ready for his afternoon shift at work. But before he left, he made sure to set up another date. He said he would cook me dinner Tuesday night.

Samantha and I spent the rest of the day cleaning our apartment. We wrote out our grocery list so that she could go shopping while I was at work on Sunday.

"Maybe we should get some breakfast foods," I suggested. "You know like bacon and eggs?"

She gave me an odd look. "Sure, I can add that to the list."

I changed the subject so she wouldn't ask any questions about my sudden interest in breakfast.

"So when are you headed home for Christmas?"

"I leave a week from tomorrow. The twenty first. Are you sure you don't want to come with me? My parents love you and they already offered to let you stay."

"No I'll be fine here. I'll hang out and try not to miss you terribly."

"Very funny. You and Ryan will be so wrapped up in each other that you probably won't even notice I'm gone."

"We'll see," I said.

I had to open on Sunday, so my alarm went off at 3:45 a.m. I liked opening and getting to spend an hour by myself, but I hated getting up so early. I let myself into the shop and my phone beeped.

Good Morning Beautiful. I missed you last night.

Yeah right. You were at work and probably too busy to even think of me.

I'm thinking of you right now. I wish you were here in bed with me.

You should be sleeping not fantasizing. LOL But I miss you too.

HA! I knew it.

Go back to sleep. I'll see you at 2.

Work was crazy busy. The owners closed for the week of Christmas, so anyone who wanted cakes or cookies had to get their orders in early. I was dead on my feet when the next shift of workers came in to relieve us. Ryan brushed past me and whispered hi. I'm glad that he didn't try to kiss me in front of the other employees. They talk about me enough as it is. He gave me a little wave as I walked outside. As I approached my car, I saw something stuck in the door handle. It was a single lily and a note. Miss you. I drove home with a goofy grin on my face.

After taking a nap, I went to the mall to get my Christmas shopping done. Samantha had been not too subtly hinting that she wanted a cute black purse from Macy's. I picked it up and then decided that I'd wrap up some small stuff and stick it inside the purse. As I was strolling around Macy's I passed a display of her favorite perfume so I grabbed a bottle. In the little girls section, I found those old school braided friendship bracelets. I bought us each a matching one. I walked out into the mall to get her a gift card to the candy store she loved but never went to.

Samantha was the only person I intended to buy presents for but I thought that maybe I should get something for Ryan. I wasn't sure what to buy him. I didn't want to get him cologne or a sweater. I wanted it to be personal and meaningful. Hmm. I decided I wouldn't find a meaningful gift in the mall, so I left. As I crossed the parking lot, heading to my car, I noticed a new store had opened up across the way. Cat's Consignment. I wonder if they might have something. I detoured away from my car and towards the shop.

I opened the door and walked inside. It was dark and a little dusty. Plus it had that old, musty smell which I hate. But if I was going to find a unique gift, it would be here. I strolled up and down the aisles. Maybe the evil, antique possessed doll? No. How about a broken pair of skates? No. He probable hates skating. Then, on the back of a shelf, I found it: a vintage microscope. I'm not sure if it would work or not but it would look cool on his desk. Perfect! I paid for my purchase and could hardly wait for the clerk to wrap it up. I wanted to head home, clean it up, and wrap it in pretty, sparkly Christmas paper.

Once I got the decades' worth of dirt off the microscope it looked almost brand new. Well, in that creepy, vintage medical instrument way. I hoped Ryan would love it. I wrapped the microscope and all of Sam's presents and hid them in my closet. I'd give Samantha her stuff before she went out of town. I wasn't sure when I would give Ryan his. I was looking forward to having dinner at his house on Tuesday. It scared me how much I thought about him and the next time I would see him.

Work seemed to drag on forever on Tuesday. I finally got off at three and headed out to my car. I planned to go
home to shower and change before going to Ryan's house at
five. I noticed a weird blue thing on the back window of my
car. Man, I hate solicitors. Stop leaving your stupid flyers on
my car. But as I got closer, I realized that it was a teal and blue
butterfly sticker. I looked around the parking lot expecting
Ryan to jump out. As I was about to climb into my car, my cell
phone buzzed.

Hope you had a good day at work, Butterfly.

*Thanks for the sticker. What if I was one of those girls who
hates stickers on cars?*

*I figured you were but you'd let it slide since you love butter-
flies.*

How does he know me so well? I loved the sticker and it
was even my favorite colors.

Thank you. See you in a little bit.

After showering and putting a on a cute pair of skinny
jeans and an oversized sweater, I decided to run to the liquor
store and pick up a bottle of wine.

Red or white?

To go with dinner? Whatever you like.

I like anything. What are we having for dinner?

*It's a surprise. Bring a bottle of your fave wine. It will be
perfect.*

With a bottle of sparkling chardonnay in my hand, I
headed for the checkout.

As I waited for Ryan to open the door, I tried to imagine
what his apartment would look like. I doubted he would have
a typical bachelor pad. It was probably sparkling clean and
designer decorated. But when he opened the door, I was surprised. His apartment was gorgeous and homey. The couch
and loveseat didn't match, but were still coordinated, and he
had a beautiful Christmas tree in the living room.

"Do you have a roommate?" I asked.

"Yeah, he went home back east to see his family. It's nice 'cause I get the place to myself for most of December."

"I love the tree. I never get one since Sam leaves to visit her family and it's just me to see it."

"What? That's wrong. It isn't Christmas without a tree." He opened my bottle of wine and poured me a glass. We sat at the table and nibbled on a plate of crackers covered with pro-sciutto and mozzarella cheese. We chatted for a few minutes when a timer went off in the kitchen. Ryan jumped up and I followed him.

"What can I do?"

"Um, you can grab these plates and the salad and put them on the table. I already set out the garlic bread and I'll bring the lasagna."

"I love lasagna. It smells amazing."

"Why thank you. It's my mom's family recipe."

My heart broke a little. My mom hadn't cared about me enough to stick around, let alone share recipes. My feelings must have shown on my face.

"What's wrong?"

"Nothing. My mom couldn't be bothered to make dinner most nights. I just wish I had someone to share things with me."

"I'll share my Mom's recipes with you. We make a mean meatloaf."

I found the corners of my lips curving up just a little.

"I really am sorry about your Mom. You seem so strong that I forget about all the shitty things that happened to you. You give off that tough girl attitude that makes people think nothing hurts you."

"That's why I give off that vibe. I want people to think that nothing they do hurts me," I said. I guess I use anger as way to hide the fact that I'm dying inside. "I don't trust anyone enough for them to hurt me. My walls keep me safe."

Ryan clenched his jaw. "I hope you realize you can trust me. I'll find a way around your walls. Come on, let's sit down and eat, okay?"

I nodded and took my seat.

"When's your next day off?" Ryan asked as he dished up platefuls of cheesy lasagna.

"Friday."

"Good. Me too. Want to go out with me?"

"Sure. Where are we going?" His eyes were bright and shining and he was biting his lower lip. "Wait, let me guess. It's a surprise?"

He laughed. "Yep. I'll pick you up at nine in the morning. Make sure you wear jeans and a warm sweater."

"Okay. So we'll be outside?"

"My lips are sealed."

I shook my head. Ryan and his surprises. He was like a little kid, so excited and gleeful.

We ate so much that we couldn't stand to look at the leftovers. I couldn't remember the last time I had eaten this much. His mom did have a great lasagna recipe.

"So I was thinking, I know you have to open and you'll head home pretty early but first do you want to watch some TV?"

"Sure. Anything good on?"

"My favorite thing about Christmas is the cartoons. Tonight is *Charlie Brown Christmas* and *How the Grinch Stole Christmas*."

"Are you serious? You want to watch cartoons?"

"It's a tradition; like having a Christmas tree."

"Okay, I guess."

I had a fun time hanging out with Ryan and watching cartoons. I had never watched them before and he was sweet and held my hand the entire time. When the shows were over he walked me out to my car and kissed me goodbye gently. I sat in my car, waiting for it to warm up. Maybe that was my problem. The Grinch and I had a lot in common. My heart was too small. Ryan should be with a woman whose heart was five sizes bigger than most, not smaller like mine.

The next day when I got home from work, I was shocked to see a bundled Christmas tree and beat up cardboard box by my front door. There was a note on top of the box.

You have to have a tree. I want you to get used to having Christmas traditions. I hope you like this one. I picked it out. In this box are some extra lights and ornaments to decorate your tree. Merry Christmas.

I carried the box in, and set it on the coffee table. Then I dragged the tree in and leaned it against the wall. It was wrapped in some kind of net. I guess I should cut it off. And then what? Maybe I should wait for Samantha to come home. I opened the cardboard box and found strands of multicolored lights, balls and bells, pretty little ornaments, and tinsel. On the bottom of the box was a bowl looking thing with screws in it. Ryan had stuck a sticky note on it.

This is the tree stand. The screws help hold the tree up and keep it from falling over. Fill the bowl with water.

Luckily, Sam walked in from work right after that and helped me set everything up. I have to admit that once everything was up and we were sitting on the couch in the dark with only the tree lights on, it was kind of magical.

Thank you for the Christmas tree. You were right. I need some tradition in my life. And it is the perfect tree.

You're welcome. I'm glad you're not mad. I thought you might think I was being pushy.

I didn't sleep well that night. I kept tossing and turning until my alarm went off. Unfortunately, work didn't do anything to improve my mood. It was busy, and we were short staffed. By the afternoon, the rush had finally slowed and I was standing at the front register when a vaguely familiar woman walked up to me. She was thin and blonde, dressed in a designer outfit and knee high boots. She strutted up and gave me the once over.

"Hi. Can I help you?" I asked in my most professional tone.

"Yes. You can stay away from my boyfriend," she snapped.

"What are you talking about? Who are you? I don't even know who your boyfriend is."

"My name is Lauren. And yes, you do know my boyfriend, Ryan. He may be having fun with you now but once he gets you out of his system he'll marry me. I'll be the perfect wife to Dr. Ryan Collins."

"Ryan told me he broke up with you months ago."

"Technically we did. Look at you. You work in a crappy coffee shop and what? Did you even graduate high school? You can't be a doctor's wife. Ryan would never be comfortable introducing you to his colleagues. I'm the kind of woman that would make him proud to call his wife. You're the girl guys call for a good time. I'm the kind of girl they marry. I don't want you to get your feelings hurt when Ryan figures out what we both already know," she said in her sickly sweet voice.

"Who said I wanted to marry him?"

"Well, good. We're both on the same page." She turned and marched out of the shop.

I locked myself in the office. She had me seeing red. But at the same time, I've always known the truth. Ryan deserved a good girl like her, not trash like me. He's going to be a successful doctor, and he would need a wife to host dinner parties and attend hospital functions. She's right. I'm the fun distraction. She's wifey material. I deluded myself long enough. I always knew I would only have Ryan for a little while. I guess that time was up faster than I imagined.

The rest of the day passed in a blur. Ryan texted me but I didn't respond. I considered telling him I wouldn't see him on Friday, but then decided it was more appropriate to tell him in person. I'd wait until he dropped me off at home and then I'd hand him his Christmas present. I had written a note and put it on the box with the microscope that told him I didn't want to see him anymore, since he deserved someone better than me.

Friday was gray and damp when my alarm went off. I had turned my phone off the night before and when I turned it on, I had four new messages from Ryan.

Are you okay? I haven't heard from you in a couple days.
I can't fix what's wrong if you don't tell me the problem.
I miss you.
Are we still on for tomorrow?

I texted him back.

See you at 9. Sorry.

Since he said to dress warmly, I threw on jeans, a t-shirt, a thick sweater and my hiking boots. I was waiting by the door at 8:50 when he knocked.

"Hi," he said.

"Hi. Sorry I've been so quiet the last few days. I haven't felt well." I guess a broken heart will do that to you.

"Oh. You should have told me. I would have made you chicken soup and used my doctor skills to nurse you back to health," he said as he opened the car door for me. I choked back a sob as he walked around to his side of the car.

"Okay, sit back and relax. We have about a three hour drive. In the bag by your feet are some super healthy snacks: beef jerky, M&M's, crackers, and chips. And I bought you a caramel latte, so we should be good to go."

I smiled at him as the knife in my heart twisted a little more. "Thanks. All my favorites." Being sweet and caring was effortless to him, and he deserved a woman to reciprocate.

We listened to the radio and I can only imagine what he was thinking about. I was picturing my life without him in it. It looked as dark and gloomy as the weather outside.

After a couple of hours the road took a steep turn as we started up the mountain. I had my face pressed to the window and every once in a while I would see a pile of dirty slush.

"Where are we going?" I asked.

"Well, I figured that since we are starting new traditions, this should be one of them. We're headed up to see snow. I asked Samantha if she had anything for you to borrow. I have a jacket, scarf, gloves, and a beanie in the trunk. Then after we play in the snow, we're having a romantic late lunch, or early dinner in a little B&B."

"I get to see snow? You planned all this for me?" I said with a sniffle. A couple of tears leaked out my eyes.

"Yes, I wanted to be with you when you got to see it. Don't cry. Today is supposed to be happy, not sad."

"I am happy."

When we turned off the main road and onto a little side road, suddenly snow was everywhere. It thinly veiled the tree branches; it coated the small bushes and shrubs, and covered the ground. I could hardly contain my excitement. We pulled into the bed and breakfast's driveway and I jumped out as soon as he shifted the car into park. I reached down and grabbed a handful, making a snowball to throw at Ryan.

"Holy shit. It's so cold. My fingers are frozen."

"Duh. Snow is cold." He laughed.

He laughed even harder when my snowball hit him in the chest.

"Hey. Wait until I get my jacket on," he said as he opened the trunk and pulled out our stuff.

Thank goodness Samantha had let me borrow her snow gear. It was so much colder up here than it was in San Diego. Once we were suited up, we went for a walk. The grounds of the bed and breakfast were so beautiful. Ryan should be here with Lauren, not me. My heart was breaking wider and wider apart with each nice and caring act he did.

We sat down on a little bench in the middle of a clearing.

"I have to tell you something. I'm so glad you're here with me today," Ryan said.

"Thanks for inviting me. It's been so much fun." He leaned over and kissed me, gently at first, and then more insistently. He abruptly broke off the kiss.

"Quinn, I love you. I have loved since your first day of work almost three years ago. Will you go out with me exclusively? My parents want you to come to Christmas dinner at their house."

I looked up at him with tears in my eyes. "I don't love you, Ryan. You deserve a good girl with a loving family and a great upbringing. You don't really want to be with me and all my problems. I'm fucked up, and being with me would only fuck you up too. You should take Lauren home with you."

His eyed narrowed. "Lauren? What does she have to do with us? I told you I broke up with her a long time ago."

"Well maybe you should inform her of that. She thinks she's still your girlfriend. She's patiently waiting for you to get me out of your system and go back to her. She came in to work yesterday. She wanted to make sure I knew my place."

"Did she tell you I dumped her because I found her sleeping with my best friend? I will never go back to her. I don't want a jerk like her. I want you." He jumped up and started pacing.

"No, she didn't. But her points about me were valid just the same. I'm not the girl for you. I'm sorry. Will you drive me home?"

"Not until you listen to what I have to say. You are the only girl for me. I want to spend the rest of my life with you."

I jumped up from the bench, tears streaming down my face.

"Quit trying to change me into something you think I should be. I'm not the social girl who likes having dinner parties; I don't even like Christmas and traditions. My life has sucked and will continue to suck. You need a good girl who will help you advance your career, a woman you will be proud to introduce to your fellow doctors, someone like Lauren, not me. I told you I build walls to keep people away. Everyone I have ever trusted has not only let me down but hurt me."

"I'm not like your Mom and all those little boys you dated," he said with his fists clenched. "I won't hurt you. I'll be patient and take down your walls brick by brick. I will never hurt you."

"Everyone says that. People come and go. Everyone acts sweet at the beginning of the relationship. But in the end, someone will get hurt. I'm not willing to get hurt ever again."

"Why can't you understand that I'm not like them? That I care for you and I'll always love you."

"No one cares for me. No one ever will. Take me home, Ryan. Now."

I walked to the car, not daring to look at him. He unlocked the doors and we climbed in. We were silent the entire three hour ride back to my apartment. As he pulled up in front of apartment, I climbed out of the car and pulled his present out of my bag, placing it on the now empty passenger seat.

"Thank you. The last couple of weeks have been great. But you deserve better than me." I ran into my apartment.

Sam was curled up on the couch. "How was it? Q? What's wrong? What happened?"

Through my tears I tried to make her understand. "He told me he loves me and wants me to go meet his family. How can I meet his family when my own family deserted me? There is no way they'll want me with their son. I told him I didn't love him and to find a nice, respectable girl."

Sam hugged me. "Oh, Quinn. You're an amazing person. He was lucky to have you. I hope you see that someday. Parents want their kids to be happy. They couldn't ask for a better girl for their son than you. I think you should try and have a relationship with Ryan. He loves you and would die before he'd hurt you."

I turned and fled into my room, slamming the door behind me.

I called in sick to work on Saturday and spent the entire day in bed. Whenever I managed to fall asleep, I had horrible dreams of Ryan being stuck in burning buildings, or in a smashed car, and I didn't save him.

Shortly before midnight, I realized that not only was I all cried out, but I was hungry.

I walked into the living room and found Sam sitting on the couch with her bags packed. I had completely forgotten that she was leaving on Christmas vacation the next day.

"I've been a shitty friend. I'm so sorry. I was so wrapped up in my drama with Ryan that I forgot you were leaving. I have a present for you." I ran back into my room and returned with the present.

"Here. I know you'll like it."

She opened it and shrieked.

"Yay, you got me the purse I wanted," she exclaimed.

"How could I not. You're not very subtle. Open it. There's more."

"Ooh, I love this bracelet."

"Look." I slid my sleeve up and showed her my matching bracelet.

"Thank you so much. I love you and wish you would come home with me. I know you keep yourself separated from people in order to not get hurt, but by doing that you're missing out on some great people. Like me and Ryan. We would do anything for you."

"I know you would and I'm grateful for it. I don't want to talk about him."

"Well, here's your present." She handed me what looked like a big, flat envelope. I ripped into the wrapping paper and then opened the envelope. It contained two tickets to an all day spa retreat.

"You and your guest can get massages, sit in the mineral spas, take mud baths, even get manis and pedis. I think you need a day to rest and relax."

"Can we go when you get back? I think we need a girl day."

"Of course. I love you. Call me if you need anything while I'm gone, okay?"

We hugged and then I went into the kitchen to make myself a quesadilla.

"Hey, I'm going to bed so I can get an early start tomorrow. There's one more present for you. I put it under the tree. Don't open it until Christmas Eve, okay?"

"Okay. The spa day was more than enough. Thank you. Have a great trip and say hi to your family from me." We hugged one last time and she went to bed.

I sat at the table a little longer and thought about what I would do with myself while she was gone. The coffee shop was closed all week so I didn't have to be at work. I had no family to visit, and if I was truthful with myself, Sam was my only friend. A tiny voice in my head whispered, "and Ryan." Yeah, Ryan had always been my friend, but I'm pretty sure I had burned that bridge.

Chapter Four

The next couple of days were spent winter cleaning the apartment. I cleaned every square inch: I washed the window sills, cleaned the windows inside and out, used the broom to remove the cobwebs, and even cleaned out my closet. By Tuesday night, my living space was immaculate, but I was bored and lonely. I decide to text a guy I knew who was always down to come over.

Josh showed up about forty five minutes later. He looked gorgeous as always. He had light sandy colored hair that made everyone think he was a surfer. He was dressed in jeans and an old concert t-shirt.

"Hey. Thanks for coming over," I said as I let him in the apartment.

"No big deal. It's been a while since you've called me. I thought maybe you had found the one," he replied.

"No. I found the one I wanted to spend a couple weeks with."

We walked into the living room and sat on the couch. He immediately reached for me and tried to kiss me.

"How about we watch a movie?" I asked.

"A movie? That's not what we do together. I thought you were texting me to come over for a booty call."

"Well, I was lonely, but I thought maybe we'd watch a movie before we headed to my room."

"Okay. What should we watch?"

I turned on the DVD player and found *Anchorman* from when Ryan and I had watched it.

"How about *Anchorman*?" I asked.

He nodded, so I turned away from the TV and joined him on the couch. We watched maybe three minutes before he tried to kiss me again. I went along with it at first but it felt wrong. I pushed him away.

"What is it?"

"I don't know. It feels weird."

"Didn't feel weird to me. Felt like every other time we

kissed."

Maybe that was my problem. I didn't want to kiss him like I did every other time. I wanted Ryan.

"I'm sorry I bothered you. Maybe you should go," I said quietly.

"What the fuck is up with you? You were never a cock tease before. Maybe that 'couple weeks' guy screwed with your head," he said as he stormed out the door.

I turned off all the lights and the TV and made sure my door was locked. Then I cried myself to sleep.

When I woke up the next morning, I had texts from Samantha and the owners of the coffee shop wishing me a Merry Christmas Eve. I decided that since today was kind of a holiday, I would go all out and make myself eggs, bacon, and toast for breakfast. I made it through three bites before I tossed it all in the trash can with a sob.

What was wrong with me? I was the one who kicked Ryan to the curb. I didn't need a man in my life. Besides, he's an amazing guy and he deserves more than I can give him.

It was another gloomy morning. I sat on the couch with only the Christmas tree lights on. I looked down and spotted my other present under the tree. Awesome. That should cheer me up. Sam told me I could open it today.

I grabbed the small gift bag and looked at the scene on the bag as I snuggled back on the couch under my blanket. It was a couple playing in the snow, making a snowman. I opened the bag and found a card and a tissue paper wrapped square.

I opened the card and started to cry. It was written in Ryan's super sloppy scrawl.

Hey, Quinn. I know you don't think we should be together and you think I deserve someone better. But I think you're the best so how could I ever settle for someone else? I know you said that you didn't love me but I hope that you only said that to push me away. I can't imagine living without you as a part of my life.

I received my letters from UCSD and Johns Hopkins. I got accepted into both. I don't know how to choose but I know that I can't leave San Diego if there is a chance I could stay and be with you. I love you. Ryan

I ripped open the white square and found a copy of Jameson Brax's CD. I got up and put it in the CD player.

I cried as I listened to him sing about looking for love and his never ending sorrow. The CD was full of longing, and described exactly how I felt. But then the next to last song talked about how the girl makes him feel better when he's upset and even when she's not around, he feels her love lifting him. The song was about his intention to never let her go, now that he finally had her.

Could this be me and Ryan? Was it possible that I deserved him? He made me happy with all his little notes and texts. The last couple of weeks were the best, even on the days when I didn't see him. I finally admitted the words I had been denying, even to myself. I loved him.

I texted Sam.

I love Ryan.

I know you do. Maybe you should tell him.

How long have you known?

Since your first date. He made you float around the house even when he wasn't there.

Shit! Why didn't you tell me? What do I do now? He probably hates me.

TELL HIM HOW YOU FEEL.

I'm scared.

It is scary but it will be okay. I promise.

Okay. Love you.

Love you more.

I decided to wait until later that night before I texted Ryan. I needed to collect my thoughts and find some courage. I listened to the CD on repeat all day, while I baked cookies and brownies and anything I could think of that Ryan might like.

By ten o'clock, I had nothing left to bake or cook in the house. Guess it was now or never. I picked up my phone and texted Ryan. I knew what I had to tell him.

Merry Christmas.

Merry Christmas.

What did you do today?

I hung out with my nieces and nephews. We finally got them to fall asleep. What did you do?

I opened your present. Thank you. I listened to the CD all day on repeat. Track 11 is my fave.

Mine too.

So you got into both your schools? Are you ready to move to Baltimore? That is such a great opportunity for you.

Why are you texting me? You're welcome for the CD. Anything else?

I'm sorry. I just wanted you to know how proud of you I am and that I know that you will be an amazing doctor. Goodbye.

How could I ask him to give up his dream school for me? It wouldn't be fair. In ten or twenty years, he'd resent me. I sat in the dark in front of the tree and cried for what I hoped was the last time. I had said my goodbyes and now it was official.

I don't know how long I had been sitting there when I heard banging on my front door. Oh shit. Should I call 911? Where was my cell phone? Then I heard someone calling my name.

"Quinn? Quinn? Open the door."

I opened the door and found a disheveled Ryan standing there.

"What are you doing here?" I asked as I invited him in.

"Your last text sounded like goodbye. I was at my parents' and I didn't have my car. Plus everyone was sleeping so I ran over here."

"You ran here? Do you want a bottle of water?"

"No. I want you." He swept me into his arms and kissed me like he was afraid he'd never see me again.

I gently pushed him away. "Ryan, I love you. But I don't want you to give up your dreams for me. In your note you said you'd stay here if it meant you could be with me. Well... what if I moved with you? That way you could have me and go to Johns Hopkins?"

"Are you sure? I thought you didn't want to leave San Diego?"

"I would rather live in Antarctica with you, than live here without you."

"What made you change your mind?"

"I realized that it wasn't fair to me or anyone else to live my life by keeping other people pushed away. I realized I did it to girls as well as the guys I dated. Sam invites me home with her every year but I won't go, staying home feeling sorry for myself instead.

"You don't try to fix me. I love that you accept me for me, flaws and all. You said you would break down my walls but you already did. I love you and I can't imagine being without you."

"I love you and I am so grateful that you're willing to move to Baltimore with me. I can't wait to start this new chapter with you."

Picking me up, Ryan threw me over his shoulder and carried me into the bedroom. I squealed and cracked up.

He laid me gently on my bed. He kissed me and started unbuttoning my pajama shirt.

"I'm going to unwrap my present early."

Hanley's Secret

by S.K. Wills

To my sweet Alabama family with their kind
hearts and welcoming arms.

Chapter One

She wasn't a smoker, but Crystal Hanley wished for a cigarette like one with a two-pack-a-day habit. She needed something to put in her hand so that the whitened knuckles on her steering wheel were forced to take a break. Didn't people pop those cancer sticks in their mouth to calm their nerves? To settle their stomachs?

The four energy drinks and king-sized Snickers bar she'd consumed during the last fourteen hours now seemed like a bad idea. The caffeine and sugar bounced around with the fear in her stomach until combustion seemed entirely possible. If only she could stop shaking, as she had been the last three hours straight behind the wheel, she might be able to settle back in the driver's seat and relax. She was halfway around the goddamn world now, or so it felt like.

She was safe.

She went back to wishing for a cigarette and looking for a place to call home for the next couple of months.

Huffing a breath, she made a grab for her cell. GPS *had* said there was a hotel or something down this road, but she should have hit it by now. She caught a glimpse of the moving arrow on the screen continuing towards a destination right before the phone beeped and went black.

"Dammit!" Did she pack the charger? Packing was a blur of stuffing a carry-on sized suitcase to overflowing. Whatever she'd forgotten, she'd simply have to buy. She took the cash at least, and that was going to burn his ass as much as her running away was. It was more than a cool hundred thousand resting in a duffel bag in the backseat, it was a new life.

"Can't wait," she said, replying to her own thoughts. Her voice carried what some would claim to be a Northern accent. She wasn't going to blend the best here, but at least it was the southern point of Alabama, along the Gulf Coast. That had to be far enough away. There was no way the dented tin she bought on her way out of Chicago was going to sputter another mile. It'd die out like her phone and then where would she be?

She didn't want to think about it, and instead focused on the darkened road, the thick oak trees twisting to block even the eerie glow of the moon. It felt like a tunnel constricting around her with every second that ticked by.

"Finally!" The weathered sign shined like a beacon calling her to safety—Lawson House Inn. She maintained her manners, no matter how much she wanted to get out of this deathtrap, and turned up the long gravel driveway with extra care so as not to wake the sleeping residents with her squeaking tires. When the car rumbled to a stop, she let her head flop back against the rest, eyes closing. She released a breath so tight in her chest it might have been held the entire trip.

Safe. The word exploded in her mind, lightening her migraine so that it was a softer pounding behind her temple. "Please have a bed open. Please, please, please." She needed a minute, two tops, to rest her eyes and let her head continue to calm, then she'd go see if the innkeeper could help her.

She took a long, deep breath. Was that quiet melody crickets? Not honking horns or screeching tires. Through the silence, there was a faint ringing in her ears, intensified by her pounding head. Country living was strange. How was she going to sleep in all this silence? Her thoughts turned hazy, the chirping a musical blending with the whisper of wind chimes that began to soothe her.

She fell asleep thinking about being hunted by crickets.

Beckett Lawson wasn't a man you'd associate with a bed and breakfast, not immediately. A quarterback or construction worker, maybe, with his broad shoulders and well-muscled 6'2" frame. Anyone who called him a sissy in high school for spending time tending his grandma's B&B soon learned to keep their mouth shut. Even if he hadn't been interested in the business side of things, he'd have had a hard time with a stranger around doing daily maintenance and whatever his sweet Gram needed after Gramps had passed.

He was that man, and he was that man with pride. He took great care in the work, from keeping the books, staffing, socializing with the guests, and more. He had a routine, a system, and it worked. Mostly. So why a piece of crap car was sitting idle in his parking lot with some kind of ruffian asleep inside, he had no idea, but he was going to find out.

The stranger was probably lost. That or his atrocious neighbor had sent them Beckett's way to kick up trouble before Christmas. It had been a while since Collin stirred up their generational feud. Either way, he would handle it.

He carried the large wrench loosely in his right hand. Though he didn't think the stranger would turn hostile with him holding a weapon of any kind, you never knew what someone was capable of.

Beckett circled the car, ignoring the bite of winter and the cold rain that had already soaked through his T-shirt on the short walk from the tool shed. He shielded his eyes from the downpour and squinted at the rope that held the stranger's trunk shut, and the piece of duct tape escaping the back passenger window, flapping wildly in the storm. His toffee-colored eyes narrowed on the luggage in the back seat before moving to make out the slumped figure in the front. Maybe they were dead? He stepped closer, aiming for a better look. It was too early for guests to rouse, but they'd be up within an hour and he hoped they wouldn't wake to some kind of crime scene.

Too small to be a man, he figured, now that he was up close. A slight rise and fall indicated that she was still breathing, though the black hoodie obscured most of his view. The hood fell over her face, but long dark hair spilled out to fan the center console. No way was that comfortable, and she'd sure be sorry when she woke.

He pressed against the window and peered down at the engaged lock. The contrast of milky skin against the black of the jacket caught his attention and he let his gaze roam where the jacket had lifted to expose one smooth side. *Definitely female.* The bit of ink on her skin interested him, and he wondered what kind of tat she had, and how low it dipped under those tight jeans. To stop his thoughts from continuing south, he rapped a knuckle against her window. When she didn't stir, he did it again, louder. Heck, maybe she *was* dead.

Stepping back, he lifted the wrench, preparing to swing it through her window, but the blur of movement caused him to pause with the wench suspended above his head. Nasty words— not proper for a lady to be yelling so easily— assaulted his ears, no doubt from the pain of her sleeping arrangement. She must have spotted him, because now she was screaming *and* swearing. His twitching lips tipped into a full-blown grin. He raised both hands and took a few steps back to show her he meant her no harm.

She flung her car door open and crawled out, wobbling on her legs before gaining her balance. Cupping her neck, she peered up at him with a weirdly angled tilt of her head. He thought of mint, fresh and intoxicating, when he looked into her green eyes. She seemed to question him without ever saying a word.

"Morning ma'am. Bit of a stiff neck, I reckon. You break down?" He motioned to the car with the wrench, then let his arm fall to his side.

"I didn't break down." She jerked her hood further over her face to stay dry. "This piece of shit almost did, break down that is, but it made it. I pulled in late hoping for a room to rent. I—I must have fallen asleep."

"We don't have an open room. Holiday season and all. I betcha' won't find vacancy for another three weeks in these parts. People like their Christmas, and we book solid every year."

She made a strangled sound in her throat that through the rain sounded to Beckett a lot like desperation. Then she tipped her face to the sky, the rain pelting and pushing her hood back. Her eyes closed now, she didn't move, and that was weird. The rain was soaking her black hair, matting it to the palest skin he'd ever seen. When she finally dropped her face and opened her eyes, they shone big and green, and definitely desperate.

"I have nowhere to go, no one to see." She stepped closer to him, and he had to drop his gaze significantly the closer she got.

"I'm not from around here." She whispered it standing close, too close. The desperation from earlier had smoldered into something else, something that had his body beginning to hum. It might have been the husky voice, or the way the green of her eyes cut through thickly lowered lashes. She tipped her chin again, demanding more attention to her pouty bottom lip. "You can't help at all?"

"I, ah..." Where did his voice go? He was half-tempted to give this pixie his bed. Feeling a little bewitched, he nodded anyway. "Well, come on then. We can't spend all day in the rain, can we?" With that, he took off for the house in hurried strides, hoping to create some distance between them. Would those lips taste as sweet as her angel face? Somehow he knew she wasn't at all as innocent as she proclaimed.

Inhaling deeply to yell instructions, he turned back once he hit the wraparound porch and found her nearly colliding with him. "You move fast for being so small," he managed once he stopped choking.

She was looking up at him through her lashes again, but this time, her lips parted and curved up around straight, white teeth. His world tilted a bit at the impact. Dear God, was she a witch? Did his neighbor hire a witch to mess with them for the holidays? Against his better judgment, he leaned the wrench against the sunny yellow siding of the house and pushed open the heavy chestnut door. Warmth, not from the heat being on, flooded him. He appreciated it, and what his home meant to him, every time he stepped inside.

Motioning for her to go in before him, he barely stopped himself from swearing when she passed by. The exotic, flowery scent – which he recognized for jasmine – mingled with the woman.

"Wow," she said, moving farther into the foyer. Shaking out her hair, she spun around to take in the rustic elegance. The chandelier sparkled, casting a bright glow despite the dreariness beckoning at the windows. A small fire crackled in the hearth, fat red candles and snowman trinkets decorated the mantle topped with the biggest Christmas wreath she'd ever seen hung above on the stone wall. Pine tickled her nose. "This is beautiful."

The droplets of water from her hair littered the gleaming wood floor, catching the light and her attention. She stopped shaking out her hair and looked back to him. "Shit, sorry. Do you have a tow—" The rest of the word burned up in her throat. The man had stepped through the door and into the light to provide her with her first really good look at him. His hair might be brown, but it was too short and too wet to tell for sure. His T-shirt was dark, but soaked and molded to his body. Her gaze dipped to where the sopping wet cotton accentuated a very deep V-line. *He might as well be naked.* Even his blue jeans were sodden, appearing black and fitted to every bulge. She sucked in a breath and raised her gaze back to his face, where he was watching her with dark eyes and a cocky grin.

The embarrassment drained away as she returned her hands to her hair and shook more of the rain onto the floor until his grin faded.

"Beckett, dear? Did Collin send us a nasty gift?"

Hanley stopped showering the floor and turned at the soft, elderly voice.

"Because if so, I'm calling the cops. Enough is enough. It's Christmas."

The voice sounded tired, but when the woman appeared in the doorway, her black apron smeared with flour, wiping her hands on a dish towel, she looked anything but. Taller than Hanley, but shorter than Beckett, with a curly cap of salt and pepper hair left to frame a face that radiated warmth and strength, despite her old age.

Beckett looked from his Nan to the back of the strange woman. He didn't quite rule her out as being a nasty gift, but he also couldn't rule out wanting to open her if she was.

Chapter Two

Hanley dragged her suitcase up and opened it on the twin bed. It was her good fortune that they sent most of their staff home to be with their families over the holidays, and Hanley could spend a night in one of the staff rooms. It beat sleeping in the car, anyway.

She pulled out the bag of items she'd bought on her way down to help disguise her. It wasn't too late to pop in the colored contacts; she doubted Beckett or the old woman would have noticed her eyes yet. Plus, brown was a much plainer color than her vivid green. She set them on the beige comforter and pulled out the short blonde wig. Too late for that, and that was too bad. She wanted to try blonde. Donovan had favored dark hair and never let her deviate from her long, black locks.

Stop, stop. He doesn't exist anymore. She stuffed the wig back into her suitcase, pulled out dry, clean clothes. A shower could wait. At least the small room had a private bath attached so she wouldn't have to share with guests. Changing quickly, she was buttoning the jeans when the knock sounded on the door.

"Yeah?"

Beckett opened her door, paused in the doorway. Now dry, his hair was lighter, more sandy brown.

"Breakfast in ten if you're hungry."

"Okay, thanks."

They stared at each other.

"Anything else?" She was hungry, but he looked like a man starving and she was on the menu. Her pulse jumped.

"Well? You coming?"

"I—you." She stopped and took a breath to stop fantasizing. Calmer now. "You said ten minutes, and *if* I was hungry. That implies I have a choice in the matter." She folded her arms, the sleeve of her tee riding up to reveal a burst of color on her bicep. He opened the door further and entered without being invited. "What are you doing?"

"What's that?" He touched a finger to the color on her

arm, and she swatted at his hand before stepping back.

"It's nothing. Eight minutes to go, see you then." When he only turned to survey her room, gaze lingering on her single suitcase, she almost stomped her foot in impatience. Why wouldn't he go?

"The room okay?"

"Yes. Thank. You." She ground each word out through gritted teeth.

"Okay, good. See you in seven, uh. I never did catch your name?" He was stalling, he knew she knew it. She was cute when she was agitated. Even cuter when she wasn't, but he was having too much fun to stop now.

She huffed out a breath and rolled her eyes. "It's Cry— " She cleared her throat. "Hanley. My name is Hanley." He raised a brow, but didn't question her.

"That's a weird name."

Her mouth popped open. "Well, it's—"

"Pretty," he finished for her. "Nice to meet you, Hanley." When she continued to stare at him, he added, "Got about three minutes till breakfast. By the time we walk over, we'll be on time." Humor flickered over her face before she controlled it. Ah well, she'd warm up eventually. Opening the door wide, he extended his arm. After a brief hesitation she sailed by him and into the hall.

"Come on," he said, leading the way to the kitchen.

She didn't need him to guide her; she could have followed the smells on her own. Maple bacon wafted, filling the halls with a tantalizing aroma and forcing her mouth to water. Closer, it began to mingle with coffee and something sweet. She nearly drooled. Her stomach growled, causing her to flush and wrap her arms around her waist.

"Good," he said. "I like a woman with an appetite." She scowled at him, so he added a wink for good measure. What a prickly peach she was turning out to be. Maybe Collin, their slimy neighbor, had sent her to them after all.

"Nan, Hanley. Hanley, Nan." Beckett walked to his grandma and kissed the cheek she offered. Nan leaned back over the hot griddle. "That's a good boy. Now, fetch the platter. No, no," she added when he opened the cabinet above the stove. "The good one in the hutch."

"Yes, ma'am." Beckett gave Hanley another wink on his way out.

Before Hanley could think of a proper reason to excuse herself, Nan was talking again. "Hanley. That's a unique name. Do you mind grabbing the maple syrup from the fridge along with the bowl of fresh berries? Oh, and the butter. Can't forget the butter," she sang out and immediately began to hum.

"Um. Sure." She moved around the woman towards the fridge, pausing as a whiff of something stirred up an old memory. Nan smelled like flowers, a little too sweet, but nice overall. "Lilac." Her own grandma used to smell like that.

"Do you like it? Beckett buys me a new bottle every year for Christmas. We have a few bushes in the backyard that are lovely in spring."

"I bet they are."

"Mmhmm." Nan resumed her humming.

At ease for the first time in weeks, Hanley turned to grab the ingredients from the fridge, and was in the process of setting them on the marbled counter when Beckett strolled in with a platter the length of Hanley's entire arm. "That's a lot of waffles."

"Nan's candied bacon waffles are a big hit. We always make more than we need, but our guests like to eat."

"We offer breakfast and dinner most days," Nan chimed in. "Most folks for the holidays spend little time here, and often don't eat dinner with us, but we make sure there's a hot meal if they want it." She slid four perfectly golden waffles onto the platter. Beckett grabbed the pan off the stove and used a spoon to sprinkle bits of candied bacon over the top. Hanley's mouth watered again.

Nan added more batter to the press and talked over the sizzle. "The McAdams come every other year, and they have family about twenty minutes from here. So we won't see much of the foursome as they tend to have breakfast with us then head out to be with their kids. Charles comes every year, and he's a doll. Only lives about five minutes away, so he's in and out. Mostly in during the holidays as he prefers some company. Then this year we've got newlyweds and we won't see them at all." She added a chuckle and plopped four more waffles on the platter next to the others. "Plates, dear. Hanley, top cabinet to the right of the dishwasher. Grab ten, please."

Hanley had to reach on her toes to open the cabinet. Her fingertips barely brushed the stack of plates before strong hands moved over hers. The heat from Beckett's body against her back spread heat to her core. If she turned to face him, her cheek would be pressed to his chest. She waited for him to grab the plates and pull away before she released the breath she'd been holding.

"Can one of you dish up the berries, please?"

"Yep," Hanley said, a bit too quick. Nan had a way of speaking softly with a firm command in her voice. Hanley had already begun to admire and like the woman, which was more than she could say for her grandson.

Time passed quickly with Hanley ignoring Beckett and helping Nan. She'd been a waitress most of her life, and serving came easy to her.

After the guests cleared, she snagged a plateful for herself and sank into one of the empty chairs. The first bite had her eyes closing on a moan, and she opened one as a male throat cleared. Reaching for her water, she swallowed a gulp. "Beckett."

"May I join you?"

The other eye popped open, regarding him warily. "Why?"

"Because it's a waste to have a beautiful woman eating alone in my Inn."

"I thought this was Nan's Inn?" There was a tick in his jaw, but his cheerful expression contradicted any sign of agitation. She used her foot to push out the chair across from her. He sat, setting a full plate on the table.

"Thanks."

"Mmhmm." She cut another bite, pushed it around in the gallon of syrup before popping it into her mouth. They ate in silence, each one watching the other. It was starting to feel comfortable when he opened his mouth and ruined it.

"So, where ya from?"

She stared at his near-empty plate, his question sitting like lead on her lungs. She knew people would ask, but wasn't prepared to tell. "You don't like syrup?" she asked suddenly. What kind of person ate waffles with bacon and berries and no syrup?

"I do, sometimes. Sometimes not."

She raised her eyes to his, noted he was waiting for her to answer his question. "Cleveland," she blurted. Cleveland, Chicago, whatever.

"What brings you down here?"

"I, uh." She stuffed a little less than half a waffle into her mouth to buy her some time. What business was it of his? Only he'd—they'd—done her a favor and took her in for a night.

"I don't have any family so I like to travel to new places for the holidays. It helps, I guess." She gripped the napkin in her lap, prayed he didn't see through her. She was quite persuasive usually, but that always seemed to be when she had a guy right where she wanted him. She had no advantage here, wasn't closing a deal for Donovan. She had to get away from Beckett.

Standing with her empty plate, she stopped before walking by him. "Would you like anything while I'm up?"

"Nope, Hanley," he said in a way that made her think there was some great joke, and she was the root of it. "I think I'm all set."

"Whatever," she murmured and hurried to the kitchen. The back door was ajar, the breeze kicking through on the cooler side, but the rain had stopped. She set the plate on the counter and walked out onto a patio to survey the lush green yard. There had been three feet of snow covering the ground when she left Chicago. It had to be close to fifty degrees here, but the skin on her bare arms still puckered with the chill. Ignoring it, she moved forward to get a better look at the gardens Nan tended.

"Hanley! What are you doing out here, child?" Hanley paused as Nan rounded the house. "You'll freeze. Get your behind back inside and grab a coat. What do you think this is, the tropics?"

Despite the scolding, Hanley grinned. "Compared to where I'm from, this might be. I mean, yes, ma'am," she corrected under Nan's steely gaze.

"Wait a second now," Nan said. "What are your plans for the holidays? Christmas is around the corner you know. Are ya heading to visit family or wanting to stick around? Because, I suppose we could offer a trade. My staff doesn't come back 'till after the New Year, so if you want a place to sleep for a few weeks, you could do some cleaning and cooking for me. Help out during serving times."

Hanley was nodding long before she ever managed to utter the word yes. "Thank you. I promise I won't be a burden. Thank you," she said again, running back through the door and nearly colliding with Beckett. He steadied her by grabbing her arms.

"Jesus, woman. You're freezing." Without hesitation, he pulled her into his arms and engulfed her with his body heat. She managed an *oof* before her face was pressed against the hard muscles of his chest. The steady beat of his heart met her ear. She closed her eyes, giving in to pretending that this was more than it was. It felt nice. Safe.

God, she smelled like the rain. Beckett rested his chin on the top of her head and drew in her scent. He had only sought to warm her up, but the slenderness of her body pressed against his was giving him other thoughts. How she would feel skin to skin, his hands on her curves, his mouth on her –

"Hey!" she shouted and pushed back out of his embrace. Though her voice had raised, there was amusement in her eyes. "Keep your boner to yourself."

He choked on a laugh, coughed to clear his throat, and adjusted himself. "Sorry. No, not really. I can't help it, you turned me on. It's your fault. Next time, don't be so appealing in my arms."

Hanley gawked at his retreating back.

Chapter Three

*I*nsufferable woman.

Beckett spent two miserable days at a hospitality conference in Georgia. On top of stuffy executives, sleeping in a secondhand, crapshoot of a hotel, and dry sessions, it had been impossible to get Hanley out of his mind.

That one fated day seemed determined to remain permanently etched in his mind. The feel of her body pressed against his in the kitchen a prelude for what he had dreamt about doing to her since. Despite her obvious efforts to be left alone, he'd weaseled his way into spending most of that first day together, and didn't feel bad about that in the least. Now that he was home, he wondered if she was still there.

He dropped his suitcase on his bed, loosened his tie. A beer and a hot meal were calling his name. Dinner would be a few hours yet, but he'd settle for that beer and a sandwich with a hot meal to follow later. He unbuttoned the top buttons on his dress shirt, left the tie loose, thinking he'd change right after he made the sandwich, started on the beer. And he'd be closer to the goal if he took the direct route to the kitchen, instead of detouring down Hanley's hallway.

Her door was shut, so he paused to listen. Quiet greeted him so he moved on. His fixation had to be due to the fact that he'd spent time with her and still knew nothing about her. She was guarding something that made him want to discover all of her secrets.

Music drifted, something upbeat and catchy filling the hall. He followed it into the kitchen and froze when he spotted her. He wouldn't normally associate sexy with the song playing, but the way she moved in tune, hips swaying while she dried dishes, made the moisture in his mouth dry up.

Hanley spotted something out of the corner of her eye and shrieked. "Beckett! Holy crap, you scared me." Her laughter held a nervous edge, but she forced herself to calm and put the dish on the counter, reach for the next. He looked disheveled, but still incredibly sexy. She'd need to be careful around him, especially since he seemed determined to be buds. "Welcome back."

"Good to be back," he said. The fridge contents rattled in the door when he pulled it open. He grabbed a beer, twisted off the cap.

Awkward silence ensued, and she stacked the last plate before turning to find him watching her. "Enjoy the conference?"

"Yep." He took a long swig, eyes never leaving hers.

She wrung her hands, uneasy under the scrutiny. What was he thinking?

"Get settled?" he asked.

"Yep." She spread her arms wide and looked around the spacious kitchen. "I love this place. It's beautiful, Nan is beautiful. The guests, at least the ones I've met are great. Hey, what are you doing?" He had set his beer down and was walking towards her. She backed up until her back hit the counter, but it didn't slow him down. His hands gripped her hips and she was sitting on the counter before she could blink.

"Beckett, what the hel—"

He silenced her with his mouth. He needed to release some of the heat before he burned up. He kept it light, testing, until the rigid way she held her body began to relax, and her mouth firm against his, began to yield, lips parting in silent acceptance.

They didn't touch each other, both not knowing if they could stop once they did and neither caring to cross the line so soon. Still, their tongues tangled, each caress igniting a flame that threatened to burn forever.

He broke apart a second before he thought he might not be able to, watched her catch her breath before she asked, "What did you go and do that for?"

"Because." He touched her then, a light brush against her full bottom lip with his thumb before grabbing her waist and lifting her back to her feet.

"Because…"

He grinned. "Because I wanted to."

"Oh, is that all. Do you go around kissing everyone because you want to?" She opened the cabinet, huffed a breath when he took the stack of plates from her hands and put them away on the shelf she couldn't reach.

"Nope, but had to with you. Just couldn't shake it."

"But—"

"No buts. Did you like it?"

"The kiss?"

"Yeah, the kiss." He'd sauntered back for his beer, found it still cold enough to his liking to drink.

"I don't know."

He tipped the bottom towards her, "Ah, ah, ah. You do know. It's a yes or no. I liked it."

"Okay, fine. I liked it." Her hands moved to her hips and she fixed him with a stare as if to challenge. "So what?"

"Didn't say it meant a thing or that it would ever happen again. Simply wanted to kiss you, I did, and I liked it. End of story."

"Is it a Southern thing? The honesty and matter of fact way of delivery?"

"Is it a Yankee thing? The mistrust and game playing?" he countered.

She stammered at that and he moved towards her again. "You should try the honesty thing. Saying what's on your mind as it's on there can be freeing."

She braced for his touch again, but he walked past her and called over his shoulder. "I'm going to finish this beer and change into some normal clothes. Then I'm going to come back and make a sandwich. Two, if you'd like to join me for lunch." Then he was gone and she was left thinking about his invitation.

Honesty wasn't the problem. It was that honesty meant trust and trust meant liking and she wasn't sure she could afford to *like* Beckett.

She moved to the fridge, started removing lunch meats, cheeses, and condiments. She'd learned a little about Beckett from Nan while he was gone, and figured having a sandwich with the man might help her to decide for herself.

Beckett followed the note Hanley had tapped to the fridge and found her sitting in the closed in porch off the side of the house. She was a constant surprise to him.

"It's amazing how warm it is here," she said once he sat across from her at the little bistro table.

"Much colder in Cleveland? Thanks." He unwrapped the plate she'd passed to him, and took a hefty bite. She'd set a pitcher of lemonade between them so he poured them both a glass while he waited for her to decide if she wanted to answer the question. He was getting used to her evading.

"Plenty of snow," she said at last while picking at her own sandwich. "Temps below zero sometimes. So cold it burns your lungs to take a breath."

"Sounds terrible. Why would you want to live in a place like that?"

She shrugged. He sensed a shutdown on her part. "I mean it gets colder here than it is now, but nothing like that. The whole city would hole up in a state of emergency if a single flurry hit."

"No. Really? That's pathetic. You'd never make it in Ch—Cleveland."

"Hanley, I don't know what you're running from, but I promise you I won't disclose anything you tell me. Believe it or not, and probably mostly not considerin' the short time we've known one another, but you can trust me."

That green-eyed gaze settled so intently on his face that he knew she was struggling to believe him.

"Tell me about you," she said.

"Not a lot to tell." He shrugged one shoulder and polished off half of his sandwich. "I've got a big meddling family and tried to leave them for a time when I was young and dumb."

"So what, you're old and wise now?"

His lips twitched, but he hid the grin by taking another

bite and nodding.

"I bet." She snorted.

"Really, I am. Gramps passed and Nan didn't want to let this place go. I can't blame her now, but I resented her and my family for a while. Why was it my burden to step in and keep this place running? Now I can't imagine doing anything else with my life."

"It's nice to have a purpose and a good home," she said quietly.

Sensing another shutdown, he pointed to the fence and neighboring property. "It is if you don't live next door to Collin Frunderick." He waited until he had her full attention before continuing. "No, he's rotten as they come and twice as vindictive. His pa wanted the property when Gramps passed. Thought they could tear the place down and build a car shop. A car shop!" Even thinking about some dirty mechanic pit sitting in place on this historical site made Beckett see red. He cleared his throat. "His pa passed unexpectedly, car crash, about three years ago and Collin blames us. Drunk drivin', though he won't admit it. That's what the rumors say, and people tend to gossip the truth most often than not around here.

"Close your mouth before I lean over and kiss it again."

Hanley snapped it shut. He grinned at her.

Would he really? Maybe she should have kept it open to find out. *Don't be stupid. You're having a friendly chat with a decent man and nothing more.* "Still, that's awful. Why's he so terrible? What's he do?"

"Goes out of his way to start trouble and calls the cops any chance he gets to report us. We want to plant trees on the property line out back, but he wrote a letter to the city council saying they'd grow and hang over his side and that's out of line. It'd increase the property value and create some more privacy between us and he doesn't want it because it'd hang over his side of the fence? Stupid son of a—"

"You'll just have to convince him somehow. Keep try-ing."

"You're a smart one, you are. Have dinner with me? I'll tell you all about this place if you'd like. We're a historical B&B,

you know. Plenty of interesting guest stories, too." He was trying to persuade her and he knew she knew it.

"I'm helping to serve dinner." She watched him over her glass while she drank. "But I suppose if you want to wait until after, we can eat together. I'd like to read by the fire tonight, so it won't be a long dinner. I've always wanted to do that." *Great, now she sounded stupid. Who wants to do that?*

"That's my favorite thing to do."

"It is?"

"Yep. I've got a bookshelf in my bedroom, and you're happy to come in and borrow anything you want."

She tried not to think too much about what else she'd like to see or do in his bedroom. "Sure, okay."

He swept up and collected their plates. "See you around seven then."

"Yeah, I guess so," she replied.

"Great. It's a date."

She started to object, but he was already moving through the door and didn't turn back. "Well, crap." She dropped her chin into her palm and stared at the pitcher of lemonade. Go on a date with Beckett? If he knew the truth about her past, he wouldn't want to mix up with the likes of her. She didn't even know if she liked herself, how was he going to?

Chapter Four

Nan's humming had grown on Hanley over the last week, and she wouldn't admit it out loud, but Beckett had grown on her too. Meals together, reading by the fire at night. It was a routine she could get used to, almost. She'd relish in it another week, then figure out what to do next. That was for after Christmas, thought. Not for today.

She hummed while bracing herself on the counter, then pulling herself up. Grabbing the stack of plates, she cradled them and opened the cabinet to put them in their place. She paused to listen for sound, thinking Beckett would chastise her for not calling him to do it, or even Nan. Short people found ways around the height disadvantages in life; they just had to be resourceful.

She jumped down as something caught her attention through the window over the sink, and she had to squint to bring the man into focus.

That had to be Collin.

Cute.

Dusting her hands off on the cloth, she moved to the back door to get a better look. He looked innocent enough, maybe Beckett was overreacting about the whole mess. She bet she could fix things for him, and now with the thought implanted, really wanted to. Grabbing her coat off the rack, she set out to see if she couldn't do Beckett a big favor.

"Hey there." Her voice was casual as she approached. Collin's head whipped up in surprise, and his blue eyes darted around her as if Beckett or Nan were going to materialize. "I'm a new guest here, just being friendly and saying hey," she added to put him at ease.

He stepped closer to the fence and his eyes raked over her figure as if she was standing naked in front of him. The déjà vu of the reaction caused her skin to crawl, and even as the shame rolled over her, she knew now how to resolve Beckett's feud.

As if a puppet on a string, like she used to be, her demeanor changed. She sauntered closer, tipped her chin so she could bat her lashes, and gave her glorious hair a flip. She drew the zipper down on her jacket slowly. Her T-shirt was nothing special, but she pushed her shoulders back, making her chest seem more impressive. "My gosh, it's so hot here. Where I come from it'd be below freezing. How do you stand it?"

"Uh, it's not too bad. I'm Collin." His eyes never left her boobs.

"I'm Hanley," she purred, then stepped back and surveyed the land. "Collin, do you know what would look sexy here?" She didn't give him a chance to respond. She knew he was looking at her ass when she turned, she could feel it, but there was no stopping now that she had him hooked. "Those beautiful Magnolia trees I see everywhere else. Yeah." She nodded as if visualizing them. When she turned back to him, she ran her nail slowly across her bottom lip as if contemplating her statement, then in a breathy whisper, added, "Don't you think? Sexy, right?"

"Yeah," he agreed in a rush.

"Maybe we can talk about it over dinner sometime?" The way his eyes lit had her stomach churning.

"Sure, sure. That'd be great."

"Great, I know where to find you." She reached out and ran a hand over his jacket. "So many strong, handsome Southern guys down here." With a wink, she turned and made her way back to the inn. At the door, she turned back to see him still staring. She knew he would be and blew him a kiss, before turning and spotting Beckett watching.

"Beckett, jeez. What the hell, you scared me." She hung her coat back on the peg and went to move by him, but he blocked the way.

His hands shook with anger, so he shoved them into his pockets. "What the hell was that, Hanley? Planning on taking good ole' Collin boy to bed? Wouldn't have surprised me if you both stripped down right there and fucked on our property line."

Her shocked expression didn't fool him, he was onto her

game now. Take advantage of anyone and everyone and he was another pawn. Time spent together was a ploy so she'd have a place to stay when she had nowhere else to go. He still didn't know her story, but he was beginning not to care. He was falling for her, whoever the hell she was, and seeing her with Collin made him crazy. "Go on, he's still out there staring after you like a sick puppy. Go get him, Hanley, since he's the man you obviously want."

"You don't have a clue about what I want, Beckett, and I don't have to listen to this from you." She elbowed him in the stomach, pushing by. Regaining his breath he was on her heel.

"What was it then, huh? A friendly welcome for my arch-nemesis?" He tipped his head to Charles in passing. The old widower said nothing, but sent a sympathetic smile that Beckett caught.

"Arch-nemesis? What a joke. You'd have no problems if you had boobs. I'm sorry you're not the right gender to play nice with your neighbor."

"Even if I did, I wouldn't stoop as low to sleep with him to get my way."

She whirled around in her doorway, causing him to stop short or run her over. When he recovered, he reeled from the sharp sting of his cheek from the slap delivered by her delicate hand. His jaw dropped, and she pointed a finger accusing at him.

"Don't judge me, Beckett. You don't know my life or what I've lived with. You don't know a goddamn thing so get off your high horse and leave me the fuck alone."

With that the door slammed in his face.

"Beckett, what's got you so bristly?

"Huh?" He paused in ladling more of Nan's chicken and dumplings into his bowl. "Nothin'."

Nan swatted his hand until he released the ladle. "Nonsense. You don't eat like a pig unless something's got you upset, and that's your third bowl. Plus, you barely spoke two words to the McAdams at dinner. Socializing is what you do best. What's got your back up?" She opened several one serving-sized bowls so the guests could grab and heat up as they pleased the next day. When he didn't respond, she kept pushing. "Did you have a run-in with Collin? No one puts you in a bad mood quicker than him."

When his shoulders stiffened, she nodded and started handing him filled containers to set in the fridge. "Don't let that boy get to you. He's trouble, that's for sure, but we've been just fine for the last twenty years." She stared out the window at the house next door. "I do have some pity for him though. He resents being left that house when his pa died. Like a chain around the ankle when he wanted to be free. Sometimes a man has responsibilities he doesn't always appreciate at the time, but they'll grow on him. He'll come around." She turned back to Beckett, patted his shoulder. "You did."

He didn't like having anything in common with Collin, but supposed Nan had a point. She always did. His brother had never wanted anything to do with the inn, and as much as fought it, his place was beside his Nan, and his home would always be this inn. "Yeah," he said and pulled her in for a hug, kissed the top of her white hair. "I did."

When he pulled away, Nan filled the last bowl and pushed it in his hands. "Take it to Hanley, and make amends. You'll feel better."

"How—"

She laid her hand on the left side of his chest. "I know your heart. You're my boy."

He shuffled his feet and put his hand over hers, gave it a squeeze. "I'm glad I have you to keep me honest."

"Someone has to." She chuckled and handed him a spoon.

"Yes, ma'am." Now there was another woman he needed to be honest with. Jealously was an ugly trait—one he didn't much care for, but seeing Hanley with Collin the way he did had it sparking until it consumed him and swallowed any rational thought. Hopefully it wasn't too late for an apology. Maybe she'd forgive him enough to join him by the fire.

The sound of running water slowed his step and he stopped in the hall to listen. It was Hanley's bathroom. His shoulders slumped. He'd have to save the apology and invitation for later. *"Dammit."*

He reached for her door, only to find it locked. Digging into his pocket for his master key, he cast a quick glance down the hall. He'd leave the food on the dresser, that was all.

"What the…" The door opened a fraction of the way and hit something solid. He shut the door then opened it again only to have it bang against the barrier. Pressing his face to the crack, he eyed the back of the dresser and swore. What did she take him for, a predator? Didn't feel safe enough to shower without barricading her door? He pulled it closed and beat on it with his fist, not caring if other residents, or Nan, overheard.

"Hanley! Open the door!" He kept banging on the surface until the shower stopped. A few minutes later, the floor groaned and creaked. Was she moving that heavy oak dresser by herself? "Shit, let me help. Stand back and I'll push the door and dresser."

"Shut up, I've got it. You'll break the door." She grunted while pushing the dresser back to its rightful place.

When the door widened, his mouth opened, ready to give her an earful, but the sight of her stole his breath.

Her hair hung dripping past her waist, the midnight black a stark contrast to the white towel fitted to her shape. Her chest rose and fell rapidly with her heavy breathing. That dresser had to weigh more than she did. Her face was bare of cosmetics and her nose and cheeks had a faint dusting of freckles. Her gaze held his, large and accusing. She never looked more beautiful to him.

When she cleared her throat, waiting for him to say something, his focus came crashing back, and all the words he had planned to say disappeared from his memory. "I would never hurt you. You don't have to barricade the door to keep me out. Do you think I would hurt you? Are you scared of me? I'm sorry for what I said earlier. I was jealous. I don't know why, I have no claim to you. You don't even know me, or I you. There's just something." He took his first breath in his long spiel, dragging it into his lungs, then out. "Something I want to explore, if you do. Why did you barricade the door?"

In the short weeks she had gotten to know Beckett, she knew he never rambled, and yet here he stood, full of nerves and holding a bowl of something in her doorway. Despite the fact that he had undressed her with his eyes, the light seduction didn't provoke the usual chill and nausea. Then again, Beckett wasn't a creep like the guys she was used to. But still, she couldn't reveal her reasons for barricading the door. It was better if he didn't know the truth. It made them both safer.

Guilt twisted around with reason as her plan formed, but she was used to this type of evasion, and she would do anything to keep her secrets her own. Her body was a vessel, her beauty a gift, isn't that what Donovan always reminded her when he needed her to seduce his associates?

She released the towel and stepped out of it.

He dropped the bowl. It landed upside down on the carpet in the hall, cream splattering his jeans and the tops of his boots.

She kept her eyes direct on his, the invitation clear. Running her hands over her breasts, her nipples puckered from the cool air. Hesitation flashed over his face, some internal struggle between desire and moral code. When he stumbled forward over the bowl, anticipation built in her stomach, surprising her. *This is a job, don't forget it.*

He kicked the door with his boot and it shut behind him, then he was in front of her and her hands were tearing at his shirt. He helped her lift it and tossed it to the side, while her hands had moved to his belt. Her fingers trembled, clumsy, but she didn't stop to evaluate why this was different. Why he was different.

She dropped, dragging his pants and briefs down with her. Balanced on the balls of her feet, she helped him kick off his boots and step free from the clothes, then she reached up and gripped his erection, running both hands the long, hard length of him. He didn't need a warm-up, but his groan had her stretching up and running her tongue along the same path her hands had trailed. His hiss of breath was the only encouragement she needed to take him into her mouth.

"Hanley…"

She purred a response, her throat vibrating around him. His hands gripped her arms and pulled her to her feet with little effort.

"Stop. I want to show you, and I won't be able to hold back if you keep that up." As he spoke, his hands had begun to massage her body, and in one swift motion she was swept into his arms, her breast in his mouth. He sucked hard on her nipple before sitting her on the dresser.

Before she could assess the situation, he was spreading her knees, moving between them. His mouth moved from her nipple to rain kisses up her shoulder to her neck, then connect with her mouth in one hot, hungry kiss the moment he slid a finger into her. Her moan was muffled against his mouth, body heating beyond anything she was used to. She lifted her hips and scooted closer, wanting more contact. Wanting more of everything.

He added a finger, and swept his thumb over her swollen peak. She broke the kiss and let her head fall to his shoulder.

"Beckett!" His name tore from her lips as the orgasm broke through her sending a tremor in its wake and leaving her dazed and sated. She was supposed to pleasure him, that's how she did this. How she *always* did this. He was changing her game and at the moment she didn't mind at all.

He drew his fingers from her slowly, and ran his hands over her thighs in a gentle caress. He would give her more later, when this blazing fire was extinguished. He gripped her shoulder and held her back to keep her from sliding languid from the dresser, and pressed a kiss to her cheek. "Don't move, I'll be right back." He let her go and dashed to the nightstand, pulled open the drawers. *Come on Thomas, it'd be the only present I'll ever ask for. Ah-ha!* He grabbed the box, pulled a foil packet free and moved back to Hanley. Unwrapping the condom, he rolled it over his length and eased back between her thighs. He met her eyes, and waited as if asking permission.

"Yes, yes, yes. More!" Her nails dug into his shoulders.

He gripped her hips, bringing her to the edge of the dresser, and filled her after one gentle push. Giving her a minute to adjust to the thickness of him, he began to move.

She wrapped her legs around his waist and her arms around his neck, pulling him closer. Her breath was hot bursts against his throat. His movements quickened, the heavy dresser rocking underneath her and banging against floor and wall alike.

"Faster, Beckett. Fuck me."

"God, Hanley. You're beautiful." He kissed her exposed neck when she tipped her head back. She bucked against him as violently as he was thrusting into her.

"Don't stop. Don't stop. Don't stop." Her mantra came in breathy bursts, until she screamed through another release.

He followed, tipping over the edge and panted keeping up with her. Bodies slick, heart rate thundering, he lifted her easily into his arms and carried her to the bed. Gently, he laid her down and stepped away to clean himself. When he returned to her, she hadn't moved and her eyes were closed. He grabbed the blanket and began to draw it over her when she stirred.

"Not sleeping. Come here." One arm lifted, fingers searching blindly for him.

He held her hand, let her pull him down onto the bed beside her. Facing her, he pulled on her arm until she rolled to face him with her eyes still closed. His gaze dipped, hand tracing the patterns of ink that covered half her body. Art, he'd think of it now, though he had never thought of tattoos as art before. The intricate design patterned her skin, black against cream. Bold sweeps of ink against soft curves. He rested his hand on her hip and let his thumb play over the sensitive skin there. He could show her more now. His body was already warming back up with her so close.

First, he needed answers, then they could see what there could be between them.

"Hanley?"

"Mmm?"

"Why did you barricade the door?" He paused, thinking

maybe he should stop there but something pushed the rest of the words out. "What or who are you running from?"

Her magnificent eyes popped up and stared at him. A moment longer and maybe he could have stared into her soul, but she started to withdraw and stammer an evasion. She managed to roll away from him before he snaked his arm around her body to hold her still and silenced her with a simple, "Please trust me."

She went limp. Trust him? Could she? Sex was meant to be a diversion from the truth and now, after experiencing what they could give each other, she felt raw and exposed and worse – willing and wanting to confide in him.

"His name is Bruce, but everyone calls him Donovan." She shut her eyes and pretended *this* was real life and the rest only a terrible nightmare. His hand began to stroke her back in soothing strokes.

"He took me in. My life hasn't been the best, but my mom and I do okay. Or do now that he's adopted both of us. My mom, she's..." She tried to think of a way to say it so Beckett wouldn't judge her, them. "She's been a victim of something her entire life, and she suffers the consequences of those bad decisions every day. Probably will forever, but she can't change. Won't get help. She's all I got." She looked over her shoulder to see if his eyes held judgment, but found them closed, his hand continuously stroking. The quiet was oddly supportive.

"Bruce—I'm the only one he makes call him that. Well, he takes care of my mom. Makes sure she has what she needs and in return I live with him now, work for him. It's not romantic," she blurted, louder than she intended to, but she needed him to understand it wasn't like that. Not that he hadn't tried, but she hadn't let it go there. She knew in time she'd have no choice, but not if she never went back.

"He's older, in his 50s, but isn't a man to cross." She couldn't think of anything else to say to summarize who he was. That he owned her maybe, and had for years. That she dressed, ate, spoke, the way he wanted her to. That Beckett had been the first man she'd been intimate with because she chose to be.

She was Bruce's powerful Queen, skillfully controlled,

and the world a board of pawns for her to use.

"He wanted me to do him a favor, to convince an associate to pay an additional ten grand for a business transaction. I tried, but the customer became violent and wanted more than I usually offer them." She trembled, remembering, and Beckett pulled her close, his hand moving to stroke her hair. She tried to focus on Beckett's heartbeat, the warmth of his skin, but with her eyes closed, she went back to that day.

She fought not to gag when the man stepped closer, the scent of the cheap perfume Bruce's girls wore clinging to his clothes. He'd already had three lap dances. Hanley knew because she had selected the easiest of their girls. Her eyes darted to his hands, to the invisible filth. Please God, don't let him touch her face with those dirty fingers. Men always copped a feel with a lap dance, it didn't matter what strip club you happened to be in.

"Sit down, please." She said it before he could touch her. Some were allowed, but not him. The way his muddy eyes stayed with her, lips tipped in a sneer had her looking to the privacy screen. She tried to draw in comfort that the two burly shadows were her guards. If she so much as screamed, he'd be escorted from the property and she'd go back to serving drinks.

Bruce wouldn't be happy with that. She had to get the ten grand somehow.

"I'm going to make you feel like a million bucks." She straddled his lap, tipped her head forward as she slid down his body so that her hair curtained her face and concealed some of the smell of him. She took a deep breath, breathing in the scent of her honeydew shampoo.

"Baby, you're going to feel like two million when we're done here," he said, making her skin crawl.

Her hands were steady when she undid his belt, popped the button on his pants. She froze when he grabbed her wrist, drew it painfully down to her side. "Sto—"

"You think your blowjobs are worth ten grand?" He laughed in her face, cigar and whiskey mingling from his breath and choking her. "Think again, and if you want the ten grand like a good girl, you'll keep your mouth shut. I know you're his prize and I want more than your pretty lips on my swollen dick. I want what no one has ever gotten from you. None of his deals, his bribes, his transactions are

worth it, but I think he's wrong. You're just a dirty slut like the rest of them, and I'm going to violate that pretty body of yours. Get a real taste for why Donovan thinks your pussy is gold."

She couldn't think. He grabbed the shimmery cloth between her breasts and yanked until the thin bikini strings snapped and her breasts spilled into his greedy hands. She cried out when he pinched her nipple, and again when he fisted one hand in her hair and dragged her to feet. Not giving a damn about Donovan's ten grand, she screamed when he shoved her onto the couch and began to climb on top.

She kept screaming even when he smacked her and covered her mouth with his hand, pushing down so hard she worried her neck might snap. Still, she kept screaming.

Why weren't the bouncers coming to her rescue? No one had ever dared cross Donovan before; maybe her screams were misunderstood. The music of the club vibrated in her ears, the heavy beat threatening to drown her into silence.

Muffled shouts gave her hope and she shoved at the man, didn't even remember his name. He released her mouth long enough for her to gulp at air, but the second strike to her burning cheek was with enough force to close her throat up.

A loud crack reverberated through the air, then the man collapsed on her, his weight crushing her. Something warm and sticky began to pour from him, the metallic tang filling her nose until she nearly gagged. His blood soaked into her hair, until she began to sob.

Someone pulled her aggressor off, and dumped his body on the floor. Though her tears blurred her vision, she looked up into Donovan's face.

Beckett shifted, rolled onto his side and pulled her back against him so she was cocooned. She reminded herself she was safe now, safe with Beckett. Her voice trembled, but she needed to tell him. "Donovan killed him. He protected me. I ran because I realized that I will never be free of him. I took his money, bought a car, and here I am. I don't know where I'll go next."

Whatever Beckett expected, it hadn't been that. A jealous boyfriend, quick-tempered dad, maybe, but not the story Hanley had shared. Suddenly, Collin made sense, and more shame for the words he'd slapped at her coiled in his gut. "I'm sorry,

Hanley, for it all. For as long as you choose to stay, I promise to protect you." And he would, for no other reason than that a woman shouldn't have to live in fear. No matter what she meant to him, or what they'd become to each other, he'd give her and keep that promise.

He'd give her everything he could.

Beckett rolled them until he was on top. He brushed the hair away from her face and bent his head to find her lips in the waning darkness. The kiss was meant to soothe, but her teeth nipped his and stroked the flames that had continue to simmer. Her hands moved over his body, exploring the hard muscle, as his mouth moved to tease her neck.

Slow and passionate, to cherish her this time. Something else he could give her. They had all night to erase bad memories.

Chapter Five

"Stop fidgeting." Hanley slapped away Beckett's hands, then because he was sulking, reached up on her tippy toes to press a kiss to his neck.

He stared over her head at their reflection in the mirror. They stood in his bedroom. "How do you know how to tie one of these nooses anyway?"

"I picked it up somewhere." She wouldn't talk about her past and spoil this moment.

"Twenty-five years on this planet and Nan has never given me a tie for Christmas. Worse, she's demanded I wear it tonight. It's my family. I see them all the damn time. What makes tonight a tie-worthy occasion?"

Hanley finished straightening the red silk and stepped back to survey her work. "Maybe she wants me to see what you look like when you're cleaned up. Show you off." Not that she was staying long-term, and Beckett didn't need to tangle up in her mess. Short-term was fine, short-term was fun. Long-term meant something she couldn't give. Didn't have it to give.

His fingers lifted her chin until she met his eyes. She offered a small, sad smile to reassure him that she was fine.

"Did it work?"

She chuckled and hugged his waist, the silk tickling her nose. "I suppose, but don't let it inflate that ego of yours."

He kissed the top of her head before drawing her back and winked. "Never. Now sit down and close your eyes."

"Beckett, it's Christmas Eve. Your family will be here any minute. We don't have time for that."

He grabbed her hand and tugged her to the bed, easing her down. "There is always time for that, but this is something else. Sit and close your eyes. I got you a present."

"You didn't have to get me anything." She shifted under his stare. "Okay, give it to me."

"No peeking." He moved to his closet, turned back to make sure she wasn't, and opened the door, drawing the dress out. He'd suggested to Nan that Hanley join the family for dinner, or Nan had suggested it. It was hard to tell. When Nan wanted something, she usually talked you into it until you thought you were the one behind it all along. Either way, he wanted Hanley with him at dinner. Wanted her to meet his family.

The baby blue Chiffon dress would be perfect for her, and long enough to hide her tennis shoes or bare feet. With a little help, he had figured out her size, but he was not a man about to contemplate a woman's shoes. The dress would have to do.

"Open your eyes," he said once he stood in front of her. As her hands slid away from her face he added, "I'd be honored if you'd join me for dinner tonight, Hanley." He watched her face closely and noted that it went from happy, to her expression darkening, to blank. "You hate it. I knew that woman in the shop was a ninny." He whirled the dress away and stalked back to the closet, prepared to throw it inside.

"No! No," she said more calmly. She moved to him and eased the hanger out of his fingers before running her hand over the shimmery material. The high-neck of lace was beautiful. "I love it. I really do." She met his puzzled look. "I don't know about meeting your family, or think that's a good idea. I can't talk about who I am, not really." She didn't want them to not like her, she realized. Gaining their acceptance seemed important for some reason. Maybe she was beginning to like Beckett more than she intended to. And wasn't that another reason not to mix up with his family and their traditions?

"Please, come." He said it quietly, and with heart.

Shit, she thought. Maybe they were both lost. "Okay." She touched his face, found it endearing the way he turned into her palm to kiss it. "I better get ready then. Thank you for my gift."

He swept her off her feet, dress and all, to plant a smacking loud kiss on her lips before setting her back down. "You're welcome, and you've got fifteen minutes." He added a wink before shutting the door behind him.

He knew he was grinning like a loon as he made his way towards the kitchen, but Hanley had, in a short time, wrapped her hands around his heart, and he knew it. He couldn't tell her, of course, not yet, not while he didn't have a solid plan to keep her there with him. But he was working on it, and having her meet his family was the first step.

Family meant a lot of things to the Lawsons. This was the one night a year where the B&B seemed like a regular household with most of the guests away visiting their own families, and the Lawsons filling the space. Beckett didn't remember when Christmas Eve had started being held here, but for as long as he could remember, it had. His mom, dad, brother, sister and family, and Nan. It was tradition, now and forever.

They'd share a meal of roast beef and all the fixings, then the family would spill into the living room in front of a fire, though it was usually too warm for one. Up next was playing a game and drinking Nan's famous boozy white cocoa. It wasn't Christmas Eve without this, only this year he hoped to add to it by spending the night with Hanley in his bed. He'd peel her out of that dress with his teeth if he had to, but he was getting his mouth and his hands on her again, and soon. He couldn't think of a better way to spend a Christmas.

"Beckett, dear, pass the mashed potatoes."

"Huh?"

"The potatoes," Nan repeated. Beckett looked away from Hanley, who was seated across from him at the large table, and did as his Nan asked. He flushed when he noticed all eyes were on him. His brother, never one to leave things alone, was grinning, and that usually meant trouble.

"She's beautiful man, I get that." Brentley's accent was thicker than his brother's. Probably because he never left for school or tried to make a life away from this place. "But if you don't stop staring at her, you're going to make Ma blush."

"Brentley James, you shut that mouth of yours." Victoria's voice held amusement, though she rapped a clean spoon against her son's arm.

Conversation ebbed and flowed, and despite the jest, Beckett risked another look at Hanley, whose soft skin was a shade of crimson he'd never seen her wear before. She pushed the peas around on her plate without looking at anyone. He'd have to get her alone for a few minutes before they moved into the living room and put her back to ease.

Hanley did her best to cool her heated skin, and took a deep drink of her ice water. While no one's attention lingered on her, she still felt like the wedding crasher and everyone knew it. She didn't belong here. She held back a gasp when a foot started to raise her dress, and lifted her gaze to Beckett's. His slight grin let her know it was him, and she tried to feel better at his reassurance.

Sure, his family had been nice during introductions. His mom had even hugged her, and his sister complimented her dress. She'd been nice and open enough until the questions started coming. Where was she from, didn't she have family to see over the holidays? Would the questions always be the same and always make her feel like such an outcast? After stumbling her way through the lies – she really needed to perfect her story if she was going to be living with it permanently – they had begun to leave her alone. While she knew it was better that way, she couldn't shake the disappointment at knowing they probably thought her weird and wondered what she was doing with their son.

Beckett caught up to her while she was carrying her plate to the kitchen. "Hey, don't let them get to you. They are a noisy, nosy bunch and you won't give them any gossip. They mean well, but they don't understand anything that's not an open book. It's not you."

"It's okay, I get it. You don't have to protect me." She rinsed her plate, started to grab for the soap, but Beckett caught her wrist. She arched a brow, and he responded by kissing her knuckle.

"No dishes. Tradition is we go play Dirty Santa now. Dishes can wait."

She really wanted to sneak off to her room and find some comfort in the solitude. "What's Dirty Santa?"

She broke away from Beckett as the rest of the family began bringing in dishes. Nan sent her a warm smile and a knowing look that instantly made her feel better. Beckett grabbed her hand again and drew her through the door.

"I'll explain while they make the cocoa. Best damn cocoa you'll ever have."

"Okay," she managed before Beckett had seated himself on the loveseat, drawing her down to sit snugly beside him. Great. If there were any doubts about their intimacy, there wouldn't be now. "Explain away."

By the time the family was crowded around in the living room with cups of white cocoa, Beckett's niece was passing around a bowl and asking for everyone to draw a slip of paper, while his nephew gathered the wrapped gifts and set them in the middle of the floor.

Hanley had every intention of nestling back against the cushions and quietly observing the action. She held her cup with both hands and brought the drink to her lips for a taste. The creamy goodness was the right heat level and rushed over her lips to serenade her tongue. "Mmm," she purred before she could stop herself. Beckett turned to her.

"Good stuff, right? Nan's secret. Be careful in drinking it or you'll forget it's loaded with liquors and wind up face down on the floor before you know it."

"The truth spoken from a man who's been there, done that," Brentley chimed in.

"Pick one please," a sweet voice rang out. Hanley eyed the pretty little girl in front of her.

"Oh no, sweetie. I'm not playing."

"You are too," Beckett said, and grabbed a slip, handed it to her.

She sat her cup down on the end table and stiffened. "But you said everyone who plays needs to add a gift to the pot. I didn't."

"You did," he said casually and ruffled his niece's curls before she continued down the line.

Hanley slumped. There went her cover. "Thank you," she muttered, and unfolded her slip of paper. A squiggly number

149

three was scribbled in red crayon on the paper, no doubt Beckett's niece's handiwork. She moved forward to sit on the edge of the couch and began to survey the different sized presents on the floor. If she was going to play, she might as well have some fun with it.

When it was her turn to draw a present, she asked Beckett's mom and sister's husband to hold theirs out again. No, she didn't want the smoothie-maker or the gift card to some local home improvement store. "Cami," she called to Beckett's niece. "Can you hand me the present in gold. No, not that one, the one with the sparkly paper. Thank you, sweetheart." She didn't care that everyone was quiet and watching her. She hadn't unwrapped an actual Christmas present since she was a little girl herself. Donovan showered her with gifts, but he figured the jeweler's box was enough wrapping.

Trembling fingers ripped through the paper in haste, causing Beckett's dad to gasp in feigned horror. Everyone teased him about taking hours to open his gifts in order to save the paper. She flashed him a grin and threw the paper to the ground where Beckett's nephew scooped it up and tossed it into a big black bag.

"What is it?" Beckett asked, leaning over her.

"I don't know yet." Her voice was breathless. She didn't know why she was so damned excited to open the small box. Lifting the lid, it was her turn to gasp. Tenderly, she lifted the silver bracelet from the box, careful of the dangling charm. She knew the snowflake wasn't really diamond-encrusted, but it sparkled as bright all the same. "It's beautiful."

Beckett took it from her hand and held it up for her wrist. She gave it, and he latched it closed around her. She shook her wrist in front of her face, admiring the way it dazzled. She'd been draped in diamonds before, but that didn't compare to what she was wearing now and the reminder she would always have of being welcomed in by Beckett and Nan.

"Let me see, Hanley," Beckett's mom said. "Oh, it's lovely. Fits you perfectly."

Hanley nodded, still amazed that it was hers, and forgetting to be dense, settled back in beside Beckett, and draped her hand over his lap. He patted it before pointing to his sister's husband.

"Give it over, Tommy. I'll take that gift card."

"Dang it, Beckett. We wanted to fix up the porch," Tommy whined, but he handed the card over.

"You can still fix it up," Beckett said while Tommy drew a new gift from the pile that remained. "Just not with my gift card."

"Yeah, yeah. You know Dad isn't going to let it go that easy."

"Yeah, he will." Brentley tossed in. "He wouldn't pass up the opportunity to torture us while taking forty minutes to open a wrapped gift." The group groaned in unison and he used the distraction to snatch the gift card from Beckett's hand. "Mine now, anyway, and second time stolen means it's out of the runnin'."

"Dam---ng it," Beckett corrected, sending the kiddos a quick glance.

"That's okay, my boys, I'll buy the supplies myself for any fixing up and you can all come over and supply the free labor."

The three boys groaned again, and again when their dad grabbed a present and brought out his pocket knife. Quite used to Grandpa's shenanigans, the kids began to boycott and ask for presents before the women got up and brought around a small stack of presents for them to open while grandpa took his sweet time opening his.

Hanley snuggled into Beckett to watch the kid's paper fly and Becket's dad tear away corner by corner in his attempt to not rip his paper at all. Remembering her cocoa, she reached for it and though it had cooled, began to sip. She liked the way the charm from her bracelet jingled against the china.

By the time Beckett's dad had opened the crystal vase, the kids were off happily playing with their new toys. Brentley leaned forward to slap his dad on the back. "Should have stolen Beckett's travel mug, dad. What are you going do with a vase?"

Their dad sent Brentley a look as if to say, 'have I taught you nothing all these years, son?' "Why I'm going to buy your beautiful mama flowers, of course." Beckett's mom leaned over and kissed her husband on the cheek.

"That's a good, loving man. Take a lesson, boys." She bent to retrieve the last two gifts on the floor. "Becca's up, guys. What's it going to be? Mystery gift or are you going to steal one of ours?"

Hanley stiffened when Becca's gaze locked on her wrist. No. Mine. As if reading his sister, Beckett sat up.

"Come on Becca, Hanley loves that bracelet and it's her first time playing. Give her a break, take a mystery gift."

"The game is called *Dirty* Santa, Beckett. Fair is fair. Hand it over if you please, Hanley."

"I'll buy you a new one," Beckett whispered in her ear while she unfastened the bracelet. She bit her lip to keep the sting in her eyes from worsening and handed it over to Beckett's sister.

"No so fast, Becca. Hand it over." Nan's voice surprised them all, especially considering Nan wore her wedding ring still and that was the extent of her jewelry. With a pout, Becca did as told and reached for the last mystery gift to open.

Hanley had already begun unwrapping her new present, and though it wasn't as sentimental as the bracelet, the shimmery scarf in blues and greens was pretty enough. She draped it around her neck to show she was being a good sport.

"That's pretty," Beckett said, fingering the material. "Even prettier on you." He grabbed her glass and stood now that the game was over. "Let me get you a refill."

Brentley followed him into the kitchen. He went about ladling more cocoa into Hanley's cup and waited for his brother to speak his mind. It didn't take long.

"What are you doing with that girl, Beckett? She's weird."

He tensed. "Is not. Maybe she just doesn't like you. I think she has great taste." He looked over to see his brother frowning. "Come on Brent, she's fine. A bit shy is all. You can't hold that against her."

"No, but isn't it ironic how she shows up here before Christmas like some charity case? Not that I wouldn't be happy if you found something outside this place to devote some time to, because I would. This was Gramps's dream, not yours. When you gonna live for you?"

"Watch it, Brent. This is my home, and my place is here as much as it ever was Gramps's place. It's not yours and that's fine. Great, even. I'm happy, and Hanley is fine. Leave it alone."

"Fine. Okay. Just don't let her weasel her way into your bed because she has nowhere else to go. This isn't a shelter, Beckett. It's a business, for Christ's sake."

Beckett paused in passing by his brother, and leaned close. Roughly the same height, they were eye to eye. "She is not some homeless nobody. She's running from an asshole in Chicago and has nowhere to go because she doesn't know where to go or what to do yet. She's scared, she's smart, and she's exactly where she needs to be."

Hanley cleared her throat, and both boys jumped before noticing her in the entry. She couldn't meet their eyes so she stared at the floor. "I came to tell Beckett I didn't want seconds." *Screw that.* She did meet their eyes now, and crossed her arms. "Don't worry Brent," she mocked Beckett's tone. "I won't be here much longer and Beckett and his wallet will be just fine." She trained her gaze on Beckett. "I understand that secrecy isn't common in your family, or a part of who you are, but you have no right to share my secrets. They are mine to tell or mine to keep." Her voice hitched, but she pushed through. "I'm sorry I ever trusted you."

"Hanley, wait," Beckett called after her when she turned on her heel and ran from the kitchen. "Dammit, Brentley. See what you did. This is your fault."

"Not entirely," he threw back. "You put yourself in this position."

"Stop it, both of you." Nan appeared and crooked a finger for the boys to follow her. She pointed to the couch where both sat at her silent command. "Attention please, attention." Minus the kids who were in another room playing, all the adults turned their gazes to Nan.

"I don't know what all of you are thinking, though I know what some of you are," her eyes narrowed on Brentley until he looked away. "Hanley is a troubled woman with a past, no different from all the others lost in this world. She has a heart of gold and has been a huge help to me this season. She doesn't ask for anything except her privacy and she's entitled to it."

When Nan's eyes lingered on Beckett, he wondered how much she knew of Hanley's past.

"Now you've all been raised good and right, and you're certainly not showing our Northern guest any Southern hospitality. I suggest you remember what exactly that is and be thankful this Christmas that you all come from and have a loving family; our Hanley does not. Until she no longer needs us, I'm going to continue to make her feel welcome, and better yet, safe here. Now you two get your behinds up." She pointed to Beckett and Brentley. "And go tackle the kitchen. The dishes alone should give you enough time to think about your wrongdoings and think up a way to fix them."

"Yes ma'am," they said in unison before shuffling to the kitchen. Nan kept her expression stern while they passed, though they were already forgiven. My, she loved her sweet, stupid, stubborn boys.

Three hours later, Beckett had helped clean up the kitchen, said goodbye to his family, and spent some time on the internet searching for Bruce Donovan. A few slaps for illegals, some trafficking, but nothing stuck and the man had never done any hard time. He'd bookmarked some articles that spoke of Donovan and his companion, Crystal Hanley. There was plenty of speculation that they were an item, despite Donovan saying the beautiful woman was young enough to be his daughter. Still, Beckett didn't like the photos in some of those pieces where a stunning Hanley was sidled up to a striking older man. The salt and peppered hair didn't remind Beckett of an old man, but a powerful one. There was dominance in the way he stood in pictures, most often, his hand around or on Hanley.

He looked down at the article in his hand that he had printed, felt the ache spread through his chest though he knew the article was a lie. Hanley was alive, and she was here. He knocked softly on her closed door. "Hanley? It's Beckett."

The voice was distant and muffled, but Beckett made out "Go away."

"I can't do that. I need to show you something." Silence hung heavy in the hall. All guests were either out with their families still or had come back and tucked themselves in their rooms for the night. He looked left to the closed door of the newlyweds. Come to think of it, he couldn't remember seeing them at all since they checked in. Nan must be delivering all their meals to their room.

He knocked again on Hanley's door. "Come on baby, please. Crystal, open the door."

It swung open, though she didn't step back to allow him to enter. "What did you call me?"

"Crystal Hanley." He said it softly and watched her face. She wouldn't meet his eyes, and didn't need to. He recognized the signs of crying. He unclenched the paper and held it out to her. She stared hard at it. "Crystal Hanley," he said again, urging her to read. "5'3", green eyes, black hair. Born April 7th, 1986. Died December 5th, 2009. Age 23."

"What!" She grabbed the paper, stared down into her own smiling face. She read her obituary on the way back to the bed. Since she hadn't shut the door in his face, Beckett followed.

"I died. *He* killed me." She began to laugh; it bubbled out of her in irregular gusts until her voice hitched and the tears began to fall again. Beckett sat down on the bed and gathered her shaking body into his arms.

"Sh, baby. It's okay. You're not dead. You're alive, and now you're free. He set you free, don't you see that?"

She did see that, she understood, but the sobs racked her body in painful waves. She didn't know how Donovan had done it, but he'd faked her death. She was safe. The world would forget Crystal Hanley ever existed and she could become whoever she wanted to be.

"Stay," he said, forcing her to come back from her

thoughts. "Stay here, with me and Nan. We can make up a new identity, find you a job. You can have a life here. With us. With me.

"Don't say anything yet," he added quickly. "Think about it." He kissed her cheek, tasted the salt from her tears on his lips. It was clear to him now. She had to stay. He'd protect her. They'd be good for each other. He stood abruptly and moved to shut her door. Undoing his tie, he sent her a grin, and kicked out of his dress shoes. He hit the switch to bring them darkness.

"What are you do-doing?" She hiccupped.

"Spending Christmas with you. You're the only present I want." With grace that didn't match his size, he gathered her in his arms again and shifted them on the bed so she was wrapped up in him.

"Tomorrow we'll think of a plan. A new life for you wherever you want it to be." God, he hoped she stayed. He'd beg if he had to.

She was quiet so long he thought her asleep, and was mostly there himself when she said his name.

"Beckett?"

"Mm?"

"Merry Christmas."

"Merry Christmas, *Hanley*."

Christmas Candy

by Misti Murphy

Dedicated to all the Wenches

Chapter One

HOLLY

"Could today have been any worse?" I holler, entering the apartment I share with Roxy. Dropping the cardboard box, which holds the items that before four o'clock this afternoon, occupied my desk, I head for the kitchen. A glass of wine is definitely in order, maybe even something stronger.

"What happened?" Roxy asks, sticking her head around the door to her bedroom, an electric shock of pink, her crowning glory today. I swear she changes her hair color at least once a week.

"I got fired." I let that hang out there for a minute. It was a big enough shock, especially on Christmas Eve. "Then some douche stole my car."

Under her stare my face heats. Those two things alone were enough to make a girl want to cry. "I called Jasper, to see if he'd come and get me. Do you know what he told me?"

Roxy, finally all the way out of her room, is barely dressed in a skimpy leopard print mini dress that shows off half of her tattoos. I say half because I've seen her naked and I know there's more than what's on display. "What?"

"That he's sorry, but he needs to break up with me because I'm too nice. What does that even mean, Rox?"

She wraps her hand around my arm, her rainbow colored nails keeping me prisoner as she drags me the rest of the way into the kitchen. I want to retreat to my bedroom and bury myself under my covers to sulk for an hour, a week, or however long it takes to get over losing my job and my car. It's surprising that Jasper's defection doesn't bother me so much.

"He's a douchebag, Hol." Roxy isn't the type to mince words, but I never saw Jasper that way. Roxy is digging in the fridge for alcohol, and I happily accept the premixed bottle of vodka and passion fruit she passes to me.

"How can I be too nice?"

She opens her bottle, and leans against the fridge for a long moment before answering. "Well, you are. Nice, I mean. You're straighter than my thirteen-year-old sister, and we both know she's a square."

"Way to go and kick a girl while she's down," I mumble into my drink while giving her the evil eye.

"You know I love you, Hol. You're too serious, that's all. You don't seem to know how to have fun. Do you realize that bottle you're holding is the first alcohol you've consumed since I moved in here?"

"What?" I raise my eyebrows and peel the corner of the bottle's label trying to remember my last alcoholic drink. "Surely not."

"Uh-huh! Isn't there a girl deep down in there who wants to have a little fun?"

"But…" I am about to say I have too much work to do, but that would imply I still have a job, which I don't, so what the hell. "What kind of fun?"

Roxy seems to ponder the question while I tentatively sip my drink. The first mouthful makes me grimace, but the next is slightly better.

"There's a bubble party tonight at Factory. That's where I was heading. You should come with me."

I crinkle my nose at the idea, but I want to prove I can have fun. "Sounds great."

*M*AX

I walk off the plane and make my way to the luggage carousels. What on earth had possessed me to take this job? Moving from Texas to Sydney, Australia almost overnight on a whim had seemed like a great idea at the time, but after fifteen hours on a long distance flight, I'm beginning to wonder if I've made a huge mistake. Of course, I had, but it wasn't necessarily this one. It had been getting involved with my boss's fiancé and the subsequent reaction when he caught us going at it in his office. I hadn't been thinking, or at least not with the head I should have been using.

I grab my two suitcases off the carousel and look around for Chase. He'd come to Australia six months before me. The way he talked about his job you'd think he'd gotten in on the gold rush. Still, it had been enough for my brother to convince me I should check it out for myself.

When I screwed up with Monica, it seemed like the perfect time for a complete change of lifestyle. Monica had been a mistake, and an expensive one at that, one I didn't plan on repeating. I'd been a playboy for so long, I'd forgotten how much trouble it could actually cause, which was why I'd made a vow while I was waiting for the plane to disembark. No more sleeping around. I was done with women.

Chase hurries toward me with a scrap of cardboard, my name written in bright red marker. By the way his lip curls up on one side, I can tell he thinks he's hilarious. I don't need the sign to recognize my 6'2" brown haired, blue-eyed brother. Other than the tattoos running over my biceps, it's like looking in a mirror when I see my twin.

"Good to see you," he says, leaning in for an awkward pat-to-the-back hug. "Glad you decided to join us."

"Where's Beth?" I ask, looking over his shoulder for my sister-in-law.

"She had to work. We'll catch up with her later."

He takes one of my suitcases, and we walk out into a wall of suffocating heat. I've left winter behind for hell.

Chase chuckles at my expression. "You'll get used to it," he says, stuffing the suitcases into the trunk of his car. "Now let's drop off your stuff, and then we'll go meet Beth."

He fills me in on Beth's job and the bubble party she's hosting tonight on the drive home. I'll be staying temporarily with Chase until I'm settled into the new job, which shouldn't take long. I'm a programming legend in my own circles, and now that I've quit women, I'll only improve.

While I unpack, I give myself a pep talk. Moving countries was a good idea. I'll start work in two weeks and forget about women entirely, at least until I'm ready to settle down. That won't be any time soon, though. I'm not even thirty yet. Once I'm settled into the spare room, I join Chase for a beer on the patio.

"What time does Beth get home?" I ask downing the beer, trying to offset the blistering heat that lingered even after the sun went down.

"Late. I promised to take you over to Factory so she could see you."

I love Beth like a little sister, but I'm not sure a club full of miniskirts and low cut tops is going to help me keep the vow I only just made today. "Maybe I should stay here."

Chase raises an eyebrow and then gets up to dump the beer bottles in the recycling bin. "No way. Beth would have my hide."

He's right, she would. She's a firecracker, and we both learned a long time ago, you don't say no to the minx. "Well I guess I'm ready then."

Chapter Two

HOLLY

"You're not wearing that," Roxy says from the bedroom door. Her arms cross in a pose I know means that I've already lost this battle.

"What's wrong with it?" I ask checking myself out in the full-length mirror behind the closet door and running a hand over my ponytail to smooth a couple of flyaway blonde strands.

"What's right with it? We're going to a bubble party. You're going to get wet. The jeans have to go, and that top is altogether too boring." She grabs my hand and tugs me into her room. "You can keep the sneakers."

Thirty minutes later, I emerge from her room dressed like a hooker. I'm wearing a gold bikini top under a white mini dress, which is obviously a singlet and barely covers my butt. Why had I thought this would be a good idea? I'm going to need a lot more liquid courage to pull this off.

Roxy isn't finished with me yet. I grab another bottle of premixed vodka from the fridge, while she stalks me with liquid liner. I open the bottle and chug half of it before sitting at the table. It is better to submit and have done with it, than to try and resist.

After she takes my look from high-class hooker to street whore, she gives a wolfish grin. "I bet you chicken out before we even get in the door."

"No. No way," I say, my eyelashes heavy from the six coats of waterproof mascara she's applied. I'm going to prove I can have fun even if it kills me.

"How about a little dare then, and a wager?"

I chew the inside of my cheek and try to puzzle out what she is thinking. "Okay."

She stands back to survey her handiwork and her smile widens. There is no way I am going to look in a mirror.

"I dare you to pick up some random hotness and bring

him home."

I swallow. I'm going to lose this dare. I've never had a one night stand in my life. "What's the bet?"

"Fifty dollars says you can't pick up the nicest nerd we can find looking like that."

$\mathcal{M}$AX

"I still don't think this is a good idea Chase. I'm trying to quit women."

Chase laughs as we line up to enter the club. "You just need to find the right woman."

There is one huge difference between my twin and me. Where I love all women, he has loved only one woman since high school. I can't blame him. Beth is amazing, but I can't imagine settling for one woman. "I'm quitting my addiction."

Chase nods. He was the only one who knew what had happened with Monica. "Maybe try playing the nice guy for a while. Girls tend to steer clear of nice."

I cock my head to the side and think it over. I did catch a lot more honey with my bad boy persona than Chase has ever managed. Maybe he's right. "I'll give it a go."

Security looks us over and we pay admission before entering the club.

It is crowded. There are people at the bar lined up three or four deep. Everywhere I look, there are girls. Most of them aren't even dressed, dancing around in barely there bikinis. I groan. This isn't helping me with my decision to quit them.

Beth is beside us in a flash of white bikini and giant gold hoop earrings. She leans in for a hug before she wraps her arms around Chase. "It's so good to see you, Max."

"You too, little one." I grin at her and she sticks out her tongue. She hates when I call her that.

"So what do you think?" She sweeps her arm out to encompass the room.

"I don't see any bubbles." I say, wondering what my sister in law had been thinking when she planned this night.

"There will be soon," she promises. "I better go talk to my boss and make sure everything is running smoothly."

I watch her saunter away. "She hasn't changed at all."

"She's perfect." Chase says, slapping me on the back. For one sparkling second, I am actually envious of what he has. "Let's get a drink, what do you want?"

I sense people looking at me and I know I'm already attracting female attention. It's only a matter of time before one of them approaches me. Am I strong enough to turn down an offer of sex? Or will my cock get the better of me?

"So how am I going to pull off the good guy act?" I ask Chase.

He turns around and chuckles. "You've already got admirers."

"I know. What do I do?" My instinct is to target the sexiest one and drag her into the bathroom for a quickie, but I'm trying to ignore it.

"Come with me," Chase says, and soon after I find myself in the bathroom with him. He takes off his shirt, a blue and white plaid button down that is better suited to the office than a club. "Put this on. Leave the sleeves down."

I shrug into it and button it up over my black T-shirt. Then he hands me his glasses. We have a similar prescription, so it's no issue to see through them, though I usually only wear them when working. Looking in the mirror, I see I've been transformed into a nerd. "Superman, huh?"

"More like Clark Kent," Chase says. "Now talk about programming and Doctor Who and I swear, you won't be able to catch a break with the girls tonight."

Chapter Three

Holly

We bypass the line to get into Factory, since Roxy works there, and make our way inside. Already I can feel guys undressing me with their eyes. I tug at the bottom of my dress and Roxy slaps my hand. "You have to act the part. Fiddling is a dead giveaway you're not who you're pretending to be."

I have never been so uncomfortable. It's crowded inside, and I try to hug the wall as they turn on the foam cannons and begin covering everyone with bubbles. Roxy pulls me forward. Her eyes dart back and forth, scanning the room for the perfect target. She's going to make an easy fifty off me tonight.

She nudges me with her elbow and points out a guy by himself in the sea of foam. "There!" she says. "That's the one."

I study him through the foam raining down on us, covering every surface. There's foam up to my knees and my dress that hadn't covered me before, is now see-through. Roxy is already dancing to the trance music, slowly making her way across the room toward one of the other employees.

He's dressed in a long sleeve shirt and his glasses have foam on them. He seems a little lost sitting on his own by the bar. I get the feeling that he and I are on the same wavelength about this party.

Making my way to the bar, I join the line and keep watching him from the corner of my eye while I wait to be served. How am I supposed to get him to even talk to me when I look like I should be paid for so much more? There is no way I'm winning this stupid bet.

I pay for my skittle vodka and sidle up next to him. I'm still uncertain how to play my part, but since he's preoccupied with the floor and not looking at me, I have time to formulate a plan. I'm a nice girl. Roxy is the sex demon. What would she do?

It doesn't take me long to realize that Roxy wouldn't

give him time to talk, and I take her lead. My stomach is full of butterflies at the idea of accosting this stranger. He's quite cute really, solidly built with brown wavy hair and blue eyes. He could be here with his girlfriend, or he might reject me. I know I would. Still, I need to prove Jasper and Roxy wrong. This girl can have fun.

$\mathcal{M}$AX

The girl standing beside me is hot. It's taking all my concentration to stare at the floor and not ogle her body, which is on display beneath a see-through mini dress. There's a hint of gold bikini clinging to her, and I appreciate that she has serious curves. If I weren't swearing off women, I'd have hit on her the minute I saw her walk through the door. How long is she going to stand next to me? The floor is boring, and I want to check her out from a distance. I'm about to get up and move away from her when she launches herself into my lap. What the hell?

"Hi." Her voice is kind of breathless and rough, as her arms wind around my neck. Her voice alone sends a flash of heat through me. Even if her naked thighs weren't wrapped around my hips, I'd still be very turned on right now.

"Hi," I mumble trying to ignore her tits pressed against my chest. Damn, this is not going well.

She wriggles on my lap, causing something to come up between us. "What about Doctor Who?"

She raises an eyebrow. "Doctor Who?"

"Yeah," I say. I don't want Chase to be right about girls being turned off by nerds, but it's my only hope if I'm going to keep my vow?

"Why? Do you want to play doctor?" she asks, rolling her hips so I can feel her against me.

I groan. There's no way I could have predicted her answer, or the way she very much makes me want to play doctor with her. She doesn't let me get another word in as she presses her lips to mine, her tongue snaking into my mouth, a sweet explosion of vodka and candy. I grab her hips tightly as she dominates my mouth like a tigress and sticks her hand between us to squeeze my cock. Who knew nerds got better action than I did?

*H*OLLY

When I jumped on his lap I wasn't expecting to enjoy myself quite as much as I am. I'd expected to get dumped on the floor while he glared at me. That would have been okay. I would have been able to go home and hide in my bed like I'd planned on doing before Roxy came up with this ridiculous idea.

Then he opens his mouth, and that sweet American drawl sends shivers down my spine. He's bigger than I thought, more muscular. The way he is gazing at me, I wonder if he can tell I'm blushing under the layers of makeup.

He says something about Doctor Who. Normally, I would be happy to talk about Stephen Moffat's excellent writing and why I think Ten is better than Eleven, but that isn't the point, so I kiss him to shut him up.

Who knew he'd be able to kiss like that? I'd thought Jasper was a great kisser. Boy was I wrong. This guy grabs my hips and skillfully explores my mouth. My blood heats and a needy ache gathers between my legs. It's no longer that I need to win this bet. I want to win it. I want to see what else this man is capable of.

I reach between us, and wrap my hand around the outline of his dick. His jeans are soaked, but I can tell, from that one touch, that he is bigger than what I've had before. "Those wet jeans must be uncomfortable. Maybe you should take them off."

He pulls back to study me for a moment, but I'm not giving him time to back out. I get to my feet, grabbing his hand to lead him outside.

$\mathcal{M}$AX

I could start my vow tomorrow. It doesn't have to be today. Besides, this girl is like me, a player, so it isn't like I'm going to be upsetting anyone with my actions. I don't even know her name, and she hasn't asked mine. She doesn't give me time to respond which is good. It's the type of play I use all the time. Don't give them time to think about their actions and you are more likely to get what you want.

We pass the packed line at the entrance and she pushes me up against a wall, her body clinging to mine she kisses me again. I wonder if her plan is to hook up right here, out in the open. Not that I mind, but some distance away from the line might be a good idea. Her mouth is hot against my skin and she runs her tongue over my jaw. "Two blocks to my house," she whispers. Then she's walking off, and I hurry to catch up.

I like this girl, which confuses me. Normally I'd be happy with this situation, but she has my curiosity piqued, and I want to know her name. I don't ask, though. Tomorrow I'm giving up girls for good so there isn't any point in getting to know her, but if I got to know her maybe I wouldn't have to give up sex. We could be buddies, the kind that are only for extracurricular activities. I decide to wait. Just because she's sexy as hell and I'm more turned on than I've been in years doesn't mean the sex will be any good.

She stops in front of a dark blue door and fumbles with her keys before letting us into the apartment. I swing the door shut behind me and then I pounce.

I back her up against the wall, pinning her with my hands in her hair. The silken strands wrap around my knuckles, giving me leverage and I tilt her head for better access to her mouth. I devour her, pushing my tongue inside her mouth to sample the unique candy taste of her. Our tongues tangle as her leg rides up around me and I hoist her up so that both legs wind around my hips. She's like skittles and vodka, and since I don't know her name I think of her as Candy girl.

She clings to me while I blaze a trail of hot kisses down her neck. My hands, free due to the support of the wall, go to her tits. Palming them, I feel the pebbled nipples only partially hidden by her bikini top. She is more than a handful, and I knead both breasts, my cock stirring against her thigh. I tug at the hem of the dress, which is nothing more than a singlet and whip it up over her head. She digs her nails into my shoulders and I crook a finger over the top of the bikini, pulling it down so her boobs fall free. My mouth waters. Even in the semi-darkness, only illuminated by a streetlight, I can see she has the nicest tits I've ever seen and they are all natural. If I were looking for a pair of tits to spend the rest of my life with, it would be this pair I've got in my hands now. It's a weird thought, and I banish it immediately. This is a one-night-only affair. I'll be gone before the sun comes up.

I suck a nipple into my mouth, running my tongue over the nub until it hardens, and nibble it playfully, making her moan. She works the buttons on my shirt and pushes it off my shoulders. She groans, and I realize she's been thwarted by the T-shirt underneath. Lowering her to the floor, I quickly shed both shirts and she yanks me into her bedroom. It's darker than in the hallway, but I don't care. I'm enjoying getting to know her body with my hands. I kick the door closed and pull her back against me. "Come here Candy girl," I growl.

My hands find her shoulders in the darkness, and I sweep her hair to one side and nip her shoulder while I run my fingers round the front of her to gather her tits and fondle them. She arches her back, which pushes her butt into contact with my groin, and I grind against her, trailing a hand down her belly and under her bikini. Soft downy hair greets my fingertips, and I layer more kisses on her shoulder and neck in appreciation. It has been a long time since I've come across a girl who didn't go for the completely bare look. Slipping a finger into her folds, I touch the slick heat gathered there. She's ready for me. I know I could throw her on the bed and fuck her now, but she has the body of a goddess and I'm off my game. What would she think if I threw off this good guy persona and went with my instincts?

Holly

Holy crap. I want to get on the bed already. When he calls me Candy girl in that sweet accent, I realize I never told him my name, but I hadn't gotten his either. It makes the situation that much hotter. His hands are so warm against my skin and I press my butt against his cock so I can feel how much he wants me. Why have I never done this before? Sex with a stranger is a total turn on. Probably because I'd been with Jasper since I was seventeen. Six years with the same guy pumping into me and then falling asleep. Shit, don't think about it. Don't destroy the moment with a guy who wasn't worth it.

His hand glides down my belly and under the edge of my bikini bottoms. I get a strange shiver low in my belly when his fingers find my nub and sweep a circle around it. My knees are weak all of a sudden, and my whole body dips when he moves his fingers a little bit faster.

I loll my head back against his shoulder. He kisses my ear and slips a digit inside me.

"Do you like that, Candy girl?"

"Uh-huh." Heat rolls through me like a wave, and I can already call this my best sexual experience ever. Boy, have I been missing out. He palms my clitoris as he adds another finger and thrusts in and out of me. One hand fondles my nipple, and he bites my neck again. There is something so erotic about what he is doing to my body, and my hips buck against his hand. My breathing picks up pace and small sounds are escaping from deep inside me. Holy shit. The orgasm washes through me so fast, I don't realize until I'm cumming. It's depressing, really, that the man made me orgasm so quickly. I've only ever been a one hit wonder, and I'm going to miss out on the main attraction.

He removes his hand from my bikini and undoes the string on the top while tugging down the bottom. I bet he can pat his head and rub his stomach too. The man is skilled. I hear the sound of him undoing his zipper and shedding his jeans, and I wonder if I should turn around and tell him that I've already come. It would probably be rude. It's definitely not fair if I don't at least get him off.

Turning, I put out my hands to find him in the dark. My hands encounter a hard chest, with a smattering of hair across the pectorals. I curl my fingers in it reflexively. I can feel his chest rising and falling with each breath he takes, and I can tell I'm having an effect on him. I run my hands lower, over the ridges of his abs. My eyes would probably bug out of my head if I could actually see him. Somewhere below is his dick, and I swallow nervously as I get closer. *Suck it up Holly. You're a bad girl remember?* There's a line near his hips and I trace it out with my fingers. A *V*, the type of *V* I haven't seen on a real man. Damn, I want the lights on so bad, and yet, if I can't see him, then he can't see me and that's what I really want. So I visualize what my hands are showing me and make do. Finally, I find his dick and wrap my hand around it, causing him to groan and shudder. He's even bigger than I thought. I run my hand up and down the length of it, feeling his pre-cum at the end and using that to lubricate my hold on him. Sinking to my knees, I take him into my mouth and suck. He's salty with a slight tang, but I don't mind. I'm enjoying being on my knees. His hips thrust forward almost immediately as I run my tongue around the head and move my mouth back and forward over his length.

"I wish I could see you while I fuck your mouth," he says, and my belly quivers. Maybe I'll be up for round two after all. He palms the back of my head with both hands and rolls his hips while I continue to work his dick. Before I can make him cum, he pulls me up and turns me around, pushing me toward the bed. I put my hands out to steady myself and end up on my hands and knees. This is so wild for me. I actually feel like the bad girl I'm pretending to be, and I'm thinking about making her a permanent part of my personality. He grabs my hips and drags me back against him. I can feel his dick between my thighs and my body tingles in response. I hear him fiddling with something behind me. "Is that a condom?"

"Yeah," he says sliding into me slowly. I'm grateful that he did the responsible thing. I'd completely forgotten about it. He pumps into me a couple times before his hand slaps against my ass. He has some weird sex moves but I'm enjoying myself too much to care. My ass stings, but at the same time it increases the sensation and I push back impaling myself on his length.

"Bad Candy," he says pulling out of me almost completely. He delivers another slap to my ass and pushes into me again. Right now, I have to agree with him. I'm being very bad. He releases his hold on one of my hips and leans down to touch my aching clitoris. He strokes it, building the pressure inside of me, before he thrusts into me again and I hear screams issuing from somewhere. It takes me a second to realize that they're mine. I have never been noisy during sex and I abandon myself to the animal in me and ride his cock until orgasm after orgasm wash through me. He shudders behind me, cumming too.

I collapse onto the bed, delirious with what I can only describe as a sex coma. The bed dips when he lies down beside me and wraps his arm around me. I should kick him out before I fall asleep. I really should, but he's a cuddler and I'll feel bad if I make him leave now. I go quiet, pretending I'm asleep until his body twitches and settles, and I know he's out of it.

I get up and go to the bathroom to pee. There is no way I'm prepared to get a UTI and ruin this whole experience. Afterward, I wash my face, removing all the makeup I can, before sneaking back into bed. Within minutes I'm asleep.

Chapter Four

Max

Waking up in a stranger's room isn't that unusual for me. Not too long ago, it used to be a regular occurrence. So much for the good guy act. It didn't help me quit women at all, damn it. I would say it was almost record breaking how quickly I'd landed in this girl's bed, but she was the type of girl who wouldn't care if I snuck off now.

Boy, am I wrong. Sitting up, I notice the room is immaculate. A window seat contains rows of books. The bedding is an off white lace number, and on the desk next to her Mac, is a row of bobble head Doctor Who figurines. I've been conned by a nerd who has probably never had a one-night stand in her life. *What the fuck?*

I jump out of bed and shrug into my T-shirt at the same time my Candy girl appears in the room. The naughty girl I met last night is nowhere to be seen. Sure, it's the same girl, same eyes, same curves, but she's clad in dark denim capris and a tank top. Her hair is pulled back into a sleek ponytail and her face is clear of makeup. She looks at me in that *I'm too scared to actually look at you, but I want to anyway*, kind of way. I smirk. I can't help it. Today she is seeing the real me. I know she sees a hint of the tattoo on my back and biceps while I try to find my jeans. She lowers her head, and her cheeks flush, and I think it might be the prettiest color I've ever seen. "Do you want to get breakfast?"

I can't believe I asked that. Did those words really come out of my mouth? I do up my jeans and tuck my glasses into my shirt. I roll the sleeves up on the other shirt, too. I'm not a good guy. I've never been him and I failed miserably at it last night.

"No," she says finally making real eye contact with me. "You were just a fuck. I'd like you to leave."

I don't think I could be more shocked if she pulled out a

gun and shot me in the chest. She is a good girl, her room and the way she shuffles from foot to foot while she waits for me to leave tells me this. So why is she knocking back my invitation to breakfast?

I cross the room and take her chin in my hand to kiss her. She's so tense, but I dip my mouth to hers and give her a reminder of how good last night was and feel a little of that tension melt. I don't know why, but knowing she one-upped me at my own game and refused point blank to have breakfast with me makes me even more interested in getting her to agree to see me again. "How about tomorrow?"

"Huh?" she asks, a little glassy eyed from our kiss.

"Breakfast tomorrow, Candy girl?"

She takes a moment to reply and I know she is seriously considering my offer. "I don't think so. It was all just a ridiculous bet."

I'd ask her to explain the bet thing, but the rejection stings. It takes me back to my one and only serious girlfriend in high school and how she dumped me by letting the whole school know she was dating one of my friends. Yeah, that sucked. That's why I've never wanted to get involved, until now.

"See you around, Candy girl," I say, knowing I probably won't. Sydney is a big city and the chances of running into her again are slim.

She doesn't say anything as I walk out the door.

*H*OLLY

He walks out the door and I breathe out in relief. Last night was better than anything I'd ever experienced before, but I'm not interested in him sticking around for breakfast. I already like him more than I want to admit. Stupid girl. Stupid sex bonding. That's all it is, my hormones are still delirious from the romp last night. Tomorrow I'll be back to normal.

In the light of day, it is easy to see he isn't the nice guy I thought he'd been last night. The glasses tucked in his tight black T-shirt, and the shirt from last night rolled half way up his biceps gave me a good view of the thick black tattoos that no doubt covered a lot more skin than I am going to get to see. Too bad I hadn't left the light on since it was the only chance I'll get.

I guess I shouldn't be surprised to learn he is a player. Nice guys didn't have sex like that. I touch my lips and revel in the slight ache in my thighs and higher up. Even if I never experience anything like it again, I can't regret winning the bet. It had been the hottest night of my life.

I find Roxy in the kitchen, nursing her head with her elbows resting on the counter. "Pay up, Rox."

She groans, and I pour two glasses of orange juice. "Have you taken some Tylenol? We're supposed to be at Perry's in two hours, right?"

"Yeah. Stupid Christmas." She sips gingerly at the juice. "So I heard you going at it like rabbits when I got in last night."

I turn to put the orange juice in the fridge. Roxy has a way with words that I'm not always comfortable with. "Can we not talk about it?"

"Oh come on, Candy girl," she says in a mock American accent and chuckles, before groaning and hanging her head. "It's a fact that it's even more fun when you talk about it, you know."

"I'm not sure that's true," I say, taking a seat beside her at the counter. "But just this once, I'm going to concede. What do you want to know?"

"Everything."

I answer all her questions, even the ridiculous ones about positions and whether he snores, and then I send her back to bed. "I'll get you up in an hour to get ready."

I decide to watch the Family Stone, the Christmas movie I watch every year. I like the fact that it makes me cry, but my mind isn't letting me enjoy it like I normally would. Instead, I'm wondering why I insisted on not going to breakfast with Mr. America. I could have. It wouldn't have been so bad. Maybe we could have come back and repeated last night's performance. These stupid hormones need to wear off already. Besides I'm not an idiot. Going out to breakfast could end up with me liking him more than I should, and then I'd be the one who got let down when he disappeared. It was definitely better this way.

I stop the movie and wake up Roxy. She looks a hundred times better than she did earlier, and she starts getting ready. I go into my room to change into my swimsuit and put my shorts and tank back on over the top.

My parents flew over to New Zealand this year to have Christmas with our relatives, and I'd stayed home since I was supposed to be working. Instead, I was going with Roxy to lunch at her boss Perry's house.

*M*AX

"So the nice guy persona failed?" Chase says from the couch when I finally make it home.

"Uh, yeah," I reply. "Did you know nerds get better action than I do? I didn't. Seriously, how is that even possible?"

Chase chuckles. "It's about quality, not quantity."

"Fair enough," I say, not sure what to make of his remark. "I'm going to bed."

"We're going to Christmas lunch in two hours. I'll wake you up twenty minutes before," he tells me as I wander down the hallway to my room.

I sink into the bed and try to relax, but I swear there are rocks inside the mattress. Candy girl's bed was so much nicer. I could have stayed in it all day. Eventually, I fall asleep only for Chase to wake me up five minutes later.

I quickly shower and change. Beth tells me her boss Perry

has a pool so I wear board shorts. The idea of swimming on Christmas Day is really strange. There should be snow, and I should be wearing layers instead of a T-shirt and board shorts. So far my new life has been surreal.

We get to Perry's, and Chase introduces me to Perry and one of the other club girls. Roxy has shocking pink hair, and the black bikini she's wearing shows off a patchwork of tattoos. If we counted mine, and then hers, I think she could definitely beat me in who has the most ink. She looks at me with her head slightly cocked to one side and an eyebrow raised, studying me, and then holds out her hand for me to take. "Mr. America. I've heard so much about you."

"It's Max," I tell her, not sure what to make of the off kilter smile and laughing eyes. "All good things I hope."

"Yes," she laughs. "Very good things."

She leaves me to go and stand by Perry who is manning the grill. I'm not sure what Beth would have told her, but I'm curious to find out. I decide to look for her and find out what has Roxy so amused.

I find her in the kitchen wrestling a turkey out of the oven. "Hey Beth, what did you tell that girl with the pink hair about me?"

I realize she's not alone when the girl steps out from behind the pantry door with her arms full of napkins and condiments. "Candy girl?"

Beth looks from me to her. "Max, Holly. Holly, Max. He's my brother in law."

Holly's gone red to the roots of her blonde hair, and I look down at the floor. This is probably awkward for her, and I don't want her to feel uncomfortable.

"Roxy's my house mate," she says, and suddenly Roxy's grin makes sense. Holly told her all about last night. It can only be a good thing. I don't mean to be cocky, but my performance last night rocked her world. The way she screamed the house down, a testament to my abilities. Now I have to work out how to repeat the experience.

She leaves me alone with Beth in the kitchen.

"Candy girl, huh? I guess I know where you were last night." She chuckles while she carves the turkey. I don't think it's funny though.

Holly flipped my world on its axis last night, and now it's a game I don't know how to play.

"I asked her to have breakfast with me," I admit stealing a piece of turkey, and Beth stops carving to gape at me. It's a weird moment where her thoughts are written on her face. She knows this is a first for me. "She doesn't want anything to do with me."

Beth frowns, and the corner of her mouth turns up. "Welcome to being a grown up," she says pushing the turkey toward me. "Time for lunch."

Holly

Everyone takes their seat at the trestle tables set up on the porch. There's all the traditional Christmas food as well as seafood cooked on the barbecue. I sit next to Roxy, and Mr. America sits next to me. I'm distracted by the proximity of him, and when he goes out of his way to rest a thigh against mine, I struggle to ignore him. I can pick out his brother immediately as he takes his seat next to Beth across the table. They're twins, which kind of freaks me out. It's like I've seen Beth's husband naked, or I would have if the light had been on.

I start filling my plate and feel Max's gaze on me. "Are you going to ignore me all afternoon?"

That was my plan, more or less, but I'm not good at being rude to people. I try to think of something to say, but I'm distracted by the pressure of his leg against mine. He picks up a bonbon and offers me one end, and I take it, grateful that I don't have to speak right now.

The bonbon pops and its contents spill onto the table. He picks up the yellow paper crown, unfolds it and places it on my head before reading the joke aloud.

Everyone breaks open their bonbons and dives into their food, the table filling with laughter and conversation.

"Have breakfast with me tomorrow," he says for my ears alone.

If I accept his offer, it's the same as asking him into my house for pudding. We'll be in a tangle of sheets long before we get to the food, and I don't think it would be a good idea to get to know him any better. How am I going to get him to stop asking though?

"Last night was... good," I tell him, even though I want to say amazing, incredible, addictive. "But you're not the kind of guy that sticks around after the event. I don't know why you're continuing to pretend like you're interested in me. Maybe it's because you see me as a challenge. If I say yes to breakfast, you're going to disappear." I snap my fingers for emphasis. "I don't want to ruin last night."

With that, I get up and leave the table. It's already stifling hot and I decide to get out of my shorts and tank and take a dip in the pool.

AX

Holly pegs me. Normally, I'd refute her claim, but the fact that after a few hours she already knows exactly who I am, throws me. The more I think about it, the more I feel there has been a shift in me, and I think she's wrong. She can see who I

180

was, but in less than a day, she's changed me. When I asked her to breakfast, I wasn't thinking about what would come before breakfast. I'm not thinking about tonight. I'm thinking about waking up next to her, and I'm thinking about breakfast the day after that, too. Even though I know her name now, I can't help but think of her as my Candy girl. I leave the table and go in search of her.

I find her in the water, looking somewhat delectable in a full piece swimsuit. She's resting on the side of the pool, talking to some guy who is trying to get close to her. The way he inches closer to her while they talk annoys me. Why would he think he even has a chance with a girl like her? She's too good for him. Hell, she's too good for me.

I shrug out of my shirt and jump into the cool water, making sure to maximize my splash. I'm not showing off. I need to break up their conversation.

Holly glowers at me when I break the surface and swim toward her. The other guy gets the hint the minute I put my arms around her and backs off, all the way out of the pool.

"What do you think you're doing?" she asks.

"How do I convince you I want more than just breakfast tomorrow?" Saying it out loud makes it reality. Candy girl is a firecracker and the one I've been waiting for to break me out of the game. I'm not in love with her yet, but I know I could fall for her. It's the head on my shoulders that realizes she's what I'm looking for. It's my head that sees the neon sign saying *this one.*

"You can't convince me." She moves to get out of the pool, but I pull her back into the water and kiss her till she's clinging to my shoulders and shaking.

"There's something great between us," I tell her maneuvering her legs around my waist. "I want to explore it."

"Your dick is between us," she says, and she's right. My cock has gotten hard from that one kiss and is pressed against her thigh. "I need more than just your dick, and I don't think you've got it in you to give me what I want."

At least she's admitting she wants more. I will find a way to convince her I do too. I wonder if sharing my inner nerd would help, but somehow, I don't think she'd believe me if I started discussing Doctor Who now. Instead, I kiss her softly, my lips against hers in a feather light touch. "I'm going to find a way to convince you, Candy girl."

Someone yells out that it's time to exchange the Kris Kringle presents, and we get out of the pool to find out towels before wandering inside.

Everyone is gathered around the Christmas tree in the living room, and Perry has donned a Santa costume to hand out the presents. I watch Holly watch the others open their gifts. She and I are the only ones who aren't in the Kris Kringle, and I want to give her something. But what?

*H*OLLY

The presents have been handed out, and Roxy is going gaga over the chunky pink skull and black bow bracelet Perry got her. I get up and head outside to get some air. It's been a nice Christmas Day, and we'll be going home soon. I should be happy to get away from Max, but I'm not really. The way he stares at me and calls me Candy girl make me want to give into his demands for breakfast, and everything that comes before it.

It was never like that with Jasper, and I don't think I'll ever find someone who makes me feel so reckless again. He's everything I shouldn't want, but if he could make me believe that he isn't just a hot sex weekend, then I'd give in to my gut instinct and get to know him.

When he told me he was going to convince me that he wanted more than another romp in my bed, my heart had fluttered. I wanted him to, but I know if I let him in, I'll fall for him because I already like him far more than I want to admit to.

I walk to the pool fence and look at the water, imagining him kissing me. When I leave here shortly, that's all I'll have, memories of the best night of my life, and a sweet kiss on Christmas Day. After this, I can't let myself get consumed by thoughts of him. I'll have to put him behind me and get back to reality. I have to find a job and find some transport with my minimum savings. Honestly, do I even have time to get involved with someone? I know if it's Max, I'll make the exception.

"We'll leave in five minutes. Is that okay with you and Mr. America?" Roxy calls out from the doorway.

Mr. America has run out of time. I turn around and shrug. "I'm ready when you are."

I stay where I am, waiting for Roxy to get her stuff and say goodbye to everyone. The year is coming to an end and I hope next year is going to be a much better year. Max steps up beside me and leans on the fence. "Holly, I wanted to tell you that I really like you. I know you can see who I am, but if you gave me a chance, you'll see that's who I used to be. For the first time in my life I want to see where this can go for more than a night or a weekend."

His words are pretty. I mean who doesn't want to swoon when a sexy guy like Max tells you he wants to change because you alone rock his world, but I'm not naive. That's all he's got, words.

He takes my hand in his. Turns it over and lays it out palm up on top of his own. "Here, Merry Christmas," he says placing a playing card in my hand. Only it isn't a card. It's a trading card of the Tenth Doctor, with the actor's autograph scrolled across it. I look up at Max. This is the first thing I really know about who he is.

"You can't give me this," I tell him, trying to hand it back to him, but he shoves his hands in his pockets.

"You can give it back to me if we go our separate ways, until then it's yours."

This is how he proves to me he wants to get to know me, and it's going to work since I'm not going to be giving him back this card. "Breakfast then?" I ask him.

"No," he says, and pulls me up against him. "Dinner, and breakfast and lunch and dinner again. I'm not giving you a chance to change your mind."

"Okay then." I wind my arms around his neck and pull his head down to mine so I can tangle my tongue with his. This is my gift to him. Me. "Merry Christmas," I say to him when we break apart. Roxy wolf whistles and yells at us to get a room. I take his hand and lead him to the car. I'm taking Roxy's advice again and going to find a room. I have a present to unwrap, so does he, and it's going to take all night.

On the Eve of Love

by Patricia D. Eddy

For all those who've overcome fear of failure. Or at least been able to work around it.

Chapter One

"Hey!" Marcus Bunch stumbled, his stack of packages tumbling into the gutter. The tinkling of broken glass heralded the vase's demise. "Shit, shit, shit. You stupid ass!" he shouted after the tall, willowy brunette who'd plowed right into him.

The woman turned, her brows furrowed over ice blue eyes. She held a smartphone in her right hand. "Huh?"

"Thanks for nothing, lady! You see that?" He gestured towards the heap of packages on the sidewalk. "I can't give my mother a broken vase for Christmas."

Her eyes went wide and she hurried back to him, dropping down to her knees and stacking his packages up one by one. When she lifted the largest box and glass slid around inside, she cringed at the sound. "I'm sorry. Really. I'm late. And my phone . . ."

Marcus snatched the short pile of packages back from the idiot and tried not to let his despair show. He wouldn't be able to replace the vase. Not now. Not after taking over payments on his mother's hospital bills. He'd bought the vase for her six months ago, when the doctors declared her cancer free. But then she'd fainted at Thanksgiving and had broken her arm. The doctors were baffled. He'd had to watch his seventy-two year old mother go from doing her own gardening to unable to get out of bed in the space of a couple of weeks.

"No one ever told you not to walk and text at the same time?" He glared at her, wishing with all of his heart that he'd taken his mother's advice and stayed home today. It was December twenty-second, and he'd had a coffee date scheduled with a friend of a friend, but he'd canceled at the last minute. He couldn't deal with dating right now and the woman was young. Twenty-three to his thirty-four. Every time they'd tried to have a text conversation, he'd broken it off in frustration because Kintie would slip into text-speak. The woman had a smartphone and couldn't manage to type out the word 'you' to save her life. He was a writer for fuck's sake. There was no way they could make it work. Even if she was hot as hell.

"Well, yeah." The woman gave him a sheepish grin. "My ma' says that all the time."

"Listen to your mother," Marcus said, his eyes burning with unshed tears. He wouldn't have his much longer. Not unless Sylvia's luck changed, and that didn't seem likely. He turned on his heel and headed back to his car. He couldn't bring the vase into the hospital. He'd hide the box in his trunk, compose himself, and then bring his mother the other two gifts: the refurbished Kindle and the crocheted shawl.

"Hey!" The rich, sultry voice of the idiot followed him.

"Go to hell." He didn't bother turning around or pausing. A tear trailed down his cheek and he dashed it away with his shoulder.

The hand on his arm was warm, hesitant, and unwanted. He jerked away. "Leave me alone."

"I want to apologize." The earnestness in the woman's eyes almost convinced him to let her say her peace, but shifting the box and hearing the broken glass reminded him that he was way too pissed off at her. At least he hadn't told his mother about the vase. He'd never live that down.

"You should have been more careful, Marcus. You're never going to get ahead in life if you don't start taking more care with things. That's what happened with your last book. And your love life." His mother's voice in his head caused his stomach to clench.

"Save it," he said, setting the boxes down on the roof of his car and fishing the keys out of his pocket. "What's done is done."

"My name's Gwen." She thrust out her hand, her brows lifting slightly.

Marcus slid his key into the lock—his car was so old he didn't have a key fob—and opened the driver's side door. Gwen's hand fell away.

"Listen, I feel terrible. Really. I was stupid and I cost you an important gift. Let me make it up to you. What was in the box?"

"A lead crystal vase," Marcus muttered. "And it's fine.

She wasn't expecting it. The other two gifts will have to be enough."

"Who doesn't wrap a lead crystal in a ton of peanuts?" Gwen asked.

Marcus shrugged. "All Things Crystal, apparently. They asked me if I was going to ship it. I said no. Apparently that meant no packing at all." He lifted the lid of the box. The vase was wrapped in a thin layer of plastic. Gwen stifled a laugh.

"That's got to be the worst packing job I've ever seen."

He couldn't help his own chuckle. "Yeah. Guess you're not the only one who should have been more careful." Once the car was locked and the other two packages tucked securely under his arm, Marcus took a second to appreciate the woman in front of him.

Five-foot-seven at least, with dark brown hair, blue eyes, and a swimmer's build. High cheekbones, plump lips with a touch of sheer gloss on them, and a delicate chin. She wore a leather jacket, open to reveal a blouse the color of her eyes. Pressed black pants, ballet flats buffed to a high shine, and a thin, silver belt. She checked her watch, and Marcus almost whistled. Movado. Not cheap. Standing next to his old reliable Ford, he was suddenly self-conscious.

"Don't be rude, Marcus Phillip Bunch. I raised you better than that!" Another imagined rebuke from his mother had him sticking out his hand. "Marcus. I'm sorry I called you an ass."

"I deserved it. Seriously. You're right about the whole texting-while-walking thing. I do it all the time and it's not like I was late for surgery or something. I didn't want to miss my chance of getting a slice of Mrs. Fitz's cherry pie." Her cheeks flamed pink and she scuffed her shoe on the asphalt of the parking garage. "Let me pay you for the vase. Please." She dug into her purse, but Marcus waved his hand in dismissal.

"No. If you want to make it up to me, do me a favor."

"Anything." Gwen smiled, dimples winking at the corners of her mouth.

Marcus's jeans suddenly felt too tight. The light angling into the parking garage gave Gwen's face a soft glow, and he'd always had a thing for dimples. He ran a hand through his hair and tugged, using the pinpricks of pain to calm himself down.

"If there's any pie left, drop a slice off in Room 3602. Sylvia Bunch. She loves pie and I can't bake worth shit. I gotta go. She gives me hell whenever I'm late." With a quick nod, Marcus rushed away, leaving Gwen standing next to his car, that pretty, heart-shaped mouth open in a little *o*.

Gwen clipped her ID badge onto her white lab coat. Multi-colored lights decorated the staff lounge and the sad Christmas tree was leaning at a dangerous angle. She knelt, adjusted the tree stand to a less precarious angle, and brushed off her hands. At least it wouldn't kill any of the other doctors now.

"Hey, Gwen." Kay Park, one of the residents, rushed in, pulling off her winter coat and gloves as she went. "I didn't expect to see you here this week. Didn't you have some epic Christmas vacation planned?"

"I did. That is until my sister found out the adoption agency had approved them and she begged me to let her and Michael go to Hawaii together as 'one last trip' before they get their son. I mean, come on. How was I supposed to refuse?"

"A son! You're going to be an aunt!" Kay threw her arms around Gwen and the two women lost their balance and nearly ended up toppling into the Christmas tree.

"Yeah. I guess I am." Gwen couldn't help her smile. Diane had shown her a photo of the little boy. He was three, with chubby cheeks, a lopsided grin, and fat fingers. He'd been in foster care for a year after his parents had been killed in a car accident, and according to Diane, he was a little angel. "Diane's over the moon. Richard too."

"I'll bet. But that doesn't explain why you're here. You're still owed vacation. You could have flown home to New York for the week. Seen your mother and brother."

"They're both painting the nursery while Diane and Richard are gone. I really didn't want to face Ma' without a buffer.

She'd spend the whole trip nagging me about my lack of a love life."

"Then you should have rented a bunch of bad movies and binged on fudge and popcorn for a week. You've worked every weekend and every holiday for my entire residency."

"Yeah, well. You know this time of year isn't my favorite. I'd rather work."

"You can't mope over Victor forever."

"I'm not moping."

Kay frowned and ran a hand through her thick black hair. "Fine. I've got rounds. But let's grab a drink after shift, okay?"

"I'm off at eight."

Gwen headed to Larry Fitz's room first. The sixty-year-old was being discharged the next day, though he didn't know it yet. His wife baked a pie every Friday for the staff and Larry always saved Gwen a piece. The man had a crush on her, or pretended to anyway. Gwen thought it was sweet. A lot of cancer patients thought their doctors walked on air and Larry was no different. He'd been in Gwen's clinical trial from the beginning and his leukemia was finally in remission, thank God.

"And how's my favorite ladies' man today?" Gwen said, flashing Larry a big smile. He was sitting up in bed, playing poker online.

"I'm winning, doll face. Up two hundred bucks."

"Good for you. Are you going to take that lovely wife of yours out for dinner tomorrow with your winnings?" Gwen slid her gaze to the pie on his side table. *Good. Still a couple of pieces left.*

"Tomorrow?"

"Yep. You're getting out of here. I got your test results back this morning. You're officially in remission."

"Hot damn! I can really go home?"

Gwen laughed and nodded her head. His joy was infectious. She loved this part of her job. The trial was getting good results, although even she and her wonder-drug cocktail couldn't save everyone. But maybe her drugs would ensure that fewer people would die. If only this type of study had been around when Victor . . .

"I saved you a piece of pie," Larry said, interrupting her thoughts. "Though I reckon Marjorie's going to bake you a whole dozen pies when she hears the news."

"You're the best, Larry. Hey, can I ask you a favor?"

"Sure, Doc Evers. Anything."

"Can I take two pieces today? I've got another patient that I think needs the pick-me-up."

"Take the rest."

Gwen picked up the pie plate and grinned. "Thanks. I'll come check on you at the end of my shift and we'll talk about your outpatient regimen. I want you on a few supplements to build up your strength and we'll need to make sure you come back for tests every six weeks. Think Marjorie can be here around seven tonight?"

"I'll make sure she is."

Chapter Two

Marcus looked up when his mother's hospital room door opened. Sylvia was resting comfortably. The latest round of tests showed that her liver was edging towards failure and her kidneys were threatening to shut down. They'd taken her to dialysis this morning and though she was mentally present enough to beat him at a game of chess, she'd fallen asleep after eating only a few bites of her lunch. His mother couldn't stay awake more than two hours these days. She was only seventy-two, not ninety-two, dammit. She should be home. Baking her famous Christmas pecan pie, not wasting away in a hospital bed.

Gwen stood in the doorway, a hesitant smile on her lips and a pie plate in her hand. Her blue eyes shifted, her gaze landing on his mother's face. "I brought pie," she whispered.

A doctor. Of course. That watch screamed money. Marcus waved her in. "Whatever they've got her on for the pain really knocks her out. We could throw a raging party in here and she'd never know."

Gwen slid the pie onto Sylvia's table and withdrew a small tablet from her pocket. It was only a little larger than her palm. She leaned against the wall and tapped the screen a few times. "Demerol. Yeah, we could probably set off fireworks and she'd sleep right through it."

"So. A doctor. I should have known." He stood, twisting from side to side to pop his back. He spent too many days in the uncomfortable visitor's chair and it was taking its toll.

Her cheeks reddened and Marcus found that he liked how her lower lip tucked under her teeth while she looked down at those long legs. His cock stiffened against his zipper again. *Calm down,* he told himself. *Nothing's going to happen.*

"Clearly I embodied every stereotype of a doctor you have in your mind. 'I should have known?' God. I never wanted to be that predictable."

Marcus laughed. "It wasn't that. It was the watch. Only

doctors own Movados. At least in my world."

Gwen looked down at her wrist and slapped a hand over her mouth. Her shoulders shook with a failed attempt at hiding her own mirth. A tear shone at the corner of her eye. She dashed it away and gasped, trying to catch her breath. "It was a gift. Shit. I can't afford this. Yeah, I'm a doctor, but I've got a hundred thousand left on my student loans. I live in a one bedroom apartment above a Chinese food restaurant and I drive a nine-year old Chevy."

"Seriously?"

"Seriously. Plastic surgeons make the big bucks. Heart surgeons. A cancer researcher? Please."

A researcher. "What are you doing working here if you're in research?"

"I developed a new treatment protocol for leukemia. Well, okay. I didn't develop it. I helped. We've got five patients in a clinical trial. Three have gone into remission." She beamed as she spoke, the pride straightening her shoulders, puffing out her chest. She glanced over at Sylvia. "Why is she here?"

Marcus shrugged. "She had a double mastectomy a couple of years ago. They took most of her lymph nodes. She had the flu before Thanksgiving and she broke her arm in a fall on Black Friday. That landed her in here. She was only supposed to stay for a couple of days, but she's gotten weaker every day she's been in here."

Gwen looked at her tablet. "Dr. Narten. He's good, but has she seen Dr. Adams? He's the head of Geriatrics."

"No."

"Let me see what I can do. Dr. Adams is a miracle worker. I've heard stories. Men and women who thought they were on death's door going on to live another ten, twenty years. If anyone can figure out what's wrong with her, he can."

"Why would you do that?"

"Because I broke your vase. And Dr. Adams owes me a favor." She smiled again, that quick flash of white teeth sending sparks down his spine. She smelled like roses mixed with antiseptic. It was . . . oddly intoxicating. A bit of normalcy in this completely abnormal situation. "So you know what I do. What do you do?"

Marcus shoved his hands in his pockets. "I'm a writer."

"Really? Anything I might have read?"

"I dunno. Do you read science fiction?"

"Yep. I'm mostly a steampunk fan, but science fiction is my second favorite genre."

"No romance?"

Gwen snorted. "I may be the stereotypical doctor, but I am not the stereotypical woman. Pul-leeze. All those alpha men who sweep the women off their feet and carry them to the bed? All tattoos and abs and kisses that leave you weak in the knees? That doesn't happen in real life."

"And aliens and steam-powered time travel devices do?" Marcus leaned against the wall a couple of feet away. *This is nice. It's been forever since I laughed, relaxed. Made small talk with anyone other than Mom.* He could reach out and touch her if he wanted. He wanted. Very much.

"No, but that's the point. I want to read something that can't exist. Not something that could and simply doesn't. Do you write under," she glanced down at her tablet, "Marcus Bunch?"

"Marco Battalion."

"Is there a story behind that?"

"Picked it out of a hat. Sounds powerful, doesn't it?" He grinned and ran a hand over his jaw. Two days' worth of stubble rasped against his fingers. His brown hair was too long. His jeans had a tear above the knee that fortunately for him, looked purposeful. He hoped he didn't smell. He'd showered this morning, hadn't he? Resisting the urge to raise his arm and sniff, he took a step back.

A little laugh escaped those pink lips. God, he had it bad if he was practically drooling over a doctor who'd cost him a hundred dollar vase. He really needed to get out more, didn't he? He stopped himself before he could shake his head and answer his own question. No. Nothing mattered now but his mother. At the rate she was weakening, he feared she wouldn't make New Year's.

Gwen was talking. Shit. He'd missed half of what she'd

said.

". . . and that's what got me hooked on science fiction."

Marcus glanced over at his mother. He heard her voice in his head. *"Ask her out. You can't stay by your mama's side forever."*

"Would—" He stopped, shook his head and shoved his hands into his pockets. "I mean, what was the last book you read?"

Her blue eyes crinkled at the edges and she smiled so widely, he wanted to lose himself in her dimples. But before she could speak, a shrill beeping from her pocket had her digging for her tablet. "Shit. I've got to go. One of my patients isn't reacting well to their chemo. I'll look up your books. It was nice to meet you, Marcus. Tell your mother to expect a visit from Dr. Adams."

With a little wave of her hand, she was gone. Marcus dropped down into the chair and stared at the pie on the table next to him.

"You are never going to find yourself a woman if you don't muster up a little courage, son." His mother's quiet words had him jerking in the chair.

"I didn't know you were awake."

"No shit. She was cute. And a doctor. How'd you meet her? She's not my doctor." Sylvia pressed the button that raised the bed up a few inches so she could look him in the eyes. Her own green pools were faded and bloodshot now, but there was still a fire in them that told Marcus she didn't want to die. Sylvia Bunch was a fighter.

Marcus told the story, minus the vase, and when his mother caught sight of the pie, the smile she gave him nearly made up for the busted vase. If only they could figure out what was making her so sick.

"Now you get out of here, Marcus. It's after five and you've got deadlines. I'm going to eat this pie. Every single bite of it, and then I'm going to watch my stories." She gestured towards the television mounted to the wall. "And the next time you see that bombshell, you ask her out, you hear me?"

"Yes, Mom."

Marcus stared at his laptop screen. Words: 3015. The number mocked him. It had been mocking him for a week. He hadn't released a book in more than a year and his sales were lagging. What was he going to do? He wasn't making enough to keep himself afloat much longer. He had a six-book series that had been wildly successful up until the last book. Reviews of that one were scathing. "Distracted," "Not up to his usual standards," and "Utter Crap," were some of the milder words used to describe *Stellar Field*. He had been distracted. He'd had to write that book while his mother had been recovering from her mastectomy and he'd thought his readers would always be there. That they'd forgive him the few editing errors, the unraveled plot points, the weak ending. He'd been wrong. He'd pulled the book a few months later and was now trying to rewrite it. It eluded him. His outline sat next to him with one phrase scribbled up at the top. *Stop being scared!*

Maybe he should take his own advice. He opened up another file. This one was complete. Edited. Formatted. The cover was done. Maybe he should go for it. *What's the worst that could happen?* He got up and trudged into the kitchen, poured himself a shot of whiskey, and downed it in a single gulp. *You could lose more fans. You could become a laughing stock.* Another shot went down even faster. *Or you could finally tell your mother that you faced your fears.* One more shot. Now he had enough courage. He could do this.

Chapter Three

Busy texting her sister as she headed for the front door, Gwen didn't see the bunched up rug in her apartment's hallway. Her foot caught. Off balance, she tried to right herself, but couldn't. She went down, twisting her ankle and landing hard on her right knee. Something popped and shooting pains arced through her leg. "Shit!"

Tugging up the leg of her pants, she grimaced. Her knee was already starting to swell. She had to get the slim-fitting pants off in the next couple of minutes and get some ice. The pain flared with each step, but she limped into the apartment, shimmied out of her pants, dropped them by the door, and retrieved an ice pack from the fridge. Within five minutes, she was on the couch with her leg propped up on pillows. Hopefully the quick ice application would stave off any serious damage.

Gwen had never been the most graceful of women. A growth spurt at fourteen had left her all arms and legs and she'd never quite grown out of it. Add in texting-while-walking and she was an injury magnet. She'd sprained her ankle more than once. The knee was a new one for her, though. At least she had tomorrow off to rest. She flipped on the TV. *It's a Wonderful Life* had just started and she settled in for the distraction.

Two hours later, she scarfed down some leftover pizza and limped off to bed. All she could see when she closed her eyes was Marcus, sitting next to his mother's bed. His green eyes sparkled when he talked about his writing. They turned to mossy water when he talked about his mother. Dr. Adams would see the woman tomorrow. Gwen hadn't spent too much time looking at Sylvia's chart, but she was on several powerful painkillers that were rarely prescribed together. For an older woman, especially one with a history of cancer, that was worrisome. Dr. Adams had a reputation for holistic treatment. Sylvia would have a real chance with him as her treating physician. Gwen would have to check on her when she returned to work on the twenty-third. And maybe run into the ruggedly handsome writer again.

The throbbing in her knee didn't lend itself to sleep, so she reached for her Kindle. *Marcus Bunch*. No, that wasn't it. He'd told her his pen name. *Marco Battalion*. She found six books listed. Five in some series called *The Outer Reaches of Humanity* and one that appeared to have been published only a few hours before. *If Only*. She clicked on that and read the description.

What if death wasn't an eventuality? Those with means are granted perpetual youth. A single shot and you will live forever. Agers want the elixir of life mass produced and distributed to everyone. When war breaks out between the agers and the ageless, who will live and who will die?

"Why not?" Gwen asked. "Let's see if Mr. Crystal Vase can write."

Gwen's knee wasn't any better in the morning. She shuffled out to the kitchen for coffee, bleary eyed. It probably hadn't helped that she'd stayed up until three in the morning reading *If Only*. That man could write. He must have written the book after his mother was diagnosed with cancer. The raw emotion of the Agers' fight resonated with her. Hopelessness, despair, the feelings of helplessness. She remembered them all as she watched Victor waste away during what was supposed to be the happiest time of their lives. As the coffee brewed, she called the clinic. She'd get her knee looked at, nap, and finish *If Only*.

"Mom?" Marcus was surprised to see his mother sitting up in bed when he arrived at the hospital after lunch on the twenty-third.

"Marcus! Come meet Dr. Adams. We've been having a delightful time together."

A handsome, older man with thick white hair and a tanned face turned a mega-watt smile on Marcus. "Mr. Bunch, it's good to meet you."

"Likewise. Um, the other doctor . . ." *Gwen. Why can't I remember her last name?*

"Dr. Evers. Yes. She asked me to check on your mother."

Sylvia patted her bed. "Come sit. I haven't had a single pill today and I feel better."

"Really?" Disbelief had him running a hand through his unruly brown hair.

"Your mother was on three different pain medications. They're not contraindicated, but I've seen them cause issues in those with a compromised immune system. Sylvia falls into that category. When she fainted a few weeks ago and broke her arm, her previous doctor prescribed the most typical cocktail of drugs, but they caused problems for her liver and kidneys. The real problem, though, was her heart."

"Her heart?"

"It's okay, Mr. Bunch. I don't think there's going to be any lasting damage. But her heart was working too hard. It's why she was always tired. Now that the arm's mostly healed, I've put her on a supplement regimen that should help her get back on her feet in the next few weeks. If we can, we'll get her home by New Year's."

"Holy shit."

"Marcus! Language!" Sylvia said, hitting his arm with a surprisingly hard thwack.

Chastised, Marcus hunched his shoulders and muttered an apology.

He spent the entire afternoon with Sylvia. She had her appetite back, and requested a burger and fries for dinner. She joked, played two games of chess, and then told him to leave her alone to watch her stories. Dr. Adams came to check on her twice and gave Marcus his email address to contact him directly, any time. The only dark cloud on the day was that he'd hoped to run into Gwen again. When Marcus let himself in to his apartment a little after eight p.m., he entered with a spring in his step and a strong urge to write.

Three hours later he'd gotten six thousand new words down on *Stellar Field*. They were good words. Solid words. Words he could be proud of. He sat back and opened up his email. "What the hell?" The first message was from Gwen Evers.

Dear Marcus,

I hope that Dr. Adams was able to see your mother today. I realize I'm being forward, but I got your email address off your website. I hurt myself last night. Yes, I was texting and walking at the same time. I'm really going to try to stop that. Anyway, I sprained my knee and spent today getting it treated.

No, that's not really true. Well, okay. I sprained my knee. And I went to the clinic. But I also napped because I stayed up reading If Only until 3 a.m. I can't tell you how much your words affected me. You're a gifted writer and I could feel the pain of your mother's illness in every word.

Anyway. I'm rambling. But I wanted you to know that the book touched me deeply. Thank you for writing it. I'll be working on Christmas Eve and I'll stop in to check on your mother.

Yours,

Gwen

Marcus rubbed his jaw. *Yours?* Should he write her back? Thank her? Tell her about Dr. Adams? What the hell?

Dear Gwen,

Thank you. You've no idea how much your words mean to me. But even more than that, I don't think I can ever repay you for speaking to Dr. Adams. He's hopeful that my mom will be home by New Year's. I'm sorry about your knee. I suppose it wouldn't be nice to tell you that I told you so?

I hope you will stop in to see my mom. I'll be with her most of the day.

Yours,

Marcus

He clicked send before he could obsess over every single word. Before bed, he checked his analytics. He'd sold thirty copies of *If Only*. Hardly enough to keep him afloat, but that was still thirty more copies than he'd sold of anything else of late. It wouldn't keep the heat on or stop him from having to declare bankruptcy if things didn't turn around soon, but it was a nice bump of sales. He looked at the reviews and nearly fell off of his chair. Nine reviews. All five stars. That was unheard of. They all carried a common theme. Readers were staying up all night to read about his pain and anguish over his mother's illness. Sure, his feelings were all hidden behind a futuristic and fictional world, but apparently that world resonated. For the first time in a very long time, Marcus went to bed with a smile on his face.

Chapter Four

Christmas Eve dawned wet and gray. Typical for Seattle. He pulled on jeans and a white button-down shirt, topped them with a maroon vest. His mother would be happy he'd put some effort into his appearance. On his way to the hospital, he stopped off at the store for a poinsettia and a single red rose. If he was lucky, he'd run into Gwen today and be able to thank her for her kind words. He tucked the rose into the top of his laptop bag and walked into the hospital with his nerves on overdrive.

"Merry Christmas, Mom," he said, finding her sitting up in bed with her Kindle. She gave him a wide smile and cooed over the poinsettia. Her color was better and her hands no longer shook. Clearly whatever Dr. Adams was doing was working.

"They got me out of bed today. I walked all the way to the nurses' station and back!" She beamed and puffed out her chest. She hadn't gotten out of bed in a week for anything but tests and she certainly hadn't walked anywhere.

"That's great." He glanced towards the door as a tall woman walked by, unable to hide his disappointment that it wasn't Gwen.

"Are you expecting someone?"

"Maybe." He stared down at his mother's hands, folded over her stomach. He never could hide anything from her. "The cute doctor who stopped by the other day."

"Gwen? She's been by twice already today. Walking with a bit of a limp. She told me all about your book. I think she's got a bit of a crush on you." His mother's eyes sparkled.

"Telling all of my secrets, Sylvia?" Gwen's amused voice startled Marcus and he whirled.

She was beautiful. Dressed in a green wrap dress that brushed her knees and dipped to expose the gentle swell of her breasts, his gaze was drawn to her kohl lined blue eyes and heart-shaped mouth. A shy smile graced her lips. "Hi," Marcus said.

"Hi yourself. I came to check on your mother."

Sylvia snorted. "Liar."

"Mom!"

"Don't you start with me, Marcus. I may be old and sick, but I am still your mother. And it's time for *The Price is Right*. Why don't you take Dr. Evers out for coffee?"

Marcus sputtered and stammered out an oath, but when he slid his gaze back to Gwen's face, her lower lip was askew, trapped under her teeth. "I have a break for an hour. Right now, in fact. There's a good coffee shop on the corner."

She wants to spend time with me? Shit. It's been so long since I've done this. What if I suck at small talk?

Gwen took a step back. "We don't have to. If you don't want to. It's okay."

"No. Wait." Marcus leaned down and snagged the rose from his bag. "I . . . I got you this. For the email. It really . . . it made my night."

A blush colored those high cheekbones. She accepted the rose, brought it close, and inhaled deeply. "So, um. Coffee?"

Why not?

"How's the knee?" he asked, noting her slightly awkward gait as they made their way to the elevators.

"It's better today. A little swollen." She lifted her skirt a bit to reveal a crisscross of tape that covered some dark bruising. "Tripped over a rug."

"While texting."

"Yep."

"And where's your phone now?" The doors opened and Marcus waved to let Gwen go first.

"In my locker. In my purse."

"So I can't give you my number."

A little laugh escaped her throat. It was the cutest thing he'd ever heard.

"You've heard of those old-fashioned things called a pen and paper?" The hospital doors opened with a whoosh and they escaped into the drizzle. Gwen hadn't stopped for a coat, so Marcus shrugged out of his leather jacket and draped it over her shoulders. She blushed and snuggled into the warmth. "But you're getting wet."

"I'll dry."

The coffee shop was packed, but they found a tiny table in the back corner and settled in with their lattes.

"I really loved your book," Gwen said, sipping her drink. Her tongue darted out to lick the foam from her lip. Marcus was mesmerized. "I was right? You wrote that when your mom got sick?"

"Yeah. She had a bad reaction to the surgery. Ended up touch and go for a few weeks. I wrote most of the book sitting by her bed in ICU. Then the end after she pulled through. Sat on it for two years. I never had the balls to publish it. I don't know what made me do it two days ago. Desperation, I guess."

"Why?"

"Mom's insurance hasn't covered everything. And my books haven't been selling. I quit my office job three years ago because I was making enough to support myself easily. But then sales dried up, my last book was shit, and Mom got sick. Kind of screwed up my whole life's plan."

"You can't plan out life," Gwen said, her pretty blue eyes darkening. "It never works."

"What was your plan?" *And what's turned you so sad all of a sudden?*

"I was engaged once. Six months away from our wedding, I discovered a lump under his arm. Cancer. He'd ignored it for a year. Thought it would go away. By the time I noticed, the cancer was everywhere. Instead of a wedding, I used our savings for his funeral. He died on December fifteenth, ten years ago."

"I'm sorry." Marcus reached out and covered her hand with his.

She twisted her fingers to grasp his tightly. "It is what it is. Or was. We had three happy years together. And you know what they say . . . 'better to have loved and lost'."

They let the din of the coffee shop fill the silence between them.

"Is there . . . anyone now?" Marcus felt like an ass for asking, but he had to know. Something about Gwen called to him. He wanted to get to know her better, but he wasn't about to worm his way in if there was someone in her life already.

Her gaze, which had been faraway and unfocused, sharpened. The corners of her lips twitched up. "No."

Change the subject, man. Before you ask her out and come across as an idiot. His brain and his mouth weren't in agreement. "Do you have plans tonight?"

A little gasp escaped her lips and her cheeks flushed again. He was really starting to like the sight of Gwen blushing. This time, the blush traveled down her neck and towards her breasts. Did she redden all over? If he put his mouth on her, on those breasts, what sound would she make? Would she scream? Beg? Or would she take control? He ached to know and his cock pressed against his zipper, begging to be let free. "I know it's Christmas Eve, but . . ."

"I don't have any plans. Unless you count curling up on the couch with another one of your books." She stared down at their joined hands, pulled away, and cupped her coffee mug. After another quick sip, she licked her lips, and then looked him in the eyes. The power behind that stare slammed him back in his seat.

Here goes nothing. "Have dinner with me."

"Okay."

"Really?" Dating had never seemed this easy before.

She smiled. "Really. You pick the place." A glance at her watch had her frowning. "I have to get back. I get off at six. Is seven too late?"

"No. Should I pick you up? *Can* I pick you up?"

"I'd like that." She reached for his napkin and dug a pen out of her pocket. "Here's my number and my address. Do me a favor and let me know what I should wear."

"You're perfect." If it was possible, he'd kick himself for that admission. But it was true. She was gorgeous, and even if she showed up wearing torn jeans and a stained t-shirt, he'd feel the same.

"And you're sweet. I'll see you tonight." She paused next to his chair, leaned down, and brushed her lips to his cheek. She smelled like roses and coffee. He reached for her hand to stop her from leaving.

"Gwen?"

"Yes?" Her breathless reply and those darkening blue eyes drew him closer.

"I'm not going to be able to focus on anything today if I don't do this." He stood, drew her against him, and slid a hand into her silky brown hair. "Tell me to stop and I will."

She parted her lips in invitation. "Kiss me, Marcus."

It started gentle, the touch of his lips to hers, coffee, velvet heat, a sweet taste he knew was Gwen. His tongue explored, hesitantly, then boldly. A purr vibrated in her throat and she melted into his embrace. Fingers tightened on his waist and the throbbing of his cock grew painful. He wanted her. Now.

"Stop," he begged, pulling away reluctantly. "Or we're going to have to find some privacy."

The look in her eyes told him she was seriously considering where they could go, but she released her hold on him and stepped back. "Tonight."

"Hell yes."

With a final smile, she left him standing there, hard as a rock and practically panting. He dropped back into the chair, needing to calm down before he could even think about returning to the hospital to see his mother.

One thing about sexual frustration, it seemed to be good for his writing. He'd spent the entire day in his mother's room, the words flowing freely, punctuated by breaks to play chess or run out for french fries and candy. Her appetite was back with a vengeance and though Dr. Adams told her she had to eat all of her vegetables, he made it a point to look the other way and wink when he saw her diving into the bag of fries from Dick's Drive-In. She was improving rapidly. The nurses got her up every hour for a little shuffle around the floor.

"If she continues this improvement," Dr. Adams told

him when he'd been chased from Sylvia's room a little before five, "we'll discharge her on the twenty-seventh. I'd like to see her have home care for another week, at least. But she's a strong woman. Now that the drugs aren't weighing her down, I'd say she's got another ten, fifteen years."

"Shit, doc. She was on death's door."

A shadow passed over the doctor's face. "I see too many patients who don't get geriatric care. It's not a sexy specialty and I only have so much time. I'm recommending, yet again, that the hospital hire more specialists. I'm just glad we caught it in time."

"Merry Christmas, doctor. Will you be around tomorrow?"

"Yep. I drew the short straw this year. Have a good night, Mr. Bunch."

Marcus cleaned his apartment in a storm of activity. He thought—hoped—that there was a distinct chance Gwen would end up in his bed before the end of the night, and he wanted to make a good impression. He wasn't a slob, but he was a bachelor and had been for years. Before he left, he checked his email. *Holy shit!* He had two dozen new messages from fans. Every one included glowing praise. *Well, let's see what sales are like.* "Oh my God."

He'd sold four hundred books. Today. Reviews were through the roof. He'd never had success like this. Even his series hadn't sold this well at release and he'd won awards for it. He left for his date whistling Christmas carols and hoping he'd be in a position to wish Gwen a Merry Christmas in person at midnight.

Chapter Five

Gwen lived in a multi-use building with a Chinese food restaurant, an accountant, and an occult shop on the first floor. She'd told him to text her when he pulled up downstairs and she wanted to pace to work off some of her nerves, but didn't think that was a good idea with her knee still tender. It was a lot better today, the ibuprofen finally kicking in and easing the swelling.

I'm here, beautiful. No parking though. I'll circle the block.

She couldn't help her smile. In the excitement of their earlier kiss, she'd forgotten to return his jacket and every time she'd thought about it during the day, she'd been paged to attend to a patient. Now, she shrugged into it and inhaled his woodsy scent. She'd be a little sad to give it back.

He pulled up in his old Ford moments after she stepped out onto the sidewalk. She'd chosen a black dress with a plunging neckline and a trio of silver chains. The French twist that currently held her hair had taken her half an hour, but her girlfriends had always told her that it was her best look. Marcus pulled into the three-minute loading zone and hopped out, coming around to open her door for her. "Wow," he said. "You're stunning. And my jacket suits you."

Gwen chuckled. "I really meant to give it back at the coffee shop."

"I don't know that I ever want it back." He trailed the backs of his knuckles along her jaw. "Not unless you come with it."

"I . . ."

"So, dinner?"

Relief spread through her. She wanted him. There was no doubt about that. But she wanted to get to know him better first. She had to know if the man in front of her was as real and raw as he appeared in his book. "Yes. Where are we going?"

"Is Italian okay?"

"Perfect."

He reached for her hand at a stoplight. "I've been thinking about this all day."

"So have I. Where did you happen to find a restaurant open for dinner this late on Christmas Eve?"

"I didn't. I thought I'd cook."

"Oh! So we're going to your place?"

Marcus looked over at her with a frown. "If you're not comfortable, we don't have to. There's a good Thai place that's in my neighborhood."

"Your mother is pretty convinced that you're a good guy. Also, she's talkative. And proud of you. I'm willing to take the chance. But I'll warn you, I'm a black belt."

"You? Miss Walks-and-Texts-and-Falls?"

Gwen pulled her hand away and gave him a playful slap on the arm. "Yes. Me. I have many hidden talents that do not involve walking."

"Maybe you can show me some moves later," Marcus said, his voice deepening.

Gwen shivered in her seat. She'd love to show him some moves, but not those. Others. Moves that would involve her slipping out of her dress. Marcus seemed to have the same idea. He grinned and said, "I'll show you mine if you show me yours?"

She wanted to laugh, or melt, or jump him in the front seat of his car, but instead, her stomach rumbled loudly, causing them both to laugh. "Do your moves involve cooking?"

"Yes. Most definitely."

Marcus lived in an older building in Pioneer Square. Gwen hesitated at the bottom of the stairs. "There's no elevator?"

"Oh shit. Your knee."

"It's okay. I'll go slow." Gwen took two steps up before Marcus stopped her with a hand on her arm.

"Turn around and climb on." He stood on the landing,

his back to her.

"Seriously?"

"Yep."

Gwen wrapped her arms around his broad shoulders and jumped. He caught her legs above her knees and held her tightly. He was warm, and strong, and between her thighs. He carried her up two flights of stairs and stopped in front of a scuffed door. She slid down his back, a little shiver racing down her spine as the friction abraded her nipples through her dress.

"It's not much, but this is me."

The apartment smelled like him, woodsy and clean, a faint hint of Scotch and wood smoke. He had a little fireplace in the corner that looked to get a lot of use and there were three logs stacked and ready to go. His writing space was obvious: a recliner in the corner with a little table next to it piled with notebooks and his laptop on the floor. The kitchen was small, with a high counter that served as a breakfast bar and a divider from the living room. Up a few steps beyond the kitchen, a loft bedroom peeked out, the dark green comforter smartly draped over the bed.

"It's nice." She moved to his large window, grinning at the sight of the stadium lights: done up in red and green for the holiday. Christmas Eve and she was on a date. With a guy who could kiss like nobody's business. And whose mind she found fascinating. When she turned around, he'd lit the fire and was moving towards the kitchen.

"Wine?"

"Mmm-hmm." She moved towards the kitchen, but he gestured at one of the stools at the bar.

"Is that okay or do you want to put your leg up?"

"This is fine. Really, it's just stairs that are the problem." She couldn't help her gaze sliding towards his bedroom. She'd crawl up there if she had to.

A throaty chuckle rumbled in his chest. "We'll make that work. Later," he said, sealing his promise with a gentle kiss.

When she had a glass of Merlot in her hand, she sipped and watched him move around the kitchen. "Did your mother teach you how to cook?"

"Mom can't cook to save her life. I dated a chef right out of college for a few years. She taught me a lot. Mostly about how to pair flavors, read a recipe, when to improvise. Baking is more of a science. That's why I can't bake at all. Cooking is art. Tracy and I weren't good together, but at least she left me with some impressive skills when she dumped me for one of her sous chefs."

"Ouch."

"Yeah. I think she'd been screwing him for months before she told me. Last I heard, they had three kids and were living in New York City. She's a big deal now. Owns half a dozen restaurants." He shrugged. "None of them Italian."

"You said that happened right after college. How old are you?"

"Thirty-four."

"Oh. A younger man, then."

"No. You can't be over thirty." He set a pot of water to boil on the stove and grabbed bowls out of the fridge: shredded cheese, crumbled sausage, marinara sauce, and a tub of ricotta.

"Thirty-six."

"I refuse to believe it. From this day forward, you're twenty-nine. And always five years younger than me."

It was easy to laugh with him. *It's been ages since you've relaxed around a man. Since you could let go enough to enjoy yourself.* "Well, we'll see how long that lasts. I found a few gray hairs the other day."

"I used to have a full beard," he said. "Until I developed a gray streak three years ago. Gray hair doesn't mean a damn thing. And you're beautiful. No matter what color your hair is."

While he assembled a pan of lasagna, they talked about their childhoods and educations, moving to the couch with their wine once the pasta was in the oven.

"Why are you single?" he asked her when he'd topped off her wine.

"After Victor died, I didn't want to fall in love again. What we had wasn't perfect. I know that now. But at the time . . . I was twenty-six, naive, thinking that this man was my entire world. And when that world fell apart, I wasn't interested in

212

rebuilding it. I became a doctor, worked hard, married my career. I don't regret it. Not really. But I think I finally realized the other night that it's not enough for me."

Marcus coughed on a sip of wine. "The other night?"

"Yes. I read something that changed my mind." She looked up at him through lowered lashes, carefully watching his reaction. "You put your life on hold for your mother. And it's admirable. But it's cost you. I read your first book too. There was so much hope in that book. A promise of a better world. But this last one, it was all pain. I think we're . . . we're the same in that. I don't want to hurt any more. I realized that it was my choice to keep feeling that pain. I loved Victor. With all of my heart. I will never not love him. But he's gone. I'm still here. And I deserve to find happiness. So do you."

Gwen set her wine down on the coffee table and eased the glass from Marcus's hand. "How long until dinner?"

"Long enough." Marcus grabbed her around the waist and pulled her into his lap. "I'm going to mess up your hair."

She beat him to it, pulling out one pin after another to let her dark tresses tumble to her shoulders. A possessive rumble in his chest shocked her, but not as much as his hand in her hair. He tightened his grip, the little pricks of sensation shooting down to her toes. "Kiss me, Marcus. Like you mean it."

That was all he needed. He lay back, guiding her down on top of him so she could feel the bulge of his erection through his jeans. Her nipples turned to hard points and scraped against his chest as he positioned her so he could ravage her mouth. His fingers in her hair held her close, and she ground her hips against him.

Tongues danced, tasted, demanded, and Gwen reached down to flick open the button on his jeans. He growled then—growled!—and snaked a hand under her dress to find her soaked panties.

"Shit, I wanted to make this last, but if I don't get you naked soon, I think I'll fucking explode," he said, rolling and coming up to standing with her in a fluid motion, barely letting her feet touch the ground. He snaked an arm under her knees and lifted her as she shrieked with surprise and tightened her arms around his neck. In five steps, they were in his bedroom moving towards the bed. "How did you think I was going to get you up here, honey? Throw you? And someone needed to prove to you that a man can and should carry a woman to bed."

"Less talk," she gasped. "More undressing."

"Got it." He laid her down on the bed and pulled off his black button-down shirt without bothering to undo the buttons.

"God."

"No, Marcus," he said with a grin, earning him a pillow thrown at his head. Gwen couldn't help herself, she didn't want to tear her eyes away. A half-arm sleeve tattoo snaked from his shoulder to his elbow. An intricate tattoo wound itself over his right shoulder, down his arm, and ended just above his wrist. The design was vaguely futuristic, with star trails, an alien skull, and thick rings, reminiscent of Saturn. He wasn't body-builder cut, but his defined chest was covered with a sprinkling of dark brown hair. A thin trail disappeared into his jeans. The start of a v angled down from his abs and as he unzipped his fly, he groaned, his erection springing free inside black boxers.

"Your turn." He crawled up onto the bed and hiked her skirt up around her hips. "How does this come off?"

Gwen wriggled and tugged the jersey knit over her head, leaving her exposed in a black lace bra and panties and her black boots. She hadn't even noticed Marcus take off his shoes and socks, but he'd somehow managed. He bent down and placed a kiss on the inside of her thigh, an inch above her knee. Moving lower, trailing his lips along her skin, he unzipped her boot, kissing as he went and finally sliding the boot off of her foot, peeling the thin sock off with it. He repeated the sensual trail down the other thigh and calf, carefully kissing around the tape that held her knee stable.

"You're perfect," he said, cupping her breasts and brushing his thumbs over her nipples. At her shudder and whimper, he grinned. "You like that?"

She could only nod and arch her back, thrusting her breasts further into his hands. She couldn't help her pout when he slid his hand around her back, but when her bra fell away and his mouth fastened onto her nipple, she didn't care.

Reaching for him, she stroked his balls, rubbing up to his shaft through the boxers, and was rewarded when he reached down and tugged the waistband down so she could feel all of him.

"Marcus, now. Please."

"Not yet."

The scent of him surrounded her, in his bed, on his skin, and she couldn't take it anymore. When he bit her, the lightest tightening of his teeth over one of her sensitive buds, she cried out and bucked her hips. He trailed kisses down her belly, to her lace-covered mound, and pulled her panties off with his teeth—his teeth! The man was sex personified. She'd been attracted to him from the first time she'd laid eyes on him, but she'd never thought he'd be like this in bed. Hell, she'd never thought she'd be like this in bed.

"I'm going to make you come," he said with a growl, and dove into her wet folds. His tongue stroked gently, and he apparently enjoyed what he was doing, for he groaned and grunted, his erection pushing almost painfully into her lower leg. When he slid two fingers inside of her, twisting, she came undone, crying out for him, out of her mind with the need to feel every inch of him.

She was barely aware of the crinkle of foil that heralded the condom, but when he nudged her with his length, she opened her eyes, smiling a lazy, drunken grin. "It's about time," she teased, and yelped when he tweaked her sensitive nipple.

"Yes, it is."

It had been too long since she'd had a man, and he took his time, letting her get used to his length little by little. When he'd seated himself firmly, he brushed a lock of hair away from her face. "You feel so good."

"Make me come again," Gwen said, "and this time, come with me."

Marcus thrust into her, grabbing her thighs and lifting her hips, taking himself deeper with every stroke. Gwen raked her short nails over his sides, eliciting a shudder and a fresh growl. "Not . . . gonna . . . last . . . long," he grunted. She matched his intensity with her own, holding his gaze, hoping he could see into the depths of her soul. She was falling for him.

Sexy, brooding, sensitive Marcus was just what she needed. And maybe she was just what he needed, too.

"Come with me, honey," he said with a gasp, grinding his thumb against the tiny bundle of nerves that had the power to send her flying.

"Marcus, yes. Yes!"

He jerked, his spasms shaking her entire body and when he'd calmed, he collapsed down next to her, pinching the condom off and tossing it in the trash.

"I hope you know," he said quietly, turning to look at her with the weight of the world written on his face, "I'm not interested in a one night stand with you."

"I didn't know," she replied. "Not for sure." Gwen raised herself up on her elbow so she could cup his cheek. "But I'm glad. I want to get to know you, Marcus Bunch. And I want to start Christmas with you."

"On one condition," he said, nibbling on her ear.

"What's that?"

"You end it with me, too."

Gwen pulled him close, tracing his tattoos with her tongue. "I think it's going to be a very Merry Christmas."

Angels in Disguise

by Jennifer Senhaji

Cheers to my lovely Writing Wenches

Chapter One

Getting Ready—Gabe

Getting ready for New Year's Eve, and I can't freaking believe the year has gone by this fast. *How can it be New Year's Eve already?*

"Gabe, you gotta wear them, man. The chicks are gonna love it."

"Dude, no way."

"Yes, way. Come on, maybe we can snag ourselves a couple of cute little angels."

How did I get roped into a costume themed New Year's Eve event? Mike. My best friend Mike. I've been friends with Mike since I was eighteen. He always has my back so I always have his. He said this event was going to be off the hook, and since I didn't have any other plans, I was in. *Of course I was.* I mean, we're going to an outdoor New Year's Eve music festival, close enough to the waterfront to see the fireworks at midnight. There are bound to be hundreds of chicks, freezing their asses off in skimpy little costumes, and I will be more than happy to help keep one or two of them warm for the night.

Two, you ask? Yeah, sure why not? I'm down for a threesome. Never gets old and I've got the stamina. *Bring it on.*

You see, I'm a connoisseur of women. I'm twenty-eight years old. I love women and they love me. I have the looks and I can charm a woman out of her skirt with a smile and a "hello, beautiful" quicker than you can say home run. I have no interest in a serious relationship, and I let the women I date — and I use that term loosely — know it upfront.

You want to psychoanalyze me and my fear of commitment? I'll save you the time. I don't do relationships.

I had my heart broken when I was eighteen. My girlfriend of three years, Krista, went out of state for college, and when I tried to surprise her in her dorm one weekend our freshman year, I found her in bed with some jerk reading her poetry, naked.

Yep, naked.

I took the high road and waited for the little punk to gather his clothes together and leave. Trying to convince Krista that we could still make it work, I swallowed my pride, and basically begged her to give us another chance. I had loved her, really loved her, but I guess she outgrew me or us or whatever. At least that's what she said.

So I dragged my sorry, heartbroken ass out of there and went home. I cried like a little bitch, then I got angry, then I got even.

I tracked down Krista's best friend Candice, who was still living back home, and told her the story of how I had caught Krista in bed with someone else, when all I had wanted to do was surprise her.

Needless to say, Candice was only too willing to console me. We spent that night tangled up in her sheets. After three days with her, I realized I didn't really like her. I had never really liked her. I had put up with her because she was Krista's best friend, but she annoyed the shit out of me. So, I told Candice that I couldn't hurt Krista by being with her best friend, even though I secretly hoped she had already told her, and never called her again.

Since then, no girlfriends, no relationships. Just fun. It's easier, and I'm happy. Most women are fine with it. I can spot a clingy woman from a mile away and avoid them easily. Once in a blue moon I meet a woman who acts like she's fine with casual, but turns out to be looking for more. I have a way of letting them down easy, building their confidence back up in the process. A glorified "it's not you, it's me" speech. They end up realizing they can do better, and I'm free to go about my merry way without guilt.

I don't want you to think that I use women to get back at Krista, I don't. I did that with Candice. But since then, I've been enjoying the single life. I'm young and having fun and I don't hear the women complaining. *Just the opposite.* Think of me as you will. Tonight, I take no prisoners.

It's on.
"Fine, Mike, I'll wear them, but I call Black."

*G*oing Out—Alex

Getting ready for New Year's Eve, and I can't believe what a long and horrible year it has been. Ugh, I mean, yeah, this last year basically sucked balls.

"Alex, you have to wear it, the guys are gonna love it."

"No way, Jamie."

"Way! You will look so hot in this."

"I don't want to look hot, I want to stay home and curl up with a good book and go to bed early."

"Nope, not gonna happen. You have been going to bed early for the last four months. You've read enough books."

"No such thing."

"In this case there is."

"Jamie, you know why. I'm in a funk. A breakup funk."

"Well, suck it up, cupcake. It's been four months. The first month was okay. Funk acceptable. Now it's just pathetic. I want to see the old Alex. The fun, dance on the tables, gives you hell Alex. Where is she? Can you please let her come out and play?"

She's right, I know she's right. Jamie is my supportive best friend, but when enough is enough, it's enough with her. I was that fun twenty-six year old four months ago, although I only danced on a table once and that was back in college. *Yep, I have lost my fun.* Lost my status as the fun friend, and have sunken to the "oh my God, when is she going to get over him" friend.

It's all because of Rick. Rick the dick. We dated for two years. Two years! I thought he was the one, turned out he was a zero. We had been happy, or so I thought. We had loads in common, we got along great. Our friends became friends — it was the perfect fit from the beginning. Except Rick, unbeknownst to me, was getting a little too friendly with Tiffany, my friend Ty's girlfriend. Needless to say, it all blew up when Ty came home to find his live-in girlfriend in bed with Rick. My Rick. The whole thing was terribly dramatic and friendships were lost when people started taking sides. My truest friends have stuck by my side. Jamie, my best friend since freshman year in college, would kill for me. In fact, Rick almost lost his dick.

So maybe I should get back out there. Maybe it's time to let loose. Maybe it's time to play the field, have a fling, who knows? *Jamie is right. It's time.*

"Okay, Jamie, you win. I'll wear it."

"Yay! Girl, we are gonna own it tonight."

"Yeah we are," I say, giving Jamie a high five.

While putting on my ridiculously skimpy costume, I try to psych myself up. *I can do this, I can do this. I can be sexy and fun again. I can do this.*

"You have to be kidding me, I can't wear these shoes, Jamie. I'm gonna kill myself in these shoes."

"You are wearing the shoes, Alex!"

God help me.

Chapter Two

The Entrance—Gabe

We end up taking a taxi to get to this shindig. The streets are packed with party goers and the traffic is miserable. A two mile drive took an hour. Mike is on his phone trying to find out where the guys are. We're supposed to meet up with Duke and Bill, but this place is huge.

The whole waterfront is covered in large white tents that go for blocks. It looks like maybe ten blocks from where I stand. *This is incredible.* I didn't realize this festival was so huge. I'm stoked now. The bass from the music is invigorating and I'm ready to get my party on.

"Okay, so Duke and Bill are already inside. They said they're in the third tent from the entrance," Mike says, as he slips his cell into his front pocket.

"Got it. Let's go, man, we're wasting time out here. We can't keep the babes waiting," I say, pointing to my watch.

The guy at the entrance attaches red wrist bands to each of us, giving us full access to the festival.

As we pass through the gates and into the first tent, Mike rubs his hands together and exclaims, "It's party time."

"Yes, yes it is."

The first tent has a place to check coats and a table, with a line a mile long, giving out party favors. Almost everyone is in costume. When a couple of naughty nurses walk by me, with skirts barely covering their asses, and smile in my direction, I give them a nod and a smirk and nudge Mike with my elbow.

"Okay, I'm cool with the costumes, bro. This is going to be an amazing night."

"See, I told you. You thought it was too girly to dress like angels."

"Well, your white wings are a little girly, but my black ones look badass, so it's all good."

"Whatever, man. I look good."

Mike is in blue jeans and a white t-shirt, basic All American boy. Blond hair, blue eyes, the man keeps in shape. His white angel wings are a little too Victoria's Secret for me, but somehow he pulls it off.

I went black all the way. I have on my black jeans, a plain black t-shirt, and my black boots. I was thinking we could just throw on our leather jackets and go as Zuko and Kenickie, but Mike had other ideas. I was against it at first, but once I put the wings on, they weren't so bad. The black ones weren't all fluffy like the white, more like rough feathers, and they lay against my back instead of sticking out. All in all, it turned out okay.

We head through the entrance to the second tent, and find a bar with a huge line. We bypass it, agreeing there are probably several bars, and head to the next tent to find Duke and Bill.

I spot Duke first. He's dressed as a fireman, which is so typical, because he is a fireman. He's chatting up a cute little brunette dressed as a pirate, and as I approach, I realize she is wearing a green wrist band, meaning she is under twenty-one. *Typical.*

Bill is wearing scrubs, with a stethoscope around his neck, going for the doctor look. He's actually a nurse, and we all give him shit about it, but he's really good at his job. He works down at General, in the ER. He sees me approach and smiles, shaking his head in Duke's direction.

"What's up man, how's it going?"

"Bill, I can't believe you took the night off. I thought for sure you'd be working and I was surprised when Mike said you would be here."

"Yeah, I worked Christmas, so they gave me tonight off. Did you see Duke, already scamming on that coed?"

"Yeah, he doesn't waste any time, does he?"

We do the traditional shake/guy hug combo all around, and when Duke drags his eyes away from his new friend's tits and comes in for the hug, I whisper, "She's a little young for you, man."

"I know. Dude, she just turned eighteen. She's totally down."

"Hey, take it easy buddy, the night is young."

The thing about Duke is, he's always looking for his next conquest. He promises the world to these young girls, playing into their hero worship because of his job. But as soon as he bangs them, he's pushing them out the door. I've seen him on more than one occasion, when he has run into one of the "notches," as he calls them, be a complete ass and even go as far as to pretend he doesn't recognize them. He's all about the wham, bam, thank you ma'am, only without the thank you. I guess I'm not in any position to judge, but at least I do it with a little more class and respect for the women I bed. He has no respect for women at all.

Bill is cool. He works so much that I don't see him that often, but he's pretty laid back. I guess if I was giving out titles, I would say Bill is the quiet one, Duke is the douche, Mike is the boy next door, and I'm the bad ass.

While Duke is distracted, his little pirate sneaks away. *I guess she wasn't "down" after all.*

"Shit, where did she go?"

Mike grabs Duke's shoulder and starts walking toward the next tent saying, "Come on, man, let's go see what's out there first, hmm? It's still early."

We decide to grab a beer and walk the length of the festival, to see what all is happening, what music is playing, and where the women that are at least twenty-one are hanging out.

The Arrival—Alex

Jamie and I are meeting Corey and Karina in tent number five. We get our red wrist bands at the entrance and make our way through the crowd. There are people everywhere and I'm feeling the party vibe. The bass from the DJ booth in tent four hits me as we enter. This tent is playing hip hop and there are lots of people dancing. As we walk through the crowd, I watch as a circle forms, and some guys and girls start a little dance battle. I stop, hypnotized by the way they move their bodies, and Jamie has to come back to drag me out.

"Did you see that guy dancing, with the zombie costume? He was amazing. And the girl, I think she was supposed to be a young Madonna, man, she was doing flips and holy cow, she was good."

"Yeah, yeah, come on. We need to find Corey and Karina. Then we can find our spot."

"Okay, but Jamie, I want to come back to tent four and watch."

"I thought you didn't like hip hop? I thought you were a rock and roll girl?"

"I am, but I can appreciate a little Eminem or Jay Z, once in a while. Those people could really dance."

We make our way to the next tent and find Corey and Karina in line at the bar. Corey has dressed up as a nurse and Karina is a Goth vampire.

"Hey Alex, you look hot, girl. I can't believe you let Jamie wear the angel costume."

"Yeah, well, she snagged it and made me wear this. Karina, I love your fangs, they look so real."

"Well, I got the kind you can attach to your teeth with putty, we'll see how long they last."

"Alex, you little devil, look at you. And you are wearing killer heels, way to step outside the box."

"Thanks Corey, hopefully these heels won't literally kill me. Yes, I'm the little red devil tonight. I'm ready to reclaim my fun, girls. Are you with me?"

"Yes!"

"Thank God."

"It's about time."

"Good for you, Alex."

We finally get to the front of the line and I grab a Corona, while the girls opt for margaritas. We amble along, people watching, commenting on costumes, walking the length of the festival to see what all is here to see.

Taking our time meandering through each tent, we stop

to dance to a little disco in tent eight for a while, which is so fun. *I love spending time with my girls.* We get a few offers, guys who come over and dance around us. After a while, we slip out and end up walking all the way down to the end of the festival before starting to loop back around. Tent twelve is playing house music, tent sixteen is playing indie rock, and tent twenty is playing classic rock. If I had my druthers, I would spend all night in the last two tents, but the girls want to head back to the tent playing house music for a while. By the time we get there, my feet are killing me. It's only 9 p.m. and I have no idea how I'm supposed to last until 2 a.m. in these death-trap heels.

I get in line at the bar to grab another beer as Jamie, Corey, and Karina go hit the dance floor, still feeling the margaritas from earlier. There are so many hot guys here tonight, one of them is bound to be good for a New Year's romp. That is, if I can find the courage to actually take someone home for the night.

Chapter Three

Hello Angel—Gabe

We slowly make our way to tent twelve, where we end up gathered in a corner, chilling for a while. It's a little after 9 p.m. and time to find a girl for the evening.

"Hey Gabe, see that blonde Angel on the dance floor?"

I follow Mike's line of sight and find her in the crowd, dancing with two other girls. "Oh, yeah, I see her. Damn, she's hot."

"Okay, I call dibs."

"You can't call dibs on a woman, bro."

"You bet your ass I can," Mike says.

"I bet I can get a number faster than you can," Duke chimes in.

"I'll do you one better," I say, taking the last sip of beer in the bottle, "I'll bet you she goes home with me tonight."

"Hey guys, I called dibs, remember," Mike says, looking back and forth between us.

Duke has that glint in his eyes. I've seen it before, but he needs to be brought down a notch, for once.

"Mike, you can't lay claim on a woman you don't even know," Duke says. Looking at me he continues, "May the best man win."

"I will, don't worry," I say with a smirk. We clink beer bottles, and I realize I'm empty. "Go ahead, man, give it your best shot. I'll be at the bar, watching you fail."

"I'll call you later from her place."

"You wish."

I make my way over to the line at the bar and take my place behind a brunette in a little red devil costume. She has a killer ass, and her legs look amazing in the five-inch heels she's wearing, but I've already set my sights on Angel Baby on the dance floor. Besides, I'm more partial to blondes than brunettes.

As we stand there, I notice how she keeps shifting from

one leg to another, making her devil's tail swing from side to side. She hears me chuckle, and turns around to find me ogling her ass.

"Can I help you?" she asks, snapping at me like a Venus fly trap.

"No, I'm good," I say, smiling. *Whoa, she's feisty. Not my normal type, in the looks department, but she is attractive. I like a woman with some fire in her. Fitting, considering her costume choice for the evening.*

"Is there something funny that I'm missing?" she asks, with an accusing stare. I'm trying to figure out what I did to piss her off so badly.

"No, but if you need to use the bathroom, there are some set up in tent ten."

"Why would you think I need to use the bathroom?"

"Well, you keep shifting from foot to foot, so either you need to pee, or you're deliberately shaking your ass at me. Either way, it's pretty amusing."

"What? Shaking my...look, the reason I'm having a hard time standing still is because my feet are killing me, alternating between numb and excruciating pain, so I would appreciate it if you didn't make fun of me."

"Sorry, sorry. It's your fault for wearing shoes like that, don't bitch at me about it."

"Wow, you are a real gentleman."

Devil Girl turns back around and we creep forward in line another two feet. *Damn, this line is taking forever.*

Another five minutes pass, and we've barely moved any further. I've been waiting too long to get out of line now, so I'm stuck here waiting behind the daughter of Satan. She keeps looking out toward the dance floor and won't stop shifting. *Shift, shift. Foot tap, foot tap, left hip juts out, then right, shift, shift. Heavy sigh.* I can't take it anymore. My feet are hurting just looking at her.

"Why don't you take the shoes off, if they are killing you so badly?"

"Why don't you mind your own business?"

"Geez, just trying to help."

Shift, shift, heavy sigh, shift, foot tap. I know she's going to lose it soon and I'm a little afraid of her, to be honest.

She looks up at me and says, "Shoot, I can't do this. I'm sorry, can you help me, please? These things have straps around the ankle and I'd normally sit down to take them off, but I don't want to lose my place in this line and I'm afraid if I try to balance and bend over to do it, I'm going to fall and break my neck."

"Ah, okay, yeah sure. What do you want me to do?"

"Just let me hang onto your arm or something for balance, while I try to get these things off."

"Okay."

She holds onto my left arm to steady herself, and brings her right foot up, bent at the knee, using her other hand to undo the strap. I'm pretty impressed with how flexible she is and how long she is able to hold her leg up like that, but in the end, she can't undo the clasp.

"Darn it, I need two hands to do this."

"Here, why don't you bend over and undo them and I'll steady you so you don't fall over, okay?"

"Okay."

I think she's going to kneel down in front of me and hold onto one of my shins for balance, but instead, she bends down, legs straight and ass up, right in my face.

"Don't let me fall."

"I won't, I won't," I say, not knowing where to put my hands. I mean, shit, I could put them on her hips, but that would be a little too familiar and I don't even know this girl's name. I end up holding my hands on both sides of her, hovering, ready to grab her if she starts to keel over.

"Yes, oh thank God. That feels so good."

I can't help it. A groan slips out of me. "Umm, excuse me?"

"I got the first shoe off and it's like my toes can hear the angels singing. One more to go."

"Okay, hurry up. The line is starting to move again," I say, my dick already at half-mast.

"Almost there, yes, oh thank God. Finally."

She stands up, shoes in hand, with a huge satisfied smile on her face and moves the three steps forward in line.

"Thank you so much. Oh my God, I feel so much better. That was torture."

"Why did you wear those shoes if they were so uncomfortable? That doesn't seem very smart."

"I'll let that crack about the heels go for now since you helped me get out of them, but believe me, I would never choose to wear shoes like that. My friend made me wear them. But I feel much better, thank you. Sorry if I was being a brat, I was in a great deal of pain."

"No problem. You're cute when you're angry."

"Oh please."

We take another few steps and there are still at least twenty more people in front of Devil Girl.

"So, are you here with anyone tonight?"

"Um, I'm here with three of my girlfriends, if that's what you mean."

"Wow, you have three girlfriends all at once? You have some serious game. Don't they fight over you?"

"That's not what I meant and you know it...you," she says, not knowing my name.

"Gabe," I say.

"You're gay? I wouldn't have guessed it, but I can kind of see it now. That pretty face and the body..."

"No, I'm not gay, my name is Gabe. As in Gabriel."

"Oh...Oh!"

Her cheeks are as red as her costume. It's kinda cute. "And you are?"

"Straight."

"No, I mean what's your name?"

"Oh, my name, sorry, it's Alex."

"Nice to meet you Alex, as in Alexandra?"

"Yes, nice to meet you too, but please call me Alex."

"So Alexandra, what do you do?"

"It's Alex and I'm a writer. What do you do, Gabriel?"

"I'm in software. So what do you write? Fiction, nonfiction?"

We take two steps forward.

"I write fiction and I blog. What do you mean you're in software? Are you a programmer?"

"Hey Alex, where have you been?" asks the Angel I saw earlier, walking over to us.

"I've been here in this line that doesn't want to move."

"Well hello there, Angel," I say, giving her friend my signature smile.

"Hello."

I take Angel in from top to bottom, and she's even hotter close up. "Hey Alex, aren't you gonna introduce us?"

Alex rolls her eyes and says, "Gabe, Jamie. Jamie, Gabe."

"Nice to meet you," Jamie says.

"The pleasure is all mine, I assure you, Jamie."

"Oh brother," says Alex, with a hand on one hip. The look on her face says it all. She has me all figured out, at least she thinks she does.

*T*he Meet—Alex

As soon as Jamie comes over, Gabe's gaze is riveted to her. I'm used to it. She's gorgeous and hey, if I was into women, I'd be all over Jamie, too.

"Oh my God, Alex, do you see that fireman standing over there to your left?"

I look and find him staring at Jamie. When our gazes meet, he winks at me and takes another sip of his drink. He's tall, built, and has a killer smile.

"Yeah, I see him. Who is he?"

Gabe chimes in, "Oh that guy, that's Duke. Yeah, he's a buddy of mine."

"Hello nosy, we're having a private conversation over here," I say, chastising Gabe for eavesdropping.

"Well, anyway, he's so sweet and he's a fireman in real

life."

"Pfft, sweet? Duke? Okay, whatever, honey," Gabe mumbles, just loud enough for me to hear him.

Glaring at my nosy neighbor, I pull Jamie around my other side so I can turn my back on Gabe and talk to her in private.

"Um, okay, so what, you like him?"

"Yeah, I really like him, Alex. He was telling me all about his job and how scary it is when he's in the middle of a fire or "The Animal," as he calls it. He says one of his friends died last year in a fire they were fighting that got out of control. Some arsonist they were tracking or something like that."

"What? He said that? Good grief, haven't you ever seen the movie *Backdraft?*"

"Um, who are you again?" Jamie asks Gabe with a sneer.

Laughing, I turn to see him squinting his eyes in Jamie's direction before he replies, "No one."

Jamie looks back at me. "Anyway, once you get through this line, come find us on the dance floor."

"Wait, Jamie, where are Corey and Karina?"

"Oh, they're over there talking to Duke's friends, Mike and Bill. Come find us, we'll all be together over there," Jamie says, pointing in the direction of the dance floor.

"Okay, fine, but I want to go back over to tent sixteen, and then see what's going on in twenty."

"Okay, okay. Oh and if you ever get to the front of this line, get me a margarita. Thanks."

Jamie skips back over to the fireman, Duke, and I can see Gabe's eyes on her ass in my periphery until she disappears into the crowd.

"What?" he asks, when he catches me watching him.

"Nothing."

We take two steps forward.

"Geez," I whine, "this is the slowest line ever. What the hell is taking so long? We've been in this line for at least thirty minutes."

"I know, this is pretty ridiculous. Should we just forget it?"

"No way, I'm committed at this point. I've been waiting far too long to give up now."

"Yeah, me too. Don't worry Alex, I'll be by your side until the end."

"That was cheesy, Gabe."

"What can I say, I love dairy."

We wait and we wait and we wait some more.

"So you said before you were a writer?"

"Oh, um, yeah."

"Well, anything I would have read?"

"I don't think so, no. So you're in software. What exactly do you do?"

"Oh, I, well… I guess the easiest way to explain it is to say I help develop the software that supports apps."

"You mean apps, like on my cell?"

"No, more like apps you can use on a website."

"Oh, okay like different plugins or widgets you can use to add to a blog?"

"Yes, exactly. I'm actually working on a Blogger website app right now."

"Where were you yesterday?"

"Pardon me?"

"Oh, nothing. I was trying to fix a couple of widgets on my website that should feed in updated information, but for some reason, they don't want to work."

"They don't work at all or…?"

"They work, but they don't update. For example, a review gets posted and the way the widget is set up, it should feed the most recent post in at the top of the list, but it feeds oldest to newest, instead of newest to oldest, so the feed never changes, you just see the same ten reviews up on the widget, all the time."

"Oh, I'm sure it's an easy fix. You probably need to adjust the HTML code."

"With that, you've lost me," I say.

"Well, next time I'm in the neighborhood, I'll stop by and take a look."

Gabe pats his pockets down until he produces a business

card with his name and cell number on it.

"Here, take this. I know it's hard when you're self-employed, getting help with computer issues and all that. There's no IT or Support Department. So yeah, anyway, next time you run into a glitch, give me a call and I'll walk you through it."

"Thanks, that's really nice."

"Don't mention it. So, you still haven't told me what kind of books you write. Is it a secret?"

We take two steps forward and I swing my shoes around my wrist after attaching the straps to each other.

"No, it's not a secret. I write romance."

"Ah, I see. The shirtless cowboy on horseback comes across a city girl lost in the country. Or the classic English gentleman falls for the strong willed ladies' maid. Or the vampire with a conscience falls in love with the human and refuses to feed on her."

"That was a pretty good list of clichés," I say with a chuckle, "but no. I write contemporary romance and a little erotica."

Chapter Four

Fantasy—Gabe

Holy shit, did she just say erotica?

We take another couple of steps and Alexandra turns back toward me as I stand there with my mouth open. *She writes erotica. Holy hell.*

Clearing my throat I ask, "So contemporary romance, as in a romance that could happen now?"

"Exactly. Do you like to read?"

"Yeah, sure, I read for pleasure here and there."

There are only about five people left in front of us, and now I wish the line was longer. *I need to get to know this woman. Stat. Erotica…*

"What was the last book you read?"

Is she quizzing me or something?

"Gray Mountain by John Grisham."

"Huh." She seems surprised. "I've read Grisham before, but it's been a while."

"So, Alexandra, how many books have you published?"

"Oh a few, but I'm hoping to publish two more this coming year."

"That's impressive. You're a full time writer then?"

"No, I also manage the bookstore on Lake Street. Being a writer doesn't pay the bills, at least not yet."

"Still, I'm impressed."

"Thanks."

"So, how do you get ideas for your books? Do you research every story you write?"

"You mean for the erotica, right?" she asks, smirking.

"Well, yeah," I admit.

"Wow, that was smooth. Are you going to offer to be my research assistant now?"

"Do you need a research assistant?"

With a frown on her face, she takes a step toward me and looks me up and down, running her fingers over her neck and collarbone. *Hello sexy.*

"I can take care of things just fine by myself, thanks," she says, dropping her voice an octave lower.

This girl—woman— is seriously turning me on. She's feisty, smart, and sexy, a triple threat. I continue to watch as her hand trails down and around her throat, then up into her hair. She closes her eyes, letting her head fall back, and a throaty moan escapes her mouth.

And now, I'm hard. What the hell is going on?

Instinctively, I take a step toward her. By the time her eyes slowly open, I'm practically panting. A coy smile slowly turns the corners of her mouth up, and she places her hand on my chest, stopping me from advancing. With her other hand, she crooks her finger at me to lean in, and as I do she speaks seductively, grazing her lips against my ear lobe.

"Men are all the same, you know. As soon as they find out I write erotica, their eyes glaze over, thinking I must be like a porn star in bed. But that is not real life. The woman you were talking to five minutes ago, that's real life. This is just a fantasy."

She pulls away, causing me to stagger forward. The sultry look on her face retreats and is replaced by the smart ass expression she's worn since I first got in line.

"It's probably been forty-five minutes that we've been standing here. They better not be out of Corona when we get to the front," she states, as if that little display didn't affect her at all. As if that was all an act...

What a freaking tease.

*R*eality—Alex

Okay, so I'll admit, I'm attracted to Gabe. He's hot, he smells really good, but he has one night stand written all over him. As much as I think that would probably be very, very enjoyable, that's not who I am.

Yes, I've had one night stands before, but I ended up feeling like crap afterward. Liking the idea of having a fling and actually having one are two different things. I like being in a relationship. I like knowing the guy I'm sleeping with is not sleeping with anyone else. Well, I guess, that's not always the case, but it should be. I mean, if you want to be single, be single. Sleep with whomever you want to, no expectations. But when you're in a relationship, you're expected to be monogamous. For me, it's a must. I do not share well, never have. If you want me, you have to want only me.

Spending the last forty-five minutes with Gabe, I can tell he's not the monogamous kind. He's looking for one night, and even though I'm seriously attracted to him, I will control myself.

Only four more people in front of us and we will be next in line. *Finally.*

Gabe taps my shoulder and asks, "So, are you dating anyone?"

"No, not at the moment," I say, turning back around.

"What happened, bad breakup? Was it your best friend or something?"

How did he know that? "Um, no." I let go with a heavy sigh, and Gabe motions for me to continue. "Actually, my boyfriend was caught in bed with one of our other friend's girlfriend. We'd been together two years at that point."

"Ouch. That's tough. That's a long time to be dating someone. It must have been serious."

Wow, he is being pretty sympathetic. It's probably all an act to get into my pants, but it's nice to hear someone say that instead of, "Get over it," for once.

"Yeah, it was."

"So if it was a mutual friend, the group was probably divided, right?"

"Yeah, how did you know that?"

"Classic tale of dating within your friend pool. Sex is the easiest way to ruin a friendship, even if it isn't you having the sex. There's always a chance, when friends get together, that they will breakup. In this case the friends had sex behind everyone's back, so I'm sure everyone was pretty upset."

"Yep, exactly. Lost a lot of friends. Really cool people, but they knew Ri—him longer so…"

"Sorry, it's a bad deal all around. No wonder you're so uptight."

"Excuse me, I'm not uptight."

"Yes, you are. How long has it been anyway?"

Chapter Five

The Gentleman—Gabe

Her face is turning red, and I can practically see the steam coming out of her ears. *Guess I hit a nerve. Good.*

"That's none of your business. For a minute there, you were actually being nice. Well, minute man, I guess my first impression was right."

"Hold it, hold it. Do not get your panties in a twist. First of all, don't ever, ever call me minute man again. I will have you know that I can go all night."

It's faint, but I can see her pupils dilate at this statement, which makes me think the thought of going all night with me has her intrigued, no matter what she says.

"And second of all, I was just asking an innocent question. The fact that you got so upset by it only proves how up-tight you are. I'm guessing it's been a few months, am I right?"

Her mouth opens and closes like a fish out of water, and I know I'm right. I don't even need her to verify it. *Yep, the woman needs to get laid and bad and I am just the man to help her out.*

Without answering, she turns around and waits behind the last three people in front of her, tapping her foot. *She is so damn sexy when she's mad.* I stand there watching her hip bounce with each tap.

"You know," she accuses, spinning around and catching me off guard, "if you were a gentleman, you wouldn't ask about my sex life. I don't know you, and I would never confide something so personal to someone I just met. Maybe the little skanks you normally date are fine with that, but I demand a little more respect from the men in my life."

She spins back around and I stand there, shocked. Most of the women I know talk about sex openly. None of them have ever been offended before. *This isn't the 50s. Who is this woman?*

"Hey, I didn't mean to offend you."

"You know what? I'm sure you didn't. I'm sure that is how you normally interact with women, and I'm sure they let you. That's part of the problem. Women rarely say anything. A gentleman, in my book, doesn't touch a woman without her consent. A gentleman doesn't proposition a woman he has just met. And the language; good God. I can't stand it when a man drops the F-bomb during a conversation. It's so disrespectful. You may think what I'm saying is old fashioned, but I'm telling you, manners matter. Opening the door, pulling out chairs, those things are all sexy as hell. The fact that there are very few men that actually do them makes it all the sexier when you run across one."

Huh, interesting, she wants a gentleman. Okay, I can be a gentleman. I mean, I'm not an animal. I have to say, it's nice to find a woman who demands respect. Dating is so casual these days, and most women are easy to get into bed. Whether you agree with me or not, that's why my weekends are always so full. I don't have to work for it. Never really have.

We finally get to the front of the line and Alex places her heels on the makeshift bar and orders.

"Three margaritas on the rocks with salt, please. And one Corona with lime."

She pulls out her debit card from some hidden pocket on her body and lays it on the counter, as I peer over her shoulder.

"Giants. You have a San Francisco Giants debit card?"

She turns her head back toward me to answer, bringing our faces really close together. I step back to give her space.

"Yes, I love the Giants. You have a problem?"

"Uh, yes. Yes I do."

"That will be $36 please, and it's cash only."

"What? Are you kidding me? I've been in line for forty-five minutes and you're telling me it's cash only? There's a sign that says you take ATM/Credit!"

"Sorry lady, our credit card machine isn't working. You can get cash from the ATM in tent one and come back."

"This is ridiculous."

I lean over her shoulder and hand the kid $40. "Keep the change."

"No. What are you doing? I can't let you pay."

"It's okay, Alex, I've got cash on me."

"Still..."

"If you want to pay me back we can walk down to the ATM, but I would appreciate it if you would take your drinks and move out of the way so I can order mine."

"Okay, sorry. And thanks."

I order a Corona and a bottle of water, and hand the kid another $10. Alex is trying to figure out how to carry all three margaritas and her beer and I step aside and let the customer behind me order.

"Need some help?"

"Yes, actually. Thank you."

"Sure, no problem."

Putting my beer bottle in one of my back pockets and the water in the other, I grab two margaritas, and Alex grabs her beer and the last margarita. I follow her toward her friends and mine, who are all chatting around a pub table tucked along the right side of the tent.

"Finally, what took so long?"

"Did you go to Mexico for these margaritas?"

"Hey, dude, where's my beer?" Mike asks.

Alex and I exchange a look, clinking bottles while everyone gives us crap for taking so long.

"Cheers!"

"Not cool man, not cool," Mike says.

"Get your own beer," I say, watching Alex as she gulps hers down.

"So what's this about the Giants, Alex?" I ask.

"The Giants rule, that's what," Alex says with a shrug.

"Uh, oh, here we go," mumbles Mike, loud enough for me to hear.

"How can you be a Giants fan and live in Santa Monica? You should be Dodgers all the way."

"The Dodgers suck."

"Oh God, everyone stand back," warns Mike as I glare at Alex, while she stands there smiling.

"I take it you're a Dodgers fan?" she asks, nodding in my direction.

"Hell yes."

"That's too bad. Sorry your team hasn't won a World Series lately. How many years has it been? I think it was 1988 the last time the Dodgers won the World Series and they haven't been since. The Giants, however, won in 2012, 2010, and 2014 and we went to the series in 2002 and 1989. So, you do the math."

"This is going to get ugly, I can feel it," says Bill.

"Duke, this is my friend Alex. Alex, Duke," Jamie says.

"Nice to meet you," says Alex.

"You too."

Jamie continues the introductions while I glare at Alex. This woman is a baseball fan who knows her stats. *That is hot as hell.* But she's a Giants fan, and that may be a deal breaker for me.

I turn to the Vampire and the Nurse and introduce myself. "Hi, I'm Gabe, nice to meet you ladies. Angel, nice to see you again."

"It's Jamie. I like your wings."

"Thanks."

"Okay, well since Gabe was nice enough to only buy his own beer, I'm going to go get in line to get a drink. Care to join me, Angel?" Duke asks, directing his eyes at Jamie's cleavage.

"Sure. I need a break from dancing anyway."

"Um, guys, I wanted to go check out the indie rock tent remember? I just spent forty-five minutes in line and am ready to get my groove on."

"I'll go with you. I could use a walk after standing still so long," I offer.

Alex gives her friends a pleading look.

"Go ahead Alex, we'll catch up with you later," Jamie says, following Duke over to the drink line. Mike, Bill, and the other girls trail along after them, talking amongst themselves.

"Wow. That was nice. They totally ditched us," Alex says with a pout.

"Shall we?" I motion for Alex to walk ahead of me.

"What the hell. I guess I need to put my shoes back on, which I'm not looking forward to."

"No you don't, just carry them. The place is all grass anyway. You should be fine."

She thinks about it for a moment, looking around at the ground.

"Actually, I think I will. I feel much more comfortable like this. Let's go."

We walk toward the end of the tent and drift through the next few, taking in all the costumes and commenting as we walk along. One guy is dressed as a genie with a big magical golden lamp wrapped around his waist. There is a "Rub Me" sign written across his groin and Alex and I both crack up as we pass him.

"So you're a baseball fan. That's cool. Except the part about loving the Giants, but let's not go there."

"Yes, let's not. I do love baseball, I'm not really a fan of other sports, but I love me some baseball. So fun to go to the stadium and just spend the day. I played a little softball too, all through school, and used to be part of an adult league, but I haven't played in a while. Now I watch."

"Really? I played baseball as well. I started playing little league when I was eight-years-old and pretty much played until I got to college. I was pretty good in high school, but not good enough to play in college, so I gave it up. But I love the sport. We should totally hit the batting cages some time. I used to go pretty regularly, but the guys always seem to be busy, and it's not as fun when you go by yourself."

I realize I just asked Alex out on what might be construed as a date. It seems, by the look on her face, she thinks so as well, but doesn't answer.

We enter tent sixteen to the sound of "Dance, Dance" by Fall Out Boy, and Alex is bouncing on her toes. Obviously, she wants to dance, so I grab her heels from her hand and throw them to the side of the tent, near the flap. Following my lead, she pulls off her devil horn headband and throws it over with the shoes. I gulp down the last of my beer and grab her hand, pulling her out toward the center of the crowd.

"Wait!"

Maybe I read her wrong and she doesn't want to dance. *Maybe she doesn't want to dance with me.*

She downs the last of her beer, takes the empty bottle out of my hand, and jogs over to throw the bottles in the trash. When she comes back, she passes me and smiles over her shoulder, motioning for me to follow.

"Come on."

Grinning, I follow her into the crowd. Catching up, I place my hand on her back to let her know I'm behind her until we get to the center of the crowd and start dancing with everyone else. She throws her hands up and lets loose. *I love it.*

*T*he Dance—Alex

We dance until we're both dripping sweat. Gabe offers me a bottle of water that he produces out of nowhere, and I guzzle it down. Stopping before I reach the bottom, I hand him the bottle while he stands there panting. He is just as hot and overheated as I am, but I drank all his water.

Hmmm, hot.

He thanks me and winks.

He is hot. Very. Why is he hanging out with me again?

He came here with a bunch of guys, and somehow we paired up. *Weird.*

Well, I don't know about Corey and Karina, but Jamie is with that Duke guy. Something about him rubs me the wrong way. I can't really put my finger on it. Slime is the word that comes to mind, but since Jamie and I came together, we will leave together, and I can make sure she's okay. Not that I really need to. Jamie is a big girl and can handle herself, but to be safe, no more beer for me. Two was enough, and right now, all I want is to get my hands on another bottle of cool water.

"Do you want to go check in with your friends?"

"I'll send Jamie a text, but right now, let's find a couple more bottles of water and hydrate, yeah?"

"Yes, I'm so thirsty. That sounds good."

We make our way through the next tent in search of short lines and cool water. We find the shortest line in tent nineteen and jog over to take our places, Gabe motioning me ahead of him.

"This seems strangely familiar," I say. "Have we been here before?"

Gabe chuckles. "Seems I keep ending up behind you tonight. Hopefully this line will move quickly so we can see what is happening next door. I can hear Def Leopard coming through. Are you up for a little banging?"

Feeling my face flame at the two innuendoes, I watch for a smirk or some other telltale sign he realizes what he just said or how it sounded, but he has a completely innocent look on his face as he waits for my response.

Clearing my throat, I say, "Yeah, sure, I love Def Leopard."

"Cool."

It only takes five minutes before we're at the front of the line. This time I whip out my card to pay for both our waters, before Gabe has a chance to plunk down the cash.

"Sorry, we have a $10 minimum for cards. Do you have cash?"

"Wow, this is not my night."

"It's okay. Here you go," Gabe says to the guy behind the counter as he pays for our waters and grabs the two bottles.

"Thanks. You should probably avoid standing with me in line, or you're liable to go broke."

"Aw, it's okay, Alexandra, I don't mind. Besides, we need to keep you hydrated. Cheers."

"Cheers." We bump plastic to plastic and each take a few gulps.

Jamie responds to the text I send telling me they're in tent four dancing to hip hop, and to come join them. I quickly text back a response that I'll see them in a bit.

Chapter Six

Almost Midnight—Gabe

It's about 11 p.m. when we hit tent twenty. I realize that I've spent most of my night with Alex, and I have to say, I'm having a really good time. When I first walked in, her friend Jamie had caught my eye, with all her leggy angelness. But, I'm really feeling Alex. She's cool, she doesn't take shit, and as the night progresses, I'm finding her more and more sexy. The way she dances with abandon, the way she taps her foot when waiting in line. The way she gulped that water down, and the little rivulets of water that dripped down her chin. She has this whole hot, smart, down to earth, tomboy thing going on, except she looks like sex on wheels. Especially in her red devil costume. *I wonder what she looks like on a normal day?*

She grabs my hand as we enter the tent, and pulls me to the center of the crowd, where we join in with everyone singing along to "Bohemian Rhapsody" by Queen.

This song is so genius, one of my all-time favorites, ever since I saw *Wayne's World*. You have to be seriously lacking taste if you don't love this song.

We both sing the slow beginning about mama, ballad style, at the top of our lungs, with everyone else in the room working up to the let me go part. Mama mia, this woman cracks me up when she head bangs full out. Her hair pins start shooting out like bullets, and I take cover behind her as "You Shook Me All Night Long" by AC/DC starts up. Her hair is half up, half down, but she's just into the music, singing as loud as possible. A little off key, I might add. It makes me like her even more. Laughing with her, I shout out the chorus, and continue to head bang at the important parts.

A few more songs and they announce the ten minutes until midnight mark. We look at each other and walk toward the edge of the tent.

"Oh my gosh, that was so much fun. I didn't realize it

was getting so late."

"I know, it's almost a new year," I say, wiping my forehead on the shoulder of my t-shirt.

"Thank God. I'm so ready for this year to be over and to start fresh."

"Is that cuz of the ex?"

"Well, no, not only him," she says, shaking her head rapidly. "Okay, yes, because of him. Truthfully, I'm ready to put that whole ordeal behind me, but I'm also excited to see what this year brings, as far as my writing career, so…yeah. So ready for the new year."

*T*he Stroke of Midnight—Alex

Gabe gives me a pity smile, and I shrug in response. I don't expect what happens next.

Taking a step toward me, he reaches up to tuck some of my now wild hair behind my ear. Just like in all the romance novels I've written, time seems to slow as I watch his hand come in and tuck, and then slowly retreat, grazing my jaw in the process. I lick my lips, a nervous habit I have, which catches his attention. We are only two feet away from each other, and every hormone in my body is screaming at me that this man has what I need.

"It was his loss, Alex, he didn't deserve you. Even I can see that, and I've only known you a couple of hours."

I feel like my stomach just dropped to the floor. I want to throw myself at him for that comment. That sweet — probably just a line, but I don't care, because that is just what I needed to hear at this time in my life — comment.

"Give me his name and address. Say the word, and I'll beat the crap out of him, then hack into his computer and ruin his credit."

"Are you serious?" I ask, beaming.

"As a heart attack," Gabe says, smiling back.

Going from lust to laughter, I throw myself at Gabe, but instead of a passionate kiss, I give him a big bear hug, and squeal when he picks me up and spins me.

Once he lets me down, I give him a friendly punch in the arm. "Thanks for the offer, but I don't want to waste one more minute worrying about the past. Nope, now I'm looking to the future."

"All right, but if you change your mind… Okay, let's go find everyone before it's midnight, shall we?"

"We shall." He offers his hand, and I take it with a smile.

I send Jamie another text and she doesn't respond, so Gabe and I walk back toward the front of the festival, stopping in each tent to look around. By the time we get to tent ten, we still haven't found them, and they are starting the countdown to midnight. The walls of the tents on the waterfront side are all open, and people are spilling out onto the grass to see the fireworks.

"Ten!" everyone shouts, and I look at Gabe, not sure if we should keep looking for our friends, or go outside with everyone else.

"Come on, we'll find them later," he says, motioning outside.

"Eight!"

I step out through the open tent walls, with Gabe following behind. Keeping my eyes on the sky, I stop at the edge of the lawn and feel Gabe place his hand on my back, letting me know he's there. It feels really nice to have this moment under the stars with this guy by my side, who has turned out to be the complete opposite of my first impression. I know it's only been a few hours, but something inside me is telling me that it's not an act.

"Five!"

I mean, I'm not the best judge of character lately, but still. There is something genuine about him, when he's not trying and is just being.

"Three!"

I close my eyes, pulling my head back, waiting for the

fireworks to explode across my lids.

"Two!"

"One!"

Gabe takes my hand in his and threads his fingers through mine.

"Happy New Year!"

A loud boom and burst of white flashes behind my lids, and I open my eyes to see the sparks in the sky floating back down to earth.

Chapter Seven

Fireworks—Gabe

The first fireworks go off, and I glance over to see Alex with her head back, eyes closed. She looks beautiful and wild, and I really want to kiss her.

As I'm wondering how she would react if I grabbed her right now, Alex opens her eyes, and I quickly look up at the sky, observing the red umbrella of sparks now overhead. I feel her shift as she gazes around at all the couples kissing and hugging, and I glance down at her when she tugs on my hand.

"Well?" she asks, with a smile curving the corners of her mouth.

"Well what?" *Did she ask me something while I was spacing out?*

"Aren't you going to kiss me?" *Bold.* I wasn't expecting that, she kind of caught me off guard. *Wait, why am I thinking about this?*

"You know, for New Year's Eve."

Her hair is wild, and she's stunning in this light. *Should I give her a friendly peck or slip her the tongue? Shit. I have no idea what she's thinking and I'm wasting time.* The smile fades from her face, and a look of rejection starts to appear as her gaze leaves mine and go back to the lightshow overhead.

"Come here," I say, pulling her gently by the waist toward me.

"It's okay, you don't have to."

"Hell with have to, I want to," I say, enthusiastically.

Quickly shifting her eyes back to mine and stepping into my embrace, she shocks me again with her response.

"Make it a good one."

I'm nervous. My heart is pounding so hard. I have no idea what this little devil woman has done to me. *Nervous about a kiss? Really, Gabe? What if we bash teeth or something equally awkward?*

I slip my left arm fully around her waist, causing her tail

to swing side-to-side. My right hand threads into her hair as she watches me, a playful smile on her lips. I study her mouth, letting the anticipation build. As she gazes back at me, and we alternate looking at each other's lips, her breathing becomes shallow, matching mine. She shifts her weight slightly forward, and now her breasts are brushing up against my chest with each synchronized breath we take. I feel myself go hard. *Hard and I haven't even kissed her yet. I am in so much trouble.*

*L*ight Bursts—Alex

A kiss is all about the anticipation, I know this from writing. When I asked Gabe for a kiss, I was expecting a peck on the lips and a friendly hug. When he hesitated, I thought, *well damn, I can't even get that.*

I didn't expect a full out real kiss, I was just kidding. But he is all in with the arm around my waist and the hand in my crazy hair, and the anticipation is killing me. It's the best part, right before lips meet, when your stomach flips, wondering what the other person tastes like. When he finally leans in, I hold my breath until I feel his velvety lips touch mine, and then *bam!* I am instantly on fire.

I bring my arms up around his massive shoulders, feeling the feathers of his wings slip through my fingers, searching for his neckline. *Yes.* I find it, and as soon as his tongue darts out and licks my bottom lip, I use my fingers, clutching the short ends of his dark hair, to pull his head closer to me so I can kiss him back, really kiss him. *Heaven help me!*

He moans into my mouth as my tongue joins his in a passionate exchange, and my stomach decides to fall down through the ground. *Holy Hell!* He tastes divine. *Yes, Gabriel. Yes, Oh God.* I want to hitch my leg up onto his hip, as his hands in my hair and around my waist tighten possessively. He's grabbing my ass, and pulling me closer, and I'm trying my best not to swallow his tongue. When we are fully aligned, his hand pulling me by my backside into him, I get a jolt as his erection rubs right against my already wet center.

I break the kiss to catch my breath. Gabe rests his forehead against the top of my head as I try to get my bearings, totally boggled. I want to climb him at this point, and I'm wondering if there are any dark corners where we could get naked. *Yep, I said it. Well not out loud, but in my head.* This guy has me so turned on, I am trembling.

"Holy shit."

"You can say that again," I mumble against his chest.

"Holy shit."

I'm about to do something I haven't done for years, but damn it, *I want him.*

Chapter Eight

Game Time—Gabe

Holy shit…

Alexandra is one hell of a kisser, and my instinct is to find a dark corner and rip her clothes off, because *damn…*

I wasn't expecting the kiss to escalate like that. Kiss her good was my mission, but then she moaned, or maybe that was me, and when I felt her yanking my hair I just lost it. I want her so damn bad right now, I feel like I'm gonna pop the buttons off my jeans. Her tits are still mashed up against my chest, and I'm not gonna lie, they look fantastic. All wench like, almost spilling out of her red corset top thingy. I feel like a fifteen year old who just touched his first boob. *I need more, I want more, but…*

Now I'm conflicted. I really, really like this girl—woman—and I…I think… *I don't want just one night.* I like her too much. Not that I don't like the women I usually sleep with… don't think I hate women, because I don't. Like I said before, I love women and they love me, just not love love. But this woman, Alex, after spending all night with her, I don't want it to be over. And I know, if we sleep together, I'll run out of there so fast, and I don't want to run out on her. I want to know her.

When Alex pulls her head back to look at me, her face is flushed and her lips are swollen, and seeing her like that, all revved up, makes me fantasize about what she would look like in my bed.

I'm chasing Alex around my living room while she giggles and easily evades me, using her legs and cute little ass to distract me. She's wearing my Dodgers jersey, just begging me to rip it off. Catching her on the side of the couch, I throw her over my shoulder, smacking her ass, and run with her into the bedroom. I end up popping a few buttons off my jersey trying to get to her, and then her nipple is in my mouth, and I'm inside of her, and she's amazing and beautiful and feels so damn good.

Blinking back to the present, I realize that was not a one night stand kind of fantasy. That was a girlfriend, relationship fantasy. *Now I know I'm in trouble.*

*I*t's A New Year—Alex

Holy moly. That was sex in a kiss. I mean, yeah. It's been a while, but I know what kind of kiss that was. That was a precursor to an orgasm. *Okay, decision made.* I'm going home with him or he's coming home with me. *Either way, I am getting in that man's pants tonight.*

I see Jamie looking for me inside the tent behind Gabe, and work my way slowly out of his grasp. Seeing him adjust himself, I snicker and then wave in Jamie's direction, finally getting her attention.

"Hey, where have you been, Alex?"

"Here, we were looking for you guys, but midnight hit, and so we watched the fireworks with everyone else. Where have you been?"

"Ugh, we've been dancing, and I'm exhausted. I'm not so sure about Duke. I think he may be a douche. He was practically dry humping me on the dance floor. Not much of a talker."

"Well, that's too bad, but I kinda had a feeling."

"What about this guy? Is he okay or…"

I take Jamie by the elbow, and walk with her a few feet away for more privacy.

"I really want to go home with him. There's something about him, and I have to say, I've had a really good time tonight."

"Really? I would have pegged him for a player."

"Oh, I'm sure he is, but there's something more there. In any case, I'm not looking for a relationship."

"Come on Alex, you're not a one night stand kinda girl."

"I know, I know, but I'm reconsidering it with him. I would regret it more if I didn't go home with him. I don't think I'll regret actually doing it at all. We kissed at midnight."

"Shut up, you did? How was it?"

"Well let's just say I liked him before that, but now, he's lucky he's still clothed."

"Okay, well as long as you know what you're doing."

"I do."

"All right, well help me get rid of his friend."

"Okay, let's go hit the bathrooms, and brainstorm."

Corey and Karina have amazingly paired off with Gabe's friends Mike and Bill.

"What are Mike and Bill like?"

"Oh they're actually really sweet. Not sure why they hang out with Duke, but yeah, they seem cool."

We start walking toward the bathrooms, and Gabe tugs on my tail before I get very far.

"Where are you going?"

"Just going to the ladies, be right back."

"Okay, don't take too long. It's time for another dance, yeah?"

"Okay, yeah, sounds good. See you back here in a bit."

As Corey and Karina follow us to the line, I start to wonder what it will be like when Gabe and I are alone.

We're at my apartment door, and Gabe is kissing and biting my neck. Barely able to get the key in the lock, Gabe presses me into the door, causing me to trip and fall over the threshold as it opens. We frantically pull at each other's clothing, until he has me naked and pressed up against the wall. He's shirtless, only the top few buttons of his jeans undone, and with wild abandon, he plunges into me over and over again, while I scream his name. I realize my front door was left slightly open in our rush, and it gives me an even greater thrill thinking that someone could catch us in the act.

Realizing I've left my shoes back in the tent, and the bathroom is basically a port-a-potty, I end up forgoing the bathroom break, and tell the girls I'll meet them back in the tent. As I make my way back to where I left Gabe, I see him involved in a heated conversation with Duke, Mike, and Bill. Before I'm close enough to eavesdrop, Gabe smacks what looks like a margarita out of Duke's hand, and then cold cocks Duke right in the jaw, knocking him out cold.

What the hell?

Chapter Nine

Wake Up Call—Gabe

As I watch Alex and her delectable tail saunter off toward the bathrooms, Duke approaches with another two drinks in his hand.

"So how's it going with the Angel, Duke?"

"Good, good. She's been hot for me all night."

"Is that right? Just don't be an ass, okay?"

"What's that supposed to mean?"

"I mean, I like these girls, they're nice, and I don't want you fucking up my game with your douchebaggery."

"Whatever dude, you're just jealous. I told you I'd get her. She's going home with me tonight."

"I don't know, Duke," Mike chimes in, "she doesn't seem that into you. I think she's been trying to ditch you for a while, she's just too nice to do it."

"What? Don't be ridiculous. I'm not letting that hot piece of ass get away."

"Whatever, man."

Mike and Bill follow me over to the bar for a couple of bottles of water while we wait, and I spot Alex's shoes and devil horns in the corner. I jog over to pick them up, and when I turn around, glancing in Duke's direction, I see him slipping something that looks like sugar into the margarita he's holding. It takes me a moment to process, but when I do, I realize what he's done, and storm over to where he's standing.

"Did you just put a roofie into Jamie's drink?"

"What? No."

"What did you just put in that drink?"

"Fuck you. I don't need to explain shit to you. Why don't you go find that little grenade of yours and get out of my face?"

My left hand flies, and I knock the margarita onto the floor, out of Duke's hand, so no one drinks it by accident. I haul back and clock him with my right fist, straight in the jaw. I don't realize Mike and Bill are standing next to me until I feel them push me back.

"Call security and get this guy out of here," I say to Mike. "I never want to see him again. He just fucking tried to roofie Jamie!"

"What?" Mike asks.

"What?" Hearing Alex's voice, I turn and find her standing behind me, her eyes practically bugging out of her head. "Are you serious? Call the police! Jesus, he could have raped her!"

"Alex, calm down."

"I will not calm down. Is this what you guys do?"

"No fucking way. I don't need to drug women, I would never associate with anyone who did, that's just sick. I caught him in the act of lacing her drink and confronted him. Please believe me, I want nothing to do with that bastard."

What a clusterfuck this is. I don't want Alex to think I would ever do something like that. *My God. It sickens me to think of what could have happened, or what Duke has possibly done in the past, but I can't lose Alex because of that asshole.*

Long Night—Alex

It's been a long night. After Gabe knocked out Duke, we called security and had him brought out to the front and held until the police got there. I wanted to file a police report. Jamie just wanted to go home. After talking to the police for what seems like forever, and listening to Gabe's statement, I can tell he really didn't realize what Duke was capable of. By 2:30 a.m., the police load Duke into the back of a car, and we're all ready to head home. I'm tired and I'm hungry and I'm disappointed. I was really looking forward to spending the night with Gabe, but now that I realize my friend could have been date raped tonight, I'm not in the mood.

"Come on guys, let's go home," I say to Jamie, Corey, and Karina.

"Hey wait. Why don't we all go grab some breakfast at the diner down the street?" Bill suggests.

"No, I don't think so. I just want to go home," Jamie says.

Mike chimes in. "How are you getting home? It's going to be tough trying to get a taxi."

"Oh hell, I didn't think of that. I guess we could walk. Wait, where are my shoes?"

Gabe pulls my heels out of nowhere, holding them out to me.

"Thanks, Gabe."

"My pleasure."

Something about the way he looks at me when he says that gets my blood pumping. *Why oh why did that ass try to drug my friend?* Scares the crap out of me when I think about what could've happened, but I still wish Gabe and I were going home together. It's pretty obvious at this point that none of the guys had any idea Duke would pull something like this.

I put my death trap heels back on, and then we all start walking out together. Really, I could probably walk home, if I had on some decent shoes, but with these on, I'll need to find a ride somehow.

We all start walking down the street together, Corey and Karina deciding they will spend the night with Jamie, just to make sure she doesn't freak out later. I live close enough to Jamie that I can get to her easily enough if she needs me, but I'll be sleeping in my own bed tonight. *Alone, unfortunately.*

Four blocks later, and we've hit 7th Street. My feet feel like they're going to start bleeding, and I'm limping now.

"Alex, where do you live?" Gabe asks.

"What? Why?"

"Well, obviously, you can barely walk, and we seem to all be heading in the same direction."

"Georgina and 20th," I say with a whimper.

"Really? Wow, we really are going in the same direction. I live on 22nd and Alta."

"No kidding."

"Small world," Gabe says with a smile. "Come on, take off the shoes."

"What? No. I'm not going to walk the streets barefoot. I haven't had a tetanus shot in ages."

"Just take them off."

It's too tempting, and honestly I was thinking of taking them off anyways and risking it. I end up holding onto Gabe's arm, while trying to balance and get the infernal things off my swollen feet.

"Déjà vu."

"Oh yes," I moan, releasing my feet from their strappy prison.

"Please don't make noises like that. It drives me crazy," Gabe murmurs into my ear, making another part of me ache.

"Thank you. I don't know why it took me so long to do that. I feel much better."

We walk another two blocks, but my feet have taken so much punishment tonight that I don't know if I can make it all the way home.

Gabe, now wing free, having left them at the festival, places his hand on my forearm, stopping my forward movement, and says, "Jump on."

"Excuse me?"

"I'll carry you piggy back, come on. I can tell you're in a lot of pain. I'll carry you for a while."

"Don't be ridiculous."

"No, you don't be ridiculous. Just get on, and if I get tired I'll let you know."

I'm too tired to argue, and give in pretty easily. I hop up onto his back, and Gabe catches my legs on the sides of his hips, pulling me up higher.

"No fair, I want a ride," Corey whines.

"Sorry hun. You'll have to find your own," I say, truly relieved to not be on my feet any longer.

We walk and walk. Well, Gabe walks, and I ride, and the girls and guys walk ahead of us slightly.

"I'm sorry about how everything went down earlier," Gabe says.

"Yeah, me too. Thanks for walking us home, though."

I enjoy the feel of his broad shoulders and chest under my hands as I hang onto him while he walks the rest of the way. When we get to 18th Street, Gabe puts me down, and Corey and Karina say their goodbyes, and head up to Jamie's apartment. After a quick hug, I let Jamie go, telling her I will call her in the morning.

"Not too early please. I want to sleep as late as possible, but let's meet for lunch okay?"

"Okay, goodnight, Jamie."

"Goodnight, Alex. Sweet dreams."

Chapter Ten

*E*nd of the Road—Gabe

After we drop Jamie and the other two girls off, Alex refuses to let me carry her, insisting that she's fine to walk the next couple of blocks on her own two feet. When we get to 20th, I hand Mike my keys, and tell him and Bill that I'll meet them at my place in a few.

"Nice to meet you Alex, and sorry about everything," Mike says, and then it's just me and Alex.

"Come on, I'll walk with you the last two blocks. I only live three blocks from you. Isn't that crazy?"

"Yeah. I can't believe we've never run into each other before."

"Me either."

We're both pretty quiet as we continue walking. I don't know if Duke has screwed everything up for me with Alex, but I really don't want to say goodbye.

Arriving at her building, Alex stops, and turns toward me.

"Thanks, Gabe, for everything. I really don't know what would have happened if you hadn't caught Duke trying to drug Jamie."

"I'm sorry he was there in the first place."

This silence is awkward between us. Luckily, my little devil breaks it.

"So, it's cool if I call you next time I'm having trouble with my website, right? I still have the card you gave me."

"Yes, please. Actually, I was going to ask if maybe I could call you sometime."

"Really?"

"Yes, really." I take a chance and add, "I really like you, Alex."

"I really like you too, Gabe."

Realizing this is a chance I may not get again, I step toward her and push a bit of her hair behind her ear, before leaning in for a goodnight kiss. I know there's a chance she'll pull away, or worse, after everything tonight, but I have to try.

She doesn't pull away.

We kiss, and when our tongues collide, it's like we're back on that waterfront, and both grasping at each other like we're drowning. *Jesus, I want her so bad, so damn bad.* It's been a long time since I felt my stomach twist like this. There is some very powerful chemistry here, and it's not easy to come by. *Oh her tits, I can feel them on my chest.* As I pull on her hips, trying to get as close as possible, she grabs my ass and grinds herself into me.

Yes.

Stay — Alex

I can't get enough of this man. He arouses me to the point where I become bolder than I've been in a long time. I'm grinding myself against his erection, and panting into his mouth, and I know by the large bulge I'm getting worked up about, that he wants me too.

Breaking away from Gabe's mouth, I say, "Come upstairs. Stay with me tonight."

He groans, and I take that as encouragement. I thought the night was lost, but I've found my second wind, and he seems more than willing.

"Give me your phone number," he says, between bites to my neck.

"What? Come upstairs and you can have anything you want."

Wow, that sounded really desperate, but at this point, I really don't care.

"Give me your phone number first."

"Oh God, yes, right there…um, I don't have a pen."

He's licking the shell of my ear now, and my toes are

curling against the sidewalk.

"Tell me, I'll remember. I'm good with numbers."

Somehow, I pant out my number, and he repeats it back twice, a lick and a bite between each number. When I confirm he has it memorized, I ask him to come upstairs again, only this time he places his hands on my hips, and steps back and away from me.

"What's the matter?"

"Nothing, you're perfect."

"Then let's go upstairs."

"Not tonight."

"What?" *No, this isn't happening. He's turning me down? After all that?*

"Not tonight."

"I can't believe this." I storm past him toward my door, with my keys in hand, more angry and frustrated than I have ever been in my entire life.

Before my shaking hand can get the key in the lock, Gabe is at my back, sweeping my hair away from my neck.

"What kind of game are you playing, Gabe?"

He lets his full weight sink into me from behind, and there is no hiding his arousal, which is just so much more confusing.

"Believe me, I want to. I want you so fucking bad right now, Alexandra, that I'm willing to suffer the world's worst case of blue balls ever."

My breath hitches at his words, but I still don't understand. I may start to cry in a minute.

"I don't understand."

He releases a breath against my neck, and then slowly turns me toward him, guiding my chin with his hand so I'm looking into his eyes.

"I don't want a one night stand with you."

"What are you saying?"

"I'm saying, let's go to the batting cages tomorrow, after you have lunch with your friends, and get to know each other."

"You are asking me out on a date? I thought you weren't the dating type?"

"I'm not the dating type, but with you, I want to be. You deserve a guy who will treat you right and I'll be damned if I'm going to waste my chance to be that guy."

"I'm not going to pretend I'm not disappointed, because I am. Very."

"Hopefully, I won't disappoint you again."

"What time?"

"What time what?"

"What time are you picking me up?"

Gabe smiles, and places a quick peck on my cheek. "How about 3 p.m.?"

"Okay, 3 p.m. Now go, before I drag you in here and tie you to my bed," I say jokingly, to hopefully relieve some of the tension.

"Oh, I'll be the one doing the tying up, if you don't mind."

And tension is back. I turn and unlock the door, and watch as he slowly backs away.

"Happy New Year, Gabriel."

"Happy New Year, Alexandra. I'll see you tomorrow."

He may just be an angel in disguise.

Miles and Mae

by A.E. Snow

To the Writing Wenches, who are by the far the loveliest, most supportive, and dearest writing friends a girl can have.

Chapter One

*M*ae leaned on the bar with her chin resting in her hand. She glanced at the tip jar for the third time in an hour. She figured she could maybe buy a pack of smokes if the rest of the customers were generous. Except there was only one customer. He sat in the back corner of the bar surrounded by piles of books. He'd been a fixture for weeks. Sometimes he had his laptop, sometimes books, but he never came in without work, which was a little odd. Determined to get some kind of a tip out of him, Mae approached the dark table in the rear corner of Acme.

"Can I get you something else? Another beer?" Mae asked.

"Um, yeah…sure," he said without looking up.

"Okay. Be right back." Weaving through the small, dark, stinky bar, Mae checked to see if there was anything else she could do.

She had big plans for Acme. The bathrooms, for one thing, needed some work. Technically, everything needed replacing. Stuffing leaked out of the sides of more than one barstool and most of the tables wobbled. Acme fit the description of a dive bar. It was so divey that it was kind of hip, with a certain crowd at least.

Mae stepped behind the bar. The door burst open before she had a chance to retrieve another beer from the cooler. A stocky, tattooed guy stood in the doorway surveying the room. "Mae!" he boomed.

"Oh…hi." Mae dropped the smile she reserved for customers when she realized it was Josh. He wore a t-shirt to show off his biceps and tattoos even though it was December and freezing out.

Josh let the door shut behind him, ambled over to the bar, and looked around. "What a dump."

Mae flushed with anger. Josh owned Acme and hated it.

Mae had been managing and tending bar six days a week for almost two years. She hated to admit that she'd spent almost an entire year of that time entangled in a relationship, of sorts, with Josh.

He came behind the bar and tried to hug Mae. She stood stiffly while he rubbed her back. "Why don't you call me anymore, baby?" he whispered, his voice full of teasing.

"You know why." Mae pulled away. "It's because you are the biggest dick I've ever met."

Obnoxious laughter burst out of Josh, and he smacked a hand down on the bar. "You kill me, Mae. Too funny."

Mae was mortified that she'd ever considered dating him at all. Theirs had been a physical relationship. Mae wasn't very good at the other stuff and neither was Josh, so it seemed like a perfect match. Really, it was a recipe for a disaster on the scale of Chernobyl.

"What are you doing here, Josh?" Mae asked and picked at a string on the hem of her shirt.

"I have amazing news!" Josh beamed. "I sold the bar!"

Mae's stomach lurched. "What do you mean?"

"I mean, I sold this dump."

Mae stared at Josh. "You can't be serious," she said through clenched teeth.

"I am. Dude is going to gut it and turn it into a wine bar. Classy, huh? This place is done as of Friday night and in a month...*wine bar*. Excuse me, I gotta make a call," Josh said and attempted to high five Mae, but she stared at him with her arms crossed over her chest. Trying to turn the high five into an awkward pat on the back didn't save it. Mae walked off to the other end of the bar and checked to see if any liquor bottles were low.

Fury bubbled in Mae's stomach. It was all she could do to keep from breaking every single bottle behind the bar, letting the clear and amber liquid puddle together on the floor. Instead, she took a bottle of bourbon and two shot glasses and plunked them down on the bar.

"Hey! You in the back," Mae called.

When the guy finally looked up, he appeared confused or maybe even irritated.

"Me?" He pointed at himself with his brows furrowed yet raised in a question.

"Yes, you. Come on!" she barked. Mae filled the shot glasses to the rim, while the guy, taller than she'd remembered, left his stack of books behind and ambled up to the bar.

"Did you, uh, need something?"

"Yeah. I need you to take a shot with me," Mae said. "Also, I'm going to need to know your name."

"It's Miles."

His eyes were brown, dark chocolate brown, which happened to be Mae's great weakness. That and the way his dark hair flopped over his forehead and into his eyes. She wondered how she'd never noticed. She found it a little surprising that her heart started beating faster and she had the almost uncontrollable urge to bite her lip and smile, which was her go-to move, both for scoring tips and dates.

"Oh shit," Mae muttered and picked up her shot glass. "Come on," she urged Miles, who spilled his a little when he picked it up.

"To fucking terrible shit."

Miles's face broke out in a grin and the dingy bar brightened. "To fucking terrible shit."

Mae threw back her shot and closed her eyes with a shudder. A slow burn crept into her belly. She opened her eyes when she heard coughing.

"What's wrong?"

Miles choked and thumped his fist on his chest. "Chaser."

Mae pulled a beer out of the cooler and popped it open. Miles's fingers brushed against hers when he took it and sent a jolt through her.

Miles chased his bourbon with almost half of a beer. "I'm not much of a drinker."

Pulling herself together, Mae brushed her bangs out of her eyes. "You coulda fooled me."

"You don't usually drink on the clock," Miles said.

How did he know? Mae wondered. "Screw it. It won't matter in a week."

"Why? What do you mean?" Miles sat down on a bar stool across from where she stood.

Mae rested her arms on the bar. "I was gonna buy this bar." Laying her head on her clasped hands, she concentrated on not crying. Sobbing in public was something she tried to avoid.

"Really?"

Mae blinked rapidly and then lifted her head. "Yeah. I've been saving up. I was gonna put $15,000 down and then make monthly payments. I've been working my ass off to make this happen."

"Oh…man." A few moments of awkward silence passed. "Should we take another shot?"

"Yes." She poured them both another round.

Josh appeared out of the back room and headed for the door. "Mae! Go ahead and close up. Let's not lose any more money on this shit hole."

Without a word, Miles and Mae lifted their shot glasses.

Mae had closed the bar but stayed for hours talking to Miles. He had suggested a big bash to celebrate the end of an era. She pondered that thought as she shivered in the cold on her walk home. None of her roommates were there when she arrived and relief flooded through her. She wanted to be alone.

In the kitchen, Mae stared at the inside of the fridge for several minutes until she realized it was empty. Pacing around the kitchen didn't turn up anything in her search for food. Eventually, she headed back to the hall, grabbed her bag, and climbed the stairs. She let herself into her small, drafty attic room and slammed the door. A space heater did little to warm her up.

Pacing around the room wrapped up in a blanket, Mae tried to process her day. A mixture of fury and resentment left her unable to sit still.

"What the hell are you gonna do now?" Mae asked herself. "What's your plan now, huh?" Frustrated, she shook her head and shrugged off the memory of Josh naked in her bed. It annoyed her to no end that he refused to cover his biceps even in the winter. They weren't even that impressive.

Curling up under the blankets, Mae hoped her body heat would warm up the cold bed. Her thoughts drifted to back to Miles. She giggled when she remembered how inexperienced he was with drinking. He'd been more than tipsy when they'd finally left the bar.

A party. Miles said she should throw a party. Mae imagined the perfect goodbye to Acme. All her favorite customers crowded around the bar. She'd hang multicolored twinkling lights and maybe stick a tree somewhere. Acme deserved one last great night. She'd invite Miles.

Mae noticed that she smiled every time she thought of Miles. She grabbed her phone and checked for missed calls or texts.

The only text had come from Tom, her best friend. Call me back asshole!!!!! She tried not to be disappointed that Miles hadn't texted even though he'd only had her number for two hours.

Realizing that she should probably let the owner of the bar know her plans, Mae sent Josh a text. *I'm having a big party on Friday night at the bar. I'm not asking your permission. Don't come.*

Chapter Two

Miles couldn't stop thinking about Mae. Not even for a second. He'd been thinking about her for months, but since he'd spent the evening with her actually speaking to her, he was dreamy and prone to blushing. Mae. Just Mae. Her long messy hair, light brown eyes, and the stud accenting her cute little nose kept him awake at night.

Miles sat with his head resting in his hand staring at the wall while he thought about Mae's tattoos. They were like the old botanical paintings of flowers, but in a badass way. He'd been astonished when she ordered him to take a shot. His heart raced and he'd fully expected his fairy godmother to appear.

Mae's phone number was now programmed into his phone. He had looked at it so many times that he had it memorized. But every time he thought of texting her, his mind went entirely blank.

"Miles?"

"Yeah?" He tried to pull himself out of a Mae-related reverie.

"Coffee?" It was Ellie, who was technically his boss. Miles was her Teaching Assistant in the Economics department.

Miles followed Ellie into her office and sat down across from her. She had two mismatched mugs already filled with coffee from the machine in the faculty lounge. Miles had coffee with Ellie once or twice a week, usually to talk about work stuff.

"How are you, Miles?" Ellie asked, smiling. She'd taken an immediate liking to him when he started the graduate program and had taken him under her wing.

"I'm fine," Miles said and nodded. "Reading essays about carbon emission policies."

"Fascinating topic." Ellie sipped her coffee. "Miles?"

"Yeah?" Miles answered, still distracted by Mae and how vulnerable but tough she looked when she took a shot with tears in her eyes.

"You got it."

It took a minute for Miles to realize what she was talking about. *"What?"*

"You're going to the Sorbonne. You are Dr. Lefevre's new Research Assistant."

Miles jumped up, standing there with his arms out, trying to speak, but nothing came out.

Ellie laughed. "Congratulations, Miles! I'm so thrilled for you." She stood up and walked around the desk to hug Miles. "You've got to be in Paris by December 26th. I know that's probably going to interrupt your holiday plans, but I spoke with Dr. Lefevre and we have your housing all arranged. It's a little flat in the 10th arrondissement, fifteen minutes from La Sorbonne."

Miles hugged Ellie again and then dashed down the hall. "I gotta call my mom!"

The bar was crowded with more people flooding in. Mae was glad that she wouldn't be the only one to miss Acme. She'd mourned two years lost, keyed Josh's car parked in the alley, and actually decorated the place a little. Christmas lights were strung around the bar top and an ugly old clump of plastic mistletoe swung from the ceiling. Mae's roommate offered her the use of a fiber optic Christmas tree and it gently changed from red to green to blue with the Ramones blaring in the background. To Mae, it felt like the perfect Christmas.

So many of her friends and customers were there. Mae wasn't much of a crier, but she kept blinking back tears. The constant barrage of orders kept her mind off of things. The last two years meant nothing now, and all she had to show for it was yet more bartending experience. At age twenty-six, she'd tended bar or waited tables in half the bars in the city and in a few more cities.

Mae had been avoiding thinking about what she would do next. She'd replaced thinking with cleaning and as a result, her apartment was spotless and the bar was as spotless as it would ever be. Avoiding thinking of her future had turned out to be easier than avoiding thinking about the way Miles's hair fell into his eyes.

"Mae?"

"Yeah?"

"Can I put you down as a reference?" James, the other bartender on duty, asked during a rare slow moment.

Mae nodded. "Of course. Have you found something?"

"I think so. Tartine?"

"Wow. That place is amazing."

"What are you going to do?" James asked.

"I have absolutely no idea," Mae said with a shrug.

"I'm tagging in," Jane, another Acme bartender, said tapping Mae's arm. "Clear out."

Mae grinned at Jane. She would totally miss her. Jane looked like Bettie Page and had a wicked sense of humor. They'd worked together for two years.

"You don't have to ask me twice."

Mae grabbed a beer and went out from behind the bar to mingle. It was clear that tough, no-nonsense Mae was everyone's favorite bartender. Probably because she was a softie at heart. She listened to everyone's stories and knew the names of their children.

She felt a tap on her shoulder. Mae whirled around.

"Hi."

"Oh shit," Mae said under her breath when she noticed the way Miles's eyes crinkled up when he smiled. "Hello."

"H-how are you?" Miles stuttered.

"I'm fine. You?" A flush crept up Mae's neck and she had the urge to ditch the party and take off with Miles.

"Fine. Good." Miles nodded vigorously.

Miles and Mae nodded at each other for too long without saying anything at all.

Finally, Miles cleared his throat. "There are tons of people here. It looks really nice too."

"Thanks," Mae said and smiled a real smile, not something that happened all that often. "Want a beer or something?"

"Sure."

"I'll meet you back there." Mae pointed to the dark, empty booth in back.

"Okay." Miles turned to make his way through the crowd.

He sat down in the dark booth, not his usual spot since the light above it was always out, and it was too dark to grade papers. He ran his sweaty palms over his jeans for the third time. In general, girls made him nervous, but Mae turned him into a stuttering mess. The butterflies in his stomach felt more like horses galloping around.

From his vantage point, he could really only see people's backs. He took a deep breath and gave himself a pep talk. "You have nothing to lose Miles," he told himself. "If she laughs at you, you can disappear to Paris." And then the wall of backs parted like the Red Sea to reveal Mae. She glowed like a tattooed angel under the multicolored Christmas lights overhead. Miles couldn't tear his eyes away from her and he died a little when she sat down and scooted around until she sat next to him. He had a hard time keeping himself from dragging her into his lap and kissing her.

"Thanks for coming," Mae said. "It's nice to see you."

"It's nice to see you, too. Thanks for inviting me." Miles cringed. Everything he said sounded stupid and Mae was so cool. He felt like an idiot every time he opened his mouth around her.

Mae wanted to slap herself in the face. She couldn't understand why she was being such a dork over Miles. So far, all she knew about him was that he was a Teacher's Assistant in Economics or something. He was certainly the opposite of her "type." Miles was tall, gangly even, with dark hair and freckles. He had kind of a big nose, but Mae liked it.

She grasped for something to say. "Why do you come here to work or study or whatever it is you do here?"

Color crept into Miles's face. "The coffee shops are really crowded. The library is too quiet. The tables here are big…"

"It's a good place to work. Quiet most of the time. Great for studying, not great for finances."

"I'm really sorry about the bar."

"It's okay." Mae smiled sadly.

"I won't ask you what you're going to do next," Miles said.

"Good. That's all anyone asks me." Mae got the urge to climb into Miles's lap. He looked at her like maybe he wanted her to. Mae was used to knowing where she stood with guys. Josh had shaken her confidence. She'd been really into him and had this secret fantasy of them owning the bar as a couple, but that dream was dashed when she found a pair of red panties in his bed one day. Since then, she'd had the chance to see Josh for what he was, a total scumbag.

Before Mae had the chance to straddle Miles, a drunk guy stumbled into the table and knocked over the beer.

Mae jumped up, grabbing the beer glasses. "I'll get a rag and more beer. Be right back." It had gotten even more crowded in the bar, and Mae had to squeeze her way to the front. She liked a crowd, but a crowd this thick would lead to drama and/ or the police being called. It never failed.

Mae had no sooner grabbed a towel and two new beers when she felt an arm slide around her waist. She turned to see Josh standing there.

"Wow! Huge crowd!" Josh said proudly, as though he had done one single thing to get ready for the party.

Mae glared at him and wiggled out of his grasp. Josh didn't notice—or pretended not to. He pulled Mae into a hug while she stood stiff with her arms by her sides.

"Why are you here?" Mae asked. She hadn't expected him to show up.

"I wanted to come and say goodbye to my baby," Josh said, grinning.

"You hate this place."

He laughed and dipped his head close to hers. "That's right, I do."

"So why are you here?"

Josh's smile faded a little. "I'm going to miss you, Mae. We had fun, right?"

"If you have to ask…" Mae said. She waited for her pulse to speed up or butterflies to appear in her stomach. Nothing.

Nothing at all. Her thoughts drifted back to Miles. "I've got to get back to my friend." Mae turned and left Josh standing there.

"Anyway, great to see you! I'm gonna mingle!" he called after her but she was already gone.

Josh stood staring at her with his mouth hanging open. How she'd ever been attracted to him, Mae wasn't sure. Yes, he was sexy as hell and covered with tattoos, but there had never been a bigger asshole than Josh. She couldn't believe the size of his balls, coming in here like he was sad and wanted to say goodbye to everyone. He wanted a boat and a new life, or whatever. He wanted a life without her. When they broke it off for good, Josh had said, "Don't worry. The bar is still yours if you want it."

"I do," she'd said, believing his lie.

Miles kept his eyes on the table when Mae returned. "Thanks," he murmured when she sloshed a beer down in front of him.

"I'm sorry that took so long," she said. "Ran into someone."

"Yeah, I saw."

Mae's mind raced. She worried that Miles had the wrong impression about Josh. *Josh. Miles. Jobless. Barless. Directionless. Alone.* The silence in the booth was surrounded by raucous laughter and loud, drunken singing.

Mae jumped up out of her seat, narrowly missing the eternally burned out light swinging from the ceiling. Miles looked up at her.

"Let's go," Mae said.

Miles stood up without a word and followed Mae through the crowd and out the front door. They stood on the sidewalk in the cold.

"Now what?" he asked.

"I haven't got a fucking clue."

Chapter Three

Mae wanted to walk, so they walked and talked. Miles peppered her with questions in an attempt to get to know her.

"Where'd you grow up?" Miles asked Mae.

"Nowhere near here."

Miles offered up information freely without being asked, no doubt hoping to start a real conversation. "I grew up in upstate New York. My entire extended family is there and there they will probably all remain."

"That's nice," Mae said.

"What about you?"

"I don't have much family."

"Family can be overrated." Miles wanted to know what happened to Mae that had made her so closed off.

Mae shivered. Her leather jacket didn't keep the cold out very well. Her lacy tank top was super hot, but coupled with the leather jacket, left her freezing with chattering teeth.

Miles cleared his throat. "Do you want my jacket?"

"No. No."

Miles was quiet while they kept on. Mae was a tough nut to crack and he was having absolutely no luck. He worried that he was screwing everything up.

"My favorite movie is *The Dark Knight*," Miles offered. "I love pizza. I'm an economics nerd, and I don't even mind reading freshman econ essays."

Mae laughed and warmth bubbled up in Miles's stomach. All around them on the street, Christmas lights twinkled. Armed with the knowledge that he was leaving, the bar was done, and this might be his last chance, Miles took a deep breath and jumped in the deep end.

"I drink so much coffee that sometimes I vibrate. I don't sleep well, probably because of the coffee. I don't get along with my father and I really love cartoons."

When the snow started falling, Miles stopped walking

and grabbed Mae's hand. She turned to face him. "I didn't go to Acme because it was a good place to study. I went because of you."

Mae smiled and Miles thought he saw a tear wobbling in the corner of her eye.

"I love the snow," Mae said.

When Miles wrapped his arms around her and kissed her, Mae let herself get carried away. She didn't know whether it was the snow or the lights but Mae, never one to give a shit about romance, had gone weak in the knees. Miles broke the kiss off first, and Mae almost gasped when he whispered in her ear.

"My apartment is a block away," Miles said. "I have bourbon and hot chocolate so I can definitely stop your shivering."

"I had no idea you were so forward." Mae raised an eyebrow. "But, I'm fucking freezing. I don't want to go home, and I'm sure as shit not going back to the bar. Let's go."

Miles lived in a loft apartment especially for post-graduate researchers and teaching assistants. It consisted of a reasonably sized living room and kitchen with a loft that presumably led to the bedroom.

"This is it," Miles said. His voice was a little shaky.

"It's nice…clean," Mae remarked. It was a lot cleaner than her house and a lot warmer than her drafty attic bedroom.

"Thanks, uh," Miles said, running his fingers through his hair for tenth time since they walked in the door.

Mae dropped her bag and shimmied out of her leather coat. She sat on the couch, leaning down to pull her boots off. Miles stood watching her, his eye twitching.

Mae crossed the room in her stocking feet and climbed the ladder to the loft. The bed was made, which impressed Mae, and she flopped on it.

"You coming?" she called down.

Miles didn't answer, but she heard the ladder creak and seconds later, his tousled head appeared and then his shirtless torso. He was hot. Mae wasn't expecting muscles but there they were. He still had jeans on but no shoes or socks.

"Very presumptuous of you to take your shirt off," Mae said with a smirk.

"I don't like to wear a shirt in the loft," Miles said, lying down next to Mae who was still sitting upright. "In fact, it's the rule. No shirts in the loft."

"Oh really?"

"Yes. I'm afraid you're breaking the rule. It's the only rule, so the consequences are pretty serious."

Mae slid her tank top over her head, and for the first time, Miles had a full view of the tattoos on her shoulders and back. Roses, pink and white, spread out delicately over her right shoulder. An orange and purple feather surrounded by more flowers covered the left side. There were poppies on her arms along with forget-me-nots. Miles traced his finger around the outline of all the flowers he could reach.

"Beautiful," he murmured.

"Thanks. I love them."

"I was talking about you," Miles said.

"So you only come to Acme to see me?" She looked back over her shoulder at Miles.

"Yes, that is true," Miles said. "Although, James is pretty cute."

Mae smirked. "I can give you his phone number." She shivered when she felt Miles's hand on her hip and he moved closer to her.

"Come here."

Mae pulled her ripped tights out from under her skirt and positioned herself on the bed next to Miles. She had always had this idea that she was only attracted to bad boys. She was, after all, something of a bad girl. She liked to be the one to leave the string of broken hearts behind her. It had been a complete surprise to her when Josh hurt her so much. She vowed it would be the last time she got her future wrapped up in someone else's. Lying in bed with Miles felt dangerous, but in a different way.

Miles pulled Mae close to him and cupped her face with his hand while he looked at her. He stared right into her eyes and really saw *her*. Mae fought the urge to close her eyes and hide all the things she was from him. It terrified her to think about what he might be seeing. She kept her eyes open when he kissed her. She liked that Miles's eyes were open too, and smiling.

His hands were warm and left a trail of heat everywhere he touched her. The tingling his fingers had left around the outline of her tattoos made the flowers come to life. The unsnapping of her bra happened so fast that Mae didn't even realize it was gone until she felt Miles's beautiful mouth on her breasts. He ran his tongue around her nipple in circles until she was dizzy. When he slid his hand up her skirt, Mae couldn't stand it anymore.

"Come here," Mae said, pulling Miles up so she could kiss him. With her lips still on his, Mae rolled on top of him and pulled her fingertips over his smooth chest. She moved down until she could reach his belt and took her time undoing the buckle and his pants.

Miles's breath came faster and he groaned when Mae leaned down and licked around his belly button on her way south.

"Take off your pants." Mae moved aside while Miles pulled off his jeans. "And your boxers." He complied.

"Get on your back," Miles said with a husky voice and a serious expression.

"Are you really turning down a blow job?" Mae asked as she lay down and moved to the top of the bed.

"I really am." Miles pushed her skirt up and her underwear aside. He started kissing her knees. "You have beautiful knees."

"Whatever." How could he think her scarred knees were beautiful? A thrill ran through her.

"It's true."

Mae closed her eyes as Miles's mouth moved up her thigh, and his hand gripped her other leg. Holding her breath, she waited for the inevitable. His tongue barely touched her and Mae's back arched involuntarily to meet his mouth.

Miles was different than anyone else she'd ever slept with. He had a goal in mind and he would keep going until she came.

"Oh God," Mae whispered and moaned softly. Her heart beat wildly. She desperately wanted Miles inside of her. "I need you…now."

"Not yet," Miles murmured into her center. Mae let her eyes flutter closed when Miles slipped a finger inside.

"Fuck," she whispered.

The finger pushed into her hard and his mouth drove her wild. She tangled her hands in his hair and let herself relax. He stopped and Mae opened her eyes. Miles climbed up next to her and reached for a box on a shelf behind her head. He fumbled the condom wrapper open. She followed his lead and pulled her skirt and underwear off and let them sail over the railing of the loft. Miles rolled on top of her.

Mae gasped when he slid in her slowly and filled her. Miles groaned and buried his face in her shoulder for a moment. Mae kissed his ear and ran her tongue around the edge.

"Now you've done it," Miles said and began pumping into her harder. His momentum built and Mae wondered for a second if the loft was sturdy enough for the level of activity. But she forgot to care. Miles repositioned her legs on his shoulders and Mae gasped as he went deeper. She was close and grabbed Miles's thighs.

Fireworks went off in Mae's core. "Oh my fucking damn," she gasped as she came.

Miles was right with her. Mae loved how his face scrunched up before he collapsed next to her and nuzzled his face into her neck.

"Where'd you come from?" Mae whispered into his dark, messy hair.

"Acme."

Chapter Four

Telling Mae about Paris was on Miles's to-do list, but he avoided it like the plague. He didn't want to tell her. He didn't want to leave her. They'd had a perfect three days. Way deep down, a small voice told him Mae should go with him.

Watching Mae doze on the couch while he made her a grilled cheese sandwich filled Miles up with happiness. When she wore his clothes, he wanted to sing. It was almost perfect. All that stood in the way of Miles and complete contentment was the Eiffel Tower.

There is no good time to tell someone news like, "I'm moving to Paris." Sometimes, Miles thought he would say no and stay where he was. Except that he'd been dreaming about La Sorbonne for years. He learned French in high school with his eyes on Paris. In the end, Miles blurted it out while they were lying in his bed, so wrapped up in each other that even their toes were intertwined.

"I'm moving to Paris." The words tumbled out of Miles at breakneck speed.

Mae laughed. "Okay." But when she looked at Miles, she saw that he was wasn't joking. Her face fell. "I'm gonna need a little more information," she whispered.

Miles smashed his face into the beautiful garden on her shoulder blade. He wanted to cry. "I got accepted to La Sorbonne. I'm going to finish my PhD there and work as a Research Assistant to one of the top researchers in the field." Mae's body stiffened.

"When?" she asked, her voice faint.

"Next week."

A tremendous silence pressed down on them. A tear slipped down over Miles's nose and onto Mae's shoulder. Mae squirmed out of his arms and searched for her clothes.

"Mae," Miles said. "Come back. Can we talk about this?"

"There's nothing to talk about," Mae said in a strangled voice. She climbed down the ladder with Miles right behind her.

"Don't leave, Mae. I really care about you and I want to be with you." Miles watched helplessly as Mae put on her skirt. She left his t-shirt on and threw her leather jacket over the top.

Mae looked at him for the first time. "I don't even know you." She slammed the door on her way out.

Miles sank down on the couch and let his head fall into his hands.

Mae didn't want to go home, but she did. Her room-mates, all guys, were in the middle of a video game marathon and didn't hear her come in. When she got to her room on the top floor, Mae crawled into bed and cried. She ignored all of Miles's texts and calls. Two days later, she finally left the house.

"Thanks for your time," Mae said to the bar manager on her way out of her third interview in as many days. Mae was a qualified bartender, but after the grittiness of Acme, nothing seemed right.

"I hate snow," Mae muttered while she tried to light a cigarette in the bitter wind. Snow blew into her face and eyes. "Maybe I should move."

Paris. The thought struck her right in the heart and tears formed in her eyes. She pretended they were from the cold and not Miles.

Miles didn't have much stuff, and what he did have

fit easily into a few cardboard boxes which had already been picked up by the movers. He hadn't thought that the small apartment would ever feel big, but it did. Without Mae, it seemed huge and empty and sad. Her Maeness had filled up the space.

A knock on the door startled Miles out of his depressed reverie.

"Hey asshole, open the door!" Miles's best friend Ben called from the other side of the door and knocked again. Miles jumped up to answer the door. He'd been lying in the floor watching movies on his laptop for hours. Ben, Miles's best friend was standing in the cold outside his door.

"Answer your phone, dickhead!" Ben said as soon as the door opened. "You look like shit, by the way."

"I know," Miles said.

"Get your life together. We're going out."

"I don't know," Miles said. He looked around the room, searching for an excuse not to go.

"You don't have a choice," Ben said. "Put on some pants. I'm your best friend. It is literally part of my job description that I send you off in style."

Three hours later, Miles understood that in style meant drunk. It also meant a tour of the bars that Ben liked while hanging out with Ben's friends.

"Don't I have any friends?" Miles asked Ben at one point.

"Other than me and a couple of geeks? Not really…"

"Hmm."

The third and last bar – Miles hoped – was brimming over with people filled with Christmas spirit. Snow on the ground three days before Christmas put the city in a celebratory mood.

As soon as Miles walked inside, he stopped in his tracks. Mae. She sat alone at the bar, a little sad island in the middle of the noise. The sudden stop caused Ben to run right into him.

"Dude! You're blocking traffic!" Ben said and whacked Miles on the back.

"It's her," Miles whispered.

"The girl you've been going on about?" Ben moved to

stand next to him and swung his head around looking for Mae.

"Yeah," Miles said. "The girl I've been going on about."

"Where is she? There are only five hundred girls in this bar," Ben said. He had a point.

"That's her at the bar. Alone. Tattoos."

"Whaaaaat?" Ben turned to look at Miles, his mouth hanging open. "I thought she was some kind of science nerd or whatever it is you do. She is…extremely hot."

"I'm in environmental economics. And, you don't know that she isn't a weird science or economics nerd. Stop reinforcing stereotypes."

"Shut up, dude. That is why you don't have any friends. Go talk to her!"

Miles had had enough alcohol for that to seem like a good idea. He made his way toward the only open seat in the bar, which happened to be the one right next to Mae.

"Hi," he said and staggered a little trying to sit on his bar stool.

"Hi," Mae said, a little startled to see him there. "What are you doing here?"

"Getting sent off or something," Miles muttered. He tried with no avail to get the bartender's attention.

"Oh." Mae returned her gaze to the inside of her glass.

"How are you?"

"Fine," Mae said, but she didn't look fine.

"I miss you." Miles moved a little closer to her. He could barely stand being so close without touching her.

"You don't." Mae shook her head.

"I do. I'm miserable, and I can't stop thinking about you."

"That's ridiculous. You're leaving for Paris in what? Two days?"

"That is irrelevant," Miles said.

"It's all kinds of relevant." Mae glared at Miles.

"I understand why you're angry."

"Do you?" Mae asked like she really wanted to know. She stood up and tossed some money on the counter.

"Are you leaving?" Miles stood up and followed Mae

back through the crowd.

"Obviously."

As soon as she got outside, Mae stuck her hands in her pockets and turned toward home.

"Mae." Miles jogged up behind her and grabbed her hand. "I'm sorry. I'm really sorry. Please listen."

Mae gave one small nod, but she didn't turn around.

Miles waited for her to say something. When she didn't, he tried to explain. "La Sorbonne is my dream. You were... *are* my dream too. But, I never thought I could have you in ten million years. Getting my PhD is actually within the realm of possibility for me. You are my wildest dream."

Mae turned to Miles. Tears threatened to spill out of her brown eyes. "Miles, I'm no one's dream. You have an incredible future. I don't even have a job! You don't want this."

Miles pulled Mae to him and wrapped her up in his arms. Her hair smelled like oranges and cigarettes. He buried his face in her soft locks, inhaling like she was the only scent he wanted for the rest of his life. He would think of her every time he smelled oranges.

"I wish you knew how amazing you are. You're kind. You make people feel like they're important, like they matter. You're not a fuck up. Owning Acme didn't work out and that sucks...maybe there's a reason it didn't work. Maybe you are supposed to do something bigger, and Acme was in the way."

Mae didn't say anything but she kept her forehead pressed against Miles's shoulder. Gentle snow fell down around them, and Miles forgot that they were standing in front of a noisy bar in the middle of the city. All he saw was Mae and the snow glistening in her hair.

"Do you have a passport?" Miles asked.

"Yeah...why?"

"Come to Paris with me."

Mae tensed up and pulled away. "What?" She searched Miles's face to see if he was serious. His eyes were full of hope, and she was about to dash it. "I can't."

"Why not?"

Miles looked at her like she was the only girl in the world

and she couldn't stand it. "I can't just up and leave everything and skip off to Paris. I need to come up with a new plan. I need to work…" Despair threatened to swallow Mae alive. A huge part of her thought that going to Paris with Miles was the most romantic thing she'd ever heard but a bigger part said it was crazy. Her mother's face drifted through her mind. Mae knew it was only a matter of time before she called needing money and help getting out of yet another bad relationship, yet another shitty situation. The only person who could help her couldn't just up and leave the country.

"Paris can be your new plan," Miles whispered.

Mae backed away from Miles while she still could. "It really can't." She turned and ran down the snowy sidewalk.

Mae ran all the way to her best friend Tom's apartment. She arrived breathless and disheveled.

"What happened to you?" Tom asked. "Is someone chasing you?" Tom glanced into the hallway.

"No. No one is chasing me. Let me in," Mae said and shoved past.

Mae collapsed onto Tom's couch. Tom had a proper couch and a clean apartment. His apartment was far nicer than hers and she didn't feel squeamish at all over sitting on the couch like she did at her own place.

"Get your boots off my couch and talk to me." Tom sat down on the end not taken up by Mae.

Mae let her feet flop to the floor. "My life is in shambles." She filled Tom in on Miles.

"Why didn't you tell me?" Tom interrupted.

"I'm not done."

"Wow," Tom said and whistled when he heard about Paris. "You should go."

Mae sat up and whirled around. "What?"

"You heard me. Don't be an idiot. Do you like this Miles

person?"

"Yes, but…he's so different from me."

"I love you, Mae, so don't be offended by this, but you need someone different than you. You make terrible choices. In fact, from now on you should listen to your instincts and then do the opposite."

"You are no help," Mae said.

"Well, what do you want to hear? I can lie to you. But I still think you should go and see. America will probably let you back in."

"I don't want to ruin Miles's life," Mae said right before she started sobbing.

Tom put his arm around Mae and touched his forehead to hers. "Then don't."

Chapter Five

Christmas Eve didn't feel like Christmas Eve even with the snow. Miles leaned against the window frame and watched the snow pile up. His suitcase lay packed by the door, and his laptop was tucked into his backpack. It wasn't the first Christmas Miles had spent away from his family, but it was the loneliest. He had pretty much given up hope of ever seeing Mae again. That thought had left him short of breath. For three days, he'd tried to think of a grand romantic gesture. Something that would change her mind. Everything he came up with was lame and all wrong for Mae.

In a moment of impulsiveness, Miles used the last of his savings on an extra ticket to Paris. He texted her one last time. *I've got your ticket. Flight is at 8:45. Terminal 2. Gate 11.* He waited all day. Nothing.

Miles waited until the last possible second to leave for the airport. He checked his phone every three minutes and prayed that she'd come around.

Finally, Miles slung his backpack on his shoulder and pulled up the handle on his rolling suitcase. He'd already given his landlord the key. He took one last look around the tiny apartment he'd called home for two years. Even though Mae had only been there for three days, she was all he saw. Mae sleeping on the couch while he made her a grilled cheese. Mae tackling him to the ground when he said he liked Taylor Swift, or demonstrating her bartending tricks with empty wine bottles. She was everywhere.

Miles pulled his suitcase through a blanket of snow down the sidewalk to where his cab was waiting. He let the cab driver put his luggage in the trunk while he folded himself into the small backseat. He held his phone the entire forty-five minute drive. For once, the roads were clear, and for once Miles kind of missed the traffic.

The ding of a text message alert woke Mae from a troubled sleep. Since the moment she'd run away from Miles, she'd had to make a concerted effort not to run right back to him. Tom's words echoed in her mind, "and then do the opposite."

A shower didn't help Mae forget about Miles or Paris. Still dressed in her towel, Mae rummaged through her closet until she found a suitcase. Heaving it onto her bed, she stared at it for a long time before putting it back in her closet and then repeating the whole process.

At noon, Mae's phone rang. "Hi Mom."

"Hey sweetie! I just wanted to wish you a Merry Christmas!" the voice on the other end slurred. Terri, Mae's mom, drank too much and always had.

"I'll see you tomorrow, Mom," Mae reminded her.

"No, honey. That's why I'm calling. I'm in Cabo with Jimmy!"

Mae's heart sank. Of course she was in Cabo. "Oh."

"Don't be mad Baby. We'll do Christmas stuff when I get back," Terri said. Mae heard her whisper to Jimmy. "She's pissed."

"Whatever, Terri. Merry Christmas! I hope you don't get dysentery." Mae wanted to slam the phone down but ending the call by violently hitting a button would have to do.

Fuming, Mae stomped to the closet and dragged the suitcase out again. After pulling it onto the bed, Mae flopped down next to the big rolling bag and dialed Tom.

"Tom," she said when he answered. "I need your help."

Grateful that the cab driver wasn't a conversationalist, Miles stared at his phone, waiting for a text to light up the screen. He willed traffic to slow down or for the cab driver to get pulled over. Anything to give Mae more time to reconsider. When the cab pulled off the freeway and onto the exit for the airport, Miles put his phone in his pocket. He took a deep breath and blinked back tears.

The first time Miles noticed Mae, Ben had talked him into going to Acme so he could serve as wingman. He'd protested that he had too much work to do and that he hated bars. Ben never took no for an answer, and Miles had walked into Acme totally irritated.

Mae had been in the process of throwing a guy out of the bar. She was firm and serious. "Get out. Don't come back or you will be thrown out of here again." The guy was angry and spewing curse words as he stormed toward the door.

"Don't forget to tip your bartender," Mae had called out with a huge smile. "Bye now."

The guy had raised his finger to give Mae the bird right before he slammed through the door, a bouncer right behind him. Not that the bouncer was necessary. Miles had seen right away that Mae was the authority in the bar, and those who didn't respect that authority got the boot. From that moment, Miles had been a regular. For months, he'd tried to gather the courage to talk to her. His heart had leapt up and lodged in his throat when she'd yelled "Hey! You!"

"Sir?" the cabbie asked and turned around in his seat. "We're here." The car was parked next to the curb at departures. Miles sat in the car for an extra minute before climbing slowly out of the cab and blinking with surprise at his driver who stood on the sidewalk next to his suitcase looking annoyed.

"Oh, right," Miles said, reaching into his pocket for his wallet. He fumbled with the money as he handed it over. With heavy legs, Miles made it to the doors, oblivious to the bitter cold. The automatic doors slid open.

Miles trudged inside daydreaming about Mae as he waited to check his bag.

"It's too heavy," the attendant said to the woman in front of him. She groaned and pulled her bags to the side to move things from one suitcase to the other. Miles stepped around her to the next available attendant and plopped his bag on the luggage scale before handing the attendant his ticket.

"One sir?" the desk clerk asked.

Miles glanced around the lobby again before answering. "Yeah."

"There are two tickets here," she said, not even looking up.

"Oh…it's just me," Miles said. The attendant, whose name tag said "Julie," handed back the extra ticket with pursed lips. She processed his ticket and scanned his passport.

Miles picked up his carry-on and trudged toward security. There were less than ten people in line. Miles took his place at the end of the line and waited. When he reached the long metal table, he grabbed two bins and put his backpack in one. He bent down to take his shoes off. His feet were cold. The hole in his sock attracted his attention while his shoes waited patiently for their turn in the x-ray machine.

"Miles!"

Miles looked around, eyebrows wrinkled, while a tiny bud of hope unfurled. He turned to see who was calling him.

"Miles!"

"Mae?" he shouted. He didn't see her anywhere and started to think he'd imagined hearing his name. The people in line around him turned to stare. Then he caught a glimpse of her, out of breath, disheveled and hesitant in front of the automatic doors which stood open, waiting. She held her bulging backpack in one hand and pulled a suitcase with the other.

Dropping his carryon, Miles strode toward Mae. Mae's face relaxed and she broke into a run up toward the rope that separated the security line from the rest. Miles ran toward her in his stocking feet. They looked at each other, the space between them filled up with anticipation.

"Sir?" a security guard called. Miles's sneakers went through the x-ray machine without him.

"I'm coming to Paris," Mae said. "I want to be with you, if you'll have me."

"I will." Miles reached out and pulled her to him with the rope still between them. When he kissed her, Miles kept his eyes open.

Happy Boxing Day

by Michael Simko

Happy Boxing Day is dedicated to the lovely Canadian who became my bride. Love you Babydoll.

Chapter One

The crunch of iced-over snow marks our walk down Front Street. Brianna and her friend compare their favorite performances of the Nutcracker. Behind them, her friend's man attempts polite conversation with me. I'd appreciate his effort more if I hadn't discarded his name ten seconds after we shook hands. It's not that I dislike him, but the forced interaction of boyfriends always feels artificial.

This is the point where most college men would duck into a bar to watch sports. Instead we pass by the taverns and continue following our girlfriends to go shopping.

"Being from the States, this must be freezing for you," the boyfriend says. He looks dapper in his black wool topcoat over a thin black tie. His accent is refined Canadian. There's no hint of an "eh" or an extended "o" in his speech. "Had you seen snow before you moved here?"

"We get lake effect where I'm from."

Brianna's scarlet peacoat stands out as she follows the crowd walking towards the new Christmas Market. A matching toque is excessive in the barely zero degree weather. Toque - it used to bother me how I switched to using Canadian terms, but after a while they grew on me. Toque does sound a bit classier than sock hat.

The boyfriend continues, "I didn't realize the States had that. I always picture the U.S. as Los Angeles or Miami. I guess some people live outside those areas."

"That's fine. When I tell people that I'm going to college in Canada, they assume Toronto or Montreal. Call them shocked that a city like Belleville has a university — much less two."

Our ladies maneuver around a homeless man sitting on the sidewalk. Brianna shoots him a dirty look for making her change paths. The cardboard sign sitting in his lap reads, "Christmas is the Season of Love." I flick a toonie into his collection hat as we pass.

"You shouldn't give those people money," the boyfriend says. "It just encourages them."

Dating etiquette dictates that I must be polite to the other boyfriend, but that doesn't mean it's not tedious. "I was rewarding the sweet sentiment on his sign."

"I didn't see it," he says. "I try not to look at those kind."

Nice compassion, good sir.

The girls continue on as the street flares to life. White lights from the trees cheer my spirits. We reach the still-standing facade of the old newspaper building that's been converted to a parking lot. This weekend it has new life, having been reborn as a Christmas market.

The boyfriend says, "I'm not sure why we're bothering to go here. Carrie and I bought gifts online and had them shipped in. Shopping in person is passé."

"We just went to a play when we could have watched the video." One point me.

The boyfriend's eyes bulge.

I blend into the crowd to ditch Captain Positivity. Excited voices pull me into the market. "God Rest Ye Merry Gentlemen" is playing from loudspeakers. There have to be thirty stalls set up. Christmas welcomes me out of the doldrums that has been my routine. The semester is over, and, for the first time in months, I can relax.

I'm on a mission to find iconic Canadian gifts to send back to family. My little sis needs something with a moose on it and mother collects knitted things. A good third of the items in the candy stall are shaped like maple leafs. I thought Americans were overboard on patriotism, but at least our gifts aren't all stars and stripes.

I buy two small maple confections and pop one in my mouth. I wander through the stalls while my taste buds are treated to maple bliss. The crystallized sugars are sandpaper against my cheeks — delicious sandpaper.

For sis, I find a sweater patterned with moose and snow-flakes. For dad, I find an Inukshuk phone charger, a modern twist on the aboriginal rock piles.

Brianna and her friend are trying on holiday scarves when I locate them. I hold my find up for Brianna's approval with the smug confidence of the hunter returning with a kill.

Her nose wrinkles at the sight. "Ewww. No, we avoid sugars. You didn't eat that did you?"

I try to sneak the sugar off my lips while nursing my pride.

"Madden. You know you need to get a few pounds off, and here you are eating that."

I move away before getting defensive. My parents drilled in my head that every criticism is an opportunity to grow. Brianna is right; my jogging routine has suffered as of late. My stomach is still flat, but I've gained a couple of pounds while finishing out the semester. But now that I have three weeks break before the winter semester starts, there's plenty of time to shed the excess.

"Good King Wenceslas" plays as I move through the booths. The sun sets and the Christmas Market takes on a magical ambience. Vendors sell their wares in the holiday glow. One stall sells donairs, the gyro-like meat treat that I was addicted to my first year in Canada. The roasted beef makes my mouth water, but the responsible choice would be a lean chicken salad.

Nothing catches my eye for mother until I return to the scarf stall where Brianna had been. There's the popular white scarf with one stripe of green, red, yellow, and black. The material has a thick weave, and it's heavier than it looks.

"That's a Hudson Bay scarf," a female voice says. I look over to a short-haired, thin brunette wearing a firefighter's jacket.

"Should that mean something to me?" Here comes the hard sale.

Her gaze travels over me. "How do you not know about the Hudson Bay blanket? You look educated."

"I'm not sure if I should take as a compliment."

"The suit, the shoes, the hair, and the nagging lady telling you to lose weight. Those are all signs of being educated."

I pull my stomach in a bit. To deflect attention I ask, "This has a significance to Canadians?"

The vendor walks around the booth. She's about my height. Her back is straight, shoulders pulled back like she's in the military. "I'm going to guess you aren't from here — that or you're a moron."

"Why can't I be both?"

Her chuckle makes me think it's not just a salesperson placating me.

Her laughing at my joke feels good. Brianna doesn't find humor in my levity.

"Where are you from?" she asks.

"Indiana." I used to say "The U.S." but everyone here knows our states.

"That's near Georgia, right?"

So much for our education system being the worst. "In the sense that Belleville is down the road from Avonlea."

She snorts. "How on earth do you know about Anne of Green Gables?"

"My girlfriend introduced me to Canadian literature. She feels it's important to learn to be sensitive to local culture."

"Sensitivity from the same skinny chick who is so understanding about you eating sweets?"

My face is hot, despite the weather. "I guess you heard our conversation."

"She must be a beast in bed for you to put up with that."

I catch the cough too late before it pops out of my mouth. "I'll take this scarf."

She wraps it in tissue paper and then wraps a copy of the Post around it. She finishes it with a couple of pieces of tape. I wrap better than that.

The girl hands me the paper and gives me a business card. Tempest Stewart: Personal Trainer.

"Call me if you're serious about getting in shape. But, do it for you and not a nag," she says. Her smile is nice, not perfect, but welcoming.

I find Brianna looking at pale blue plates with white paintings. Her friend has disappeared.

"Where did your friend go?" I ask.

"You forgot her name, didn't you?" Brianna has the

grandmother over-the-glasses look down. She's going to be fearsome when she reaches that age.

"I'm not good with remembering names." It's been at least a week since I've received a lecture about paying attention to names. Dad says not remembering names will be a career limiter, but that I can work on that after getting through my MBA.

Brianna touches my hand, the way she does when trying to make a point. "Learn to remember names. It's a basic matter of respect." She leads me over to a bench facing the Moira River. "You can remember the most obscure facts, but you forget the most important thing about a person? Forgetting makes it look like you don't care."

Pressure fills my temple the way it does when I need to relax. I lean back and pay attention to "Joy to the World" playing over the loudspeakers. Heaven and nature may sing, but that has to wait while Brianna makes her point. This is not how I want to spend our last night before Brianna goes to England with her family for the holidays.

"It was a long semester," Brianna says. You need to focus on recovering. Come on, walk me to my apartment."

We hold hands and walk in silence. We leave the Christmas market behind and make our way to the Old East End. This area is known for its Victorian homes. Working couples buy the big homes and then rent rooms or apartments to get their mortgages down. We have to take the bus to campus, but it's worth it to live in this neighborhood.

The yard in front of Brianna's house is littered with plastic toys.

I help gather up a couple of them and ask, "Do you ever think about how life will be like with kids?"

"Of course. Children will be important once we're established in our careers, and once we've moved to a big city. That should be our late twenties, thirty at the latest."

"It seems so preordained."

Brianna spins to look at me. "People who fail to plan are setting themselves up for failure. Those who wish to succeed have faith in order."

I grunt while I grab a bicycle off the lawn. I'll carry it in so it doesn't sit in the snow tonight.

"I didn't realize that the weight you've put on is from stress," Brianna says. "You need to keep healthy. Take the holiday break at the gym to get back in the flow — and lose the gut."

"May I come in and have some Christmas Joy?"

She ponders my request for what feels like minutes before answering, "It's a long flight. I need my rest. Have a good holiday, Madden."

Chapter Two

*I*n the morning, I look up gyms and find an article on the paper's website about a new club on Dundas Street. Thirty minutes later, I'm standing outside it and debating if I can afford a membership. The snow isn't bad today so I can probably find a cleared jogging path at the park. Or I can see about borrowing a pair of skis and take up cross-country.

"Fella, you aren't getting in shape by standing out here." A man with a gray-speckled mustache wearing a Canadian Air Force jacket puts his hand on my shoulder and tries to lead me to the door.

I hold my ground. "I'm debating expenses."

"Money is temporary. You'll earn more," he says with a French accent. "No one is getting rich running this place. But we are getting in shape. Come on, what do you have to lose?"

Uhhh, the money. But the soldier is so damn likable that he has me walking into the gym. "Why not?"

"That's the spirit." He ushers me through the door.

A blast of heat greets me as I step in. I can't imagine their hydro bill to keep it this hot. I snicker at how another Canadian term feels natural: hydro means electric here.

The gym is double the width of a normal strip-mall store. There's no register or welcome counter, instead it opens right into the gym. In the middle of the floor is a maroon mat emblazoned with "Trojans" that covers about a third of the space. Around it are those interlocking colored rubber floor tiles that auto shops have.

"Where are the barbells, or better, the treadmills?"

The solider slaps my back hard enough to pop ribs out then points to a set of old duffle bags. He walks into the back where a couple of guys are stretching out. They are fit, but not muscle-bound, and for some reason, have their shirts off. Their ripped stomachs make me question giving up jogging to study.

A titter comes from the back. Tempest, the girl from the market last night, struts out of a back room. "Happy days. It's the Indianian from last night."

"The term is Hoosier — and no, I don't know why."

Her toothy grin answers. In a winter coat she's average, but in her workout clothes she's shredded. She's wearing a tight jogging bra, and then a couple miles of toned abs before painted-on yoga pants. Two other women follow her out, both in skimpy workout clothes. They're fit, but not as strong looking as Tempest. That girl has swimmer's shoulders.

"I'm glad you came by. Did you find the place off my business card?"

I pause. "Well, umm. No."

"Good — you're honest. I hate when people lie to me."

My confused state switches to bewildered.

"My card didn't list this place. So either you're a stalker or it's fate."

I notice a couple of the guys watching us. No doubt they can hear. I don't need a beating from the hockey crowd. "I'll go with coincidence. I was standing out front when the soldier shoved me in here."

"Jacob is good for that," Tempest says. "He doubles as a carnival barker."

I laugh along in case that was a joke. I hope she wasn't serious. "Where are the weights or the cardio machines?"

"The weights are in the bags on the pallet there. And you don't need machines to do cardio. So are you interested in LGN?"

"Lagoons?"

"Looking Good Naked. Your lady said you have a couple of pounds to drop. But is that all you want? Or do you not like the thought of women drooling over you."

My face burns from the blood rushing to it. "I have four weeks before the semester starts again. What's possible?"

"Get the shirt off and let's see."

"Mine or yours?" slips out before I catch my tongue. My parents would disapprove. Brianna would be mortified. Why did I say that out loud?

Judging from the laughs in the room, others appreciate the humor. Tempest's eyes light up. "That depends on how good the show is. Now, shirt off — boy."

Never have I been so self-conscious in taking off a shirt.

Tempest walks around me like I'm a used car. "If you're willing to devote the next few weeks, we'll have you ripped. Are you up for that?"

My mind screams to run, but my body is jumping with adrenaline. "I can do that."

"And we don't mean that you come work out for an hour or two. You devote yourself to this, and we'll have you where you want. It will not be easy, nor pain free."

"Let's go for it," I answer with more bravado than I feel.

The soldier claps then starts shadow boxing.

Tempest says, "Get your shorts on. We start work out in five minutes."

"Oh, I didn't bring workout clothes. I was just coming to investigate."

"Then borrow from someone, or work out nude, I don't care. But you aren't walking out of here without being sore."

A cop loans me a pair of mesh shorts. Despite the un-washed musk, I'm grateful since that saves the embarrassment of wearing only my boxers.

The workout uses duffle bags full of sand. Whoever came up with the idea of using sandbags as exercise equipment is an asshole. By the end of the workout, my fingers are rubbed raw and I'm having trouble seeing. We do squats, lunges, jumping squats, and a whole host of horrible exercises. Sweat pours off me to where I feel like I just left a pool. The room is hot enough to be a sauna; the only thing missing is the uncomfortable wood furniture.

Tempest walks to the middle of the mat holding a two foot-long rubber tug-o-war bone. It may be the lack of blood in my head, but she is the hottest thing I've ever seen. Her jog bra and pants are soaked with sweat and leave nothing to the imagination. Too bad she must be a firefighter's girl. They aren't known for appreciating people looking at their ladies.

She holds the bone over her head. "Challenge to end it. Two people grab the bone. On my mark you pull. Winner is the one who gets it off the mat. Pair up."

The others find partners.

The bone must be slippery as the matches are fast. One guy passed the bone and tackled his opponent but lost his grip. His opponent tossed the bone off the mat.

Everyone goes but me. Jacob takes the bone from where it landed after the last match and steps into the middle. "I will give a countdown, you go on three."

The only other person on the mat is Tempest. That's when I notice everyone looking at me.

"You've got to be kidding?" I stand straight and puff out. I'm not a beast, but she's only a girl.

One of the women must sense what I'm thinking. "Get out there. Tempest is going to kick your butt."

I walk onto the mat, offended to have to do this. We each take a hand on the bone. On the count of three, I spin and try to snap away. Tempest tackles me. She lands on me. I spin to my stomach to try to get space to flip the bone. Her forearm smashes on my chin and grinds across my neck.

I try to pull her arm away but can't get the leverage while still holding the bone. I force myself up but she hangs on and rides along on my back. I stumble the ten feet to where the mat ends.

The impact on the floor is rough. The pressure on my neck releases and air burns as it rushes back into my lungs. God, I hurt. I try to roll onto my back but Tempest is still on top of me. Her sweat drips onto me, joining mine. The taste of salty pickles slips into my mouth.

Tempest whispers in my ear, "Well done. Underneath that beat-down exterior is a fighter. I can't wait to see what you can do." She lays on me longer than she has to before rolling off.

Everyone else towels off, but of course I didn't bring a towel.

Tempest hands me a small hand towel. "That's the best I can offer you. Bring it back once you wash it."

"Thanks. Is it like this every day?"

"Nah. Tomorrow is chest and cardio. We are going to see you again, right?"

I am in pain, and have been beat and smashed. I feel like

crawling in a hole. I also feel more alive than I have in years. "Hell yeah, I'll be back."

Chapter Three

By the sixth day of training, the pain has subsided into numbness. Thank God Tempest taught me how to ice sore joints. After each workout, I spend twenty minutes in an ice bath, then twenty out, then another round in the tub. It takes a large bag of ice each day, a cost I'm happy to pay.

The sixth day ends with a Paramedic crushing me with a homemade pugil stick. It seems when you spend all your days helping people, you build up some frustration. I roll off the mat and watch the remaining contestants.

Tempest and a nurse compete hard. The nurse's handle catches Tempest and a small cut starts bleeding next to her eye. Bad move, nurse. Living up to her namesake, Tempest becomes a flurry of attacks. She is a beast when she wants to smash. The nurse falls and covers up while Tempest lands a few more hits. After their fight they hug, and then the nurse bandages the cut.

"Now that's sportsmanship," I say.

The Paramedic says, "I'd hug you too — but that's not happening."

"Thank God for little miracles." Sweat pours into my eyes, but I'm used to it now.

"She deserves a hug since she put up a better fight."

"If I had the energy — or ability — I'd smack you for that."

The Paramedic helps me up. He's a good guy. I wish I could remember his name.

Tempest catches me as I'm dressing. "Do you have plans after this?"

"No."

"Wrong. You have plans. Let's roll."

She towels her sweat off then slides on a tank top. As we near the exit, she pulls on wind pants and the firefighter jacket she's always wearing.

"Do we have time to clean up before whatever torture you have in mind?"

Tempest pulls me out the door before I can finish zipping up my jacket. The winter air gropes me. It pulls the breath out of me and feels wonderful at the same time. I finish zipping up as we reach her farm truck. She walks around and unlocks my side before going to hers.

"No auto locks?"

"Nah, it wasn't worth the extra cost. I saved the splurging to get four-wheel drive. You know, something practical." She throws it in gear. The truck responds with a metal girding cry as we lurch out onto Dundas.

"Do you have your wallet on you?" she asks.

Please tell me she doesn't want me to buy raffle tickets. "Yeah."

"Good. It's time we kick your training up a notch."

A cough beats me to the laugh that was coming. "Should I worry?"

"You promised to do as told." She downshifts and puts on her blinker. "Now it's time to up your ante."

She pulls us into a fire station. My neck tightens. I'm pretty sure she has a firefighter boyfriend and this could be bad if he's the jealous type.

On the walk in I'm coming up with excuses. "She was just driving me to — to I have no idea."

Four hulking brutes are in the station's kitchen when I come in. They're the type of guys who have chests bigger than cattle. Oregano and bacon compete for my attention. I'd make a jibe about their cooking aprons, but I want to continue breathing without a tube.

"Hang here," Tempest says, "I need to grab something." She skips up a metal spiral staircase leaving me with the firefighters.

The firefighter making pasta says, "How do you know our Tempest?"

Uh. Hi to you too. "She's leading the workouts at the gym. I need to get in shape over the holidays."

The firefighter working on the grill washes his hands, and then takes his apron off. He walks too close to me, which by definition is within an arm's reach. He offers a paw to shake. I'd call it a hand if it wasn't thicker than a brick.

I wait for the inevitable crush.

Instead it's firm, but doesn't leave broken bones. I look at his graying eyebrows and speckled handlebar mustache. He waits until our eyes meet. God, I hate when people want to do direct eye contact.

"Do you know much about firefighters?"

"No, sir."

"We're a family. Firefighters are a tribe of our own. We take care of each other. We risk our lives together."

I bite my lower lip. Please tell me this isn't her boyfriend's father.

I sense more firefighters coming in behind me. Crap, I'm going to die.

"That means Tempest has brothers — lots of brothers. Do you understand?"

"I'm not sure what's going on."

One behind me says, "That means anyone who upsets Tempest causes us distress. We don't like that."

"I would never—"

The one still shaking my hand says, "See to it that you don't."

He still hasn't released my hand.

Tempest returns, saving me from whatever this is. "Oh, I see you boys got to meet Madden. He's from Illinois," she says, pronouncing the "s".

It's Indiana — but I prefer her brothers not know this.

"We did get to meet Madden from Illinois. We had a nice talk," the handshaker says.

"Great. Now that you finished trying to scare him we can go. Here," she says while handing me a set of white shopping bags with brilliant red maple leafs on them.

I follow her out. A glance back shows the firefighters still watching me. Most have their arms crossed. I make a mental note never to come back here.

Back in the truck, Tempest says, "They get a little protective. Like I need their help. I can totally kick your ass."

"Jesus. Can you let me pretend to keep my masculinity

intact?"

She throws her head back in laughter. "I'm not one for the traditional male/female roles."

I gasp as loud as possible. "Say it isn't so. Anyway, where are we heading?"

"It's time to take your training to the next level. You want to look awesome before your break is over, right?"

"That's the goal."

"Then it's time to change up your diet. But first, Timmy's."

If I needed proof that Tempest is Canadian this is it — they all love this chain. Of course there is a line, there's always a line here. We hang out while I stare at the donuts that I'm trying to ignore.

When it's our turn I order a double-double.

Tempest jumps in and says, "He'll take that with sweetener and skim milk."

"I prefer—"

"You said you'd do whatever. That means cutting the useless calories and sugars."

We grab our coffees and Tempest leads me back to her truck. The coffee is less sweet and creamy than I prefer. How do people drink this plain?

Tempest grabs the reusable bags from behind her seat and leads me into the grocery store.

"Let me guess? Sports drinks and nutrition bars?"

She looks like I tried to hit her. "Hell no — that stuff is garbage. For the rest of this year you are authorized to eat leaves, berries, and meat."

"Authorized?"

"I'm in charge — remember?"

There's something exhilarating about a woman with this much confidence. My gaze lingers as we pass the milk section.

"Don't even think about it."

"I'll miss the milk in a bag. The only liquid you buy in soft plastic."

A small smile creeps onto her face and grows into a high grin. "What else would milk come in?"

Tempest loads me up with kale, chard, spinach, lettuce, mustard greens, and cabbage. In other words: rabbit food. She adds half a dozen types of berries to my cart, and then loads chicken, pork, and beef.

"I'm going to get ripped eating meat?"

"It's lean and you'll add muscle, which burns off fat. Trust me."

I pay, and Tempest drives me to my apartment. She helps me carry the items in.

"Wow — this is Spartan," Tempest says as we enter my apartment. "This is so tiny."

My two-room apartment is little, but it's not that bad. The kitchen is in the living room, but I live here to study instead of entertaining.

"Did you get robbed? Where is the television?" Tempest sets her bags down near my refrigerator then takes off her coat.

I guess she's staying. "I don't own a TV. I came here to study. I'm not great at school so I have to focus to get through. As my father says, 'where smarts fail effort succeeds'."

"That's inspiring and saddening at the same time. What parent tells their kids that?"

"Mine did all the time when I lived at home." I load up the empty vegetable tray. "They were trying to motivate me."

"Did it work? Is that why you escaped to Canada for college?"

I laugh, hoping it's not true. "I came because getting a degree here is cheaper and faster. Canada has three-year Bachelor degrees. In the time I'd finish a baccalaureate in the U.S. I'll have a bachelor's and Master of Commerce degrees."

"Which gets you off and working faster. Let me guess, that way you can work your butt off for decades and then retire early?"

I start to put the meat away. "Something like that."

"That doesn't seem like much of a life," she says while still looking around. "Where do you sleep?"

"The center closet is a Murphy bed — an efficient use of my space."

She bumps me out of the way and starts taking food out

of my fridge and putting it an extra bag.

"What on earth?"

"Out of sight, out of mind. If it will expire in a month it's gone. I'll drop it off at the food bank. Why do you have two packages of butter tarts in here? You don't eat that, do you?"

Good thing she didn't know about the Nanaimo bars last night.

Tempest clears out most of the items in my fridge. She leaves hot sauces and my sugar-free water flavorings. She even pours out my milk. "There you go. There's nothing to tempt you. At least nothing in the fridge."

I have to concentrate to get in enough air. I put the remaining groceries away while Tempest moves around the place. It doesn't take her long in my one room apartment.

"Okay, man up."

"Excuse me?"

"I want to see what I'm working with. Get that shirt off."

It's not like I'm a prude, but that one took me aback.

"Do it, boy."

Well, she is a trainer. I pull my top shirt off revealing my dried-sweat self.

Tempest walks close to inspect. "Back is looking stronger. Your posture is improving. Ribs are nice. This diet will kick start getting you to that super-hot body."

My fingers tingle. "Gee, thanks."

Tempest grabs hold of my wind pants and pulls them and my mesh shorts down to just above my junk. "Okay, the V is coming. This is what I couldn't see in class. I love the V that guys get next to their abs. The diet and a couple of weeks will get this perfect."

Having a gal grab your pants and pull down like that is much less erotic than I would have thought.

She turns her back and walks to the bed. "How does this thing come down?"

I'm not feeling right about this. Out of the country or not, I have a girlfriend. A man should remain faithful to his lady. "The doors open and then you have to pull the bed down."

Tempest opens the doors and stares at the bed. Then she

walks back across the room to where she's well within my personal space. "Is that clock accurate?" she asks while pointing at one on the wall.

I peek to make sure. "It's radio controlled. That's the one I use to make sure I make my classes."

"Good. So, I have sixty minutes. Let's play a game."

"Okay."

"The game's name is: Do you love your girlfriend?" Tempest's imperfect smile glows with mischief. "The game is simple. You say you love her and I leave — or we pull that bed down and make magic. Which is it?"

My mouth is a desert. Tempest pulls off her tank top so she's back to her sports bra. She flexes, showing her toned body. It would be so easy and right to be with her. My stomach is in knots.

Being the good man wins. "Option three. I'm not sure if I love Brianna, but I am in a relationship with her. As fantastic as sex with you would be—"

Tempest closes the distance to me and leans in. She kisses me on the cheek. Her lips are soft like a flower where they meet my skin. My body screams to touch her. Conflict rages inside me.

"Good boy. You may make keeper material as soon as you figure out what you want in life." Her eyes meet mine. "You're the one who has to decide if you're going to live your dream — or someone else's. Have a good evening."

Tempest puts on her shirt and jacket, and then grabs the bags of my food she's throwing away. Before reaching the door, she turns back and says, "You better be at the workout — or I'll tell the station that you were mean to me."

Chapter Four

A warm spell makes for a soggy walk to the gym. As gorgeous as Belleville is when snow covers it, like everywhere, it's depressing when the snow melts and the brown returns. I guzzle from a water bottle to keep the hunger at bay. This is the fifth day since Tempest made me switch to a fast-cut diet. That was also the day I managed to restrain my desires and kept true to my girlfriend when a hottie wanted to screw my brains out.

Mozart's violin concerto plays from my pocket as I'm closing in on the gym. I pull out my phone. "Globe Theater, how may I help you?"

"Madden, hey, it's me." Brianna's voice is cracking and I don't think it's the line.

"Are you okay?"

"I'm fine. No, I'm not. Look, calling from my cell so I can't talk long. We need to talk. Will you be available later?"

Something bad must have happened. "I'm going to the gym. I'll be available in two hours. Are you sure you're okay? Do you need me to call the police or anything?"

Brianna gives her contemptuous laugh, the one with a half gasp. "I'm wonderful."

She doesn't sound wonderful.

"I'll call you later."

"Okay, then. Hope you're enjoying England."

"I am. Bye."

What the hell was that? Brianna doesn't call when she's in town, much less when she's in Europe.

My mind wanders through the workout as much as it can when your partner is throwing a forty-pound sandbag at you. The session ends with Tempest having us split up and do handstand pushups. Winner is the one with the most in three minutes. In related news — those are impossible when you don't train crossfit. Those mats are rough on a head when you collapse.

As usual, I'm one of the last to leave. The rest have places to go and families to get home to. I have a girlfriend in a different country and no classes — this is the only place I go until classes start again. Then I'm back to the madness that is finishing college while doing all the right things that a young gentleman should do.

As I head for the door, Tempest shouts, "Wait up." She jogs over with her usual exuberance.

"Hey, Tempest. Thanks for the workout. Sorry I wasn't so into it today."

We step outside and she locks up. "I noticed, what was going on? It's not me is it?"

"What?"

She turns so she's facing me. "I did offer to fuck your brains out and you said no. With how your girlfriend was acting I figured she was more of a date than a permanent addition. Sorry. I don't want that to come between our friendship."

My toes start to cramp.

She must see my look. "That was an apology — how about I get an okay?"

I stretch against the wall before the cramp spreads to my calves. "Okay. But that wasn't why I've been moping today."

"No? So what is?"

Brianna would flinch at that abuse of our language. And when I'm with her I become her, so I would have objected as well. But in this case, it seems freeing. "I don't know. My girlfriend called to say she'd call later. She said we have to talk."

Tempest bellows, "Get out. She met someone on vacation?"

"What? No. She needed to talk. Maybe she got into a different grad school and wants me to go there instead of Toronto."

"You don't believe that, do you?"

"I did until you asked it like that."

"Come on. Let's grab a bite to eat, then you call her. She's your girlfriend. If something is going on then she owes you an explanation."

I don't feel much like eating.

Tempest drives to a steakhouse named after a U.S. state that no American would ever associate with good steaks. Guess it sounds like a place with cows to Canadians.

"Don't think for a minute that you're off your diet mister. You're getting salad and a steak."

"And if I eat the bread?" These places always have the best bread.

"Then you get to walk home." She hops into a bad movie accent, "Choose wisely, grasshopper."

Brianna would cringe at the implied racial connotation. I was too busy noticing how Tempest raises inflection on the last syllable that makes every sentence these Canadian girls say sound like a question. She can't quit that.

"Too much? Does that offend your enlightened sensibilities?"

I shrug.

"I may sound like a bitch. But I say, embrace it."

"What about you? I thought for sure you had a firefighter boyfriend?"

"Based on what? That I have a jacket?"

I take a bite of salad.

"You doofus. The jacket is a woman's cut. So even if I did date firefighters — and I don't — then the jacket would fit him and not me."

"Well, you do have a muscular build."

"I'm about to kick your ass, cowboy."

Steaks arrive in time to keep me from putting my foot further into my mouth. Roasted meat merges with garlic and mushrooms to form a scent few men can resist. I cut to reveal the pink goodness inside. Before I can put it in my mouth the violins start playing.

"What the hell is that?" Tempest asks.

"The Magic Flute," I respond as I debate answering.

"If that's your girlfriend you better pick up."

I put my fork down and answer.

Brianna's voice is chipper. "Madden — I have great news."

Pinning the phone to my ear I start to slide out of the

booth. "Wonderful. What's that?"

"You won't have to worry about forgetting my friends' names any longer."

I stop getting up. My throat goes dry. "That means you're no longer going to have friends?"

Brianna sighs. "I met someone."

"That's funny. So why did you call?"

"I'm withdrawing from college and staying in England."

I stand up and walk to the lobby.

My voice rises. "Two days before Christmas and you break up with me? What did I do to deserve this?"

"Don't play the victim, Madden. You've been trying to sabotage our relationship. We've been hanging on until one of us meets someone better."

"Damn it, Brianna. What are you talking about? All I've done is do exactly what you want. I have bent over backwards for you."

The hiss of her breath leaving is loud even through the static of the call. "That's the problem, Madden. You never embraced what I wanted. You tolerated it, placated me, and let me know that I was inconveniencing you the entire time. There is a world of difference between playing the role and embracing it."

I pace in the lobby. "I cannot believe you're doing this."

"Goodbye, Madden."

The teenager greeter offers me a sad look. The bartender is laughing with a waitress. They had to have heard.

I step out for a quick walk, but without a coat I'm driven back inside. I'm an odd mix of embarrassed, pissed off, and relieved.

Tempest has a drink waiting for me by the time I get back.

"What's this?"

"Rye. Sounds like you need it."

"What happened to the diet?"

"I added rye to your acceptable list tonight. Was that the call I think you just got?"

I gulp down half of the caramel tasting drink. I let the warmth flow into me. She dumped me. These last two years down the drain. "It appears that I no longer have to worry about being nit-picked."

She takes my hand in hers. "I'm here if you need anyone to do that for you. Speaking of that, eat and you'll feel better."

A second rye and the steak did make me feel better. I'm not sure if I felt bad about losing Brianna or about losing. No one likes to compete and fail.

On the way to my apartment, we swing by the Beer Store and order a two-four of something strong. I love how in Canada there's a different phrase for everything. The twenty-four pack whooshes out on the metal roller table like the ones that grocery stores used to have.

We gun it to my apartment. Tempest bounds up the stairs. I fly up them much easier than I did last month, and this while carrying my gym bag and the beer. Following her amazing backside is enough incentive to hurry.

We crack open the beer and start swigging.

"I'm afraid I'm a lousy entertainer. I don't have a television and I only have a couple of games. How are you at decade-old Trivial Pursuit?"

She wears a bemused smirk. "Let's start by moving these TV trays out of the way and getting the floor cleared."

"Should I ask?"

"You don't think you get to drink without having some punishment for going off the diet, do you?"

I move the stack of library books off the trays and then collapse them down.

"Why were you reading Little Women and Helen Keller?" At my lack of answer she continues, "That girlfriend made you read them?"

"She said it would be good for me to better understand women."

"How's that working out for you?"

The laugh jumps from my throat. "So what is this? Time for some plyometrics?"

Tempest kicks off her shoes and pulls off her sweatshirt so she's standing in only yoga pants and her jog bra. "This is a challenge — boy. Gear up. We're going to go a round or two."

"Are you sure? I'm not the nerdy weakling I used to be."

"You mean like last month? Come on, on your knees. Do you want to pull guard or get in wrestling start position?"

The righteous indignation rises. "You want to wrestle me? I'm a man. There is no way—"

Tempest tackles me. I roll over to get up and she is on me with powerful arms. Her forearm dives under my chin.

"Nice try," I grunt. I'm not a great fighter, but I know enough to put two hands on her wrist to stop the choke.

"Remember that part when you said you're a man and I won't be able to beat you?" she whispers in my ear.

"Yeah," I grunt back as she tries to tighten the clamp on my neck.

Red. My hands release as pain explodes from where her heel clanked into my balls. She tightens the choke and I fade. Feeling worthless, I tap the rug hoping she knows what that means.

The pressure releases and air flies back into my lungs. It burns coming in. I gasp between tears. "I'm pretty sure kicking someone in the nuts is against the rules."

"First, we didn't set any rules. Second, I just gave them a tap. Third, I don't deal well with people doubting my abilities because I have a vagina."

I roll into my back and stretch my hands over my head to get in more air.

Tempest grabs my shorts and pulls them down to the last possible point before my gear comes out. She then slides my shirt up. "There you go. Now you have the true V going."

"The what?"

Her hands trace the sides of my abs, over my hips, and down to where my belt line starts.

"You have a nice V." My breathing returns to normal as I drink in the sight of Tempest. Her long torso is tan and smooth. Her stomach is strong without having the chunky abs that guys get. She is strong, confident, and pure woman.

Tempest rolls onto her back and says, "Help slide these off."

Through my drunken haze, a sense of the prude I pretend to be comes through. "Excuse me?"

"You don't have any reason not to. And judging by how you watch me at class, you aren't gay. You said she broke up with you."

"I did."

"Then let loose. And if I do say so myself, I'm like the perfect celebration."

I grab either side of her pants and pull down with as much force as I can muster. Her shaved nether region greets me as I pull past. Desire screams from every part of me.

I am free of Brianna.

I am free of expectations.

I fling the yoga pants to the side. Tempest pulls her jog bra off to reveal perky tan breasts with the darkest nipples I've seen in person.

I cup her breasts and engulf one in my mouth. She is the most perfect being I have ever seen.

I start to slide off my shorts.

Her hands pull my head up so we make eye contact. "Hold on, cowboy. To the winners go the spoils."

My eyebrows rise in question.

Tempest scoots out from under me until her crotch is in my face. "Maybe next time you'll work harder to win the match." Her smooth left leg wraps around my head and pulls me down.

There it is, sitting in front of me. How hard can this be? I've seen dirty movies where the girls did this for each other. I kiss down her salty thighs to the holy land. Then I start in. Tongue wiggling, I move around and judge from her moans to figure out the right spot.

It is so hard to breathe down here. Her legs alternate between shoving straight out and wrapping my head so hard that I worry she's trying to kill me. The heat is oppressive, and I try not to pay too much attention to anything but her. At one point I gag but hold it in. My jaw is killing me, and my tongue is aching by the time she bellows a war cry and finishes. Her legs release me from the spider prison.

I kiss my way up her body, along that flat stomach to

those wonderful breasts. Then I move on to her neck.

"I'm so glad that bitch broke up with you."

Now that's a mood killer. I start to get up.

"I'm sorry," she says pulling me back down. "I know you hurt. Grab a condom and work the pain out."

I fumble through my closet until I find the multipack I bought when I moved here. Despite having a steady girlfriend for the past two years, the pack still has a few left.

Tempest is watching, smiling. "Are you getting out the bed or are we doing this where you basked in the shame of your loss?"

"It'll be your back that takes the pain."

"Oh, you think you get to be on top. That's adorable. Grab a towel."

I lay down a beach towel. Tempest pulls off my shorts. "There's that V. You're getting ripped."

"Thanks."

"On your backside, boy."

Tempest puts the condom on for me — which is nerve-wracking. Those little hairs do not like being pulled.

We make sweet love. As violent and aggressive as Tempest is in the gym, she's the opposite in bed. She licks my nipples and brings my mouth up so I can reach her breasts while we engage in rhythmic sex. Time slows to where each heartbeat feels like there are minutes between them.

Afterward, we lie on the floor. I trace along the muscles in her body.

The conversation may lack compared to being with Brianna, but this is a thousand times more satisfying.

Chapter Five

On Christmas Eve, I grab my bag and head out the door to walk to the gym. Brianna is sitting on the garden bench outside my apartment. Our eyes meet. It takes me a minute to register that she's not an apparition. There's no reason for her to be here if it wasn't to see me. My teeth grind and I have to fight away an urge to scream at her. I'd rather leave than give into such base thoughts. I cut left and jump a small fence to the driveway.

"Madden Jones. You will stop and talk to me."

I have to resist the urge to take off at a jog. I want her to see me walk away.

Brianna huffs after me and catches up in a block. Her makeup is streaked and her hair looks like she hasn't fixed it in a week.

"What do you want, Brianna?" I ask while continuing to walk.

"I want you."

Fuck my life. "To do what? To go to your boring ass plays? To read the boring drivel you like? You want me to move to Toronto with you and buy an overpriced condo with a view of the lake and work the next three decades to pay for it? Maybe we can save up and be on one of those house shows?"

"God damn you." Brianna runs in front and pushes my chest. "I flew all the way back after realizing what a mistake I made, and you respond with taunts?"

"Was it an oversight when you broke up with me before Christmas, after telling me that you were just holding on until you could find someone better?"

Her jaw drops open. I step around her and resume my pace.

"I was running away from myself — not you. I'm under a lot of pressure. You don't know what it's like to live for someone else's expectations."

I almost pee myself from the shock. I stop. "What would

you know about that? Everything you do is easy."

"That is what I mean. Everyone thinks I succeed natural-ly. I work my ass off to be the best person I can be."

"Self-induced pressure is different than being hounded to do what everyone else wants." I stride off toward the gym.

Brianna calls after me, "Madden. I know this is going to sound weird, but I called your parents."

The heartbeat in my ears roars. I circle back to her. "You did what?"

"I explained to them how you have been struggling with doubt. About how you didn't want to get married until you were through with school. And how you were afraid they'd be disappointed if you stayed in Canada."

The bitch called my parents.

Brianna continues, "I told them I'd never let you fail. Your parents are marvelous. They welcomed me into the family and said how they'd love to have me for a daughter-in-law."

"Unbelievable."

"It is." Brianna's eyes are watering. "Fear was keeping me from being a good partner. Now I realize that settling down with you is the right thing for me. We should start planning."

"Did you just say that I'm the best thing in your life?"

"Well, there's no reason to act superior because of that. I did fly across the Atlantic to tell you my decision."

"And what if I tell you that I've not been happier since you left?"

She tugs at her hair. "I wouldn't believe it. You're happy to be out of class and to not have any responsibilities. It's the break you enjoy." She runs her hands up her arms. "You had a happy little vacation. And now we're back together and can resume our life plan."

"Yeah, well, my life plan is to keep a clean slate. Sorry, Bri."

Her nose wrinkles at the nickname she hates.

"I'm sorry to disappoint my parents again, but I have other plans."

A bread truck rattles past. She says something, but it's lost in the ruckus.

Her body stiffens. In an almost inaudible high-pitch she says, "I'm sorry, it sounded like you said—"

"My life is better without you in it. I didn't realize how unhappy I was. You forced me to move on."

Tears stream down her cheeks. The same nervous laugh she gave the one time I took her on a Ferris wheel escapes. "What about all our plans?"

"The plans were anchors holding me back. I'm glad you left me. I'm free. Take care of yourself, Bri." I cross Dundas and head for the gym. My feet are lighter than they have been in years.

I look back before walking into the building. Brianna is still standing there like she thinks I'm going to change my mind. Sorry dear, but once you've tasted a dutchie you aren't satisfied with a plain doughnut.

The door to the gym is still locked by the time I arrive. I check my phone. I'm ten minutes early, but there are always folks here early. After fifteen minutes, Tempest drives up and grabs two buckets and cleaning supplies from her truck. "Oh hey, I was wondering if anyone else would be here."

It's been two days since I saw Tempest. She, and the other first responders, had to miss the workout yesterday. Our nurse said there was a big fire at a trucking company up on the 401. We led our own workout, but I hadn't realized how much of my motivation was lusting over Tempest. I texted her a few times to no avail.

"You'll never guess who came back today?"

"The girlfriend?"

"The ex-girlfriend. She tried to get me back and failed. I've moved on." I feel like a mountain of a man.

Tempest opens the door and doesn't bother going in the back to change — not that I'm complaining. "I was thinking of skipping the workout and cleaning the equipment instead."

"Do you have big plans or can we do both?"

Her eyebrows squish together. "I suppose we can do both. I wonder if any of the others will show up?"

I'm thrilled they aren't here. Since Tempest left the other night, all I can think about is touching her again.

The gym is still burning hot. She pulls off her hoodie, under which is a silver jog bra. Like every third girl in our generation she's wearing yoga pants. Thank God for that fashion trend.

I walk in the back and change into my forest green mesh shorts and gold tank top.

For the workout, Tempest lines up to the side of me, which makes staring at her harder.

An hour's hard sweating ends with me asking what the challenge is.

"Let's see who can bleach their part of the mat first."

It takes an hour to get the mat cleaned. I fight through the smell of bleach neutralizing whatever is in our sweat to win this round. "Boom, done. Winners get to choose right?"

"It was that memorable?"

"If that was losing then I want to see what winning is like."

Tempest turns away and starts cleaning the equipment. Salt and grime coat the sandbags. We rip the duct tape off the bags and empty out all the smaller bags of sand that form the weight in the canvas duffle bags. We make a big pile of the sandwich bags wrapped in duct tape.

"Help me get these out," she says while scooping up a pile of the empty duffle bags. We put on shoes then scamper out to her car and throw them in the trunk. We race back in before the sweat freezes to us. It's not bad for December in Ontario, but in soaked workout gear that's still brutal.

We finish off cleaning the ropes, hammers, and an assortment of outdoor tools that we haven't used since I started coming.

"Want to grab something to eat?" I ask when we're done.

The air hisses through her teeth as she lets a breath out. "No thanks."

"Okay, how about tomorrow?" I press, but I'm not feeling confident. I catch myself licking my bottom lip.

"It'll be Christmas."

"I can't think of a better present than to spend the day with you." I say it. There I am, taking the big risk.

Tempest puts on her socks and boots. "Christmas is for family. Speaking of, I should find out what mine is doing. Let's close up."

"What about my victory?"

Tempest puts on her sweatshirt in a deliberate manner. "Look — I'm not going to be your rebound girl. I'm sorry you put so much time into that twat, but it's making you reckless."

"Maybe impulsiveness is what I'm missing."

Through gritted teeth she says, "Just because one person needs something doesn't mean we all do."

My stomach is in knots.

We walk outside in silence. Tempest locks up. As she gets in her truck she says, "Madden — have a Merry Christmas."

"You as well." I stand outside the gym as she drives off.

I'm worthless. I turned away the woman who wants to be with me only to have the one I want reject me. Tempest didn't even offer me a ride, something she would have done before we had sex.

The walk back through the slop doesn't release my tension. The deserted streets tease me. The only sound is from the wind cutting through pine trees. I'm ready to admit defeat by the time I get to my apartment but Brianna isn't there. I expected to see her, the old reliable option waiting on me. Instead, there is the empty bench where she had waited for me.

My sparse apartment feels emptier than it has before. No sense giving in to melancholy. What the hell, I was happy she broke up with me and now I feel like a failure for not having someone.

The answering machine has a message waiting. Please let that be Tempest. My mouth waters as I move to hit play.

"Madden," my father's voice says from the machine, "What are you thinking, breaking that poor girl's heart? Are you trying to ruin your life? Of all the things you screw up this is the one you put extra energy in ruining."

The message ends without a Merry Christmas. All I'm left with is the taste of bile in my mouth.

Happy Holidays indeed…

Chapter Six

Christmas was spent working through James Joyce's Dubliners, an assignment for next semester. Christmas morning saw a dumping of snow, so I grabbed my e-reader and walked to the Rose Garden. There's peacefulness in being out on Christmas Day. Everyone else is off with families leaving the city to me. The only people I saw in the park were heading to relatives' houses. They carried in their presents and raced into embraces. If they noticed the man reading on the bench they made no indication of it.

The next morning I'm heading back to the Rose Garden. I pack a bigger lunch this time and trudge through the snow. Some of the residents were even kind enough to shovel their walks. I dive into James Joyce's short on a college student trying to fit in. Great, like that doesn't explain my life. Today, I'm more troubled and having issues focusing. I stave loneliness with progression. Between scenes I look around. Brown thorns stick out of the pristine snow; in every beauty there is pain.

My focus is on getting my life on track. For the last year and a half I was on autopilot. I went to class because of expectations. I did what Brianna wanted because she was forceful in her decisions. Now I only have the plan to graduate in summer, then finish off a first masters, so I can get into the MBA program. With luck I'll be debt free by the time I'm twenty-five. The hollowness inside reminds me that the rationalization isn't working. That plan belongs to my parents, not to me. I want to be happy and experience life.

Over lunch I stare at the old architecture that used to bring me such joy. But the welcoming feeling has left given the events of the past few days. Instead, the happy lives remind me of how pathetic mine is. Shouts from a party reinforce how I don't have a life here — Brianna does.

My phone beeps with a text notification.

"You missed workout. Are you okay?" It's from the cell phone that was on Tempest's business card.

I check the time, four-thirty, I hadn't thought about the

workout.

"I was studying."

"You should spend Boxing Day with friends. Mind if I come over?"

I forgot Canadians call this Boxing Day. Last year Brianna dragged me around to visit all her friends.

I reply, "I'm out but can be back in twenty minutes."

"I'll be there."

I finish off the story then stroll the few blocks back to my apartment.

Tempest's truck is in my building's little lot. One of the spaces is mine, though only Brianna ever used it. Tempest climbs out when I walk up. She's wearing a long white coat with the green, red, yellow, and blue stripes like the scarf I bought from her at the Christmas Market. She has on red and green striped wellies with white fur sticking out of the top. I've never seen her wear anything other than runners before. She has on a matching stripped ski hat.

"You didn't come to the workout today," she says as way of greeting.

"I didn't think it was on."

"It wasn't. But I was there," Tempest says. "May we go in?"

I lead her into my little apartment. I hadn't noticed how small and empty it was before Brianna left for Britain. Now that I'm here all the time, the space feels like a prison. One more semester in this place, and then I'm on to either Toronto or Ottawa for the first masters. What's sad is that this apartment will feel monstrous compared to what I'll find in either of those places on my budget.

"Care for something to drink?"

"No need," she says, "We need to talk."

For fuck's sake, she already rejected me, what else is she going to do, inform me that I stink?

"Okay then. Do you want to take off your coat?" My apartment is hot. The winter has been mild for Ontario, but the neighbors below are still pumping on their heat. I have to keep the window open to get any sleep.

Tempest still has her coat wrapped tight. She kicks off her boots at the door, and puts her hat on a hook, but still has the coat on. She's not wearing socks. I bet those boots smell great after the day.

"The coat depends on how you answer."

"The anticipation is killing me," I say, trying to force a smile.

Tempest sits down — not talking. She has to be sweating in that coat. She eyes the e-reader where I had set it down.

"I spent Christmas reading, a wild bachelor's holiday. What did you do for Christmas? Make it over to your family?"

"No. We got called out to the County just before midnight." Her voice cracks. She runs her hands up and down her covered legs. "A family farm went up. The barn caught fire and it spread to the house. They were so far apart it shouldn't have jumped, but the wind was wicked last night. Three generations living together lost everything."

I feel for them. "That's horrible."

"It was beautiful. I'll never think of the smell of wood and carpet burning quite the same. It changed me."

My throat tightens up. If she pulls a pistol out I'm going to be upset. "In what world is that beautiful?"

Tempest wrings her hands together. "The family wasn't upset. Everyone was fine. They even got the pets out. They're thrilled to be together. When the boys offered condolences for their loss, the family said everything was perfect. That the only thing in this life that matters is family."

I have never felt more alone in the world than now. I have no one who cares that much.

She continues, "It got me thinking about who I know. I focus so much on my goals that I forget about people. Hey, are you crying?"

Damn unmanly tear ducts. My lungs hurt from the emotion.

"I know you took a chance the other day, and I tried to save us from risking embarrassment. Then the universe shows me a better way." She leans close, "Now that you had a day to think, do you feel the same way about me?"

My feet feel warmer than normal. "Are you asking what I think you are?"

"I'm not asking for anything more than to see if you want give this shit a try. I want to see if we work together."

Every instinct warns me not to risk again. Those defenses are there to keep the pain away. Fuck that. I bound from my chair toward her. "Yes, dammit. I'd love to see if we could make it."

She stands and gives me a sweet kiss. Her gentle lips, with the hint of playful tongue, dance against mine. Spearmint fills my mouth. Then she steps back to the door.

"Then, do you mind if I stay?"

"I insist."

Tempest opens her coat and lets it slide to the ground. She is wearing a mini skirt in that same white and stripped pattern — and that's it. The sight is so amazing I almost collapse from shock and blood loss.

"Yes — we should give this a try."

Winter's Gift

by Kay Blake

I want to dedicate this story to my Mother, My Cubs
and My Other Half
& A Very Special Dedication to my favorite writing
group, Writing Wenches. I love you all so much.

Chapter One

Mel

I checked to make sure I packed everything that I would need for this three-day ski trip. Just before Christmas. Frankly, I wasn't really in the mood to do anything this year. I wasn't in the holiday spirit. The school administration had let the school out a few days early because of a boiler issue. The entire basement had flooded. I was looking forward to reading some good books and drinking a glass or two of wine. Okay, maybe more than two glasses. I needed to unwind. Badly.

When you're an elementary school teacher, things can be quite a hassle, sometimes. Whether it was a new rule or an unruly child, there was always something new to overcome. Though I loved my first graders dearly, the closer we came to the holidays, the more they wanted to goof off and not do their work. Of course, I appreciated their young hearts and minds, but I have grown quite a few gray hairs constantly repeating myself. The flood was an answered prayer for both me and the children.

I looked at my cellphone. Several missed calls from my best friend, Joanne. Jo was the reason I was leaving the comfort of my home: to go skiing with her, her fiancé, and some friends of his. Usually she would head out to her parents' house for Christmas. They did the whole shebang. Baking, caroling, the works. This year, her parents were away at a sunny beach and would be back on Christmas Eve. I couldn't blame them. Sunny beaches beat snow every time. My parents have been dead for years, so holidays were never my favorite time of year. It was always painful. Lonely.

I didn't want to be in the company of Jo and Jackson because it was another reminder that I was the single girl who occasionally got bitter around the holidays. Jackson smothered

Jo with affection. Don't get me wrong, I was happy for her. It just sometimes made me a little envious. I've been on my own since I found out that Danny—the man I was supposed to marry—already had a wife. Outside of Jackson, all men were snakes. There was a small part of me that wanted to swear off love. For a while I did. I was hurt and embarrassed. Danny and I had worked together, and it was very uncomfortable until he decided to move to a different school. Things got a little easier after that, although I still had to endure the accusatory stares of some of the other female teachers. I suspected it had to do with the fact that they wanted him for themselves.

I went to my closet to pull out my second pair of snow boots. They were much better for hiking in the snow. My phone vibrated again, and I hurried to answer it.

"Hello!"

"Please tell me that you're ready." Jo's bubbly voice filled the speaker.

"Yes. I'm getting the last of my things, and I'll be downstairs in five."

"Well, please hurry up. I'm expecting you to be there in five minutes. If not, I'm coming up there and getting you." She hung up, and I sighed.

This trip couldn't be that bad, right?

I grabbed my bag and headed downstairs. Jo stood there waiting, with a white winter jacket and earmuffs covering her ears. She reminded me of when we went through our matching phase as teenagers. Everything had to be color coordinated.

"Glad you finally decided to make your way down. It's cold."

"Well hello to you, too. Why didn't you just wait in the car for me?" I asked. It was very cold out and it didn't look like Jo was dressed warmly enough.

"I had to show off my outfit," Jo replied with a wink. "Your hair looks great, Mel."

I didn't do anything special to my hair. Never did. My dark brown hair naturally fell down just under my shoulders.

"Thanks." I smiled and went to the trunk.

Jackson got out of the car and gave me a bear hug. His

arms swallowed my petite frame.

"Hey, Jackson." Letting me go, he took my bag and placed it in the trunk.

"Hey, Mel. I know you don't really like the holidays, but you're family. You're like the sister I never had, and I have a sister." He grinned and I laughed. "I don't want you to spend it alone," he continued, and placed my bag in the car.

"Thanks, Jack, that means a lot to me." And it did. He was a great guy. He treated Jo like a queen. He was right about one thing: he always treated me like I was his sister. I climbed in the backseat. Maroon Five was playing and it calmed me.

Jo got into the car and smiled. "I love this song. Adam Levine is so sexy. Not more than you, Jackson, but he is *definitely* sexy."

I chuckled. She was right.

"Babe, you can think anyone you want is sexy because I get to take you home at night," Jackson said, not batting an eye.

We all shared a laugh as he pulled away from my apartment building.

We drove through the city, and surprisingly, traffic was light. That was a miracle. I knew from looking online that the drive would take about two and a half hours. I gazed out the window at all the holiday decorations, and the people who were scattered outside seemed more patient than usual. Maybe even cheerful. In the city that never sleeps, that was a good thing to see. New Yorkers sometimes didn't know when to slow down and just enjoy life. I can't even remember the last time I just slowed down and enjoyed life. This was my way of doing that. All I did was work and watch romantic movies that had me in tears by their endings. My eyes started drooping. It would be a bit before we got there so I welcomed the sleep.

The car ride got a little bumpy and I jolted awake. The sun was beginning to set, painting the sky in several shades of oranges and reds. I snapped a picture with my cell phone. After twenty more minutes we arrived at the cabin that we would be staying in. It was in close proximity to the Brookes Ski Lodge—the perfect escape from the tourists, but with enough beauty to be mesmerizing.

Jackson pulled the car up in front of the cabin and cut the engine. From what I had read online, the resort had been started by a married couple, and it had become quite a success. The reviews on it were great. The pictures had shown a gorgeous little cabin, but it looked ten times better in person. It was oak, or appeared to be, with wood stacked high on the porch. From what I saw, it would be just as beautiful in the summer. Lights surrounded the outside of the cabin, giving it a holiday feel. There was already a decent amount of snow on the ground. I was in a small wonderland. There was a spacious front patio, and from looking at the cabin from the outside, six people should have enough space to be comfortable.

For a moment I was transported back to a time when I went skiing with my parents as a child. Life was easy than. They used to make sure I could do things like go to museums and watch plays. They always let me know there was something in life to enjoy. I missed them so much.

I got out of the car quickly and stretched my legs. I usually had no problem with a nice long drive, but my legs had surprisingly fallen asleep on me. I didn't like it. An icy drop touched my face and I realized that it was starting to snow again.

Jo got out of the car and spun around in a small circle. "Yes! The more snow, the better. This is just perfect for skiing."

"See, I told you not to worry. This ski trip will be great," Jackson said. He touched her arm just enough to stop her twirling and placed a kiss on her lips.

I faked a gag, then laughed. "You two need to get a room."

"I am quite sure you will be just as in love as I am. Very soon even, if everything works out," Jo said, giving me one of those looks that she only had when she had a secret that she wanted to share.

I tilted my head to the side, puzzled. What did she mean by 'if everything worked out?' She was up to something. Jo was always up to something.

Realization dawned on me, and just like that, I was annoyed. "Is this some kind of weird blind date you set up for this ski trip, Joanne?"

Jo gave me a sheepish look, but said nothing. I knew it.

"You know I hate blind dates. I hate blind anything. They always wind up being disastrous. I don't like being set up. I really could have stayed home for this. I'm going to be stuck in a cabin with a guy whom I don't know. I'm not saying he's a psychopath or anything. It's just, Joanne, you know I don't like feeling like I'm some kind of charity project." I was fuming.

Jo came over to me and tried to give me a hug.

"I'm sorry, Mel. I really am," she said.

I shook my head in response. Usually hearing her say sorry was enough, but not this time. I wasn't letting her out of this so easily. All I wanted to do was head back home and have a couple of glasses of wine. Maybe something stronger.

"Please, let's just get this week over with." I sighed. I grabbed my bag from the car, and headed to the door of the cabin.

Jackson walked over to me and gave a small smile. He knew that I hated that Jo always wanted to meddle in my love life, but he also knew not to try to talk her out of anything she had her heart set on. Even if that meant I might end up with a broken heart and more of a complete mess than I already was. He had her back.

Jackson opened the door to allow me and Jo to go inside. There was a fireplace with a roaring fire already going and a nice sized chaise sectional. I was liking the cabin already. I dropped my bag and took my coat off. It was getting a bit warm.

"Oh, I guess they beat us here," Jackson said, as he walked further into the cabin and out of sight.

Jo came up to me. "I really am sorry. I know you hate the whole blind date thing, but I hate that you're so sad around this time. I know why. I understand. I just want you to be happy. I really do. You're too good of a person not to be. I thought maybe with Scott here, you wouldn't feel like a fifth wheel. Well, a third wheel, considering how everything else played out."

My anger subsided. I could never stay mad at her for too long. "I know you meant well, Joanne. You always do. That's one of the things that I love about you. Even if sometimes you drive me half-batty by always trying to fix me up. I love you."

We hugged. Jo was my best friend for a reason. I knew from the beginning that she didn't mean any harm because that was the kind of person she was. Good-hearted and caring. I also knew that if I had my heart broken, she would be right there for me.

Jackson walked back in with someone else behind him. My interest was piqued as I watched him approach. He was quite handsome. Okay, maybe more than quite. He was hot. He stood about six feet tall. A good nine inches above my five-foot-three-inch height. He had dark brown hair that was brushed back in a messy sort of way. It gave him a dangerous but boyish look. His jaw was strong. Hell, from the look of all his muscles, everything was probably strong on him.

His dark gray eyes glanced to me, and the color rose on my pale cheeks. Damn, he caught me staring.

"My name is Scott, and you are?" he asked. His hand reached out to mine. For a moment, it felt as if it was just the two of us in the room. He looked like trouble. Trouble in a good way. A really good way.

"I'm Melissa. Everyone calls me Mel," I replied. I shook his hand and backed away a little. He was freaking sexy. I really needed to clear the thoughts that were running through my head. He *screamed* player. He seemed like a guy that would break my heart into a million little pieces. Though the longer I stared, the more I determined that maybe it wouldn't play out as badly as it surely was in my head.

"Nice to meet you as well, Scott."

"Amanda and Kevin weren't able to make it. Amanda wasn't feeling well," Jackson interrupted as he came around me to stand next to Jo.

"Really? That's too bad. It would've been fun. I haven't seen Amanda in ages." Jo made a face and quickly returned to smiling. "Oh well, the four of us can still have a great time," Jo said.

I gave Jo a patient look. Sometimes she was just too obvious in her attempts to fix me up. Sure, Scott was *hot*. I just wasn't sure if I was ready to find out whether he was worth the trouble.

I excused myself, and hurriedly walked to one of the empty bedrooms. Dropping my bag and coat in the corner of the room, I sat on the bed to give myself a moment to process what was going on. I played with the brown strands of hair that fell across my face, something I did anytime I was nervous.

Jo stood at the door. "I know this seems like some double couple type of thing. That wasn't the intent."

"I know, Jo. I wish you were bunking with me instead of Jackson. I know it's a bit selfish, but it would have been nice to bunk with you, like our younger days."

"Well, just say the word and if you need me, I am here." She winked and strode out of the room. I changed into a sweater and walked out of the room.

Everyone was standing in the kitchen. They all seemed so comfortable. Scott looked at me and winked. I averted my gaze. Heat instantly colored my cheeks.

"I hope you don't mind. I brought pizza from the resort a few blocks from here. It may be cold now, but I know how to heat it up so it should still taste almost as good as it did earlier," Scott said, his gaze still on mine.

"Oh, that's fine. I'm not picky when it comes to food."

"That's good to know," he quipped.

Jo and Jackson went to sit on the couch. A soda sounded good, so I headed for the fridge. Scott moved a little to allow me to pass and I got a better view of him. His toned arms were nicely showcased in his plaid shirt. He wore a white tee underneath. I noted the small hoop earring he wore. It was a play on the nineties. Normally, I didn't find men with an earring attractive, but it worked on Scott. His good looks all of a sudden felt stifling. My throat was starting to get dry. I really was going to need that soda.

When I opened the fridge and reached for the soda, Scott

leaned in at the same time. He brushed my hand as he gently moved me to the side to grab two sodas. He placed both cans on the small table and leaned towards me. He had a look in his eyes that I couldn't read.

"I'm going to make love to you, Mel. I promise I'll have you begging for more. After that I'll make love to you again."

"Excuse me?" I asked. I knew that I'd heard him right.

"You heard what I said, Mel," he responded.

"Is that is how you pick up women?"

He smirked. Without replying, he grabbed one of the sodas and walked out of the kitchen.

If any other guy had said that to me, I would have slapped him. I wasn't what you would consider easy. I didn't know whether to feel offended or excited. Scott was quick to assume that something would happen between the two of us. For a moment, I considered what that something could be. I started to think that maybe he was joking, but then again, who jokes around like that? I shook my head. This trip was going to be hard. Grabbing my soda and a slice, I walked out to where the others were sitting.

Of course, there was a space right next to Scott. I decided the best course of action would be for me to go all the way to the opposite side of the room and sit beside Jo. She was going to be my safe place. There was no way I was sitting by Mr. Love Machine. He made me nervous.

"So Mel, what do you do?" Scott asked, after I took a couple bites of my pizza. I tried to think of a way to act like I didn't hear the question. I couldn't even look at him without blushing. All I kept thinking about was the comment he made in the kitchen.

"I'm a first grade teacher," I finally said.

"Sounds exciting. You must love kids, huh?"

"Yes. Kids are wonderful. Especially my kids. I mean my students." I wanted to look away from his gaze, but his dark eyes were piercing mine.

"Scott is a firefighter," Jo said, interrupting the silence. She looked between the two of us. She couldn't be any more obvious that she was trying to set us up.

"That's a brave thing to do. It's quite honorable," I said.

"Thanks. My dad did it. At first I didn't want to, but things happen," Scott said, his gaze still on me. I felt like I was under a microscope. Not that it was a bad thing, but it did feel a bit weird.

"Well, I'm tired," Jo said, stifling a fake yawn. I rolled my eyes. I was going to kill her. I didn't want to be alone with Scott, but I wasn't going to be rude either. Jackson got up and gave me an apologetic shrug as he left the room.

"Joanne, you can't be that tired," I said, sounding quite desperate. I needed her here. She was my buffer. I didn't trust the things that Scott would say with her gone. I was split between wanting to go to my bedroom and wanting to get to know Scott without doing something I may regret.

"Yes, it's been a long day. I'm tired. I am sure Scott will keep you company." Still smiling, Jo got up and followed Jackson out of the living room.

An awkward silence fell after she left. Scott grabbed two beers from the kitchen and came back to sit next to me.

"So what brings you to the cabins during the holidays?"

"Well, Jo wanted me to come. My plan was to stay at home and just relax, you know?"

He nodded. "Sure I get that. I haven't had a real vacation in years. My mother and stepfather left town for the holidays because I usually don't have the time to stop by. So when Jackson asked me to come, I decided why not? I was hesitant at first. The past few months have been exhausting. Now, I'm kind of glad that I came."

I raised my eyebrows, but said nothing.

"I'm surprised a pretty woman like you isn't somewhere cuddled up naked with some guy." He smiled while taking a sip of his beer.

"Why must everything go there with you? Sounds like you are trying to pry out of me if I'm single or not."

"Where is everything going exactly? I'm not prying. If you had a boyfriend, you wouldn't have come here alone. You would have probably stayed home to be with him or you'd be doing what Jackson and Jo are doing right now." Sarcasm laced his words. "Since you didn't respond, I know I'm right. What I really want to know, is how long is it going to take for you to let me make love to you? I promise after I wear every part of your body out, I will hold you until you fall asleep." He shifted closer to me. I smelled the faint hint of the beer on his breath. His voice was husky. I wasn't trying to go there with him. At least not yet.

I backed away from him, and took a swig of the beer. I felt the best way to avoid everything he said was to quickly change the subject. So I turned the tables on him.

"May I ask why you don't have a woman up here with you?"

"Honestly, I have tons of girls. Well, I used to. Too many maybe. The last one was borderline crazy." A serious expression graced his handsome face for a split second.

"Tons of girls? Why are you worrying about me when you have tons of girls? I'm sure one of them is free," I said, failing to keep the jealousy out of my voice.

What the hell was wrong with me? He wasn't mine. It didn't make any sense.

He laughed. "Ah, so you *are* interested. I said I used to. As in not anymore. I haven't had a woman in the past four months, which I am quite proud of."

For some reason, I was satisfied with that answer. I took another sip of the beer as I looked at my cellphone.

"Four months? That's not too long. Try two years," I said, half sarcastically.

"Two years, why?"

I debated if I should tell him. This wasn't the kind of information you gave to someone that you barely knew. Scott looked genuinely interested. What could be the harm? The most that would probably come out of this was some pretty amazing sex. And I needed that kind of sex.

"I had a relationship with a man who was already married. I didn't know. Not at first. I started seeing signs eventually, but I ignored them. We met at work. He was one of the fifth grade teachers. When the whole thing was out in the open, he made me out to be a desperate woman. He told his wife that he slept with me once. Which was a lie. He never mentioned a wife. I would have never slept with him if I'd known he was married." I paused every time I thought about it, I felt stupid for falling for the lies he spewed effortlessly.

Scott looked at me with sympathy, so I continued.

"His wife called me and told me. He never wore a ring. He slept over. He never tried to hide his phone. It didn't make sense. Why not tell the truth? Why lie to me, and more importantly, your wife? I felt like some kind of whore and worse, I invested two years in a man that was never really mine."

Scott was quiet for a moment. He placed his beer down and grabbed my hand. "I am really sorry that happened to you, Mel. I mean, I admit I wasn't always the best guy to women. I was never married though." He gave a small laugh, placing his arm around my shoulders and pulled me closer to him.

For a moment, I debated if I should move away from him or stay. It felt kind of nice. Who was I kidding? It felt wonderful. Safe. There was a quiet that settled around the two of us.

It felt good to be near a man who seemed interested in me. Well, maybe he was just interested in sex. It had been two years. He could probably go all night. Wait. What the hell was I thinking? He was dangerous territory. He was the one who was used to having tons of girls. I didn't want to get burned a second time.

I glanced at my phone and realized that it was later than I thought. If I didn't get some sleep, I'd be horrible to be around. Besides, this was the perfect excuse to get away from him and avoid doing anything I may regret.

"I think I'm going to bed. Jo said she wanted to head to the slopes early tomorrow," I said, slowly removing myself from his arms.

He nodded. His face was locked into an expression of deep thought. I wondered what he was thinking.

As I rose to get up, he grabbed my hand and pulled me to him. I could smell his sweet, musky scent. He moved my face towards his, and kissed me softly on the lips. He barely kissed me, but it was one of the sweetest kisses I have ever had. He pulled away and winked at me. I didn't want anything to happen. Well, maybe a one night stand wouldn't be *that* bad.

"Sleep well, Mel," he said softly, touching my face and sitting back on the couch.

"You too." I got up and walked away. I felt his gaze burning a hole in my back side. My thoughts were jumbled.

I closed the bedroom door and undressed. Finding one of the night shirts I packed, I sat on the edge of the bed. There was a part of me that wondered what it would be like to fall asleep in his arms. The other part warned me that he may not be any good for my already fragile heart. I lay down and closed my eyes, hoping for sleep to find me quickly.

Chapter Two

Mel

I found myself up earlier than I planned. Usually, in peace and quiet, I could sleep well into the day when I didn't have to be up for work. I went to the bathroom so I could shower. I had no idea how long hot water lasted up here in the cabin so it would be best if I was quick in getting myself ready.

After choosing what to wear and getting dressed, I walked out to the kitchen area. Scott was standing there with navy pants on and a t shirt that showcased his muscles. He turned when I walked in. His face instantly brightened into a smile.

"Good Morning, Mel. How did you sleep?"

"I slept pretty well actually. You?"

"I slept like a baby. I'm a heavy sleeper."

I sat on the stool by the table that separated Scott from me. Distance was good for right now.

Soon, Jo walked in, followed by Jackson. They were smiling. They probably got in a morning quickie.

"Morning, Mel. Morning, Scott. What time did you did you two go to bed?" She added those invisible quotation marks, which really weren't necessary. I knew exactly what she was trying to imply.

"Good morning to you, too," I said. "I think the real question is what were you two doing before you came out here?" I smirked. Jo blushed, and Jackson went to the fridge.

I knew if I told Jo about the kiss Scott and I shared it would do nothing but fuel the fire in her matchmaking hands. As if she needed any more of a push. I couldn't even be sure how I felt about that kiss. Besides, I really wasn't ready to share that yet.

I wanted to know what he thought about our kiss, but I was afraid to ask. Maybe I was overthinking.

Scott cooked, and we ate, laughing as Jackson told us one of his infamous stories of his childhood. It was nice to laugh. For the first time in a long time, I felt a bit carefree.

Soon, we were ready to head to the slopes. I was covered in a ski suit and boots. It was quite cold. Jackson elected to drive us to the ski slope. Scott sat next to me and squeezed my hand. His hands swallowed mine. I smiled at him, and he winked.

It didn't take us long to get to the lodge. Jackson pulled into the parking lot and we got out. We could see all the beautiful mountains covered with fresh snow. The trees had traces of white all in their branches. I was in awe.

We walked inside the ski lodge to get our rentals. Jo and I had been skiing before, but we were far from experts. We decided to do the beginning courses together, and then explore some of the intermediate routes.

After two hours on the easier courses, I decided that I was ready to do one of the tougher ones. When I wanted to, I could be quite the daredevil.

"Jo, I think we should try this course right here." I pointed to the map. It looked like there were enough turns and surprises, but nothing too advanced.

"I would love to, but I'm hungry. Why don't you and Scott go and meet us back at the inn's café," Jo said. For once, she wasn't smiling. She got irritable when she was hungry.

"Okay," I said, and turned towards Scott. "Are you down to go do this last course before we head back?"

"I am down to do many things with you." He winked, and though it was cold out, the heat rose on my cheeks.

"Okay, Jo, we'll meet you back there," I said, choosing to ignore Scott.

We headed to the ski lift that would take us to the top of the course. The ride would be about fifteen minutes over to the other side. One of the workers strapped us in and we were up. The lift moved slowly up the cable. Not too long after there was a small shake, and then a pause. After ten minutes with nothing moving, I assumed we weren't going anywhere anytime soon.

"You have got to be kidding me," I said, sighing. I wasn't afraid of heights. That didn't mean that I wanted to be stuck on a ski lift.

"You know I'm not going to let anything happen to you, right?" Scott asked.

"I know you won't." I sounded so sure of myself, which was funny, because I wasn't certain of anything when it came to him.

A few moments passed, and an announcement that the ski lift would be fixed as soon as possible and they were sorry for the inconvenience came over the loudspeaker. I bet they were sorry. Of all the luck in the world, I would get stuck on a ski lift with a guy who made me feel things I hadn't felt in a long while. I turned towards Scott and studied his face. I had to admit that Jo got something right. I was really attracted to him.

I decided to break the silence.

"You mentioned you didn't want to be a firefighter at first. Why was that?"

Scott's brows drew together and lines of pain crinkled at the corners of his eyes. This wasn't a comfortable subject for him.

"My dad was a firefighter. He said there was nothing more important than having someone else's life in your hands. That you could be the very reason they lived another day. I thought he was a bit narcissistic when I was younger. He walked out when I was sixteen. For a man who said he liked to feel like he helped someone and it was important to save lives, he ruined mine. My mother was never the same after that. I did a lot of shit I'm not proud of. I acted out, and once I lost my virginity, I slept with tons of girls. Anything to numb the pain. Anything that would take my mind off the fact that my mother and I weren't good enough for him."

Scott looked away for a moment. I got the impression he was trying to hide his emotions and I understood that. I did it quite often. The only person who really knew when something was bothering me was Jo.

"Eventually, I decided to become a fireman to prove that I could be better than my father ever was. I wanted to make my mom proud of me. I enjoyed being with the guys and knowing that I could save a life. That was one thing my father was right about. I liked it, though. I admit it got me lots of girls, too."

I frowned. I didn't like that part. He gave me an apologetic look and grabbed my hand.

"Well, it seems like you realized you liked doing it, so why do you seem so down about it?" I made no effort to move my hand from his.

"Two months ago, we got this call for a three-story house on fire. We were able to get everybody out. At least I thought we did. I heard crying from the top floor so I went back. I tried looking for him and calling out to him, but it was very hard to see with all the smoke in the house. I was too late when I found him. The smoke had killed him. I brought his body downstairs. That was my first loss. I felt like I failed him. Like I failed his family. The chief told me that it happens sometimes, and that it would get better. It didn't get better. It was all I could think about. His small face. His body, lifeless. I couldn't stop blaming myself. I needed a break, and here I am." He struggled to keep the pain off his face. His brow was knitted together in a mask of anguish.

This was a different side of him than the side that he showed me at the cabin. The side he showed at the cabin was cocky and so self-assured. I had a new-found respect for him.

"It doesn't sound like it was your fault. You did your job. Even your chief said that it happens. He's in a better place now." I squeezed his hand.

Something felt different now between us. He shared his deepest secret with me. My attraction grew.

A few moments later, the ski lift started moving, and we finally made it to the top of the ski trail. We skied down together. We skied, we stumbled a little, and we laughed. I was having fun, something I hadn't done in a while. Towards the end of the trail, I tripped over one of my skis and rolled down the hill a couple of feet. Scott skied to me. Quickly taking his skis off, he knelt in front of me.

"Are you okay, Mel?" His eyes were dark and locked on my face.

"I think so. I hit something, but nothing feels broken." A part of my leg did hurt, but I knew if I broke something I would be in more pain. I tried standing up and stumbled a bit.

"You sit right there. I'm going to ask one of the workers to get our skis. I'm taking you back to the cabin."

"But what about Jo and Jackson?"

"They'll be fine. I'll text them and inform them of the situation. My priority is you." He seemed so protective of me. I liked it.

"You're quite bossy, Scott."

"Only with those I care about."

Wait, what? How was that even possible? I'd only known him for one day.

I waited as he walked off to get help. A few beats later he was back. He bent down and scooped me up. I felt like a doll. Safe. Quickly, I brushed those thoughts aside. I didn't like what I was feeling this close to him.

"I can walk, you know," I said stubbornly.

"I know you can, but if something is wrong I don't want to risk making things worse."

I watched his face with the concern carved into his expression. His brow was furrowed. He still looked amazing, and I felt myself staring at him in adoration.

The ski resort workers came and helped me into one of the small Jeeps. I laid my head on Scott's shoulder as we were driven back to the cabin. He smelled good. Not overly manly, but good enough that I wanted to snuggle against his chest and stay there.

Chapter Three

*S*cott

Once we got back to the cabin, I lifted Mel out of the car, and carried her into the house. She was light as a feather to me.

I wonder what it would be like to carry her into the bedroom.

Mel uttered a small chuckle and shook her head softly.

"What's so funny?" I asked, my eyebrows raised.

"Nothing," she said, trying not to smile.

"You can tell me. It was funny enough that you laughed."

She gave me a look, her brown eyes sparkling, and then she shrugged. "I guess I can tell you. The worst thing you can do is laugh. I was thinking that this looked like you were carrying me over the threshold," she said.

I looked down at her and smiled. "Honestly, I don't think I would mind if I did carry you over a threshold one day." I was surprised that I said that. I didn't think marriage was anywhere in my future. My ex-girlfriend said that once, and I wanted out quickly. But I could see Mel in a white dress, looking stunning, and afterwards, spending our whole honeymoon making love. I didn't know what it was, but Mel had me opening doors I swore would be forever closed.

She quieted. I wanted to know what she was thinking, but decided not to pry.

I sat her down in the room she slept in. She backed up a little on the bed.

I took off my jacket so I could check her leg. Placing my things on the chair on the side of the room, I walked back to her. I noticed her moving her leg around a little. She flinched.

"How is your leg feeling?" I asked.

"It hurts a little. I'm not dying or anything."

I knelt in front of her. She smelled so sweet. I wanted to devour her lips.

"Is it okay if I check it out?" I asked, instead.

She nodded.

I rolled up her pants leg partway, but it was too tight. "If you want me to check, you're going to need to take your pants off so I can see your leg better. I promise I won't do anything you don't want me to. Boy scout's honor." I didn't know why I said that. I couldn't promise I wouldn't touch her. I wanted to. I felt myself getting hard as I thought about it.

She nodded again. She slowly stood up and stumbled a little. Her cheeks turned a bit red. I didn't know why she was embarrassed, because it was cute. I said nothing as she shimmied out of her pants. She took them off holding on to the bed, and she was left in her shirt and her red panties. Sexy red panties. She looked down at the floor, avoiding my gaze. This was going to be harder than I thought.

Mel sat back down on the bed. I bent down and examined her leg. There was a bruise that looked pretty bad, but nothing looked broken. That was a relief.

"What's wrong with it?" she asked, a bit alarmed.

"Didn't mean to upset you, it just looks worse than it is."

Mel grimaced, the corners of her mouth tightening.

"I can put a little ice on it."

"I'm fine, Scott. No worries," she said softly.

She looked stunning. Her eyes were bright, her pouty lips ready, I needed her.

"Scott?"

"Yes?" I asked, looking at her.

She reached out, cupped my face with her hands, and pulled me towards her until our lips were pressed together. I was taken aback for a moment, but I recovered quickly, and I kissed her back. Everything I'd been feeling since the first time I laid eyes on her came bubbling to the surface. She had me seeing stars. I stopped and pulled away from her. Shit, what was I going to do now?

"What's wrong? Why did you stop?" she asked.

"Are you sure you want to do this, Mel?"

She looked perplexed. "I thought you said you wanted to make love to me?" Uncertainty laced her tone. It sounded sexy.

"I did. I do. I really like you, Mel. More than I thought I would. I don't want to hurt you. Your leg…" I was making excuses. She wanted me just as badly as I wanted her.

"And that's a problem, why? If you're worried about my leg, it will be fine. It's just a bruise, right?"

"I'm not used to feeling like this." Most girls were nothing more than a quick fling, and I let them go. Relationships equaled broken promises for me. Just like my dad with my mother. Mel had my head in another place. She was vulnerable. She needed protecting. I wanted to be the one to do that. I wanted to make sure she wouldn't hurt like she did when she was in that relationship with the guy who never mentioned he was married.

"So why not do something about it?"

She kissed me again, pulling me on top of her. I hungrily devoured her lips, and all felt right with the world. There was no possible way that I could feel everything that I was feeling, but I was. I never felt anything remotely like what I was feeling for Mel. My walls were coming down.

I placed small kisses all over her neck. Moving to her breasts, she let out a small sigh. I kept my kisses slow. I wanted to tease her. I wanted her to beg for me. She kept her gaze on me, her lips trembling.

Eying me with a look of hunger, she let me pull the shirt over her head. Wanting to satisfy her every need, I lifted her up gently so I could unclasp her bra. Her breasts spilled out, and I was momentarily dazed. Perfect round mountains of flesh. I greedily placed my mouth on them, sucking and biting softly on her nipples. She gave tiny moans and writhed against me. I caressed each nipple as my tongue licked eagerly around them. No, I was no longer playing fair.

"Scott, please. I need you now," she said in small breaths. Oh, I was ready to penetrate, but I needed a condom.

I stood up quickly and her brows raised. Her lips went into a small pout.

"Don't worry, beautiful, I'm going to get a condom," I said, as I hurried out of the room to get one. I took my shirt off and came back, the condom in my hand.

Mel reached for me, a keening sound escaping her lips. I would fulfill her wishes right after I did one more thing. I placed the condom beside her and traced the lining of her panties with my finger. I slowly pulled her panties down and around her ankles. I lowered my lips, and greedily let my tongue explore. She moaned and squirmed. I wasn't letting her go anywhere.

"Scott, I don't think I can hold on much longer."

"So let go," I mumbled into her folds. I felt her body shudder and she released. It was such a sweet orgasm.

I got up to take off my pants. Once I was down to my boxer briefs she smirked.

"I would give you lots of money to do that again," she said with a laugh.

"I would do it for free," I quipped back. And I would. I would do anything she asked. I had it bad already and all because of a kiss.

I grabbed the condom, put it on slowly, and placed myself over her.

"Are you sure you want to do this?"

"Yes, Scott," she whispered.

My erection probed her opening and I slowly slid into her. She gasped and clung to my chest.

"Shit," I muttered. She was so tight. I wasn't going to last long at all.

"You weren't lying when you said it had been two years, huh?" I said, as I waited to catch my bearings.

I was throbbing inside of her. There was a fire between us. A fire I desperately needed to put out. We moved together in perfect sync. Matching each other's pace.

Her body tightened, and I watched her face as she wrestled with her orgasm. She shook her head.

"I can't. This is too much," she whispered.

"It's okay, Melissa. I'm right here with you," I said. Her full name sounded beautiful on my lips. *She* was beautiful.

Her body got tense. My balls tightened and I swore. A fire shot up my erection, sending my release flowing. Hers matched mine, and we came together.

I rolled over, and she laid her head on my chest, breathing shallowly. I was falling for her. Everything about her was different than I was used to. That was something I never experienced before. I wasn't sure how to process all the emotions that were playing around in my head.

"That was absolutely amazing," she said, her voice soft. She seemed tired.

"It was. How's your leg?" I tried to be as gentle as possible, but looking at her body had me unable to restrain myself.

"It's okay. I don't feel the bruise too much," she replied, snuggling her head against my chest. Everything felt right.

After a couple of beats Mel sat up and stretched.

"I guess we should go take a shower before Jo and Jackson get back," she said.

"I have another idea of what we can do in the shower."

"I bet you do." She smirked. Getting up and grabbing a towel, she beckoned for me to follow her. I trailed behind her compliantly. I wanted to touch her soft skin again. I was getting addicted to her quickly.

Mel turned on the water in the bathroom and the mirror fogged almost immediately. She got in the shower and I saw the silhouette of her body as she let the water run over her. I wanted her again.

I stepped into the shower and she smiled slyly. She grabbed my member. That was all it took to get me hard again.

"I owe you one." Bending down, she placed her hands on my erection and did clever things with her mouth. The blood rushed to my head and I groaned, steadying myself to avoid dropping to my knees.

"Mel. Shit."

She said nothing, but hummed against me, her breath and tongue doing a dangerous tango.

"Damn... I'm going to burst, babe," I said, my voice husky. She continued concentrating on the task at hand. My erection tightened in an overwhelming rush of pleasure and I released. She kept her mouth over me until I'd finished.

I stumbled against the wall of the shower, trying to catch my breath. She stood up and continued to wash as if nothing had happened. When she was done, she got out to brush her teeth and I rushed to finish showering. I was falling for this woman and I was falling hard and fast.

I got out and she was wrapped in a towel. She looked at me. Her face locked into an expression I couldn't read. She gave me a soft smile, sighed, and walked out the bathroom.

"Okay, that was weird," I mumbled, as I dried off. I walked out the bathroom, towel wrapped around me, just as Jackson and Joanne were walking in. Jo gave me a strange look.

"I got your text. How is she?" she asked.

"She's fine. She has a bruise, but she's okay. She should be in her room," I said, trying to keep the confusion I was feeling out of my voice.

Joanne nodded, and walked to Mel's room and that left me with Jackson. He took his ski jacket off and turned towards me.

"So what really happened?" he asked.

"I had the most amazing time of my life, but I don't know. She just walked out like that was it. I don't get it," I said.

"Well, you can tell me more after you put some clothes on, dude," he said, and I laughed.

"Sorry, I'll be right back."

Quickly getting some clothes, I put some sweats on. When I emerged, Jackson was sitting on the chaise and Joanne was nowhere to be seen.

"So what happened with you and Mel?" he asked.

I sighed. "I took her back here because she fell at the ski course we were on. We had sex. It was amazing sex."

"You know we're cool, Scott. We have been for years. But Mel is like a sister to me and Joanne will kill me if you do anything to hurt her." Jackson's face was more serious than I'd ever seen.

"You don't think I know that? I know my past isn't necessarily the best, but I care about Mel. I know that's crazy considering that I haven't known her long, but I do. She's amazing," I said.

Jackson nodded, understanding written on his face. "Okay, man. I believe you. I think maybe you need to tell her that," he replied.

"I plan to, whenever she decides to come out of her

room," I said bitterly. I didn't know what was going on with Mel.

At that moment, Mel walked out, dressed and with her bag in her hand. I jumped up immediately.

"What's wrong, Mel? Why are you carrying your bag?" I asked, panicked.

Mel looked at me, her brown eyes clouded with an emotion I couldn't read. She said nothing. Joanne gave me a sympathetic look. I watched as Mel walked out the door.

"Joanne, what's wrong with her? Why is she leaving?"

"I don't know exactly. She doesn't want to talk about it. I'm driving her to the bus. She wants to be alone," Joanne said, looking stressed.

All that was running through my head was that I needed to get to her. I needed to make sure she was okay.

"Scott, just give her a little time," Joanne said, and walked out the door.

What the hell was I supposed to do now?

Chapter Four

M el

It was Christmas morning and I was alone. I tried to tell myself that I wanted to be alone. I sat on my couch looking at the small tree that I put up as soon as I got back from the cabin. I know it was crazy to have Jo get me out of there when we were supposed to be enjoying our trip, but after the shower I needed to get far away from Scott.

I couldn't deal with my emotions or my feelings, and I thought it was best that I leave. Jo called me nonstop to make sure I was okay, but I didn't want to talk to anyone right now. I sent a text to her and told her I was fine, and I would call her soon.

I went to the kitchen to get some egg nog and my bell rang. I wasn't in the mood for any carolers. Not today. I ignored it and continued to pour my egg nog.

"Damn it, Mel, I know you are in there. Open up! Please." The voice was familiar.

It couldn't be him. How did he know where I lived? I debated ignoring him or opening the door. The logical thing would be to open the door and see what he wanted. But part of me didn't want to face him. I wasn't ready.

After a few more moments of debating, I finally walked to the door and opened it. "Why are you here?" I asked. I wanted to get this over and done with.

Scott looked amazing. His hair was brushed back. His gray eyes were just as dreamy as they were when I first saw him. I almost lost the willpower that made me leave in the first place. He walked inside and paced around.

"I tried to leave it alone. I wanted to give you space, but I couldn't. I needed to see you. To make sure you were okay. I don't understand why you left after what happened, what we did together. What did I do wrong?" He stopped pacing and his eyes were dark with confusion. He was so sexy, even with the worry and aggravation plastered across his features.

"You didn't do anything wrong."

"So why did you leave like that, Melissa?"

"I couldn't be around you."

"Why not? Didn't you enjoy what we shared?"

"Of course I did. Couldn't you tell?" I shook my head and took a seat on the couch.

"How would I be able to tell? One minute you were okay. You did this amazing thing in the shower, and then you were gone, just like that." He snapped his finger. Anger was creeping into his voice.

"Listen, Scott. Everything we shared was special. I enjoyed it. I just didn't know what to do about my feelings. I was overwhelmed. I don't even understand what you see in me," I said, finally.

Scott's facial expression relaxed, and he came to me. Sitting down, he pulled me close. I tried resisting, but it felt good to be in his arms again. He placed his chin on top of my head.

"What are you feeling? You don't have to hide your feelings from me," he whispered into my neck.

"I think I am falling for you. I know it's insane. We barely know each other. Just a few special moments, but I never wanted anything as much as I wanted you. It's too fast, even for me. I felt something with you that I never felt before with anyone else."

Scott laughed. I bristled.

"Why are you laughing?"

Scott laughed harder. He held my face in his hands and placed a gentle kiss on my lips.

"Mel, I'm not laughing at your feelings. You're cute when you're mad. I feel the same way. I know no one would understand how or why, but I'm okay with that. All that matters is that we know, and we understand." He looked at me. "You don't think I felt overwhelmed? I wanted to talk, but you left. You pushed me away and all I wanted was to be closer to you."

I looked up into his eyes and got lost in them. His striking gray eyes. I shook my head softly. He was right. He kissed me again. I was consumed by his feelings, by mine.

"Merry Christmas, Melissa," he whispered, as he pulled away from my lips.

I smiled brightly. "Merry Christmas," I replied.

I laid my head on his shoulder. It was a great Christmas indeed.

Declan's Special

by Jennifer Ray

To my hubby, you are my forever.

Chapter One

The tinkling of the little bell tied to the bakery's doorknob draws Evie's attention to the front. She comes out from behind her desk and out to the shop's counter expecting to see Jack, one of her two employees. Instead, a sultry, feminine chuckle reaches her ears before the woman comes into view.

Declan O'Connor and his woman of the week. She should have known. It is Monday morning after all. A coffee and pastry from her bakery is Declan's parting gift after what she assumes is a sex filled weekend.

"Good morning, Mr. O'Connor." She turns her gaze to the tall, gorgeous brunette. "And ma'am." The woman doesn't acknowledge her. She's too busy stroking Declan's arm and giggling. Rolling her eyes, Evie looks back at Declan, whose grin doesn't mask the mischief gleaming from his gaze.

"Good mornin', Evie." That thick Irish accent can melt the panties off the most prudish of women. "How was your Thanksgiving weekend, love?" The brunette shoves her hand inside his suit jacket and purrs. Purrs?

He's laying the accent on thick this morning. Evie politely smiles. "It was great, thank you. A Declan's Special this morning, sir?"

"Oh, wow! Do you own this bakery too, baby?" The brunette finally looks at Evie, but not without an air of superiority.

Evie can't help but laugh. A frown starts creasing the smooth skin above the brunette's eyes, and Evie quickly wipes the smile from her face and clears her throat. "No, he does not own this bakery, ma'am. I do. He has a special because he is a frequent customer and always brings his… um… special guests here." Subtlety is lost on the brunette as she grins from ear to ear at the smirking Declan.

"Aww! Am I a special guest, baby?" The brunette runs her fingers through his fashionable, messy, chocolate brown hair.

Evie snorts.

Without taking his gaze away from Evie, Declan removes the brunette's hands from his hair and his person and clears his throat. "Of course, love." Not missing a beat, he winks at Evie and continues to grin.

The doorbell tinkles, ushering in Jack. "Sorry I'm late, Evie. Oh, good morning, Mr. O'Connor. One Declan's Special coming right up." Jack removes his coat, hat, and gloves and places them inside the office doorway. He grabs an apron and his baseball cap and goes to work getting the order together.

"That's okay, Jack." Evie turns back to Declan and his brunette. "That will be ten dollars and fifty-three cents, Mr. O'Connor." The satisfaction of ending the encounter causes an unavoidable small smile to form on Evie's face.

Declan hands her a twenty as his grin begins to falter.

"Thank you. See you next Monday." Evie turns on her heel to go back to her office as Jack hands over the two coffees and danishes.

The doorbell tinkles again and the brunette's giggle fades as the door closes behind them. Evie releases the breath she only now realizes she's holding. Declan always makes her fidget, and his parade of women is infuriating. She clenches her fists, trying to release some of the built up tension that his visit brought. Even though she's Southern, born and raised, there's only so much politeness she can muster, and Declan's visits exhaust her reserves. He only comes in on Monday mornings, and if she's lucky, Jack is around to take the order and deal with the bimbos. At least she doesn't have to think of him again until next Monday. She unclenches her fists as she sits behind her desk, only to then have her thoughts interrupted by baby blue eyes and a lopsided grin. "Ugh!"

Chapter Two

*H*ow does she continuously get under my skin?" Declan sighs and attempts to finish the email he started a half an hour before. "Now I'm just talkin' to m'self." He shakes his head and clicks send, hoping for the best.

"Mr. O'Connor?"

"Yes, Misti?" Declan's assistant peeks her head into his office. "Come in."

"I just wanted to remind you about the Christmas party and gift baskets. You never gave me the information of the bakery you wanted to use so that I could place an order, sir." Misti smiles at him.

Momentarily distracted by Misti's low neckline and tight skirt, Declan's gaze moves to the Young Entrepreneurs magazine framed on his wall over Misti's shoulder. This issue contains the article that lists his monetary worth and achievements, which his grandmother had framed. He shakes his head. "Thank ya for remindin' me, love." He winks and pulls his wallet out of his back pocket. He flips through the various business cards until he finds Evie's. Staring down at the baby blue card with Sweet Spot Bakery in big script letters, he flips it over repeatedly while picturing the petite, spitfire redhead. "Just give me the list of the sweets we need, and I'll give the shop a ring."

"Oh, okay." Misti hands over a sheet of paper from inside the yellow file folder she always carries close to her spilling cleavage.

"Thanks. Is that all?" He watches Misti as she clutches her folder to her chest, pressing her breasts higher, and slowly begins to sashay back out of the office.

She turns and leans over to pick up a non-existent item and slowly stands back up, offering him a spectacular view of her cleavage. The view leaves nothing to the imagination. "You wanted me to remind you of your grandmother's arrival. Her flight lands at 9:23 tomorrow evening. I've arranged for her car service for the month she's in town." Misti steps completely out of the office.

"Thanks, love." He stops himself from winking as he watches Misti smile and shut the door. He rubs his forehead with one hand and his gaze drifts over to his cell phone. Eight missed calls. Picking up the phone, he scrolls through the names, all women. They either want to set up a dinner with him, which they hope will lead to more, or they want to pick up where they left off and continue the affair. He deletes all of the voice messages without listening to them and then deletes all of the missed calls. It's easier to ignore them than to explain his lack of interest. After three years of endless women, maybe it's time for something more.

He picks up the business card and stares at it again, but he doesn't see the blue card, only the bright green eyes that crinkle at the corners when the owner smiles. Shaking his head, he shoves the card back into the wallet after noting the closing hour.

Chapter Three

"Yes, Mother, it was a lovely dinner." Evie holds the phone to her ear with one hand, while the other hand rubs her temple.

"Julia's son, Mark, is moving back to Roswell. Isn't that wonderful news? You two used to play together as kids. You know, he's single. I know Julia would love for you two to get together." Evie can picture her mother sitting at the kitchen table in her childhood home with a list of eligible men held tightly in her grasp, hoping her extremely single daughter will be interested in one of her carefully selected choices.

"If I remember correctly, Mother, Mark is gay. I think Julia needs to come to terms with that instead of pawning him off on the single women she knows." Her hand still holding her head, Evie drags her hand down her face, stifling a groan.

"Oh! I thought that was just a rumor. Well, heavens, let's scratch him off."

So there really is a list.

"I really don't think you should be worried about my dating life. I can do this on my own. Please, let me handle my love life, Mother." Evie waits for the irritation to explode from her mother.

"Well! I am only trying to help, dear. I hate to see you so sad and lonely. I will keep my mouth shut from now on. Not another word. You know Sarah's daughter who is twenty-four, three years younger than you, I might add, is already pregnant with her second child. Tick tock, Evie." Her mother tries to twist that knife, but she doesn't help her cause.

"I know my age, Mother, and, yes, let's discuss Lizzie. I don't need to remind you that this pregnancy is her *third*, Mother. Remember, she had a baby at sixteen. So, I think Lizzie's breeding isn't relevant." That little reminder thrills Evie. Triumph!

"I'm not arguing with you, Evie. I'm merely pointing out that people your age are already married and having children.

It has been, what? Three years since you broke it off with Colin? But, that shouldn't make you sad, my dear. We'll find someone for you!" Clearly, her mother is going to ignore her previous promise of not speaking of Evie's love life.

"Colin cheated on me with my best friend, Mother."

"Yes, yes, dear, like I said, three years. But, don't worry, I'll find someone of marriage quality. So, chin up, sweetie."

"I'm not the one who is sad about my marital status," Evie mumbles.

"What was that dear? What did you say? Speak up."

Evie hears a knocking coming from the front of the shop. She glances at the clock on the office wall. It's one minute to closing. Jack must have locked the doors early. "Mother, I need to go. A last minute customer is here. I'll talk to you later. Love you. Bye." She hangs up the phone after her mother's goodbye and reminder to call her again soon.

She turns off her desk light and walks out of her office as Jack exits the kitchen, investigating the same knock. The street lights are bright enough that she can just make out a figure standing in front of the shop door.

Jack unlocks the door and cracks it open as he peers around. "Mr. O'Connor, what are you doing here so late?"

"I apologize. I thought I made it in time. Am I too late? Can I still place an order?"

Evie immediately recognizes the Irish brogue. Jack steps to the side so that Declan can walk into the bakery.

Standing at the counter, Evie frowns as Declan makes his way to her. "Is there something wrong, Mr. O'Connor?"

"I apologize for being an arse, but I tried to arrive before closing…" Declan's eyes momentarily glaze over before shaking his head and focusing back on Evie. "I'm being rude. I'll come back tomorrow." He starts to turn away to leave.

Evie reaches out her hand, almost touching his arm. "No. That's okay. You're here now. What can I help you with?"

"I need to place an order. This can wait until tomorrow. I got held up in rush hour traffic. I'm sorry." He turns to walk back out.

"It's okay. Please, come sit down." Evie points to one of

the small circular tables opposite the counter and display cases.

Declan pulls out a chair and gestures for Evie to sit. Once she complies, he walks to the other side of the table and takes a seat. "First, call me Declan. I need to place a Christmas order, and I know it's late to be doin' that. Do ya think ya can fit in another one?"

"What do you need and by when?" Evie shifts in her seat. Declan's ruggedness, his scruff and purposefully messy hair, are at odds with his polished and fashionable dress, yet together, they add to the allure of this man. When she adds his seductive, Irish drawl, she has to shove her hands under her legs to prevent any embarrassing fidgeting. His sky blue eyes and their intense stare make one feel special and unique, which adds to his charm. It's no wonder he's able to attract gorgeous women into his bed on a weekly basis. Although he's still wearing his winter coat, she can see the expertly tailored dark gray suit underneath. It fits snugly to his athletic build. Too snugly.

Her mother's pestering pops up in her mind, but Declan isn't the dating type. He would impress the socks off her mother though. She mentally starts ticking off his assets. Gorgeous, owns his own architectural firm, smart, featured in the Young Entrepreneur magazine, gorgeous... Did she already list that?

Declan clears his throat, drawing her attention from her list to his face. His expression is amused as he waits for her answer.

Evie pushes the thought of dating Declan from her mind. "I'm sorry. What did you say?" Her cheeks begin to heat when she realizes she's been caught perusing his body. Stupid lists. She can only imagine how red she must look to him, which makes her cheeks feel even warmer.

"I need desserts for a party of 100 guests in three weeks, and I would like fifty gift baskets made up for some of my clientele. I will need the baskets in a week. Can ya do that with such a short notice?" Declan gives her a lopsided grin, which deepens her blush. Thank goodness her hands are still stuffed securely under her legs.

"Mr. O'Connor, I mean, Declan, we would be happy to take care of your order. Today is your lucky day." At the quirk of his eyebrows, her blush intensifies. "What I meant to say is, we are available to fill the order. Is there anything in particular you want in the baskets or for the party?"

"No, just a selection of treats will be fine." Declan stands up and rights his coat. "Will ya be needin' anything from me? I don't want to keep ya from your fella."

Evie stands up to walk him out. "Oh, just a deposit, and I don't have a fella… umm… boyfriend." She walks over to the register to take his deposit and finalize the details in writing. *Boyfriend?* She slides her hand off the counter and pushes it into her stomach, trying to stop the flutters.

Chapter Four

Declan glances at his watch. It's fifteen minutes until closing. He pushes opens the shop door. Once he reaches the counter, Evie comes out of the kitchen wiping her hands on a towel. "Evenin', Evie." He gives her his most charming smile as he studies her face.

"Hello, Declan. Can I help you?" Evie frowns at him, seemingly unmoved by his smile.

Smile gone, he clears his throat. "I thought about what ya asked on Monday." At Evie's confused look, he continues. "The question about wantin' anything special in the gift baskets."

"Oh, okay. Did you come up with something?" Evie brushes a loose red tendril out of her face, leaving a fresh flour smudge on her cheek.

A smile tugs at his lips as he clasps his hand behind his back, the urge to brush away the flour almost too tempting. "My nan always cooked and baked for us kids. Two of my favorite things were soda farls and gypsy creams."

"Hmm… I haven't heard of these. What are they like?"

He has her full attention. Her gaze sharpens at the challenge, intrigues her, as he hoped. The thrill of the small win sends electricity through his body and straight to his groin, as an image of her in his bed appears in his mind. He clears his throat, focusing back on their conversation. "The soda farls are a bread-like scone, very dense. The gypsy creams are a sandwich cookie. Both are excellent with tea." His mouth waters, and he swallows as he thinks about the gypsy creams. When did the idea of licking off the icing become sensual? The image of Evie, with her deep red hair flowing around her, teasing him with the strands barely covering her nipples takes him back to his bedroom. Now, he wants to lick the icing off what he suspects are pert pink nipples. He stifles a groan. *Get a grip, you dope.*

Unaware of his inner turmoil, Evie gives him a determined smile. "That sounds delightful. Come with me." She crooks her finger and turns to go back in the kitchen.

This time, Declan groans out loud. He shakes his head, determined to think straight, and not straight to the bedroom. He follows Evie through the kitchen and into a back room. The small, rectangular, closet-like room is solid bookshelves except for the furthest end, which has a desk that is as wide as the shortest width of the room.

Evie points to the desk. "Have a seat. I'm going to pull out a few cookbooks."

He stands over by the desk, placing his coat down and leaving the chair available for her, as he watches her scan the collection. "Are all of these books...cookbooks?"

"Pretty much. You never know what people will want to order, or what wild idea I may get." Evie looks over at him as a breathy giggle escapes her lips. "I'm a bit of a collector, I guess." She shrugs her shoulders and goes back to searching.

This is Evie in her element. Declan is watching someone completely at ease and happy with her career. She glows. It reminds him of himself, which only intrigues him more. "I have to admit, in my office at home, I have quite the collection as well." Evie, with a raised eyebrow, looks over her shoulder as she reaches up to grab a book on the top shelf. He walks the three steps to her side and reaches up to retrieve the volume just out of her grasp. "The only difference is my collection is of architectural magazines, journals, and drawings. When I'm feeling uninspired with a project, I only have to look at something from my collection to make that connection again." He hands her the book.

Evie stares at him, her eyes momentarily wide. A small smile creeps up at the corners of her mouth. Her emerald green eyes sharpen in awareness. "I know what you mean." She sweeps her available arm at the filled shelves. "These are my inspiration. No two recipes are the same." She opens the dusty tome and flips to the index. Declan watches as her finger slides down the page, looking for a recipe to suit his needs. "Is soda farls like the Irish soda bread?"

"Yes and no. It's cooked in a skillet instead of the oven and has very few ingredients." Declan watches her read through a couple of pages. He moves to stand beside her and reads over her shoulder. She smells like vanilla and something fruity. It makes him curious if she always smells like the bakery or if she has her own sweet scent. At the end of the second page, he sees the recipe she's searching for. He steps closer while reaching around her shoulder and points. His free hand holds on to the other side of the cover, grazing her hand and effectively trapping her between him and the cookbook.

Evie tenses at his touch, but doesn't move or say anything. She turns her head to where he is pointing, and a few moments later, she nods her head as she mumbles, "Thanks."

Declan releases his grasp on the cookbook, freeing her from his makeshift trap. He watches her walk toward the desk and lay the book down, opened to the recipe. Evie pauses, looking down at the book. He half expects her to ask him to leave. He could just make out her deep intake of breath as she turns and meets his gaze.

"Tell me how you decided to move to America and open your own company?" Evie walks to another wall of books and starts a new search.

Declan, surprised by the question, searches for the right words. "How does anyone come to that decision? I graduated from university and wanted a new challenge. I had visited America several times in my life because of extended family livin' here. So, I made the decision rather easily. I packed up and moved across the pond, as they say. I applied and was accepted into a graduate program. I worked part time and went to university part time. Once I received my duel master's degrees, I knew it was time for a new challenge. That challenge became openin' my own company. I had the experience, so nothin' was holdin' me back. I think I did okay for m'self." Declan smirks, knowing his words sound cocky. "What of ya? Did ya always want to own a bakery?"

Evie smiles to herself while flipping through pages of another cookbook. "Yes." She replaces the book on the shelf and pulls out a new one.

"And?" Declan leans against one of the walls of shelves, crossing his arms and one leg over the other. "That can't be all to the story."

"Well there isn't much to it. As far back as I can remember, I knew I would open a bakery. I went to college and earned my MBA, and then I went to culinary school. Once out, my parents helped me by investing some money into opening Sweet Spot. And, here I am. I don't have any Young Entrepreneurs magazine recognition, but I do well for myself."

"Is there anyone who hasn't seen that fecking article?" Declan reaches up and rubs the back of his neck.

"Probably not. It was a great article. You should be proud." Evie flips to a page in the new cookbook.

"I am proud of what I have achieved, but I didn't want the silliness of my worth and such plastered over magazines."

Evie snorts. "I'm sure the attention hasn't been that bad." Declan can tell by the scarlet settling onto her face, she means the parade of women.

"You would be surprised," Declan mumbles. *Will she ever see past the women?*

Evie lays the new cookbook out on the desk and starts to untie her apron. "Well, this has been a lovely chat, but we should get going."

Declan follows Evie into the kitchen where she hangs up her apron and turns off lights. She grabs her things from the office while he pulls his coat over his shoulders. "Have you tried the new diner on the corner?"

"Yes. They're great." Evie pulls on her coat and gloves.

"What's good there? I think I may try it out one night." Declan waits as she flips off the main light and he holds open the door.

Evie turns to lock the door. "The chicken and dumplings are divine. Oh. And, the Shepherd's Pie is great too." Evie stops in her tracks, mumbles under her breath, and turns back to unlock the door. "I forgot something inside. I'll make a trial of both recipes tomorrow, so stop by tomorrow night before closing for a taste test." Evie smiles at him as she walks back in to the bakery. "Goodnight."

"Oh, okay. Goodnight, Evie." Declan, hiding his disappointment in having to leave without her, turns on his heel, shoves a hand into his pants pocket to retrieve the key fob, and walks up to his car. Pausing at the car door, his stomach growls, he glances down the street toward the glowing windows of the diner and changes his mind. He drops the key fob back into his pocket and heads to the diner.

Chapter Five

After watching Declan walk away, Evie turns her back to the door, leans against it, closes her eyes, and hugs herself. When Declan's arms were around her, it had taken every ounce of her willpower to not lean into him. She wouldn't have minded turning around and running her hands up his chest and around his neck, bringing his head down so their lips could meet. And, his scent… He smells like a man fresh out of a cologne ad.

"Dear lord," Evie says on a groan. He's just what she has always imagined in a man. He has a bit of scruff, a little more than a five o'clock shadow, but less than a beard. He never wears a tie. His immaculately pressed button-down shirts are always unbuttoned on top, which he wears under a dark gray or dark blue suit. She shivers from thoughts of running her fingers through his messy, chocolate brown hair while staring into his baby blues.

Evie shakes herself out of her reverie. She walks back to the office and grabs her purse. Although not intentional, she's glad she convinced him not to wait. He weaves a tempting spell, and she's starting to get wrapped up in it. She reminds herself, again, that Declan is not a man who sticks around longer than a weekend and probably not someone who would be interested in her.

A buzzing in her purse stops her before leaving the shop. She digs around until she finds her cell phone at the bottom. Seeing that it's Jack, she answers.

"Hey, Jack. What's up?"

"Hey, Evie. Sorry for calling you so late, but I forgot to ask you earlier if it would be okay to take off this Friday too?"

"So, you need Friday and Saturday off?" She walks to the kitchen to look at the order schedule for Monday. Only Declan's order was written in.

"Yeah, I know Ashley won't be there Saturday either, but she will still be in on Friday."

"That's fine, Jack. We only have Declan's order for Monday morning, which I already planned to do on Sunday." Saying Declan's name reminds her of his embrace again, sending fresh warmth coursing through her.

"Thank you, Evie. I'll see you in the morning. Bye."

"Goodnight, Jack." She ends the call, drops her phone in her purse, and slides her gloves on.

Stepping back out into the cold air is a blessing, as the warmth of her thoughts are causing her to overheat. She has a standing order at the diner every Wednesday night for her favorite chicken and dumplings, and tonight will not be the exception.

Evie walks up to the counter of the diner and waves over Marcy. "Hey, Marcy. Are the chicken and dumplings ready?"

"Hey, sugar. Not yet. Cook had to make up a fresh batch. It should be ready soon. Have a seat and I'll get you a hot chocolate." The deep southern rasp of the gray-haired woman's voice brings a smile to Evie's lips. Shoving her pencil back behind her ear, Marcy returns the smile and goes back to the other customers.

Evie is about to sit at the counter when she hears, "Evie?"

There is no mistaking the voice with the smooth Irish brogue. Her pulse quickens as she turns toward the voice and is met with a wide grin and blue eyes. "Hi Declan. I didn't realize you were coming here tonight."

"I couldn't pass up the Shepherd's Pie recommendation. Please, come join me." Declan points to the empty booth seat across from him.

She can't tell him no without seeming rude, especially since her order isn't ready. "Okay, thanks." Evie pulls off her coat and gloves and slides into the booth. "I'm glad you're enjoying the pie. It's my second favorite here. Oh, and the chocolate pie. Cook won't tell me his recipe." Evie makes a mock sad face, drawing a chuckle out of Declan.

"I know what I'll be havin' for dessert." He winks at her

while shoveling another fork-full of food in his mouth.

Marcy brings the hot chocolate, but Evie's blush is keeping her more than warm at the moment. "Cook said it would be five more minutes, sugar."

"Thank you, Marcy." Evie looks up at Marcy, but the woman's attention is focused on the gorgeous man across from her.

"Tell me, sugar, where are you from?"

"Northern Ireland, love." Declan winks at her and goes back to shoveling. Marcy sighs and walks back to the counter.

"I think Marcy is in love with you." Evie bites her lip to stop the giggle from bubbling out.

"I get that a lot after that article. Makes me want to gamble away my money." Declan frowns at his pie. "Sometimes."

"It can't—" Evie's sentence is lost as a loud female voice interrupts her.

"Declan? Declan O'Connor? You dirty man. You never called me back. How's a girl supposed to move on from you, Declan?" A gorgeous blonde wearing a tight mini dress and six inch heels struts up to the table.

Evie is stunned, momentarily mesmerized by the blonde's striking beauty. She watches as the blonde slowly sits down next to Declan, sliding as close to him as she can get.

"Barbie. Nice to see ya. I apologize, but I have been extremely busy. I will make sure to give ya a ring soon." Declan looks back at Evie. "Ya were sayin', Evie?"

Evie is at a loss for words. He can't possibly be interested in talking to her now that Barbie is plastered against him. Really, who names their child Barbie? Before she has an opportunity to form words, Marcy walks up with her takeout order.

"All set, sugar. Just come up to the register when you're ready." Marcy gives Barbie a once over and snorts as she walks away.

"Will ya stay, Evie?" Declan smiles at her as Barbie rubs his back and gives Evie a death stare.

"I really should be going. Thank you for asking. I'll see you later." Before he has a chance to respond, she bolts out of the seat. She throws a ten dollar bill on the counter and calls out to Marcy. "Thanks, Marcy. See you later." Marcy nods in acknowledgment as Evie rushes out the door.

Chapter Six

The tinkling doorbell draws Evie's attention away from her supply ordering. She glances at the clock. Almost closing. She strains her ears for the voices of Jack and the customer, expecting to hear Declan. She isn't disappointed.

"Evie wanted me to taste her test batches. Is she here?" Declan's voice filters through her closed door.

"Yes, she is. Let me go get her," Jack says.

Jack's dirty blond hair covered head pokes in through her office door moments later. "Evie? Mr. O'Connor is here for the taste test."

"Thank you, Jack. The samples are in the cookbook room. Can you grab them for me, please?" Evie clicks the purchase button on her last order. After putting away the receipts, she walks out to the shop counter. "Hi, Declan." She starts to grin, but then an image of gorgeous Barbie enters her mind and her smile falters.

"'Ello, Evie. Did ya enjoy your dinner last night? I'm sorry ya had to leave." Declan gives her his charming lopsided grin.

"Yes, thank you. Did you have a, um, pleasant evening too?" Evie tries again to give him a smile, but she's afraid it will end up being as a sneer.

"Well the company was lackin', but the food was good. Thank ya." Declan's scrutiny makes her fidget with her apron and blush, which seems to cause his smile to widen.

What a gorgeous smile. *Evie, focus.*

"Here you go, Mr. O'Connor." Jack places a Christmas tray with the fresh treats on the counter between Declan and Evie. Jack returns to the kitchen to finish cleaning up for the night.

"They smell divine, Evie." Declan's tongue darts out and licks his lips as his hand hovers over the tray. "I can't decide what to try first." Declan glances up at Evie, smiles again, and goes back to staring at the tray.

"Try the soda farls first, I think."

"Do ya have some jam?" Declan grabs one of the triangular pieces of bread and starts to split it in half.

"Um, yes. I'll go get it." Evie turns to walk into the kitchen and almost slams into Jack.

"Sorry. I forgot to bring the strawberry jam." Jack hands her the jar and goes back to the kitchen.

"Thanks," Evie calls after Jack. "Here you are." She hands over the open jar of jam.

"Mmmm… this is delicious Evie. Have you tried it?" Declan's eyes are closed and his face betrays his bliss. Evie stares at the emotion on his face and can't help but grin.

"Yes, but not with the jam." Evie scoops up a spoonful of jam and takes a large bite. Delightful. She needs to add this to her menu, for sure. She closes her eyes and savors the bite. "Mmm… delicious." She lathers on more jam and takes another bite, licking her lips. After finishing the last bite, she starts sucking the jam off her fingers and looks up at Declan. He is staring at her with an intensity that sends a chill up her spine.

Declan's gaze darts over to the corner of her mouth. "Ya have a bit of jam, right…" Declan reaches his finger up to the corner of her mouth and touches her at the same moment her tongue darts out to lick the jam.

Heat flows to Evie's cheeks. "Thank you," she says without meeting his gaze.

Declan clears his throat. "Shall we try the gypsy creams?"

"Yes, please." Evie musters her courage and looks up at him. The heat and intensity that meets her gaze makes her cheeks feel like they are blistering, she is so hot.

He bites into one of the cookies and frowns.

"What's wrong?" Evie grabs a cookie and bites into it. The crunchy sweetness is still the same from when she tried one earlier.

"Hmm… They are good, don't misunderstand me, but they are not what my nan makes." Declan finishes up the last bite of cookie.

"Oh," Evie frowns. "I can try another recipe."

"Ya don't mind?" Declan actually blushes.

"No. You're the customer, and the customer is always right. I'll do some more digging."

"My nan is comin' back into town tonight after visiting a friend, so I will get her recipe and bring it by tomorrow mornin'. Will that be acceptable?" Declan looks like a kid in a candy shop, his excitement barely contained.

"Yes! That will be great. I love collecting old recipes." She clasps her hands together, preventing her child-like clapping and the ensuing embarrassment.

"Great. I'll see ya tomorrow mornin'." He pulls his coat back on, winks at her, and leaves.

Evie fans herself. She needs to check what the thermostat is set to. She's been overheated for two nights in a row.

Chapter Seven

Declan parks in front of Sweet Spot. Walking up to the shop's door, he wipes his palms on the outside of his long trench coat. A woman hasn't caused his palms to sweat since he was a teenager. Put it on the list of ailments Evie produces.

Evie greets him at the counter with a smile, her dark red hair not yet up in her standard work ponytail. The crinkles at the corner of her emerald green eyes always make him happy. The mere presence, hell, even the thought of her, makes his pulse quicken and sends blood straight south. He either needs to sleep with her or find some alternative to get her out of his system. But once the thought of sleeping with her to end this obsession filters out, it's replaced with the fear of never being able to get over her.

She intrigues him. While every woman he meets throws herself at him, Evie barely notices him. But her fidgeting, which appears to be motivated by his presence alone, makes him believe that she is aware of him far more than she lets on. Now, how to convince her to come home with him?

"Mornin,' Evie." Declan pulls a folded piece of paper out of the interior pocket of his coat. "Here is my nan's recipe for the gypsy creams. Hopefully ya can work with this." He hands it over.

Evie studies the paper as her eyebrows knit together. "Wow. She doesn't like to use measurements, does she?"

Declan snorts. "She has been makin' this recipe for as long as I can remember and longer, so her measurements are probably habit. A little more of a challenge for ya, I apologize."

"Challenge accepted." Evie's eyes twinkle with confidence.

Her attitude and determined expression draw a bark of laughter from him.

"Thank you for this." Evie waves the paper in the air. "I'll work on it today. Feel free to stop by tonight to try them, if you like." Evie's expression changes from determined to unsure.

Maybe he does have a chance with her. He needs to bring out his A-game. "I wouldn't miss seein' ya and tryin' your new creation for anything." Declan gives her what he hopes is his best smolder, while still smiling. He's rewarded with her scarlet cheeks and fidgeting hands. Perfect.

"Um, well, I'll see you tonight then. Thank you again for bringing this by." Evie's cheeks turn a deeper shade of scarlet.

Time to sink this ball. "Anything for ya, darlin'." Declan winks. He hears her gasp and knows he's made a hole-in-one. He hopes today goes by quickly.

Chapter Eight

Evie puts the mop back in the closet. She grabs her bag from the office, sits at one of the shop tables, and pulls out a book. She scans the page for where she left off and finds the steamy kissing scene between the two main characters. Why did she read the male main character's voice in an Irish accent when he was born and raised in New York? She really needs to get Declan, his delectable lips, and that sexy accent out of her mind. Slamming the book shut, she glances at the clock. It's five minutes until closing. She tries to ignore the disappointment as she shoves the book back in her bag and gets up to start locking everything up. "You shouldn't be disappointed, silly."

"Why are ya disappointed, Evie?" a familiar male voice replies.

Evie releases a shriek as she starts to twirl around at the sound of the unexpected voice. Her foot catches on a chair leg mid-turn and she tries to catch herself. She reaches out to grab the chair, but her fingers can't find purchase, sending her careening toward another table. She closes her eyes bracing for the impact and the pain. Instead of hitting the table, though, she slams into a hard, muscular chest. Opening her eyes on impact, she wraps her arms around Declan's chest to right herself and is greeted with a groan. One strong arm secures her to him while the other stops their falling momentum on the table behind him.

"Sorry, I didn't mean to scare ya." Declan's other arm, no longer needing to hold them up, joins the first in securing her to him.

Her ear is pressed against Declan's chest, listening to the tempo of his heart. It double thumps quickly, the only sign of his exertion and quick reflexes. She breathes in deeply, smelling the mixture of cologne and laundry detergent. She lets go of her embrace and starts to pull away, while swallowing the moan that almost escapes her lips. "Thank you for catching me. I hope you didn't hurt yourself."

Declan slowly releases her and drags his hands to Evie's

upper arms, preventing her from moving too far from him. "I'm fine. I apologize for scaring ya. I didn't realize ya hadn't heard me enter the shop." Declan gives her one of his charming lop-sided grins.

"I guess I wasn't paying attention. I was focused on closing up." Declan drops his hands and steps away leaving her disappointed by the lack of contact.

"Is it too late to taste test? I could come back tomorrow if ya want to get home." A little frown creases at Declan's eye-brows.

"No, it's fine. Come with me to the kitchen." Evie rushes over to the shop door and locks it, then gestures with her finger for him to follow.

Evie opens the small container of cookies and holds it out for him to take one. Declan grabs one and inspects it. "It certain-ly looks like my nan's creams." He smiles at her and takes a bite.

Evie watches Declan as he chews and continues to in-spect the cookie. Even chewing, he is sex on a stick. He holds the cookie up to his mouth and licks the cream filling and then his lips. Dear Lord, how she wants to lick those lips. She chews on her bottom lip, trying to stop the tingling void.

Declan glances at her as he brings the cookie up to his lips. Before the cookie makes it to his mouth, he lets out a long sigh. "Bloody hell," he mumbles.

Her gaze follows his hand as he puts the remains of the cookie on the kitchen counter, and then he's before her, those same hands reaching up to her face, drawing her in as his head comes down to meet hers.

Evie's eyes instinctively close when his moistened lips touch hers. Declan kisses softly at first, his tongue lightly touch-ing where her lips meet, trying to convince her to open up to him. She sighs and runs her hands up his strong chest to his neck. She shoves her fingers into his hair and opens her mouth to him. He deepens his kiss, ripping a moan from her chest. He slides his hands down from her face to her hips, and he then wraps his arms around her waist, crushing her to him.

Their tongues tentatively touch each other, letting the heat slowly build. Declan breaks their kiss, trailing down Evie's chin to her throat where he licks, sucks, and nibbles. A chill running up her spine sends a shiver through her body. He moans in response.

He slides his hands from her back up her sides, and picking her up under her arms, he sits her up on the cool, stainless steel kitchen counter. He opens her legs and stands between them, going back to work on her neck as she shoves her fingers into his soft hair again.

Declan makes his way to each of her collarbones, licking the dip in between them. He reaches up between their bodies and unbuttons the buttons of her blouse, opening her shirt down to her breasts. He continues lavishing kisses on her skin until he reaches the edge of her bra. He pulls the shirt wide, exposing both satin-covered breasts, and leans down to suck the tightened nub of one through the thin material.

Evie's head falls back as desire surges through her body. She bites her lip to keep from groaning. Declan moves to the other breast, sending new waves of desire through her.

Declan releases the tormented nipple and pulls her off the counter letting her body slide down the length of him. The evidence of his desire drags up from the top of her thighs and settles at her stomach when her feet reach the floor. Declan groans at the contact. He grabs her face to give her one last deep kiss, rendering her senseless.

He breaks the kiss and holds her at arm's length. He squeezes his eyes shut, catching his breath. "I'm sorry. I shouldn't have done that."

Holding her shirt closed, Evie looks down, afraid to look at him. How had she lost control? She must be a terrible step down from the other women he's been with. She buttons up her shirt, trying to come up with something to say. "How are the cookies?" Her voice warbles, which makes her wince.

"The cookies?" Declan glances over at the container of cookies. "They are fine. Not quite how I remember them, but they are good. Do you mind if I take some to my nan?"

Evie nods her head, still not looking at him.

Declan leans down and looks into her face. "How much do I owe ya?"

Evie's eyebrows shoot up and her eyes widen, now looking squarely at Declan. "What?"

"How much do I owe ya for these cookies?" He points to the container of cookies.

"Oh. Don't worry about it." She blushes.

"Thank ya, Evie. Will ya be here tomorrow?" He brushes a loose tendril behind her ear.

She is stunned by the contact. "Um… yes."

Declan pushes her chin up to look at him. "I, unfortunately, have dinner plans, so I need to go. Thanks again." He leans in and pauses nose to nose. Still holding her chin, he rubs his thumb over her bottom lip, looks up at her eyes, and smiles. He leans in and gives her a tender kiss. He tears his mouth away and rests his forehead on hers. "I need to leave now before I won't be able to." He drags his head up and kisses her nose. As he pulls away, the muscles in his jaw begin to clench. Deflated, he turns on his heel and stalks out.

After hearing the door open and close, Evie sinks to the floor. "Stupid, Evie. Stupid, stupid, stupid. He's not interested in you. Hell, he's got a dinner date with another woman, and that doesn't even stop him from making out with you first. Stupid!"

Chapter Nine

The doorbell hits the glass as the customer leaves. Just inside the kitchen doorway, Evie is grabbing a stack of bags to restock underneath the counter at the register.

"Evie?"

Evie peaks her head out hoping her ears deceive her. They didn't.

"Hi, Declan."

She walks out with a stack of bags and stuffs them under the counter. When she stands, she can't stop herself from staring at him. He smirks while removing his aviator sunglasses. Her gaze makes a slow descent, starting at the intentionally messy hair, over his sky blue eyes, and pausing at the usual scruff on his face and throat. She continues on over his form fitting, gray, knit shirt with the buttons unbuttoned exposing a small smattering of hair on the muscular chest, over the black fashionably worn leather jacket, and ending at his olive green cargo pants.

By this point, her lips tingle and her nipples can cut glass, as the memories of his kissing expertise makes her body crave his touch. She's only ever seen him in suits. Today, though, he's wearing casual attire, and he's even more gorgeous, if that's even possible. *Damn.* She licks her lips. The movement draws Declan's attention to her mouth. He glances back up to her eyes, his gaze sharpening.

Movement out of the corner of her eye draws her attention away and she realizes that Declan isn't alone. She smiles at the elderly woman. "Good afternoon, ma'am."

"Good afternoon." The elderly woman gives her a lopsided grin that strongly resembles the man next to her.

"Evie, this is my nan, Siobhan O'Connor. Nan, this is Evie Barnes." Declan puts his arm around his grandmother and guides her up to the counter.

"Nice to meet you, ma'am." Evie shakes her hand.

"Nonsense. Call me Nan." Nan gives Evie a devilish grin, not unlike her grandson's.

Evie giggles. "Okay, Nan."

"Me luvie tells me, ya are makin' him my gypsy creams for some holiday baskets."

"Yes, I am." Evie looks at Declan, chuckling, amused by his grandmother's use of his nickname. Declan shakes his head and laughs.

"Well I tried those creams last night, and yer measurements be off." Nan grabs Evie's hand and pats it. "I want ya to come over tonight for dinner, and I will show ya how it's done the way my luvie likes."

"I can just bring you back to the kitchen, and you can show me there." Evie points the thumb of her free hand over her shoulder.

"Nonsense. Ya come over for dinner. I won't be havin' no for an answer." Nan pats Evie's hand again and turns to Declan. "Come along, luvie. Let's leave the lady to her business. We be in the way here." Nan starts waddling to the shop door.

Declan pulls out a business card and pen from his leather jacket. He leans over the counter and starts writing. "Sorry about that. When my nan gets an idea in her head, there's no deterrin' her." He slides his business card over to her. "Here's my address. The house is a couple blocks away from here. Is seven o'clock okay with ya?" Declan gives her the family lopsided grin while his eyes twinkle.

Evie's throat goes dry, and she's only able to nod.

"Great. See ya later, Evie." Declan winks and rushes to hold the door for his grandmother.

How will she make it through dinner in one piece? Get it together, Evie. Yes, he's gorgeous, but you don't have to melt every time he smiles at you.

Chapter Ten

At five minutes after seven o'clock, the doorbell rings. Controlling his excitement, Declan answers the door. Declan clears his throat. "Hi, Evie."

"Evening, Declan. I brought some wine to go with dinner. I wasn't sure what we were having so I decided on a Shiraz." Evie's voice is a little strained, and she doesn't quite meet his gaze.

"Sounds good. Thank you. Come in. I promise not to bite… yet." A soft chuckle escapes, as he tries to ease her nerves.

Evie rolls her eyes and walks in.

"Nan's almost ready with dinner. Let's have some wine." Declan leads the way to the kitchen.

"Hello, Nan—"

Nan swoops in for a tight hug. Evie's words are cut off as a swoosh of air is squeezed out in their place. "'Ello, Evie! I'm so glad ya be joinin' us tonight."

"Thank you for having me." Evie smiles and is finally released from Nan's grip.

"We be havin' pork, potatoes, and carrots tonight. Then we'll be havin' the gypsy creams for dessert." Nan shifts her focus back to making dinner, glass of wine in hand.

"Sounds delightful." Evie takes the offered wine and steps out of the kitchen, into the family room. She looks around the open space, admiring the wall hangings and knick-knacks. "You have a nice place, Declan. Very warm and homey." She smiles at him over her shoulder.

"Thank ya, Evie. Come, let me show ya my office. Ya can see my collection." He grabs Evie's hand and laces his fingers through hers.

She stiffens for a moment, but relents and walks with him, hand in hand.

He stops at his office door and gestures for her to enter first. He leans against the door frame, not fully entering the room, and watches her take it all in. She walks over to the large mahogany desk and absently drags a lone finger across the top edge while looking at the books and other items crammed into the floor to ceiling dark wood shelves. She walks along the furthest wall of shelves, looking at everything that's at eye level, occasionally stopping and pulling something out. He can't help but smile. She is absolutely stunning, more so than any of the other women he's been with. She's petite and slim, but curvy in all the right places. She's wearing tight jeans that accentuate those lovely curves, all the way down to her black ballerina-like shoes. Her black, low-cut sweater is a little looser than her jeans, but there is no denying her luscious curves don't skimp on top either.

Declan licks his lips, remembering getting a hold of those luscious breasts. His pants feel a bit snug, so he adjusts himself while Evie's head is turned, and tries to stop thinking about her breasts.

Evie stops as she reaches the corner with a plush leather chaise jutting into the room. She runs her hand along the soft leather, walking around the chaise. She tucks a strand of her deep red, breast-length hair, and all he can see is her lying in his plush bed, her hair flowing out over the pillows waiting for him to join her. He stifles a groan and turns to look down the hall. It's time to go back before he decides to shut the door and show her what he stopped himself from doing last night.

"I think dinner is ready. Come, let's eat. I'm starvin'." Declan reaches out his hand, waiting for her to take it.

Evie frowns, but walks over to take his hand. "I'm hungry too. It smells so good."

Walking down the hallway, he can't help but notice how well her hand fits in his grasp. She's the perfect fit in every aspect he can see, and he's sure that will translate into other areas as well. He especially enjoys that her head only comes to his shoulder, instead of being almost as tall as him like the others. In fact, thinking about those women makes his stomach churn.

He really needs to convince Evie to give him a shot.

Chapter Eleven

While the first batch of cookies are in the oven, the three of them sit in the family room, enjoying after dinner cocktails.

"So, ya goin' to remember how to do this fer tomorrow, Evie?" Nan takes a swig of her whiskey.

"Yes, I definitely have it down now. Thank you for taking the time to show me. And, thank you for cooking such a lovely dinner." Evie takes another swallow of her wine. She is definitely going to feel this in the morning. She doesn't know how she is going to get home, either.

"Good. Well, luvies, I'll be gettin' home then." Nan throws back the remaining contents of her glass and stands up. She makes her way to the kitchen to leave her glass.

Declan follows her to the kitchen. "Nan, you're not leavin' now, are ya? Don't ya and Evie have some more bakin' to do?"

"Aww hell, luvie, she's got it now. No need for me. Besides, my driver is already waitin' outside. I think ya two will do just fine on yer own." Nan winks at Declan and pats him on the chest. "See ya later, Evie." She turns and walks toward the front of the house.

"Bye, Nan. Thank you," Evie calls after her as she walks to the kitchen to check the cookies.

Declan rejoins Evie after walking Nan to the car. "She said to tell ya she had a lovely time." He grabs his drink off the kitchen counter, walks over to the couch, and sits on the opposite side from Evie.

"It was fun. I really like your grandmother. I think she thinks we're dating." At Declan's confused look, she continues. "She told me how you've never introduced her to a girl in all of your thirty years, and that I must be very special." Evie releases a nervous laugh.

Declan studies her face before responding. He scoots closer to her on the couch, never breaking eye contact. "Evie, ya are special."

Evie chokes on her wine. "That's not what I mean, but thank you."

"I think your missin' the point, Evie. I think you're special, and," he takes a large swallow of his whiskey, "I want us to get to know each other better."

"You can't be serious. I'm sure that works on all of your other women, but I'm not interested in a fling, Declan." Evie gets up and starts pacing. "I need some coffee. Do you have any coffee?"

"Yes, of course." Declan gets up and walks to the kitchen. She follows him but doesn't enter the room. She stops in the dining room, with the table between them.

After starting the pot, he joins her in the dining room. "Evie, I'm serious. I'm not tryin' to get a fling out of ya." He starts to walk toward her.

"Stop. Just stop." Evie puts more space between them and walks around the table, away from him.

He looks hurt by her reaction. "Don't ya believe me?" He starts to slowly inch toward her.

"Declan, you have brought a new woman in to my bakery every Monday for over a year. And, if I'm not mistaken, you were doing the same thing long before you moved to this neighborhood. Where else do you have a Declan's Special?" She takes a side step away from him.

"How can I prove to ya that I'm serious? How do I woo ya?" Declan continues his slow creep toward her.

"I don't know. I don't know I can believe that you suddenly want to reform your womanizing ways. What about Barbie, or last night's date? If I say yes, you'll get bored with me within a day, just like all of the other women. And, what then? Are you going to buy me a Declan's Special?" Evie stops walking away from him, and now, he is standing next to her.

"Nothin' happened with Barbie. She's desperate and pathetic. If ya had stayed and joined me for dinner, ya would have seen me send her on her way. And last night, I had dinner with Nan." He leans in, smelling her hair. "Tell me, Evie. How can I win ya?" He whispers this into her ear as he brushes her hair away from her neck. He feathers light kisses down her throat.

Evie shivers at the contact. "This isn't disproving my preconceived notions."

"Yes, but I rather like the idea of this happening between us." He leans forward and starts to kiss her neck again. His hand, at her waist, starts to slowly move up. Reaching his destination, his finger and thumb pinch the tight nub of a nipple through her shirt.

Evie lets out a small moan. She turns fully toward him, and standing up on her toes, she reaches for his head and brings it down to hers. She immediately parts her lips and lets him invade. He wraps his arms around her and crushes her to him. Their tongues play and caress each other. His hands find the bottom edge of her shirt and pull it up, exposing the skin of her back and stomach. His gentle touch sends a shiver down her back, and she breaks the kiss.

She rests her forehead against his while letting their pulses slow down. "If you truly want to try this, then you have to act the perfect gentleman and also let me make the next move. But, I won't make it unless I really feel you are interested in longer than a weekend."

Declan picks up his head from hers and kisses her forehead. He pulls away from her, keeping her at arm's length. "Deal."

Chapter Twelve

$\mathcal{E}$ vie closes the oven door on the next batch of gypsy creams, as her cell phone begins to buzz and play her favorite Christmas carol. She glances at the caller ID and answers the call. "Hey, Declan."

"Afternoon, Evie. Come unlock the shop door. I've brought lunch."

"Okay." Evie ends the call and walks out to the front door. Declan sees her approaching and raises a full restaurant bag. He gives her a goofy grin while sucking on the straw in the drink he's holding.

Evie can't help but smile. When she issued her deal last night, she never expected Declan to follow through with it—and so soon. First, he followed her home last night to make sure she was safe, then he showed up with breakfast and coffee this morning before she went in to the bakery, and now, he's standing outside with lunch. Every time she expects him to kiss her or make some kind of move, he surprises her and stays away. He is definitely leaving the next move up to her.

Sitting down at one of the small tables, Declan pulls out the food boxes. "I hope ya like Chinese take-out."

"Yes, I do. It smells great." Evie picks up the containers as he pulls them out of the bag and peers into each, figuring out what he brought.

"This restaurant is a hidden gem. Their food is wonderful, but their eggrolls… just wait." Declan places the bag on another table and hands her a fork. "Dive in!"

After eating what she can honestly say is the best Chinese food she has ever had the pleasure of tasting, she lays her fork down and licks her fingers. "Where is this hidden gem?"

"That, Evie, is a secret. One I won't share with ya unless ya come on a date with me." Declan's eyes twinkle with mischief as he stuffs in another bite of food.

Quirking an eyebrow, Evie shakes her head and chuckles. "I'll think about it."

"How is the bakin' comin'? Almost done?"

As if on cue, the buzzer for the cookies in the oven starts chirping. "One more batch in the oven, and then I'm done." Evie stuffs the last bite of eggroll into her mouth and makes her way to the kitchen. She places the last batch into the oven and rejoins Declan at the table.

"Everythin' done now?" Declan leans back in his chair, watching her finish up her lunch and clean up her plate and fork.

"I need to spread on the icing and sandwich the cookies. Want to help me? I may even let you sneak a few cookies." Evie laughs at him when he jumps out of his chair.

Declan holds out his hand and, once she lays her hand in his, he drags her to the kitchen. "Ya don't have to ask me twice," he says over his shoulder.

He watches her make the first few sandwiched cookies. He eats a couple and then starts to help. As they finish icing the cookies, she can't help but scoop up some icing on her spatula and rub it on Declan's cheek. She starts laughing uncontrollably at his shocked expression.

"Bad decision, darlin'." Before Evie has a chance to move away, Declan wraps an arm around her waist. He scoops icing with his free hand and rubs it down her neck and exposed chest.

Evie squeals and squirms, trying to get free, but Declan's hold tightens. She grabs up some more icing in her hand and slaps his clean cheek with it and drags her hand down his neck.

A devilish grin breaks out on Declan's face as he growls at her and lowers his face to her neck. He licks her from her collar bone up to just below her ear.

A moan escapes Evie's throat as a shiver runs up her back. The mood immediately changes from playful to lustful.

Declan moves his head lower and starts licking from the edge of her shirt up to her chin. He continues to lick off all of the icing he spread on her.

Once he raises his head, she bends forward and starts sucking the icing off his neck. Between sucks and licks, Declan pushes her slowly toward a side table. He backs her all the way to the table and then swoops in and catches her mouth in a fiery kiss. Their tongues, which still taste like the icing, mingle. She breaks the kiss and licks his cheek.

"Mmmm… I think we need some chocolate." Evie scoots around him and makes a dash for the refrigerator. While she leans into the refrigerator, Declan comes up behind her, grabbing her hips, rubbing up and down her sides. She stands, her back to his front, feeling the warmth of him while standing inside the open door of the refrigerator. A smile spreads across her face and she whips around to face him, squirting the chocolate on his neck watching it run down the front of him, plastering his shirt to his skin.

"You little devil!" Declan crushes her to him. He grabs her hair and gently tugs, forcing her face up. He swoops in for a fierce kiss, but she starts to laugh, ending the kiss. He rubs a finger over his throat, coating it in chocolate, and wipes it across her nose.

Giggling, Evie leans in and licks in between the two sides of his unbuttoned rugby shirt, licking all the way up his throat.

Releasing a groan, he grabs her face and kisses her again. He bends her back, deepening the kiss, the cool air of the refrigerator doing nothing to reduce the heat coursing through her veins. He removes one hand from her face. The sound of a metal ball knocking around inside an aluminum can drags her out of her bliss. But before she recognizes the sound, her neck and side of her face is covered in cool, creamy sweetness.

"Mmm. Whipped cream is an excellent addition."

Evie straightens up, wipes her face off, and closes the refrigerator door. When she turns back around, she is greeted with more whipped cream and a deep chuckle. She squeals and starts backing away from Declan. She squeezes the chocolate syrup bottle and douses him again. He tries to get her with the whipped cream, but it doesn't reach her. A cackle escapes her lips, as the predator slowly starts stalking her.

They both circle the long, stainless steel island in the middle of the kitchen, laughing and trying to squirt the other with food.

Rounding the corner, Declan loses his footing and crashes onto the floor. "Bloody hell! My arse!"

Evie, pinching her lips to stop from laughing, loses the battle and snorts out a laugh. She carefully walks back to Declan, bends down, and kneels in front of him. Evie clears her throat to momentarily stop her chuckling. "Are you alright?" She squeezes her lips together in a tight smile as she wipes the tears from her eyes.

"My bloody arse hurts like hell. I think I broke it." Declan reaches behind him and rubs said arse. "Can you break your arse?"

"I don't know." Evie's laughter starts bubbling back up to the surface.

"Bloody hell. I think I deserve a kiss." He cocks an eyebrow at Evie, still kneeling in front of him.

"I'm not kissing your ass, if that's what you're asking." Evie sits back on her legs and crosses her arms in front of her while releasing a "humph."

"I'll take one on my mouth then." Declan winks and starts to lean forward to collect his kiss.

Before Declan's lips reach hers, Evie holds up one finger and puts it to his lips. "Only if you help me clean up this mess."

"I promise to lick ya clean." Declan sucks in the finger that is still pressed to his lips and waggles his eyebrows.

"Mmm...while I wouldn't mind the licking, I meant the kitchen."

Declan pauses. "Deal." He reaches out for both of her arms and yanks her to him. Her mouth slams into his, and he swallows her gasp as his tongue enters her mouth.

Evie relaxes into Declan's hold and scoots over to sit in his lap, never breaking contact. She wraps her arms around his torso. The sweetness of the whipped cream draws her in, pushing into him and deepening their kiss, lapping him up.

"Damn it! My arse really hurts, love." Declan breaks their kiss and pulls back from her.

"You probably bruised yourself. Let's stand up, but be careful, the floor is still slippery." Evie helps him stand up. "How's that?"

"Much better. I would love to pick up where we left off." He gives her a wicked grin.

Chapter Thirteen

"Can I convince ya to come home with me and let me cook dinner for ya?" Declan doesn't know if she's changing her mind about him yet, but she did seem to enjoy his company this afternoon. He can't remember the last time he had this much fun with a woman that didn't involve sex.

"I should probably go home and get cleaned up." Evie bites her lip, not quite meeting his gaze.

"Ya can take a shower at my place. I'll find something ya can put on and wash your clothes in the meantime. Come on, I make a mean fettuccine alfredo." Declan lifts her hand and kisses the inside of her wrist, watching as a shiver shakes her shoulders.

"Okay, as long as you throw in some garlic bread." Evie leads the way outside, not even waiting for his response.

This woman can definitely keep him on his toes. He chuckles to himself. He's up for the challenge.

At his house, Declan leads Evie to the master bathroom. "Ya can take a shower in here. Let me look for a shirt and pants for ya." Declan digs around in one of his massive dressers, finding his favorite sweatshirt and a pair of pajama bottoms and hands them over to her. "These pants have a drawstring, so ya can tighten them up." Declan watches Evie for a moment, but she won't look up at him. She's chewing her bottom lip again. "I'm goin' to take a shower in the guest bath and then start dinner. Feel free to take your time. There are towels in the closet and plenty of soap and shampoo." She finally meets his gaze.

"I don't want to take your shower. I can shower in the guest bathroom." She clutches his clothes to her body.

"This bathroom is much nicer. Don't ya worry about me." Declan winks and then leans in to kiss her on the forehead. If he doesn't leave soon, he'll join her in his massive shower and show her how much better his shower is to the guest shower. "I'll have some wine waitin' for ya."

After dinner, Declan leads Evie out to the living room where they sip on Irish coffee. He can't stop staring at Evie tonight. With her long, deep red hair curling with its dampness, her warm pink cheeks, and wearing his favorite sweatshirt, it takes all of his control not to lean in and try to convince her to come back to his bedroom. It also doesn't help that she isn't wearing a bra, and he's pretty sure she doesn't have on panties either. Bloody hell, just thinking that causes him to clear his throat to cover a moan that almost escapes and his dick grow even harder, if that is possible. At this rate, he is going to need another cold shower tonight.

"Where is your grandmother tonight? She really doesn't stay with you?" Evie peaks at him over her mug.

"She left for Savannah today for a weeklong trip to see my brother and his family. They won't be able to come here for Christmas this year, so she's spending time with them now. Whenever she visits, she likes to stay at a hotel. She doesn't like bein' a burden on anyone." Declan concentrates on staring at the floor.

"So we're alone for tonight?"

Declan coughs, choking on his coffee.

"Are you okay?" Evie leans over and pats him on the back.

He clears his throat a few times, trying not to get his hopes up. "Yes, I'm fine. And, yes, we're alone. Dare I ask why you want to know?"

Evie grabs his coffee and sets both cups on the table next to her. She turns back and leans toward him again. Before she gets all of the way to him, she stops and searches his eyes. Having zero patience, he closes the gap and grabs her, sitting her on his lap.

"I like the way ya think." He finds her lips and picks up where he left off in the bakery. He wraps his arms around her, finding the edge of the sweatshirt and tucking his hands underneath it. A soft moan vibrates in her throat, so he slowly starts to moves his hands up her back. Once he gets as high as her shoulder blades, he starts to drag his hands around her sides and toward the front. When he finds her breasts and her tight little nubs, he gives each a pinch. Evie shifts where she sits, sending a new rush of sensation to his dick. She breaks their kiss and moves to straddle his lap. Declan takes the opportunity to pull the sweatshirt over her head and throw it to the floor.

Evie's hair falls over her shoulders, just barely covering her pink nipples. "Sweet Jesus, you're beautiful."

She's more gorgeous than Declan ever imagined her to be. Her scarlet blush runs from her face, to her neck, and ends at her chest. Her bashfulness is quite possibly the sexiest thing he has ever seen. He leans in and sucks a pert nipple into his mouth. She groans and wraps her hands around his head, threading her fingers into his hair. He licks, sucks, and nips until she's breathing heavily, and then he moves to the other nipple to continue the torture.

Evie starts to rock back and forth, making his dick unbearably hard. He shoves a hand down the front of the pajama pants, searching out her heat. He slips a finger into her folds. She jumps at the contact. She is so wet and ready for him that he stands, keeping her legs around him, and carries her to his bedroom.

Declan lays her on the bed, her legs dangling off the side. He reaches up and pulls off the pajama pants. She squeezes her eyes shut, afraid to see his reaction to her naked body. She isn't one of those gorgeous model-like weekend flings that she's seen him bring in on Monday mornings. She swallows her nerves and peeks open first one eye and then the other. She mentally kicks herself for almost missing him removing his clothes.

As he pulls his t-shirt over his head, she watches his ab muscles flex and ripple. She licks her lips in anticipation of touching those tight abs. After he throws his shirt to the floor, he unbuttons his fly and shoves his thumbs into the waistband of his worn jeans. He pauses, looking up into her eyes. Something she recognizes as desire flashes in his eyes and he pushes his jeans and underwear down, and steps out of them. Her gaze slowly moves down to his groin. Damn!

Evie pushes herself all of the way onto the bed. She finds the end of the covers and climbs underneath them. She lies on her side and holds the covers back, waiting for him to join her. Declan grabs a condom from the nightstand, tears open the wrapper, and pulls out the rolled up rubber. His hands are shaking so much, it takes him two tries to get the damn thing on. Could he really be as nervous as her? He's with a new woman every weekend, but the last time she was with a man was three years ago. Her stomach flips. Evie pushes that thought out of her mind when he turns back to her and she gets to feast her eyes on his lickable body. The light sprinkling of dark hair covering his defined chest, abs, and the trail leading down to his dick, makes her fingers itch to touch. She really could stare at him all day.

Declan joins her under the covers, pushing her down onto her back, while his body covers hers. Her nervousness is forgotten once his lips suck in one of her nipples. Her back arches and she fists handfuls of sheet. She needs to feel him inside her now. "Please," she groans.

Declan releases her nipple and moves up to her mouth. He kisses her gently and slowly, their tongues tasting each other. He moves to the side and caresses her free breast with his hand. He alternates between kneading the mound and lightly pinching the tight nub. She starts to move her hips against his erection, wanting the fullness inside her.

Declan's breathing comes faster and heavier. He reaches between them, and finding her moisture, he slides in a finger. A deep groan fills the room. Declan is back on top of her and leading his dick slowly in as she wraps her arms around him. He stops halfway and pulls almost all the way out. "Jesus, Evie. You feel so good." He shakes in her arms.

Before he even has a chance to plunge back in, she wraps

her legs around his hips and pulls him toward her, thrusting him into her body. They both groan in unison. She unwraps her legs, hikes them up to the side, and spreads them wide, deepening his reach. With most of his weight supported on his forearms, Declan devours her mouth, as his hips start to push forward again.

Evie slides her hands down to his ass. She grabs on to both cheeks while he slowly pumps in and out of her. The tension builds and she breaks the kiss, breathing heavily. She tightens her grip and he picks up the pace.

Her back arches and her body tightens around him while pleasure explodes through her. Within seconds, he is joining her, after one final thrust and a deep groan. Declan lies on top of her, trapping her in an embrace, and rolls to his side, taking her with him. She nuzzles her head against his shoulder and drifts off in a satiated sleep.

What feels like several hours later, Evie wakes up with a naked man wrapped around her. She moves to get more comfortable causing her hips to rub up against his dick. A moan escapes his lips and he has her pinned down and panting for round two before he even comes fully awake. Within minutes, he is pounding into her, hard and fast. It's only seconds and they are both screaming out in pure ecstasy. Spent, he collapses next to her. He wraps her in a full body embrace and she sleeps until morning.

Chapter Fourteen

$\mathcal{E}$vie is filling the displays with Ashley's fresh baked pastries when the doorbell tinkles. Her stomach jumps and she is too afraid to look up to see who entered.

"Good morning." Jack breezes by her to put away his coat and gloves.

Relief and disappointment wrestles within her. Is Declan going to come in this morning and give her the Monday morning send-off like he has every other woman? Maybe he won't even bother since it's her bakery.

The bell tinkles again. Evie swallows and looks up from her task. It's Declan. He doesn't give her his usual charming, lopsided smile. He fidgets with his keys. She is about to say something when Jack beats her to it.

"Good morning, Mr. O'Connor. I guess you don't need a Declan's Special today?" Jack turns to look out the front windows, his gaze searching.

"Ah, no, lad. I came to speak with Evie." His gaze never leaves her.

Realizing both Jack and Declan are waiting for her to say something, she clears her throat and acknowledges Jack. "Thank you, Jack. Can you give us a minute?"

Jack's eyes grow round and his eyebrows rise. "Of course." He speeds off in the direction of the kitchen.

Evie, finally able to move from the spot to which she is rooted, walks out from behind the counter. "Would you like a coffee?" She leads Declan to a far side table against the wall. All morning, she's been playing out different scenarios in her mind as to how Declan will drop her. She even thought about how she would miss their Monday banter when he stops coming into the bakery.

"Ah… no, thank ya." Declan pulls out the chair, gestures for her to sit, and then sits across from her. "Actually, I need to talk to ya."

Great. Here it comes. "Yes?" Evie steels herself, waiting

for the blow.

"Well… ya see… that is… dammit." He takes a deep breath and the words tumble out. "Evie, will ya have breakfast with me this mornin', and then, I thought that maybe I could cook us dinner tonight. We could stay at your place instead of mine tonight. And, I want ya to come to my company's Christmas party next week…" He looks down at his hands resting on the table.

"You don't want the Declan's Special?" She holds her breath.

"What?" He looks up at her, confusion clouding his eyes. He blinks and then his lopsided grin slowly creeps up on his face. "No, love, I don't want the Declan's Special with ya. The Declan's Special is a goodbye. I don't want to say goodbye to ya. Ya deserve a breakfast, lunch, and dinner, every day. But, I do rather enjoy your desserts, if ya will be so kind as to provide that." His expression changes from playful to sultry.

She can't help herself, she matches his smile with her own. She jumps up from her seat, easily clears the short distance, and lands in his lap. She wraps her arms around his neck as they face nose to nose. "Yes, to everything."

"Everything?"

She nods, so he continues. "Mmmm… I do look forward to your dessert." He kisses down her neck, dragging out a throaty laugh.

She turns her head to catch his lips. She sucks in his bottom lip and gives it a little nibble. He groans, which sends a thrill through her. He opens his eyes and gives her his charming smile. Seeing the crinkles around his baby blues makes the butterflies flutter in her stomach. "We should go get that breakfast."

"And, Evie, darlin', don't ya leave without saying goodbye to me in the mornin' again." He kisses along her jawline.

"Mmm… I won't again. I promise. Can we go eat now?"

He kisses down her neck. "Mmmm… hmmm…"

"Declan?"

"Yes, Evie?"

"Breakfast." Her stomach growls in response.

He removes her from his lap and stands up. "Right ya

are. I'll fetch your coat."

Ashley and Jack peek their heads out of the kitchen. Blushing, Evie walks up to the counter. "Declan and I are going to go get breakfast. I'll be back later."

Jack smiles and walks up to the counter. "We've got it handled." He looks up behind her. "I gather we need to remove Declan's Special from the menu?"

Declan, standing behind Evie, helps her into her coat. "Indeed, lad."

Rhythm of Love

by Keisha K. Page

For Lisa, who always knew I could.

Chapter One

Leslie walked into the conference room, vowing to herself that she wasn't going to stand there with her mouth gaping open, looking like a fangirl. Resistance had been her favorite band since she discovered them in high school. Try as she might to look cool, calm, and collected, her heart was beating quickly at the thought of photographing the band she had idolized for twenty-five years.

Leslie had been taking pictures for most of her life. She stumbled into a photography job for an art professor her first week on campus, and managed to put herself through college by photographing pieces for him and his students for use in their portfolios. When she graduated, she moved back home and started working for a local weekly alternative paper, and helping more artists build their portfolios. When she had spare time, she started taking the type of pictures she had always wanted to. She experimented with lenses and effects and film types. She learned by trial and error.

A few years passed, and Leslie picked up better gigs, but still not enough to support herself with only the type of photography she wanted to do. She found a husband, had two girls and a little boy, and struggled with that balance of being a mother and having a career. After maternity leaves and sleepless nights and unpaid time away from work, she found it difficult to get back into photography. The alternative weekly she had been working for was under new management, and by then Leslie was a soccer mom in her thirties. She wasn't cool enough to work for them anymore.

Now, at forty, Leslie had fought her way through freelance work, awful clients, and a divorce. She was finally getting regular work from some national magazines, although senior portraits and weddings paid most of her bills. When the posting had come through to photograph Resistance in New York City, she had begged, cajoled, and called in some favors to get the job. She also had to line up three other gigs while she was there to justify the cost of the plane tickets. Now, she was standing in a conference room trying not to look like the bowl that held her marbles had just fallen off of her head.

Resistance had been the biggest band in the world when Leslie was a teenager. If you could think of a cliché that described a rock band, it fit Resistance at some point in their career. Selling out stadiums? Check. Wild, drunken, drug-fueled orgies on the tour bus? Leslie wasn't a betting woman, but she was sure she had the odds on that one. She'd heard rumors. The band had almost broken up and then reconsidered a dozen times in their twenty-five years together. Each of the band members had been married more than once, and they had all been in rehab at one time or another.

Tim, the drummer, stood up and walked around the conference table. As he reached her, he held out his hand. From her research, Leslie had discovered that Tim had battled a drinking problem, and had only gotten sober within the last few years. While he always had it together on stage, there wasn't a candid picture of him on tour without a glass of wine in his hand. He was a huge man, standing well over six foot and built like a Viking on steroids. His shaved head gleamed in the florescent light, and his blond goatee didn't detract from the Viking image.

"Hi, I'm Tim," he said.

Tim seemed sweet, but she knew his past was a bit dark, too. His first marriage had been to an actress, and they were relentlessly stalked by the paparazzi. While the rest of the band had stayed relatively private, even with their problems, Tim's life had largely been played out in front of the cameras, and not by his choice. Tim and his wife had three children, all stillbirths. Each hopeful pregnancy was played out in full detail on entertainment shows on TV, and in captured moments as the paparazzi stalked them. They would try to keep things secret, but their secrets were always public. With each pregnancy, Tim and his wife had bought a crib, and baby clothes, and diaper bags. With each pregnancy, the cameras had chronicled when the charity truck came to take away the unworn clothes and unused diapers.

Leslie smiled, reached out her hand to take his, and was

pulled in for a hug. It was comfortable, familiar, and gave Leslie a chance to take a breath and get her feet back underneath her. She smiled and introduced herself, turning her head to include everyone in the room. One by one, the band members came around and introduced themselves, although no one but Tim tried to hug her.

Resistance's singer, Greg, looked far younger than his band mates. Leslie could see the telltale signs of plastic surgery. She thought it must be difficult for a man who spent a large chunk of his life being the sexy frontman of a successful rock band to be aging out of sexiness. The band had won two Grammys, and Greg had won two others for his solo work. He was a prolific writer, not only for the band, but for various other artists across different musical genres. He could get to the heart of your emotions, make you want to laugh, cry, fight, fuck, or everything all at once. And his voice was like ice water on a hot day—bold, invasive, everything you wanted, leaving you breathlessly wanting more. But he had never seen that talent within himself. Somewhere along the line, Greg became convinced that it was his looks that sold records. As he got older and his looks changed, Greg found himself struggling.

Alex, the bassist, was the bad boy in the band. In all of the candid shots, there was always a bottle of Jack Daniels in his hand, despite multiple stays in rehab. Their record label had once hired a "sober companion" for Alex, to try to keep him from drinking. It took all of seventy-two hours for their tour manager to find them both passed out drunk in the hallway of a hotel in Houston. Both of his marriages had ended in divorce. He narrowly avoided going to prison when he pulled a gun on a venue security guard one night after a show. He had spent several months in jail on minor charges ranging from public drunkenness to assault.

Tomas was small. At 5'6", he was the shortest member of the band, and he looked like the skinny kid that got sand kicked on him at the beach. He always seemed to be on the defensive, and he had been in lots of fights through the years. From her outside point of view, it seemed like he had developed a reputation as someone who fought his way out of being picked on, and people couldn't resist testing that theory. He had gone to jail a few times on misdemeanors, and three stints in rehab had helped him kick a nasty heroin habit about fifteen years ago. When he picked up a guitar, the sound was magic.

Tomas leaned forward as Leslie sat her camera bags on the table. "So whose side are you on?"

"There's a side?" Leslie asked.

"Everyone wants to paint us as assholes. The guys that got away with everything. The rich dudes who should have retired. Even our record label didn't want us to make this album. They were afraid we had lost our edge."

"I'm just here for pictures, Tomas. Your record company asked me to be here, so I'm guessing they have at least a little bit of faith in you."

Leslie realized in that moment that it wasn't easy being Resistance. Every album that they had released, since their debut back in the 80s, had gone platinum, except the last two. Sales had been strong, but certainly not up to their prior levels. But, to be fair, Resistance's fan base now had mortgages and failing 401k's to worry about. That had to be at least partially to blame for the falling record sales.

Every record company is concerned about a band's last album. That's the one that they shouldn't have made. The one that doesn't sound like the old stuff, that isn't music the fans love, and that shows that the lead singer doesn't have the range he used to. It's the album that record companies pour millions of dollars into, with promotions, tours, and recording costs. And it usually ends up being a financial nightmare.

Resistance's record company had thought every album was their last for the last ten or twelve years. The guys had to fight each time they were ready to start recording. They could have moved off label, but that would mean new contracts, and it would have been expensive. After twenty-five years in the music industry, and with their past, they were a risky bet in today's market. Leslie understood why Tomas was being so defensive.

Chapter Two

The room that the record company had provided was huge, with great backdrops, and floor to ceiling windows for perfect lighting. Leslie set up her equipment and got the band into position. She spent several hours posing them, both as a group and one-on-one, taking shot after shot after shot. During the shoot, they told stories, leaving Leslie laughing so hard she had to stop the shoot at one point because she had tears in her eyes. They had lots of fun stories to tell. This was one of the best shoots that Leslie had ever been on. As the clock passed noon, Leslie decided it was time to take a break.

"So, I'm in New York for the first time ever, and it's lunch time. Where do I need to go for pizza?"

All four guys stood up together. "Luigi's."

Hours into this photo session, and Leslie still couldn't get over the fact that she was about to go out for pizza with the guys from her favorite band ever. *Being a photographer sucks.*

Now that she'd gotten them started, they were in the mood for storytelling. As they walked into Luigi's, Tim was telling her about "This one time in Denver," and everyone was laughing. Since Leslie was from Denver, she recognized all of the locations. She had been at the concert they were talking about. They led the way to a table in the back, and Leslie got the feeling that they were regulars. She sat, surrounded, as they told their stories. She enjoyed just listening, hearing the laughter as they recalled the good times.

When they were done eating and the stories were slowing down, Leslie looked around at the restaurant. Mirrors lined one wall, and if she looked carefully, she could tell that before it was a pizza place, Luigi's had been a bar. She asked about the history of the place.

Alex spoke up, "My parents met here. Some of my earliest memories are of coming to dinner here. My mom says that my first food was salsa, but my second was pizza crust from Luigi's. We used to hang out here, after school, before we started the band, but I never heard about what it was, before it was Luigi's. It's been Luigi's since before we were all born. Of course, the current owner is the third Luigi, but it's been a family business for a very long time."

Leslie's eyes lit up, "Do you think he would talk to me? I love this sort of stuff. I would love to get some pictures here."

Tomas laughed. "Maybe another time. His daughter is getting married this weekend. Should we head back?"

As they were walking back, Leslie took in the sights. The record company's offices were near the Bronx Terminal Market, and they had walked about a mile to get to Luigi's. The Bronx was like many areas in New York—parts of it were newly gentrified and had had millions of dollars poured into them, and parts of it stood abandoned and forgotten. Even coming from Denver, Leslie was awed by the magnitude of what she was seeing. New York was beyond anything she had imagined. Alex, walking beside her, followed her gaze.

"So you've really never been to New York City?" he asked.

She shook her head no. Leslie told Alex that she had always wanted to see the city, but her husband had never wanted to travel. Now that she was divorced and supporting the kids, she only got to travel for work, so she took advantage of it when she could.

"What should I see while I'm here?" she asked him.

Alex smiled. "If you're going to see New York, it should be with a New Yorker. Otherwise, you'll miss all the good stuff. If you're not doing anything this evening, I could show you around."

Leslie laughed. "You sure you're not going to be tired of me after spending all day with me?"

"Well, I might be, but it's my duty as a New Yorker to show you around."

Leslie couldn't decide if Alex was joking or not, but the thought of him showing her around New York City was captivating.

After lunch, the guys changed into street clothes and started wandering around the Bronx. The record company wanted candid shots of them in the city. Most of the shots were silly, but Leslie managed to capture a few great ones. The guys kept talking as they made their way through their hometown, pointing out places where each had gotten into trouble, or first made out with a girl.

Their stories evolved, sometimes getting dark. Greg shared a lot. Leslie got the sense that he was kind of haunted. It had taken a lot of work to get him to commit to this album. He felt a huge sense of responsibility toward the other guys in the band, and at times, that had turned into feelings of animosity. It wasn't so much that he hated them, but he hated that he felt like he was responsible for them. Before they had recorded this album, Greg had to dig himself out of a pretty deep pit of self-loathing. It took long hours of rehearsing before the band really clicked together again.

Once they got past the initial rough spots, the guys enjoyed the process of recording the new album. But months of stress had strained some of them, and some were near the end of their ropes. Tomas was struggling financially, and Alex's second wife had left him when they were writing the songs for the album. Recording some of the words he had helped to write when he was in so much pain had gotten to him. Tim remained the bright and shining ray of sunshine, trying to get everyone to move forward. Some days, that was harder than others.

As Leslie listened to them telling their stories of this struggle in their lives, she could feel their heartache. While the album had gotten recorded, and the mentions Leslie had heard were favorable, she knew that it had been a struggle for them to get it done. But now that it was in the can, they were looking forward to being back among their fans.

Leslie could sense their excitement as they talked. Their voices got louder as they talked about what they had been working on. Tim, in particular, talked with his hands. The more excited he got, the more he gesticulated. At times, Leslie had to suppress the urge to duck. The upcoming album was full of promise, and being talked about in the rock media. They had years to write this one, and once the record company had realized that they had something good on their hands, the band had broadened their horizons, and promised an album that would blow everyone away. Tomas, in particular, was looking forward to seeing the record company eat crow, after their initial hesitation. The band's excitement was contagious, and as Leslie followed the animated conversation around the room, she couldn't wait to hear the album.

Chapter Three

Leslie took a few final shots, then started wrapping things up. She told everyone she was going to work on the photos over the next few days, but might need to follow up with them. She handed out her cards, and encouraged them to call her if they needed anything from her. As she was packing her camera bag, Alex was at her side. She turned to look up at him, and was caught by his eyes. She had never really been into brown eyes, but his were deep, and she felt like she could see forever. She blinked to break the spell, then smiled.

"Where to first?" she asked.

"I need to pick up my kid and take him to his mom's house. Can I meet you at your hotel?"

That was perfect for Leslie. She wanted to drop her cameras off in her room, backup her files, and call to check up on her kids. She liked the idea of Alex doing regular dad things, too. Leslie realized that her impression of him had certainly been clouded by the media's portrayal of the band. He really didn't seem all that different from her. Well, other than the fame and musical talent. They promised to meet in the lobby of her hotel in a few hours.

Once Leslie was up in her hotel room, with the pictures backed up and her phone calls made, she began to get anxious. *Oh my God. I'm actually going to be hanging out with the bass player from Resistance!* Her high school self would have been squealing out loud by now. Leslie hoped her high school self wouldn't make an appearance tonight.

Should I take a shower? Should I change clothes? Should I do something different with my hair? In the end, Leslie changed into her comfortable suede boots, perfect for walking around the city. She grabbed a jacket, just in case, and made her way down to the lobby. She found Alex waiting for her there. He smiled when he saw her.

"What did you want to see?" he asked.

"Everything. I've never been here before."

When they got outside, Leslie was surprised to see a nice Harley waiting for them. She turned to look at Alex, her eyes wide.

"It was this or my minivan. We can take the train if..."

"No, this is okay. I just haven't been on a bike in twenty years, at least. Do you really have a minivan?"

Alex blushed, and handed her a helmet. "Yeah. I really do. I have kids, you know? They stay with me a lot when I'm home."

He chuckled, "I've blown that image of a sexy rock star right out of your head, haven't I?"

Leslie settled the helmet on her head, suddenly glad she hadn't done anything different with her hair. "Yes, yes you have. All of my fantasies, up in smoke."

Alex smiled up at her from the bike, his brown-eyed gaze fixed on her.

"I promise, you'll feel better before we've gone ten miles."

Alex is kind of adorable. Leslie climbed on the Harley behind him, and settled her arms loosely around his waist.

It was a perfect summer evening in New York City. There was a good bit of traffic, but the heat of the day had backed off a bit. They weren't sweltering when they were stopped, but it felt great to be going. Alex had been right. She was having a great time riding through the city with him. After a few minutes, Alex turned onto the expressway, and she enjoyed the sights as they made their way into Manhattan.

Traffic slowed once they left the expressway. Over the roar of the bike, Alex told her about some of the places they passed. Through Harlem, he pointed out great restaurants and places she should stop by if she had time. It wasn't until they were right on top of it that Leslie realized he was bringing her to Central Park. They drove down Fifth Avenue, and then he found a parking garage. A short bus ride and a bit of a walk later, and Leslie found herself at the Central Park Carousel. Leslie was thrilled as she walked up to the ticket counter. Of all the places that he could have brought her in New York City, he'd chosen perfectly. She loved carousels. They had made it just in time—the carousel was loading up for its final ride of the evening. She bought tickets for them both.

Leslie was enchanted as she wandered around the carousel, looking for a horse to ride. She chose a black one with a green bridle and climbed on. Alex picked the horse right next to hers. They had to wait a bit for the other riders to get on board, and Leslie asked Alex about his kids. He had four, ranging from nineteen to eight. He had been divorced for two years.

With a lurch, the carousel started. Leslie hung on—a bike wasn't the only thing that she hadn't been on in twenty years. She and Alex teased each other as they rode round and round on the carousel. She enjoyed the sound of his laughter, and thought that he was alluring. Alex was confident, easy to talk to, and had a great sense of humor.

"Our next stop is going to be it for the evening. We'll hang out there for a while. There's lots of stuff to see in New York, but this is one place you should see at night. If you want to do more sightseeing, we can go tomorrow night if you're not going to be busy."

Leslie nodded, still trying to grasp the enormity of Central Park. She had spent most of her married life in a town that would have fit comfortably within its borders. As they made their way back to Alex's bike, they talked about her kids. She had a thirteen-year-old, a ten-year-old, and an eight-year-old.

As they rode, they ran into traffic a few times; the stop and go made Leslie nervous. She tightened her arms around Alex's waist, thought she heard him laugh. She trusted him, but speeding over New York City expressways on the back of a Harley was definitely out of her comfort zone. He grabbed her hand a few times and gave it a squeeze to reassure her.

As traffic thinned out, Leslie relaxed. She didn't realize that her hands were on his thighs until he reached down and squeezed her hand again. As soon as he let go, she moved her hands to the sides of his waist, embarrassed.

"Almost there," he yelled over his shoulder.

When Alex finally pulled into a parking spot, Leslie was thankful. Her ass had gone to sleep, and she really had to pee. She got off the bike and looked around. She had no idea where they were, but thought she could smell the ocean. A short walk, and they were standing in front of Nathan's Famous.

"You brought me to Coney Island." Leslie squealed. "You are the coolest tour guide ever!"

Leslie was really looking forward to exploring Coney Island. With an excited "Come on!" Alex grabbed her hand and led the way, asking about Leslie's work. As they waited their turn in line, she told him about the museum opening she would be shooting later that week.

When they got up to the register, Alex turned to her.

"Do you trust me?"

"Y-yes," Leslie stammered.

Alex turned to the cashier and ordered chili cheese dogs, bacon ranch fries, and beers. When their order was up, he grabbed everything and pushed his way through the crowd, trying to find them a table.

It's weird that eating a chili cheese dog in Coney Island is only the second coolest thing I've done today. First, riding on a Harley through New York City with Alex, and now this.

When they were done eating, Alex led the way to the boardwalk. They walked for quite a while, and talked about everything from their childhoods to the different places they had traveled. Alex had been all over the world. New York was the furthest that Leslie had ever been from home. Alex shared a few amazing stories with her, telling her of the exotic things he had eaten in Japan, and about surfing in Australia.

They made their way over to Deno's Wonder Wheel. The Wonder Wheel had been a Coney Island tradition since 1920. They bought tickets and joined the line. Leslie was a little nervous. She had always been scared of heights. The sun was setting, and the entire atmosphere of the amusement park changed as the lights came on. The bright neon lights cast their glow over everyone. The delighted faces seemed even happier bathed in the festive lighting. As they made their way through the line, Alex got excited.

"My favorite part of Coney Island is being on the Wonder Wheel after dark. You can see for miles, into the city and even New Jersey, and the lights of Coney Island all up and down the beach. And then, that sudden, deep dark of the ocean. Whenever we came here when I was a kid, my mom would get us all packed up and ready to leave after we had dogs at Nathans. And my sisters and I would always beg to stay so we could ride the Wonder Wheel after dark."

"Did it work?"

Alex smiled, "Most of the time. It was the only time mom ever let us get away with anything like that. I bring my kids at least once a year."

Finally, it was their turn. Not the intimate little cars built for two that Leslie was expecting, but large, ugly cars built for six. Alex ushered her inside a blue one, and then sat, pulling her down next to him. She was growing more nervous, but her excitement was outpacing her nerves. She wasn't sure if her heart was beating faster because of the Wonder Wheel or because Alex put his arm around her shoulders and pulled her even closer to him. When she realized that someone else would be sitting next to her, she tried to make herself smaller.

As the Wonder Wheel began moving, Leslie experienced that mixture of fear and excitement that you feel when something incredible is about to happen. Half excitement and half fear of death. She thought it must be what people felt before they jumped out of an airplane, or dived off a cliff into the ocean. Leslie had no intention of trying either of those things, so she thought that this might be as intense as that feeling would ever get for her. The car she was in was not on the outside of the Ferris wheel, but rather on a track that caused the cars to move according to the spinning of the wheel. Each time the Wonder Wheel stopped, the car would swing, and if it gained enough momentum, begin moving along the metal track. Once gravity took over, the car could get some decent velocity, and move pretty quickly, sometimes swinging out over the cars on the outside of the wheel. Leslie had never seen a Ferris wheel built that way.

Leslie tried to will herself not to scream. She told herself that she wasn't going to lose it on the Wonder Wheel while she was sitting next to Alex. But the moment their car picked up momentum and seemed to be rushing toward the outside of the

Wonder Wheel, she lost her resolve. It wasn't one of those loud, horror movie screams, but everyone in the car knew she had a good set of lungs. When the car reached the end of its forward motion, swinging out over the car below it, Leslie started laughing and trying to catch her breath. She leaned against Alex, wondering if she was in over her head. As the wheel moved, the anticipation built. By the time Alex reminded Leslie about the view, she was practically in his lap.

It was, as he had promised, breathtaking. The lights of Coney Island were spread out underneath them, and then Brooklyn and more of New York City. She was certain that part of the lights she saw were from New Jersey. And then, on her other side, the ocean was dark, like ink. It was unlike any dark she had ever seen. She was staring into the dark when the ride started moving again, and her car shuddered forward. She jumped, and felt Alex's arms tighten around her. He moved, and then she was on his lap, his arms around her waist. She put one hand around his shoulders, and he leaned his head forward. She used her other hand to pull his long hair out of the way. As their car descended, Leslie was able to take in more of the view from her more secure perch.

Back safely on the ground, Leslie was elated. It was like everything was magnified. The slight breeze bringing the tang of the ocean, the smells of the food stands, the heat radiating off of the asphalt underneath her feet.

"It's beautiful here. Thanks for showing me."

On the way home, Leslie found herself snuggling against Alex's warmth. It had been cool at Coney Island, and the ride back into town, on the back of Alex's Harley, was a little chilly, too. They pulled in front of her hotel, and she slid off the bike. He grabbed her hand.

"I'll see you in the morning?"

"Yeah." Leslie smiled. "I meet with you guys until lunch for the album cover shots, and then I have to go take care of some of the other stuff I lined up to photograph while I'm here."

"If you don't have plans for tomorrow night, I would love to show you more."

Leslie nodded. "That would be great."

Alex held her hand a little longer than he needed to, and then let her go. Leslie walked into her hotel, smiling.

Chapter Four

The next morning moved a little quicker. The band already had an idea of what they wanted for their cover. It had been almost five years since their last album, and there had been a lot of rumors about their imminent demise. A lot of the talk centered on Greg's voice, and whether or not the Grammy winning band could still write songs that moved people the way they used to. For the album cover, the band wanted shots that symbolized their unity.

After makeup, wardrobe changes, and three hours, she had hundreds of shots, and several that both she and the band thought would work. She would pick out the best and send them on to the band's publicist and marketing team.

She parted from Resistance at noon, with her camera bags, a copy of their newest CD, and lots of laughter. She had a concert itinerary, which included a stop in Denver. She was already on the list, and would be getting an advance ticket. She also had a promise from Alex to meet her at her hotel later that day. She ran around like a mad woman to get most of her other stuff done, including photographing an exhibit in New York's newest museum.

By six, she was walking through the lobby of her hotel. Alex was already there, waiting for her by the elevators. His face lit up when he saw her, and she imagined that her own must have, too. She couldn't understand what was going on. She had actually felt that butterfly feeling in her stomach when she turned the corner and saw him standing there. *What are you doing, Leslie? You are entirely too old to be having a crush on a rock star.*

"Hey," she said, trying not to sound as excited to see him as she felt.

"There you are. I was just about to text you. I'm starving."

Leslie couldn't wait to hang out with Alex tonight. She realized that she had laughed more in the last few days with Alex and the guys from Resistance than she had since her marriage had fallen apart.

"Where are we going?" she asked.

"Well, you can't really say you've been to New York City until you've seen Manhattan. Not just Central Park, either. It's what everyone wants to see. It's what you see on TV. It's everyone's image of New York. Times Square is there. You will never, ever, in your life, be in a place with more people in such a small space."

By the time they got to Times Square, it was a little after seven. They grabbed food from a street vendor and walked around. Leslie didn't know where to look first. Alex hadn't exaggerated about the number of people. On a summer evening in New York, Times Square was crowded. After the third time they got separated, Alex grabbed her hand and didn't let go. She had never seen so many people.

It was bright in Times Square, even as the sun began to set. The ads kept changing and flickering, and the constant buzz of chatter in what seemed like a hundred different languages was like a whirlwind to Leslie. She had spent a good bit of her life in Denver, thinking that she lived in a major metropolitan city. Times Square showed her that she couldn't have been more wrong.

It was like being in a giant outdoor mall. She had never been into a Sephora store, and hadn't even heard of some of the stores that were there. She felt like a back country hick in the crush of the crowd. She couldn't imagine what it would be like to work here, with the constant influx of people.

Despite being completely out of her element, she had a good time, and she knew that part of that was because of Alex. He pointed out stores she should see, and sights she shouldn't miss. They made their way out of Times Square and hopped a bus to see more of Manhattan. She saw places she had only seen in movies.

As they passed by Madame Tussaud's, Leslie grabbed Alex's hand and turned him around. She had always wanted to go inside the wax museum. She took pictures of Alex standing next to the wax figures of Marilyn Monroe and Muhammad Ali. After, he took her to Grand Central Terminal, still full of people even as it got late.

They headed back toward Times Square. Alex stepped into the doorway of a closed shop, and brought Leslie with him. He wrapped his arms around her. His lips met hers with a fierceness, hungry, seeking. Her arms reached up, her fingers meeting behind his neck. She was urgently aware of the heat of his body as he pulled her against him.

It was like taking the first bite of a food that you haven't been able to have for a long time. All at once, she wanted him, needed to feel his skin, knew that she wasn't going to be able to stop with just this kiss. She needed more. He moaned into her, and it felt like she had to put every ounce of strength into her knees, so they didn't buckle beneath her.

By the time he broke the kiss, Leslie was breathing hard, her chest heaving against his. His fingers were tangled in her hair, and he was leaning back against the wall, surrounding her with the warmth of his body against hers. It was dark in the doorway; she couldn't see his face. She hoped he was wearing the same goofy smile that she was.

She stepped away from him, but his hands were still on her, keeping her from moving far away. He leaned forward, resting his forehead on hers.

"Hotel?" he breathed into her, almost, but not quite, pleading.

She didn't trust herself to form words yet. She nodded.

He took her hand, walked back out onto the sidewalk. Leslie was almost running to keep up with him. He stopped at a sign that indicated a bus stop, took a quick look, and then was on the move again. They stopped at the next sign, about a block away.

"About ten minutes."

He looked around and started heading for a drugstore. He walked through fast, pausing at each aisle, until he found what he was looking for. He grabbed a box of condoms, and headed for the cashier. He threw them on the counter, tapping his foot impatiently. The cashier took one look at both of them, rang up the condoms, and bagged them as Alex dropped some cash on the counter.

Back at the bus stop, Alex leaned on the back of the bench and wrapped his arms around Leslie, so that her whole body was up against his. His weight was solid against her, his hand at the small of her back, supporting her. His other arm was casually over her shoulder. With his lips on hers, Leslie forgot that she was standing at a bus stop in the middle of Manhattan. She hadn't been kissed this thoroughly in a really long time. At first, Alex had kissed her like a man who's dying of thirst drinks a glass of water. Now, he took his time, exploring her, teasing her with his tongue. She had to keep reminding herself to breathe.

Leslie heard the bus pull up. *Had they really been standing here, on the street in Manhattan, making out, while they waited for the bus to come?*

The trip on the bus seemed to last forever. Public transportation had seemed a really good idea when they left the Bronx. Now, sitting in the bright florescent lights next to Alex, it felt like they were creeping along at a snail's pace. Leslie hadn't just stepped out of her comfort zone, she had deserted it several miles back. Suddenly, she was unsure. *What am I doing here? What is he doing here? I mean, really, women must throw themselves at him. Younger women. Women with better bodies. Women who didn't nurse three children. What the hell am I doing?*

Alex chose that moment to put one arm around her, and the other hand on her thigh. Leslie was so lost in her thoughts that she jumped when he touched her, and then dissolved into a fit of nervous giggles. She felt drunk, almost. She turned to look at him, and saw that goofy smile she had been hoping to find earlier. He leaned toward her, his long hair falling forward.

"You okay?" he asked.

"Yeah, I just...I didn't expect this to happen. It's like I'm back in high school, riding home on the bus from a field trip where we hid behind the bushes and made out."

His hand was stroking her thigh, lightly touching, almost tickling.

"Yeah, but now we actually get to do something about it," he said.

Leslie leaned against him. Maybe they couldn't make out on the bus, but she could touch him. She hadn't touched a man like this since the one fumbling, disaster of a date she had been on after she had left her husband. Knowing that her track record wasn't so hot added to her anxiety. She really didn't want to screw this up. But she wanted Alex so badly she could taste it.

It seemed like the bus stopped at every street corner, for every stoplight, regardless of color, and to let every single little old lady cross the street. *Because there are so many little old ladies roaming Manhattan this late at night.* The ride wasn't a short one to begin with, and when you paired that with the urgency that Leslie felt, it seemed endless.

She felt modest, and awkward. She was certain that he would change his mind, there in the harsh lights of the bus. He would remember that he was a rock star and he could get women that were younger, hotter, who didn't have stretch marks and whose boobs were still perky. She knew that they were going to get to her hotel and he was going to drop her off at the elevator, and that would be that. The long bus ride gave her brain time to voice every negative thought she ever had about herself.

Finally, Alex leaned forward to hit the stop button. The bus began to slow, and Leslie focused her attention outside. The bus was passing by her hotel as it made its way to the next bus stop. Alex stood up, and led her to the back door. As they got off the bus, he pulled her over to the side of the building and wrapped his arms around her again.

His lips tasted like sweet iced tea on a hot day. His tongue teased hers, drawing her into his mouth. When he tightened his lips around her tongue, started sucking on it, she was grateful for his arms around her. Otherwise, her knees would have buckled, and she would have fallen. She hadn't made out with anyone like this since before she was married. When Alex kissed her, she wanted to forget the rest of the world existed.

He broke the kiss and pulled away from her, then grabbed her hand and started walking toward the entrance of her hotel. Straight through the lobby, to the elevators. He was like a dog on the scent of something. Once in the elevator, blissfully alone, he wrapped his arms around her, his hands cupping her butt. In one smooth motion he lifted her up, and she got her legs around his waist. His mouth was on her throat, wet and hot, leaving a trail like fire where he kissed her.

When the elevator stopped, Alex set her down. Leslie turned toward the door. She was lightheaded, giddy, and glad she was wearing clunky boots instead of heels. She never would have made it to her door. She started digging through her purse, trying to find her room key. She slid it into the lock, her hands shaking. *Am I really bringing Alex Torres back to my hotel room?*

She walked into the room, and Alex followed closely on her heels. He kicked the door shut. She set her purse down on the table, trying to take a moment to calm her nerves, but Alex was behind her, his arms wrapped around her. She leaned against him, closed her eyes, and took a few deep breaths. She wanted to still her heart and calm her breathing and make her brain shut up so she could enjoy every minute of this.

Alex turned her around so he could kiss her again. Leslie couldn't get over how his kisses tasted. She was certain that if she only kissed him, that would be okay for hours. She wanted to touch him, though, to feel his skin, and the memory of how his mouth had felt on her throat made her squirm as that feeling in the pit of her stomach intensified. She pulled his shirt up, ran her hands up his back, and around to his chest. He lifted his arms so she could take his shirt off.

The skin on his chest was light brown, like the color of fudge before it hardened. His chest was broad, and smooth, and Leslie couldn't stand it any longer. She moved her head forward, kissed his bare chest, and then moved to flick her tongue over his nipple. He moaned, and his movements became more urgent. He pulled up her shirt with one hand, and she helped him pull it over her head. As she took his nipple into her mouth, his hands were at her waist, unbuttoning her jeans. He slid his hand inside, over her panties, and she whimpered, wanting him. She pulled away from him, moving to the bed.

She sat down, and then reached up to unbuckle his belt. Her hands got in the way of his as he was trying to get his jeans off and she laughed, and then he was standing there, naked in front of her, his hard cock inches from her mouth. She wrapped her hand around the base, leaned forward, and took the head into her mouth, sucking gently at first, then slowly increasing the pressure until she heard him moan and felt his fingers in her hair. She brought her other hand up to cup his balls as she took him deeper.

"Oh, fuck, Leslie. No. Stop," Alex whispered, as he pulled away from her. She looked up at him, unsure, but he was bending down to kneel in front of her. He kissed her neck as he reached around behind her to unhook her bra. He pushed her back onto the bed as his mouth moved down her left side to her breast. He licked her nipple, flicking it with his tongue, then, started sucking intently. Leslie was trying to wiggle out of her jeans when he bit her. She couldn't move. The feeling was so intense. Her eyes closed. All she could concentrate on was his teeth on her nipple, the exquisite mixture of pleasure and pain making her blind and deaf to anything else that was going on.

He released her nipple and helped her slide her jeans down her legs. She was trying to move up onto the bed when she realized she still had her boots on. She started giggling, mostly from nervousness, as she leaned forward to unlace them. Alex sat down next to her, his own jeans drooping around his ankles, also caught on his boots. Finally, there was a pile of jeans and boots and socks on the floor next to the bed. Alex pulled Leslie over so that she was straddling his waist as he lay on the bed. He reached up, both hands on her breasts. Leslie closed her eyes, enjoying the feeling of his hands on her, of his skin under her fingertips as she stroked his chest. He moved his hands to her waist and she bent forward, lying on him, to kiss him again. Her mouth moved to his neck, tasting him, and then down to his nipple once more. He gasped.

"Oh shit." Leslie said, as she moved away from him. "I forgot about the condoms."

Alex helped her find the bag, and she ripped the top off the box. She was jittery and in a hurry, but she didn't want to look nervous. She pulled a condom out of the box and tore open the wrapper. Her hands shook as she pulled it out. She positioned it over the head of his dick but kept getting it crooked. He took it from her and smoothed it down his length in one smooth, practiced motion. Leslie straddled him.

She wiggled her hips, trying to get into the right spot to

slide him inside of her without having to move her hands. After a moment, she felt the head of his dick slide inside. She settled herself, and then moved so that he slid his full length into her wetness, gasping as his cock filled her.

"Oh, fuck," he moaned, his hands on her waist, helping her move up and down. She sat up, and his hands moved to her breasts again, stroking and lightly pinching her nipples. She leaned back a bit, arching her back, her orgasm building. He propped himself up on one elbow, quickly wrapping his arm around her waist. The movement put more pressure on her clit, and when he bit her on the side of her breast, her breath caught in her throat as the orgasm hit her, hard and fast. Her hips moved back and forth, her moans mingling with his. When she could breathe again, she couldn't really lift her arms.

He moved them around so that she was lying on the bed and he was on top of her. Her nipple was in his mouth again, and his cock slid in and out of her. She arched her back, wanting to touch all of him, every inch of his skin against hers. She had one leg propped on his waist, and one hand was grabbing his ass, pulling him hard into her every time he thrust. Her other hand was playing with his nipple as he suckled and bit hers. His moans got louder and louder—or were those hers? Caught in the moment, she couldn't tell them apart. She couldn't catch her breath, couldn't control the way her hips were moving, couldn't form coherent thoughts. She just knew she didn't want him to stop.

Stop is exactly what he did, and all she could do was moan as he pulled away from her. He moved her toward the edge of the bed, pulled her toward him so she could stand.

"Turn around," he breathed into her ear.

She did, and he bent her over at the waist. His knees nudged the back of her legs, and then his cock brushed against her. He eased inside, put his hands on her waist, and then began to thrust his cock into her. She put her hands on the bed pushed against him, wanting every last millimeter of him inside of her. He leaned forward, over her as he fucked her, long and deep, and moved his hand to her breast. He grabbed the pillowy flesh, squeezed, and moaned loudly as he came. He finished those last few strokes and she collapsed on the bed, her knees finally giving way. His weight landed next to her on the bed.

She was trying to move to a better spot on the bed when he shifted. He stood up, moved the blankets, and then picked her up and laid her back down with her head on the pillow. He covered her, then moved to the other side of the bed. He climbed in next to her, wrapped himself around her, and was snoring almost immediately. Leslie let herself enjoy the feeling of having his arms around her for just a moment before she joined him in exhausted, dreamless sleep.

Chapter Five

When she woke up the next morning, he was gone. She checked her email, then started getting ready to shower. Today was her last full day in New York, and she still had work to do before she left. She told herself, standing there in the bathroom, staring at her naked body in the mirror, that she wasn't going to cry. There had been no declarations of love; there weren't even declarations of like, or declarations of intentions to spend more time together. They had hung out, he had shown her some cool stuff in New York, and then they had crazy sex in her hotel. Of course she had put emotional overtones on it—that one date had been so bad, and sex with her husband had been dull and monotonous for years before they got divorced. This was the first great sex she'd had in years. She couldn't expect it to have been the same for him. She tried to tell herself that his leaving said nothing about her. But she still cried in the shower.

She walked out of the bathroom naked, to find coffee, croissants, and orange juice sitting on the table, and Alex on the bed, reading the paper. *Who reads the paper anymore?* Leslie grabbed a cup of juice, feeling sheepish. At least she had closed the bathroom door, so he hadn't heard her crying. Probably.

"I have kid stuff to do today, can we hang out tonight?" he asked. Leslie was surprised to hear that he sounded eager, excited even, to spend time with her.

As she got ready for work, they decided to meet back at the hotel for pizza and a movie in her room. Her flight left tomorrow afternoon, and she would need some time to tie up loose ends in the morning before she left. This would be their last night together.

She finished up her photography and research, and took a cab back to the hotel. She wanted to get back faster, so she could see him sooner. Leslie tried to tell herself that this was just a fling, a novelty, something to enjoy while she was here—and to talk about when she was wheelchair bound in the nursing home. But she knew that if it was just a fling, she wouldn't have that feeling in the pit of her stomach as she waited for him to text her back to let her know he was coming.

He said he was on the way, so she called and ordered pizza. He knocked while she was still on the phone; he must have been close. She opened the door, and he pushed his way inside and slammed the door. He kissed her on the cheek, his hands already on her, sliding up her back under her shirt, to unhook her bra. She laughed, and tried to move away from him so she could concentrate on the phone. Alex walked with her, step by step, guiding her toward the bed. She had to start over with her order twice, as Alex helped her down to a seated position and began unbuttoning her shirt, his mouth on her neck. She finally finished the order and ended the phone call. Alex helped her move back onto the bed. He very quickly and skillfully stripped her clothes off. She felt like a fumbling idiot as she tried to pull his shirt over his head. She wanted the weight of him, comforting and close, on her body.

This time was hurried. They both needed the other, quickly. Sometimes, what you need is someone else's skin against yours, knowing the thrill of the touch of a live body. Knowing that someone wanted to touch you, as much as you wanted to touch them. Anything else that happens is a bonus. That's how Leslie felt from the moment Alex started touching her. As he moved over her, his mouth on her neck, her breasts, her stomach, all she could think about was his skin against her fingers.

So intent on touching him, she hadn't noticed that he had managed to get his pants off, until she felt his hands on her thighs, moving them apart. She brought her legs back so he could easily slide inside of her. Even his cock was warm, filling her with him. His hands were on her waist as he slid into her, again and again. She was on the verge of orgasm already, from the urgency in his touch and the warmth of his skin, when he flicked his thumb over her clit. She kept her hands on his arms, and closed her eyes, as the orgasm took her.

As her climax subsided, Alex moved forward so he could kiss her. She wrapped her legs around his waist, pulling him closer. He moaned, moving faster, and Leslie sucked his tongue into her mouth. As much as she tried not to, she knew her fingernails were biting into the skin on his back, but she was so lost in how he was moving that she couldn't have stopped if she had wanted to. It didn't take him long either. He collapsed, wrapping his arms around her.

Her breathing was just starting to slow when she heard the knock at the door. She laughed as she realized that it must be their pizza arriving. Then she blushed, remembering how loud they had been as they finished. She hoped the delivery driver hadn't heard anything. Alex got up, slid into his jeans as he yelled, "Be right there."

They found a movie and ate mostly in silence, curled up around each other on the bed, the pizza box balanced on their legs. During the second half of the movie, Alex pushed the pizza box to the floor and made love to Leslie again. The movie hadn't really been all that interesting anyway. She took him, welcomed him, wanting more of him, but not able to keep her eyes open once they were done. When her alarm went off at five, they showered together, enjoying each other's touch one last time.

"I wish you were here longer," he said as he got dressed and she packed.

"I know. But I can try to come back. Maybe I can book some other photography. If the record company likes what I did, they may ask me to come out again. And you'll be in Denver in December for your concert."

"Yeah, our last one before Christmas, too. Maybe I can stay a few days."

"That would be great," she said as she looked him in the eyes. *I'm not going to cry. Dammit. You are not going to cry, Leslie.*

"Text me as soon as you land."

"I promise."

He put his hand on her face, his pinky finger against her neck, his fingers curled in her hair. He leaned in to kiss her, whispered in her ear.

"I don't want you to go."

Unbidden, her tears spilled, giant, fat tears, rolling down her cheeks. Leslie didn't want to leave, either. She wanted him. She wanted to touch him, to smell him, to kiss him, to fuck him.

She knew that if she could stay for months, it wouldn't be enough.

"I wish I could stay," she said.

He leaned forward, his forehead resting against hers, his eyes closed. Then, without a word, he turned and walked out the door.

Leslie sat down on the edge of the bed for a few minutes, trying to gather her thoughts. *How could this happen?* She could understand her feelings if this had been a rebound fling, but she had been divorced for three years now. She had never been one to jump head first into a relationship. *How could she have feelings for someone she had known for three days?*

Shaking her head, Leslie got up to finish packing. She had a few things to throw into her backpack, then she grabbed her jacket and suitcase, and walked out of the room. When she got to the elevator, Alex was standing there.

He wrapped his arms around her, his eyes searching. Leslie was afraid she was about to get lost in them. His voice was low, gravelly, and thick.

"There's got to be something we can do here."

"What do you mean?" Leslie asked.

"Did I misunderstand things? Am I the only one that felt something in your room this morning?"

Leslie tried to shake her head no, but then he was moving toward her, his lips on hers. His hand slid back along her jaw line, tangling in her hair, and Leslie could only stand there as he took her with his mouth. There was no other way for her to describe it. It was the hottest, most sensual kiss Leslie had ever had. He had claimed her. By the time he finally stopped, Leslie was panting.

Alex's lips were against hers, his voice almost a growl. "Well? Did I misunderstand?"

"No. But I can't stay."

Alex took a step back. Leslie reached out, wrapped a finger in his belt loop. She didn't want him moving too far away.

"I know you can't stay. But dammit, Leslie, I am not just going to let you walk out of my life. I...I don't even know what I'm doing here. But what I do know, is that I couldn't even stomach the thought of getting on that elevator, knowing that you were ten steps away. I'm not just going to leave right now. I can't."

"I don't want you to leave. I don't want to leave. But the real world, Alex, is an entirely different matter. You have kids, I have kids. You have a tour to rehearse for. My kids went through a divorce, and then I moved them from a tiny little town to a big city. They're just now getting adjusted and I can't move them again right now. I'm fairly certain that you don't really want to move yours, either. And considering that the bulk of your work is here, it's going to be hard for you to live anywhere else, anyway."

"Are you always this practical?"

"Yes."

Built up tears finally spilled over her eyelashes. She rested her head on his chest. It fit there, like his chest was sculpted for the exact shape, size, and location of her head. She closed her eyes, breathed in his scent.

"I'll text you when my plane lands. We can talk on the phone when you're not in rehearsals. I'll see you in Denver in a few months. You can spend Christmas there, if you want." Alex's arms came up, around her, pulling her even closer against him.

"Yeah. We can talk anytime. Maybe I can come out before the tour starts. It's not going to be enough, Leslie. I couldn't breathe, standing out here, waiting for you."

"I know, Alex. I sat on my bed, willing myself not to cry. But," she said, pulling away from him. "I have to go."

She pushed the elevator button. Feeling him take her hand, she turned toward him as he pulled her fingers to his lips, and gave them a quick kiss as the elevator doors opened. He let go of her, and she stepped into the elevator. She managed not to really cry until she got on the plane.

Chapter Six

She texted him when she got clear of the airport in Denver, and they texted back and forth as she rode home on the bus. She told him about the guy who sat next to her on the flight, who fell asleep before they left the ground and who farted until they landed in Denver. He told her about the amazing bagel that she had missed out on.

For the next few weeks, they texted back and forth, regularly. They kept their conversations light, each focused on making the other laugh, or talking about work. The photographs Leslie had done in New York had been well received, and Alex and the band were rehearsing for their tour, and getting great reviews for the album. School was starting and they were both getting busy, so they rarely talked on the phone.

Alex stopped returning her texts around the middle of October. Their first tour date was supposed to be Halloween night, so Leslie thought that maybe rehearsals had just been grinding him down. He had mentioned being tired the last time they talked. But she kept trying to text him for a week after Halloween, and never heard a word. After a long, teary, bourbon soaked night, she gave up, and called herself stupid for falling for a rock star.

Things didn't slow down for Leslie. Thanksgiving came and went, and before she knew it, it was December. Her kids were going to spend the holiday with their dad; they were leaving the morning of Resistance's concert. She had been unsure about going, but decided that they were still her favorite band, even if Alex was a stone-cold prick. The record company's press office had mailed out her ticket a while back, and she had it ready to go.

Once the kids had left, she started getting ready. Part of her wanted to get there early, so she could pin him down and get some answers. She had believed everything that he said the morning that she left, and she thought that she deserved some kind of explanation for why he had said those things if he didn't mean them. It wasn't like he needed to say them to convince her to sleep with him. The deed had long since been done by then.

The other part of her still wasn't even sure about going. She didn't know how she was going to feel, standing there watching him play. She hadn't even resolved her own emotions. In some ways she wanted to beg, to plead, to understand what happened and ask him to make her feel the way she had their last night together. The rest of her wanted to throw a drink at him like a film noir drama queen.

She dressed carefully. It would be cold outside, but warm in the venue. She chose jeans, knee high suede boots with a low heel, a black top, and a floor length cardigan sweater. She looked good, and she knew it. When she arrived at the small arena they were playing at, it was three hours before show time.

She sat in her car and tried to decide if she should go in now, or wait. She was certain they were in there, doing their sound check, and whatever else it was that bands did before a show. She was certain that her press pass from one of the local publications that she worked for would get her in the door early. She was certain that if she went in now she would say something that she would regret later. She was not certain that she cared.

In her head, she had rehearsed what she would say to Alex a million times. She wanted to be mad; she felt used, and betrayed. She had wanted him, and slept with him without needing to hear words of endearment, or commitment. The things he had said that last morning, when he was waiting for her at the elevator, that was the part that hurt. If he had never suggested trying to make a relationship work, she would have gone home, and accepted the fact that she had a great three days with a nice guy, and that was that. Even feeling the way she had that last morning, was on her. She accepted that.

On the other hand, she also wanted to be aloof, to act like his not returning her texts hadn't bothered her. She had even considered bringing a date, but had decided not to. She didn't want to put some poor innocent guy in the middle of her history with Alex.

Lost in thought, she didn't notice when Tim walked up

to her car, and she jumped when he tapped on the window. She opened the car door, and found herself swept up in a hug.

"The pictures were great. You made us look ten years younger," he said.

She laughed. It had been one of the more fun photo shoots she had been on in a long time, and she told him that.

"Are you coming in? It's getting cold out here."

"I was just thinking about it. I'm not sure I should come in early..." She didn't know if Tim knew that she and Alex had slept together.

"Alex has been talking about seeing you," Tim said.

"Oh yeah? I find that kind of surprising. I haven't talked to him in months." Leslie felt the tears building in her eyes. She hadn't told anyone at home about what had happened with Alex. At first, she had wanted to respect his privacy. Afterwards, she had been embarrassed.

"He told me everything a few weeks ago. We got stuck in Chicago because of weather, and we spent a long night at the hotel bar. Hadn't done that in years. He feels really bad."

"I don't know what to say. I should go." Suddenly, Leslie wanted to be anywhere but standing a few hundred feet away from Alex. The thought of seeing him brought that anxious feeling to the pit of her stomach. It wasn't that pleasant little twinge of excitement you get when you're going to do something really awesome. It wasn't that slam you in the gut feeling like when you're falling or you're watching a baseball come flying at your face. It was visceral, somewhere between butterflies and vomiting.

"I'm not going to try to change your mind. But I think you'll be making a mistake if you leave. At least talk to him. He should know how you feel. Clearly, you're hurting. You need him to know that."

"When did you become a philosopher?" Leslie smiled.

"Actually, I'm a yoga master. Philosophy is a big part of that. I used yoga to find my own balance, after so many things in my life went to shit. It was what I clung to. I had lost faith in everything, including myself. But the spiritual side of yoga got me through. Now, I try to help people find balance. You were balanced when we met in New York, but I don't think you had been for long. Now, you're all off balance, and you're not going to get back there unless you talk to him."

Leslie wouldn't have put it that way, but she knew that Tim was right. It would be easier to leave, and let her feelings abate with time, and a good bit of bourbon, but she had never run away from a fight. She wanted him to know that he had hurt her.

"All right, let's go. But you're buying me a drink after the show."

"Deal," he said. He put his arm around her shoulders and walked into the club with her.

As they stepped into the small arena, she was assaulted by bright lights and warmth, a big contrast to the drizzly, gray coldness outside. She heard the sounds of guitars echoing through the halls, and Greg talking into the mic. Resistance no longer sold out stadiums, but they could manage smaller arenas, and had sold out the 4000 tickets to tonight's show.

As they were walking, Tim said, "I want to tell you something. I've known Alex all my life. I've watched him struggle with legal trouble, ex-wives, and addiction. I've watched him beat every struggle in his life. He's always reached a point where he was just done and got busy and fixed whatever problem it was. Serving his time, doing what was right by his kids, going to rehab. He's always known what to do, and gotten it done. The other night was different. He knows he messed up. But he has no idea how to fix it."

Leslie nodded. She was afraid that she didn't know, either.

Tim opened the door. "He's in there," he said, guiding her inside. He shut the door behind her, leaving her standing there by herself.

She saw Alex running hard on the treadmill, his long hair braided down his back. She knew how hard he was running, because she'd run that hard at the gym that morning. It still hadn't been fast enough. She moved against the wall, careful to stay out of his line of sight so she didn't startle him. He had lost weight since August. It looked good on him. He didn't have that puffy look that heavy drinkers get, so she guessed, despite his binge in Chicago with Tim, that he'd managed to mostly stay sober. He kept on for about five more minutes before he changed his pace. As he slowed to a stop, she moved so he could see her. His eyes met hers, then dropped to the ground. He moved off the treadmill, towards her. She took a step back, ready to flee. She wanted him to come to her, crying, begging forgiveness with his arms around her, but she knew that if he touched her, she would run. Otherwise, she would be the one crying.

"Jesus, Leslie, I'm not gonna hurt you."

"That's about the one thing I know for sure right now."

"I'm sorry," he whispered.

Leslie snorted. "For what?"

"I don't know. Everything!" Alex yelled.

"That's not good enough, Alex. I need you to know. I need you to care. I need you to figure this shit out and then give me a real apology, if that's actually what you intend to do."

"Do you know how many times I've been married?"

Leslie knew the answer, but decided to let him talk.

"Twice. I loved both of them. I felt like part of them was engraved on my soul when I was with them. With you? I felt like my soul was being ripped apart when I wasn't with you. I couldn't stand watching you get on that elevator, walking away from me, knowing that even if I fucking begged you, you couldn't stay. You didn't look to me as a trophy, or a savior, or a bank account. You are this strong, independent woman who doesn't need me to clean up some mess or make her life better. You don't need me. But because of that, I can't have you. Because that, apparently, is all the good I am."

"Now you wait just a fucking minute here. Don't go judging what happened between us because of what happened in your past. Here I thought you were supposed to be the big bad guy, and you're standing in front of me whining because life is unfair? You think it didn't kill me to get on that elevator? It did occur to me, for about half a second, to uproot my kids and go to New York and be happy with you. But we're grownups, Alex. With responsibilities. So it can't be like that. So you chose nothing, instead of trying to make something, anything work? How's your nothing working out for you?"

"It's not. Is that what you want to hear? I'm miserable. I have wanted to pick up that phone every day. Every damn day. And yeah. I do judge what happened between us by what's happened in my past. There's a pattern, in case you haven't noticed."

"Yes, Alex, there is a pattern. But the one I'm noticing isn't the one you're noticing. You need to ask yourself a question. You know the answer. What do I need from you?"

Alex was silent. Leslie took a step toward him, wanting to look into his eyes.

"What do I need from you?"

"Nothing."

It was so quiet in the room that she was sure she heard her own heart, pounding in her chest.

"Wrong, Alex. You're wrong. I do need something from you. And if you can't figure that out, we're done."

Leslie walked out of the arena, got into her car, and drove home, sobbing the entire way.

Chapter Seven

It was Christmas Eve, and Leslie was baking. The house was quiet. With the kids gone, she really didn't need to bake, but she took the break during the Christmas holiday to stock the freezer with cookies and brownies and other treats for the days when she was busy with work. Her kitchen was small; the apartment she and the kids had moved into after her divorce wasn't huge, but it was her space, and she loved it. She moved through the kitchen in her bare feet, dancing to the radio, as she slid several bread pans filled with banana bread batter into the oven.

It had been a week since the concert. Leslie had forced herself to work, updating her website and sending out proof sets to two brides. While she enjoyed being paid to travel around the country to do the photography she loved, it was the stuff like weddings and large public events that paid most of her bills. She was sought after, and well respected, but she still had to work her butt off. Saving for a house was no easy feat.

Lost in thought, she almost hadn't heard the knock on the door. She turned down the radio, and went to the door, expecting to find a neighbor, or her brother, maybe coming to take her to dinner. Alex was the last person she expected to be standing on her doorstep. She let him in and closed the door. She had no idea what she was going to say. She turned around and he was there, wrapping his arms around her.

"You need me. Only me. Not my status or my fame or my money, but me."

"Like I need to breathe."

Leslie wanted to be mad. She wanted to hate him. But she couldn't. She had waited months to feel his arms around her, and she needed him. She took a deep breath, inhaling his scent, drinking it in. Drunk, on him, before he had even kissed her.

She wrapped her arms around his neck, bringing him down to her, so she could taste him. She closed her eyes, and let him take her with his mouth. She wanted to touch him everywhere at once, to feel the warmth of his skin under her finger-tips. She tried to pull his shirt off, couldn't get it out of the way fast enough. She wasn't sure she could wait until they made it to the bedroom. She just needed to feel him. All of him.

She walked backward, trying to guide him into her bedroom without breaking the kiss. Finally, she could go no further, and she pulled away, took his hand, and pulled him with her. Her bed was unmade, clothes scattered on the floor, and her purse was thrown in the corner. She cared about the mess for about half a second, before she felt his hands on her again. She couldn't think of anything else except getting him into her bed, and feeling him inside of her. She fumbled at his belt, trying to loosen it, and almost sobbed when she couldn't make it.

"Shh, Leslie. Let me do it." Alex moved her hands away, undid his belt, and then reached for her, grabbed at her t-shirt, and pulled it over her head. They moved back onto the bed, and he unhooked her bra. Immediately, she felt his mouth on her nipple. She gasped, and then moaned. It had been months since New York City.

She couldn't think, couldn't remember what she had been doing just a second before. She let him touch her, enjoying the sensation as she trailed her fingers across his back, as his tongue flicked her nipple and made her moan. He tried to un-button her pants, and got just as frustrated as she had been. She reached her hands down, undid the button, and slid her pants over her hips.

His fingers stroked her pussy lips, and she spread her legs. He brushed his finger over her clit, and she pushed against him, wanting more. She was trying to get her legs out of her pants, and he was doing the same. There were legs and arms everywhere. They were giggling.

When they were both undressed, Alex moved so that he was lying beside her on the bed. She wanted him, badly, but he was taking his time. He stroked her belly with his fingers, occasionally brushing the undersides of her breasts. She reached down, wanting to touch his cock, but he moved away from her. Clearly, he planned on tormenting her for a while.

Leslie had a different plan. She sat up, pushed Alex down

on the bed, and moved so that she was straddling him.

"We can play later. I don't know about you, and I really don't want to know, but for me, it's been a long time since August."

She reached down, wrapped her fingers around his hard cock, and guided him inside of her. He moaned loudly as she settled herself on top of him. She leaned forward, rested her hands on his chest, and began moving her hips. She loved hearing the sounds that he made when he was inside of her.

Alex wrapped an arm around her waist, and reversed their positions so that he was on top. He started fucking her harder, and faster, and Leslie knew it wouldn't take long for her to orgasm. Alex's mouth on her nipple was all it took. It started deep in her belly, and her orgasm triggered his. She was senseless for a few minutes after they had finished.

Leslie thought she must have drifted off. She heard Alex say something, but she couldn't quite make out his words.

"Leslie, I asked what you're cooking. Whatever's in the oven smells great," he said.

"Oh shit!" Leslie jumped out of bed, and ran through the apartment, naked. She opened the oven, and pulled out the banana bread. It was really done. Not quite burned, but definitely done. She pulled the loaves out and set them on the counter to cool. She turned around to see Alex standing in the doorway, laughing.

"I guess it's a good thing we were in a hurry."

"Yeah. Hurry. It's what we do, I guess. Why are you here?"

"Do you want me to leave?"

He was on the defensive. That wasn't how Leslie wanted to start.

"No. I'm sorry. That came out wrong. I'm glad you're here. But what are your intentions about us?"

"My intention is to pack up this apartment and move you and your kids to New York with me and live the perfect little life. But I know that's not your intention, so I guess we're going to have to figure out another solution. Working, spending time away from you is something I'm going to have to adjust to, I guess. It's better than not having you at all. I can't do that anymore. I need you, too. You were right. Anything is better than nothing."

"Alex, I don't need perfect. But I do need you to be around once in a while. I want to show you around Denver, and discover your favorite books, and watch campy movies with you. I want to show you my favorite spot in the mountains, and see yours in New York. I just want you. I want to go to New York with you. We just have to do things slowly, responsibly. It sucks and I'm sorry, but it's the way it has to be. Can we make this work?"

In that moment, Leslie was afraid he would say no. She was afraid he would walk away, but she had offered everything she had to offer. She hadn't realized she was holding her breath until he smiled and took her hand, and her breath left her in a rush.

"We'll make it work, I promise."

Fixing up Christmas

by Melody Barber

To my best friend, who told me I could write a book, and to anyone who ever thought they missed their chance in love.

Chapter One

The lump in her throat was the size of a softball. She hadn't seen most of her old classmates in ten years. Apparently, it was a unanimous decision to wait until mid-December for a reunion to ensure people could attend. Her class president scheduled it close to the holiday when everyone would be traveling home already. Amberly didn't take part in any of the planning or voting that happened over social media in the prior months. There had been better things to do, like painting the cedar shakes on the Jacobs' House.

Amberly got out of the car and immediately regretted her choice in attire. The brisk air hit her long, bare legs, and she walked towards the door as fast as she could in her heels. "Why did it have to be formal? Don't these people remember it gets cold in the winter in New Hampshire?" A chilly forty-six wasn't as bad as it could be, but it certainly wasn't warm. Especially to someone that spent the last four years getting accustomed to the warm temperatures of southern California. She stopped short of the door upon hearing someone mention a familiar name. Sawyer Jameson. That name sent a chill down her spine and made the butterflies in her stomach chug a Five-Hour Energy. He was the love of her life – or had been. Sawyer had been the captain of the football team, popular, and voted most likely to succeed. If only he'd known she existed. The softball from earlier made a triumphant return to her throat with the intention of cutting off her airway. Now, on top of seeing the people who made fun of her weight, talked behind her back, and couldn't be bothered to include her in anything, she had to deal with seeing the one man that got away.

Holding her breath, she opened the door to the banquet hall and stepped inside. Luckily, there was a bathroom to the immediate right so she could slip inside to do a quick check before making a real entrance and hopefully catching a glimpse of Sawyer.

A large mirror rested atop the granite vanity. Stormy

blue-gray eyes were adorned with black, wing tipped liner and light brown shimmering shadow that complimented her deep red lips. She didn't usually wear this much makeup, if any at all, but her makeup artist was a friend and taught her a few tricks before she left. She fixed the buckle on her strappy heel, and adjusted the deep red satin dress that draped over her curves to her mid-thigh. She thanked God that she was no longer the quiet, awkward girl who spent more time in shop class, alone, than having lunch with her "friends" who never seemed to notice if she was there, anyway. Not that she regretted her decisions. In fact, shop class was the best part of high school. It opened the door to her passion. Additional classes in woodworking, construction, interior design, and real estate shaped her into the most sought after contractor/rehabber of historical homes in Pennsylvania, and that reputation landed her a TV show on cable and a new home on the west coast. Who was the nobody now?

He adjusted his tie. Looking in the mirror, Sawyer wondered why he was bothering to go to a reunion where everyone would know his story. Word traveled fast when probation and jail came into the conversation. No one had talked to him since he came back. He was an outcast now. The boy once voted most likely to succeed was now labeled a "bad seed" and a "druggy," whether it was true or not. Even so, he knew why he was going: to see *her*. Even if it was from afar, it would be worth it.

It had been ten years. He wondered if she looked the same, or if she was completely different. They weren't friends, nor had they dated. Hell they'd barely spoken two words to each other, but he had loved her. She was quiet, always kept to herself, but there was something about her. If only he'd had the guts to talk to her back then, maybe his life would be different now. Then again, what would have been the point? They went to college in different states. Still, it would have been nice to start something when he had a chance. He was one of the few people he knew that never got into social media. He'd had a Myspace account for all of two weeks then deactivated it. Unlike the rest of the world, which seemed to be addicted to Facebook, he had no idea what anyone was up to. She was probably married with kids now.

Leaving his house, he set off for the banquet hall. If he hurried, he could be out of the cold in less than forty-five minutes. Walking in the cold was less embarrassing than getting a ride from his parents. Only two more months and he would be able to get his license back. He'd been off probation for a few years now, and his fines almost paid off.

The lights on the banquet hall were visible when he turned the corner. He hurried towards the door, partly because he was shivering, but also in anticipation of seeing her, of seeing Amberly.

Amberly left the bathroom with a thin veil of confidence, if only for a moment, when she spotted her best friend behind the table, handing out nametags.

"Amberly Jenkins, it's been forever since we've talked. Seriously, it's been like four hours." Unable to keep up the stern façade, a smile spread across Kelsey's face. "Hang on a sec. I'll grab your nametag."

"I know, way too long; that shit is unacceptable." She laughed as she walked over to give Kelsey a hug.

Although they'd never spent time together outside of school, now that they'd graduated and moved on with their lives, Kelsey Sherwood was one of the few people Amberly spent time with when she was in town. She was happy to call this five-foot-two-inch spitfire her best friend. They lost touch for a few years after graduation, but reconnected in their early twenties and had been best friends ever since. Even when Amberly was given the job of a lifetime and moved, she and Kelsey remained close and visited each other several times a year. They were overjoyed when her career brought her home for an extended stay where they could spend quality time catching up outside of Skype and Facebook.

Kelsey handed her a white sticker. *Amberly Jenkins, Valedictorian.* With that, she walked through the double doors into the crowded room. It was bustling with the sounds of her classmates' conversations, footsteps, and chiming plates as waiters prepared a table for food in the middle of the dance floor.

Walking towards an empty seat, people she didn't know, or never associated with greeted her. She hadn't counted on people recognizing her from her TV show. She even overheard someone call her a hometown hero.

Hometown hero? She snickered at the thought.

She might accept that title if this deal she had on the table for a house on Fourth Street worked in her favor. Saving the oldest house in the town seemed like a heroic act, to her anyway. The old woman that lived in it passed away a few years ago, leaving it without anyone to take care of it. Now Amberly's dream house faced demolition. It needed major repair work, a new foundation, replacement support beams, and a fresh roof. She was willing to pay the funds needed to bring it back to its former glory, and if everything fell into place, she might just move into it afterwards.

The sight of a familiar face and dirty blonde hair pulled her from her thoughts. She met his intense gaze and almost lost her balance, bracing herself with one hand on the nearest table.

Was he walking towards her? Was he looking at her? Was she breathing? She took in a deep breath and forced it out at the realization that she, in fact, wasn't.

Chapter Two

She was more beautiful than he remembered. She had the same blue-gray eyes that reminded him of the sea on a cloudy day and her dark brown hair framed her face in curls. Although she had lost a noticeable amount of weight, that didn't matter to him, she was beautiful at any size. He stared from across the room as she talked to their classmates. Once she set her purse on a table, he decided it was now or never; sucking in a deep breath he started towards her.

Time seemed to stop as he made his way towards her table. His stomach was doing flips, nervousness washing over him, as he got closer to her. The look on her face didn't help the matter. It was too late to turn back now.

"Amberly Jenkins. Is that you?"

"Y-yes, that's me," she stuttered through her answer.

He grinned as they both took a seat.

She jumped when his deep husky voice spoke her name. He knew her name? He had to have seen her show; surely he didn't actually remember her. She was invisible back then, why not now?

"How've you been?" he asked.

This wasn't happening, not really. Was it? *The* Sawyer Jameson was talking to her. Moreover, he was talking to her like an old friend.

"I've been good." Assuming he knew her from her show like everyone else, she continued. "The show's next season starts filming in a few days."

"Wait, show? You're on TV?"

"Uhh yeah, isn't that how you know me?"

"No, that's cool and all, but we've been in the same

homeroom since Junior High. I know who you are."

Under the table, Amberly pinched her arm, just to make sure she wasn't dreaming. What kind of alternate universe did she step into? "Right," she mumbled.

Amberly leaned back in the chair and took in the sight of the gorgeous man talking to her. He had a strong jawline covered by a five o'clock shadow. His eyes were a unique and amazing combination of blue and brown specks that everyone swore were contacts. Although, she knew better; she memorized those eyes long ago. He was tall and lean, but muscular. The vision of him without his shirt had her cheeks flushing crimson. He was in a black suit, white shirt, and red tie that was a perfect match to her dress.

"Are you okay?"

Oh great, he noticed…

"I-I'm fine, just a little warm. I need to get some fresh air, and then I'll be okay." As she rose from her chair, he followed. When his hand touched her arm, the spark ignited something low in her belly that had been dormant for the better part of a year. She expected him to wait for her at the table while she ran and hid in a corner until her mortified state passed. However, to her surprise, he escorted her the entire way. Once they were outside, she realized that she was alone with him, for the first time ever.

"Can I be blunt?" she asked, twisting her hands together and praying she wouldn't throw up. It'd be easier to get the hard part over with if the conversation was going to last. The worst case would be him taking offense and her going back to life as normal.

His shrug shouldn't have been sexy, but it was. Maybe it was the smirk that followed it. "Sure," he said. "Ask me anything."

"Why now? If you knew who I was in junior high, then why wait ten years after graduation to say one word to me? Unless you looked me up from my show and put two and two together that we would have had homeroom together." She waited as he stood staring at her with a dumbfounded look.

"Well…" he said. "Honestly, I didn't think you liked me

very much. Every time I looked at you, you'd turn your head the other way. Plus you were always so quiet and were never around at assemblies, so I guess I figured you didn't want to be approached."

She wanted to kick herself. His statement made perfect sense. She never thought how her actions would appear to the outside world. She did look away if he looked at her, but only because she thought he would catch her staring from afar, and she didn't go to assemblies because she hated the cheerleaders and most of the jocks that graced the halls of her school. They were the ones who called her "Stay-Puft Marshmallow" and other mean names because of her weight. She didn't want to find out that Sawyer was the same so she kept herself away from him.

"Oh." She looked anywhere but at him. "I did like you." She wasn't sure if he'd even hear her with how small her voice was. She shifted and turned away so he couldn't see her blush.

A cold breeze swept through the bushes that lined the patio area where they stood, causing her to shiver. Her thin shawl was no match for the winter air.

"Let's get you back inside before you freeze to death."

She hadn't noticed that he'd removed his jacket until his strong, rough hands grazed her shoulder, wrapping the jacket around her. Walking back inside, she snuck a deep breath into his jacket without him noticing. If he did catch sight of her, he didn't say anything. The scent of his cologne and an aroma that vaguely reminded her of her dad after he'd change the oil in the car, a comforting, manly scent of sweat and grease, filled her nose.

"So what have you been up to over the last ten years?" he asked as they took their seats again.

"Well, I went to Penn State, majoring in architecture with a minor in business. I took side classes in construction and real estate. I started building new houses until I fell in love with an old house slated for demolition. I knew I had to save it, so I chained myself to the door and wouldn't move until they made a deal. I had six months to fix it up to code, or I had to pay out of pocket for the demolition myself. I raised a lot of media attention and got a lot of help from volunteers." Being so close to him had her babbling. "At the end of six months, it was up to code and fully restored. When the city inspected it, they decided they wanted to keep it as a historical piece and paid me three times the amount I put into it. I found my passion in that house and used the money to buy another house to restore. Three more houses and I was approached by the network to start filming, moved to Southern California six years ago, and the rest is history." *God, he didn't want her life story.* She needed a drink so she would shut up.

Panicking, she rose from her seat and excused herself to the bar. "Do you want a beer? Yes? No? I'll just get you one anyways." She returned a few moments later carrying two beers. Passing him one, she almost immediately retrieved it. "Shit, you're not an alcoholic or anything, right? I don't want to mess with any twelve step programs." *Did she just say that out loud?* "I mean… I'm an insensitive idiot." Leaning her forehead against her hand in embarrassment, she hoped the floor would open beneath her and swallow her whole.

"So, what have you been up to?"

Shit. He thought she already knew his story, and wouldn't have to worry about the conversation shifting to him. Although, since she didn't, and she wouldn't be there long enough to matter maybe he could make himself a better person.

"You're not insensitive or an idiot, although you are cute when you're nervous." He flashed his smile when he saw her blush, and continued. "For the last few years I've been here working at my dad's shop since he hurt his back. I'm sure I'll be taking it over fully soon since he's been talking retirement lately."

"What about football?" she asked.

"Well I blew out my knee and lost my scholarship, so I switched to business before coming back."

At that moment, Kelsey interrupted them.

"Amberly, sorry to interrupt, but you're up next for your speech and we'll need to take your photo and get your bio for the newsletter we're giving out at the end of the night."

Amberly excused herself and walked towards the group of people in the hallway.

Sawyer took the last drink of his beer and got up to head towards the bathroom. On his way back, he saw Amberly and Kelsey talking quietly amongst themselves. He overheard his name and ducked around the corner before they noticed him.

Kelsey started, "What are you doing, Amberly?"

"What do you mean? I was just talking to Sawyer Jameson. Do you remember him?"

"Yeah I remember him. Who could forget Francistown's resident bad boy?"

"Bad boy? What are you talking about, Kels?" Amberly asked.

"You don't know? He was arrested." Kelsey's tone painted him as a disgusting piece of shit.

Before he could hear any more of the conversation, Amberly was called to the stage.

"We'll finish this after my speech. You can tell me what this is all about." With that, she started towards the stage.

The jig was up; as soon as Kelsey got a hold of Amberly again, she would know he was a complete failure. Struggling with what to do next, Sawyer stayed out of sight and listened to her speech, but quickly made his exit before she could find him.

Chapter Three

After her speech, Amberly didn't see Sawyer anywhere. She pushed him to the back of her mind and continued her night of reminiscing with her friend, as well as answering and dodging questions about being a *celebrity*.

Towards the end of the night, she asked Kelsey what she meant about Sawyer. To her surprise, she got a completely different story about what happened with his life after high school. He did lose his scholarship due to a knee injury, but it was because he crashed his car and injured himself in an attempt to get away from the cops. They found drugs in his car and arrested him for it, along with illegal street racing. He served some time but was let out on good behavior, put on probation, and allowed to come back here and work off his debt to society.

"Why would he lie to me about that? It doesn't make sense."

"Probably to get in your pants; if you were impressed maybe he could get somewhere with you."

"Damn it, and I fell for it. Thank God you were here and set things straight; I was starting to wonder if I had a chance."

She kicked herself for thinking there would be any real reason he would talk to her. She should have known; she guessed some things never changed. Still, she couldn't shake the spark she felt and the obvious attraction to him that never went away.

Her drive back to her parents' house was boring and too quiet. She had too much time to think. Sawyer couldn't have spent that much time coming up with a detailed story just for sex. There had to be more to it. At least she hoped. Either way, she was determined to find out what. There was plenty of time. She'd be around until after Christmas.

"I'm going to that shop first thing in the morning to straighten this whole thing out. This time his charm won't faze me...I hope."

She wondered why she was still interested, and wanted it

to be a misunderstanding, that she would still have a chance to make something of it. Still she knew better, she couldn't pursue another liar, and people never change. Steering clear should be the only option, but her pounding heart had her questioning it. She went back and forth the rest of her drive home, finally deciding to leave it alone and avoid him the rest of her trip. It would be easier to go back to not knowing him than try to figure this whole thing out.

Pulling up to her parents' house, she noticed the kitchen light on; it was almost midnight, they were never up that late. Turning the key in the doorknob, she quietly crept into the house in case they left it on for her and went to bed themselves. Not that she needed it. This was originally her grandmother's house. She spent every summer here until she left for college. Not long after, her grandmother passed away and left the house to her parents. Amberly completely restored it for their anniversary in her first season on the show.

Walking towards the kitchen, she heard a familiar voice. What was Sawyer doing here at this hour? Especially after everything that happened, how could he show his face? And why was her heart beating faster?

"Amberly dear, there you are." Her mother sounded cheerful. "Your friend stopped by looking for you; we told him you were still out, but he could wait here until you got back."

Her mom was one of the town's favorite people. She was a friend to everyone and brought her southern hospitality with her after she and Amberly's father moved from South Carolina. She never lost the slow pace, the need to talk to everyone, and of course, the Southern drawl.

"Mom, can I talk to you in the living room for a minute?" Amberly smiled, hoping the apprehension didn't come through in her voice.

Speaking as quietly as she could so he wouldn't overhear, she turned to her mother. "Mom, it's late. You should have told him to come back tomorrow."

Because tomorrow, she knew that she would have come up with *something* that made it impossible to meet up with him.

"Don't be silly dear. You're not a little girl anymore. You

can have friends over at a later hour. I'll let you two talk; your father and I are going to bed. I'll see you in the morning. Come on Harold, let's give these kids some time to talk."

"Okay, goodnight pumpkin." Her dad's voice got louder as he walked in from the family room.

"Goodnight Sawyer, it was nice chatting with you." Her mother said loud enough for him to hear from dining room.

With a kiss on the forehead, Amberly's mother left the room. Amberly didn't have a chance to object.

She walked back into the kitchen and sat at the table.

"Please tell me Kelsey was misinformed," she pleaded. "You were arrested for drugs and illegal street racing?"

"She was right. It's true, and that's why I wanted to talk to you," he answered.

"Why would I want to talk to you after you lied to me? Ugh! Why am I bothering? It's not like you're going to be honest with me."

"I'm sorry."

He hung his head and there was silence for a few minutes.

"That's it? That's all you have to say for yourself? You're not forgiven. Goodnight!" She stood, but he started speaking again.

He ran his hand through his hair. "I didn't want you to know I was a failure." He paused and she could see the torment in his eyes. "Everyone else here wants nothing to do with me, like I'm some kind of murderer."

As she was about to speak, he started again. "What did you want me to say? Oh, I'm glad you're doing so great. I screwed up my life, there's no point in talking about it. Technically, I didn't lie. I just left out the bad parts." His fist bumped the table, causing her to jump in surprise. "What Kelsey told you was true. I was street racing. I got into the crowd thanks to my roommate. He was making tens of thousands of dollars a night and he took me along when I needed some fast cash. When my dad hurt his back, he lost a lot of business to the dealership that opened down the street. He was about to lose everything, I had to do something."

Wringing his hands, he continued. "So I raced and I won. It was an adrenaline rush and the money was great. I sent it to my dad in spurts so he wouldn't know where it came from. Eventually, I ended up getting my own car. One night, my roommate and I got drunk and decided to bet pink slips for the next race. I won." He shook his head at the memory. "He called the cops on me and left. When the cops showed up I panicked and ran. But they followed me because their tip also said that my car was holding thousands of dollars of illegal drugs. My roommate planted them when my back was turned." He sighed long and deep. "I took a turn too quickly and lost control of the car, crashing into a light pole. The impact tore three of the four major ligaments in my knee. When they released me from the hospital, I went straight to jail. I pled out to reckless driving, fleeing the scene, and possession. I lost my license, received several thousand dollars in fines, and served six months, followed by eighteen months of probation. My parents convinced the judge to let me serve my probation here, under their eye, working off my debt in my dad's shop. Most of my hours went straight to paying my fines." He held up his hands, palms to her. "That's the whole truth, I swear it."

She didn't know what to say. She hadn't expected a full confession. His honesty had her reeling. She couldn't help the feeling that she wanted him to take her right then.

This can't happen. It's not a good idea, Amberly. Pull yourself together. Getting mixed up with a guy like him, misunderstood or not, will only complicate things.

"Well?"

His voice cut through her thoughts as she realized she had been sitting there staring at him like an idiot.

"Sorry, I need some time to process this. I don't know if I should even consider believing your story."

The shame on his face was apparent, and she felt in her gut that he was being genuine. Besides, that was one hell of a detailed story, and not in his favor, for that matter. If he was lying, he should be an actor.

"Okay," he said, standing. "I can give you some time." She stood with him. As she moved to walk him to the door, he stepped forward forcing her body to collide gently against his. "I had no nerve and no luck with you before. This time has to be different." His hands stroked her arms, and she trembled with desire. "So, you can have your time. All the time you want, but I'm not leaving before I do this one thing I want. What I've always wanted."

His gaze bore into hers with an intensity that made it hard for her to swallow. What was he talking about? She was sure his lips were moving, but the sound that met her ears was the clumsy thud of her accelerating heartbeat. He was going to kiss her. It registered one second before his soft, warm lips pressed to hers and the world went blissfully dark. Who needed to see when you could feel? An electric current soared through her, surging into a burning heat, so hot she was sure they would both go up in flames.

He cradled her face in his hands and took the kiss deeper. Her lips parted, and as his tongue invaded her mouth, a quiet moan escaped her. There was no way this was really happening; she must be dreaming. She would have pinched herself had her brain not gone into complete shutdown. Thinking escaped her; what were thoughts anyway? She leaned into his kiss as he slowly pushed her back to the wall, and pressed himself against her. She felt the hard muscles of what had to be a six-pack at the very least. Her brain jumped in to rescue her as his arousal pushed into her leg. She pulled away from him, even though every part of her screamed to keep going. She was breathless and struggling to regain control.

"As much as I hate to cut this short, if you don't go, I may do something I'll regret later." She let out a breathless laugh, partly because she knew she must be mad for stopping this, and because that was a hell of a kiss. She was punching herself in her mind. She'd been waiting for this moment, ten years in the making, and she was giving it up, just like that. She knew him, what was so wrong with sleeping with him on the first night?

"I understand, thanks for hearing me out." He turned towards the door and she wanted to stop him and drag him to her room. Even if it was weird that it was her parents' house, and that their room was right next to hers.

Instead, she grabbed his shoulder. "Are you free for lunch tomorrow? I would love to continue the conversation."

His face lit up. "Yeah, how about the little deli, say around noon?" He didn't need to explain where it was, there was only one deli in town.

"Sounds great, I'll walk you out." She turned to follow him to the door and gave him a quick kiss before she shut the door. It was hard not getting caught up again.

She turned, leaning her back against the door, sliding down against it to the floor. *What are you doing? What happened to leaving it alone?*

She hoped she wasn't grinning like an idiot the whole time. Who was she kidding? There was no emotional control going on in the empty space between her ears. Her brain had long left after that first kiss, only making a brief and unwanted return to keep her from sleeping with him.

He should have been freezing. It was a twenty minute walk back home from Amberly's house, but he didn't feel it. He was warm all over. She kissed him back, and even more, she asked to see him tomorrow. He barely contained his excitement as he turned the knob and entered his house. Things might just turn around.

He switched on the light in the hallway as he headed for the kitchen to grab a beer. He was sure he looked like an idiot with the grin on his face, but he didn't care. The feelings he'd harbored for years never went away. He'd finally done the one thing he'd never got a chance to do back in high school.

He took his beer with him into the bathroom and started the shower. There was no way he could sleep. Not now, his heart was still racing. Stepping into the warm water relaxed him. He stood under the stream of water for a long time before reaching over for his body wash. He couldn't help thinking about that kiss, and the feel of her body against his. His hands traveled across his body. Were they his hands? Or hers? When he started washing the trail from his stomach down to his inner thigh, his body responded. Grasping his erection in his hand, he started to stroke back and forth. His breathing deepened with each movement. He thought of Amberly, pressed against the wall, him possessing her mouth, feeling the curves of her body with his hands. He stroked faster, imagining her underneath him, naked, screaming his name, and as his balls clenched with need, he found his release. Grabbing the showerhead and washing away the evidence of his need, he leaned against the tile until he could think again. With the tension fading, he thought of their lunch date. She was giving him another chance and he wouldn't fuck up again. From now on, she would know everything. After that kiss, he would do whatever it took to see where this could go.

The blurry red lights came into focus as she looked at the clock on her side table. She shot up as her mind registered the time. "It's eleven! Fuck!"

She jumped out of bed and ran for the shower. The warm water was enticing her to stay and relax but she knew she couldn't stay long if she wanted to look good. As quickly as she was in, she was finished and plugging in her straightener and hair dryer.

It was the fastest she could recall getting ready. She decided on her tightest jeans, a deep red sweater, and black boots. Grabbing her phone, purse, and keys, she ran out the door.

The deli hadn't changed since she was in high school. The simple, family run business had been in the town for generations. Deep, golden walls offset charcoal colored countertops, tables, and chairs. The sandwich case held all of their crowd-pleasing desserts, and the giant chalkboard behind the counter was the home to the daily specials neatly written in multi-colored chalk.

Looking around, she didn't see Sawyer yet, so she grabbed a table and checked her phone. There was a text message from her best friend.

"Your mom told me you went to meet Sawyer. What are you doing? He's bad news Am, please be careful."

Even Kelsey knew this was a bad idea. So why was she here? The psychotic butterflies answered her question when he walked through the door.

"Hey, have you been here long?" he said, a concerned look on his face.

"Oh no, not at all. I just got here a few minutes ago and scooped up a table. Shall we go order?"

An awkward silence hung between them as they placed their order and awaited the food. She wasn't sure what to say when they got back to the table with their sandwiches. Hoping last night wasn't a fluke, but not knowing how to begin, she waited for him to start the conversation.

"So, about last night..." He finally broke the silence. "I'm sorry for lying to you, and coming by uninvited. And I'm sorry if I got too carried away. I couldn't help myself. I had to kiss you, even if it was to find closure for the last ten years. You looked sexy as hell, and to be frank, it's been a long time since someone gave me the time of day. With my reputation, people around here tend to avoid me like the plague."

She secretly wondered if they had the right idea. She knew she shouldn't be getting mixed up with him, but God. Did he have to look so hot in his tight black t-shirt, tattoos peeking out, and dark jeans?

"It's okay, I appreciate that you came all the way to my house to explain, and probably against my better judgment, I've decided to forgive you. All I ask is that you don't make me regret that decision, and answer me one question."

"Anything," he answered.

"Was that night the last time you raced, or have you done it since?" She needed to know if he had any regard for the law before she would even consider talking to him again.

"I haven't since that night. I want to race, but not illegally. I want to do stock car races. I've got a buddy at the racetrack in Weare. He said he might be able to help me get a racing license, and a car. I've been saving up for a few years now, and I'll make my last payment in January. I know that's probably more than you expected, but I don't want to hide anything from you again." With his head down, his eyes raised to meet hers.

She didn't know why it was so easy to talk to him.

"About last night," she continued, "I'm not sure it's a good idea to pursue anything more than friendship. Not that I'm not interested, it's just, I live across the country and I don't get much opportunity to come home unless I have a project or it's a holiday. I don't see it going anywhere, and I don't do casual relationships."

She held her breath waiting for his response. Thinking she finally found her way out of this mess, she sat back, trying to hide the smirk that threatened to cross her face.

"Well, I don't do casual relationships either, and while I believe that long distance relationships do work when you both put in the effort, I think it takes time to build to something like that. But, you're here now. I don't see why we can't find out if we can turn this into a relationship before you have to go." His words brought her back down from her smug cloud nine.

"I don't know, Sawyer," she said, wringing her hands. "I just don't know that it's a good idea."

"I'm not going to force you to date me, Amberly. I'd just like the opportunity to hang out, even if it's only as friends while you're here. I missed out on you once, and I'll take you in my life anyway I can. All I want is for you keep an open mind and don't shut this down right now."

"Okay," she choked out. What else could she say? He wanted to date her. Every fiber of her being wanted to jump up and down and scream yes; her brain, on the other hand, was a spoilsport.

Chapter Four

$\mathcal{B}$uttoning her only blazer, Amberly walked towards her car. It was D-day; today she would find out if she was staying and working on the house of her dreams, or if she was going back to California to find a new list of houses to be saved. The drive was too quiet. She thought of her conversation with Sawyer. If she got this house, she would have a few months to fix it. If she did, would they see where a relationship could lead? Or would they stay friends?

The meeting lasted forever but she didn't care, she got the house. With only a few more papers to sign before the closing after Christmas, it was unofficially hers. She pumped her fist as soon as she was out of sight from everyone. Had she not been in her best clothes, she would have done a cartwheel.

She managed to talk her way into getting the keys a little early so she could start cleaning up right away and assess what needed to be done. Rushing home, she ran to her room and changed into jeans and a sweatshirt, threw her hair into a long ponytail, and grabbed her work boots. The crew and her best workers wouldn't be there until after the holiday. Eddy, her main cameraman, was visiting family close by and offered to record the meeting and the initial walk through. He was heading over to meet her at the house.

This drive was quiet too. Turning the corner, she saw the house. It was beautiful. It needed some TLC, but she could already see its potential. Grabbing her phone as she got out of the car, excitement flooded her, and she almost fell as she started sprinting towards the door.

The click of the lock sent goose bumps trailing up her arms; this happened every time she bought a new house and went through the initial walk through. Her fingers swiped over the phone screen as she brought up the camera app and immediately started taking pictures of her surroundings. This was her dream house. She had loved this house ever since she was young. When it went up on the demolition list, she put in an offer, sight unseen. This was her first walk through. She could tell she had her work cut out for her, but if anyone could save it, she could. It was going to be a lot of hard work and late nights. A pang of guilt washed over her, she would be too busy to spend time with Sawyer during her stay. But, it was probably for the best, she had trouble focusing on what she needed to do when he was around.

Another oil change. Today was dragging. Talking to Amberly would have brightened his day, but she told him at lunch the day before that her stay depended on the result of a meeting she had today. He wasn't sure how long those things lasted. While he had a few minutes before his next car, he decided on a quick text.

I hope your meeting is going or went well. I would love to see you tonight. Let me know if you're free.

Hitting send, he put his phone away and went back to work. The workday crawled by. He checked his phone every time he got a break, but Amberly never responded.

"What's wrong, Sawyer?" Carmen, his only friend in town and favorite co-worker, came up behind him. They tried dating for a while when he came back, but there was no chemistry, for either of them, and they decided they were better off as friends.

"It's nothing." He didn't think it was appropriate to discuss the girl he liked with an old flame.

"Oh come on, it's me. Is it a girl?" She gave him a look that let him know there would be no getting out of this conversation.

"How do you do that?" he asked, waving another car into the oil change area. As they worked, he told her about Amberly.

"She's probably just busy. Depending on how her meeting went, she could be working. My best advice is to grab some beer or whatever she likes to drink and head over after work. Best case scenario is you celebrate with her, worst case you're there for support." She winked at him and dodged a playful push.

"You're a bigger perv than me," he joked. "But you're right, that's a great idea. Thanks." *Thank God, the day is almost over.*

Finishing up with his last customer, he tossed his oil change rag into his toolbox. Before he left, he checked his phone.

Hey there, I can't hang out. I'm up to my eyeballs in work, sorry. On the bright side, I got the house.

It was a cause to celebrate, or at least he thought so. Leaving work, he stopped at home for a quick shower, set off to the liquor store on the corner for a six-pack of beer, and headed towards Fourth Street. Even if she was too busy to have a drink with him, he could leave it with her for her own celebration later.

Cleaning up before the camera crew arrived was her favorite part of these projects, especially old houses like this that were still completely furnished. The old furniture, the pictures on the walls, and the little trinkets, told the stories of families, love, and past lives that time seemed to have forgotten. Like reading a book, going through old houses transported her to another world.

The knock on the door startled her. It was almost nine o'clock, and Kelsey was out with her husband for date night. Brushing her hands on her pants, she turned the knob.

"Sawyer, hey. Come on in." She was surprised and unexpectedly excited to see his face.

Why was he so alluring? He brushed against her as he entered the house, causing her knees to go weak, like they would buckle at any minute.

"Wow, this place is amazing, look at all this stuff,"

he said, looking around the room. "Congrats on the house, I brought you this to celebrate." He held out the beer. As she took it from him, her hand grazed his and a spark raced up her arm. She was fighting as hard as she could to be casual, but her heart thumping in her ears made it very hard to concentrate.

He broke the silence. "I'll leave you to your work, I just wanted to drop those off."

She stopped him as he turned to leave.

"You should stay, have a beer, and celebrate with me." Her hands were trembling, but she hoped he didn't notice. Placing the cardboard carrier on the side table, she grabbed two of the beers, twisted off the caps, and handed one to him. They both took a minute to take a drink before she asked, "Do you want a tour?"

She led him through the living room, into the kitchen and formal dining room. There was a sitting room off the back connecting a small hallway that led to a flight of stairs.

"Three of the bedrooms are up there. I'm excited that the furniture is still in great shape; a lot of it is period appropriate." She started up the narrow staircase and as her heel slid backwards off the top step, she clenched the rail to stop herself from tumbling backwards. Her face flushed as her ass brushed against him.

"Whoa, you okay there? Do I need to cut you off already?" he joked.

She reached the top of the stairs and turned on her heel to give him a witty comeback, not realizing he was right behind her. Her breath hitched and before she had a moment to think, he leaned in and kissed her.

It was a needful, wanting kiss, and this time she kissed him back with an insatiable hunger. His hands were moving slowly from her hips over her ass, and a light moan escaped her lips. With that, he grabbed and pulled her towards him. His erection pressed against her thigh. He trailed his hands to the hem of her t-shirt. Pulling upward, she raised her arms to allow the fabric over her head. She met his lips for another kiss as she fumbled with the button of his pants. This was really happening. She was going to sleep with him. There was no turning back, and she didn't want to. He unbuttoned her jeans with what seemed like no effort, and with a slight pull, her jeans fell to the floor.

He kissed a path from her mouth down to her throat. As a moan escaped her lips, his hands moved to her breasts. With a flick of his fingers, the front latch of her bra came undone and the material slipped off, exposing her. Her nipples hardened in excitement as the warmth of his breath swept across her neck. Trailing his lips past her collarbone and further down her chest, he covered her nipple with his mouth and rolled it between his teeth.

"Sawyer," she moaned.

She barely noticed the silky material of her panties sliding down her legs until she felt his hand on her bare mound. With a groan, he slipped a finger inside of her. Kissing a trail back to her mouth, he reached into his pocket, withdrawing his wallet, and retrieving a condom. Sliding off his pants, he used his teeth to rip open the package and rolled the condom over his shaft. With that, he picked her up and walked over to a chair in the first bedroom. The scent of him, motor oil mixed with the clean musk of his aftershave, surrounded her.

Sitting, he placed her on his lap and continued kissing her. Her pulse pounded on her ears. Holding his shoulders and leaning back, her breath hitched as he adjusted and the hot firm length of him filled her. Her heart raced as she leaned forward and started grinding against him. Running her hands along his back, she relished the feel of him. He squeezed her ass, encouraging her to go faster and pushing into her, he rasped against her most sensitive spot. Quiet grunts and sweet breath dancing against her ears. As she quickened her pace, her moan filled the air and she shuddered as they both found their release together, falling into each other.

He kissed her forehead and helped her stand. Walking over to the hallway, he grabbed their things.

She accepted her clothes. "Thanks, the bathroom is down the hall. First door to the right, if you need it."

He grinned at her and nodded, heading down the hallway.

She leaned against the doorframe. Her head was swimming. Did that really just happen? *Holy shit.* Those two words continued to repeat in her head while she got dressed.

"Hey there, gorgeous." The voice from behind her startled her even though she knew who it was.

"Hi," she replied with a shy laugh as she turned to face him.

"Do you have more work to do tonight?" he asked.

"Not really, I was just doing some light cleaning. The camera crew won't be here until after Christmas." She ran her fingers through her tousled hair.

"Well, if you're hungry, would you like to grab a late dinner and go back to my place?"

"Sure, sounds great. Just let me close up." They headed downstairs, and she grabbed her coat. Before they left, he grabbed her in an embrace and kissed her.

"Sorry, just had to get that out before we go." He beamed. "Shall we?"

Chapter Five

*H*er eyes fluttered open. Looking around the room, she smiled knowing that she was in his bed. He was breathing softly beside her, still asleep. His arm draped over her naked body, pinning her in place. She knew she needed to get up and go home. It was Christmas Eve, and she had a Christmas party tonight. She should be home to help prepare food and clean before her aunts, uncles, and cousins arrived. She slowly removed his arm from her stomach, careful not to wake him. She grabbed her clothes and walked into the bathroom. Leaning over the sink, she splashed her face with cool water. Getting dressed and throwing her hair in the elastic band she kept around her wrist, she went back for her shoes.

"Hey beautiful." His voice was soft as he rolled over to greet her.

"Hey, sorry. I didn't mean to wake you. I was trying to be quiet." She wasn't sure why she was whispering since he was awake. Clearing her throat, she continued in a normal volume. "I have to go prepare for the family Christmas party tonight. I was just going to leave you a note."

"Well, now you don't need a note, you told me. And bonus, you can give me a goodbye kiss." He winked at her, sending chills down her spine. She walked over and brushed her lips against his, but he grabbed her, rolling her back onto the bed with a moan. Maybe a quickie wouldn't be too bad before her hectic morning.

She grabbed a meat tray and a few bottles of wine out of her car. Her arms full, she walked to the door and leaned down to ring the doorbell with her elbow. The bustling volume increased as the door opened.

"Harold, will you go wake up… oh, I thought you were still sleeping. Never mind Harold, she's at the door," her mom said, reaching to grab some of the supplies in Amberly's arms.

"I've been up for a while. I went to the store and grabbed some goodies for tonight." She followed her mom into the kitchen.

"I didn't hear you get up. I would have come with you." Muriel put the meat tray in the refrigerator.

"You wouldn't have heard me. I didn't come home last night." She grinned into the wine cooler, thinking about her night.

"Oh, okay. How is the house looking?" her mom asked.

"It's great. I got a lot of cleaning done. It needs work but I'm excited to get started. Sawyer came by last night and got the tour." She and her mother always had an open relationship. No subject was taboo. She was thankful for that, because she hated keeping secrets.

"Kelsey told me about that boy. I hope you're being careful, Amberly. I don't want to see you mixed up in a situation you can't handle."

"I am, Mom, I promise. I don't think he's as bad as everyone believes. He got tied up in a bad situation." She smiled at the realization; he wasn't a bad person. She could be with him; she wanted to be with him.

"Well, invite him tonight. If you like him that much, I want to get to know the man you've fallen for."

"I didn't say anything about falling mom," she said, looking away.

"You didn't have to dear, it's written all over your face."

Amberly pulled her mom into a tight hug. She had to call Sawyer.

Hanging up the phone, Sawyer could barely contain his excitement over seeing Amberly again. His family always celebrated on Christmas Day, and spending the day with her sounded like a perfect evening.

To his surprise, Amberly was walking towards him when he opened the door. "What are you doing here?"

"Well, I wanted to see you, so I thought I'd pick you up." A grin was painted on her face as she opened her arms for a hug.

"Thanks." He wrapped his arms around her and kissed her forehead.

He kept his arm around her and together they walked to the parking garage where her car was parked.

"My mom is excited to see you," she said as she turned the corner.

"It will be good to see her too, but why is she excited? She doesn't really know me." His stomach did a flip as nervousness set in. Amberly had probably told them about him.

"She doesn't usually get to interact with guys I really like." Her face flushed bright pink.

"Wait, guys you really like? Are you saying what I think you're saying, Amberly?" His heart started pounding against his chest like a drum.

"Um, yeah." Her voice was quiet. "I started thinking about it, and in talking to my mom this morning, came to the realization that I do like you, and while I'm here I want to see where this can go."

He tried his best to play it cool, and caught her glancing at him, since he didn't respond.

"You have nothing to say?" she said before biting her lip.

"Well I am pretty likeable." He winked.

She playfully slapped his arm.

As soon as she turned off the car, he removed his seatbelt and leaned towards her. Gently framing her face, he turned her head towards him and kissed her deeply.

"I'm so happy to hear you'll give us a shot. I know it's early, but I think we can make something out of this. Even after you go back."

He smiled at the way she fumbled when she was nervous, and her ear-to-ear grin. He wanted her, more than just sexually. He was in love with her. He never wanted this to end.

Impressed by how well he'd gotten along with her family, she couldn't keep her eyes off of him. It had been a rocky start, because they all knew the stories of his past, but he won them all over. He cracked jokes with her dad, and wouldn't allow her mom to refuse help with the dishes. He gave her cousins piggyback rides and listened to her Aunt Margot's latest divorce story. As the night wore on, she fell even deeper for him. He would look at her from across the room from time to time, and his grin made her giddy. When dinner was done and it was time for presents, her mom surprised him by having a gift ready. It was like a scene out of an old Christmas movie, her family gathered in the living room. Amberly's dad sat by the tree and made sure everyone had a gift to open. They waited for a signal and opened their gifts at the same time. His face lit up as he opened the small box with a blue silk tie; he didn't expect anything since it was short notice.

She had a gift for him too, but decided to wait until they were alone. While he was engaged in conversation with her family, she ran his present out to the car, figuring she would give it to him at his apartment.

After everyone left, the four of them talked with her parents until after midnight. "Okay guys, it's about time I got him home. It's Christmas after all, and I'm sure his parents will want to see him at a decent time."

"Thanks again for having me over." Sawyer stood to shake her dad's hand.

"Of course, any friend of Amberly's is welcome here, and I needed to know who to kill if you hurt my girl." Her dad winked.

"Dad!" She rolled her eyes.

"I'm just kidding, sweetheart. Sawyer can take a joke. Right, Sawyer?"

"Yes, sir." He smiled, but she noticed the scared look in his eyes, making her giggle.

Together they walked toward the car, and he opened the door for her.

"Who says chivalry is dead?"

"As long as you're with me, it won't be," he answered, gently closing the door. The drive was short and quiet, with the exception of the Christmas music playing through the speakers. She pulled into the guest spot in the parking garage and turned off the car. She stopped him before he opened the door to get out.

"Wait, I have something for you. It's not as cool as the tie my mom got you," she said with a laugh, "but I saw it when I was at the store this morning, and it made me think of you, so I bought it." Reaching into the back seat, she retrieved the small box and handed it to him.

"You didn't have to get me anything," he said, taking the box. "I feel like an asshole. I don't have anything for you."

"You cancelled your plans and spent the evening with my entire family. That was present enough for me, now open it."

Untying the ribbon and removing the lid, he peered into the box.

"Amberly, I love it. Thank you." He pulled the small race-car shaped keychain from the box.

"You did say you wanted to race stock cars when you got your license back. I thought it was time to stop turning racing into a bad thing." Before she could say anything else, his lips were on hers.

Chapter Six

*S*he was singing along to "Silver Bells" when she pulled into Kelsey's driveway. Getting out of the car, she grabbed Kelsey's present, and walked into the house. She set the gift under the tree and headed into the kitchen where she was almost certain her friend was getting a cup of coffee. The clink of the spoon against the mug confirmed it.

Walking through the archway, she called out, "Merry Christmas, Kels."

Kelsey turned around with tear stained cheeks. Amberly rushed to her side.

"What's wrong? Kels, are you okay?"

"Yeah," Kelsey answered, wiping her cheeks, handing Amberly a cup of coffee. "I have some news. Things might be a little difficult for me for a while."

"Why, what's the matter?" Amberly set the cup back on the counter and hugged Kelsey.

"Because I can't have any coffee for a while, nine months to be exact." She laughed through her tears. "By the way, you're going to be an aunt. Merry Christmas."

They both squealed, bouncing up and down, still intertwined.

"Since when? How long have you known? Is that why you weren't drinking at the reunion?" Amberly scolded, as she pulled away from Kelsey, and grabbed her coffee.

"No, I wasn't feeling well during the reunion. Although, now I know why I felt sick." She laughed, putting her hand on her stomach. "I just took the test this morning, and kind of freaked out. Can you believe it, Am? I'm going to be a mom."

"This is great, where is Jason? I want to congratulate the daddy." Narrowing her eyes and lowering her voice, she continued. "He is the daddy, right?"

"Yes, he's the dad. You think I would cheat on my husband?" Kelsey asked, feigning offense. "He's in the basement, telling all his gamer friends."

"I'll leave him be, you'll have to relay the message. I love you, but I'm not walking into that. We both know how he gets with those games." Amberly smiled. "Oh, I left your present under the tree. Are you ready to exchange gifts? Although, I don't think I can top yours. I'm not getting pregnant any time soon." She chuckled.

Kelsey opened her gift first: a basket of microwave popcorn, plastic popcorn buckets, movie theatre candy, white chocolate cocoa mix, chick flicks, slippers, and a robe.

"Amberly, I love it. Before you leave, we're having a sleepover and using all of this. Open yours."

Amberly pulled the ribbon tied onto her gift and opened the box, revealing a basket of coffee, two mugs, muffin mix, her favorite creamer, a robe, and slippers. She couldn't help but laugh.

"I love it, Kels, great minds think alike. Now I have a robe and slippers for sleepover night, and breakfast is on me."

She hated to rush off, but if she wanted a shower before dinner with her parents, she had to. Her mom would be expecting her help. The girls hugged. "Since Jason didn't make an appearance, tell him I said congratulations, and don't forget we have a date tomorrow night."

"Will do, love you, Am, I have to go call my mom and let her know the news."

"You didn't tell your mom yet? Hop to it girl, and I'm honored you told me first," Amberly said with a laugh. "I'll talk to you in a bit." With a wave, she walked out the door and headed home.

Back at her parents' house, she jogged up the steps to her room, grabbed some clothes, and headed for the shower. Once her hair was dry and her makeup perfect, she slipped into a red sheath dress and an old robe, knowing she was a mess when she cooked. An apron never kept her clothes food-free. Heading downstairs, she met her mom in the kitchen.

"Merry Christmas, Mom."

"Merry Christmas, honey," her mother answered. Her mom always went all out for the holiday. Amberly grabbed the bowl and mixer and got to work on the peppermint pie. It was her specialty after all. She'd been making it since she was fifteen.

Cheery Christmas music played in the background as they worked to prepare the meal. They moved around the kitchen like a well-oiled machine. After years of working together for the holiday, they had a system that kept them out of each other's way in the smaller kitchen.

Dinner was full of conversation about nothing in particular, followed by their tradition of poker over dessert. In true tradition, Amberly and her grandfather teamed up to take down the others, and then he cheated to win the last few hands, but gave her the winnings anyway. She loved Christmas with her family; it was her favorite time of year, but it always went by too quickly. Before she knew it, she was saying goodbye to family that she wouldn't see for months and heading upstairs, putting on pajamas. After turning off her light, she climbed into bed and grabbed her phone to send a text to Sawyer.

I hope you had a good day today. Merry Christmas.

Her phone lit up in a matter of seconds.

I did, thanks. I hope you did too. Merry Christmas, Amberly, I'll call you tomorrow.

With that, she rolled over and drifted off to sleep.

Waking up at seven in the morning to a phone call was not the way she wanted to start her day. The deal on the house fell through. All of the paperwork, the meetings, and the work she'd already put in were a complete waste of time. She lost her dream house, all because the network decided a house in South Carolina would make for better television. Tears filled her eyes as she started packing her suitcase. Her vacation cut short, she had to catch a plane and prepare for this new house.

Hey beautiful, I hope you're having a good day today.

How was she going to explain this to him? They never had a chance.

Hey, do you think I could come see you at lunch?

Figuring it was better not to give it away on the phone, she hit send. She sat on the bed. They weren't together long enough for it to hurt this bad. She had to get herself together. There was no way she could break it off painlessly if she started crying.

We can meet up any time. I'm not working today. The shop's closed until Monday. I'm home if you want to come over.

Her hands shook as she typed.

Okay. I'm on my way.

She threw on her boots and headed for the car. Her heart ached and she was nauseous. She didn't want to do this, but there was no point in continuing anything if she wouldn't be around long enough to build a relationship. It wasn't fair to either of them. Going over what she would say to him while she drove, she thought she had it down pat, but when he opened the door and enveloped her in a big hug, she almost lost it. How was she going to do this?

"Amberly, what's wrong?" He instinctively stepped aside so she could come in.

"The deal fell through on the house." A tear made its way down her cheek.

"Oh no, I'm so sorry."

"That was my dream house, and now it's gone." Her tears flowed gently as she walked to the end table, grabbing a tissue. "Anyways, now I have to fly home tomorrow, I just wanted to say goodbye in person."

"What do you mean? You're leaving?" He grabbed her, holding her still.

"I am. I have to get back home, they already have me lined up with another project to work on. I'm sorry." Her voice trailed off. She could see the hurt in his eyes.

"Don't give up. Maybe you can talk to them. You can't throw in the towel just like that. On the house, or me." She cut him off.

"I tried to fix it, but the network withdrew their offer on this house days ago. The news was delayed because of the holiday, I called them and fought but they told me if I'm not on the flight back tonight I'm in breach of contract, and I'll lose my job." She didn't mean to yell. "I think it would be best if we quit while we're ahead. It's been an amazing few days, but it's not fair to either of us."

"You can't leave, I just got you. I can't let you go yet." His voice cracked.

"You don't have a choice, I have to go. I would love to stay friends if you're willing." She walked toward the door. "I can't stay. I have to drop off the keys and meet Kelsey in fifteen minutes to return my rental car. I'm so sorry, Sawyer."

Before he could say anything, she was out the door. She held it in until she was a safe distance from the apartment. Tears flooded her eyes, forcing her to pull over to regain her composure.

When she met Kelsey at the rental car agency, she avoided eye contact and put her luggage in Kelsey's back seat.

"I'll tell you in a few minutes, I have to take care of this before I lose it," she said, walking into the building and up to the counter. It felt like an eternity before she signed off and turned in the keys.

Kelsey met her with a hug as soon as she was outside, causing her to cry again.

"Everything is ruined Kels, they took away the house." Her sobs cut her off from finishing.

"It's okay, honey," Kelsey said. "There will be other houses, I know it was your dream, but I'm sure you'll find another."

"It's not about the house, Kels, I mean partly it is, but it's more than that." Amberly said into her friend's shoulder.

"Sawyer?" Kelsey asked.

"I think I love him, I know it's early but..." She couldn't finish, her tears flowed down her cheeks.

"Shh, it's okay. Let's get you back to the house. I have ice cream, movies, and popcorn, the breakup essentials. We'll get you through this." Kelsey gave Amberly one last squeeze before letting go.

The next morning came too soon. Sawyer called and texted throughout the night until Kelsey lied, telling him Amberly was asleep. When Kelsey dropped Amberly off at the airport, she said, "Don't forget you need to be finished with your season and back here by August. I'm going to miss you. Be safe and call me when you land. I love you."

"You have to let me go first." They both chuckled as Kelsey let her go. "I'll call you when I land I promise. I love you too." She grabbed her luggage and headed for security.

Waiting for the flight gave her too much time to think. She regretted avoiding Sawyer, and hoped he didn't hate her. Before she had to shut off her phone, she sent him a text message.

I'm so sorry for everything, I hope you can forgive me one day. I'm getting ready to take off but if you want to call me tonight, you can.

She sent the message and powered off her phone before the flight attendant made it to her seat.

He called her that night, but there was no answer. He didn't know why he was bothering. She left. She didn't even let him try to talk her into staying. Who was he kidding? He knew she didn't let him try because he would have succeeded. Why else would she avoid him? Having her friend lie to him about being asleep may have worked had she not been sniffling in the background. It was then that he decided to leave it alone. He knew what he needed to do to get her back, and he wasn't wasting any time. He sent her a text message in lieu of a voicemail.

I understand why you did what you did. I'm sorry. I'll take your friendship over nothing any day. It may be hard at first, but I'm sure we'll find a balance. I hope your flight wasn't too long. Please call me when you get this.

He may have offered friendship but he wasn't giving up without a fight and he had a plan. He grabbed his phone and dialed Kelsey's number.

Chapter Seven

She would have sworn the months dragged by, but she knew it was no time at all before she was boarding the flight back to New Hampshire for Kelsey's baby shower. The network ended the season early, giving her time off. With the success of this season, she was able to renegotiate her contract and they agreed to follow her to the east coast for the next season. She was excited to see Kelsey and her family, but was nervous about seeing Sawyer. They talked here and there, but it wasn't the same. She hoped it was because he didn't like talking on the phone.

As hard as she tried to deny them, her feelings for him never dulled. Thinking about him had the butterflies in her stomach fluttering out of control. She didn't know how things would go between them, or what to expect. It had been seven months and she doubted that he was still single. That would explain the strange way he'd been acting over the last few months.

They'd stayed friends, but she could see him not wanting to break relationship news over the phone. She was lost in her thoughts until the pilot's voice pulled her back to reality. They would be landing in a few minutes. *Had it really been almost seven hours?* Excitement flooded her. She would finally get to see Kelsey and her ever-growing baby bump. She couldn't wait to tell her friend she would be staying because the show had agreed to follow her.

Anticipation built inside of her as she neared the baggage claim and caught a glimpse of her best friend. She nearly ran over the people in front of her running to Kelsey for a hug.

"You're the cutest pregnant woman I've ever seen. I've missed you." She hugged her tighter.

"I've missed you too, Am." Kelsey's belly jiggled as she laughed.

"So, I have some news," Amberly started, but Kelsey cut her off.

"I do too. I have a lot of news, actually, but we'll talk

after we get your luggage loaded. Holy crap girl, talk about over packing. Did you bring the entire contents of your closet?"

"Well, sort of. The rest of it wouldn't fit so it's coming with the movers." She grinned as her words resonated with her best friend.

"Wait. Movers?" Kelsey squealed.

"Yep, I'm moving back. I need to be here for my new niece."

Kelsey started crying in the middle of the airport, "I'm so glad to hear you say that, considering you'll need to be here for the christening as her godmother." Her words were almost inaudible from the crying, but given their history, Amberly understood.

"Godmother? Oh Kels, I'm honored."

"Don't act like you didn't figure it would be you. Who else would I entrust with my child?"

Amberly beamed and hugged her again, this was exactly what she needed. She may not even need to worry about seeing Sawyer. This might be the best excuse to avoid him. They'd already agreed to meet up for coffee, but beyond that, maybe she could avoid him.

"So, what is your other news?" Amberly couldn't wait any longer to ask, Kelsey would have to try hard to top godmother.

"Well, the other news isn't really good news." Her heart sank with those words and she immediately thought of Sawyer, but Kelsey continued. "It's about the Fourth Street house." Trailing off, Amberly realized they weren't heading for Kelsey's.

"Please don't take me by the wreckage, Kelsey. I can't bear to see where it used to sit," she said, wringing her hands together, but stopped when she saw the top of the house. "It's still standing? How is that possible?" She was opening the car door before it had fully come to a stop.

"Well," Kelsey said. "Some idiot went and paid twice its worth to save it, but doesn't know the first thing about fixing a house."

Turning to face her friend, Amberly narrowed her eyes. "Kelsey, you didn't, did you?"

"God no, I have a child on the way, remember? My money is tied up."

"Then who?" As she turned back toward the house, she saw him. Sawyer walked out the front door.

"I really wish you would stop calling me the idiot, Kels," he said, flashing a smile that made Amberly weak in the knees.

"Kels? What are you two up to? I thought you didn't get along." She glanced back and forth between the two of them.

"How could I not help him? He obviously cares about you," Kelsey said.

"So?" Sawyer asked. "Will you restore this house?"

"I will, of course I will, but how did you do this?"

"Well, let's just say I'm a little further away from my stock car and trailer than I was before."

A tear fell down her cheek as she met his gaze. "You did all of this for me?"

"Please tell me you didn't move on, it would make my grand gesture really awkward. I'm still not over you, and I don't think I ever will be. I love you, Amberly, and I will do anything to have time to prove that to you. And if flipping this house it how I can do it, then it will all be worth it."

She jumped into his arms and kissed him. "I love you too, Sawyer, more than you'll ever know." She let go and stepped back, wiping her face. "Now there's only one matter left to attend to." She had to fight the smirk that was trying to make an appearance.

"Anything that needs done, I'll do it, but you have full creative control." He was cute when he babbled.

"Anything?" she teased.

"Anything," he replied.

She grinned. "Okay then, I'll need to change the small room at the top of the stairs into an office."

"An office?"

"Of course, you'll have the garage with your stock car, that I'm replacing by the way, and I'll need my own space to get some work done. I'm staying for the long haul this time."

He kissed her again, and she knew she was exactly where she wanted to be forever. She was home.

Noah Cane's Candy

by Christine Cacciatore

This story is dedicated to my sweet Honeybear. He is my muse, my best friend, and my love. In short, everything on my Christmas list.

Chapter One

You can't fire me. It's almost Christmas!" Candace Mahoney's face flushed with anger.

Rick Purcell, Candace's supervisor, threw his hands up in the air. "What am I supposed to do, Candace? Last in, first out. Anyway," he continued in his mewling voice, "not my decision. It came down from Corporate."

Candace fumed. The timing was not only disastrous personally but a little too suspicious for Candace's liking. Several months ago, she had sent a memo to the Chief Financial Officer letting him know that receipts weren't balancing with sales. There had been several odd phone calls lately, too, in which customers were indicating they had paid invoices and had canceled checks to prove it, and yet they were still showing unpaid on the company's aging report.

For being an accounting office, nothing was adding up, and Candace made sure someone knew about it.

"Oh, really? Something stinks here, Rick. My work has been accurate; you know that. Does Corporate know that I have a three-year-old son to support?"

"Probably not. Remember, you're still a temp. You haven't even been hired in yet. There's really nothing I can do."

"I'm technically only days from the six month mark. I was counting on the medical insurance for my son and for me. Is there anything available in any other departments? I'd even take a small pay cut..." She couldn't really afford a pay cut, no matter how small.

"I'm sorry," Rick said, sounding not sorry at all. "Your last day here is Friday."

Friday. With rent to pay, groceries to buy, and a sitter who needed money just as much, if not more than Candace. She looked at her supervisor, a man she had merely despised before. Now she absolutely loathed him. She could feel the words bubble up in her throat and tried to close them off.

Don't burn any bridges. Don't burn any bridges. Don't burn any bridges.

She thought she had her mouth under control as she turned and walked out of the office, but twenty-seven years of being a redhead gifted her with a sharp, if unoriginal, retort. She gave him a half smile.

"Rick? Tell Corporate I said Merry fucking Christmas."

Candace hit the total button on her calculator, peered at the paltry sum, and pushed the paper, pen, and calculator away in disgust. She was still paying off student loans for her recent accounting degree; how was she going to keep the two of them afloat for another week? Seven days had gone by since she had lost her job. She had kept Ben in daycare and paid the sitter because she didn't dare lose her—it was difficult enough to find one you could trust. But one to trust and one you really liked? Rarer than hen's teeth.

Besides, Ben loved it there. Their sitter, Ronnie, was Ben's one constant and Candace put him first. His happiness was paramount.

Feeling one hundred years old, she shuffled over to the teapot, filled it, and put it on to boil. She leaned against the counter. It was 11:00 p.m., probably way too late for a cup. Didn't matter anyway, she had no job to go to in the morning. Her bedtime wasn't exactly a priority. She tiptoed down the hallway of her tiny apartment and peeked in on her little blond-haired son. Her heart swelled with love as she smoothed his sweaty baby curls off his face. How was she going to give him any kind of a Christmas when she could barely afford to put food on the table?

There had to be some type of job she could find, something online or in the newspaper she could apply to. She had to find something, or it would be another in a string of bad Christmases.

She crept back down the hall into the kitchen and caught the teapot as it broke into song. She poured water over the teabag and started into the living room, thought better of it, then turned back to the kitchen. She opened a tall, high kitchen cabinet and grabbed a small bottle of whiskey. Candace poured a healthy dollop into her cup with a half-smile.

She settled on the couch, where she stared at the twinkling lights on their Christmas tree. Little Ben moved the ornaments around all the time, meaning there was a haphazard row of homemade and wooden painted ornaments all along the bottom of the tree. The middle was mostly bare except for lights. The top of their little tree had a couple of expensive ornaments, leftover from her blink-and-you-missed-it marriage.

Ben was the sole good thing to come out of it. She had received some child support after they divorced when Ben was one, enough to fool her into being comfortable enough financially to rent an apartment. The joke was on her, though, as her child support dried up when her ex disappeared off the face of the earth. Since then, despite Candace working full time, it was mostly a hand to mouth existence.

And now this. She took a long sip of her Irish tea and leaned her head back against the couch cushions. Oh—the paper—that's right. She had taken a cursory look at the job listings before but most of them were sales jobs, or third shift warehouse jobs or—here was one, good for a laugh—an elf for the mall Santa.

Like that would ever happen. Her? An elf? Not in a million years.

Chapter Two

*N*oah Cane watched a very angry female elf stomp around the Winter Wonderland that was the center of the Midtown Mall. The mall was not quite open yet—there were mall walkers galore, but none of the stores had pulled up their security gates for the morning shoppers. Cheerful Christmas music was being piped throughout the large structure, though. Noah knew after a few years of playing Santa how to tune the repetitive music out so he didn't go crazy by the end of the day.

His attention was drawn back to the new elf, wandering past him with a box of candy canes. "I'd support the bottom of that box, if I were you," he said, gesturing to the box. They don't make the boxes very sturdy and it tends to…"

"Keep your comments to yourself, Santa," the sassy little elf ground out. "I can handle a box of candy." Of course, the box split at that exact moment, dumping hundreds of small candy canes on the floor. The look on her face was absolute outrage and Noah thought it was the funniest thing he had ever seen. *If she stomps her foot, I'm going to lose it.*

Sure enough, the diminutive red-headed elf pounded a pointy toed shoe on the white carpet of "snow" near the small Santa house he was sitting in.

"Oh, for heaven's sake!" She surveyed the candy all over the ground. "Half of these little things are broken."

Noah snickered. "I tried to tell you." He rose up from his Santa chair, with the intent to help her pick up the candy.

"Can it, Kris Kringle." The woman in front of him began the task of gathering up all the prepackaged candy. "And sit down. I can handle some candy canes."

Have it your way, he thought, as he settled back down in his chair. He watched her kneel and twist, scooping them back up. At one point, she turned her backside directly in Noah's direction, affording him a marvelous view of her shapely bottom encased in green velvet as she picked up the treats.

You don't want any help? Fine. I'll sit here and enjoy the view.

"The kids start arriving soon," he sang out.

"I can only go so fast," she sang back.

Enough was enough. He had been Santa at this mall four years running and a stampede would soon hit their area. He rose, brushed off his red pants, and made his way over to his elf helper, taking his time to admire the efficient way she moved. Her short red hair was tucked behind her ears, which had been accentuated by the pointy costume ears the Santa company required all the elves to wear. He flipped the ruined box over, expertly tucking in the bottom to make it usable again. She thrust her hands full of canes towards him.

"Don't put the broken ones in here," he cautioned.

"Why not?" she asked, green eyes flashing.

"Would you want a broken candy cane?"

"I'd throw it in a cup of cocoa," she shot back.

"All full of Christmas spirit, I see. Kids don't like broken candy canes."

"I have a three year old. He doesn't care if his are broken." She made to toss a couple of them into the box, but Noah's hand stilled hers.

"Well, I care." Still holding her hand, he said, "Noah Cane. And you are?"

"An elf." She turned away to pick up more spilled candy.

"No, what's your name?"

She looked down at the nametag on her outfit. "This one is good enough." One red tipped fingernail tapped the plastic.

She was adorable, Noah decided. His eyes dropped to look at her tag. "Sparkle?" He laughed. "Sparkle? Really? Hm. I don't know that it fits you so well. I'd go for Klutzy. Clumsy." He dodged an airborne candy cane. "Crabby? Grumpy?"

She frowned at him and he knew he needed to dial it back a bit.

"Your eyes are like emeralds," he said. "They do sparkle. Okay, Sparkle it is."

The past four years Noah had played Santa, his elf helpers had been of varying shapes and sizes. The first year was Jenna, who filled in one day as Santa without needing padding because she was as wide as she was tall. One year it was Katelyn, who was arrested for shoplifting two days before Christmas. Last year was Rowena, who looked as if she dabbled in the dark arts and was by far the most Goth elf he had ever seen. She had even pierced the faux elf ears and had visible tattoo sleeves under her green velvet costume.

So to have someone like his current elf, Sparkle, a redhead with a pixie cut, luminous green eyes, and an ass that could stop traffic…well, it really was beginning to look a whole lot like *his* Christmas wish would be granted.

After work, Candace knocked on the door to her babysitter's little ranch home. From inside, she could hear, "Tyler, go see who's at the front door. I think it's Miss Candace."

The door opened. Candace smiled down at Tyler. "Hi Tyler! Did you have fun playing today?" She could hear her sitter, Ronnie, calling faintly from the other room. "Ty, is it Candace?"

"Friss Miss, mommy."

Ronnie turned the corner. "Miss who? Oh, you mean Christmas!" Both women laughed. "Let her in, Ty. Hey, Candace, how was the North Pole today?"

"Oh, funny. It was chilly in the mall." Except for a pair of brilliant blue eyes that put her in mind of hot temperatures, naked bodies, warm beaches, and turquoise water.

"Mommy!"

"Hi, BenBen!" Candace's son flew into the room. "You're an elf, mommy! Still!" She scooped him up and breathed in his little boy scent.

Ronnie leaned forward and whispered to her. "Are you working with that really cute Santa? I'm telling you, they've had a real cutie the past few years."

"What do you mean, a real cutie?" Candace whispered back.

"Like, I'd do him once a day and twice on Sunday. That kind of cutie."

"Oh, I didn't see his face. He was Santa, remember? Besides, you're not supposed to date someone you work with. No matter how "cutie" he is."

Dinner, bath time, and Legos gave way to bedtime. Once Ben was sleeping, Candace talked to her mother for a few minutes, reassuring her that everything was still okay. She spent the remainder of the evening pinning virtual things onto virtual bulletin boards and was surprised when she finished that she had pinned far more Christmas related things than ever. More specifically, hot Santas.

The internet was certainly a wonderful invention.

The patience Santa had with the children was amazing. So many shapes, sizes, and temperaments that Candace could hardly process them, yet she watched Noah pull one child after another onto his lap and talk to them as if they were the only child in the world.

She shifted on her feet. She'd have been better off in pumps than these pointy-toed elf shoes. They were pinching her feet so bad. A quick glance at her watch told her that three minutes remained until lunchtime. She could make it that long, surely.

"Smile!" she said from behind the camera, to a particularly fretful little boy about Ben's size. He paused long enough to put the end of the candy cane in his mouth and look at the camera with teary eyes. Candace took the picture at that exact moment, smiling as she did so. His mom and dad would love this one.

The last little girl in line freaked out on her parents before she could even come down the approach to Santa's lap. That was the last child for an hour. Candace rolled her neck and studiously avoided Noah's gaze. Not fair, she thought. He had seen her, but she had yet to see what face was lurking under his white bushy beard. Was he the adorable Adonis Ronnie referred to? She walked slowly around the Winter Wonderland, picking up discarded candy cane wrappers and watching Noah talk to the father of the little girl who fled. He handed the embarrassed father a candy cane to give to the girl.

"That was nice," Candace said, when he wandered back over to her. "Take off your beard."

"You need to add subtlety to your Christmas list, young woman." Noah waggled a finger in her direction.

"I'll add it. Right under 'High-paying, full-time job'."

"Is that why you're here, elfing it up this holiday season? Because I could tell it certainly wasn't your holiday spirit."

"That's in short supply right now, sadly. I just got fired."

"That's never good around the holidays. Where did you work?"

"I was a temp worker in accounts payable. You wouldn't know the place. And take off that beard."

"Ho, Ho, Ho. Santa can't take off his beard," Noah said loudly, for the benefit of a young family walking past where he and Candace were talking. He lowered his voice. "And I will take off the beard, but not here. Let's not ruin it for the youngsters. I don't want the kids to see."

"Ah. Good plan. You don't plan on wearing that…" she motioned to his white beard and moustache "…while you're having your lunch, though, right?"

"Actually, if you wait here, I'll treat you to lunch at the food court. Let me change." Noah walked over to the tiny Santa house and grabbed a large gym bag from inside, then walked toward the bathrooms.

Candace sat on the bench provided for weary husbands and swung her legs like a kid, impatient for Noah's return. What did he look like without the entire costume on? Lost in thought, she was oblivious to the admiring glances of the male Christmas shopping population.

Five minutes went by. Where was he? She looked at her watch and turned her head back toward the bathrooms where she she'd last seen him. No one heading her way except some-one who must be one of the mall models; surely that wasn't Noah. No, that guy was probably here at the mall buying twin-kling diamonds for his high-society girlfriend.

Candace grew a tiny bit uncomfortable. The tall, well-built man was walking directly toward her as if he knew her. He had on a red plaid flannel shirt covering up what looked to be scandalous musculature. His shirt was tucked into well-worn jeans and he had on a pair of black Doc Martens.

The closer he came to the bench, the drier her mouth became, and quite suddenly, she realized the man standing in front of her was Noah. The white Santa beard had been replaced by a scruffy dark beard and the red Santa cap was removed in favor of slightly mussed brown hair. The gleaming, white smile and those eyes were the same. Her Pinterest boards included a lot of hot Santas, but this one took the candy cane cake.

"Ready?" Mr. Lumberjack Model Man held his hand out to help her up.

Her heart pounded. *Not in the least,* she thought. *I'm not ready for you in the least.* She could practically feel herself falling for him right here, right now, in the center of the mall, dressed in an elf costume.

"So, Sparkle, what's your real name?" He was conscious of the feel of her smaller hand in his. She wasn't making any move to pull away as they ambled through the Christmas-deco-rated mall toward the food court.

"You have to guess. You won't ever get it, though."

"Well, unless you're Rumpelstiltskin, I'll figure it out eventually."

"Perhaps." She gave him a mischievous smile. "Starts with a C."

"Claude. Charles. Courtney. Carla." He laughed as she shook her head.

"Clodhopper. Charlemagne."

"Nope. Hey, let's split a sub!" She pulled him over to the sub shop. Mindful of the time, they shared a meatball sub and tried to eat quickly. They talked about the hot toys the kids seemed to be asking for and the naughtiest children they'd seen come through the line. She mentioned she was divorced, her son was named Ben, and despite never having seen a real dinosaur, he was obsessed with them.

Noah wondered if she had someone near to support her, even if it was only emotional support. He was also curious about her divorce. He watched her finish the last bite of her sandwich and brush a stray crumb off her lap.

What kind of man would walk away from this woman? *If she were mine,* he thought, *I'd never let her go. I'd wake first to see that silky cap of red hair on my pillow, to touch her soft, pale skin. Slide a necklace around her slender neck and a diamond ring on that small, capable finger.*

He told her that his brief marriage was tenuous from the beginning—an unexpected pregnancy pushed them to marry before they were ready, and the marriage did not survive when their tiny daughter failed to draw her first breath. He tried everything he could think of to make his young, despondent bride happy but it seemed the harder he worked to try to keep their marriage from falling apart, the further apart they grew. The one thing he knew was that he gave it his all, even when the sadness in his wife's eyes told him that it was a losing proposition.

And that was why, looking at the vibrant woman in front of him, he couldn't understand why the man once married to her didn't bother trying harder to keep his marriage together and take care of his son the way a real man should.

It dawned on Noah that he was very, very glad "Sparkle's" husband wasn't in the picture. That man's loss was Noah's gain.

"I guess we'd better be heading back," he said; although he was loathe to let the lunch hour end. "Kris Kringle calls."

"Well, then, he should probably have my number, don't you think?" the red-headed elf said. She held her hand out for his phone, and he wordlessly handed it to her. Smiling, she punched some numbers into it.

"You never did tell me your real name, Sparkle."

"You'll find it later. Come on, Santa, let's get back to work."

Chapter Three

Later that night, with Ben tucked into bed and Candace showered and reading a good book, she felt like a girl in high school. She had seen what Noah looked like out of costume, and hot damn, he was about the most handsome man she had ever seen. And now he had her phone number. Granted, she had given him her phone number that afternoon, and *granted*, it was only 8:30 p.m., but she was sixteen years old again, waiting for her crush to call her so they could play the "no, *you* hang up!" game.

She couldn't believe her own daring when she had asked him for his phone then put her number into it. What was she thinking? She had never been that bold in her entire life with a man. Generally, she bided her time and waited for the man to make the first move. It gave her time to form her own opinion of him before accepting his advances.

Well, I'll tell you what you were thinking, she thought. *You were thinking of those dazzling blue eyes. You were thinking of those broad shoulders and how it would feel to run your hands up and down those muscular arms, of how strong his hand was as he held yours walking to have a sandwich in the food court.*

You definitely were thinking about his fine ass when he bent down to pick up the napkin he dropped.

Her phone played its soft tune, startling her. She levered up, grabbed it from the coffee table, and looked at the number. It was a local area code, but it wasn't a number she recognized. *Well, that didn't take long.* It pleased her. She took a deep breath and forced herself to let it ring one more time before she picked it up.

"Hello?"

"So your name is Candace, eh?" *Oh My God, it's him.* His warm voice sent tingles up her spine.

She smiled even though he couldn't see it. "I have a quick question. How long did you wait until you looked at your phone to see what name I put my number under?"

"When I went into the bathroom to change after lunch."

She laughed out loud. "Ten whole minutes? Wow. I admire your restraint, Noah."

"It was a very long ten minutes, Candace. What are you doing right now?"

"Talking to you."

"And being silly. I, too, can be silly."

"I already know that. You dress up in a red suit and white beard every day and listen to little kids tell you what they want for Christmas. That's pretty silly."

"Hey, now. I happen to think it's one of the most important things one could possibly do during the holiday season."

"It's admirable, I'll give you that. I didn't get to really ask you at lunch about your real job. Do you have another job, or do you play Santa for a living? What do you do January through November?"

"I'm a business owner."

"Well, what kind of business? You have a lot of flexibility if you can go play Santa for a whole month."

"I do it every year, yes."

"You didn't answer my question. What kind of business do you own?" Obviously someone who owned their own business should be proud of it, right? It seemed odd to her that he wouldn't say. "Do you own one of those telemarketing firms? A golf course? Run a strip club?"

"Fear not, fair lady. It's a legitimate business. Nothing as nefarious as a strip club. Although, in that green velvet, I bet you could give the other girls a run for their money....you know, shaking your mints and all that."

"Don't worry. I'm not that good a dancer. Neither are my mints."

"Let me be the judge of that. Let's go dancing tomorrow night. One of my friends is in a band that plays at Duke's on Saturday. Would you like to go?"

Candace practically purred at the thought. She had a slinky, long sleeved gold lamé dress that she had rarely worn. It would be so good to be out dancing with anyone, but the thought of being held in those strong arms, looking up into his blue eyes, being kissed by those lips…

"…so, I'm figuring around 7:30, if that's okay with you."

Oh, God. She was so busy thinking about his mouth that she failed to hear the words that were actually coming out of it. "I'm sorry, what?"

"I was wondering if you could get someone to watch Ben so that I could come get you around 7:00, so that we could get to Duke's around 7:30. Would that be okay?"

Noah had no way of knowing it, but he just scored major big points. Not only did he remember her son's name, he made sure she was comfortable making plans for his care while she was gone.

"Yes, that would be fine. That sounds really nice, Noah. I'll brush off my dancing mints. I mean, shoes."

Noah laughed. "Careful, girl. I might take you up on those mints."

"I'll give you a candy cane tomorrow at work."

"Not a broken one."

Candace laughed, remembering how angry she'd been when the box containing all the candy canes had spilled all over the floor. "That was a bad day. I'll make sure you get an unbroken one tomorrow. Maybe two."

"I'll hold you to it," Noah said, "Better get some rest tonight…Saturdays at the mall during Christmastime is absolutely nuts."

"Don't I know it. I'll see you tomorrow, Noah."

"Looking forward to it, now that I know your name, Candace. 'Night." Noah hung up the phone.

Candace clicked off, breathless upon hearing her name in that throaty voice of his. Well, how do you like that? Eighteen months without a date and suddenly she needed a sitter because she was going out dancing, with a cute guy, on an honest-to-goodness date.

Perhaps Christmas wasn't a complete washout after all. *Now, if I could only get a hold of the corporate guy at Robertson's who decided I should lose my job right at Christmas. I've got some coal I'd like to stick where the sun don't shine.*

After a lengthy, but rather enjoyable day at the mall taking pictures and handing out candy canes to youngsters, Candace ran home and poured a hot bath. Noah had offered to pick her up to go out, but Candace really enjoyed knowing her vehicle was available, should she need it. He was going to meet her at Duke's. Her mother had been considerate enough to watch Ben all day and offered to keep him overnight so that Candace didn't have to come and pick him up so late. "Or at all," her mother hedged. "Have a little fun."

"Mom, it's just dancing. It's the mall Santa, for crying out loud."

Now, however, having a glass of wine and soaking in a warm bubble bath and picturing Noah's face, she was very happy her mother had Ben for the night.

She washed her hair and shaved her legs. She did her makeup with a steady hand then smoothed on her dancing dress, pausing briefly to admire the view. *Not bad,* she thought, *for an elf. Anyway, it's only a night out dancing. Nothing more than that.*

Just a night out? A little voice teased as she left her apartment. *Not that anything would happen, of course,* she argued back. *My goodness, I've only known him a few days.*

Really? If it's nobody important, why did you wear your best bra and panty set? Why did you stop at the salon with your birthday gift card for a fresh wax on the way home, if it's "just" the mall Santa?

Chapter Four

The club where Noah's friend was playing was dimly lit and packed with young people ready to dance the night away. The opening band was playing something with a catchy, thumping rhythm, setting Candace's hips in motion before she even made it over to the table where Noah sat, watching for her. As she approached his table, she could see the frank male appreciation on his face as his gaze took in her sleek hairstyle, form fitting short gold dress, bare legs, and heels.

"You made it! You look fantastic!"

His slow appraisal left her feeling both shy and bold at the same time. "You look good too, Noah. Love the cowboy boots." He was wearing a brown Henley, blue jeans, and brown boots. She grinned at him like a fool. Inwardly she rolled her eyes. *Candace. Get a grip.*

They ordered drinks—a Corona for him and a glass of Riesling for her.

"What's your Christmas shopping list like this year?" she asked. "Has everyone on your list been a good boy or girl?" She was digging, she knew, and didn't care.

"My parents, for starters. They make out like fat rats this time of year; they just celebrated their thirtieth wedding anniversary a week ago, and now Christmas is coming up. That's okay, though, I like spoiling them."

"Brothers? Sisters?" *Anyone special?*

"Two sisters. Nicole and Nancy. Teenagers. Twins. I play it safe with gift cards." As if he was reading her mind, he added, "No one special."

"You're lucky to have both of your parents. My dad died when I was twelve. I don't have any brothers or sisters. You're lucky there, too."

He nodded and took a long swallow of his beer.

"I have a pretty small Christmas shopping list, although Ben is starting to see things on TV now that he wants. I don't stand a chance against the commercials anymore. He stares at the screen or comes running in when he hears the jingle. It's why it really sucked when I lost my job. I mean, being an elf with you is fun and everything," she tapped invisible elf ears, "but I was good at what I did. I liked working there."

I'm yammering on too much. "Well, at any rate, they couldn't wait to get me out of there." She turned and looked toward the dance floor. "Your friend's band is really good." The beat switched from a salsa-like tune to a slow, seductive song. She turned back and held out her hand to Noah. "Let's dance."

She led him out onto the dance floor, then turned and settled into his arms.

The moment she did, she didn't ever want to leave.

The man could dance. The way he held her was so natural, like they had danced this close together in this lifetime and lifetimes before. She reveled in the way his strong hands gripped her hips. She loved the way he'd grab her hand and ruthlessly spin her away, only to spin her back as if he never wanted her to leave his side. He held her so close that she could feel his breath on her hair as his thumb made circles on her back.

Her heart skipped a beat as an even slower song came on and he pulled her closer yet. It had been far too long since she had desired any man. Longing surged through her and obviously him as well, as she could feel an interesting bulge against her pelvis. The wine she drank decided to have its turn talking. "Is that a Yule log, or are you happy to see me?"

He pulled back a little bit and laughed, surprised. He looked down at her. "A little of both, I think."

"Well," she whispered, "I heard I've been a really good girl this year and if you can believe this, a Yule log was really high up on my Christmas list."

Her breathing hitched as she watched his face come closer and closer to hers until his lips were a hairsbreadth from hers. She stood stock still, breathing in his scent. Finally he spoke.

"I'm parked two blocks down. Let's get out of here."

They didn't speak on the way back to his home. In the dark, Candace got a brief look at a long driveway and a garage door opening for them. He opened her door, and to her surprise and delight, leaned over her to undo her seatbelt. He physically lifted her out of the car, his gaze hot on hers. Still carrying her, he brought her into the house, slamming the door behind him with his foot.

Candace had never been so turned on in her entire life. This man meant business.

He brought her through the foyer and down a hallway to a bedroom door and elbowed the door open, finally allowing Candace to slide fully down his body to stand on the floor. She had barely gotten her bearings when he put his hands on her shoulders and pulled her to him, a thumb gently caressing the side of her face. "You're an amazing woman. A little spitfire. I knew there was something special about you the moment I laid eyes on you, Candace." He let his arm slide down her shoulder to her back and pulled her even closer to him. "I have wanted to know how your mouth tastes since I met you."

She stroked his shoulders. "It's time to find out. Kiss me, Noah."

He needed no further encouragement. His lips came down on hers, soft at first. Testing. Feeling. Tasting. She fought for breath as he touched his tongue to her bottom lip, urging her mouth open. She obliged willingly, running her hands up and down the arms that she had so admired as he had walked to her in the mall. It had been so long since she had felt such desire for a man.

She grabbed his hand, brought it up to her breast and pressed it there. She moaned when he kept kneading and pressing, finding the nipple and toying with it. "Oh, my God, yes. Noah, please," she said, between scorching kisses. His hands shook as he fumbled at the zipper up at the back of her neck. "Yes," she whispered, urging him on.

He pulled her zipper down, replacing fabric with his hands. Sliding the dress off her shoulders, he touched every inch of her that was revealed, breaking the kiss only long enough to pull her dress down over her hips and onto the floor. She was now standing in front of him in black panties and a fancy bra and heels and had never felt sexier in her entire life. If the look in his eyes was any indication, he was not only appreciative of the view but ready to ravish her.

She stepped out of her dress, kicked it to the side, and then tossed her head, feeling strong and feminine. She moved back into his arms. "Want to know what the very first thing on my Christmas list was?"

He had one strong hand on her back and one on her butt, squeezing her ass. "I have a really good guess."

"You'd be right. But you know what…you need to be as naked as I am." She tugged the hem of his shirt up and out of his jeans, and with his help, pulled it over his head while on tiptoes in her heels. She reached for his belt and unbuckled it, then unbuttoned his pants and undid his zipper. When his jeans began to sag down his legs she leaned forward to touch his erection, amazed at the length and breadth of him.

She quickly looked up into his eyes. "For me?" she whispered.

"Every bit of it. Come here." He lifted her effortlessly into his arms, and once again, settled his lips onto hers, hard and hot to match his erection.

He walked over to the bed, leaning her back, kissing her as he did so. He grabbed a scrap of material on either side of her hips and pulled her thong down and off, tossing it onto the floor. Candace leaned up and undid the clasp on her bra. When she completed that task, he playfully pulled the bra up and toward him, tossing it onto the floor as well.

This woman had the most beautiful build he had ever

seen. He knelt on the bed before her, pausing a moment as he looked at her body in its full glory. Although she was small in stature, her figure was full and lush, beautiful breasts tipped with strawberry colored areolas and pert nipples. Her waist was small and her hips flared out giving her that hourglass shape that was always described in books. He admired her legs.

"You're beautiful." He hadn't even realized he'd said it out loud until he saw the pleased reaction on her face. "You are," he reaffirmed. "You're like a dessert. I don't even know where to start with you because I want to eat you all up."

"Most people who like desserts start with the cherry." Her voice wavered slightly. He could tell that it took courage for her to say that, but the words encouraged him. They were apparently both on the same wavelength.

"You're right. That's exactly where I should start." He held her knees and gently pulled them apart, then settled down between her legs. He kissed one leg from her knee up to her hip, loving the way she shuddered and writhed under his lips. He hovered over her mound, letting his hot breath warm her skin before kissing his way down the other thigh. She squirmed on the bed, and he worked his way back up before fastening his mouth directly on her core, licking and sucking gently, allowing her movements to guide his tongue and mouth exactly where she wanted him for her pleasure. His erection thudded harder with every one of her moans.

He delighted at the touch of her hands on his head, and her sinuous movements as she took her pleasure almost threw him over the edge. He licked, nibbled, and sucked, both of their worlds reduced to that tiny bud of sensitive skin. Moments later, she came hard, thrusting her hips even closer to his mouth. She pulled him up and over her, but he paused briefly with a shy smile to grab a condom out of his nightstand and roll it on.

He settled himself back in the cradle of her hips, then using his fingers; he rubbed inside of her, fondling the place he had licked, wetting her even more. She arched her back, moving closer, seeking his touch. He wrapped his fingers around his cock, running the sleek head of it up and down her slit. Teasing. Prolonging the play, until he couldn't wait any longer.

"Are you ready?" He forced himself to stop, to make sure she was just as ready for this as he was.

"God, yes. Please. Do it."

He eased in halfway, hot and heavy, then back out. "Okay?"

She nodded, green eyes looking directly into his.

A little smoother now, he thrust back in, over and over, finding his rhythm, finding hers, until he could feel her tense around him and milk him from inside as her second orgasm found her.

"Oh, my God. So good, so good," Candace murmured.

Watching her movements, the muscles of her stomach tensing and flexing as she took all he had, he could feel his own release coming and thrust a final time. He ground his pelvis to hers, using his thumb to brush over her clit, extending her orgasm a little longer as he came down to earth.

He fell forward, catching himself on his elbows and pressed his forehead to hers. They were both glistening with sweat and exertion. He kissed her soft lips until he could feel she had recovered, then he quickly discarded his condom in the wastebasket. Rolling back over to her, he tucked her into his side and toyed with her hair, smoothing it off her brow.

"Wow," she said with a little laugh.

"Wow is right," he breathed.

They both spoke at the same time.

"I don't normally do this."

"This is so unlike me."

They laughed together. Noah was amazed at how comfortable he was with her lying there in his arms and planned to keep her there as long as he could.

I could get used to this, he thought.

He must have said it out loud, though, because he heard a sleepy reply from the woman next to him.

"I could get used to this, too."

Chapter Five

He woke up and stretched, wondering why he felt so different. Candace. He reached out for her, but she wasn't there. "Candace?" he called out.

"I'm in here, the kitchen. Do you want a drink of water, sexy?" she called.

He sat up, ridiculously pleased. "I would." *What a night,* he thought. He peered at his phone on the nightstand for the time. It was 3:00 a.m.

"Do you need to get home?" he called. "Or would you like to work on that Christmas list and stay here?" He waited for a reply but there was none forthcoming. "Candace? Are you finding everything okay?"

When there was still no answer, he padded out into the kitchen, naked. "Do you want to, uh, continue the festivities?"

Candace was standing in the kitchen. She had thrown on his Henley to get a drink of water and she was standing there, looking down at his mail on the counter, white as a ghost.

"Candace? What is it, are you okay?"

"Robertson's. You work at Robertson's?" She held up an envelope that clearly was addressed to him, as CEO of Robertson's Distribution Center.

"It's my company, yes. Why do you have that look on your face?" Noah recognized angry when he saw it, and the woman in front of him was downright pissed.

"It's your company? The place that fired me two weeks ago? You own that company?" She took the rest of the glass of water and threw it in his face, then tossed the plastic tumbler in the sink.

"There's your water. I'm getting dressed. Take me back to my car, right now." She stomped back down the hall to the bedroom.

Robertson's. The second she said the company name Noah wanted to shrivel up in a ball. Robertson's. His company. Well, he was never there in late November, early December. He entrusted the running of it during that time to his Chief Operating Officer, but ultimately, yes, it was his company. And it was his company that had fired the very woman he had just slept with. He wiped the water off his face with a dishtowel.

Now what?

Candace refused to look at Noah or even talk to him on the way back to her vehicle. When they finally pulled up next to her car, she got out, but before she shut the door, she leaned against it, obviously determined to give him a piece of her mind.

"Christmas has been ruined for me in one way or another for the past four years, Noah. This, losing my job, this was the latest in the long line of bad Christmases for me. I don't know what your reasoning was for having Rick fire me, when I was doing such a good job for your AP department. I didn't get any kind of explanation except for 'last in, first out'. So now I'm an elf. Helping others celebrate the one holiday I would prefer to forget every year. And you helped that happen too. So thanks, Noah. Thanks for giving me one more reason to hate this holiday."

With one last venomous look, she slammed the door.

Noah watched her drive away. It was a long time before he put the car in gear and drove back to his house, to where hours before he and Candace had made such sweet love.

Sunday at the Winter Wonderland was even crazier than Saturday had been. People were coming to the mall dressed in their church clothes to have their kids' pictures taken with Santa. Candace pointedly ignored Noah, all the while being overly polite to the parents and playful with the youngsters.

When the two of them had a lunch break, Candace sat on the bench right outside the winter wonderland, deleting all of her hot Santas on Pinterest, getting more ticked off by the minute at the poor internet service the mall provided.

As she looked down at her phone, a pair of black Doc Martens came into view. "You can just keep walking, Noah. I'm not talking to you, Mr. CEO." She shot him a look full of venom before she gazed back down at her phone.

"You don't need to talk to me. But I'd like it if you listened. That Rick Purcell guy? Your supervisor? He had a specific list of people that were to be terminated. You were not on that list."

"Ha!" Candace scoffed. "He already told me, last in, first out."

"He had three people he was told to let go, Candace, and none of them were in the AP department. They were all in shipping, and they had all failed two drug tests. We administer random drug tests, as you know, and if they test positive, they're fired."

He had her attention now and she looked up at him. "Then why was I really fired?"

"The AP department has been under review. My accountants have been watching Rick with an eagle eye, because our audit showed that the books haven't exactly been adding up."

Realization dawned on Candace's face. "You know, I knew there was something shifty about that Rick guy. I mean, he's a jerk, but that's nothing. The receipts didn't always add up to what the sales showed."

"And that's why the accounting firm was watching him. Turns out, he was stealing from the company." He sat down next to her on the bench. "Since I take the Christmas season off to play Santa every year, I was trying to let the Vice President handle everything and stay out of it. Had I known...well, let's just say that apparently I need to take more time meeting the temps in my own company. Especially the ones who unwittingly expose the very person stealing from me." He reached for Candace's hand, kissed it. "Can you ever forgive me?"

"Of course, but it looks like right now I have a job." She looked down at her elf shoes and rotated her ankles.

"Well, as CEO of the company, I would like to let you know that you're officially hired back in at Robertson's. In fact, you're being put in charge of the accounts payable department and the accounts receivable department. If you'll have the job back, that is."

Candace forgot her Pinterest app entirely. "Does that include medical insurance?"

"Medical and dental insurance, of course. And since you're hiring in, a raise as well."

"Well, I did mention that a high paying, full time job was on my Christmas list."

"If I recall correctly, there were several other things you mentioned last night that were on your Christmas list. Perhaps we need to revisit that list."

Candace laughed up at him. "Yes, we definitely should." She looked down, then back up at him, serious. "I'm sorry too, Noah. I overreacted."

"You reacted the way anyone would. You have a lot at stake. You have nothing to be sorry for." Noah stood. "I need to get the costume back on. We have a few more hours of kids yet. Walk me over?"

She stood with him and walked arm in arm over to get his bag at the little Santa house to change. "Noah, thank you."

"For what? Getting your job back? You should have never lost it in the first place. You should have been rewarded for exposing that scumbag."

"No, for taking what was a holiday I dreaded and turning it into something wonderful." She leaned up on her tiptoes, in her elf shoes, to give him a resounding kiss on the lips.

Noah headed to the bathrooms to change into his Santa costume. He stopped several feet away and turned back to her. "Candace, I had a thought."

"What?" Candace asked, her head cocked.

"This is down the road, of course. But I was thinking… did you know that if we got married your name would be Candace Cane?" He laughed as he turned the corner and disappeared from view.

Christmas, thought the future Mrs. Candy Cane. *I think I could totally get on board with that.*

A Fresh Start

by Sonja Fröjdendal

To mom for teaching me to read and for always being in my corner.

Chapter One

The sight of her made my heart race. Ever since we were kids, I'd had this reaction. She always wore jeans and a tank top, you know the tight fitting kind? I'm pretty sure she did it on purpose to make people insane. Don't get me wrong, she doesn't have a big rack, she's just so bloody fit. And beautiful. Her blond hair was still long, her eyes the same deep blue I sometimes dreamt about.

Watching her through the window of the coffee shop made me feel like a peeping Tom. She didn't know I was watching her eat the ice cream like she was making love to it. Okay, she probably wasn't, but it looked like that to me. Everything about her made me think of sex. I had never had sex with her and probably never would, but you can't blame me for thinking about it. Thinking isn't illegal. Yet.

I had never told her how I felt; she wouldn't like knowing her best friend was in love with her — had loved her since childhood. The love of my life and I couldn't say anything. When she left Sweden, I cried for a month. Come on, I was just a brat back then. I was sure she would stay in the UK. I was right, she'd stayed fifteen years. Talking on the phone and writing letters were the only ways of staying in touch back then. Even Facebook, emails, and Skype aren't the same thing as in person. But now I had made it myself, from Sweden to the UK. Freaking life had been throwing obstacles in my way for the last six years, ever since graduating high school. Well, no need to dwell on the past. Time to get inside and say hi. I was clever, even if I didn't know it at the time, and had made her tell me her favorite places and hideouts during our phone calls. Trust her to find the best place in Walsall to have a cup of tea. Knowing Sam, she was probably on her third cup. I couldn't help smiling at that thought. Sam would be so surprised. She didn't know that I had found the money and time to come.

As I opened the door, I could smell the scones and the

cupcakes, the sweet scent of fruit tea. The sound of people talking and laughing was peaceful. I understood why she chose this shop. It wasn't the place I would go for a relaxing time though, I would feel so out of place here. No matter how old I get, I worry what people think when they see me. Would they judge my tattoos or the way I dress? I love my style, but many people don't. I let a couple pass me and went to the counter to place my order. I looked around to see if my pen pal had arrived.

I pretended I was only here to see Sue, but I knew Sam was here. Sue understood; I had told her about Sam in our letters. I scanned the room and found her in the corner. I took my cup and went over.

"Hi gorgeous, where have you been all my life?"

Sue turned her head and beamed. "You're so funny. I've been watching the door, when did you get here?"

"Just now, there were a few others that came at the same time as me." After a hug, we sat down. It was hard to believe that I had only known Sue for a year. I needed to find her a Christmas gift before I left town. After Sue checked Sam out over my shoulder, she agreed that Sam looked good. "When are you going to talk to her? You can't sit here all day."

"I know, but I don't want it to be too obvious that I'm here to see her. And besides, I just got here. I have you here and it would be bad if I let you sit alone and went to talk to another woman." A little wink made sure she knew I was joking with her.

"I'll fix that." Sue took our empty cups and went to the counter. How would buying more tea make Sam see me? Just then, Sue turned and asked in a higher tone, "What do you want this time, Alex?"

What I really wanted was a beer or a whisky, but it wasn't that kind of establishment. "I'll have the elder tea again, thanks, with some honey, please. If they don't have any, just dip your lovely self in it, and I'm good." With a wide grin I looked at Sue. That line worked every time; Sue blushed and shook her head.

"Alex! You never told me you were coming to the UK."

Sam's soft voice hit me like a hammer. *Breathe and pretend to be calm.* I turned towards the voice. Sam looked me up and down, and then grabbed me in tight hug before pushing back and holding me at arm's length. "Why are you dressed so over the top on a Thursday?" I had on low rise black pants, tight over my ass, with a myriad of straps and chains hanging. I topped the look off with a black leather corset, decorated with green velvet, showing my assets under a leather jacket.

"Sam? Hi. I'm here in the UK to see Sue, and you, of course. I thought you worked Thursdays. What are you doing here?"

"I am working. Didn't I tell you I work from home Thursdays? Well, from here, technically. Their Wi-Fi is much better than mine." Sam let out her thousand-volt smile. Sue made her entrance with our tea.

"Hi, I'm Sue. "

"Oh, hi, I'm Sam." She shook hands and curtsied like the polite girl she was.

"Hi Sam, why don't you join us?" Sue pointed at an empty chair at the table.

"Sure, I'll grab my things and come over." Sam rushed over to get her things.

"Don't glare at me like that; you know you want to talk to her. Do you really need to wear the jacket indoors?" Sue asked. "Is that a fashion statement? I want to see those tattoos of yours, Alex."

I hadn't known that Sue had an evil streak in her. That never showed in the letters. I liked it though, even if she was pushing me toward Sam. I wasn't ready to talk to Sam, not here in public anyway. Would I be dumb and do nothing but gaze at her, or were words going to come out of my mouth? Time would tell; there was no backing out now.

After a bone crunching hug from Sam, I put the jacket over the chair and we sat down. "Okay, I know that you said you had lots of tattoos but I didn't think you would be covered in them." Sue leaned closer to take a look at the tattoo on my lower right arm.

"Is that a Celtic sun?"

"Yeah, it is. Some things you don't say in letters or on Facebook. And I'm not covered yet, I still have a few empty spots on my body. Not saying you're one of them, Sue, but some people think of me as being a tramp for having a lot of tattoos."

That got Sam and Sue talking about idiotic people who judge others by their looks. It was a good thing Sue was here doing most of the talking since I was kind of busy looking at Sam. Savoring everything about her: her eyes, her lips, her voice. Yeah, I was deep under; how could one person mean so much to me?

Sam looked good, even better than when she left Sweden. She aged well, like fine scotch. Yeah, yeah, I know she was only fifteen then, but she was still foxy. The kind of foxy that made you want to cover her whole body with yours and make her melt in your arms. I'd never had the guts to make a move before. I knew I loved her, but I was still figuring out my sexuality then. Nowadays, I'd simply go down on her and then, when she was exhausted, I'd start all over and make her melt like chocolate.

"You finally got the money to come over to England? How long will you stay?" Her voice was as smooth as whisky.

"What did you say?"

"I asked how long you would be staying in England. "

"I'm here to stay for good. Well, not right here really. Scotland, to be more exact."

"When did you arrive? Wait, what? You are here to stay? You're moving to Scotland? How cool. Where are you going to live?" In her excitement, Sam's voice got higher. A huge grin spread slowly and her eyes twinkled.

"I came yesterday and I stayed outside Sue's house."

"What? Outside the house?" Sam glared at Sue and me.

"Alex has a camper van to sleep in. Stop frowning at me like that. I offered her a bed inside the house, but no. You should know how Alex is when an idea pops into that wonderful head of hers." Sue watched Sam to gauge her reaction. Sam didn't disappoint, her gaze flew to mine. "You're still living in that van?"

I wanted to ignore them, but I knew it would only get

them more fired up. "I can't leave the van alone when I don't know the neighborhood. Someone might break in and steal my belongings. What's in that van is all I own in this world. Do you really think I'm going let someone steal it?"

"What do you mean all you own? What about your furniture? Your things? Have you sold all your books? Sam looked really shocked at that last thought. As though it was an unbelievable thing. Okay, I admit that it was.

"I didn't have lots of furniture and things to begin with, Sam, you know that. Did you forget that I've been living in my camper van for years now? Easiest way to move on when you're finished with a place." I couldn't help but smile at her. "My books are still mine, can't sell the kids, you know." The expression on her face made me laugh out loud. She glanced at me and frowned.

"You know I love you, don't you?" Did I say that out loud? Please let there be a God so she didn't hear me.

"I love you too, Alex." Sam tilted her head in that love-me-because-I'm cute way.

"I know you do, honey." Quick change of subject needed. Think Alex, think. "Sue, when was it you had to be back at work?"

"Oh, work! Need to go now, honey. See you back home."

I gave Sue a quick hug before she rushed out, leaving a slightly awkward silence in her wake.

"So, how long are you staying here in Walsall before you move on? Where in Scotland are you moving? How did you get money to move over? Are you really..."

"Sam. Can you breathe so I can answer your questions?" Yeah, she still blushed when told off, and yeah, it was still really cute. "I'm staying in Walsall until Saturday, then I'm driving up to Edinburgh, Glasgow, and then to Oban. I'll be living in Oban for three months while I help a lady on her small farm." I put a finger in the air to let Sam know to keep quiet because I wasn't finished. "I've been saving every little penny I could spare and working off the books as much as possible. And yes, I'm really staying in Scotland. This is not a holiday. So, your turn to answer questions. How's work going? Is the boss still an asshole?"

"The work is perfect; I can work more or less from wherever and whenever I like. As long as I have an internet connection, that is." She shrugged, as though it didn't really matter. "The boss is still a big ass. But I've talked to the regional manager and I may be able to report directly to him, then I wouldn't have to go to the office at all. Perks of being a copywriter that kicks ass."

"When do you know if you get a new boss?"

"He said he would call me today and let me know how it went. Fingers crossed that I get him as a boss, 'cause then I can move."

"Move? I thought you liked it here? That's what you have been saying, anyway." When she turned her head away I put my hand on her arm. "Sam, talk to me. What's wrong?"

"I do like it here, Alex. That's not the problem. The asshole boss is the problem. He shows up everywhere I go. It's like he is stalking me, but I can't prove anything because he's never alone. He always has friends with him, so it could be a coincidence. But it gives me the creeps and I don't want to take any chances on him going mental."

Ah, so that was why she kept glancing at the door. "Fingers crossed that this new boss is taking you under his wing. Where are you moving then, do you know that? Any ideas?"

"Well, I was thinking about Edinburgh since you have been rambling on about it for the past few years." A little crooked smile in the left corner of her mouth appeared. "I thought that you would move there if you got the chance. The way you talked about Edinburgh you would think it was the only big city in the world."

"It is the best city of all. But can you really see me living in a big city? With all the stress and rush?" I couldn't control the snort from escaping.

"I'm only in Oban for a short while and then I'm moving to a small holding between Drumnadrochit and Newtonmore. Before you ask, it's my land and I paid for it in full. I sent Sue to check it for me and she sent me a film of it. I'm meeting the seller tomorrow, signing the papers, and handing over the money." I couldn't help smiling over the thought. Tomorrow this time, I would be a homeowner.

"Where and when are you signing the papers? Why are you signing them here and not in Scotland?" Sam's voice pierced through my thoughts.

"I'm signing them here as the estate agency, Bairstow Eves, is just at the crossing and the seller actually lives here now. I have to be there at 1:30 p.m."

"I thought we could have lunch." Sam always bit her lower lip when she was nervous or worried. It was a huge giveaway about her feelings. If you added in the bags under her eyes, that weren't quite hidden by her make-up, I knew something was wrong.

"Sure I'll lunch with you before the meeting. Where? Know any good places?"

"The Brewers Fayre is a good spot to grab a bite. Unless you want to go to McDonalds instead?"

"Okay, seriously. You ask me if I want to eat at McDonalds? Have you ever seen me at a McDonalds? I wouldn't get caught dead in that place. Tired much, Sam?" Raising my eyebrows always got her giggling, this time too. It helped her relax and that made me happy. I didn't like seeing her this tense. If that freaking boss of hers could be so kind as to come in to the café I'd beat his sorry ass. I had to remind myself to breathe, I couldn't let Sam know what I was thinking. It always bothered her when my temper flared up.

"So if we meet at Brewers at noon, that will give you enough time to eat and still get there."

"Okay, Brewers at noon. See you then, I have some shopping to do for the trip. I promised Sue I would be back in time for dinner. I know you have work to do so I'll leave you to do that."

"I can't believe you would choose to stay with your pen pal rather than me. I thought we were best friends." Sam pouted and it nearly killed me.

"Sam, you live in a tiny apartment complex, where would I park my van? I promise we'll see each other soon." Ignoring Sam's sad look, I gave her a hug and left her at the table.

Chapter Two

The next day, I showed up at Brewers ten minutes late. I was always late. Sam knew that about me but never held it against me. Yet one more thing I loved about her, and another reason why I had no luck with relationships. I hadn't been able to find anyone, besides her, who would put up with all my quirks. Never found anyone, never wanted anyone. I only wanted Sam, but knew I couldn't have her. So I stuck with one night stands that didn't force their feelings on you, but never gave more than temporary satisfaction. The bump on my shoulder woke me up from my thoughts. The dude apologized. Brits are so polite. I found Sam at a corner table, unsurprisingly, as corner tables had always been her thing. When Sam got up to hug me, I saw she was wearing a short, tight miniskirt and heels. She had always liked to wear heels, even when she wore pants. She was short and always complained about her height. The heels made her feel better.

"You're dressed to kill today, is it for me? I can't remember ever seeing you in a skirt before."

She still couldn't take a compliment. "I'm not going to kill anyone, at least not on purpose. I felt like celebrating by dressing up." Her voice trembled with excitement.

"What? You got the other boss?" Sam nodded. "Congrats, honey!" Maybe it wasn't such a smart idea to hug her so tightly when she smelled so wonderful. Feeling those breasts against mine, even with clothes between, was making me a bit hot. *Better to let her go now or she would find out that she turns me on when I undressed her, in a public place, during rush hour. Better get those thoughts out of my head.*

"Since we are celebrating, it's my treat. What do you want?" Could she tell by my voice that I wasn't calm?

"Well, if you're buying, I'll take the salmon."

"Sam, if you order the same thing you normally do, it's not celebrating." I waggled my eyebrows in hopes of making her laugh.

"I've not eaten salmon here often and it's my celebration, right?"

"Yeah, yeah, salmon it is. Make it two, will ya? And two Cokes." The waitress left, and Sam dove right into discussing where to move. I nodded once in a while and said okay here and there. Listening to her talking about the pros and cons of every city I ever mentioned was kind of fun. She had really done her research. Did she know that she drove me crazy by rubbing her knee against mine under the table? It was subtle, but I wasn't sure if it was intentional or not. Lucky for me I had an appointment, so it wouldn't be suspicious when I shortened this lunch. What I hadn't planned for was the fact that Sam insisted on coming with me to read the contract.

"Come on, Alex! You know I have more experience reading and writing contracts than you. I might only be a copywriter, but I've written a few contracts in my time." Standing outside the restaurant, I had relaxed knowing that I would say bye to Sam. Her insistence on coming made me tense up a bit again.

"You have work to do, Sam. I can't let you get crap from your asshole boss, even if you're changing bosses soon."

Sam shook her head. "I don't have anything to do for them for the next four weeks. Okay, my holiday officially doesn't start until after four p.m., but all my work is done. I am coming with you to the estate agency and that's that." She still had that stubborn streak in her that I knew so well from childhood.

"Fine, you can come." Why the hell did I always say yes to that woman?

"Afterwards we can celebrate that you're now a grown up." Sam smiled and danced on her way to the office. *Damn woman, you got me wrapped around your finger. Just like you did when we were kids.* "Are you coming, then?" Sam's voice sounded odd, I wasn't sure if I liked the tone in it. "Getting old are you?" She giggled.

"Old enough to buy my own place. Come on." I shooed her inside the door. "Let's get this over with."

Driving at night always put me in a good mood. Driving with Sam in the passenger seat made it perfect. I just had to remember to drive on the left side of the road and not to sneak peeks of Sam sleeping too often. We were supposed to have left early this morning, but Sue wanted to give us a proper English breakfast. And then we stayed for lunch and dinner for some reason. But I always preferred driving at night anyway, fewer people and traffic. It was still hard to accept that Sam was following me. That she would live in the same town, well at least the same shire. The town would depend on the internet access and speed, considering she worked mostly from her laptop.

She looked so innocent and sweet sleeping, although I knew she couldn't be comfortable in that seat. I wondered if she knew that she snores. It's not one of those loud, annoying snores, and even snoring she was cute and adorable. I, on the other hand, looked like a grizzly after sleeping badly. If my Mum was to be trusted, and she normally was, I was as grumpy as one before I had my coffee. Arriving in Edinburgh early in the morning, people were still out and about, either on their way home from the pub or going to work. The city wasn't showing its best side this morning. The rain drizzling down from above made it look a little sad, and in parts, abandoned. I parked the van outside an apartment house in their parking lot. It looked so weird with a modern parking lot outside a house built 200 or 300 years ago. Since Sam still hadn't moved, I decide to go for a little walk, stretch my legs, and get the blood flowing again.

Walking down the Royal Mile made me feel at home, for the first time ever in a city. The only other time I had felt anything like this was with Sam when we were teenagers and she had fallen asleep on my shoulder. That had made me feel at home and whole then and I had never stopped looking for the feeling again. Now, I found half of that in Edinburgh, a city I wouldn't live in, just occasionally visit. Maybe it would be a good idea to buy a flat here and use it when I was in a city mood. And when I wasn't here, I could rent it out and get an extra income. It might be useful in the future now that I was changing my life around. The salary would be much less than I currently made. If I really got my business started well, with a bit of luck I could grow my salary back in a few years. A good investment plan: spend lots of money now to get some later on. The flat in Stockholm gave me a good sum of money every month, so why not Edinburgh? I had to research a good real estate company that could do all the work, finding tenants and doing the maintenance. Sam was probably awake now and hungry, so it was time to head back and eat. And to find out if she was staying or if it was Glasgow she wanted to live in.

By the time I got back to the camper van I was soaking wet, one thing I probably would have a problem getting used to: Scottish weather changing by the minute. Time to dig out the umbrella and start using it. Or at least get a rain poncho. Sam was awake and watched me when I entered and started stripping off my clothes.

"Never seen a wet woman before?" Every single piece of clothing was wet. How the hell could you get your undies soaking wet in five freaking minutes? The damn jeans got stuck at my hips and wouldn't budge no matter how much I tried. That made Sam giggle hysterically so I glared at her.

"Need any help, Alex? I've got an extra pair of hands if you need them." The giggling exploded into outright laughter that left her wriggling in the bed.

"Sure, you can help me. Seems like I forgot how to undress myself." Snorting, Sam came over and helped me drag my jeans off.

"Why do you have to wear those tight jeans? Wouldn't it

be easier to wear looser fitting trousers?" Sam's voice was muffled, pulling my pants down, her face had gotten covered.

"They make me look sexy and show off my ass. Why do you think I wear them?" I grinned at her when her head popped up to see if I was serious. "They seem to do the trick too, got you pulling them off and making you all red and hot." In retaliation, she pulled extra hard and I ended up on my butt.

"Seriously? That's all you think about? Sex, sex, and more sex. Don't you think you could spend time thinking about something else?"

"What? I'm not allowed to think of sex because I'm a woman? Forget that. If I want to think of sex I do, and I do it with whomever I like, when I like. Spare me the goody-two-shoes speech, I've had it before and don't care for it." I really needed a shower so I could get warm and calm down. Sam didn't deserve the telling off.

Coming out of the shower, I smelled food. Sam had obviously gone shopping. "It's my olive branch for not thinking before speaking. I have a habit of doing that. Sorry," she said.

"Well, I'm sorry too for lashing out at you because of everyone else's opinions. It smells delicious, you bought beans and toast?"

"Let's eat. You can tell me if you think it's good. "

It did taste good, beans on toast and sausage was always a good choice. Scots knew how to cook warm food for chilly days. The sturdy breakfast made you ready to tackle anything. Not that I needed to tackle anything worse than the weather, but anyway. I wouldn't care so much about the weather with a full stomach.

"You look like the Cheshire Cat with that grin. What are you thinking about?"

"I'm enjoying the food." I let the grin grow wider. "What are you going to do today? Look for a B&B to live in while you get sorted?"

"Nope. I'm going to see if I can find new shoes and then I'm going shopping to see if I can find a market. I only got a few things earlier, for breakfast. This kitchen is tiny, makes it hard to cook. I want to find some easier foods that we can take with us. Or are you planning on eating out?"

No way in hell was I going to eat out when there was a chance to get a home cooked meal. "We can eat here. You're doing the cooking? I don't have to help?" I had never been a great cook.

"I'll do everything, you just have to show up and eat." There was some emotion in her face I couldn't read.

"Great! See you later then. I'll take the garbage out from breakfast." I escaped. It was the only word for it. She didn't realize how it affected me, being so close to her.

Happy that she didn't ask to come with me, I dumped the garbage in the nearest bin. I needed to get my freaking head under control, it had felt too much like a home. Like our home, and that was not the reality. Now I had to figure out what to do all day in Edinburgh. Maybe I'd see if I could find the coffee shop that J.K. Rowling sat in while writing her books. Don't judge, you read them too. I couldn't believe my luck when it didn't take me that long, just two hours, to find the coffee shop. The Elephant House. I wondered if they ever thought of kicking Rowling out for taking up a table all day. She didn't have the money in the beginning to buy lots of coffee. On the way, I had bought a pen and a notebook. Okay, pens and notebooks. Useful tools when you completely change your life. And you could always use a spare one in case one broke or disappeared. The notebook might even get full. I had bought a Christmas gift for Sam at the same time. A book by Diana Gabaldon, *A Leaf on the Wind of All Hallows Eve.* I knew she wanted it, she had said so last time we spoke on the phone.

Sitting down with a coffee and looking out of the window made me relax even more. The walk around looking for this place had settled me, but now I could feel the calm filling me. This was what I needed, to be alone with my thoughts. I opened the notebook and stared at all the blank space in it. Page after page of blank space. What would I fill it with? Could I fill it with something good and useful? At the moment it didn't feel like it; I felt like a fraud. Why would anyone read what I had to say?

"Are you a writer?" It was the waitress cleaning off the next table.

"No, I'm not sure I'm good enough."

"Well, staring at the paper won't tell you if you are good or bad. Putting the pen to the paper and writing the words will. Your story is new and no one has told it before; no one has heard it before. It's your story and you are the only one who can tell it. You owe it to the story to tell it the best way you can. Refill is on the house." She left as abruptly as she had intruded in the first place.

I owed it to my story? Really? Well, better test her theory. I put the pen to the paper, hesitated for a second, and then I started writing. The only breaks I took were to refill my coffee and to buy something for lunch. Four hours later I got a text telling me Sam had started dinner and would be finished in an hour. I hadn't realized that that much time had flown past while I was caught up in writing. The first notebook was full and I had started the second one. Now I hoped I could read what I had written in my daze. A first glance didn't give me much hope of that part. Well, that would have to wait; it was time to gather my stuff and go back. Dinner and Sam awaited my arrival.

Chapter Three

Three hours later and I still felt full; it was almost uncomfortable to move. It made me sleepy and the darkness outside didn't help. Luckily Sam had a driver's license, and was used to driving on the left side of the road. The sound of the engine made it even harder to stay awake, it was so monotonous. I should probably talk to Sam to help her stay focused. Just have to yawn first.

"Close those blue eyes of yours, Alex, you are really tired. I slept on the way up to Edinburgh so I'm fine. You, on the other hand, drove all night and have been up all day. Sleep for a few hours, I'll wake you when it's time for bed." A little twinkle in her eyes made me feel all mushy and warm, like she loved me as a lover, not just as a friend. It made me hope, and hope was not a good thing when you knew there was no chance. I did as she asked and closed my eyes. A few minutes of shut eye would be good. No sleep though, otherwise I would have problems sleeping when we got to Glasgow.

Focusing on the lyrics coming from the radio and trying to figure out the next line in the songs kept me awake. I still got a rest and felt less tired than before. Sam sang along to the radio, not the best voice but who cares? She enjoyed it and I enjoyed listening to her. Having Sam staying in the camper with me would make it hard not to show how I felt. It was nice though; it made it feel like a home. The home I had always wanted but never thought I would have. It felt good when she touched me, when her hand caressed my knee. Her hand caressed my knee? I had to be hallucinating. I opened one eye to see if it was real or not. There it was. Why was Sam's hand on my knee? *Okay, Alex, breathe, just breathe.* Closing my eyes again, I tried to really enjoy the feeling. If it weren't for the fact that I was turned on, I would have loved having her hand on my knee. It couldn't be comfortable driving like that. Should I say something or should I pretend to sleep?

"Alex, if you are going to make believe you have to

breathe. At least a couple of times." Sam could barely get the words out, she was laughing so hard.

"First of all, I'm not pretending to sleep. Second of all I am breathing. Why are you holding my knee and laughing at me?" That made Sam really lose it and laugh hysterically; she even snorted a few times trying to get it together. "Seriously, why are you laughing?" The upside of her laughing was that she had to take her hand away from my knee. My breathing slowly returned to normal and my brain started to function properly. Well, somewhat properly anyway. With her around it never worked as expected. Would I ever be able to think straight with Sam around or should I just sign in to an asylum?

"I'm sorry, Alex." Sam giggled. "It's just that you looked so peaceful and sweet, I wanted to know what was going through your mind. Touching you seemed like a good idea. I wasn't aware that your breathing was connected to your knee." She lost it again, tears streaming down her face.

"Pull over here at the rest stop. You can't see anything laughing like that so I had better drive." Without arguing, she pulled over and stopped the van. Changing places in the cabin didn't help my arousal. It might be bigger than a car but it wasn't that spacious. Feeling her rub her body against mine got my hands moving of their own accord. Stroking her hips instead of holding them to move her, making her catch her breath while I was holding mine again. Breathing was over-estimated in my opinion.

"Is this payback for me touching you?" Sam's voice cracked.

"Payback? No, I just wanted to reciprocate the favor." I can make sounds that form words, impressive! "Why would you think it's payback? Do you like it, does it turn you on?" I let my hands follow her hips up along her body, stopping just under her breasts. It made her inhale. Taking that as a signal to continue, I let my right thumb graze the underside of her breast. She grabbed my hips and pulled me closer as a moan slipped through her lips. That nearly drove me over the edge. I settled for nibbling my way up her neck. Trying to press her against the wall, we lost our balance and fell into the living quarters of the camper. Not the most romantic moment ever.

The fall woke us up from our daze. Not knowing what to say, I sat up on the floor. Sam seemed bewildered. She studied her knee and smoothed out her jeans. A nervous reaction I would bet. I fought the urge to drag my fingers through my hair. "So, are we going to keep on?"

"If that's what you want, sure."

"Good, you said you would drive." Sam moved to the passenger seat. Of course she meant the driving and nothing else. With a deep breath, I got up and went to the driver's seat. As I started the van, I gave Sam a quick look, she was staring out the window. Would she give me the silent treatment all the way to Glasgow? Maybe if I said I was sorry and promised to never do it again? Leaving the rest stop, I strangled the thoughts that were leading me nowhere. If I was lucky, she would think about what had happened and decide that she liked it and wanted to do it again. Dream big and aim high my Mom used to say. Most likely she was thinking up a good excuse as to why she had let it go on, or how to end our friendship in a nice way.

I'll give her a few minutes or more to calm down. Letting her be in her own world would let me get my thoughts and feelings under control and give me the opportunity to think of what to say to her. I had to make sure she understood that I didn't intend for it to happen but that I'm not sorry it did. That would be a balancing act worthy of a medal. Hell, it would be worth the Nobel Peace Prize. I hadn't missed Sam's tendency to overreact and twist words and their meaning around in her head. Sometimes it didn't matter if you were careful with what you said, she read tones and words that weren't there and got upset. Listening to my own thoughts got me wondering if I should give up women and become a nun. Or at least give up Sam.

It wasn't like I was perfect and without flaws. Throwing stones in a glass house was never a good thing, I needed to stop doing that. Back to the original thought, how to talk about what happened without making a mess of it. It would be a miracle if I made that happen. Want a smart remark or a witty comeback? Then I'm your woman. Sensitive, thoughtful, and that sort of thing isn't my game. It usually got me in trouble and caused lots of pain. Pain because then the lady I was with in those moments threw whatever she had close by, usually something of mine. Why did every woman I chose have to be neurotic and aggressive? Most importantly of all, why did they have to take their problems out on me? Did I have a sign on my forehead that said 'easy pickings'?

The sound of raindrops on the windshield brought me from my thoughts and forced me to pay more attention to driving. The rain soon changed to hail. We needed to get off the road.

"Sam? Can you check the map for a place to stop and get out of this weather?"

"There should be a road coming up in a mile or so. It's the only thing I can see." Sam started scrolling through pages on her phone.

"Who are you calling? Got friends in the area?"

"I'm not calling anyone; I'm checking the GPS to see if there's anything closer. Slow down, Alex, it should be just ahead."

Creeping down the road due to the hail, I still would have missed the sign if it wasn't for Sam. *Moving to Scotland in December was a smart idea, Alex? Don't answer that, I know the answer. Celebrating Christmas with Sam sounded better than Christmas alone.* "I guess it's a good time to have a tea break. What do you think, Sam? I'm starting to get hungry again."

"Really? We didn't eat that long ago."

"Dinner was four hours ago. Do we have any leftovers?"

"No leftovers since you ate everything. You have a bottomless stomach and a bad memory. Maybe you need a note app on your phone like an old lady. Maybe then you won't forget to take a shower or to not eat so much."

"What? Are you saying I stink?" I knew I didn't smell but still I had to check, making Sam giggle.

"Yep, bad memory. You took a shower earlier today."

Watching her in the galley made me happy; she looked as though she belonged there. Yesterday had been the first time I'd seen her in my camper but now I wanted her to stay forever. I wanted her to come with me when I traded camper living for an actual house. On my land. I owned land. How my life had changed.

"What are you smiling at?" Sam looked up at me, pausing her setting of the table.

"I can't really believe that I own a house with land. How do you live in a house? I'm used to small spaces; this house has four bedrooms!"

"It's easy. I'll teach you. Oh! You need to shop for furniture. Yeah, you need my help with that. We probably have to check online. I don't think the middle of nowhere will have a good shop."

I could count on Sam for shopping. She scribbled on a piece of paper with a dopey look on her face. I'd let her help me and she'd stay longer. It felt good knowing that.

"Okay, Sam. You can help me decorate the house on one condition."

"And that is?"

"You eat something and drink the tea you poured yourself." I crossed my arms, trying to look intimidating.

"No problem, I can do two things at the same time." Sam waved her hand in my direction. I wasn't sure that she was really listening to me.

"Have you noticed that the hailstorm stopped? We can probably continue after this."

"You're right. I missed that. Good. I can't wait to see Glasgow."

This conversation felt stilted, almost like we weren't communicating at all, and I had no idea how to start talking about what happened earlier. I'd hoped to use the hailstorm to force us to stay here and talk. Now I only had a few minutes while Sam ate to clear the air. Not the easiest when you aren't used to talking about feelings with someone you care about. I guess I had to just blurt it out. Unless she addressed it, which didn't seem likely. And I had better stop staring at her before she noticed. What was wrong with me? Staring out of the window wasn't any better. I could still feel her behind me. I tried to ignore her and focus on the window. The snowflakes made the world look magical. Wait, snowflakes?

"Sam, is it snowing or am I hallucinating?"

"Snowing? Is it?"

"I don't know, that's why I asked you."

To confirm my suspicions, I opened the door. It was indeed snowing. Obviously for a while going by the snow covering the ground. We must have sat there in silence longer than I had thought.

"We are not going anywhere tonight, hon. Soon it will be a blizzard with limited visibility. Glad to be in a campervan and not in a regular car?" I couldn't help smiling, you had to love Mother Nature. "So, what do you want to do? Read, play cards, get a tattoo, or get naked?"

"What? Get naked? Why should we get naked?"

"I guess you don't remember that I sleep in the nude. You used to do that too. Has time changed you that much?"

"Oh, yeah, no I still sleep nude. Don't like to get tangled. But it's too early for sleeping, it's only eight. You don't have a TV? How can you get tattooed in the middle of nowhere?" Frowning, Sam looked at me.

"You want a tattoo? I can do one for you, free of charge, too. It could be a Christmas present from me to you." Leaning over the table to get the box out from under the bench, I saw her watching me. It felt like I was under the microscope. Was I dangerous or harmless? "Decided yet?"

"Decided on what?"

"On what kind of tattoo you want." Opening the box, I revealed ink bottles, needles, and tattoo machines.

"You brought them with you?"

"Of course I did, they are mine and it's my livelihood. I have my certificate with me so I can tattoo wherever I like. As long as I have a work permit of course." Smiling at her, I picked up one of the machines. "Should I break the seal on a needle and give you one?"

"Does it hurt a lot?"

"No, I don't think so. But it all depends on how you tolerate pain. Arms, legs, and over the spine will hurt more. Doing it on a more meaty part hurts less. Trust me, I have a few."

"But if it hurts on arms, why do you have so many

there?"

"Because it doesn't hurt that much on me; everyone has a different tolerance for pain. I like the pain. It lets me know I'm alive. And I love the sound of the machine so I get a kick out of it. I can make a small butterfly on your ass or one of your boobs. It won't show unless you get undressed." I winked at her as I hooked the needle to the machine. "The boys love when girls have hidden tattoos."

"I wouldn't know."

"If you don't have tattoos you wouldn't know that unless you had talkative girlfriends. And I guess by what you said, you don't."

"Oh, I have talkative friends but I have never been with a man. It's not my cup of tea, as the Brits would say."

"You have never complained about girlfriends over the years. Have you been lucky and gotten the good ones?"

"I've been single, and no, I'm not a virgin." Being Sam, she stuck her tongue out. "You shouldn't talk about not talking about girlfriends, I have never heard you mention one. Don't think I can give good advice?"

"You know I'm lesbian? And you're okay with it?" If she had said she was a killer I wouldn't have been as shocked. How could she know?

"It's not a secret. You've never looked at boys in the same way you look at girls. Everyone knew when we were growing up. Did you get different friends after I left or did they just not mention it? Why would I not be okay with it? You're my best friend and I don't care who you love. As long as you still love me." Sam winked.

"I still talk to some of our childhood friends but they have never mentioned it. My new friends know, considering we met in a lesbian group on the internet. I will always love you no matter what. You should know that."

"You never said anything."

"Aw, Sam." I went over to the bench and hugged her. "I'm sorry if you felt unloved by me. You've always had a place in my heart. No one can ever take it from you."

"So, do you have a girlfriend?" Her voice was muffled

against my neck.

"No girlfriend, single as always."

"Why are you single? You look good and are a great catch."

"Thanks for that, Sam, I'm single because I choose to be. The one I want isn't for me."

"Why? Doesn't she love you back? Have you told her?"

"She doesn't love me and no, I haven't told her how I feel. That would be pointless, wouldn't it?"

"Why do you get to decide what others feel? If you haven't told her, you don't know if it's pointless or not. She might feel the same as you but doesn't have the guts to tell you. You can appear a bit harsh and standoffish sometimes." Sam lifted her head and pinned me with a look I didn't recognize.

"Hmm, true. I don't know, but I wasn't aware that she was into girls." This conversation gave me hope. Could it be that simple? Would she, could she mean…?

"I never took you for a coward, Alex. Will you tell her or are you going to suffer for the rest of your life?" A mischievous smirk appeared in the corner of her mouth.

"What do you mean?"

"As a kid and teenager you went for what you wanted. Now you tell me you don't even try to get the woman of your dreams? You are going to force everyone around you to tell you how they feel first, aren't you? Such a coward." Without warning she leaned in and kissed me. And it wasn't one of those friendly kisses. It was a kiss that you felt down your spine. A kiss that made you forget everything else. Which was exactly what I did.

The only thing I cared about was Sam, what she did to me, and what I did to her. How it felt when her hands touched my skin as she undressed me. That tingling feeling running through my body when her kisses moved down my neck. Making her moan as I teased her. Her skin under my hands felt like heaven. It sent shivers down my spine, in anticipation of what was coming. Was this real or a dream? Her hand on my breast made it clear I wasn't dreaming. When her other hand found its way between my legs, I definitely knew. This was going to be the ride of my life. I had to stop her before I came; I wanted to make it good for her. Flipping her around in the bed made her stop and start laughing. I had to get the upper hand on the situation. Kissing her breathless was a good start, and I worked my way down her body. I took my time to memorize every part of her, every noise she made. Could I make her scream? Time to find out.

The Perfect Christmas

by Tami Lund

Dedicated to my Writing Wenches family. Thank you for the support, the inspiration, and the laughs.

Chapter One

She would always remember the moment she fell in love with him.

It was at a pharmacy, the big box kind that sat on the busiest intersection in every town. Anna North was a cashier, had been working there for a few years now, and was going nowhere fast. On that particular blustery winter day, she'd snuck outside for a smoke. It was a filthy, expensive habit, and she smoked so infrequently that she ought to just quit all together. But every now and then, the urge to get away from it all, to hide in a corner somewhere and suck that soothing poison into her lungs, was too damn hard to resist. Considering Anna rarely bothered to resist anything that wasn't good for her, she wasn't concerned with quitting this particular vice.

She leaned against the side of the building, one arm wrapped around her torso, holding her coat closed because she was too lazy to zip it, while the other held the burning cigarette as far away from her body as possible, in a pointless attempt to keep the stench from permeating her clothing.

Her gaze scanned the scene, taking in the slush-coated parking lot, the handful of cars parked there, the colorful, bright lights covering every building, practically every tree and bush within eyesight.

Christmas. Her least favorite holiday. It was even worse than Thanksgiving, because not only was she expected to show up and mingle with her relatives, but she was expected to bring gifts, too. Anna didn't even like her family. The only good thing about Christmas was that she'd get to see him. That thought was spiraling through her mind when she spotted him.

Him.

He was probably fifty feet away, standing next to the staggered brick half-wall that lined the sidewalk in front of the pharmacy. He wore a knit cap over his shaggy brown hair. It was black with gray trim.

"You gave me a black hat to wear with my brown coat," he'd teased her last Christmas. But his bright blue eyes had been crinkled at the edges and there was a smile on his face, and he'd ruffled her hair before tugging the cap over his head and wearing it around the house for the rest of the day.

And he still wore it, a year later.

There was a little girl with him. A few months away from her third birthday, little Cora Patterson wore an adorable pink-and-chocolate-brown coat with matching mittens, matching hat, and matching boots. Anna knew her mother had dressed the little girl just by looking at the painfully coordinated outfit.

Wisps of pale blonde hair stuck out from under the stylish winter hat. Her right hand clung to her daddy's fingers as she struggled to walk along the top of the wall. There was a look of pure, unadulterated joy on both daughter and father's faces.

I love him.

The thought hit her like a sloppy, slushy snowball to the chest. She could even feel her face flushing, as if someone was listening to what was going on in her head.

No, Anna, no. You can't. That is the one thing that you cannot screw up. You can't.

She continued to stare as she waged the internal battle, until his head turned, as if he really, truly *could* hear her thoughts. Their gazes locked for several seconds. Anna's breath hitched, and then she held it, afraid that if she released it, the moment would be shattered.

"There you are."

It was shattered anyway, by a high-pitched nasally voice that had taken the owner years to perfect, and that grated on Anna's nerves more than almost anything else in the universe.

"They've been paging you and paging you, inside," the blonde beauty queen added. Her baby blue gaze, perfectly outlined with black liquid liner and heavy black mascara, dropped to Anna's hand, before she could move it behind her back. Not that it mattered. The stench of burning nicotine was hard to hide.

She wrinkled her flawless pert nose. "I can't believe you're still smoking, after the last time Mom caught you."

Probably exactly the reason I still smoke. "What do you want, Jessica?"

Her perfect sister waved at the brick building behind Anna's back. "Well, I'm trying to make a purchase, but you are too busy trying to develop cancer to come inside and use your employee discount to ring me up."

Of course. Jessica and her husband lived in a tax bracket so far away from Anna, she couldn't even imagine what it must be like, and yet her sister refused to buy anything at full price. But then again, that probably helped ensure they stayed in that far-away tax bracket.

"I'm coming," Anna muttered, and stubbed out the cigarette under her sister's disapproving gaze. She deliberately flicked it into the parking lot. She intended to head toward the back entrance, to meet Jessica inside, but as usual, her older sister quelled her with a look. Between Jessica and their mother, it was no wonder Anna had turned out the way she had.

"Damn it," she grumbled under her breath, when she spotted Jesse and little Cora heading their way. She adored her niece, to the point of worship, and her recent revelation about her brother-in-law had her still feeling off-kilter. She was not ready to be near him yet, at least not without the safety of the cashier's counter between them.

"Auntie Annie," Cora squealed. Despite her trepidation, Anna couldn't help the grin as she watched the toddler twist and turn in her father's arms, trying to get free, so she could rush over to greet her favorite aunt. Jesse grinned back and waited until he stepped onto the sidewalk before letting her go. She toddled over and threw herself at Anna's legs. Anna obligingly lifted the little girl into her arms. Cora wrinkled her pert little nose, just like her mother.

"You stink," she announced.

Anna flushed. "Sorry, sweetie." She never, ever smoked when she knew she was going to be around her niece. Today, she hadn't expected to see them.

"No she doesn't," Jesse admonished his daughter. "Cora, that's not very nice."

If Anna were the heroine in a romance novel, she would

surely have swooned at this point. Jesse was so damn nice. Her bitchy older sister did not deserve him. Anna had often – *often* – wondered how the hell Jessica managed to snag someone who was so incredibly unlike her.

"Can we go inside already?" Jessica demanded. "It's cold out here, and I have places to be."

"Oh, I forgot to tell you, Jess. My parents can't watch Cora tonight. My dad came down with a nasty cold, and my mom doesn't want to expose her."

"Do not call me Jess," she snapped. "It sounds too much like *your* name."

Jesse rolled his eyes before winking at Anna, his lips quirking into a small, knowing smile.

Jessica turned to her and said, "I'm sure you aren't busy tonight. What time do you get off work?"

"Um, seven."

"Good. Come straight to our house. I will probably be gone before you get there, but Jesse can wait until you show up before he goes to his thing. Now, can we *please* go inside so I can purchase my items and leave?"

Jessica walked inside. Jesse pulled Cora out of Anna's arms and said, "Hey, if you can't or don't want to, it's okay. I can stay home."

"No, it's fine. She's right. I didn't have any plans. Besides, I love hanging out with Cora."

The little girl rewarded her with a happy grin. It occurred to Anna that her niece was the only female in her immediate family who actually liked her. She doubted the feeling would last – not if Cora's mother and grandmother had anything to do with it – so she was happy to enjoy it while she could.

"I really don't mind," she insisted, before ducking her head and hurrying into the store to ring up her sister's purchases.

Chapter Two

*E*very time Anna visited her sister's house, she was blown away by the extravagance, the lavishness, the freaking beauty of it all.

Jessica was the top salesperson for a company that owned luxurious resorts all over the world. Jesse owned his own carpentry business, catering to their peers. Together, they were the ultimate power couple.

Anna sat in her fifteen-year-old sedan, parked in the circular drive in front of the towering, arched, brick-faced front entrance, working to get over the feeling of not belonging. She felt this way every time she was in her sister's presence, or her mother's presence. She was a black sheep, an outcast. She did not belong in this family.

She remembered asking her mother once – in all serious-ness – if she had been adopted. Her mother and sister were both flawless, with Scandinavian blonde good looks, whereas Anna had dark hair, olive skin, and was petite and more rounded than their tall, elegant statures.

"One would think," her mother had replied. "But no, you came directly from my womb. I promise you, the pain of deliv-ering you was far too hard to ever forget." Leave it to her moth-er to make her feel guilty for having been born at all.

"Too damn bad," she had retorted, provoked by her mother's tone. "I had hoped that if I ever had kids, they wouldn't stand a chance in hell of having *your* genes."

"If karma has anything to do with it, your children will be just like you," her mother replied, completely nonplussed. Anna sure as hell hoped so.

The right side of the double front doors opened and a fat evergreen wreath swayed to and fro for a moment before Jes-se's upper body popped into view. He was so damn gorgeous. Anna hated herself for thinking that way about her brother-in-law, but she couldn't help it. Most women fantasized about actors or rock stars or models. Anna fantasized about her sister's husband. Every night, as she lay in bed alone, she stimulated herself, while in her head, she and Jesse did all sorts of naughty acrobatic exercises. Sometimes, she tried to tell herself that she had created such a solid fantasy of the man that there was no way he could ever live up to it, so she ought to just get over her crush, but she was never very convincing.

Obviously, since that very afternoon she'd had the revelation that she was in love with him.

He held a phone to his ear, listening to whoever was on the other end. His hair was tousled, like always. He wore a simple Henley button-down, long-sleeved shirt over a white t-shirt, and a pair of faded jeans. With his right hand, he beckoned her inside. Anna gripped the steering wheel for a moment, giving herself a mental pep talk regarding self-control, with a reminder that even if she actually did hit on her brother-in-law, he would turn her down flat. He was married to the flawless, gorgeous Jessica. Why would he ever consider giving Anna a second thought?

Especially tonight. Having come to his house straight from work, she wasn't exactly dressed to impress, not that she ever really did, she supposed. Still, while she'd stripped out of the red and white polyester uniform shirt she had to wear at work, her black slacks and white long-sleeved t-shirt didn't exactly scream sexy.

With a resigned sigh, she grabbed her purse, tugged her hat more firmly over her messy hair, and climbed out of the car. She walked up the wide, brick-paver steps until she stood under the portico that protected calling guests from the elements.

"Hey," she said, striving to push away the image of Jesse pulling her into his arms and greeting her as if he couldn't bear not to touch her for one moment longer. She should be a romance writer. She had the imagination for it.

He nodded, mouthed something that she took to indicate he would be off the phone momentarily, and then moved to the side so she could step into the spacious entry, with shining wood floors and a staircase with a banister that curled into itself at the bottom. A Christmas tree, decorated with red ornaments and white lights, was tucked into the area under the staircase, and evergreen garland, dotted with tiny red bows and more white lights, ran the length of the banister.

As she was her sister's go-to babysitter – her price was right, after all – she visited this house frequently. So she knew, without actually investigating, that there would be a decorated tree in every single room. Even the bathrooms would have miniature trees perched on the counter tops, decorated in colors to complement the space.

Three years ago, during the first Christmas season after Jessica and Jesse were married, Anna had been surprised to learn that it was Jesse, not his wife, who did the holiday decorating. As it turned out, he loved Christmas, and his carpentry business had a professional decorating division. Learning that little bit of information about him had probably been when her crush had begun to simmer, slow and steady, until the day Cora had been born, and it had turned into a raging fire when he'd held her in his arms and swiped a tear from his eye.

Anna didn't normally date sappy, sweet guys, so the crush had been something of a surprise, in the beginning. But the more she got to know her brother-in-law, the more she realized her crush was completely justified. He was well and truly one of the good ones. And her sister had snagged him.

Story of Anna's pitiful life.

She toed off her boots and pulled the hat off her head. As she ran her fingers through the brown locks, she deliberately avoided looking into the mirror strategically placed right next to the door. After hanging her coat in the closet, Anna made her way toward the sound of the television. She found her niece snuggled into a corner of a wrap-around suede couch, a fleece blanket tucked around her person, her thumb in her mouth and her eyes riveted to the screen of the giant television affixed to the wall across the room.

"Auntie Annie," she said, joy radiating in her voice. "Look. Puppies. Come sit with me." She pulled her thumb from her mouth to point at the screen and then patted the cushion next to her.

"I love *101 Dalmatians*," Anna assured her, as she obligingly sat and tugged a corner of the blanket onto her lap. Jessica kept the house far too cold for Anna's taste. As soon as Jesse left, she planned to increase the temperature, at least in this wing.

"Yeah, that's why Cora insisted on watching it tonight," Jesse explained from where he'd appeared in the doorway. "You must have told her that once, and she never forgot it."

Self-consciously, Anna lifted her arm and again ran her hand through her hair. She should have pulled it back into a ponytail.

"Your hair looks fine," he admonished. He sounded almost annoyed. Anna dropped her arm and glanced at Cora, who snuggled into her side.

"It really is one of my favorites," she assured him.

"Hey, Cora, let Aunt Annie up for a minute. I need to talk to her."

Cora pouted, but she shifted so that she lay against the couch cushions instead of her aunt's arm. Anna climbed off the couch and followed Jesse out of the room. When he reached the base of the stairs, he turned to face her.

"Listen, my buddy cancelled for tonight. A couple of us were supposed to go to his house to play cards, but his wife is sick and she's refusing to let anyone come over because the house isn't clean, or some shit like that." He ran his hand through his hair, sending it into disarray and stirring up her never-entirely-suppressed fantasies. She did not miss the irony that she was so self-conscious of her own sloppy hair, when his looked so utterly gorgeous.

"I swear, everybody's getting sick lately," he added.

Anna shrugged. "It's the time of year. Everybody's inside, lots of socializing going on, germs are spread more readily." She worked at a pharmacy. She knew the drill.

"I'm sorry I didn't find out before you drove all the way over here."

All the way was an understatement. Her tiny, one-bedroom apartment was nearly an hour away and on the other side of the world from Jesse and Jessica's luxurious neighborhood.

"It's okay. No big deal," she said, hiding the lie with a smile. She started toward the coat closet.

"You don't have to go. I mean, if you don't want to. You

can hang out for a while. Watch the movie with Cora or something."

She hesitated. "What are you going to do?"

"I'll watch too," he said. "Well, sort of. I'm actually going to grab my laptop and do a little work. I've seen that movie about a billion times," he said with a smile.

"You're going to work on a Saturday night?"

He nodded, and practically vibrated with enthusiasm. "Yeah. Come on, I'll show you." Without waiting to see if she would follow, he headed up the stairs and turned left at the top. She hurried after him.

He led her to the master bedroom, which was actually a suite of rooms. Jesse had converted one of them into his office. Jessica had a home office too, but hers was on the main level, on the opposite end of the house.

Anna felt strange walking into Jesse's bedroom. She'd never been in this room before. She and her sister were not the type of siblings who shared clothes or got ready for a night out together or even sat and chatted while the other put on makeup.

She smiled and indicated the Christmas tree, decorated with multi-hued lights. "Nice tree."

"Thanks. It's the only one Jessica doesn't get a say in, so it's the one with the most color. Everything else has to be monochromatic, per her specifications."

"They all look nice." Anna felt obligated to say it. "Although this one does look the most... casual," she said, settling on the word after a moment's pause.

"That's exactly how I see it," Jesse said, his thrilled grin so wide and bright, Anna was certain she was being bowled over by a steamroller. She grasped the doorframe, half afraid her knees might buckle. Just from a smile. God, she had it bad.

"Come look," he said, beckoning her to his desk. He powered up his laptop, pulled up what looked like a variety of pictures of a house, along with drawings, renderings of, she assumed, proposed renovations. The house was on the small side for Jesse's typical clients, but it definitely had character, and lots of potential.

"New client?" she asked, wondering why he was so enthusiastic, and why he wanted to show *her*.

"Yeah. Myself." He said it with a chuckle. "I bought this place a few weeks ago. I couldn't resist. It was dirt cheap, and although it needs a lot of work, it's just so…"

"Perfect?" Anna supplied, studying the images on the computer screen.

"Exactly. I knew you would understand."

"I do," she admitted. It was just the sort of house she fantasized about living in – when she wasn't fantasizing about doing naughty things with the man standing next to her. Anna really spent far too much time fantasizing. Of course, if her reality was a little more interesting, maybe that wouldn't be the case.

"What are you going to do with it?" she asked.

"I don't know yet. I'm going to fix it up, probably sell it. Look, here are some of the ideas I've worked out so far. I'm going to do it all myself. I have the time right now, since this is my slowest time of year. Maybe we'll keep it as a second home. It sits on a small, private lake. I figure Cora would love it during the summertime. You know how she loves the water."

Anna smiled. "Yeah. I could see Cora hanging out there, running down the hall in a wet bathing suit and sandy feet," she teased.

"Which is why I'm planning to do hardwood floors. No carpet, not next to a beach."

"Good idea."

There was an awkward pause. At least, it felt awkward to Anna. But what else was there to say? Yes, the house was beautiful. Yes, she could picture the warm beach home with the happy memories. She could picture herself, too, and Jesse, running down the hall in bathing suits and sandy feet, except she was missing her bikini top because Jesse had untied it and then run away, laughing, heading toward the bedroom, where he intended to tackle her when she ran through the door, tossing her onto the bed and…

"Anyway, you want to go back downstairs and finish watching the movie with Cora? I'll make popcorn, and there's plenty of beer in the fridge."

Anna shook off the fantasy and swallowed. Hard. "Yeah. Sure. Um. That'd be great."

He shouldn't have invited her to stay. He should have apologized, offered to give her some gas money – he knew it was a freaking long way to her apartment and that she barely eked out a living working as a cashier at that pharmacy – and sent her on her way. It pissed him off that Jessica always called her first when they needed a sitter, and then never paid Anna for doing it. He knew if he offered, Anna would refuse his money, which only made him respect her more, but it was the principle of the thing.

Instead, he practically begged her to stay. And then he'd been so excited over showing her his plans for the beach house that he'd taken her upstairs to his office – the office that was connected to his bedroom. He'd watched her face as she admired the pictures, soaked up the ideas he'd sketched, and expressed her appreciation for his plans. Her natural beauty glowed, especially when she was absorbed in something she liked.

He wanted to kiss her when she looked like that. Okay, he wanted to kiss her all the damn time, but especially when she was truly, honestly impressed by his work.

Jessica was never impressed by his work, at least she never expressed as much. Not that he was comparing the two women. Who was he kidding? He compared the two women all the damn time, and his wife always came up short. Always. Every damn time. What the hell would she think if he told her that he thought about her sister on the rare occasion they actually had sex?

If he was a bastard, he would have thrown that in her face by now.

Jessica hated her sister, and her reasons were as fucked up as she was. The perfect, fucked up, glamorous doll.

She hated Anna because she was jealous. Because Anna

was normal, natural, made mistakes, owned them, and moved on. Jessica lived with her head so far up her perfectly fucked up mother's ass that she could never make any mistakes. Ever. Their entire lives, Jessica had always blamed Anna on the rare occasion she did fuck up. And Anna took the hit, dealt with it, and moved on to live a completely average, normal life.

Exactly what Jesse wanted. And could never have. He'd made his bed. Three and a half years ago, he'd made his bed when he got so fucking drunk that he slept with Jessica without using a condom. He didn't regret a single moment of his daughter's life, but he sure as hell wished he'd made such a colossal mistake with some other woman.

Like Anna.

He sat next to her on the couch – more self-induced torture – and drank his beer and watched her, while she snuggled with his daughter and watched a movie he knew damn well she'd seen too many times to truly be so engrossed. But if Cora liked it, then Anna was happy to indulge her. It was more than Cora's own mother ever gave her.

When the movie ended, at Cora's bidding, he and Anna both went upstairs with her, watched as she obligingly brushed her teeth, and then they both tucked her into bed. It was the idealistic family moment that Jesse had been craving since the first moment he held his daughter in his arms. His own parents had tucked him into bed, together, as a team, for practically every night of his childhood. He wasn't sure Jessica had ever tucked Cora into bed. Half the time she was off at one of her work functions, entertaining clients, ensuring her exuberant commission checks continued to pour in. Without Jessica's income, they'd never be able to afford the gilded castle in which they lived. Maybe that's why he bought that little house on the lake. Because if he ever worked up the nerve to tell Jessica he wanted out of this sham of a marriage …

He never would. Cora's happiness was too important. And he selfishly liked having Anna in his life. He figured if he divorced Jessica, he'd probably rarely, if ever, get to see Anna anymore. At least this way – married to a woman who was forever jet setting all over the country – he got a steady dose of the quiet, introverted sister, even if he could do no more than to admire her from afar.

"Want another beer?" he asked as they headed back down the stairs together.

"Probably shouldn't. It's a long drive home and I'm already tired."

It was on the tip of his tongue to say, "Don't go." It was always on the tip of his tongue.

"I was thinking about that house you just bought," she said, and he admired the faint blush as it stained her cheeks. Her expressions were so different from Jessica's. He liked that he could practically figure out what she was thinking just by watching her face.

"Yeah? You have some ideas?"

She nodded, her gaze dropping to the floor. She was embarrassed to give him her ideas. She had no idea that he loved every tip or idea she'd ever expressed in the nearly four years he's known her.

"Tell me. I want to hear it. I'll probably use it."

"I don't know about that. It's just ... I was thinking about that house you showed me. The room, the one that opens out onto the lake. It has that wall with the sliding glass door, but it's so plain, compared to the rest of the house. I thought French doors might look better. It's a big enough wall that you could do two sets."

"That's great," he enthused, getting overly excited, like he always did, about his work. "Wait, come back in here with me. I want to make sure we get this right, while it's still fresh in your mind."

Instead of walking straight to the couch and sitting down next to where his laptop was perched on the coffee table, she walked over to the wet bar he'd built into the darkest corner of the room. She grabbed two bottles of beer out of the mini fridge and then headed to the couch.

As she handed him one of the beers, she said, "I figure, knowing you, I'll be here for a while longer." There was a twinkle in her eye and a smile tugging at her lips. Jessica could have said the exact same thing and it would have been an insult. Hell, his wife *had* said the exact same thing before. Yet Anna found his fascination with carpentry and design work interesting.

He noticed that she shivered slightly, and he leaped off the couch and headed over to the thermostat, tapping the screen to up the temperature a few degrees. Jessica always wanted to save a buck by keeping it at a barely tolerable temperature in the house, and it always pissed him off because she was practically never there anyway.

"You didn't have to do that," she protested. "I'm fine."

"You're freezing," he replied, and he walked over and sat down next to her on the couch. He leaned back, opened the laptop and pulled up the plans for his little house on the lake.

"That is exactly the sort of house I would love to live in," she said, and his fingers froze, hovering over the keyboard, while his mind attempted to formulate a response that wasn't along the lines of, "Me too. Let's run away and live there together." How did she feel about having sex in a lake? Would she be open to doing it on the couch, facing those French doors he now planned to install?

Why the hell was he torturing himself with these questions? He'd never get to find out.

Jesse grabbed his beer and downed half of it in one, long pull. Then he sucked in a breath, blew it out slowly and said, "Okay, let's talk French doors and walkout basements. So when you say two sets of doors, do you think..." She leaned toward him while they discussed renovating first the walk out basement, and then the main level.

Several hours later, Anna had fallen asleep, while he'd outlined the rest of the floor plan. Her head lay against his arm, her hand rested on his thigh. He closed the computer and very gently, so as not to disturb her, leaned forward, placed the laptop on the coffee table, then leaned back again and lifted his arm, so that she fell into the crook. Feeling slightly guilty but utterly unable to resist, he wrapped his arm around her sleeping form and held her.

They fit together perfectly. She was a couple inches shorter than Jessica, and where his wife was sleek and toned, Anna was soft and round in all the right places. He imagined grabbing her ass while he pressed into her, or cupping her breasts, kneading and massaging them, burying his face in her cleavage. He shifted in his seat, adjusted his swollen package, while Anna slept on, oblivious to his self-induced discomfort. Still, he did not wake her. Torture it may be to be so close to her and know he could never, ever do anything more, but it still felt too damn good to wake her and send her home.

He never got this from Jessica, this comfortable relaxation. She was always on, always made up, always ready for... something. She never fully turned it off, and thus was never fully engaged with Jesse, even when they were getting it on. He knew damn well she faked it half the time that they had sex, but he'd long ago quit caring. It was infrequent enough that he got his own rocks off. If she didn't want to enjoy herself enough to have an orgasm, why the hell should he bother trying to help her along?

He imagined that when Anna had sex, she did it with pure abandon. He bet she was wild, uninhibited, purely focused on giving and receiving pleasure. He'd bet her partners loved being with her. Thinking about her with some other guy sent a surge of unjustified jealousy through his system, so he stopped that train of thought.

Well, not entirely. He just shifted it. He wondered if she had a steady boyfriend. He had never heard her mention someone, but then again, Anna wasn't a big talker, at least not when he was around. He knew she had a terrible relationship with her parents and her sister, and he wondered if that made her gunshy about relationships in general. She was only twenty-five, so she had plenty of time to figure it out. He hoped that when she did, it was with a guy who deserved such a special woman. He spared a moment to wish it could be him, but that was stupid, so he told himself not to ever think like that again.

He must have dozed. When he woke, it was well after two a.m. and he was lying on his back on the couch, with Anna's sleeping form sprawled across his body. The house was utterly quiet, save the faint *tick tock* of the grandfather clock out in the entry. Jessica must not be home. Surely she would have come in here and raised a stink about finding the two of them laying in such an intimate manner.

Not that she had any right.

Anna moved, shifted her body slightly. She lifted her leg and draped it across his lap and somehow the V of her thighs managed to end up cupping his dick, which swelled instantly. She smoothed her hand over his shirt until it curled up under her chin, and as her hips rolled, rubbing over his dick and making him wish they didn't have any clothes on, he swore he caught a faint smile on her lips.

Except she was Anna, and he was married, and it wasn't to her. Fuck, his life sucked sometimes. Hell, his life sucked all the damn time these days. The only rays of light were his daughter and the rare occasions he got to spend time with his wife's sister.

Anna moved again, her hips ground against his groin, and she let out a breathy little sigh, while her fingers curled into his shirt. He stared down at her, willing her to do it again and wishing she would stop at the same time.

She did it again, and he realized she was dreaming. It was a hell of an erotic dream, at least from his standpoint. The way she shifted and moved her body... He should slide out from underneath her. He should do something that involved putting a little distance between them. Instead, he lifted his arm, placed his hand on the small of her back and very slightly mimicked her action. Her fingers tightened on his shirt, her hips shifted again and a tiny moan escaped her lips.

Guilt hit him as he responded, rolling his hips too, but it didn't stop him. This felt too damn good. She was his forbidden fruit, the one person with whom he wanted this more than anything in the world, yet he knew he could never have her, other than right now, while she was asleep, oblivious, believing she was all alone, having what equated to a wet dream. At least, Jesse was suddenly determined to ensure it was. If he could do one little thing for both of them, it was to give her an orgasm in her sleep.

She didn't wake up, or at least she didn't become conscious enough to realize she had help, as he rocked them both, dry humping her, holding her in place as her body reacted to the friction and moved faster and harder, her hand clenching his shirt, her breath coming out in short little spurts, her body tensing, tighter and tighter, until suddenly she gasped, her entire body went rigid, and her eyes flew open. She pushed against his chest, lifting her torso, staring at him with lust-glazed fear in her eyes.

"Oh my God, please tell me that did not just happen."

Chapter Three

"It's okay," he started to say, and when Anna's faculties returned, she struggled, tried to get off him, to get the hell away from him. Jesse snaked his arm around her waist and held her in place.

"No. Don't leave. Not yet."

"I – I was dreaming. And – and…"

"Yeah, I figured that out."

"I'm so sorry."

"Don't be. Are you kidding? That was the most fun I've had in a hell of a long time."

"Oh please. Jessica acts like you two are sex-crazed rabbits."

"Not hardly. Trust me, our relationship only *appears* perfect. But appearances, in this case, are far from the truth."

All was not perfect in the land of Jessica? Lying on the couch with her felt good to Jesse? Was Anna still asleep, still dreaming?

"Let me up."

"No. Not yet. It feels too good holding you like this. Will you tell me something? And be totally honest?"

Had she not woken from that spectacular orgasm after all? She lifted her hand and pinched her other arm. "Ow."

"What are you doing?"

"Checking to see if I'm still asleep."

He chuckled. She felt the rumble roll through her body, especially that part of her body that still tingled from when she'd dry humped him a few moments ago. The fresh memory caused her cheeks to flush with renewed embarrassment.

"You aren't asleep."

"Let me up." She needed to get out of there, needed to go home, to hide in her apartment, alone, away from Jesse and this little piece of heaven that she could never have.

"No. Answer my question first."

She stared at her own thigh, head bowed, hair hanging

like a curtain, hiding her face from view. "What question?"

"Who were you thinking about?"

He had to ask *that* question. And she couldn't possibly tell him the truth. It was bad enough that it happened at all, now he wanted to dissect it?

"No one."

She tried to push away from him again, but he refused to relinquish his hold. "Tell me," he begged. "Please."

"Why? What are you going to do with that information? Tell my sister, so my life can be an even bigger hell than it already is?"

"I would never tell Jessica. This is between you and me, Anna. We're the only ones here. Just us."

She let out a bitter, hollow laugh. "What time is it, anyway? Shouldn't Jessica be home by now?"

"It's shortly after two, and I doubt she's coming home anytime soon. My guess is, we've got a solid eight or nine hours, maybe more, before we see her again."

His bitterness was as strong as hers. Momentarily distracted from her own humiliation, Anna peered into his face. "What's wrong, Jesse?"

His gaze shifted to the side, and she felt his hand stroke her back, almost absently. The apex of her thighs still tingled and her panties were soaked through. She should be more forceful with her insistence that he let her go, so she could go to the bathroom, clean up and then rush home and pretend this never happened. Instead, she lay there, allowed him to stroke her back, secretly enjoying the way his erection was still pressed against her hypersensitive nerve endings.

"She's cheating on me."

Anna gasped, and his arms tightened around her, as if he was afraid she would once again try to leave. But at the moment, she was too stunned to do anything but lie there and stare at him.

"Jessica?" she blurted. Of course it was Jessica. Who else would be cheating on him? Who else would be so stupid?

He nodded. "I told you, our perfect life is only perfect on the surface."

"Does she know you know?"

He shrugged. "Not sure. I mean, she still comes up with excuses when she stays out all night like this, but they're definitely getting more and more feeble. Either she doesn't care if I know anymore, or she's losing her game. Knowing Jessica, she's definitely not losing her game."

He was right. Jessica would never, ever lose her game. His hand stroked down, boldly inching low enough to brush over the curve of her ass. She arched her brows.

"I wish it was you." He said the words so quietly, she could almost convince herself that she'd imagined them. Almost. But when she looked into his eyes, there was no denying what he'd said.

"I married the wrong sister."

She forced a laugh. "You didn't even know me until three days before the ceremony."

"I know. But I started crushing on you at that moment. When Jessica lectured you on what to wear, and you just rolled your eyes and said, 'I think I'll wear black.' I remember thinking, 'She's so fucking cool. That's the kind of girl I'd want to date.' Only I couldn't, because Jessica was pregnant and we were about to get married."

"Don't be ridiculous," Anna scoffed, because she needed it not to be true. Otherwise, how could she possibly curtail her own fantasies? Not that she was doing a particularly good job without knowing he had feelings for her.

"Jessica's gorgeous. And successful. And… and perfect."

"She's also a raging bitch who's sleeping around on her husband. A husband who, by the way, was always more than willing to give her whatever she needed in that respect. And don't knock yourself, Anna. You are far more beautiful than your sister ever will be."

"Okay, now you're just being stupid."

"No, I'm not." He lifted one hand, touched her chest, just above her left breast. "You are beautiful in here. As well as on the outside. And don't look at me like that. Looking like a runway model is not everyone's cup of tea. It's not mine, that's for sure. Give me natural, *real*, any day of the week."

"Then why'd you hook up with her in the first place?"

She felt it as his chest rose and fell with his deep exhale. "I screwed up. I got so drunk that I thought I was sleeping with my girlfriend at the time, only I slept with Jessica. Without a condom, no less. Nine months later, along came Cora."

"Eight," Anna reminded him. "Remember, she was a month early."

He smiled fondly. "She was so beautiful. The moment I held her in my arms, I knew it was worth it. Whatever the hell happened between Jessica and me, it was worth it to have that child in my life."

"Jessica is so stupid," Anna said fiercely. "To not realize what a good thing she has. You're – you're the perfect catch."

He pressed his hips against hers and offered a teasing smile. "So does that mean it was me you were thinking about in your sleep?"

Her cheeks reddened and Anna averted her gaze. Damn him for bringing it up again. Even though they hadn't changed their position, she had thought they'd moved on from such an embarrassing subject.

"It was so hot," he whispered. "I wish ..."

"Me too," she admitted. Why the hell not? He'd already guessed as much. What did she have to lose?

Everything.

His hand roamed south and cupped her ass, pressing her more firmly against his erection. "I want you, Anna. Why shouldn't I get what I want? Jessica does. All the damn time."

"Because you're married. And I'm her sister. And we..."

"Just tonight, Anna. The next hour. We're already half-way there. Can't we ... live the fantasy? For a little while."

"Jesse..." Did he have any idea what he was asking? Clearly, he did. He lifted his head, kissed her collarbone. She automatically raised her chin, giving him more access. He nibbled his way along her jawline to the other shoulder, then down to the edge of her sweater.

"Please, Anna," he begged, his voice muffled because his lips were pressed against her skin. His hand lifted, cupped her breast. His thumb skimmed over her erect nipple. She arched, pressing her breast into his hand. God, she wanted this. She wanted this so badly, she was seriously considering…

And why the hell not? It was nothing less than what everyone in her family would expect of her. Jesse was one of the good ones, and *he* was willing to do it. Everyone assumed she was the bad seed anyway. Why not prove them right?

"Jesse…"

He paused in the process of lavishing kisses along the neckline of her sweater. "Yeah?"

"Kiss me."

She gave in to the temptation. He wrapped his arms around her again and suddenly rolled, so that she was pressed into the couch cushions, covered by his hard body. He balanced himself on his forearms, cupped her face with his hands and leaned down, kissing her so tenderly, she had the ridiculous urge to cry.

"My fantasies have nothing on the real thing," she admitted.

"We haven't even gotten very far yet."

He remedied that soon enough. He kissed her again, this time nibbling and biting her bottom lip before his tongue swept into her mouth, searching for her own, so that they could perform a mating dance. While their tongues made love, his hands slipped under her sweater, unlatched her bra. He broke the kiss so that he could pull her sweater and bra over her head, and then he lay there, staring down at her, as if seeing her for the first time. She supposed it really was the first time, at least for him to see her breasts.

"So beautiful." He cupped each one, almost tenderly, before he skimmed both thumbs over her nipples. She groaned and arched into his touch. He leaned down and kissed first one, then the other, before returning to the first and sucking the nipple into his mouth.

Anna panted and ground her groin against him, already worked up from her earlier, half-asleep orgasm. He pulled his mouth away from her nipple with a popping noise, and then nuzzled her cleavage before moving on to suckle the other nipple.

"Jesse, *please*," she begged after only a few moments.

"I love it when a girl begs," he teased. "Especially you. I didn't think you ever begged for anything."

"I've never felt anything quite like this before."

"You sure know how to give a guy a swelled head."

They both barked out a laugh at the unintended pun.

"Let's get these pants off you," he said, and he sat up, straddling her thighs, while he tugged both her pants and panties down her legs. He lifted her panties, letting them hang from the end of his finger. "Looks like somebody has already had a hell of a good time."

She grabbed the panties and tossed them over the back of the couch and then smirked. "Maybe this time, we can *both* have a good time."

"Definitely," he promised, his gaze raking over her body, making her feel … special. That was it. Whether Jessica was far more beautiful was beside the point at the moment. Anna was special. Jesse cared. He cared about her.

He pulled his shirt over his head and then extracted his wallet from the back pocket of his jeans. "Don't ask me why, but I actually have a condom in here."

The whys of him having a condom handy hardly mattered at the moment. Just so long as he did, and she could feel the length of him, inside her, filling her, within very short order. Anna snagged the small square package from his hand and gave him an impatient look.

"Got it," he said as he struggled out of his jeans. "Less talk, more action."

"You're good."

"Give me a minute. I'm hoping to change that 'good' to 'great.'"

Anna snickered. Jesse managed to get his jeans off, grabbed the condom, and sheathed himself. He sat on his haunches, looking down at her, a mingled look of anticipation and, oddly enough, satisfaction, on his face. She opened her legs and lifted her arms, a silent invitation.

He lowered himself onto her body, expertly situating his erection so that it slid through the wetness pooling at the apex of her thighs. She hissed, her body tensed, and she grasped his biceps, her nails digging into his flesh. He balanced himself on one hand while positioning his erection with the other, and then he paused, the tip a hairsbreadth away from her opening.

"Are you sure?" he asked, sounding as if he would actually really and truly pull away if she said no.

She choked out a laugh. "Don't you dare stop now," she demanded.

His eyes burned with an intensity that might have frightened a lesser woman, but Anna knew she could handle whatever he intended to do. They'd come this far. There was no turning back now. She had no doubt they would both regret their actions come morning, but for now, she intended to be that girl her parents and sister always thought she was. For once, she was going to take what she wanted, consequences be damned.

When he didn't move, she dropped her hands, grabbed his ass – damn, he had a fine ass – and pulled him toward her. He wasn't expecting it, and lost his balance, collapsing on top of her and not – as she had intended – pushing into her.

Chuckling, he pushed himself back up onto his elbows and gazed down at her. "One of the things I like so much about you is your ability to make me laugh," he said.

"Know what I like? Your ability to make me moan."

He chuckled again and obediently grabbed his erection. "Point taken." And then he pressed into her, and the mood instantly shifted to pleasure. He slowly worked his way in, then pulled nearly all the way out and quickly filled her again.

"Yes," Anna cried out, her arms clinging to his back, her knees pressing into his waist. She lifted her hips and he sank deeper into her, groaning loudly as he did so.

He continued the slow, steady rhythm for a few moments, until she felt him swelling inside her, getting even bigger, and stiffer. His hand slip between them, his finger grazed her clitoris, and she cried out again as her orgasm swamped her. Jesse gritted his teeth and picked up the pace, pressing into her faster and faster, like a man possessed, until his entire body stiffened, and he wrapped his arms around her and held her to him while he found his own release.

"Oh Anna," he murmured, just before he kissed her ear and then his body went lax, as he fell almost instantly asleep.

Chapter Four

*S*hit!"

Jesse jerked from sleep, pulled by the faint sound the alarm made when it was disarmed and someone opened a door. In the course of just a few seconds, he comprehended that he was asleep on the couch, that Anna was underneath him, and that they were both naked. Pale, pre-dawn light filtered in through the windows. Thank God he'd woken before Cora, or they could have had a real mess on their hands.

"Fuck," he blurted, because while Cora was still asleep, Jessica had just arrived home, and her discovering the two of them in this compromised state was no better than if his daughter had. He jumped off the couch, snatched his jeans and began stuffing his legs into them. "Anna, wake up. Wake up. Anna!"

She blinked, squinted, and then stretched, and he spared precious seconds to stare at the spectacular sight of her naked and preening like a cat. Damn, she was beautiful. But then reality intruded.

"Jessica's home," he hissed, and he grabbed her shirt, her bra, her pants, and shoved them into her lap as she sat up on the couch. "Go. Go. Over there – there's a powder room. Hurry." Her eyes were wide and confused, but she stood and did as he said. He pulled his shirt over his head a scant second before Jessica walked into the room.

She hesitated on the threshold, her gaze sweeping the room, clearly trying to figure out why he was downstairs in the entertainment room at – as if on cue, the grandfather clock in the entry began chiming the hour – six o'clock in the morning.

He supposed he could see why Anna thought her sister was so beautiful. On the surface, even at six in the morning, when she had yet to see her own bed, Jessica was utterly flawless. But Jesse knew what was on the inside, and Anna was far more beautiful than her sister could ever be.

"What are you doing home so early?" It was undoubted-ly his own guilty conscience that caused his greeting to sound so gruff.

He hadn't expected to fall so deeply asleep after making love to Anna. He wasn't sure exactly how things might have worked out had they stayed awake, but he knew one thing: he did not want Anna to take the fall for whatever the hell hap-pened from this point forward.

Last night had been spectacular. He didn't regret it in the least. Well, except for one aspect. The only thing he regretted was not having the balls to tell Jessica to go fuck herself, so he could be with Anna every night, for the rest of his damn life.

Jessica arched perfectly shaped blonde brows, gave him a cool look, and ignored his question. "What are *you* doing up so early?"

"Fell asleep on the couch." He yawned. He didn't have to fake that.

"Is that Anna's car out in front of the house?"

"I got home really late, so I told her to stay the night."

Those blonde brows lifted higher on her head. "Why do I get the impression I'm missing something?"

"I don't know."

She started to walk into the room, and he jumped into her path. "What are you doing?" he demanded.

"I was going to get a bottle of water," she said coolly.

"Oh. Right." He stepped out of the way. Jesus, he sucked at the whole cheating routine. Good thing it wasn't something he made a habit of doing. Although if Anna approached him and offered to be his girl-on-the-side, he knew without a doubt that he'd accept her offer.

He stood next to the couch, his hands stuffed into the front pockets of his jeans, while Jessica walked over to the wet bar and pulled a bottle of water out of the mini fridge. She twist-ed the cap off, lifted the bottle to her lips and drank. When she pulled the bottle away from her mouth, her gaze fell onto some-thing lying on the floor behind the couch. She and Jesse both realized what it was at the exact same time. He bolted, but she was closer, and scooped up the panties before he could reach them.

"These don't quite look your size, Jesse," she remarked, ice dripping from every syllable.

"Give them to me." He grabbed for the panties, but she jerked them out of his reach.

"Where is she?"

"Who?"

"The whore who owns these goddamn panties, you jackass."

"She isn't a whore," he retorted, defending Anna's honor, despite the fact that he wasn't even sure if Jessica realized precisely with whom he'd made love last night. Although he'd told her that Anna spent the night, it was perfectly conceivable that he'd hooked up with someone prior to coming home, and had brought her panties as a souvenir or some shit. Didn't people who cheat do stuff like that?

"You are such an idiot," she sneered. "Any woman who sleeps with a married man is a whore."

"What about married women who sleep with men who aren't her husband?"

He could tell by the surprised look on her face that she hadn't realized he had become aware of her infidelity.

"I don't know what you're talking about. And besides, this is about you, not me. Is she still here? Is your whore upstairs in our bedroom?"

"No. There's no one here." Except Anna. And Cora. He hoped to hell their raised voices did not wake her. His daughter did not need to experience this side of their marriage.

"How long has this been going on? How long have you been screwing around on me?"

It amazed him that she was able to ask these questions, to be so outraged, when she had been screwing around on him for months now. Hell, for all he knew, she'd been screwing around for as long as they'd been married.

"It was the first time. Last night. I've never been unfaithful to you, Jessica."

"Bullshit," she spat. "Who the hell is it? Do I know her?

Are you going to potentially ruin our social standing?"

"Jesus Christ, listen to yourself, Jessica. How about focusing on our marriage instead? Who the fuck cares about our social standing? What we should care about is what we're doing to our daughter."

"We? *We* aren't doing anything. It's all you. You and your – your whore."

"For the last fucking time, she isn't a whore."

"You care about her."

"No." It was a knee-jerk response, said in defense. But it was a lie. He would gladly – *gladly* – walk away from it all for Anna – so long as he could have Cora too. But that was the kicker.

"Who are you fucking, Jesse?"

"None of your business, Jessica. Now, let's talk about our marriage. How are we going to make this work? I know you've been screwing around for God knows how long, but in my mind, we're even now. So why don't we start over? Let's figure out how to make this work, for Cora's sake."

"Who is it?"

She hadn't heard a damn word he said. None of it. She didn't care about him, about them, about their marriage. It was all about Jessica, and how this would adversely affect her life, her social status, her extracurricular activities.

"Fine." He threw up his hands. "Fine. You want to keep sleeping around? Do it. Maybe I will too. Maybe that's the answer to this fucked up sham of a marriage. If we both keep a piece on the side, we can tolerate living together." He hated the idea even as he said it. He didn't want Anna as a piece on the side. He wanted her, all of her, only her. He wanted out of his marriage. He wanted the freedom to choose the better sister.

He just had no goddamn clue how to make it happen.

"Target," she sneered, looking at the panties. "You're screwing a two-bit whore who can't even afford quality underwear. You have perfection, but what you really want is to go slumming. You're pathetic, you know that? Pathetic. I should never have married you. You weren't even that good in bed. In fact, you were pretty damn lousy. I faked it, Jesse. Every damn time. I was faking it. All those moans and screams and saying, 'Yes, yes, yes,' it was all a lie. I never wanted you. If I were a guy, I wouldn't even be able to get it up for you. That's how lousy you are."

His temper flared. "You think I give a fuck about what you think? I quit caring about you a long time ago, Jessica. Hell, I'm not sure I ever cared. I was doing what was right by my daughter. You were just the goddamned vessel. And trust me, I was fully aware you faked it, and I didn't give a rat's ass. All I cared about was getting my own rocks off."

"Does your slutty little girlfriend know that? Did she have to fake it too? What is she getting out of this? You going to put her up in a penthouse suite somewhere? Even you have to realize that the vast majority of our income is mine. Your stupid little carpentry business doesn't make squat compared to my salary. You want to end this marriage? You're going to walk away with nothing. *Nothing*."

"I don't care about any of this," he replied, waving to encompass the room. "All I care about is Cora."

It was the wrong thing to say. He knew instantly, but he couldn't take it back.

She didn't quite smile, but he could tell she was fighting it. She had him by the balls and he knew it.

"Who was it?"

Fuck. "Jesus, Jessica, why the hell do you care?"

"Because I do. I want to know what kind of woman my husband turns to when he can no longer have the goods."

"How the fuck are you able to even walk through a goddamned doorway with that gigantic ego of yours?"

"Who is it?"

Shit. He didn't know what to do, what to say. "No one. Insignificant."

"Bullshit. Who the hell are you sleeping with? If I didn't know her, you would have given me her name by now."

Goddamn it, she was so much better at this game. His gaze shifted to the closed door to the powder room. Jessica caught the look.

"She's still here? In the fucking *powder room?*" She

stormed across the room and grabbing the doorknob, she jerked it open.

At least Anna was dressed. The look on her face was devastated, though. She'd heard the entire exchange, right down to him saying she was insignificant. And her self-esteem was shot, thanks to years and years of her sister and mother being such bitches to her. Jesse could only imagine what she was thinking right now. He wanted to go to her, to comfort her, to tell her he didn't mean any of it, but he couldn't.

He couldn't, because Jessica was standing in his way, staring at her sister as if she was a particularly horrific science experiment gone terribly wrong.

"Anna?" She sounded utterly disbelieving. "Anna?" she said again. She slowly turned her head to look at Jesse. "You fucked *my sister?* You let her worm her way into your bed?"

"No," he shouted, because that was not the way it went down. Anna had been innocent in this entire charade. He was the one who'd asked her to stay. He was the one who convinced her to have another beer, to talk through his latest plans. He was the one who let her sleep in the crook of his arm, who let her cum all over his leg while she was having an erotic dream. He was the one who pulled the condom out of his wallet, who tempted and teased her until she had no choice but to say yes. He was the one who was married, and never, ever should have done it in the first place, even if his wife had probably been doing the exact same thing, at the exact same time.

"I seduced her," he swore, stabbing at his chest for emphasis.

"Bullshit. I know my sister."

"I did," he insisted. "I – I did it … because it was her," he said, speaking the absolute truth. He knew, without a single doubt, that he would never have forsaken his wedding vows – however fake they may be – for any other woman. It was only because it was Anna that he'd done it. She had been worth it.

Because he loved her.

The sound of a sob caused him and Jessica both to turn their heads, to look at Anna. Her right hand covered her mouth, and there were tears pooling in her eyes.

"Anna…" He reached for her, but she batted his hand away, forcefully shoved her sister out of her path, and ran through the room.

"Shit." He started to chase her, but Jessica's fingers wrapped around his arm and pulled him back. He started to throw off her grasp, but then she said, "Let her go. Trust me. I know my sister. You won't be able to reason with her right now."

Chapter Five

"Wow."

The word was out of Anna's mouth before she could bite it back. She hadn't seen nor spoken to Jessica since that fateful morning three days ago, yet she couldn't help the shocked greeting. She had never seen her sister in such a state before.

The woman had never been anything but perfect, all the time, all her life. Even when she was sick, she was beautiful. She never went through the awkward stages that everyone else in the world experienced. She was a living doll.

Except this morning.

Her hair was disheveled, her makeup smeared. Her lips were naked. There were bags under her eyes. Even her clothes were rumpled.

"Is he here?" she asked, looking over Anna's shoulder, into her tiny apartment.

Anna shook her head. "I told him we couldn't see each other again."

He had been calling and calling, begging her to listen to him, to let him explain. She had refused. As much as she often hated her family, the idea that she had ostracized herself from the lot of them by sleeping with Jessica's husband made her heart ache. The fact that Jesse had done it deliberately, had used her to seek revenge against Jessica, nearly caused that particular organ to seize up and refuse to function.

"Of course," Jessica muttered. "Only you would choose to be a martyr in this situation. Do you have a cigarette?"

Anna gasped, her mouth popped open, her eyes bulged. "You don't smoke."

"Yes, well, Valium makes me loopy and it's too damn early to drink." She looked at the slim gold watch on her wrist. "Or maybe not. You don't happen to have any champagne and orange juice, do you?"

"Not exactly something I keep stocked in my fridge."

"How about tomato juice and vodka? I can make a mean bloody, even with the meagerest of ingredients."

Anna could not manage to formulate more than, "Um…" She was still reeling from how far her sister had fallen.

"Move out of the way and let me in already. It's cold out here."

Anna's gaze swept over the red wool overcoat, covering what looked like obvious bar attire.

"You don't have a knife or gun or something under there, do you?" she blurted.

Jessica rolled her eyes and shouldered her way into the apartment. While Anna closed the door behind her, Jessica pulled off her coat and let it drop onto an armchair, revealing a sparkly top and the micro mini she wore underneath. She kicked off four-inch heels and sighed.

"I might have to borrow a pair of shoes to get home. I'm not sure I'll be able to get my feet back into those heels again. Look. They're already starting to swell."

Anna didn't notice any difference whatsoever, but she didn't say so. "Why are you here?" she asked instead. Jessica rarely visited her apartment at all, and the fact that she was here now, so soon after… what happened … was disconcerting. At least now that she'd shed the coat, Anna felt reasonably certain her sister wasn't hiding a weapon on her person. That outfit didn't exactly offer many hiding places.

"Vodka? Tomato juice? I really need some hair of the dog right now."

"Umm… In here." Anna led the way across the room into the tiny kitchen built into the corner.

"Where's your Christmas tree? There's not a single decoration in this apartment."

Anna wasn't about to tell her sister that she'd come home after sleeping with Jesse and cried herself dry as she striped the apartment of every single reminder of what was supposed to be a cheerful, happy holiday. There was no cheer left in Anna's life.

I should have said no. Why didn't I say no?

She knew the answer. She had been in love with her brother-in-law almost from the first time they'd met, when Jessica introduced him to the family and said, "We're getting married in three days. Clear your calendars."

Jesse should have said no, too. He was the one married to another woman.

But Anna understood why he hadn't, either.

It was deliberate. He used me. He knew sleeping with me would be the biggest insult to Jessica. It was the perfect plan.

She should be angry, furious, and desperate to seek her own revenge. Instead, she was a heartsick puppy dog, hiding in her apartment and licking her wounds, refusing to acknowledge the outside world.

"I called your job. Told them you've come down with some stomach bug and you're going to be out sick for a few days," Jessica commented.

"Um … Thanks," Anna said, feeling awkward and unsure of herself. Not that this wasn't the normal state of things when she was around her sister. But usually, Jessica wasn't being *nice*. Or what constituted her version of nice.

Jessica did not acknowledge her expression of gratitude. Instead, she began opening and closing cupboards as she asked, "Toothpicks?"

Anna shook her head. Jessica gave her a reproachful look and then stabbed a few olives with a fork and dropped them into her drink. She lifted the pint glass, took a sip and then sighed. "Every time. I don't know what the hell it is about tomato juice and vodka, but it always makes me feel better after I've overindulged the night before." She lifted the glass, offering it to Anna. She shook her head. Jessica shrugged and wandered back into the living room area. Anna followed.

"Why are you being so…" What was she doing, precisely? She wasn't exactly being nice, but she wasn't screaming or threatening to kill Anna, or really, acting in character at all.

Jessica sat gracefully in the armchair where she'd dropped her coat a few moments ago. "I've been thinking," she said. "Well, in between shots. And sex." She leaned her head back against the chair and let out another sigh. "Danny is so much more creative than Jesse ever was. And he takes these little pills that make him last all night. I'm going to be sore as hell on a regular basis, but it's going to be worth it."

Anna was completely at a loss for words. Jessica trained her gaze onto her sister, sipping her drink while she studied her.

"It's really amazing," Jessica said, "when you think about it. Out of the two of us, you're the one who wants the picket fence and the boring suburban lifestyle. All our lives, our parents always expected it to be the opposite."

Anna wondered if her sister hadn't popped a couple of pills as well. She certainly wasn't making any sense.

"I have a few confessions to make. I am making them only to you. So if anyone else ever finds out, I will know who told them."

When she was younger, Anna used to wish her sister would confess to her. Confess how to please their parents, how to look pretty, how to be... *her.*

"Why would you tell me anything?"

"Because you are the only person who will know what to do with the information I'm about to tell you."

"Jessica, I think you're still drunk. Or high. Or something. You aren't making any sense."

"I'm making perfect sense. You're just afraid to believe me because of how our relationship has been for, well, ever. I suppose I should apologize for being such a bitch for all my life, but you have to admit, you managed to be equally as bitchy on many occasions. How many holidays did we ruin because we ended up in a screaming match halfway through dinner?"

"Not very many, because I was always sent to my room, so that you three could continue your meal in peace."

"And the holiday was ruined, because you were no longer there."

Anna didn't quite know how to respond to that. She had always assumed they were happier without her there.

"I'm divorcing Jesse."

She didn't think that was a very big revelation, given what happened three days ago. Her parents would be furious, of course. And it would be Anna's fault. Just like always.

"And I'm giving him Cora."

Anna's gaze shot up to catch her sister's. *"Giving* him?"

She nodded. "This parenting gig is not for me. I've never been very good at it. And frankly, I don't really like it."

"But... But she's your *daughter."*

"Yes, I know." She abruptly leaned forward, and as she stared into Anna's eyes, she said, "But she isn't his."

Anna decided it was a good thing they were both sitting down. Otherwise, her knees surely would have buckled. Not Jesse's? Cora wasn't Jesse's? But hadn't they gotten married because Jessica was pregnant – with Jesse's baby?

Despite how everything ended between them, Anna felt a pang of sadness for Jesse. He adored that child more than anything else in the world. He would be devastated when he found out.

"She's actually Danny's."

"Who's Danny?"

"My boyfriend. The guy I've been sleeping with on the side. He's a rock star. Well, kind of mid-level, but he will be big, someday."

"Wait a minute. Jesse said you'd only been sleeping around for the last few months."

"I've been sleeping with Danny on and off for over seven years. Every time he breezed through town, we hooked up. And every time, he breezed out again, and I was always bitter, because I wanted to go with him. I didn't want to be here, living this life, doing the stupid, boring suburban thing. But that's what our parents expected, and God forbid I would ever go against our parents' wishes. That was your job."

"I didn't exactly mean to sign up for that job."

Jessica's unpainted lips curled into a wry smile. "I know. I admit, I have always appreciated that you took so much heat off of me. I was able to get away with so much in life, because they were always so focused on keeping you in line."

"You're welcome," Anna said, the bitterness loud and clear.

Jessica waved away her sarcasm. "The summer I got pregnant with Cora, I did it deliberately."

Anna gasped. Jessica nodded.

"I figured that way, Danny would be forced to take me with him."

Anna stared at her.

"But when I told him I was pregnant, he informed me that he hated kids and had no interest whatsoever in being a father. Then he left, and I didn't speak to him again until well after Cora's first birthday."

Anna tried to wrap her mind around the fact that her sister deliberately got pregnant to try to manipulate her rock star lover into taking her on the road with him. "I don't even know what to say. Except, how does Jesse fit into all of this?"

"I knew Jesse through a friend. Well, she *used to be* my friend. Actually, the two of them were dating at the time, and she was forever gushing about what a sweet, wonderful guy he was. 'A keeper,' she kept saying. At this point, I was getting desperate, because I could not very well tell our parents that I was pregnant, without having a man in the picture. I decided Jesse was the perfect solution. So I seduced him."

Anna's insides twisted into a knot as the truth slammed into her. When she slept with Jesse, she had thought he never cheated before, that she was the only time. Now, if Jessica was to be believed, he'd done it with her, too.

"Don't go and compare what we did to what you and Jesse did," Jessica said, guessing Anna's thought process. "It isn't even remotely the same. In fact, Jesse didn't even know he was sleeping with me until the next morning. Maria had invited a bunch of us up to her parents' cottage on the lake. Of course, we all got rip roaring drunk, but then again, I deliberately fed Jesse drinks. He got so drunk, I had to practically carry him upstairs to Maria's bedroom. Maria had already passed out an hour before. He thought I was her. He kept calling me Maria."

She paused. Anna felt a strange sense of relief combined with revulsion. Jesse hadn't cheated on his girlfriend, not intentionally. Jessica, on the other hand…

"Yep. I totally and completely took advantage of him. Although I will say that I was almost not successful. He was so drunk, I thought he'd never finish. But finally, he did, and then he passed out cold. When he woke up the next morning, he was lying on his back, naked, with a sticky, limp dick and me sleeping next to him. No condom in sight. The poor man was convinced *he'd* taken advantage of *me.* He felt so guilty, it was almost too easy to inform him a few weeks later that he was going to be a father and then to convince him that we should do the right thing and get married."

"That is absolutely appalling, even for you." Anna pushed off the couch, too agitated to sit still any longer. She paced the length of her tiny apartment, clenching and unclenching her fists. She had no idea what to say, how to react. She had always known her sister was a self-centered person, but she had no idea Jessica was so … conniving and devious.

Jessica waved her nearly empty glass. "Oh stop already. You cannot possibly be that surprised by any of this?"

Anna flung around and stared at her, frozen in place, in the middle of the living room. "Are you kidding? Everything you just told me, and you expect me not to be surprised? First of all, the fact that you are telling *me,* of all people" – Jessica cut her off.

"I told you, you are the only person who will know what to do with this information." She was as cool as a cucumber. Just like always.

"What the hell do you expect me to do with all of this?" Anna shouted, her arms flapping, her eyes wide, nostrils flaring.

"I expect you do to what's *right,*" Jessica hissed. She narrowed her eyes and stabbed her finger at the couch. "Now *sit.* And listen to me."

She sounded so much like their mother, Anna found herself automatically walking over to the couch and dropping down, slouching back and crossing her arms, glaring at her sister, waiting to be told what to do.

Jessica took a deep breath and let it out slowly, as she leaned back and crossed her legs, looking as serene as Anna undoubtedly looked sloppy.

"Yes," Jessica said. "What I did *was* appalling. And yes, I do regret it, but not for the reasons you think. Mostly, I've regretted losing my freedom. But really, I've regretted having to sneak around when I finally managed to convince Danny to sleep with me again."

Anna leaned forward, shocked yet again by her sister's words. "This guy knows Cora is his, and he's letting some other guy raise her?"

"No. He believes I lost his baby. He believes Cora is Jesse's."

"Jessica, you have to tell him. You can't–"

"No, I don't. I told you, Danny isn't interested in being a father. His stance has not changed over the years. And frankly, I'm not particularly interested in being a mother. Which is where you come into the picture."

Anna slowly leaned back again, giving her sister a wary look.

"I want you to make up with Jesse. I want you to admit that you're in love with him – and tell him as much – and then I want you two to get married and raise Cora as your own."

"You want... *what?*" Anna leaped off the couch again, scrambled backwards until she bumped into the wall. She pressed her palms against the smooth surface and stared at her sister as if Jessica was transforming into an alien right before her eyes.

Jessica remained as calm as ever, nodding with a look of pure satisfaction on her face. "It's perfect, really. Cora loves you more than she loves me. And Jesse definitely loves you more. He's regretted our marriage every step of the way, too. He's just too nice of a guy to admit it, or do anything about it."

"He did something about it three days ago," Anna replied, unable to hide the bitterness in her voice.

"I think you are confused about his reasons, Anna. He slept with you because he is in love with you, not because he wanted to get back at me."

Anna stared at her. "But... But..."

"But nothing. Go talk to him. Listen to him explain why he did what he did. And when he tells you it's because he loves you, believe him. And for the love of God, do it before Christmas. You'll ruin him forever if you make him suffer through Christmas without you. That man loves this holiday almost as much as he loves you and Cora, and that is saying something."

"He … he loves me?"

Jessica rolled her eyes. "Cora is young enough that she won't even remember me in a few years."

That pulled Anna out of her confessions-of-love induced stupor. "Wait a minute, what do you mean, she won't remember you?"

Her sister stood, placed her empty glass on the coffee table. "I'm leaving. I really am going with Danny this time. It's what I've wanted since the first time I ever slept with him, on my twenty-first birthday. Now I'm closer to thirty than twenty and I'm sure as hell not getting any younger. It's time to realize my dreams. It's time you realized yours, too. Go talk to Jesse." She slipped her arms into her coat and winced as she slid her feet into her heels, and then walked toward the door. With her hand wrapped around the knob, she paused and turned to look at Anna.

"Oh, and Anna? I'll take the hit for this one. For once."

"What does that mean?"

"I'll tell our parents the entire thing was my fault. I'll figure out something. Maybe I'll tell them I stole Jesse from you, four years ago. Actually, I kind of like that angle."

"But what about Cora?"

"I'm going to sign away my rights, so that you can adopt her."

"But… But what about Jesse? You said he isn't her father."

"There are now only two people on the entire planet who know this fact. What you choose to do with that information is up to you. I know what I would do. I have confidence that you'll do the right thing, Anna. Despite what we all have always thought, you always do."

And then she was gone.

Chapter Six

He got it right this time. He'd married the girl of his dreams. Well, it would be right, as soon as he figured out how to untie the damn silk laces on the back of her wedding gown. "Who the hell came up with this contraption, anyway?"

"Jessica bought it in Italy and shipped it to me, remember?"

"I think she deliberately chose this, in an effort to try to ruin our wedding night." But a moment later, he found success, and announced it with a triumphant, "Aha. Finally. Come here. I want to see what you have on underneath there."

He pushed the dress over her shoulders, down over her hips, until it pooled on the carpet at her feet. Then he stood and simply stared at his new wife, breathtaking in nothing but a lacey white bra, matching panties and sexy as-all-get-out white garter belt with complimentary garters.

"Can we leave these on?" he asked hopefully, his eyes riveted to the seductive contraption.

"It's your wedding night," she replied.

He grinned and pulled her into his arms, kissing her senseless before leaning his head back and looking down into her eyes. "Are you happy?"

"Completely."

"Do you love me?"

"Of course."

"Do you want to have another baby?"

He'd shocked her with that one, which made him laugh.

"We haven't even had one yet."

"Yes we have. We have Cora. She's *yours* now, just as much as she's mine."

Her smile was wistful, so he kissed her again, and reassured her. "Jessica signed over her parental rights. The adoption is final. She's yours. No one will ever take her away from us."

"I know," his new wife whispered. He cupped her face, used his thumbs to swipe away the tears.

"Don't cry, baby."

"I'm sorry. I really am happy, I swear. It's all just catching up to me, I think. My parents have been so supportive. My dad walked me down the aisle. Jessica and Danny showed up after all. The reception was perfect. Your parents are keeping Cora so that we can go on a honeymoon—"

"And work on making another baby. They are rather fond of their granddaughter. And her mother. They'd be thrilled if we gave them another."

She laughed and hiccupped at the same time. "I still can't believe I'm standing here with you, that we're married. That I found my Prince Charming."

"You sure know how to butter a guy up. But I want you to know that you didn't get the best end of this deal. I did. I got you. And I don't care what you say, I'm never letting you go, Mrs. Patterson."

Anna smiled. He loved her smile.

"Let's go to bed, Mr. Patterson. I got this cool book at my bachelorette party. An entire book full of sexual positions. With pictures."

Jesse quickly shed his tuxedo. "Yep. I definitely got the better end of this deal. Without a doubt."

Loving Mondays

by K.R. Wilburn

for Ben
with all of my heart for all of our tomorrows

Chapter One

*J*esus, I hate flying coach," grumbled a voice next to me. "I swear the only way to get through flying in the cheap seats is Xanax and gallons of spiked eggnog."

My gaze slid to the young woman crammed next to me in the too-small seat ,and I took a sip from my plastic cup of ginger ale. Flying always made my stomach do flips no matter which section of the plane I was in, but the headache I had brewing had nothing to do with hurtling through the air in a tin can while choking on the clouds of cupcake scented perfume my seatmate had obviously bathed in. No, this headache had sprung up the moment I knew I would have to go back to Texas, back to the one place I had never wanted to see again and face the one girl I never could escape.

"You look really familiar to me, have we met some place?"

"I doubt it." Or rather I really hoped not. There were plenty of women roaming around Florida who knew me in a biblical sense, but none that I was interested in seeing ever again.

"Are you sure? Because I could swear I've seen your face somewhere before." She cocked her head to the side and pursed her lips while she stared at me. It made her look like a deranged cocker spaniel and it was everything I could do not to promise to scratch behind her ears if she'd just quit yapping at me. "Oh! I know! You're Cody Jackson aren't you? You play for Florida State! My brother drags me to all of your games, I just didn't realize it was you with your helmet off. Oh-em-gee! My sorority sisters are going to just die when they realize that I got to meet you!"

Her lips kept moving, but I was no longer listening to her, searching instead for the flight attendant. If I was going to be forced to listen to this woman the entire flight to Dallas, I was going to need something stronger than my ginger ale or I would stop pretending that I was calm and let loose with all the turmoil bubbling inside me. With the way things were going this week, the whole thing would get live-tweeted and wind up on ESPN before I even landed. I could just see the headlines now. "Heisman winner Cody Jackson verbally assaults woman on flight, ruins Christmas for everyone on board, invitation to carve the Whoville roast beast rescinded amongst allegations of general grinchiness."

I sighed and instead of saying what I wanted to, I forced my face into what I hoped was a passable smile while she took a half a dozen selfies with me, all while hinting not so subtly how willing she would be to keep me company for the holidays instead of going home to see her parents. I could practically see her calculating the easiest way to land herself a future NFL pro for a boyfriend and just how many holes she could poke into a condom before getting caught. I just wanted to land and get as far away from this chick as I could.

I didn't even want to think about what was going to happen after that. Luke had offered to pick me up at the airport, but I had hung up before he could finish his offer. Going home to scatter the ashes of the last family member I had left was hard enough; there was no way in hell I was sitting in a truck with my former best friend for the two hour drive back to the ranch from Dallas on top of it. I had been planning on spending the holidays in Key West with some of the other guys from the team just so I could avoid going home to see Gran for the holidays like I had every Christmas for the last four years. My guilt would eat me alive if I didn't go home to honor her final wishes.

My chest ached. Gran was dead and I would never get to spend another holiday with her again. I was such an asshole. I knew she wouldn't leave the ranch, but I still hadn't been back to see her since I left for college. I should have made time, but I had been avoiding going home and having to see Luke living happily ever after with the love of my life. She understood that I didn't want to see them, even if I had always steadfastly refused to tell her why. Gran was good like that; she always took my side no matter what. And where Luke and Monday were concerned, I couldn't even begin to talk about what had happened that would make me cut them out so thoroughly that any mention of their names was strictly avoided.

"So what do you think?"

"What do I think of what?" I growled at my seatmate, irritated to find that she was still talking.

"Of dinner? Or maybe we can just grab a few drinks if you like? I can hold off going to see the family for a few days. I've been an awfully good girl this year and if you play your cards right, maybe I can sit on your lap and tell you what I want for Christmas."

Helen Keller could figure out what this girl wanted for Christmas and I could feel my patience waning. Where the hell was that flight attendant?

"Somehow I doubt you've ever been a good girl in your life. I appreciate the offer but I'm going to pass. I'm not much for company right now."

"Well, if you change your mind," she simpered, batting her overly made-up eyes at me, and scribbling a number on the damp piece of napkin that sat on my tray, "you just give me a call. I'm sure I can put you in the holiday spirit."

"I'll keep that in mind." I tucked the napkin in my pocket, thinking it would be rude to just toss it out in front of her and waved at the flight attendant when I finally caught her eye.

"What can I help you with, sir?" The flight attendant smiled as she approached.

"I need one of those little bottles of whiskey," I told her, pulling my wallet from my pocket. If I was going down I might as well go down in flames. "And a couple more on standby."

Chapter Two

Time stood still on the ranch, as it always had. While the rest of the world marched forward with progress, life in west Texas remained. Turning the rental car down the long dirt road that led to my childhood home, I couldn't help but feel overwhelmed with the memories of growing up here. Memories of Gran, of Luke and me running through the fields planning out the day's mischief, and memories of her. Memories that I had spent the past four years running as hard as I could to get away from suddenly were drowning me.

I pulled up in front of the two-story yellow house that had been the only home I had ever known, lined with cheerily blinking lights and the same evergreen bough hanging from the from door that had been there every Christmas for longer than I had lived. It looked so cheerful and welcoming, disguising the sad reason I was really home. I turned the key in the ignition and clutched the steering wheel with both hands, knowing I needed to get out of the car and walk up those wide country steps, but unable to do so. Regret and remorse welled up in my chest and lodged in my throat as I let my gaze sweep over the places that were burned into my memory. Seeing Gran's wicker rocker empty cut to my core, and I inhaled deeply and closed my eyes to ward off the tears I could feel building.

"You just going to sit in that car all day or are you going to come inside?"

I started at the sound and time froze. Monday leaned down to the open window, her honey blond hair blowing lightly in the breeze, filling the air with the clean citrus scent that had haunted my dreams. I hated that my body turned towards her instinctively, like a flower turning towards the sunshine.

"Come on inside, Cody," she said gently, her warm golden eyes filled with concern. "You must be exhausted. I know how much you hate flying. Let's get you inside and get you something warm to drink."

I wanted to say something cutting, something so cruel

that we would both remember that I hadn't forgiven her for running off with my best friend as soon as I left for college, but as soon as I turned to face her, the words died in my throat. I hadn't expected to feel my heart well up at the sight of her again, my arms twitching with the need to wrap around her slender form and pull her into my chest. Four years away from here, convincing myself I was over her, and the first sight of her told me that I still loved her, that I would probably always love her. My heart was broken and scarred, and each time it beat out the rhythm of her name it throbbed angrily, but still it couldn't heal. Not while she still held all the pieces in her delicate hands.

Unable to trust my voice, I nodded and opened the car door and climbed out. My fingers tingled with the need to touch her, to comfort her for the pain that I knew she felt as keenly as I did at Gran's loss. If anybody loved my Gran as much as I did, it was her.

"Monday," I whispered, the taste of her name in my mouth familiar and alien at the same time. "I—"

"I know," she interrupted me, stepping into me and draping her arms around my neck. Before I could stop myself, my arms encircled her waist and crushed her to me, hoping that she couldn't feel my body trembling beneath her touch. I buried my face in her hair and inhaled deeply, amazed at how much my body remembered the feel of this, of her softness against my chest. Even though I knew she was nothing but trouble, my body cried out for her. This was what home felt like, and no matter how I tried, I couldn't deny her. I hated her for that. Why couldn't I let her go?

"There you are." A familiar gravelly voice interrupted my thoughts and I stiffened, icy anger sliding down my spine. I released Monday and stepped back, putting distance between us. I clenched my hands into fists at my side to keep from pushing her behind me and shielding her from Luke. She wasn't mine anymore. I had to remember that, and standing before me with a broad grin like nothing had ever changed between us, like he hadn't buried a knife so deep in my back it was still lodged there, was the reason why. "I was wondering when you were going to get in. I wish you would have just let me pick you up at the airport."

"I needed the time to think." I focused my gaze over his shoulder, unable to meet Luke's steely gray eyes. Once he was my best friend, and the only person in the world besides Gran and Monday that I trusted. In a small town in Texas, being the high school quarterback meant everyone wanted to be your friend. You couldn't know who had your best interests at heart and who was out to ride your coattails. Being an all-state quarterback committed to a division I college with every major sports network calling you the one to watch meant that everyone wanted a piece of you, everyone but the three of them.

But as it turned out, Luke had wanted something from me after all—my girl. And now Gran was gone and the girl I loved was his, and I truly was all alone in the world. I felt a dark anger building in me at the sight of him and I flexed my hands to keep from plunging them into his face.

I needed to get the hell out of this town first chance I got, and never come back. I thought I had put all this behind me, but seeing her here, seeing them here together, just dragged it all back up. I wasn't there to rekindle old flames, or make nice with long lost friends. I would spread my Gran's ashes over the ranch like she wanted me too, and lay to rest all the hurt and anger alongside her. I was here to free myself from this town and the people who still had an inexorable hold on me, and then get back to Florida as fast as humanly possible.

Unable to meet Monday's questioning gaze I busied myself pulling my suitcase from the trunk.

"I'll take this to the bunkhouse for you," Luke insisted, taking the handle from me and gazing meaningfully from Monday to me. "Give you two a chance to talk."

"There's nothing to talk about," I insisted gruffly, but he was already walking off along the edge of the property. Looking back at Monday, whose lips turned up sheepishly, I pointed at Luke's retreating back. "Why am I staying in the bunkhouse instead of the big house?"

"You can always stay in Annie's room if you want," Monday offered, her hands fidgeting with her hair, looking nervously around the yard so she didn't have to look at me. She hadn't changed at all. Her long fingers twisted through the gleaming blond strands, a nervous habit, though the worry and grief etched on her heart shaped face was new. "I thought it might be easier on you if you were in the bunkhouse without being surrounded by her things."

"Is there something wrong with my room?" I frowned at her.

"It's occupied."

"Occupied? By who?"

"Me," she said matter-of-factly, meeting my eyes, her jaw clenched challengingly.

My eyes widened in surprise.

"You?" I asked, my confused feelings and anger at being forced back to Texas finally bubbling to the surface. "Why are you staying in my room, Monday? I come back to town and you think you can climb back into my bed like you never left it? Fuck it, if that's what you want I'm down for the ride, just don't expect anything to change between us come morning. You'll still be a cold bitch and I'll still be on the first flight out of here."

Her eyes flashed and my head snapped back under the force of her palm connecting with my cheek. I deserved it.

"That's your one," she said angrily, her voice trembling, "And you're only getting that out of the kindness of my heart and respect for Annie's memory. If you ever speak to me like that again, Cody Jackson, it'll be a closed fist and don't you think for a minute that I won't knock the smart out of your mouth and take your front teeth along with it."

"Well aren't you an angry little elf," I chortled. "If my Gran hadn't raised me to be a gentleman, Monday, I would tell you exactly what I thought of you and your little boyfriend setting up house in my family ranch. Like the two of you haven't taken enough from me already. I'll sleep in Gran's room tonight because I'm too tired and too pissed off to deal with you and your bullshit. But tomorrow you and Luke can pack your shit and get the fuck off of my land and I'll be satisfied to never see either of your treacherous asses again."

Her nostrils flared and she stepped into my personal space.

"First of all, I told you when we were twelve not to call me an elf and I meant it." She jabbed her finger into my chest painfully, punctuating her words. "Secondly, I don't like what you're implying about Luke and me, and if I wasn't so damn happy to see you I would demand you explain yourself. So instead of beating some sense into you like you deserve, I'm going to go put some clean sheets on Annie's bed and try to be glad that you're finally home. I just wish it hadn't taken something like this to get you to do it, and sorrier still that the one person who should have been at Annie's side was too busy being a big city jerk to do right by her."

My shoulders slumped and I felt my anger dissipate. Gran would tan my hide if she heard me yelling at a woman the way I had been, no matter what they had done to me first.

"Look Monday—"

"I don't want to hear it," she said on a sigh, her eyes wounded. "I'll go put some linens on the bed, you go have Luke bring your things up to Annie's room. Whatever problem you have with him, you need to fix it before you take off again. You hurt him something terrible when you cut us off, Cody. You hurt all of us and you'll never get to tell Annie that you're sorry for it. Don't wait until it's too late to mend those fences with Luke too."

Damn.

She always did know how to go for the kill shot.

Chapter Three

The house didn't look like much had changed since I had left. There was a new sofa in front of the fireplace, but the same photos hung on the walls and the Christmas tree in the corner had all of the ornaments Gran had painstakingly collected over the years, and the stockings hung from hooks on the mantle. Gran's beat up red stocking, my blue and white stocking with my high school football number, seven, embroidered in the crushed velvet, and a delicate red stocking with *Monday* stitched in dark green swirls on the snowy white cuff next to it.

Dragging myself up the stairs, I took a deep breath and opened the door to Gran's room. Monday was bent over the bed, tucking in the white wedding ring patterned quilt that had been on Gran's bed since it was given to her as a wedding gift some sixty years ago.

Monday's shoulders were shaking quietly and I froze, uncomfortable and torn between not wanting to bear witness to her private grief and wanting to hold her in my arms and comfort her. She sniffed delicately and turned towards the door. When she saw me, her spine stiffened and it was her turn to freeze.

"Cody," she said softly. It was so difficult to be close to her and not touch her. Her face crumpled and I stopped fighting the need and tugged her into my chest. She buried her face against me and her shoulders began to shake with the force of her sobs. I ran my fingers over her hair with one hand and whispered platitudes, feeling my resistance crumble with every tear that fell from her eyes.

"Why weren't you here, Cody?" She cried against my shoulder, her tiny fists pressing into my chest. "Why weren't you here when we needed you? Did she mean so little to you? Did I mean so little to you? I waited for you to come back, but you never came..."

I held her close and let her continue to cry as every word stabbed deeper and deeper until I knew she would draw blood.

"You meant everything to me, Monday," I said as I held her tight against me. "I just couldn't bear to see you and Luke together, so I stayed away. I knew it would hurt too much. I never meant to hurt you, I only meant to protect me."

But that wasn't exactly true. I had meant to hurt her. Every time I went out in public with sorority clones on my arm, smiling for the cameras, I knew that she would see it and I wanted her to hurt as much as I was hurting. The truth was, I had stopped answering her calls and reading her letters because I knew if she asked me to forgive her, I would have, as much as I didn't want to.

"What the hell are you talking about?" She pushed herself away from me, her chest heaving. "I think this is the part where you explain exactly what you were implying about Luke and me outside."

"I know about you and Luke." My gaze moved around the room, darting this way and that, anywhere but on her. I couldn't bear to look at her while she crushed me. "About two months after I left for school Madison Wylie called me and told me that she had been seeing you and Luke together all the time. At first I told her she was imaging things, that neither of you would run around behind my back. But then she texted me a picture of you sitting in his lap in the front seat of his truck. You had your face tucked into his neck and his arms were around you. I almost called you a thousand times to demand you explain yourself, but the guys on the team made me realize it was best if I just let you both go. And so I did. I couldn't bear to hear you tell me you loved me when I knew I wasn't the only one, or worse yet, tell me that you loved him. So I just stopped answering your calls."

I watched as a range of emotions played out over her face. Confusion, shock, disbelief, and finally, rage.

"So you're telling me that you broke my heart, and Luke's, and your Gran's for that matter, because you were too much of a coward to pick up the damned phone? I thought you knew me better than that, and you owe Luke an apology. It's too late for you to apologize to Annie now and you'll have to live with that regret for the rest of your life, but let me tell you something, Cody Jackson, you were lied to."

"How was I lied to?" I demanded. "Pictures don't lie, Monday!"

"Because you were stupid enough to believe Madison Wylie, the girl who always wanted you and never got you. That girl has been looking for a chance to sink her claws into you since the seventh grade, and you bought her bullshit by the pound. Pictures may not lie but it's only a moment in time, out of context, and if you would have called and asked me I would have told you what was going on."

"So tell me now," I demanded, moving close to her, my fingers curving under her chin and forcing her to meet my eyes. "Tell me what the picture didn't. Tell me how it wasn't what it looked like."

"The only time I ever curled up in Luke's lap was the day I found out my momma had cancer. I was crying, and he held me while my heart bled out. And when I tried to call you to tell you what was happening, to tell you that I needed you, you never picked up the damn phone."

If she had punched me, she couldn't have slammed into me as hard as her words did.

"I needed you and you were off hiding like a coward, and when we put my momma in the ground, you were off at college partying it up and giving interviews to ESPN. When the bank took my house and I had nowhere else to go, Annie took me in, and when she got sick I took care of her, too. You're not the wounded party here, Cody, you're just the narcissistic asshole who made everyone else's pain about him. And that's something you'll have to carry your whole life through because you've chased off anyone who would have shared your burden."

Her chest heaved as she dragged in a ragged breath, and she pushed herself away from me and left the room without another word. When her steps echoed off the stairs as she ran down them, I sank to my knees on the floor, all the righteous anger that had been carrying me deflated, and I was left alone on Gran's floor. The reality of everything I had lost to stupid pride burying itself in my chest like a dagger.

Chapter Four

The next morning I awoke to something I had never expected.

Snow.

Sure, it occasionally snowed in West Texas, but rarely did it ever stick around long enough to actually enjoy it, and it was rarely anything more than a light dusting. This was a hefty blanket of snow, and from the looks of the dark clouds and the chill in the air, it wasn't going anywhere. Who knew if it would be there in the morning, but I'd take a white Christmas Eve over nothing at all. I pulled on a pair of flannel pajama bottoms and rubbing a hand over my face, I stumbled down the stairs in search of the coffee pot. I had tossed and turned all night playing Monday's words over and over in my head and coming to the same conclusion every time.

I had fucked up, but that didn't mean I couldn't fix it.

I had to win her back, no matter what it took. She had loved me once, I could make her love me again. How hard could it be?

Monday was standing over the sink staring out the window at the glittering snow that had blanketed the property, a fresh cup of brew in her hand. I let my gaze trace the soft curves of her figure. Her tiny waist, her rounded hips and up to the slender line of her neck, exposed by the messy bun of her hair were so heart-breakingly perfect. Her oversized shirt and tiny sleep shorts showed off long slender legs, leaving me with images of those same legs locked around my hips dancing though my head. I never could figure out how someone so short in stature could have legs miles long, but somehow she pulled it off. She was so much better than the girls who followed me around at school. They seemed so shallow and fake with their salon tans and bleached hair. Monday was real from the tips of her unpainted toes to her sun-kissed hair.

My lips curled up into a smile as I padded up behind her, placing a hand on her hip and pressing myself against her back while I reached up into the cabinet beside her for a coffee mug. I felt her tense underneath my hand and chuckled darkly, closing my eyes and inhaling her heady scent. It sent a jolt through my body and when she stiffened, I knew she could feel my arousal pressing against her.

"Morning," I said huskily into her ear, and my smile spread when she shivered.

"Morning," she replied, her voice stilted as she turned away from the window. I put my hands on the counter on each side of her, caging her in and invading her personal space in all kinds of awesome ways. Two bright pink spots appeared on her cheeks, letting me know that my nearness was affecting her. "Um, would you mind putting a shirt on or something?"

I glanced down at my bare chest, my body well developed from years of football conditioning, then looked back at her. "I would, actually. The heat is up pretty high for me this morning."

"Well if you didn't notice, it's kind of cold outside, the heat was necessary. It's always warmest in Annie's room, but you know that." Her gaze darted about the kitchen, looking everywhere but at me. My own was fixated on her full lips, lips that I hadn't kissed in four years. Lips that I knew as well as my own and suddenly I felt the wild desire to claim them again. If it hadn't been for Madison's lies and my fears, I could have been kissing those lips for years. There was a swift stab of pain when I thought of the lost time, but I pushed it off.

I needed to make up for lost time, not mope over it.

I leaned in close to her and paused, letting my lips hover just above hers. I felt her breath pick up, tickling my lips, and her eyelids fluttered closed. I knew she wanted me to kiss her, as much as I wanted to kiss her. I inhaled deeply and plucked the cup of coffee from her hands. I leaned back and drank. It was so sweet it made my teeth ache. I much preferred my coffee black, but she had always been a three sugars kind of girl. Her eyes opened wide and she glared at me, snatching her mug back. I smiled sweetly and moved to the coffee pot with my own mug, filling it up before leaning against the counter and watching her.

I had flustered her, and it made me feel like yelling with delight. If I could do that, it proved that I still affected her. It meant that there was always a chance, no matter how small, that I hadn't lost everything after all.

I had spent the previous night wallowing in regret and anger before I came to the conclusion that there was no reason we couldn't just pick up where we left off. I still loved her, and I had known that when I had flown here. I just needed her to realize that she still loved me, too. Gran would have been pleased as punch to see us make up and I had every intention of making things right with Monday, of begging her to take me back if necessary. There was no way I was letting her slip through my fingers a second time.

I had loved Monday my whole life, or at least since the first day of kindergarten. Her long, golden pigtails had fascinated me. They were so different from my dark hair, and the citrusy scent of the shampoo she still used and so I had reached out and touched one. I had only meant to feel it, to see if it was as silky as it looked, but she had jerked away and my fingers had tightened down instinctively. She responded by slugging me so hard she gave me a black eye. We were both suspended, but once we had returned to school, I had followed her around like a lost puppy until we were both preteens and a lifelong crush had turned into full blown first love. What were four years of heartbreak and loneliness when we had fifteen good years before that and countless years stretching out before us? I would spend every waking moment apologizing to her for the wrongs I had done her. Second chances were rare, but I was going to take this one. Monday and I were meant for each other, I just needed to remind her of that.

"Cody?"

I blinked and realized she had been talking to me. I had picked a really bad time to space out. "Sorry, what's up?"

"I asked what time you wanted to drive out to Twin Peaks to scatter Annie's ashes? I don't know what time your flight is, but I figured we could get it done relatively early since I have to be at the church this evening to help set up for the Christmas pageant."

"They still do that? What am I saying, of course they still do that. I thought I could see some old friends while I'm in town, maybe mend some fences with Luke. Why don't we do it tomorrow before I fly out? And I can take you to the Church this evening to get ready for the pageant. I haven't seen a good Christmas pageant in years. Do Reverend Donnelly and Mike Campbell still fight over whether or not to use real livestock?"

"Yes." She snorted and dropped her gaze to her cup, a frown marring her perfect face. "The Reverend will never forgive him for letting that sheep do his business in the rectory. Look, Cody, I'm not trying to be an inhospitable host, and I know that technically this is your house and all, but I'm not sure, given our history, that it's such a good idea for you to stay through the holidays. I'm sure you've got someplace else to be."

"Nope." I grinned as I reached for her free hand and entwined our fingers. "There's no place I would rather be. It's been a long time since I've spent Christmas at home and it's been even longer since I've had a Monday when I didn't feel like I would rather fall off the face of the earth than climb out of bed and face the day. Look, I know I screwed things up between us, and while I hope like hell you can forgive me, I just want the chance to say I'm sorry. Give me the chance to prove to you that we can still be friends at least. Let me learn to love Mondays again."

She blinked, and her gaze slipped down to my lips. "I, uh, I don't know, Cody," she said breathlessly, wetting her lips instinctively, a subconscious invitation that I had every intention of accepting.

"I think it's a great idea." I stepped closer to her, lightly fingering a tendril of her hair that had fallen loose from her messy bun before pushing it behind her ear. She inhaled shakily as she reached out, tracing a finger along my jaw, and a shudder ran down my spine. All hesitation fled as I leaned forward and claimed her lips with my own, cupping the back of her head with my broad hand and holding her to me.

She stilled underneath me and I pulled away, concerned that I had moved too fast. I searched her eyes for a sign, for encouragement, for anything really that would tell me I hadn't just ruined everything. Before I could ask if she was okay, she shocked me by pressing herself against me. Her kiss sent the pit of my stomach into a wild swirl of heat and desire. The feel of her mouth on mine rocked me to my core, and I encircled her with my arms, crushing her to me. She responded by moving her arms around my neck and tangling her fingers in my hair, tugging gently.

I knew in this moment that whatever fire had existed between Monday and I had never died down completely. There was a spark there, a small flame, quietly banked through the years but never burned down to embers. If nurtured right, it would come roaring back to life with the force of a wildfire. I groaned against her and moved my mouth, tracing a path down her neck and her shoulders, tasting the sweetness of her flesh with my tongue and moved my hand from the back of her head to the small of her back, sliding up under the hem of her shirt and pressing against the warm flesh there. My body surged beneath hers as I moved back up her neck, reclaiming her mouth.

"Monday," I groaned as her teeth nipped at my lower lip. "Fuck, I've missed this. I missed you. I almost forgot how good it could be between us."

That, apparently, was the wrong thing to say.

She moved away from me forcefully, holding her hands out as if to ward me away. "No, you haven't," she said angrily, pressing her fingers to her swollen lips. "You abandoned me, and if you think I'm going to let you waltz back in here like everything is okay and pick up where we left off, you've got another thing coming. If you missed me you would have called, but you didn't. You left me here with my world falling apart. You threw me away, Cody. You threw us away. You can't just kiss me and tell me that you missed me and undo the last four years."

Her eyes filled with tears and the sight was a sucker punch to the gut.

"I know I can't," I lied. That's exactly what I had wanted, but, as always, she could see straight through my bullshit. "I wish I could take back every mistake I made. I wish I could have been here with you when you needed me at your side, and I wish I had been able to help you and Gran, and to not be such a selfish asshole. I know that I can't just say I'm sorry and fix everything, but Monday, I am sorry. Sorrier than I can ever explain. Just give me a chance to prove that to you before you give up on me completely. I don't deserve your forgiveness, but I'm asking for it anyway."

The tears slid down her face, sparkling like jewels and I leaned forward, brushing them away with my thumbs.

"Please, Monday, just give me this chance to make things okay between us. I don't want to lose you. Show me how to fight for you, tell me what I need to do and I'll do it, just don't give up on us as easily as I did. You're better than that. You're better than me."

"I can't show you how to fight for me, Cody," she said sadly, swinging her gaze to meet mine. "Especially when I'm not even sure it's something that I want you to do."

I was speechless as I watched her leave the room, fear smashing into my chest and rendering me incapable of breathing.

Chapter Five

Monday had avoided any contact with me after our kiss this morning, like my bad judgment was catching, and so after agreeing to meet up in the afternoon to scatter Gran's ashes, I decided it was time I paid a visit to Luke. I needed to talk to him, to apologize for assuming the worst, and to mend those fences. Okay, I also wanted to pick his brain on how to win Monday back and see just how bleak things were looking in that department.

Unlike Monday, Luke didn't seem to have any reservations about welcoming me back into his life. Monday had called him to let him know I was on my way, and he met me at the front porch, a hot cup of coffee in his hands and a smile on his face. Like most people around these parts, Luke still lived on his family ranch, helping his father keep it running smoothly and training for the day that he would take over the property. There were nearly as many memories lurking here as there were at Gran's. He ushered me into the house and a familiar face greeted me.

"Tanya!" I grinned, pulling her in close for a bear hug. "Good lord, girl! It's been forever. What the hell have you been up to?"

Tanya swung her gleaming dark hair over her shoulder and beamed at Luke. "Oh you know, this and that. I'm studying Nursing up at the community college for now, and Luke's mom and I are busy planning the wedding, so that takes up large chunks of time. You know how my mom is about these things."

Luke groaned as he moved behind Tanya, pulling her back into his chest and pressing a kiss into her hair. "Don't remind me. I swear running off to Vegas looks better every day," he muttered, lifting his brows at me.

"Don't even joke." Tanya twisted to give him a stern look. "You'd break my momma's heart, and your momma's too. They want a big wedding, and they're getting a big wedding. Just give them their day and we'll save ourselves years of grumbling about how tacky it is to get married by Elvis around the dinner table."

My eyes darted from Tanya to Luke and back to Tanya.

"You guys are engaged?" I asked, not disguising the surprise in my voice. "When did this happen?"

Luke had always had a thing for Tanya but never had the sack to pursue it. I was happy for him, but I felt like an even bigger fool for believing there could be anything between Monday and Luke. How could I have forgotten how much Luke had loved the raven-haired beauty before me? But then I never could understand how anybody could fail to be in love with Monday.

"I popped the question about a year ago." Luke grinned.

"Which you would have known if you could be bothered to call home once in a while." Tanya's eyes narrowed at me. I hung my head and stared at the floor and flushed. "Monday called over here last night and filled me on what's been going on. I ought to smack you upside the head for thinking that my Luke would do you dirty like that. If I ever get my hands on that Madison, I'm gonna set her ears ringing for a week for spreading filthy lies. She was always green with envy whenever you and Monday were together."

"I still shouldn't have believed her," I muttered, my cheeks heating from embarrassment, lifting my gaze to meet Luke's. His expression was tight and I knew that I had wounded his pride. "I'm sorry, Luke. I should have known better. You're the best friend I ever had, and I sure turned out to be a piss poor one in the end."

Luke just shook his head and walked to my side, clasping my shoulder in his hand the way his Dad used to do to us both when we had fucked up and he wanted to impress upon us the severity of our actions. "It's water under the bridge. But still, I wish you would have just called me, or at least picked up the phone when I called. It would have saved everyone a whole lot of heartache in the end."

I rubbed my face with both hands. "Yeah, well, hindsight and all that. I'm happy for you and Tanya. You have no idea how good it is to see you both. I missed ya'll a lot more than I thought I would. So when is the wedding?"

"May." Tanya smiled and settled herself on a chair across from me. "As sorry as I am for the reasons you finally came home, it sure saved us on airfare."

I looked at her questioningly.

"I was going to fly up there and put the invitation in your hand myself." Luke grinned. "You think I could get married without you at my side? Even if I had to drag your sorry behind all the way back here I was going to do it, so why don't you save us both the hassle and come of your own free will. Traditionally the shotgun should be held on the groom, but don't think I won't use it on the best man."

I snorted. "I'll be here, no kidnapping necessary. I just wish fixing things with Monday was this easy." My heart dropped when I realized there was a good chance I couldn't fix things with Monday. What if she never forgave me? Would I have to keep moving through life with this hole in my chest like I had been doing?

I thought of the women that had tried to take her place over the years. None had ever come close. Even when I thought she had betrayed me, I could never give another my heart, not when it wasn't mine to give.

Luke gave Tanya a meaningful look and she muttered something about needing to check on dinner and left the room. He sat down on one couch and I sat down across from him, bracing myself for whatever he had to say. My heart sped up as the worst case scenarios started rolling through my mind.

What if she loved someone else? Obviously not Luke, but that didn't mean that any of the other guys in town wouldn't have jumped at a chance with Monday once they knew I was out of the picture. It had only been the knowledge that I would have buried them somewhere on the back forty of my property that had kept them away when we were growing up.

"So am I right in assuming that you want Monday back?"

I nodded. I didn't just want Monday back, I needed her as much as I needed air.

"The good news is that she's still in love with you. She never stopped."

"Oh thank baby Jesus," I muttered, running a hand over

my face, feeling my shoulders sag in relief. If she still loved me, there was a chance I hadn't fucked everything all to hell after all.

"You hurt her something fierce, Cody, and she's been nursing that pain for a long while. So I would be doing both of you a disservice if I didn't warn you. If you hurt her again, best friend or not, I will bury you so deep that archaeologists won't be able to find your bones for another thousand years."

Startled, I looked at Luke. His eyes were stone-cold serious and his jaw was tensed up like he was waiting for me to argue with him. I wasn't going to because the look he gave me let me know this wasn't an idle threat.

"I won't hurt her ever again, Luke, I swear it. I'd rather cut my own heart out and stomp on it."

"Good." He inhaled deeply and climbed to his feet. "Because I'll be right there next to you handing you the knife and critiquing your field dressing. Some hurts go soul-deep, and what you did, it left a wound that hasn't come close to healing yet. So you go fix it, and then you spend every day for the rest of your life making it up to her."

"I'm planning on it," I swore.

Chapter Six

*M*onday was an angel. Or rather, she was dressed like one. I watched, transfixed, from the same pew that my ass had polished every Sunday morning and Wednesday night as a boy while Monday moved around the stage. Dressed as the Angel of the Lord in a glittering white gown with huge gossamer wings affixed to her back, she moved about the stage, telling the shepherd boy and the audience of the coming of their savior.

It was a part she had played every year since we were teenagers and the good Rev had thought her blond curls made her look heavenly. Really, it was just her. There was something about her that forced the eyes to follow her movements on the stage, a light that filled her and spilled over to everyone she touched.

Jesus, I had been a fool to let her go.

Her eyes met mine and she blinked, startled to see me there. I smiled at her and lifted my eyebrows when she missed her cue. Her face colored brightly, and she angled her body so that I was out of her line of sight. It was rare to see her off her mark, and knowing that I could still unsettle her lifted my heart a bit. I chuckled and let my own gaze move about the church, startled to see how people had changed in such a short time.

I had always held this view that the people here would stand as still as the town itself did, as if it were caught in a vortex that prevented anyone from moving forward. Seeing guys that ran the field with me in school with small babies in their arms made my heart stop beating momentarily. Is this where Monday and I would have been had I never left for college?

My heart warmed briefly before I remembered our conversation in the kitchen that morning. Whatever track we had been on, Monday had made it obvious that she wasn't ready to pick that back up. Luke had said I shouldn't give up, but right now the whole situation seemed hopeless.

The sound of applause startled me from my thoughts,

and I joined in as Monday smiled and moved off stage, her gaze clinging to mine. I stood up in the pew and slid to the aisle, meaning to head through the hall to the anteroom where all the players always changed into their costumes. I only made it as far as the hallway before I realized I hadn't made it out unseen after all.

"Fancy seeing you here, Cody Jackson." A sultry voice caught my attention. I turned to find a tall, beautiful girl leaning against the doorway. She tossed her glossy dark hair and crossed her arms under ample breasts that seemed far too exposed for a Christmas Eve church service.

"Madison," I replied coldly. I had never hit a woman in my life, but that didn't mean that I hadn't visualized it a couple times since I found out that she had lied to me about Monday and Luke. I tucked my hands in my back pockets to keep from throttling her in the house of God.

She leaned forward and ran a finger down my chest, looking up at me from under heavily made-up lashes. "Football has done you good." She smirked, biting down on her lip and grinning at me. "I'm sorry to hear about your grandmother. She was a sweet old lady. How hard it must be for you to lose her so close to the holidays."

A stab of pain bloomed in my chest again as I thought of Gran.

"Yeah," I muttered, closing my eyes against the tears that threatened to fall and ducking my head.

"Poor Cody," she purred, stepping closer. She rested her hands on my forearms and I stiffened uncomfortably as I felt her breasts brush my chest. "I'm sure things are mighty awkward for you staying up at the ranch, what with your ex-girlfriend living there now and all. You're more than welcome to stay at my place while you're settling things. My couch is a mite small for you to be crashing on but you can always take the bed and I can bunk on the couch if you like."

"I appreciate the offer, Madison," I stuttered, scratching the back of my neck uncomfortably, "But I'm not about to kick you out of your bed."

"I suppose it is big enough to share." She grinned licentiously as she leaned towards me.

"That's not what he meant, Madison." Monday glared at the girl. "He was trying to say no without hurting your feelings, but as usual, you're oblivious. Cody never cared much for the scent of desperation and bad choices, and Lord knows your sad little apartment is probably reeking with it. Now, if you don't take your trashy hands off of him you're going to pull back a bloody stump."

Madison whirled around and shot a withering glance at Monday, still wearing her white gossamer gown, now missing the wings and halo that she had worn on stage. "Please, I'm surprised he can smell anything with your skanky scent all over his house. Cody is a grown man and he ain't yours anymore, honey, so if he wants to spend the night in my 'sad little apartment', he's welcome to. It can't be easy sleeping under the same roof as your cheating ex. That's so pitiful they wouldn't even put it in a country song."

Monday flashed a brilliant smile and Madison blinked at her, confused until Monday's fist barreled straight at her face, slamming her head back before she crumpled in a heap on the floor.

"Didn't your momma ever teach you not to tell lies, Madison? I think that was the lesson that came between not letting your mouth write checks your ass can't cash and not spreading your legs for every man that looks at you crossways. Although I see she completely skipped over how not to dress like the town slut at a church function."

Madison climbed to her feet and stamped one stiletto heel before turning tail and stomping off. My shoulders shook as I struggled not to laugh at the look of satisfaction on Monday's face. I wiped away tears of mirth until Monday fixed her glare on me. I held both of my hands up in surrender.

"I swear I was only back here looking for you."

"I know. I was wondering what was taking you so long. I wish I could say I was surprised to find Madison trying to trap you with her vagina, but I'm not."

"I can't believe you hit her in church."

"Well, she had it coming," she muttered. "I didn't like her

before, but knowing that it was her lies that started this mess pushed that from a soft dislike to a hard hate."

"And me? Am I at a hard hate, too?"

She shook her head. "No. I keep trying to hate you, Cody, but I never can seem to pull it off. But I am disappointed and I'm not sure which one is worse."

To be honest, I wasn't sure either.

Chapter Seven

"This is beautiful." Monday sighed, looking out over the expanse below us from where we stood on Twin Peak, high above the town nestled in the valley below. Twin Peak was a misnomer. There's only one peak, and it doesn't have a twin anywhere in sight. There was some legend somewhere that involved twin sisters who were separated and used this peak to search for one another or something. But local legends aside, Monday was right, the view spread out in front of us was nothing shy of amazing.

"That's part of the reason Gran chose it, I think. She used to come up here when she said she needed to see the big picture." It was hard not to see the big picture from up here. Below the peak, the valley began and stretched out as far as the eye could see in a blanket of glittering snow and twinkling Christmas lights. Everything looked so tiny from up here that surely nothing could be insurmountable in comparison, not even the distance that lay between us. Down in that snow covered valley, families were exchanging gifts, and sitting down to break bread together, thankful for another year they were blessed to share.

That's where we should have been, Monday, Gran, Luke, and I. Instead, Monday and I were up here, dressed in thick layers against the cold, preparing to say goodbye to someone we loved.

My gaze swung back to Monday. Her eyes were focused on the box that holds Gran's ashes in her hands. She was shaking, but I didn't think it was from the biting cold of the wind as it whipped around us, stirring up the flakes of snow that were falling again. Resting one hand on the back of her neck, I tugged her forward gently, pressing her into my chest and wrapping myself around her, letting her know silently that I would shelter her from this pain if I could.

"I don't know how to say goodbye," she whispered, and my heart cracked a little more.

"Gran used to tell me that the hardest part of loving is letting go, but sometimes it's the best thing you can do. Sometimes it's the only thing you can do so you're not walking wounded through life, bleeding out little bits of yourself as you go."

The irony of that thought was not lost on me. I knew that Gran would tell me that the best thing for Monday would be to let her go and give her a chance to heal, but I didn't know if I could do it. I'd lost her once because of my own pride and my fears, and coming home had reminded me of everything that I had lost. I wasn't sure I could lose her again.

We stood there in the silence for what seemed like forever, the snow falling gently to the ground around us until she stopped shaking. Together we opened the box and watched as a strong wind scattered Gran's ashes out over the countryside, mingling with the snow and flying into the distance.

"Now there will be a piece of her in every place that she loves." Monday smiled though her tears and I had to agree with her.

I lifted my hand and moved a loose blond curl from her face, tucking it behind her ear, but leaving my hand against her cheek, feeling the warmth against the cold of my skin. "Thank you."

She looked up at me, startled. "For what?"

"For taking care of Gran when I didn't. For taking care of Luke when I didn't. For being everything I couldn't be. For being everything I'll never be."

Tears formed in her eyes and she ducked her head, trying to avoid my gaze. My fingers slipped under her chin and tilted her face back, capturing her eyes with my own. "And I'm sorry, Monday. I'm sorry that I didn't turn out to be the man that you needed me to be. I'm sorry that I let my own insecurities destroy something so beautiful, something so pure. And I'm sorrier than I can say that I wasn't here for you when you needed me most. I'm sorry for every single tear you cried over me. I always swore I would protect you and love you and I let you down instead."

Tears slipped down her face and I brushed them away with my thumb, leaning forward and resting my forehead against hers. I took a shaky breath and closed my eyes, reaching for the strength I needed.

"But I won't ask for your forgiveness, because I don't

deserve it. If you hate me forever, I'll understand, but it won't stop me from loving you. And even though I know I don't deserve you, I can't walk away from you. Being without you has been slowly killing me. And all the drinking, and the partying, and the bad decisions numbed the pain, but it never made it go away. We only get one life, Monday Munroe, and mine belongs to you, whether you want it or not."

I opened my eyes and gazed down at her, fear blooming in my chest when I saw that her face had crumpled and she was sobbing quietly. This was not the reaction I had wanted from my declaration.

"Why can't I let you go?" she cried. "I shouldn't still want you. You didn't just break my heart Cody, you broke *me*. You abandoned me. How can I know that you'll be there when I need you? How can I trust that I won't wake up one morning to find you gone again?"

If she had stabbed me in the heart she couldn't have cut me deeper because I had put those fears there. I had taught her not to trust.

"Because I know what it is now to live without you, because I know —"

She gripped my shirt in her hands and tugged me closer, fastening her mouth on mine, and every thought I had fled. I slid a hand through her hair, cupping the back of her head and pressed her even closer. It wasn't a tender kiss; it was raw and full of emotion. I could feel her anger, her desperation, and her hope in the glide of her tongue against mine and the feel of her fingers fisting in my hair.

My heart soared and when she finally broke away I was speechless.

"Just shut up, Cody," she whispered, the corners of her mouth turning up. "I've always been a foregone conclusion where you're concerned. The hardest part of loving isn't letting go. It's forgiving and moving on. Just consider yourself damn lucky that I'm strong enough for the both of us."

Numb

by Sheri Williams

To my family, for loving me. To the wenches, for laughing with me.

Chapter One

*J*ohan stared up at the sign above the door: Pink Ink. He stomped his feet to knock off the snow before he stepped through the door for his appointment. The first time he'd seen the shop, six months ago, he hadn't noticed the name. All he'd seen was the neon tattoo sign blinking, and he'd pulled over on a whim. Now, he was addicted. Not only to the numb feeling it gave him, and the time to let his thoughts drift as the needle worked its way across his body. It gave him time to think of Marnie.

He hoped it didn't show; he hoped she hadn't realized he didn't just come for the art anymore, but to see her. Marnie of the ever-changing rainbow hair. The woman whose tattoos were so stunning, he couldn't wait to catch the next glimpse. She wore black t-shirts, and sometimes the v-necks were dangerously low. She knew what she had was spectacular, and she didn't hide it. He had almost been caught, once or twice, staring when he shouldn't have been, but it was hard. She was so beautiful, and he couldn't help himself.

There had been little real beauty in his life before he'd met her. Planned from day one by his father, his life was never his own. "Typical whiny rich boy," the voice of the school bully replayed through his mind.

His soul lightened at the sound of her laugh.

"Hey Johan, I'll be right there," she yelled from her station.

She had a monitor above where she kept the ink, so he didn't wonder how she knew it was him. He was never late for an appointment. He sat on the big comfy couch in the front room and waited for her.

Whoever was talking in her stall made him angry. She laughed at something, and a tightness came over his chest. Jealousy. Despite having no claims on her, he couldn't stop the feelings she brought out in him. Ever since the first time he'd seen

her, his feelings had grown. He was already halfway in love
with her, and to her, he was just another customer. Granted,
he had been spending a lot of money there so he was at least a
very good customer. He still hadn't told anyone about the tattoos
that now covered one bicep and the top of his back. He was on
his second sitting for the back piece. Another six hours in close
proximity to Marnie. It was torture for Johan, but he couldn't
stop now.

Moments later, Marnie walked out, laughing with another woman. The second woman was pretty, her skin an exotic
dark color, but she paled in comparison to Marnie. The telltale
plastic wrap peeking out from under the woman's shirt revealed she was a customer.

"Ma'am." He held out his hand to the other customer.
"What kind of art did you get done tonight?"

She was eager to show it off and lifted her shirt. "Oh my
God, it's amazing, Marnie is amazing. Here, look."

The tattoo was lovely, an old wire birdcage with petite
roses. He could feel the blush creeping up the back of his neck
as a woman he didn't know stood there with her shirt up, casually showing him the underside of one of her breasts.

His face was getting warm and he backed up a few steps.
He cleared his throat. "That's some incredible work."

In his pocket, his phone vibrated. Thank God, he
thought, saved. Holding his phone up with an apologetic smile,
he went outside into the biting cold.

"I'll be ready for you in a minute," Marnie called after
him.

The cold calmed him as he looked at his phone. He
wanted to be furious but all he felt was rejected. He had known
it was coming, deep in the back of his mind. It still hurt though.
To be groomed for only one thing your whole life, and then
to have it snatched away. It hurt. He was a failure; this newest
development proved it. Sliding his phone back in his pocket, he
walked into the warmth of the studio. The other customer must
have left out the side door as he didn't see her. Marnie sat at the
counter flipping through a magazine.

She looked up as he came in. Something in his face must

have alerted her to his troubles. She gave him a quick hug, and smiled. "We're at that point, yeah? You look like you need a hug."

Johan couldn't say anything. The contact had been brief but electrifying. He was afraid he might stutter if he tried to talk.

One eyebrow arched, she took him by the hand. "You ready for your session or do you need a minute?"

He had to stop himself from physically shaking off the stupor her touch had caused. "I'm okay. I can start now."

Marnie held his hand, and walked him around the counter, back to her private stall. He kept his eyes on their hands, still locked together. How could she not feel the electricity jumping between them? Maybe it was all in his head. Maybe it was nothing more than her just being friendly to a customer.

He knew the drill. He pulled his shirt off, and sat backwards in the chair. He wrapped his long arms around the back of the chair so Marnie could work on the scroll across his upper back.

She chatted as she normally did, but he couldn't hear a word she was saying. His body was still in overdrive from all the physical contact. With all the upheaval in his life lately, he hadn't been touched by a woman in a long while.

His brain snapped back to reality when she laid her hand on his shoulder. "Hey, you've not heard a word I've said, have you, Johan? Off in space?"

He turned to look at her, and found her all set up and ready to start. "Sorry, Marnie. I have a lot on my mind. I'm ready."

He dug his chin into the back of the chair and prepared himself for the first sting of the needle. Tattoos were amazing. They hurt like crazy at first but after a few minutes, the numbness takes over. He had started simply. A small Valkyrie on his shoulder. Since then, he had been back to get the lines from his favorite Poe writing on his opposite inner bicep. For two months he had been working on the scroll across his shoulders that held his family motto. It struck him odd getting a permanent reminder of his family after that phone call.

All of sudden, he was drawn from his thoughts by a crash of something metal, and Marnie swearing a blue streak.

"What happened?" He moved to get up, but her hand flew up in the middle of her kneeling amongst the mess.

"Sorry, Johan. A stupid fucking spider crawled over my toe."

Untangling himself from the chair, he knelt down next to her. They each grabbed at the paper towels to clean up the spilled ink at the same time, fingers bumping. He laughed and backed off. "Sorry. Here, you get the ink, I'll get the bowls."

Marnie wiped all the ink off the tiles, the best she could without a mop, sat back on her haunches, and watched him get all the tiny ink cups that littered the floor. Her grin was fast. "So quick to help. I wish all my clients were so considerate."

With a handful a clear plastic cups in his hand, he sat back, mirroring her position. "I was raised to be a gentleman, ma'am."

Another giggle broke from Marnie's lips as he tipped an invisible hat.

The rest of the session went smoothly. He let his mind shut down as she finished the piece on his back. When she was done, he stood, fighting against the need to roll his shoulders and get the stiffness out. Marnie wrapped his shoulders with the plastic wrap. "Now you remember what to do, right?" she asked. "I don't have to give you the proper care spiel again?"

He pulled his shirt back on gingerly, wincing a bit as he moved his shoulders against the fabric. "No ma'am, I remember."

She patted him low on his shoulder as they headed out of the small room into the main area. "Such a responsible guy you are, Johan. I'd ask if you ever loosened up, but I guess the tats give me that answer."

Johan hung back a few steps, letting Marnie walk ahead and to his left, fighting his urge to stare at her behind. Suddenly, she skidded and toppled right into him. "Son of a fucking, cock-sucking whore. My fucking shoe."

Johan let out a grunt as his newly tattooed shoulder hit the wall behind him.

He froze.

He was absolutely certain it had been an accident, and he wasn't going to say anything, but damn. Her hand was on his dick. And it was rising, fast. He all but shoved her off of him and stood up, holding out an arm for her to steady herself.

As she held on to him with one hand, she took her now broken shoe, and threw it across the room. "Shit, those were my favorite shoes."

Johan didn't say anything. He was still willing his erection to go away. Hoping she wouldn't notice.

Marnie let go of his arm and inched closer to hug him before he could protest. "Sorry. I can't believe the night I'm fucking having. I really loved those shoes."

He held her back, he didn't want her to feel his arousal. "Hey, we all have bad days now and then."

She let him go and bent over to take off her other shoe. When she stood up, she was a good couple of inches shorter than before. He towered over her, and it was one more thing about her that turned him on. She was short, but all plush and curvy.

He knew he should say something, but wasn't sure what. Three times tonight she had touched him in a very familiar way, and it had really taken its toll on him.

The silence was too much. "I know a shoe place," he blurted. Marnie looked at him like he spoke a different language. "I know a place that fixes shoes. If only your heel came off, then I'm sure this guy I know could fix it."

"Oh you know a guy, huh? Should I be jealous you're spending time with another craftsman besides me?" she said with a half-smile on her face. He couldn't tell if she was serious or not. Surely she couldn't be jealous.

He walked over and picked up the red plaid high-heel shoe. The heel itself was dangling off, attached only by a few strands of the fabric that covered it. "I'll take it to him tomorrow. See what he can do."

"You'd do that for me?" she asked, approaching him again. Johan was backing up against the door, but she didn't stop until he couldn't back up any farther. "You are the sweetest man ever." Johan could see the gleam in her eye. He thought he might know what was coming. She leaned in. He turned to offer his cheek. Reaching up on her tippy toes to grab him by the chin, she kissed him full on the mouth. When she let him go, he almost slid down the door, his bones melted.

His reaction was enough to have her grinning like a loon as she backed out of his personal space. "Just the sweetest man."

Chapter Two

*J*ohan was sitting at his desk staring at the wall, waiting for something, anything to happen, when his cell phone rang. "Hello, Exports office. This is Johan." He didn't hear anything on the other end and was about to end the call when a breathy voice he didn't recognize spoke.

"What are you wearing, Johan?"

"Wha-a-a-t?" Johan stuttered and almost dropped his phone.

"I said, what are you wearing? Is it that black suit?"

He was trying to figure out how the person on the phone might possibly know anything about his wardrobe choices when there was a telltale giggle.

"Marnie...what... why are you calling?" Johan couldn't keep the shock out of his voice or the blush from creeping up the back of his neck. She wasn't even in the room with him and she was having an effect.

"I was calling to see what you were wearing, wasn't that obvious?"

Johan couldn't respond. Sitting in his air conditioned office, he was sweating as if he was in a sauna. He tried to speak, but his mouth was dry. Clearing his throat a few times, he tried again.

"Are you still there? If you really want to know, although I can't guess why you would care, I'm wearing a black business suit."

Marnie giggled. He was really growing to love that sound. "I figured as much. Belt or suspenders? What did my favorite businessman pick out today?"

This was the oddest conversation Johan could recall having. He wasn't about to stop it though. Marnie was definitely the highlight of his day.

"Belt. I never knew you were so interested in the daily attire of a lowly businessman." Johan leaned back in his chair, twirling around like a girl on the phone with her first boyfriend.

Or at least, that's what he imagined this was like.

"Well, I do have a special attachment to at least one lowly businessman, as you call him. He happens to have my favorite shoe." Her voice was teasing, but it stopped him cold mid-spin.

"Oh right, I should have known you would be wondering about that. The guy I know said Friday at the latest." Johan heard her clapping through the phone.

"That's perfect. Absolutely fucking perfect. Friday. That leads to my other reason for calling." Johan's heart started beating faster again. There was another reason? He couldn't think of anything else.

"What are you doing on Friday night?"

Johan almost fell out of his chair. Was she asking him out? No. No one ever saw anything in him. "Um…Friday is the day before Christmas Eve, right? Probably hanging at home."

"Yes! I knew it!"

Johan coughed, a little uncomfortable over her enthusiasm. Of course his life was boring. *He* was boring.

"Oh shit. Sorry. What I meant to say was, you want to come to a Christmas party? If you have nothing better to do?"

Johan's jaw dropped. She asked him out. That was what had just happened, wasn't it? His little knowledge of women was going to kill him one of these days.

"A party?" he asked. "Whose party is it?" *Please let it be a party for two at your house? Please?*

Marnie could probably hear the desperation in his voice, but he didn't care.

"Well, I throw one every year for the shop and our best customers. It's down at The Whale and The Squid on 2nd Ave. What do you think? You could bring me my fabulous shoe and we could walk down from the shop together."

Holy shit, he almost dropped the phone. "Yes," he blurted, but tried to control his excitement. He pictured her wiggling her toes as she sat on that big ugly couch in the shop's front room. "That's great. What should I wear?"

"Do you own a tux?" she asked.

"Yes ma'am, I do." He would break the tux out of mothballs if it would make her happy.

"Oh good, I'll keep that in mind for later. You don't have to dress up. Whatever you want to wear is fine."

They said their goodbyes, and Johan glanced down at the screen of his phone. Only ninety seconds. The best ninety seconds of his life. He had to physically restrain himself from dancing in his office. Probably no one would care. He was just a figurehead now. No power, only a name to keep the company family-friendly. It was Tuesday. He only had to find a way to occupy himself for three days before he got to see her again. He could continue going into the office and doing nothing, but he would be getting paid no matter what. He didn't actually have to show up. His sorry excuse for a father had given him that at least. A paycheck for life, even if it wasn't as the CEO, which was what he had always been groomed for. No. That went to a board member. His father's will left him rich, but empty in every other way.

The days dragged. He couldn't stay in his office for more than four hours at a time. He tried the gym, but his new ink kept him from everything but the treadmill. Occupying himself was impossible.

Finally, Friday arrived. He had already picked up the fixed shoe. His friend had finished repairing it early. He had chosen what he would wear after agonizing over it all week. It had gotten to the point where he had broken down and asked for help at a department store.

The man at the store had been very helpful, once Johan was able to explain the situation. He wanted to impress Marnie, but he didn't want to seem as if he had tried too hard. He landed on new black jeans, a button down white shirt, and black and white checkered suspenders. She always commented on his suspenders when he wore a pair under his suit. The pair he bought had a rockabilly feel to them. A perfect match to her red plaid heels.

By the time he made it to Marnie's, snow was falling. The snow two days before Christmas had him feeling festive. He had flowers and her shoe, both red. Pushing through the door of the shop, he saw Marnie sitting on the couch with her feet bare. She had a bright red dress on that sparkled under the soft glow of the lamp.

She stood as he closed the door.

A blush crept up the back of his neck. Sure he could hear his blood roaring, he thrust the flowers at her. She made a beautiful picture standing there in the half-light. She laughed as she took them from his hand.

"Cat got your tongue, Johan?" She sniffed the flowers. "Do I not look okay?"

"Okay?" Johan said, and walked up behind her as she tried to find something to put the flowers in. He held her shoe. "Okay is not the word I would use. Stunning maybe, beautiful as always. I brought your shoe. All fixed."

Marnie's eyes lit up as she snatched it out of his hand. "Oh, my baby. Mama has missed you."

She caught his raised eyebrow, smiled at him, and sat to put her shoes on. "What? You don't talk to your shoes? I guess it's a girl thing."

Johan found her coat and held it out for her.

She slid her arms into the sleeves. "Always the gentleman, Johan."

She stayed on his arm until they walked into the bar. Johan was bombarded by noise unlike he'd ever heard before. Almost all of his previous social experience was in business circles. Sedate affairs with lots of classical music and waiters with silver trays. The Squid and the Whale was not that. It was hot and loud, the music hitting him square in the chest, and he loved it. Marnie slipped off his arm, and waved. She shouted a name he didn't recognize and was off.

Unsure about the whole situation, Johan made his way to the bar, and ordered a whiskey and soda. He sat at the long expanse of wood, sipping on his drink until Marnie bounced back up to him.

"Sorry, an old friend. Come on, let's dance. Don't be

shy," she said into his ear, and dragged him onto the dance floor. It was a fast-paced song, and he felt awkward with Marnie grinding against him. She moved so much he didn't know what to do with his hands, itching to touch her but unsure what was appropriate, he kept his hands to his side. She kept rubbing her breasts against him but the contact was fleeting. He'd almost worked up the nerve to grab her by the hips but it was too late. The song ended and they made their way back to the bar laughing and a bit sweaty.

"I need a drink, Johan, will you grab me one? I'm gonna run to the ladies'." Johan's gaze was locked on her as she walked away. Her body was humming with energy. She was becoming like a drug to him. He couldn't get enough of her.

Turning to the bartender he ordered them new drinks. By the time she came back from the bathroom, he had drank both of them. The bartender had told him they were complimentary tonight so he figured there was no better night to break his normal two drink rule.

She had a huge grin on her face as she plopped down next to him. "Are you having fun?"

He felt a lot braver with the extra drinks in him. "It's more fun now that you're back."

"What?" she screamed over the noise of the club.

"I said, do you want to dance?" A slow song came over the speakers and he thanked every god he could think of.

The bartender placed two new drinks in front of them with a wink. Whiskey, neat for her and another whiskey and soda for him. She downed her drink in one shot.

"Shall we?" He held his hand out and pulled her onto the crowded floor. There was really no choice but to hold her close, or at least that's what he told himself. With his arms wrapped around her, and her head on his shoulder, he was in heaven. Or was it hell? The alcohol and the music worked together to bring another part of him to life. He tried to think of baseball, but that was apparently a cliché and didn't work. He didn't want her to feel his erection, to be embarrassed, but the only way to hide it would be to push her away.

"Marnie, I, uh, let's get another drink." He tried to loosen her grip around his waist, but she was holding strong. "Marnie. You're killing me. Let's go sit down."

She giggled. His discomfort amused her. His carefully imposed control snapped. He grabbed her hand and spun her around, pulling her across the dance floor. She didn't say anything as he pushed through the back door and steered her into the alleyway. He backed her against the brick wall, one hand holding both her wrists above her head as he ravaged her mouth. Johan pressed his erection into the apex of her thighs. One of her legs wrapped around his waist, pulling him closer.

Dragging his mouth from hers, he began to nibble along the curve of her throat. The sounds she made were so sexy and they spurred him on, giving him courage he didn't know he'd had. He rocked his cock against her and growled deep when he heard her answering moan.

"We need to stop," he said. "But God, if you moan like that again, I'm liable to take you right here, right now." Johan's voice had a rough edge to it. Marnie slid her leg down and pushed her wrists against his hand.

"Damn. You talk like that buddy, and I may let you fuck me right here, right now."

He let her hands go, and she reached down to grab his ass and pulled him even closer to her. "But here's the thing. My shop is two blocks away, and there is a softer, more horizontal surface and no snow."

Johan fought to control himself. He knew she was right. They were in public. At any moment, someone could come out that door and into the alley. It took every ounce of control he had, but he backed off and ran his hands through his hair. "Yes. Your shop. That's good. I'll go and get our things."

He went to grab the door handle, but she snagged one of his back pockets before he could. "Whoa there, stud. You don't really want to go in there with your little friend standing at attention, do you?" Johan looked down and found his pants still tented. Backing off hadn't calmed him down at all.

"You stay right here. I'll be back in two seconds, and then we can continue this." Marnie smacked him on the ass before she slipped through the door. While he waited for her to come back, he shivered in the cold. He dropped his head against the brick wall. What an ass he was. He had gotten so caught up in his own need he hadn't noticed that she must have been freezing. She came back quickly, ending his mental flogging. Both of their coats draped over one arm and her purse on the other.

His posture straightened up as she walked back over to him. "You must be freezing. Here, let me help you put your coat on."

Her shoulders dropped. "Oh shit, are we back to polite, Johan? I was only gone for two fucking minutes. What happened?"

"I was cold. I figured you must have been, too. What do you mean *polite?*" He couldn't understand why she sounded disappointed in him.

"Polite Johan is the guy who comes to my shop, and tries his best to not stare at my boobs no matter how low my shirt is. He's the guy who gets my shoe fixed." She had her hand on his chest, and had backed him up to the wall again. "Polite Johan is not the same guy who almost fucked me against the wall. While I like the polite version, I'd really rather have out-of-control Johan back. At least for a little while."

Chapter Three

*S*tunned into silence, all he could do was look at her. Disappointment colored her face and he hated that he put it there. Upset but still processing, he couldn't believe what she had just said. "So what you're saying, what I'm hearing, is that you are interested in me. In something happening between us. Something more than this?" He stood there waiting. Hoping she'd say anything. Give him a nod, a smile, anything to let him know that she really was interested in him. Leaning into him she wrapped one hand around his suspender and pulled herself up to kiss him on the mouth. It took his breath away. Another trademark giggle escaped as she tried to break away from the kiss and he tried to follow her with his mouth.

"I love it when you talk all proper and polite." Marnie ran her hand down his chest, and with a wicked smile on her lips, she cupped his dick. "Hmmm. Not nearly as hard as it was earlier. What can I do to bring that bad boy back to life?"

Any control Johan thought he might have left vanished. The ability to think left with the control. Grabbing her hand he ran for her shop. It was still two blocks away, but he was running on pure adrenaline and lust. Marnie had to sprint to keep up with him, her heels and his pace made it hard for her. They barely made it to the back door before Johan had her back up against a wall, his hands in her hair and his mouth on her hers.

The need to have his hands everywhere had him shaking. Only being able to get to her arms and her neck was frustrating him, until it hit him that her neck was a perfect place to be. Quick nibbles on the curve above her shoulder had her moaning.

"Hurry up," she ground out, as he took the key out of her hand and fumbled with the lock. His hands shook. She wasn't helping matters by grinding along his already-hard cock.

"Damn it. Where the hell is the hole?" Unable to hold

back the giggle, she turned to take the keys from him. It was her door; she knew where the lock was. Finally pushing into the shop, she grabbed him by the hand and pulled him toward her private stall. Feeling the wall for the light switch in the hallway, she left her room shrouded in semi-darkness. At the doorway, she spun him around and grabbed his head, pulling it down to hers.

She nipped at his bottom lip before kissing him, hard. It was quick but enjoyable work to slide off his suspenders, so she took her time with his buttons. Running her hands over his chest. The shirt stuck in his pants. Marnie tried pulling it again, this time harder, but her fingers were fumbling in her excitement.

"Help me out here. I haven't seen the whole package yet. You keep teasing me. It's time to show me what you got."

Johan had to catch his breath. It was all happening so fast. He grabbed her hands and put them on his hips. "Just give me a sec. I need to...God. You're killing me."

There was no gently pulling his open shirt out of his pants, instead it was yanked out and his pants undone while she stripped in front of him. His pants were almost down when he looked up and saw her standing there in just her bra and panties. He'd assumed she was covered in tattoos, but the reality was stunning. The floral piece on her right arm was longer than he thought and covered her from wrist to shoulder. Added to that was a cameo on her thigh and some lovely script on her ribcage. What really drew his attention though, was the angel that peeked out from the dip of her panties.

He reached out, his pants dropping to the floor, to trace the angel wings with his fingers, and watched as she shuddered. That was all he needed. He scooped her up and laid her on the table behind them. She sat up on her elbows as he lowered his head. It was so tantalizing, all that creamy white skin with the beautiful gray and black art. He had to lick it. He dipped his tongue down and she almost jumped off the table.

The sudden wave of tenderness she felt was unexpected. They had been flirting for months now, and she was just looking for a bit of release. But this, this was sweet. One of his hands stayed right under her breasts as he traced the tattoo all the way down under her panties with his tongue. He got so close to her core without actually touching it. She was already dripping wet and was sure he could feel it before he even touched her there.

"I love that I did this to you. That I could make you so wet for me." Johan kept teasing her with his tongue.

"I'm glad that makes you happy. I really and truly am, but if you don't put your mouth on me right fucking now, I'm not liable for the pain you'll suffer." The roughness in her voice was new but he appreciated it.

She lifted her hips and Johan pushed her panties down. Stepping between her thighs he held her pelvis up slightly. Her back arched as he lifted her up to his mouth, his tongue darting out to taste her for the first time. Taking his time, he explored her wet folds. Short quick licks followed by longer deeper ones had her moaning and her hips arching even more to meet his talented strokes. "Oh my God, Johan. I swear I'm about to fucking explode," Marnie said through gritted teeth, which was enough encouragement for Johan to go deeper.

He ran one finger up the length of her slit and then eased it inside her. Keeping his tongue on her, he pumped in and out with first one, and then two fingers. It only took a moment and then she came apart. Her whole body shook in spasms as she pounded one fist on the table. Johan removed his fingers as she lay limp on her tattoo table. Running his hands over her skin, now covered in goose bumps, he slid up to her head and laid a soft kiss on her collarbone.

His earlier urgency gone, he stood back, almost rocking on his heels as he looked down at her. Skin glistening with sweat, wearing nothing but a lacy black bra, and with one leg dangling off the table, she was gorgeous. "You look like art. So beautiful. I could stare at you for hours."

Marnie cracked one eye. "I was totally gonna rock your world, but now… now you are going to be screaming my name by the time we leave this room."

She sat up and pulled him to her by the waistband of his boxers. "Let's lose these. I really want to see what other talent you've been hiding."

Johan toed off his shoes and his pants, which had pooled around his ankles. Skimming her hands down his hips, she slid his boxers down and he stepped out of them as well.

Eyes wide, her mouth formed a silent 'O', and he hoped that was a good thing. Sliding off the table, she stood before him and trailed her fingers down his chest stopping only to wrap them around his hard cock. "Oh my, all this is for me?"

His cock jumped under her grasp. Johan couldn't take much more teasing. "Please, please tell me you have some form of protection? I was not at all prepared for this to happen."

Every inch of him was ready for action, but he couldn't do a thing if they weren't safe about it. He hung his head in the silence. Her hand was still wrapped around him and the feeling was exquisite. It was also painful. He needed release, and soon. With his eyes still closed, he felt her hand leave him. She rummaged around in her purse, and he opened his eyes to see her holding a silver package.

"You mean one of these?" Marnie winked at him as she tore it open and rolled it over the length of him. "I stuffed a few in my purse before I left my house."

"Thank God,' he choked out a laugh, "it's good one of us was prepared."

Standing back she smiled at him. "How do you want me? I don't care which position, I just want that bad boy inside me. Now."

He grabbed her by the hips, and she held onto his shoulders as he lifted her up. Her legs wrapped around his waist, and he drove into her in one thrust.

"Oh fuck." Marnie's voice dropped about two octaves as he filled her completely. Bracing himself against the table as he lifted her up and down, it was the perfect amount of leverage. His movements were slow and controlled, but that didn't stop him from reaching the brink of orgasm faster than he liked. One last pull of her onto him and he had to still his movements. "Marnie, I swear I can do this better, but right now I really need to cum. What can I do to get you off with me?"

Marnie ground her pussy on his cock, and he jumped in her slickness. "Oh. Oh," she groaned. "I can't see how you could do any fucking better, but if you're that close, I can get there fast." She disentangled herself from him, wobbling a bit, and another surge of lust hit him. He had done that to her. Her knees were weak because of him. She grabbed his hand and pulled him away from the table. Stepping into her, he bent his head and kissed her like his life depended on it. Like he had wanted to since the first day he'd met her.

Marnie leaned into his kiss. She snaked one hand around him to grab his ass and pull him in closer. Her fingernails digging into his ass pushed Johan to his limit. A groan broke through, and he ended the kiss and spun her around. Bending over the table, she rested her head on her arms with her ass in the air, smiled up at him, and wiggled. "How did you know?"

He stepped up behind her, his fingers gripping her hips. "I didn't know, I really fucking hoped, though." Leaning over her, he pushed her hair to one side so he could nibble on the back of her neck and whisper in her ear. "If you had any idea how many times I pictured doing this while you were working on my tattoos…." He didn't finish the thought. Instead, he lifted her up a few inches and slid into her. His need hadn't lessened any and she was still wet.

With a strength he didn't know he had, he pumped in and out. Hips slamming into her ass had her moaning. Back arched as he kept pounding, her body was taut as a bow. There was no letting up. Every thrust he got closer and closer to the explosion he knew was coming. The release he needed. Right as he was about to let go, one hand slid down and found her clit. With a tiny bit of pressure, he rubbed. Marnie bucked against him, but he never let up. His fingers and his cock pushed her to her climax. She screamed, and her pussy convulsed around his cock right as he came.

Johan stood there, a bit shell-shocked. Even though he had been the one doing it, he couldn't believe that had happened. He ran his hands up and down her back, bemused when they crossed her bra strap. She didn't say anything, and he wasn't sure if he should, so he didn't move. His cock was still twitching inside her. It felt weirdly amazing, but he needed to throw away the condom. Gingerly he drew out of her and took care of the mess. She still hadn't moved or spoken, and Johan was getting nervous again. He pulled his boxers and pants back on and walked around to the other side of the table.

Crouching down, he was surprised to see her with a giant smile on her face and her eyes a little glazed over. "Are you okay? I'm sorry I was so rough." He smoothed her hair out of her face.

Her eyes cleared a bit. A small groan slipped out as she lifted her head. "Sorry? You're sorry? That was the best sex of my fucking life. Ever. We need to do that again. A lot." Getting up, she stumbled, giggling like she always did, and held onto him for support.

Johan was shocked. Best sex ever? There was no way. He had such limited experience.

He found her panties and handed them over, then her dress. While she fixed herself, he retrieved his shirt and suspenders. Both back to rights, they stood there, the two of them, not saying anything. Johan had no idea what she was thinking, but she had liked the sex. Hell, she had said best ever, and he had to agree with her.

"So, um, would you..." Johan couldn't finish the question. He looked around the room and all he could see was him bending her over that table. The memory was only minutes old, but it still made him turn red. After what had just happened how could he still not be able to ask her out? He *could* do this. No longer feeling numb, his outlook was much brighter. And that was thanks to the beautiful woman next to him. Turning slightly, he smiled at her. "Would you go out with me sometime?"

Marnie giggled, then outright laughed. She squeezed his hand back and looked up at him, smiling. "If by go out you mean have lots of amazing sex and then maybe eat some cold Chinese take-out, then yes. I definitely want to go out with you again. And again."

Johan's jaw dropped. "Seriously?"

Marnie started to drag him out the back door. "Seriously. Asking the bartender to give me your bill was the cheapest Christmas present I have ever bought for myself."

Marnie tried to keep walking, but Johan had stopped. "You...you paid my bill? Why the hell would you do that?" His mind staggered. He wouldn't have kept ordering drinks had he known. "I thought all the drinks were free."

"What? You aren't mad are you?" She poked him in the chest. "I've been watching you drool over me for six months now. I would have had gray hair before you worked up the nerve to actually say anything, so I sort of, gave you a push." Marnie ran her hand over his cock, causing it to start pulsing against his pants. "A few drinks you didn't have to pay for and you loosened up nicely. You can't tell me you didn't have fun."

Johan looked down into her wicked smile. He could get mad. But why? He ended up exactly where he wanted to be. "I'm your Christmas present, huh?" He smiled. "Does that mean you're mine?" He closed the gap between them and kissed her, their tongues dancing as he held her close. In his pants, his cock was coming back to life. Breaking the kiss he looked for the nearest surface.

"My apartment is eight blocks away. It will take us fifteen minutes to get there." He nipped her bottom lip with his teeth. Her smile turned him on even more.

"Yeah," she said. Her smile widened. "My apartment is ten steps up. I have a very large box of condoms up there."

He grabbed her hand again. "Really? Then why are we still standing here. I feel like unwrapping my present early."

First Position

by Quenby Olson

To my husband, for showing me what a great love
should be.

Chapter One

Coffee. Therese should've stopped and grabbed a coffee before coming in to work. Her plastic water bottle crinkled in her hands. What good would plain water do for her today? Forget hydration and healthy kidneys. She needed caffeine, and plenty of it.

A loud buzz of voices greeted her as she pushed through the heavy glass doors that marked the entrance to the Southern Ohio Ballet Academy. Luca must already be here, she realized.

Inside, the halls were lined with young girls and boys. Most of them sat on the floor, the girls in black leotards and the boys in white t-shirts and black bike shorts. The girls' hair was immaculate, pinned and sprayed and twisted into neat buns and braids. Most of them had their dance bags open, piles of legwarmers and ballet slippers and granola bars spilling out onto the floor while the kids chattered and giggled with excitement.

She stepped around two girls stretching and a third buried in a mound of homework. A group of boys stood around the soda machines, half of them still dressed in their street clothes.

"Hey, Miss Therese!" one of the older boys called out, a fifteen-year-old who had yet to grow into the gangliness of his arms and legs. A couple of the other boys waved, and Therese gave them a nod in return.

She tried not to let her irritation get the better of her. It wasn't their fault she was in such a bad mood, or that she hadn't gotten more than three hours of sleep the previous night, or that she would give serious thought to tackling her grandmother for the chance at a piping hot chai latte. They were just kids. Extraordinarily talented kids who were about to get an amazing, once-in-a-lifetime opportunity.

The classroom was already full. Mirrors lined two of the four walls, while waist-high barres ran along three. Over twenty students were busy stretching, chatting in whispered voices, or adjusting the satin ribbons that crisscrossed their ankles. Therese dropped her bag on a chair and began rifling through it for her CDs and class notes. Behind her, the students shuffled to their places. The soft sound of legwarmers and sweatshirts stripped off and tossed into piles along the edges of the walls whispered. By the time she turned around again, eighteen girls and four boys, none of them over the age of seventeen, were ready to dance.

They knew the steps, but she ran through them anyway. *Plies, tendues, degage battement.* Every movement was accompanied by the sound of creaking pointe shoes, of hips and knees and ankles that popped and protested against the movement and the cold, gray weather outside.

With each exercise, the lines became longer, the positions deeper, the extensions higher.

"Come to the center, please." Their warm-up finished, a few of the dancers snagged sips of water from bottles stashed behind their clothing or tucked away on the windowsills.

Therese turned back to her notes. She didn't need them today. They were beginning rehearsals after warm-up, but she looked at the pages anyway. The words scrawled across them blurred in front of her vision as she tried not to think about the next few weeks.

Behind her, the hum of whispers and giggles rose again. Of course they were wound up, she realized. Rehearsals about to begin, the weather threatening snow, school vacations on the horizon, and then there was that eensy little matter of Luca...

The voices lifted again before almost everyone in the class stopped talking at once. Therese shut her eyes as a kind of prickling raised the goose bumps on the back of her neck. A part of her wanted to be stubborn. She would simply not turn around, wait for him to go away, and then everything would go back to normal.

Except she knew that wouldn't happen. And she was standing in a room full of mirrors, so refusing to turn around seemed like it would accomplish about as much as breaking out an umbrella during a hurricane.

She set down her notes. She raised her chin. She didn't turn around.

"Marzipan variation," she called out, while she picked up the remote for the CD player and began searching through the music. "Boys, you can take a break. Girls? I want you to separate into groups of four, please."

The four boys grabbed their things and shuffled out of the room, past the man in the doorway. Therese glanced at the mirror nearest to her, and bit her lip. Luca was still in his coat, a heavy black wool thing that boasted the glint of a few raindrops—or melted snowflakes, even—on the arms and shoulders. There was a thick, blue muffler wrapped around his neck, and his gloves...

She looked away again. What was she doing, looking at his clothes? Stalling, that's what she was doing. She waited for the girls to line up, for the first group to step into the center of the room, and then she pressed play.

The dancers moved through the variation, shaky at first, but gaining more confidence as they went along. Therese knew they were nervous. They were being watched. They were being watched by one of the greatest dancers of the last fifty years, so no doubt they weren't exactly keen on making a mistake in front of him.

While the girls switched groups, Therese chanced another glance in the mirror. This time, she ignored his clothes, and instead she looked at him.

Goodness gracious, she needed some coffee.

Luca looked older than she remembered. Well, of course he looked older. What did she expect? That he would remain in some sort of physical stasis for the seven years since she had last seen him?

His hair, a dark brown that could almost be mistaken for black was longer than he used to wear it. His eyebrows still cut the same straight creases of shadow above brown eyes, and the lines that fanned out from the corners…

Well, there were actually lines there now. And also lines flanking his mouth, deeper than the dimples she knew were there when he brought out his smile. And she remembered that smile, and how often he'd switched it on to better charm the women he danced with.

But not her, of course. She had always seemed to be the exception to the rule.

Therese glanced away again, and gave her attention to the quartet of dancers in front of her. They were behind the music, struggling to stay on top of it. So she began to count for them, pushing them along, and all while tossing out corrections and compliments together. She wanted them to do well. They were her students, and when the group finished the variation in perfect unison, she felt a swift rush of pride.

The last group stepped forward to dance. The music began again, and the soft sound of pointe shoes striking the floor underscored Tchaikovsky's melody. Therese chanced one more glance in the mirror, and she caught Luca's gaze then, focused on her.

She turned away. She could feel the perspiration on her hands, making the remote for the CD player slick. The girls continued to dance, every movement precise, not a single ounce of energy wasted.

"Very good," Therese found herself saying once the final group had relaxed out of their last poses and were wiping the sweat from their faces. "I think some of you have partnering class next? So I'll let you go, give you all five minutes to catch your breath."

The girls greeted this news with broad smiles, some of them already laughing as they grabbed their things and ran towards the door.

"Thank you, Miss Therese!" one of the younger students called out, before ducking around Luca and skipping into the hallway.

Therese turned back to the CD player. One by one, she gathered up her things: CDs, notes, the second bottle of water she'd dragged from the bottom of her bag. She had another class in the second studio, and she wanted to have a chance to pop into the restroom before…

Her thoughts were interrupted by the sound of footsteps behind her. All of a sudden, the chattering of the students in the other parts of the building seemed to be a thousand miles away, and all she could hear was each step, one after the other.

She picked up her bag and slung the strap over her shoulder. Perhaps she could pretend that she didn't remember him. It would be a long shot, but it had been seven years, and they had only danced together that one time...

"*Miss* Therese?"

His voice... Okay, forget coffee. What she needed was something infused with a healthy amount of alcohol. His accent was subtle, but there was no denying the warmth of his Florentine upbringing that made his voice somehow richer.

"Vasily insisted on the titles," she said, referring to the school's partnering and men's class instructor. "It's the same for all the teachers." Her gaze again drifted toward his face and then back to the buttons on his coat. His jaw, she noticed, had shed the roundness of youth, and everything about his face seemed to be made of angles now, rather than the softer lines of a man only a few years into adulthood. "He thinks it makes the students respect us more."

"Ah, Vasily." Luca rubbed his jaw with the back of his hand, the corners of his mouth turning upward, revealing a deep dimple in his cheek. "He's old school."

"Very much so," she admitted, while resisting the urge to smile along with him. For goodness' sake, less than twenty words of conversation and he made her feel like she was eighteen years old all over again. But she remembered being eighteen, and it was definitely not an era in her life she had any interest in revisiting. "Well, I guess I should thank you for agreeing to come here and be the Cavalier in our Nutcracker. Our oldest boy is only fifteen years old, and he's small for his age, so I doubt he'd be able to lift any of the girls onto his shoulders. At least not without seriously hurting himself."

Luca's smile faded a little. "It's no trouble. I'm about to have more time on my hands soon, so when your director came to me about helping to fill out your cast, I didn't have to give it more than a moment's thought."

"That's very kind of you, and I know the kids are looking forward to the experience of sharing the stage with you."

Therese readjusted her bag and gave him a polite nod, the kind intended to put a cap on the end of the conversation. "Well, it was nice seeing you again, Mr. Durante, but if you'll excuse me, I'm almost late for another class."

He put his hand on her arm, beneath the cuff of her sweatshirt, so that his fingers grazed the bare skin of her wrist. "What's this? Mr. Durante? You used to call me Luca."

"That was a long time ago," she said, and pulled her arm away from him. "I was just a kid, and you were..." An artist? A charmer? A conceited bastard with an ego the size of a small nation? "Excuse me," she said again, and ducked her head before walking away from him.

As she left the room, she sought out her wrist with her other hand, her fingers skimming the area where he'd touched her. Seven years, she reminded herself. It had been seven years since any part of him had come in contact with any part of her.

So why, she wondered, did that single touch feel so familiar on her skin?

Chapter Two

*S*even years, she thought to herself. Seven years ago, she had danced with Luca Durante.

As an apprentice member of the American Ballet Company, she had taken classes with him for months, but she'd rarely spoken to him. He had always been a little too far above her, and a bit too charismatic to spend time on a quiet thing like her.

While she stood in the back, never putting herself forward, never making waves, he did everything he could to be seen as well as heard. She'd watched him argue with company directors, with dancing partners, even nearly coming to blows with the conductor of the local philharmonic orchestra when Luca threatened to shove the man's baton where only a surgeon would be able to retrieve it. He had a reputation as a hotheaded perfectionist, a reputation he took great care to defend.

Of course, when he wasn't picking a fight with someone, he was charming them. Especially women. He knew exactly what to say, how to act, and most of them—the ones who hadn't already sworn off ever standing in the same room with him again—melted like butter when faced with that gorgeous smile.

Well, all except for her. She'd seen him flirt and laugh with the other girls, watched him layer on the compliments so thick that she'd rolled her eyes at his behavior. But never once had he tried any of it on her.

And it had stung, she had to admit. She'd been eighteen years old, a brand new apprentice plucked from a round of national auditions, and her self-esteem didn't take kindly to the fact that while he sweet-talked all her fellow dancers, he hadn't bothered to send even a hint of a smile in her direction.

Therese shook her head at the memory, her morning cup of coffee clutched in her hand. She raised the rim to her nose and breathed in the scent of it as she shouldered her way through the glass doors, cutting her off from the wind and light snow that whirled across the sidewalk.

Only twelve hours had passed since Luca's arrival the

evening before as Therese made her way to the office amid groups of kids huddled inside their sweatshirts, yawns stretching their sleepy faces, some of them even using their dance bags as makeshift pillows as they curled up for a quick nap before their first Saturday class.

The office was bright with artificial light, while the hum of a microwave oven was the first thing to reach Therese's ears.

"Morning!" Audrey, one of the administrative assistants—and one of the few to agree to work on a blustery Saturday morning—piped up from her place in front of her computer. "Do you want some oatmeal? I'm heating up water for a second cup."

Therese shook her head and brandished the steaming cup of coffee in her hand. "No, thanks. Breakfast of champions, right here." She sidestepped around boxes of printer paper, stacks of posters and old programs, and a broken desk chair to get to the wall of cubbies that housed the teachers' mail and various bits of paperwork. She picked up her paycheck, dropped it into her bag, and was about to leave the office when Audrey waved her over to her side of the room.

"So, have you seen him yet?" Audrey's eyes gleamed as she stirred her instant oatmeal.

Therese took a sip of coffee and winced when the hot liquid scalded her tongue. "Who?" The moment she said it, she regretted it. She could play stupid all she wanted, but everyone here knew she had a history with Luca. "Oh, you mean Mr. Durante? Um, yeah. He was here last night, I think."

"I heard he's taking class today," Audrey said, her words carried on a dreamy sigh.

"Is he?" Therese's fingers tightened around her cup. Not her class. Please, not her class...

"Not until later this afternoon, though. He and Julia have rehearsal with Vasily at the end of the day."

Therese released a breath she hadn't realized she was holding. "Ah, well then. I have rehearsals with the beginner and intermediate groups all afternoon, so I guess I'll miss him."

"Shame, that." Audrey shook her head as she blew across a spoonful of steaming oatmeal. "But do you think he's going to be difficult?"

"Who? Mr. Durante?"

"Yeah, you know his reputation. And I heard he's not with the National Ballet Company anymore. Rumor is they refused to renew his contract."

Therese cleared her throat and took another sip of superheated coffee. "No," she said around a mouthful of pain. "I hadn't heard that."

"And I saw him talking with Bruce last night," Audrey went on, referring to the ballet school's director. "Whatever they were discussing, it seemed pretty serious."

"Maybe Bruce was asking for advice about expanding the school," Therese said. "You know he's been talking about adding on, growing into a professional company attached to the school for years now. Luca would probably have some advice about that."

"Maybe." Audrey straightened in her chair, a dollop of oatmeal sliding off her spoon and plopping back into the bowl. "But you've worked with him before, right? So… what was he like?"

Therese glanced at the office door, only a few steps away. She knew this would happen. As soon as the announcement came that Luca Durante would be their guest artist for this season's production of The Nutcracker, she knew she would spend half her time fielding questions about what it had been like to dance with him, to have known him while he was still a rising star.

"He's…" She cleared her throat again, finished it with half a shrug. "He's a perfectionist, that's all."

"Is that all?" Audrey slumped down again and began stirring her rapidly congealing breakfast. "Oh, before you go, I need your RSVP for the fundraiser next week."

"Next week?" Therese blinked, feeling stupid. "It can't be time for that already, can it?"

"Seven days from today." Audrey tilted her head towards the calendar pinned to the wall. "I expect to see you in high heels and something sparkly. And your hair cannot be pulled back into anything that even slightly resembles a ponytail."

Therese sighed. Every year, in the weeks leading up to the Nutcracker, the school and the local theater joined forces to raise money to help support their projects for the future months. For the last two years, Therese had managed to wiggle out of attending, but the administrative staff—Audrey in particular— were not going to allow her to make it three for three.

"I'll be there," Therese said, as if the words were pulled out of her with a pair of tongs.

"Good." Audrey settled back in her chair, satisfied. "And no scrunchies!" she warned, before shoving a spoonful of congealed oatmeal in her mouth.

Chapter Three

Therese set her coffee on top of the CD player and dropped her bag on the floor at her feet. She took a deep breath, in and out, and then again, before rolling her shoulders backwards. A few weeks. That's how long Luca would be here. And then the performances would be over, and he would be gone from her life, probably forever.

She shook her head, chiding herself. As if he'd ever really been a part of her life to begin with.

Her notes were in a crumpled ball at the bottom of her bag. She dug them out, smoothed the pages, and spread them flat beside her coffee cup. Then, she reached for a bottle of Tylenol, shook a few into her hand, and washed them down with another scalding sip of coffee. Her knee had already begun to twinge this morning, and the first class hadn't even started yet. Probably stress, she thought. A career-ending injury had a tendency to flare up at times like these. And when it was cold. Or damp. Or any day of the week ending in a "y."

Behind her, the students finished up their pre-class stretches and conversations. Therese was so engrossed in her own thoughts that she didn't hear one of the students say her name.

"Miss Therese?"

She glanced over her shoulder and saw a group of girls, advanced students, trying to snag her attention.

"What is it?" she asked as she walked over to them.

The girls looked at each other, all of them sharing a smile and a few of them giggling before their spokesperson, Rebecca, swatted playfully at the others and stepped forward.

"Miss Therese, is it true you danced with Mr. Durante?"

Here we go…

"Yes," Therese said, and stifled a sigh before it could drag down her shoulders. "Yes, I did. But only once."

"Well, what happened?"

Therese licked her lips. It had been such a long time ago,

or so she told herself, even while every detail remained crystal clear. "There was a workshop," she began. "I was eighteen years old, an apprentice with the National Ballet Company, but one of the leads got sick—fever, chills, the whole deal—and I...I was asked to step in."

"Why you?" one of the other girls, Sarah, ventured to ask. "If you were just an apprentice..."

Therese shrugged. That part had always remained a mystery to her, as well. "I don't know. But I knew the part. I had rehearsed it in class a hundred times. We all had, but for some reason, they asked me."

Rebecca leaned forward. "And so you and Mr. Durante...?"

"Yes." Therese nodded once. "Romeo and Juliet. I knew the solo variations, but I had never learned the pas de deux. You know the one, from the famous balcony scene? So I was called in to an emergency rehearsal, and they taught it to me in a few hours. And then it was showtime."

"And?" This, from Rebecca. "That can't be it. What was it like to dance with him?"

What could she say? They had heard all the stories, that Luca Durante had a temper, that he was notoriously difficult to work with, that there were some female dancers who absolutely refused to share the same stage with him.

But that hadn't been her experience. From the first moment she'd stepped toward him, his hands gliding across her skin, her body curving against his...

"It was nothing remarkable," she said, and watched the girls' excitement deflate at her words. "In fact, I hardly remember much about it."

"And then you hurt your knee, right?" Rebecca's question sounded so innocent, so matter-of-fact. But Therese's breath still hitched.

"Yes," she said. "In class, a few days later. And because of that, I am now your teacher and not some famous ballerina currently performing in Paris or Rome." She attempted a smile, and tried to inject as much humor into her voice as she could manage. "So go to the barre. It's almost time to start."

It was then she realized how quiet the classroom around her had become. She knew, before she even turned around, that he was there. A glance over her shoulder confirmed it. Luca stood at the side of the room, her side of the room, a black gym bag slung over his shoulder.

He was dressed for class, she realized. Gone were the designer coat and the expensive shoes. Clad in old sweats and warm-up clothes, he looked like any other student in the room. Except... he didn't. No one else had that same aura of self-assurance, of easy confidence that Luca wore as comfortably as a second skin.

A dozen thoughts flitted through her head as she watched him set down his bag and prepare for class. The most prominent one was that he wasn't even supposed to be here. Hadn't Audrey said he wouldn't be in until later this afternoon? His first rehearsal wasn't scheduled until four o'clock, so why would he show up now, and in her class?

She returned to the front of the room, jammed the CD into the tray, and jabbed at the buttons on the remote. "First position," she said without preamble. Another button pressed, and the music began.

The students knew all the combinations. She went through nothing for Luca's benefit, leaving him to follow the kids on either side of him. It was cruel of her, she knew it, but his unexpected presence in her class had so rattled her that she didn't trust herself to even run through the sequences correctly.

For the first ten minutes, she kept to the left side of the classroom, away from Luca. The other students had given him a large amount of space in which to work, and so it was easy for her to simply avoid him. But when she saw Rebecca, only one place away from Luca at the barre, struggling over a complicated step, she drew in a deep breath and moved to the other side of the room.

"Here, like this," Therese said, as she went through the combination again with Rebecca. She watched the girl's progress as she reversed the step, but all the time, she could feel Luca's eyes on her, like a faint prickling of awareness that raised the hairs on the back of her neck. "Okay, other side."

She remained where she was, near Rebecca, but this time, Luca had his back to her, allowing her to watch him.

He had stripped out of his sweats and gym pants, she realized, and was down to only a pair of bike shorts and a sleeveless shirt. The thin white cotton of the shirt stretched across the muscles of his back and shoulders as he moved, and her gaze latched onto the tattoos she hadn't seen yesterday, hidden by his heavy coat and scarf.

One circled his left bicep, while another, a design she couldn't quite identify, peaked out above the collar of his shirt, between his shoulder blades. Her eyes traveled down then, along the narrowing of his waist, over his hips, and along the taut muscles of his thighs. She swallowed quickly, and wondered how anyone could think of ballet being a feminine art, when it took only a single glance at Luca to recognize the amount of control that was necessary to keep so much strength and power in check.

The music ended, and the dancers relaxed. Therese heard their rapid breathing and saw several of them reach for water bottles or for towels to wipe the sweat off their necks and faces. Luca turned around, his own dark hair soaked with perspiration, his shirt clinging to the lines of his chest. She waited for him to say something, anything, but the only change in him was a slight lift of his right eyebrow as he looked at her.

"Right," she said, her mouth dry. "Let's see that one again."

Chapter Four

herese glanced at the windows. The sun had set an hour
or so before, but she could make out the faint glow of
the street lights through the wet panes of glass. If she held her
breath, she could hear the sharp strike of sleet on the panes. As
much as she loved The Nutcracker, she despised the weather
that often came along with it.

She grabbed her bag and switched off the lights in the
room. The last of the students had gone home for the day, and
only Luca and Julia, their Sugarplum Fairy, remained with Vasily in one of the smaller classrooms. Even through the walls, she
could hear the music. The pas de deux from Act Two, between
the Sugarplum Fairy and her Cavalier.

The hallway, stuffed with children and teenagers only a
few minutes before, was now deserted. There were bobby pins
scattered across the carpet, along with the wrappers from candy
bars and a few empty potato chip bags. She shook her head and
began picking up the mess, along with a couple of stray pointe
shoes and a lone legwarmer she tossed into the lost and found.

Her keys were already in her hand when she walked
past the last classroom, the lights and music spilling out into the
hall. She was going to walk straight through the door, across
the parking lot, get into her car, and drive home. That was her
plan. And then, she raised her chin, and looked toward the open
classroom door, and her carefully laid plan fell apart before it
even had a chance.

She stood outside the doorway, her gaze switching between the mirrors and the two dancers reflected in them.

"Again," Vasiliy said, and tapped his cane on the floor.
"Again, again, again. Until it is right."

The music started over from the beginning. Julia stepped
forward, her long legs seeming even longer beneath the stiff,
white tutu she wore. Luca came up behind her as she moved
into a pirouette. He would put his hands on her waist, Therese
knew, playing out the choreography in her mind. She would

continue to turn, and then he would lift her, as if she weighed nothing, and carry her halfway around the room before setting her down on the tips of her right toes.

At least, that's what was supposed to happen. Julia went into the pirouette, but the timing was wrong. The lift quickly fell apart, and Vasiliy turned off the music, leaving only the sound of Luca's cursing to fill the room.

"You're anticipating everything," Luca growled, running his hands through his sweat-soaked hair. "You're supposed to wait for me, not try to do all of it on your own!"

Julia looked down at her shoes. Therese followed the girl's gaze. They had been rehearsing for several hours already, and Therese thought she could see blood from Julia's overworked feet staining the pale pink satin. "I'm sorry," Julia muttered, her voice quiet.

Therese bit her lip. Julia was a strong dancer, a strong young woman, but being in the presence of someone like Luca was apparently too much for her.

"You have to trust me," Luca said, his voice still irritable. "Or this is never going to work!"

"Well, what do you expect?" Therese took a step forward before she realized what she was doing. "She's seventeen years old," she said, gesturing to an exhausted Julia. "Her only dance partners so far have been young boys who barely have the guts to touch her, let alone the strength to lift her over their heads. So of course she's trying to do it all on her own. She doesn't know anything different."

Luca's eyes blazed. They seemed to grow darker when he was angry, and yet there was a gleam in them that had probably sent other people running the other way. But Therese wasn't about to turn tail and shuffle back the way she'd come.

"This is your first rehearsal," Therese pointed out. "She needs more time."

"She doesn't need more time. She needs to listen—"

"To what? You yelling corrections at her? And that's going to make her trust you, after you berate her—"

"I'm not berating her!" Luca snapped. His accent, she noticed, grew thicker when he was irate. "I'm simply trying to tell her—"

"Talk, talk, talk," Therese interrupted, her own voice growing louder. "Words won't help you here. You can't simply tell someone to trust you, and you can't expect someone to fall completely in synch with you the first time you dance together. It doesn't happen like that."

He exhaled slowly as he ran his fingers through his hair a second time. But his eyes never left her face. "I disagree," he said, his voice lower now, as if he were speaking only to her and there was no one else in the room. "Sometimes… sometimes it does."

Therese opened her mouth to speak, then closed it again. She didn't know what had come over her. She never raised her voice. She never got angry, but for some reason, Luca was able to show up and, in only one day, bring out some shouty, temperamental version of herself. "I'm sorry," she said, and finally tore her eyes away from him. "I-I was just leaving."

She turned to go, desperate to slip away before she made any more of a spectacle of herself, but Vasily spoke up before she'd taken three steps toward the door.

"No, no. You come back," he said in his imperfect English. "You help us."

But she didn't want to help. She wanted to stick to her plan. Leave building. Get in car. Drive home. Snarf down half a container of ice cream with a potato chip for a spoon.

And then… she remembered Julia. Whether Luca brought out the worst in her or not, Therese couldn't run away and leave one of her best students in the lurch.

"All right," she said, and turned on her heel. "What do you need?"

"You do this," Vasily said, gesturing vaguely to the room around them. "Show her how to move through the steps, how to allow him to catch her."

Therese's lips parted as realization struck. "Oh, oh. You want me to dance…" She glanced at Luca. His expression was guarded, giving nothing away. "I'm not… I mean, I'm not dressed for it. And my shoes…"

"No matter." Vasily waved away her arguments with a

quick flick of his hand. "You'll do well."

"Okay, then." Therese heaved a sigh and dropped her bag against the wall. She stepped out of her sneakers, pulled her sweatshirt off over her head, and searched through her bag until she found a barrette for her hair.

She thought she would feel cold in nothing but a tank top and leggings, but the air in the room carried a touch of humidity. Inside her chest, her heart thudded against her ribs. She pulled in a deep breath, and then another.

And then one more, for good measure.

"From the pirouette," Vasily said from his place at the front of the room, and then he gestured toward Julia. "Come. You watch, you see how to do it."

Therese wiped her palms down the front of her leggings. She hadn't even taken a single step, and already she was sweating everywhere. What was she thinking? This was stupid. How was this going to help Julia? And Luca, she hadn't danced with him for years. Seven years, and they were supposed to simply—

He placed his hand on her waist. It was the lightest of touches, but she had an overwhelming urge to lean in to that touch, to feel his fingers press more firmly against her body.

Vasily began to strike the floor with the end of his cane in a steady rhythm. "And five, six, seven, eight!"

There was no music. Only the sound of Vasily's counting, of his cane tapping on the floor. Therese moved, feeling too cautious at first. She didn't dance anymore, at least not more than demonstrating the occasional step for one of her classes. Her arms were stiff, and when she began the pirouette, she wasn't certain if she would be able to stay balanced.

But then Luca was behind her, his hands on her waist, his fingers fanning out above her hips. For a moment, she shut her eyes, took a breath, and allowed the room to disappear around her.

She didn't need to think. They moved from the pirouette into the lift, and then his hands were at her back, and the world turned upside down before he set her on her feet again. The next step came, and then the next, and before they finished, he held out his hand to her, his fingers beckoning.

Trust me.

He said it, not with words, but with every part of him. She remembered how it had felt seven years ago, when she had been scared and so, so nervous, an apprentice filling in for an experienced member of the company. And he'd held out his hand to her then, and she'd let herself fall into him.

She breathed, and placed her hand in his.

There was a gentle squeeze to her fingers, and she thought she noticed something like relief course through him. But then they were moving into the final step, and she didn't have time to dwell on it.

Another turn, his arm around her waist, and then he tipped her backward. Her back arched over his forearm, and yet he held onto her as if it were the easiest thing.

A second passed, maybe two, and then Luca helped her stand up again. He was too close to her, she thought. She could smell him, the tang of his soap mixed with a day's worth of sweat. And she could hear his labored breathing, could even feel it, stirring the hair above her right ear. His hands were still on her ribs, his thumbs tracing the low-cut back of her top, grazing her bare skin. For a moment, he pulled her toward him, her back against his front, until all she could feel was the rise and fall of his breathing together with the rapid beating of his heart.

"Well done," he whispered in her ear, his mouth so close to her skin that a shiver went through her.

"Aha!" Vasily clapped his hands together in satisfaction. "You see?" He gestured to the two of them, while beside him, Julia nodded enthusiastically. "Like two halves of whole. That is how you must be."

Chapter Five

Therese stood inside the hotel's main entrance, still huddled in her coat and scarf. Behind her, the doors swung open, letting in a draft of cold air that raised a fresh layer of goose bumps on her bare legs.

She could be at home, she thought. Warm and cozy in her fleece pajamas, while she ate take-out Chinese food and watched a marathon of mind-numbing action movies. But instead she had braved the sub-freezing temperatures, in a little black dress she'd dragged out from the back of her closet, and a pair of strappy high heels that had still boasted the original price sticker from when she'd bought them over a year ago.

After checking her coat, she made her way toward the banquet room, further into the hotel. She passed several other doors, and one room that appeared to have housed a wedding reception earlier that day. The space rented out by the ballet school was decorated with twinkle lights, Christmas trees that bore ornaments boasting various donors' names, and displays of antique Nutcrackers and wooden toys.

Therese dodged a waiter carrying a silver tray of empty champagne flutes, and sidestepped her way toward a table of edible delicacies. She nibbled on a piece of marzipan, and eyed a tower of petit fours made to look like miniature Christmas gifts.

The room buzzed with conversation, but Therese kept herself off to one side. She didn't know most of the people here, these wealthy patrons of the arts. She had never been one to socialize much, her evenings and weekends eaten up by her teaching duties at the school. Grabbing another piece of marzipan and a glass of champagne from a different waiter, she began a slow circuit of the room, her gaze sweeping over the mingled guests.

"Oh, you made it!" came a voice from behind her, and she turned to see Audrey, decked out in a gorgeous gold cocktail dress with ruby drop earrings glittering from her ears.

"You look great!" Therese said, after quickly swallowing

the last of her marzipan.

"You mean this old thing?" Audrey did a little half-turn and raised her hand to her head to primp her curled hair. "How often do we get to dress up, honestly? I wasn't going to pass on an opportunity to show off my best duds." She stepped back, and looked Therese over from head to toe. "But what about you? I can't remember the last time I saw your legs. And your lipstick! I just love that color on you."

Therese ducked her head before a blush could flood her cheeks. She didn't realize that so many years of wearing nothing but sweatshirts and scrunchies would be enough to make people goggle at her when she swiped on a bit of mascara. "Thanks," she said. "So, have I missed anything important?"

"Not at all," Audrey told her, and took a sip of champagne from her own glass. "Unless you find listening to other people talk about their golf vacations to be scintillating conversation."

Therese made a face. "No, I think I'll pass."

"Good idea. But there is the auction coming up in a few minutes, and I know Bruce is planning some sort of announcement or presentation about the school. Something to do with Mr. Durante, I think."

Therese pulled in a sharp breath. In the back of her mind, she had known that Luca would be here tonight, but it wasn't something she had allowed her thoughts to dwell on for any length of time.

It had been a week since their demonstration in Vasily's rehearsal. For an entire week, she had not spoken to him. And yet he seemed to seek out her classes, never drawing any attention to himself, keeping to the back of the room, working silently, and then leaving again as soon as she dismissed her students.

He wasn't avoiding her, if he made a point to take one of her classes every day. But he hadn't made any attempt to speak to her, and she had to admit she wasn't doing much to approach him, either.

And what was she supposed to say if she did? *Gee, Luca. When you touch me, it's like the world stops and I can hardly breathe for wanting to feel more of your skin against mine. Why do you think that is?*

She closed her eyes for a moment and drained the last of the champagne from her glass. Classical music had begun to play from somewhere, and just when she thought about sneaking back to the hors d'oeuvre table for another handful of treats, she caught a glimpse of Luca, all the way on the other side of the room.

He was dressed in an impeccable suit, all black, with only the hint of a white dress shirt peeking out from beneath his buttoned jacket and tie. The tailoring accented his height, along with the breadth of his shoulders and the lean lines of his hips and thighs.

Therese watched him, all smiles and easy confidence as he chatted with Bruce Jordan, the school's artistic director. He gestured with his hands, and she imagined the movement of his muscles beneath the layers of fabric, the patterns of the tattoos that he kept hidden away under his everyday clothes.

For a moment, she thought he had spotted her across the room, but she ducked behind Audrey and turned her face away before his dark gaze found her.

"Excuse me for a minute," Therese said to Audrey, and plopped her glass on a waiter's empty tray as he whisked past her. "I'm going to use the ladies', and then I'll…" She waved her hands in a vague gesture, hoping Audrey would finish the thought with whatever she liked.

"Of course. See you at the auction!" Audrey called out as Therese slipped behind a group of older guests and began to make her way toward the doors.

Once outside of the banquet room, she took a moment to breathe. She should be able to face him, she thought. It wasn't her fault that her body had gone traitor and decided to become infatuated with Luca after only a few minutes of dancing together.

But that wasn't exactly true, she reminded herself as she walked through the hotel. She passed the ladies' room and ducked into the deserted banquet room she'd seen earlier, the one that still boasted swathes of tulle and a mass of crepe paper bows and leftover wedding favors.

The room was dark, but the light that poured in from the hall behind her was more than enough with which to see where she was going. Round tables were still set up throughout the room, and she moved through them quickly enough, until she arrived at another set of doors that opened onto an empty brick courtyard.

She checked to make sure it wasn't an emergency exit before she pushed through the doors and into the cold, outside air. The chill was a shock at first, but she ran her hands up and down her bare arms, while her breath escaped from her mouth in puffs of steam.

The hotel's lights were too bright for her to see any of the stars, but she tilted her head back anyway, the thought of knowing they were there helping her to breathe more easily.

Her mind had been a jumble of confused thoughts ever since Luca had arrived. For so many years, she'd successfully managed to push him to the back of her mind. Except when her knee twinged. Or when she heard a bit of Tchaikovsky's Romeo and Juliet playing somewhere. Or when...

Okay, so not quite as successful as she'd hoped.

The first time she'd danced with him was a memory so vivid, it was as if it had burned into her mind. From the first moment he had touched her, it was nothing short of electric. But yet it had been more than that. She'd only been eighteen at the time, but she recognized the attraction she felt, how it left her breathless every time his hands moved over her body.

"Juliet," she sighed. To Luca's Romeo.

And then, two days after the performance, she'd twisted her knee while taking class. What was supposed to have been a minor injury sidelined her for months. And that was before the physical therapist's final prognosis was delivered.

The joint couldn't handle the strain of a full-time career in dance. She would either have to quit, or risk a surgery that would guarantee she'd never be able to set foot in a classroom, even to teach. And so she quit, and she didn't see Luca again.

Chapter Six

Therese wrapped her arms around her upper body and took a deep breath, the cold air filling her sinuses and making her shiver all over again. She didn't know how long she'd been out here. Twenty minutes? An hour? Even with the heat lamps that lined the courtyard, she knew she would have to go back inside at some point. She would drink some more champagne, and chat with strangers, and she would avoid Luca. Because she was a coward. A coward with a body that yearned to feel his fingers trail across her skin.

"Dammit," she muttered, and turned back to the doors.

But Luca was already there, blocking her way.

"Therese," he said, his voice soft.

She dropped her hands down to her sides. "I was about to go back in," she said, and started to walk past him.

"Wait."

He didn't touch her. He didn't do anything to stop her. She could've continued walking away from him, if she'd wanted. But her feet stopped moving, and she turned around to look at him.

In the dim light of the courtyard, he seemed to be made of shadows. The black of his suit, combined with the dark of his hair and his eyes, forced her to glance down at the glimpses of white at his chest to assure herself he was real.

"What are you doing out here?" he asked, a note of concern in his voice.

She shrugged. "I needed some air."

"It's a bit cold tonight."

"Freezing," she clarified, and chanced a smile. He didn't return it. "Well, um, is there something you wanted?"

Luca sighed and rubbed his jaw. She noticed the stubble there, adding even more shadows and smudges to the lines of his face. "I can't… here." He shrugged out of his jacket and stepped forward, closing the distance between them.

His jacket was still warm from the heat of his own body,

and as he draped it over her shoulders, she caught the spicy scent of him that clung to the fabric.

"Better?"

Therese nodded as she pulled the jacket tight around her body.

"What I want to say, it's not easy." He licked his lips, and she watched his Adam's apple rise and fall as he paused to swallow. "I'm retiring at the end of this season."

"Oh." At first, she was surprised, but then it began to make sense. A dancer's career was often a short one, most taking jobs as teachers when their bodies couldn't handle the constant stress any longer. "I had heard your contract wasn't going to be renewed."

"At my request," he added. "Though I'm sure you've heard rumors to the contrary."

Therese bit her lip. She wasn't about to divulge the bit of gossip she'd shared with Audrey the other day.

"And I've been offered a job," he continued, his gaze locked with hers. "Here. At your school."

"Oh," she said again, and this time, the shock of it lingered.

"Your artistic director, he's looking for a new ballet master. Rumor is that he'd like to build up a performing company that would be associated with the school."

"I'd heard that. And you... you've been offered the job of ballet master?"

He nodded.

"And have you accepted?"

He was close to her, so close he could've reached out and touched her. But he didn't move, and...

The space between them pulsed with tension. "I haven't decided yet."

"Well." Therese fidgeted inside his jacket. "I don't know why you're telling me about it. I mean, I'm not—"

He closed the remaining distance before she could draw another breath. His mouth met hers, firmly, and yet his lips teased hers, the tip of his tongue searching for entry until she gasped, and he slipped inside.

His hands came up to cradle the sides of her face, and she had a dim awareness of something timid in his touch, as if he were afraid to go too far, too fast, in fear of driving her away. But she leaned toward him, her arms lost for a moment in the oversized sleeves of his jacket before she placed her hands flat against his chest.

He stiffened, and she wondered if he thought she was about to push against him. So she slid her hands lower, down across the taut planes of his abdomen, and then around his waist, her fingers gliding possessively over his back. His reply was a moan, almost a growl, as he nipped her bottom lip with his teeth and then dragged his mouth along her jaw, to the sensitive hollow beneath her ear.

"I… wanted you." Luca breathed the words against her skin, and she shivered as the heat of him warred with the cold all around them. "Romeo and Juliet. There were twenty other dancers they could've chosen. But I wanted you. Only you."

She drew in a quick breath as his hands trailed over her shoulders, inside the jacket, his thumbs catching on one of the thin straps of her dress and tugging it aside. He kissed her there, beneath her collarbone, and then above, before his mouth returned to hers, all the former timidness gone.

For years, Therese realized, she had wanted this. Not merely to dance with him, to move through a series of choreographed steps together. She had wanted this: His hands, his mouth, the line of him pressed against her, his sharp intake of breath as she unwittingly shifted her thigh between his legs.

"You never looked at me," she spoke against his shoulder, her heart thudding inside her rib cage as his hands continued to slide over her back, down and down, until his fingers grazed her hips, and down again until his palms moved across her upper thighs. "I would see you with the other girls, flirting with them like it was nothing. But with me…"

He placed his hand beneath her chin and lifted her head from his shoulder. His breath shuddered against her cheek as he caressed her bottom lip with the edge of his thumb. "Yours was always the first face I searched for in every class, every rehearsal. I watched you as if I were some lovesick puppy. Which, I admit, I was."

"Why didn't you ever say anything? I mean, I was right there, a few feet away from you, every day."

He closed his eyes. When he opened them again, they were liquid, dark and shining in the boughs of twinkle lights that decorated the edges of the courtyard. "Because I was young, and I was stupid. And then, after the performance, when you disappeared…"

"I twisted my knee in class," she said, and shook her head. "It was a small injury, but it was enough. I had to stop dancing full-time, and so I started teaching."

"I know, I remember." His thumb made another pass below her mouth, and then he dipped his head down, kissed her where his finger had been only a moment before. "And I didn't go after you," he said, his words sweeping across her cheek. "Because I was young, and I was stupid. But I always knew you were here, and I always told myself I'd come here, too. At least, when I was old enough to realize I'd finally grown up a bit."

She quirked an eyebrow. "So, you're not getting into fist-fights with conductors anymore?"

Luca smiled at that, and lowered his head until his hair fell across his forehead. "Not as long as a suited monkey couldn't do a better job."

She laughed out loud. There was a slight tremble in her voice, and she knew that if he stepped away from her now, she couldn't trust that she'd be able to remain standing. "We should go back inside," she whispered. She didn't want to return to the fundraiser, to the stuffy room filled with stuffy people, while trays laden with champagne and caviar twirled about her head. She started to shimmy out of his jacket, but his hands moved down to her upper arms and stayed there.

"No," he said, and dropped another kiss on her forehead.

"But they're probably waiting for you!" she said, feeling more anxious as she thought about how long they'd been out here. "Isn't there going to be some kind of presentation?"

He kissed her again, this time on her cheek. "First, I need some advice."

"Advice? From me?"

"What would you say," he went on, ignoring her questions. "If there was a famous dancer, someone who had performed with all the top companies, traveled the world, garnered praise and prestige from—"

She placed the tips of her fingers on his mouth. "Ego much? I thought you said you'd grown up."

He smiled behind her hand. "Sorry. Old habits. But what if that person wished to leave that life behind them, and settle in some place... smaller?"

Therese tilted her head from side to side, as if thinking something over. "Smaller meaning... Ohio?"

"Ohio," he echoed. "And had an offer to work at a small dance school. An amazing school, but one still hovering on the cusp of something more?"

"Something more, " she said, repeating his own words back at him. "I'd say he's crazy. I mean, Ohio? Really?" She clicked her tongue. "Definitely certifiable, that one."

Luca didn't smile. He looked into her eyes, searching, she thought. But for what, she wasn't quite sure. "And what if he wanted to leave everything behind... for you?" He lowered his head and kissed her, a kiss so sweet and full of yearning that she thought she might pass out from the need it stirred inside of her. "Just you," he said, his voice nothing more than a soft push of air on her lips.

Therese swallowed, and bit back a giggle that threatened to bubble up from inside her. Her hands were still around his waist, her fingers digging into the waistband of his slacks for support. "I'd say he was still crazy," she told him, and let herself lean against him, simply because she could. "But I'd also tell him to go for it."

He sighed, his relief palpable in every limb. "Good advice." He wrapped his arms around her and held her, she guessed simply because he could. "I'm glad I came to you."

"Well, I have worked with some difficult people in the past, so I'd like to think I know my stuff."

His laugh vibrated through his chest. "I think you're right, we should go back inside. I'm starting to lose feeling in my fingers."

"It's supposed to snow tomorrow," she said, as he pulled away from her so they could walk back toward the doors.

He made a sound of disgust in his throat, but she glanced up quick enough to see the smile at the corner of his mouth. "Snow and ice," he grumbled. "And it's not even Christmas yet."

"Christmas?" she scoffed. "I hate to break it to you, but we once had a foot of snow on Halloween."

His steps faltered as he reached for the door. "But that's in October, right?"

"Luca, welcome to Ohio," she said, and put her arm around his waist as they went inside.

A Little Snow Music

by Melina Dillies

For my beloved Pip, whose endless humor and encouragement knows no bounds, and for DG--my true north, and the co-creator of my best works--F&E, the brightest stars in my sky.

Chapter One

You will not tell me how to raise my son."

The leather of Jeff McAllister's gun belt squeaked as he turned from the window, a layer of thick frost obscuring the snowy yard beyond his shoulder.

"I wouldn't presume to, I—"

"I know what you presumed, Ms. Watson," he cut in. "The point is, you won't be including my son—end of story."

Emily Watson swallowed hard, forcing herself to maintain eye contact with the unnerving ice-blue stare that bore into her. Rising, she stepped out from behind the ancient aluminum desk, keeping a hand on the gray metal to steady the quake in her legs. Standing with arms crossed across his broad chest, Officer Jeff McAllister of the Fergus Falls Police Department was certainly at the top of his game when it came to intimidation. Emily's palms began to sweat, and she could now understand the swirling rumors of "dirty cop" which had followed McAllister since his arrival in town. She took an unconscious step back, and his eyebrows arched though he didn't move his position. Emily took a deep breath.

"Officer McAllister, I know you may think that Danny is wasting his time in my music class, but I promise you that he has talent—and he loves to sing. The holiday concert will only require six after-school practices, so if time is a concern I can assure you that his commitment will be minimal."

Emily took her hand off the desk and raised herself to her full five-foot-seven frame, which was still dwarfed by the much taller figure of the town's newest patrol officer. *And local jerk-face*, Emily thought.

"The answer is no, Ms. Watson."

"Is it because he's a boy?" Emily asked. "Not many boys can sing like that I assure you, especially with a song like Ave Maria. Given his age, he'll likely only have—"

"I do not have to explain my parenting to you—or anyone else."

"Maybe not—but the other kids are depending on him."
Emily raised her chin.

"Well, they'll get a better education out of a little disappointment than they ever will in a sixth-grade, amateur music
class. Good night." Jeff strode through the classroom door without a look back.

"Damn." Emily collapsed against the desk, giving her
unstable knees a break. *The man certainly has the looks category
nailed down*, Emily thought. She listened to the hollow thump of
boots on old wood as Officer McAllister retreated down the hall.
If only his attitude matched his smile. Sighing, Emily gazed around
the expansive music room, which was like a vertical time cap-
sule. Colorful foam baffles dangled in a cheerful rainbow from
the ceiling signaling groovy days gone by, retreating to the tops
of the same ancient desks her grandmother had used, and the
antiquarian floors below. It smelled of old brass and spit and
Emily loved every inch of it.

There was a time that she would have said Fergus Falls,
Minnesota was as lame as the day is long. Now though, it was a
world away from the broken engagement she left in Minneapolis, which made it paradise on earth. *So much for life in the big
city.* She padded around and placed tomorrow's music books on
each tall, black stand. While moving to Minneapolis did provide
her with an excellent education, staying there in order to satisfy
someone else's vision of perfect was the height of immaturity.
Returning home to Fergus Falls was like being wrapped in a
homespun quilt, warm and welcoming, though one particular
officer could use a lesson or two in manners. She gathered her
things, pushed the old hurts away for another day, and headed
out of the room, pulling the door closed behind her.

The school was silent, the halls losing light to the long
winter night which darkened the floor to ceiling window panes.
Emily hurried through the double doors at the end of the hall
and descended down the stairs, missing the last one. She stumbled into the opposite wall, bashing her elbow on the corner of
the railing, and her sheet music scattered in the breeze like an
errant snow squall.

"Double damn." She stopped to scoop them up, fumbling with the sheaves, attempting to put them back in order.

Danny McAllister seemed to be perched on the forefront of her mind, refusing to budge. The boy had the voice of an angel and was well-liked by his peers. Emily couldn't understand what objection any parent would have to showcasing a natural gift like Danny's. It was bad enough that the entire event fell on her rookie shoulders without the star player being pulled so close to the event. *Maybe if Mr. Machismo could let his gender stereotypes go, then he might see how happy his son is.*

Emily tapped the thick stack of papers against the floor and stood. The light from the front doors was gray and muted. Emily swung her body against the heavy door and trudged out into the blowing snow. The light faded fast in the throes of winter, even faster when it was miserable weather. Ice pellets stung her skin and she dug her chin into her zipped parka and plodded through the ice-covered parking lot. Clutching her sheet music in one hand, Emily cried out when a passing car sent a wave of cold, slushy water down her side.

"Come on!" Emily shouted as her calm demeanor trickled away like the ice water running down her leg. Tears stung her vision and she squeezed her eyes hard to halt the flow. The deep thrum of an engine roared down the street and Emily straightened, wiping her eyes with her free hand. The streetlights buzzed into action in reaction to the last daylight fading from the sky, and Emily picked up her pace. Danny McAllister—and his judgmental dad—would have to wait until another day.

Chapter Two

Halfway home, Emily was startled out of her stupor by an apple-red Mustang, weaving precariously from one side of the road to the other. Her heart sank like a stone when the car slowed beside her.

"Need a lift?" the grating voice of Dennis Adams, town mechanic and first-class creep, called out from the open window. The reek of hard liquor was unmistakable.

"No thanks." Emily didn't slow her pace.

"Wait up," Dennis called, cutting the engine and struggling out of the car. Emily cringed at the squeak of metal as the door slammed shut and she lowered her head, plodding on. "I said wait up!"

"I'm late, Dennis," Emily replied, hoping that he didn't hear the catch in her voice. She prayed for some traffic on the deserted road. *Anything for another human being,* she thought as she slogged through the deepening snow. Her thighs burned.

"Well darlin', all the more reason for me to give you a lift," Dennis said as he fell into step beside her. "Why haven't you ever given me a call?"

"I don't recall asking for your number. And I'm not your darling."

"Don't be like that, love, I slipped my number to you at the pub last summer—or don't you remember?"

The vision of a drunk and sweaty Dennis Adams pawing her in a crowded bar flowed back like the stale beer he had spilled on her dress. She had been taken out by a fellow teacher to celebrate her new position at Jefferson Public School, and had been enjoying a great night until Dennis appeared, relentless in his unsavory pursuit. Given the fact that he was the Mayor's nephew, a position which provided him a certain level of indemnity, no one had challenged him, and Emily had cut her night short. She left the bar and made a mental note to avoid Dennis Adams at all costs, which included walking when her rickety old car decided to misbehave; such was the case this evening.

"I remember." She gripped her sheet music tighter.

"Well then?"

"Well what?"

"Why don't you let me show you around—starting to-night?"

"Dennis, I grew up here—remember?"

"Well, you went all city-girl for a while—just trying to be hospitable." His alcohol soaked tongue struggled with the last word.

"No, thank you." She glanced over her shoulder to ensure her reply was received as intended and was met with a menacing smile.

"I don't think so darlin'," Dennis slurred. His large hand gripped her arm, pulling her around to face him.

"I'll call the police," Emily squeaked with less authority than she intended, and her stomach began to churn. She tried to unzip her purse and prayed she would be able to locate her phone in the cavernous tote.

The laugh that escaped from Dennis was chilling at best, and Emily cried out as his hold tightened around her arm. He slid the purse off her shoulder and tossed it to the side. "No one turns me down twice."

Dennis attempted to pull her closer and Emily pushed back with all her might, holding her breath to force more power into her arms and to stifle the scotch-laced breath which was so close it dampened her skin.

"I don't think so." An ominous voice cut in and Dennis Adams was hauled away from her body.

She stumbled away from the sickening thud of bone on flesh which rang out behind her. Various grunts and curses permeated the still, winter air and Emily began to shake. She willed her feet to turn around. Bile rose in her throat as she spied the dark trail of red, leading straight to the crumpled form of Dennis Adams, already handcuffed and squirming like a worm on a hook. Looming over him was a furious looking Jeff McAllister.

"Don't. Move. A. Muscle." Jeff looked at Emily until she nodded understanding, the rise and fall of his shoulders highlighting the aftermath of his exertion.

"But—"

"Not a muscle, Emily, you got me?" Jeff hauled a still cursing Dennis from the ground and moved him across the street where Emily could now make out the dark lines of Jeff's cruiser.

The two struggling shadows reached the car, and Emily heard a loud thud, followed by a repeating screech of "Police Brutality" that was muffled by the slam of the car door. A few lights lit up the adjacent apartment building, and Emily cringed. Grabbing her purse, she ran, and by the time she reached her apartment complex she was clutching her ribs, breathing in short, erratic hitches. Her tears turned to ice as she ran, and she could feel the cold trail that they had left across her cheeks. She dug her keys from her purse, dropping them twice in a shaky attempt to undo the front door lock of her building. The cylinder emitted a satisfying click on the third try and Emily burst through the door into the quiet lobby. She bypassed the elevator and headed for the stairs, afraid of how she would handle an unexpected encounter with one of her neighbors.

Reaching her apartment on the third floor, she unlocked the door, hands steadier this time, though the cramp in her side had returned. She flicked the switch, bathing the tiny entranceway in cheery light, and slammed the heavy door behind her. Chest burning, she twisted the deadbolt and slid the chain lock into place, exhaling only when she had tested the door. Emily stood very still, heart jumping at every sound that echoed around her. She closed her eyes and forced herself to focus on the hum of everyday life in her building. The muffled sounds of televisions, meowing cats, and a crying child permeated the walls, and Emily began to breathe steadier, taking comfort in the regular goings-on around her. Her heartbeat receded out of her eardrums beat by beat and found its rightful place in her chest. She took a few more steadying breaths.

"Shit." She took a few tentative steps away from the door and made her way into the kitchen. Plugging in the kettle, she grabbed a clean cup from the drain board and reached for the canister of tea. "Double shit." She dropped the limp tea bag into her mug and slunk to the kitchen floor, sobs racking her petite frame.

After what seemed like an eternity, Emily dragged herself up off the floor and headed for the sanctuary of a hot shower, avoiding her swollen eyes as she passed the bathroom mirror. The icy pit that had settled in her belly overpowered the need for burn protection and she cranked the lever as far left as it would go and hopped in. A steady stream of water thrummed over her brow as she leaned her head against the wall, shaking. Her elbow ached and she could feel a tender patch forming on her temple.

"You stupid fool," Emily whispered as she considered the ramifications of leaving the scene of the crime. *Is that even a thing?* She scanned her scant knowledge of criminal law. She knew leaving the scene of an accident was one thing, but being saved from a drunken creep, did that require a statement?

Emily already knew she wouldn't press charges, no matter what the problem, given Dennis Adams's status as the Mayor's favorite nephew. In the arcane rules of small town politics, that would create a scandal that would keep the barber shop gossips busy for years.

Emily tested her rusty joints, skin warm and reddened like a boiled lobster, and turned the water off. Satisfied she was warm enough to coordinate her movements, she stepped out of the shower and dried off. The bright red smatterings of blood against the snowy sidewalk forced their way into her memory, landing on the fearsome glow in Jeff McAlister's eyes as he stood over Dennis. The man unnerved her at the best of times, and Emily wondered, not for the first time tonight, if the brutal incapacitation of Dennis Adams was a textbook protective measure—or something more ominous. Given Jeff's reputation, and if the rumors were true, the mysterious disappearance of his wife in Boston, Emily didn't know what to expect.

She stuck her discarded clothes in the garbage, knowing she would never be able to don them again without thinking about Dennis Adams, lamenting briefly over the loss of her favorite blouse. She threw on a pair of tights, an old Ohio State Sweatshirt, and a Snuggie. In need of warmth and comfort with no thought to appearance, Emily wrapped the Snuggie, a gag gift from Monika, around her and was grateful tonight for her friend's odd sense of humor. Padding into the kitchen, Emily re-started the kettle and slumped down in a kitchen chair to wait.

A loud knock sounded at the door, and Emily's heart slammed against her ribs. Before she had a moment to round the corner, the knock came again with much more force.

Emily stopped short of the door, rising on her tip-toes to peer through the peep-hole. She spotted a stern looking Jeff McAllister staring right at her and gasped in surprise.

"I heard that—open up," he said

Cursing under her breath, Emily released the deadbolt but left the chain lock intact and eased the door open a crack, leaving her foot wedged against the door to prevent further movement.

"It's not really a good time," Emily replied.

"I'll say—and it's about to get worse. Did you not hear me tell you to stay put?"

"Well, what the hell did you expect me to do?" Emily could feel the burning in her cheeks. "I was a bit out of my mind at that moment."

"I expected you to do as I said!" Jeff glanced back as one of the neighbors opened their door across the hall. An old woman with beady eyes glanced out, apparently assessing the commotion.

"Look—" Jeff lowered his voice, the velvety undertones of his speech making short work of her nerves. "—I get it. Really. Let me in and we can figure out what to do about it, okay? Believe it or not, I'm here to help."

Emily glanced at the peering Mrs. Mitchell across the hall and sighed. Closing the door, she hesitated before for a moment before sliding the chain lock off. She pulled the door and stepped back to allow Jeff to enter, giving Mrs. Mitchell her best attempt at a smile. *At least someone knows he's in here,* she thought, closing the door. Jeff had already retreated into the living room where he inspected each window, testing each lock as he went. Emily's palms began to sweat and she wrapped the Snuggie tighter around her body. *What did you do, you fool?* She attempted to hatch an escape plan if the rumors about him were true. His muscles flexed, straining against his t-shirt looking no less intimidating than he had in her classroom that day. *Was that only this afternoon?* Emily pinched the bridge of her nose in an attempt to compress the throbbing pain forming there.

Images swirled through her head of Jeff, disposing of her because she'd seen him use brute force on the job. Those visions, however, were outweighed by lack of probability, and Emily glanced at Jeff who was watching her with an amused look. She took a step back.

"You realize your face reads like a book right?" Jeff laughed and Emily balled her fists at her side.

"Well, apparently that trait didn't translate for Dennis Adams."

"That's because Dennis Adams is a drunken idiot who can't read," Jeff snapped. "Look, you shouldn't have left to-night—you know that. It put me in an awkward position that wasn't easy to talk my way out of, believe me."

"I'm sorry," she murmured.

Jeff stepped forward and touched the bottom of Emily's chin, tilting her face upwards. "You have a bruise on your forehead." His face was creased with concern as he assessed her, and Emily began to breathe a touch faster.

"Yeah. I think I got elbowed when you grabbed him." Emily tried to back away, but her heels were already against the wall. Her eyes widened and Jeff took a step back, though he still held her gaze.

"Any other injuries?" he asked, clearing his throat. The emphasis on each word held the cut of steel and his meaning was clear.

Emily shook her head. "No—I'm fine. Thanks for helping me." She looked away before her eyes spilled over. It had been a taxing day, and the last thing she wanted was to let Jeff get the emotional upper-hand. Emily scooted to the left and edged to the kitchen door.

"Can I make you a coffee?" She sniffled and ducked through the doorway before he could answer. Her pulse beat furiously in her ears. She crossed to the small window above the sink and cranked it open. Closing her eyes, she inhaled the icy blast that sailed through.

"Are you sure you're okay?"

Emily jumped, banging her damaged elbow on the counter. She crumpled to the floor, cursing through racked breaths which made her laugh instead of cry. "Ow, shit, ow," she repeated, rocking back and forth.

"Not so funny bone, huh?" Jeff said and hauled her off her feet, depositing her at the kitchen table. Emily sat down and nodded, unable to form any coherent words.

Jeff filled the kettle and plugged it in, following Emily's wordless commands to the can of coffee. She was glad his back was turned when she heard him apologize for his behavior in the classroom. She was certain her jaw hit the table. He set the can of coffee on the counter and continued, "Danny's just—well I wouldn't expect you to understand."

"Danny's very special," Emily said, the edges of her speech still laced with pain.

"Like his mother." Jeff turned to her, his jovial eyes now laced with ice. "I'm sorry, I really am, I just can't allow it."

"Officer—"

"Jeff," he said. "Call me Jeff."

"Jeff," Emily continued, "I'm sure you think that a boy singing falsetto is somewhat emasculating, but it really is an extraordinary thing. If you're worried that he'll be teased, I can tell you the other boys in the class are in awe of what your son can do."

"I wouldn't expect you, of all people, to understand my motivations, but if you think they're that shallow then you've got another thing coming." Jeff's eyes narrowed to slits and Emily swallowed hard.

"I assumed—"

"Exactly. You assumed."

"Will you stop cutting me off?" Emily stood now and placed her hands on her hips. "You haven't exactly been the easiest person to navigate, and given your naturally abrasive personality, what did you expect me to think?"

"I don't know, Emily." Jeff sighed. "I'm sorry—look, can we just start over?"

Emily huffed, blowing the auburn bangs from her eyes and saw Jeff's mouth twitched in a crooked smile from beneath her fringe. She noticed how it highlighted the cavernous dimple in his right cheek. Her breath caught and she doubted how anyone could label this man a bad anything.

"Fine," she said.

"Fine?"

"Yes—now take it or leave it."

"Okay, okay—I'll take what I can get." Jeff extended a hand, which Emily regarded for some time, eyes narrowed in shrewd assessment of his sincerity.

She gripped his callused hand and shook it, hard. Jeff nodded in approval. "Nice handshake—didn't expect that."

"Well, there's a lot of things about me you wouldn't expect."

"Why do I get the feeling you're absolutely right?" Palms still placed firmly together, Jeff stroked her wrist with his middle finger. An electrical impulse rippled across her skin and Emily gulped, reclaiming her hand and placing it in its former position as a balled mass at her side.

"I don't date the parents of my pupils," Emily blurted.

Jeff maintained his composure, though his eyes glistened with the satisfaction of a man who had just gained the upper hand. "Who said anything about dating?"

"I, uh—"

"Do I unnerve you, Miss Watson?" Jeff sidled closer, the heat from his body making her vision cloud.

"I think you should go," she whispered, tearing her eyes free of his gaze. She stared at the cracked linoleum and tried to upend her heart. She fought against her hands, which were itching to cross the mere inches between them and cleared her throat.

"You don't need to be scared of me, Emily."

She raised her chin to argue, but his steel-blue gaze pinned her in place, leaving her once again weak-kneed and slack-jawed—though for very different reasons from that morning.

"Please, Jeff."

"Fine." He stepped back slightly, giving Emily a wounded look. "I only came here in the first place to tell you that I've taken care of it. Dennis Adams won't bother you anymore, and no other officers at the station know about it. I told them I found him lying on the ground, drunk, and that it looked like he had been in a fight—knowing Dennis that's pretty much par for the course."

"You forgot to mention that your version of the events will also serve to keep you out of trouble," Emily said.

"You too, huh? Bad cop cheats the system, gets away clean? Yeah, I've heard the rumors—one of the reasons I keep my life—and that of my son, out of the spotlight."

"Well, I—"

"Look, lady, I have no problem taking my licks. Given the size of this town, your role as an educator and the fact that Dennis is in the Mayor's back pocket—I don't know, Emily. I figured you might also want to stay out of the spotlight." Jeff huffed and walked past her to the door. "Look, you want to report him, fine by me—you know where to find the Chief. Nice Snuggie, by the way."

By the time Emily recovered enough to lob the first swear word, it had soared through the empty doorframe, missing its target by a long-shot. Jeff McAllister was gone.

"Shit."

Chapter Three

The next morning, every muscle in Emily's body screamed in pain, trampled like the school football field after a big game. She rubbed her throbbing temple, raw from the bruise, head pounding from a sleepless night. Each bump and sound had seemed to echo through her in the dark, and twice she had thought she heard someone trying to come in through the living room window. Her thighs burned from the frantic run home, and she sported a large welt on her elbow from stumbling in the stairway.

She showered, dressed, and ate breakfast in quick succession, doling out silent pep talks about getting back to normal as she went. Bile rose in her throat when she heard the final click of her apartment door and by the time she reached the lobby she had to convince her legs to step outside the door. Every movement caused her eyes to dart, each peripheral movement holding the possible shadow of Dennis Adams. Breathing the wintry air did nothing to calm her senses, and the world around her began to sway.

"That's enough." She clutched her bag to her chest and headed for the school with renewed intent. "You will not let him get the better of you."

"I sure hope you don't mean me."

"Geezus." Emily jumped and she dropped her bag. She spun around, scanning her surroundings with blind panic until her gaze rested on Jeff McAllister, leaning casually against the side of his rusty pickup truck. Denim, boots, and a work jacket did nothing to hide his muscular form, and Emily bit her lip. She silently debated whether he was better looking in uniform or out, but had to remind herself she was still angry with him. Blushing, she lowered her gaze to the muddled pile of sheet music in his hand and cried out in relief.

"I thought you might need these."

Stunned, Emily stepped forward and accepted the bundle, bound in a black shoelace. "Thanks. I'm sure they weren't easy to find."

"They weren't. I think I got them all, though I can't promise they're in order." Jeff turned around and paused before looking back. "I can give you a lift if you—"

"No! I mean no, thank you," Emily replied. "You must be off today?"

"You could say that. You sure you don't want a ride?"

At Emily's narrowed gaze, he held his palms up in submission. "Okay, you win. I'll see you around then." Jeff offered a nod in her direction before hopping in his truck and rumbling off.

Mouth agape like a deceased carp, Emily followed the blue truck until it receded into the distance. She took her time walking to school, though given the amount of snow that had fallen, she doubted she could move much faster if she wanted to. Thoughts of Jeff McAllister bounced around in her head as she walked, and for the life of her, she couldn't figure out why she didn't despise the man. *Well, not fully, anyway.*

For some reason, she wanted to peel back his layers like an onion and find out what made him tick. His inability to avoid sarcasm intrigued her and she wondered what other qualities lay under the bravado and attitude. Most of all, his ability to get under her skin made her want to figure out why. *Having a conversation which didn't involve him berating her was a great start,* she thought as she assessed the lopsided bow around her sheet music, made with an old shoelace, and smiled.

She pictured Jeff up to his knees in snow, picking up each sheaf of paper, scattered like leaves in the night breeze. As she approached the site of her encounter with Dennis, goosebumps assailed her arms. The scene in her mind changed to one of Jeff, creeping through the snow, frantically trying to remove the evidence that would suggest she, and maybe he, was ever there. The question of whether he did that to protect her—or himself— lay untouched like the fresh snow beyond the sidewalk.

"What's up, chica?" Monika handed Emily a soda from the staffroom fridge and motioned to an empty table. "Why do you have your hair in front of your face?"

"Thanks." Emily took the soda and sat down, shrugging. "Something different I guess."

"Out with it, girl," Monika said. "I haven't seen you this distracted since you found out that cheating ex-fiancée of yours was getting married."

Emily pulled the tab on her can and stared at the tiny bubbles that exploded from the rim. "Trust me, that pales in comparison."

"Well then?" Monika leaned in close.

Emily sighed. She looked at her fellow teacher and most trusted friend and laid everything that had happened from the night before out between them. Monika grabbed her hand, listening intently, and squeezed it harder as Emily scooped her hair behind her ear, revealing her bruised temple. Monika's doe brown eyes magnified like a full moon as Emily detailed her uncomfortable conversation with Jeff, including her suspicions about the sheet music and Jeff hiding what had happened. When she was done, they both sat in silence, while the laughter and hum of the staffroom buzzed around them.

"Well, dirty cop or no, there's worse men to have interested in you." Monika broke the silence with a smile.

"Seriously? I bare my soul and that's how you reply?"

"I'm just saying, I'd hit that." Monika laughed. "Don't be such a prude."

"This is not helping me."

"Okay—if you want the truth, I'll give it to you." Monika glanced around to make sure no eager ears were listening in and lowered her voice. "Do not whisper a word to anyone, you hear—or Rico will kill me."

Emily nodded, remembering Monika's cousin Rico was a detective with the Boston PD and wondered why she hadn't thought to press her for information before.

"Well, I can't promise the man's not dirty in bed—but I can tell you he's not a dirty cop—he's one of the good guys,

Em."

"Monika..." Emily said, her voice low in warning.

"Okay fine, no more sexual references—but damn, you gotta admit he's hot!" Monika said. "When Danny told me after Spanish class last term that his mom had disappeared back in Boston, I was concerned for the kid and called Rico to find out what he knew."

"And?" Emily's question came out in a rough whisper.

"Well, turns out she didn't disappear; she was banging his *staff sergeant* of all people and left him for the dweeb. One night when Jeff was working, she hired a babysitter for Danny, packed her stuff, and moved in with the new guy—talk about humiliating."

"Wow."

"Yeah, like what kind of mother just abandons her kid?" Monika huffed. "Anyway—Jeff couldn't go back working for the guy. I'm sure that's a hard pill to swallow, especially for a guy like that. When he transferred here, and the rumor spread that his wife disappeared, it's no wonder he didn't try to counter it. Plus the fact that he left Boston so quickly meant he came here with a shadow over his head—hence the bad cop thing."

"Poor Danny," Emily said, her heart aching for the boy. "But that doesn't explain why Jeff would lie about what happened last night."

"Maybe he really did want to protect you. Parents in this town are vicious, you know that. Most of them haven't changed since high-school."

"Yeah, I guess."

"Look, first off you need to go and talk to the Chief, regardless of what Jeff did. You owe that to yourself so you can sleep at night."

"I don't know..."

"I'll take you myself after school. Jeff's not a bad guy—but he can't protect you twenty-four hours a day. You gotta take care of you. What happens the next time Dennis shows up around you drunk? What if he comes to your apartment?"

"I know—just let me think about it first, okay? The last thing I want is a bad rap with the Mayor." Emily rose and tossed her can in the recycling bin, looking for an end to the conversation. "Whatever happened to Jeff's wife anyway—after she left I mean?"

"As far as I know she's living the life of Riley with the douchebag sergeant. Apparently she's a big shot classical singer—Clara Hughes—you've probably heard of her, seeing as you live and breathe that stuff."

The silky blond tresses of Clara Hughes invaded Emily's memory and she recalled having seen her perform once, years ago. At the time, she had been in awe of her angelic voice. She remembered being held in rapture as she sang her signature tune—Ave Maria. Emily cursed, and several of the older teachers cast sideways glances in her direction.

"Ave Maria," Emily said. "Mon—do you know what this means?"

"Um, what?" Monika said through a mouthful of salad.

"Ave Maria—that's why Jeff doesn't want Danny to perform. Not because he's afraid of a boy singing falsetto, but because it was Clara's song." Emily turned and strode to the door, turning back as she heaved it open. "Thanks, Mon."

"Yup," Monika replied. "But don't forget what I said. Your safety comes first—I'll come and get you at your classroom after school."

Emily nodded, striding through the door and down the long hallway, weaving through the throngs of bouncing kids. She knew Monika was right about Dennis, and about protecting herself. The first time was a nuisance, but the second time—well she knew what would have happened if Jeff hadn't shown up, and her stomach started to turn. As she entered her classroom, the telltale black spots began to appear in her vision, and she doubled over to force the blood back to her head.

"Shit," she whispered, raising her body to full height. She crossed the room to her desk and the spots ebbed with each step. Her fingers were like ice, and she grabbed her yellow cardigan off the back of the chair, wrapping it around herself. She doubted she would ever feel warm again. Pulling her chair out, she noted a folded piece of paper on the seat and she unraveled it.

The cops can't be around all the time.

Emily dropped the note on her desk and collapsed in her chair, a fierce tremor racking her frame. Before she had time to contemplate the absolute violation of the note's words, the bell rang and the sixth-grade class burst through the door. Chatting, yelling, and pushing, the children filed. Emily sat stone-faced in her seat. Danny McAllister passed her desk and then backed-up a few paces until he was eye-to-eye with her.

"Are you okay, Miss Watson?" Emily concentrated hard on his voice until she could focus on his eyes, concerned and holding too much awareness for a twelve-year-old boy.

"Yup! Fine, thanks," Emily replied, hoping her voice hadn't betrayed her fear.

Danny's gaze drifted from hers to the scrawled note, sitting face-up, on a pile of papers. Emily grabbed it and shoved it in her desk drawer. "We're wasting time—what do you say we get started, only two weeks to the big concert!"

Emily molded a plastic smile out of her fear and managed to get through the rest of the class—and the following two—with robotic intent. By the time it was over, she had absolutely no recollection of what she had actually taught or if her classes had sounded like synergetic choirs or packs of strangled birds. Saved by the bell, Emily ran to get her coat and purse from behind the door. She stared at her desk drawer—picturing the nefarious note inside—and felt the ache of guilt at the trouble Jeff would have to deal with if she contradicted his story. Shaking her head, she took a deep breath, and pushed Jeff just past the point of self-preservation in her brain and opened the drawer. The note was gone.

Crying out, Emily rifled through the small drawer and the three below it, even dumping out the waste bin in her search. As she was digging through the discarded contents, Monika walked in.

"What on earth are you doing?"

"Paper," was all Emily could say, her trembling hands unfolded each piece of paper she came across.

"It's okay, Em." Monika walked over and steered Emily by the shoulders towards the door. "Let's get going."

"But the paper."

"School can wait Em—whatever it is, I'll help you find it in the morning, okay?"

Monika grabbed her hand like a lost child and led her to the staff lot, where she opened the door of her rusty white sedan and helped Emily get inside.

Monika thrummed her fingers on the steering wheel and gazed out at the fat snowflakes that blanketed the windshield. Emily hadn't spoken since they left the school and sat now, eyes trained on the brown metal doors of the police department.

"You've got to do this, Em, you know that."

Emily turned her head and nodded, the lump in her throat continued to choke her words. "What the hell." She shook her head and tears slipped, unbothered, into her lap.

"Hey." Monika placed a hand on her shoulder. "Don't let that drunken slob get the better of you. Let's go in there and get your life back, come on."

They exited the car and shaky legs spirited Emily into the division, where Monika asked to see Chief Brown. The female officer manning the desk, who went to school with the two women, took one look at Emily, nodded to Monika and said, "Come on back."

Chief Brown rose when they walked into the room and greeted Emily by name. It didn't hit her until after she had sat down that she had never met Chief Brown before, let alone been in a position for him to know her name.

"I was wondering if you were going to come in and see me." Chief Brown gestured to a pitcher of water on the credenza. "May I offer you a glass of water?"

Emily nodded and accepted the water with two hands. "Thank you. Forgive me Chief Brown, but how do you know my name?"

"Why, from Officer McAllister, of course."

"But—he told me no one knew," Emily said, dismay lacing the edges of her speech.

"I believe he meant no officers knew. I, naturally, am not included in that group. You know, he risked a lot to protect your privacy, even volunteering for an unpaid suspension while the... er, incident with Mr. Adams is investigated." Chief Brown concentrated on Emily's face. "You do know that Mr. Adams is suggesting he was unfairly treated by Officer McAllister."

Emily's thoughts retreated to Jeff, shrugging casually that morning when she asked him if he'd had the day off. The gravity of the professional risks he took for her settled in, and the coldness in Emily's belly began to melt. She glanced at Monika, who was sitting in astonished silence.

"So, what is it you would like to tell me, Ms. Watson?" Chief Brown asked.

Emily opened her mouth to answer when a loud commotion rang outside the door. Jeff burst through with a folded piece of notepaper in his hand.

"Chief, I'm sorry to interrupt but—"

"My note!" Emily rose and took the paper from Jeff's hand. "How did you get this?"

Jeff reddened, stood at attention, and addressed the Chief. "My son—he read it in class this afternoon and brought it home to show me." Jeff turned to Emily. "He said Miss Watson looked sad and he thought I could help."

"I see." Chief Brown raised an eyebrow, his tone holding an edge of insinuation. He motioned to the note in Emily's hand. "May I?"

Emily handed the note to the chief who placed a thick pair of reading glasses on the tip of his nose. "I see," he said again and glanced at Jeff. "Thank you McAllister, but seeing as you are not on active duty, I think we can take it from here."

Jeff turned a pained glance to Emily, the unspoken anguish lighting a fire in her belly that dispelled the rest of the cold, and nodded to the chief. "Yes, Chief."

"And McAllister, I hope you have spoken to that boy of yours about theft of property, regardless of the intention behind it." Chief Brown raised an eyebrow at Jeff, who had his hand on the door.

"I have, Chief."

"Good." Chief Brown nodded. "Good day, Officer."

Jeff retreated, strong shoulders held high. Chief Brown shifted in his chair and placed the note flat on the desk. Monika read the words and cursed audibly, grasping Emily's hand.

"So tell me, how exactly did you manage to come across this?"

Emily spent the next hour regaling Chief Brown with every detail she could remember from the unwanted approaches months ago in the local pub to receiving the note on her chair that afternoon. Monika's eyes misted and Chief Brown nodded, jotting scrawling notes and asking the odd probing question. When she was done, the three sat in silence, the tick of the wall clock the only sound in the room.

"You realize this changes things a bit?" Chief Brown removed his glasses and placed them on the desk. "We have a written statement from Mr. Adams on file, but I'm going to hand this note over and have it sent for analysis. In the meantime, we have enough information to arrest Mr. Adams, and given the violent nature of this crime, and his past history, I will seek to have him detained. But, given his unique connections, I imagine the DA may try to order a release."

"I understand." Emily nodded.

"I would recommend that you might want family or friends to stay with tonight—for your own peace of mind, of course."

"She'll be staying with me," Monika said.

"Good." Chief Brown rose and extended a business card to Emily. "If anything changes, please call me as soon as possible. Would you like me to contact Principal Harris on your behalf to—"

"No," Emily cut in. "I'm really okay. Thank you, Chief Brown—for everything."

Emily took the business card and shook Chief Brown's hand. "Strong Handshake." Chief Brown eyed Emily's small frame in surprise.

"So I've been told," Emily replied.

As they reached the door, Emily paused, turning to face Chief Brown. "What will happen to Officer McAllister?"

"He will remain on suspension until the conclusion of the investigation," he answered, surprised. "The Mayor has already called, asking for his head, but like I said, given the violent nature of the crime he encountered, well—it changes things."

Emily nodded. "Thank you, Chief."

"Oh—and Miss Watson—it might be a good idea to limit your conversations with Officer McAllister until after the investigation is complete. I realize you teach his son but..."

Emily colored, a hot flush staining her cheeks. "I understand."

Emily was spirited away to a young officer who helped her fill out the necessary statement and then headed straight for the lobby, where Monika waited. Once outside, she took a deep breath to steady herself. Monika touched her elbow and steered her towards the car.

"Seems like I'm not the only one who noticed you and the fine officer have the hots for each other."

"Shut up Mon—"

Monika's deep laughter pealed through the crisp air. Their boots crunched through the new fallen snow as they walked. "Let's go pack your stuff. Good thing it's Friday, I sense an epic weekend of wine and sappy movies heading our way."

Chapter Three

O n Sunday night, Emily shut the door of her apartment behind her and inhaled the comforting scent of wood cleaner and spiced apple. She exhaled, happy to be home, and in a place where every square inch of floor space wasn't covered in magazines, clothing, or food containers. As much as she loved Monika, her housecleaning habits were less than ideal.

She hadn't spoken to Jeff, though the man had left an indelible stain on her mind the last three days. She felt desperate for an opportunity to thank him—and to apologize for ever doubting his motivations for protecting her privacy. Most of all, she wanted to let him know that she knew about Clara and that she would pull the entire finale from the Holiday concert if that meant he would let Danny participate.

Sighing, she dropped her bag and padded into the kitchen, plugging in the kettle and grabbing the tea canister off the shelf. Returning to the living room, she sat down at her piano, by far the most expensive thing she would ever own, and a gift from her parents after obtaining her teaching degree. She flexed her fingers and placed them on the keys, playing with reckless abandon. She let each note thrum through her soul, winding its way like a golden thread around her heart, mending the holes and placing the shattered pieces of herself back together.

The kettle forgotten, she played until the sky was black outside, but for the silver moon broadcasting its light through the large living room windows. Her fingers ached and her back was stiff, but Emily played until she could picture every inch of her, whole again, even if she were a bit maimed. By the time the last note faded from her ears, she was thankful for the gift of music and how it had always healed her worst hurts, time and again.

Over the course of the next two weeks, Emily hardly had time to consider Jeff, though his face peeked in from the recesses of her mind from time to time. Preparing for the Holiday concert was all-consuming, and she had her work cut out training Danny's replacement for the finale. She spoke to Danny about replacing the song so he could participate, but Danny had shaken his head, saying his Dad wouldn't like it. Instead, she instructed Danny to work with his classmate Samantha to help prepare her for the piece and somewhere along the line; contentment began to settle over Emily.

By the night of the concert, Emily's nerves were crackling with electricity. She sat alone in her darkened classroom and was hopeful about her talented group of students. She always preferred a silent moment to herself before a performance. A knock on the door startled her, and Monika's dark curls poked around the corner.

"You only have an hour to change. You're not wearing that, are you?"

Emily glanced at her slacks and sweater and shook her head. "No, I brought my suit, I'm going to change now."

"Okay, well hurry up girl. People are already starting to file into the gym."

Emily blanched at that and she swallowed hard. She could almost feel the color drain from her face. "Oh."

"Don't worry Em—you'll do fine, they'll do fine." She waved a hand to the music stands around the room, "and before you know it, you'll have your first concert under your belt."

"Yeah," Emily replied as she followed Monika out the door, though her palms were sweaty and her knees were knocking.

Chapter Four

By the time Emily stepped into the crowded gym, the placed hummed with excitement. The heat level had already begun to rise given the number of bodies in the room, and Emily was glad she'd decided against putting her suit jacket on. Her emerald green blouse fluttered with her movement, and she winked at her pupils who were making their way to the stage. After giving them all a quick pep talk, she located Stephanie, waiting in the wings for her turn at the Finale. She threw Emily an enthusiastic thumbs up. Laughing, Emily repeated the gesture and climbed up to the makeshift podium. She squared her shoulders, grabbed her baton, and turned to face the crowd.

Principal Harris approached the front of the gym and held one hand in the air. The crowd slowly came to order among the scrape of chair legs and laughter, quieting down to a happy semi-silence.

"Welcome everyone, to what promises to be the most incredible holiday concert Jefferson has ever experienced." When the crowd died down, he continued, "This year in particular we are thrilled to have the concert conducted by Miss Emily Watson, our newest teacher—and an alumnus of this very school."

A loud whoop came from Monika, in the corner, and Emily stood with a smile frozen on her face, trying to convey her displeasure to her embarrassing friend. A few scattered claps came from the crowd, and Emily turned to her pupils who were at the ready. Tapping her baton, she guided each grade through stilted versions of "Frosty the Snowman" and "Let it Snow," with squeaky brass instruments and tiny voices. By the time the sixth-grade vocalists took to the stage for the finale, Emily was engrossed in the music, her frayed nerves long since tucked away.

The lights dimmed and the crowd hushed into silence, gasping in unison as the bright spotlight snapped to life. Samantha stood, basking in an angelic glow. For such a young girl, Samantha held an air of maturity and calm and Emily swallowed a small lump in her throat as she watched her emit opening strains of Ave Maria with a crystalline voice.

Emily descended the podium and took her seat at the piano for the point in the song where she would provide dramatic accompaniment. She took her seat and glanced up at the stage, stifling her cry with her fist. Danny McAllister was entering from stage right with all the composure of a pro. He took Samantha's hand, to the collective sigh of the crowd and belted the second verse of Ave Maria as he offered a wink to someone in the crowd. Emily didn't have to turn around to know it was Jeff he winked at. His voice pierced the silent gym like an arrow and the hair on Emily's arms stood straight up. A collective wave of appreciation swept through the crowd as Danny and Samantha turned towards each other and continued the song in perfect, practiced harmony.

Emily attempted to play, but she couldn't see the keys through her blurred eyes. "It's an e-minus," Jeff whispered as he appeared beside her. He discreetly squeezed her shoulder and nodded at her to continue before slinking back into the shadows.

She missed her cue by a beat but snapped back to her keys, struggling to catch up to the melody. The crowd didn't seem to notice, and a few hands clapped when the remainder of the stage lit up and the rest of the choir chimed in for the last heartbreaking notes of the song.

Emily reveled in the perfect split-second of silence that's borne of the best performances. The crowd erupted into a standing ovation for the group and Emily joined in, digesting the proud faces of her pupils. Danny caught her eye from the stage and elbowed Samantha, who glanced down and shrugged. Emily laughed and wagged a teasing finger at the two of them before joining the kids on stage for a bow.

As Emily straightened and the lights came up she found Monika, who was eyeing Jeff with evident appreciation as he stood beside her looking like a pig being sent to the slaughter. Jeff nodded to her with a shrug and a half-smile, and Emily laughed, enjoying the fact that the tables seemed to be turned, if momentarily, on the over-confident Jeff. The next few minutes were a blur as Emily congratulated students, shook hands with their parents, and wished everyone a happy holiday break. She glanced toward Monika but saw no sign of Jeff. At her wave, Monika began to weave her way through the crowd towards Emily. Principal Harris cut in front of Monika, who made a sour face and changed direction, melting into the fray.

"Well done, my dear," Principal Harris said and shook her hand, "Quite the finale. Those two young kids sing with amazing soul don't they? And the duet—brilliant, Emily."

"Thank you," Emily smiled, "though I can't take credit for the duet. That was a surprise."

After Principal Harris had taken his leave, Emily snuck through the thinning crowd and made her way through the silent halls to her classroom. She took a cleansing breath and stepped through the door, but squeaked in surprise when she saw Jeff, leaning against her desk.

"You did great, Emily," Jeff said as he stood and stepped towards her. "It was a great show."

"Uh, thanks," Emily said. "Aren't we not supposed to be talking?"

"The investigation is over." Jeff took another tentative step in her direction, "I'm back on shift, slap of the wrist and all that."

Emily released the breath she hadn't realized she'd been holding. "That's good to hear."

"Yeah, well, given the new information that came to light, the mayor backed down, and according to his lawyer, Dennis Adams just checked himself into rehab."

Emily nodded. A warm tear slid down her cheek and she squeezed her eyes to stem the flow. "Thanks, Jeff."

"Hey now." Jeff finished crossing the void and pulled her against his chest. "I know it sucks, but you'll get stronger because of it."

Emily sniffed and backed up a bit, wiping her eyes. "I know, I'm just—emotional, I guess."

"Well, you should be, those kids you have are incredible."

"Why did you let him do it?" Emily asked.

"Sometimes you have to make a choice—let the bad memories go, you know?"

"I know exactly," Emily replied, keeping her knowledge of Clara to herself.

"He really does have talent, doesn't he?"

"Boatloads." Emily straightened with pride. "He's a special kid."

Jeff nodded. "Special enough to score a sleepover at his best friend's house. I don't suppose you would be up for a celebratory drink?"

"Oh Jeff, I—"

"Don't date parents of students. I know." Stepping forward, Jeff laid his hands on her shoulders and placed a kiss on her forehead. "I can wait."

Emily swallowed hard as she watched Jeff stride out the door and fought every muscle twinge that begged her to run after him.

Monika burst around the corner and ran smack into Jeff, crying out in alarm. Her eyes looked like they would pop out of her head as Jeff steadied her. "Oh, hello Officer," she said. Jeff nodded and continued on his way. She tilted her head as he retreated out of sight, in visible assessment of his rear-end, and Emily cleared her throat.

"So? Did you two kiss and make up?" she asked, snapping back around and dodging Emily's swatting fingers.

"No." Emily glanced out into the empty hall and her heart sped up, each beat pulsing through her blouse.

"Why the hell not?" Monika asked. "Besides the fact that you guys are nuts about each other, who cares that he's a parent? Is Danny even taking music next term?"

Emily shook her head.

"Well then? Get out there girl, before I do."

Emily smiled at the throng of butterflies that danced in her stomach. Before she lost courage, she stormed past a laughing Monika as fast as her high heels would take her, losing her footing on the stairs and clutching at the handrail to keep upright. Her heart hammered and she slowed her descent, thinking of how mad she was at Jeff the last time she tripped down these stairs. *Gives head over heels a whole new meaning,* she thought as she reached the bottom and raced through the door.

The parking lot was nearly empty but for a small collection of concert-goers trudging to the sidewalk on foot. Jeff was halfway to his truck on the far side of the lot. *Damn, the man makes good time.* The lot was slippery and she stumbled like a new foal across the black ice. She labored to catch up, offering a few unplanned hollers as she skidded, and Jeff turned around, the look on his face a mixture of pain and amusement. Emily didn't care. She careened into him and grabbed the lapel of his jacket to pull him down to her height, planting a thorough invitation on his lips.

Breaking the kiss, she raised her head and loosened the grip on his lapel. Jeff stood silent, solid as a sentry, and regarded her through drawn eyebrows. The butterflies in Emily's stomach began to take nosedives. She backed away, heat rising through her blouse, but slipped on the ice and careened backward.

"Whoa!" Jeff grabbed her around the waist and pulled her in. "You're supposed to fall towards me, not away."

"Apparently I like to be difficult." Emily smiled and Jeff leaned down, answering her invitation in kind. The warmth of his lips on her wind-chilled skin made Emily shiver, and Jeff wrapped her tighter in his arms.

"Geez woman, did you not think a coat was appropriate?"

"Is it cold outside?" Emily replied through tingling lips.

Jeff unbuttoned his wool overcoat and wrapped Emily against his chest. He gasped at her icy fingers through his thin dress shirt and leaned down to capture her lips. A car rumbled past with holiday songs blaring from the cracked window. Thick snowflakes were trickling from the deep gray sky and Emily reveled in the feel of Jeff's heartbeat under her fingers.

Breathless, Jeff stood tall and smiled, "Now, how about that drink?"

Emily nodded. "Let me get my coat."

They walked in silence back to the school, and Jeff placed a protective arm around Emily's waist. She glanced up into his stormy eyes and wondered how she ever could have doubted him.

"You know — we could always have that drink at my place…" She stepped with care through the slushy parking lot.

Jeff's surprised laugh was muffled by his kiss and Emily reveled in the feeling of Jeff's arms around her, warm as the summer sun filtering through a windowpane.

Jeff leaned his forehead against hers and they stood in silence, the muffled sounds of the winter snow swirling around their bodies like a symphony.

All Wrapped Up

by Beth Stanley

Dedicated to my parents, who always made Christmas a magical time of year; and to my husband, who continues to do so. Special thanks to my mother for teaching me the beauty of a perfectly wrapped present.

Chapter One

Ivy

"If I hear 'Deck the Halls' one more fucking time, I'm gonna deck someone's halls, all right." Ivy slapped a bow on the box in front of her, and the cardboard sagged under the pressure. She shoved the present across the counter to a wide-eyed woman who shook her head.

"I'm not accepting that," the woman said. "The box is deformed now, and you missed a corner."

"Lady," Ivy hissed. "It's a free gift wrap station. If you want it perfect, do it yourself. With the way you're bitching, I'm sure there's gotta be a pair of scissors or something wedged up your—"

"Here, let me fix that." Merryn plucked the package from the counter and ripped off the dancing Christmas tree paper wrapped haphazardly around the broken box. The bell on her green hat jingled as she taped the cardboard and began applying a shiny red paper coating around it.

When the woman finally huffed off with her gift, Ivy hopped onto the counter. "Thanks for the save, Mer. Even though I think you should've let her take the broken one."

"I thought you needed this job," Merryn said. She swiped the bits of leftover paper into the trash at the end of the table.

"I do. I've been fired from almost every other store in this shitty mall."

"Well, then you'd better start acting like it. Mr. Stanton's a perfectionist. He insists the presents go out looking perfect."

"I don't think Mr. All-Hands cares about the presents themselves. It's just an excuse to come down here and flirt with us. I guess he hasn't heard of sexual harassment in the workplace. Besides, no one pays for this crap." Ivy pulled at a stray thread on her ridiculous green dress. At least she'd swapped the ludicrous elf shoes for combat boots. There was no way she was jingling every time she took a step. "I don't get why he cares."

"Because he just took over as manager of the mall," Merryn said. "He wants us to look good so he looks good. Speaking of, you should be wearing your hat."

"No way." Ivy shook her head. "That shade of green totally clashes with the purple in my hair. Besides, hat or no hat, no one is going to believe I'm an elf. I'm almost six feet tall."

She kicked up from the counter, showing off her long legs and the fishnet stockings she sported instead of the black and white striped things her boss asked her to wear. Those things had looked like something the Wicked Witch of the East wore before a house flattened her in Oz.

"Ahem."

A cough made both women jump. Ivy's eyes widened, and she bit the inside of her cheek to keep from licking her lips at the source of the sound.

The man on the other side of the counter was all kinds of hot, even if he clearly wasn't her type from the neck up. The horn-rimmed glasses perched on his nose shouted, "comic book nerd," but the chest muscles straining against his button down shirt screamed, "Gym membership."

The man ran his hand through his chocolate-colored hair and smiled. "Can someone help me?"

Merryn stood frozen in place, her jaw practically hitting the floor. Ivy shook her head and hopped off the counter. "What do you need?"

The man produced a box from the overly priced department store at the other end of the mall. "I'd like this wrapped, please."

Please. He was polite, too. So *really* not her type, then. That was too bad. It might've been fun to see how she could fog up those glasses as she ripped off his shirt.

Blinking away the thought, Ivy took the box and pulled a scrap of paper from the stack beside her. "Fine. Just write down who it's for, and give us your name for pick up."

The smell of musky aftershave wafted across the counter as he bent over to scribble on the sheet. Ivy bit her lip, wondering why her heart had suddenly increased its pace and why she couldn't get the image of throwing him down onto the counter and taking him right there out of her head. What the hell was in those free candy canes she'd been sucking on all day?

He slid the paper to her and she sucked in a breath as their fingers touched. He grabbed his hand back as though she'd electrocuted him and shoved it in his pocket.

"Thanks, uh, *Mal*," Ivy said, reading his name off the bottom of the sheet. "Do you want to keep shopping and come back in a bit?"

"Sure. I'll pick you up in like an hour?" His face turned the color of the crimson paper Merryn had used on the last gift. "I mean the present. I'll pick the *present* up in an hour?"

God, he was even hotter with red cheeks. Ivy cleared her throat. "Plenty of time. See you then."

He left the booth, the musky smell trailing behind him. Ivy pressed her hips into the counter; grateful it shielded her from jumping after him. Or jumping him at all.

Really not my type. Such a good boy. He probably doesn't even have any ink. Though, I certainly wouldn't mind inspecting him to verify…

Ivy shoved the bowl of candy canes to the other side of the counter. *No more of those. Just in case.*

She glanced at Merryn, who still hadn't moved. "Are you gonna help me with this or what?"

Merryn's head snapped to her, and she blinked. "He's coming back in an hour?" She smoothed her hair and righted the hat on her head.

"Don't get all excited," Ivy said. She glanced at the names he'd written. His script was neat and precise, like his appearance. "According to this, the present is for some chick named Jenny."

Ivy peeped in the box and spotted enough sparkle and satin to tell her it was a dress. Her food court lunch threatened to climb back up her esophagus at the bubblegum pink fabric. She frowned and slammed the box shut.

"Lucky Jenny," Merryn said with a breathy sigh.

"Yeah." Ivy sorted through the rolls of paper before deciding on gold foil with holly embellishments. She chose to ignore the way her hamburger and fries soured in her stomach. "Lucky Jenny."

$\mathcal{M}$AL

Mal made the mistake of glancing over his shoulder after he left the gift wrap booth. As he focused on the woman with the purple hair and the word IVY on the nametag pinned to her breast, he slammed into an elderly woman loaded down with purchases. Gold tissue paper and brown paper bags fluttered around his feet.

"Watch where you're going," the woman chirped.

"I'm so sorry about that. Here, let me help." Mal bent to collect the strewn bags and boxes. He grabbed a gift basket from the bath store that had settled between his boots. It reeked of strawberries.

She grunted and whisked it out of his hand. Without another word, she pushed past him, toddling with her bags towards the mall exit.

Mal glanced again at the gift wrap booth. The girl with the name that matched her eyes stared at him, her lips quirked up. He tried not to notice the way the slopes of her breasts peeked over the too-tight costume, and how they strained against the bodice with her laughter. She caught him staring and the laughter stopped. She raised an eyebrow.

Mal coughed and spun away from the booth, his head down until he reached the elevators in the center of the mall. When he made it up to his brother's office, Mal struggled to catch his breath, as though he'd swam the entire way there.

He couldn't figure out why the gift wrap girl unnerved him so much. Sure, she was intimidating. She was taller than him, which wasn't something he was used to. Tattoos covered every inch of her arms as far as he could see. She had purple hair and smelled like grape candy. She was so unlike any woman he'd ever been with. Not that there was a long list. But the way her green eyes lit up when she laughed, even though she had been laughing at him, he wanted to see that again. Mal rubbed his temple. She didn't matter. She couldn't. He had Jenny. There was no room for the gift wrap girl anyway.

He walked into his brother's office without knocking. Jeffrey looked up when he entered, waving him to a leather chair across from the desk. He spoke rapidly into his phone, and Mal tuned him out as he slid into the seat.

Beige file folders strewed across his brother's desk, and Mal found his gaze drawn to one in particular. His breath hitched in his throat. *Ivy Gilbert.* It had to be the girl from the gift wrap booth. Mal couldn't think of a lot of girls named Ivy. As his brother yapped into the phone and typed on his computer, Mal slid the folder closer.

The girl at the booth was twenty-three. Four years younger than him. Though, he wouldn't have known it. The sadness drifting behind her emerald stare aged her beyond her years.

Mal raised his eyebrows as he absorbed the rest of her profile. She'd worked a lot of jobs in the last year. Almost every store in the mall. She'd been fired for things like smoking in the stores, frequently showing up late for shifts, swearing at customers, and there was one unconfirmed report of theft.

"Quite the girl, huh?"

Mal jumped. He hadn't heard Jeffrey hang up the phone. His brother stared at him with raised eyebrows and a smirk.

"Why did you hire her for the gift wrap booth?" Mal asked. "Looks like she has a pretty long rap sheet. I thought you'd be happy to get rid of her."

Jeffrey sat back in his chair and studied his brother. "Have you *seen* her? She's easy on the eyes. Smokin' body. Legs that go for miles. And those eyes…I'd love to see them begging for mercy beneath me some time." He leaned on his elbows and pressed his fingers together so they formed a point. "Besides, she came to me crying. Pleading with me to find her another job. Saying she had to have the work. I guess I felt sorry for her."

A deep chuckle vibrated through Mal's chest. "Right,

because you're so caring. Are you sure it's not because you just wanted to get in her pants?"

"You know me too well, little brother."

"Because you're a pig, *big* brother."

Jeffrey chortled. "Just because I don't let myself get tied down doesn't mean I'm not enjoying life. Speaking of being tied down, how's Jenny?"

Mal sat back in his chair, the leather squeaking beneath him. "She's wonderful. Loves the new house. Loves this town. She's beautiful as ever. And I hardly think of her as tying me down. She makes my life better."

"Yeah, I can see that. You light up like a freaking glow stick when you talk about her. I can't believe you moved all the way to the 'burbs for her, but I'm glad you did. It'll be nice to have my little brother around again." Jeffrey stood and came around his desk. He leaned against the wood and crossed his arms. "And I'm honestly happy for you, Bro. I mean, all this tail chasing I do is because I want what you have, someday."

"You're just going to bang gift wrap girls till then, huh?"

"Only the ones who'll let me. I had no problem with the other one. Mary or something like that. Surprisingly, the tall one is playing hard to get."

Mal frowned at the warm sensation that flooded his insides at those words. He wasn't quite sure why he was relieved to hear Ivy had no interest in his brother. Not that she'd have any interest in him, either. She obviously wasn't the kind of girl who was into guys who sat at home on Saturday nights and binge-watched *Battlestar Galactica*. She probably didn't even know what a Cylon was.

"I was hoping to find something in her file that would give me a clue to the girl," Jeffrey continued. "But all I've got is a bunch of terminations and no emergency contact info. It's kind of sad. In the 'in case of emergency, please contact' box, she wrote, *'no one'.*"

Jeffrey held up the sheet, and Mal studied the handwriting of the mysterious girl. Jagged and dark. Kind of like her.

Mal shook his head, as though he could clear her from his mind. "Maybe she's just a private person."

"Maybe." Jeffrey tossed the folder back onto his desk and patted his brother on the shoulder. "I'll crack her. You'll see."

Mal grimaced. "Good luck with that. She seems like a tough one."

"You know me. I like a challenge."

"Is that why you took this job?" Mal gestured to the bare office walls. "Re-hauling this place is definitely a challenge. I've gotta admit, I was pretty surprised when you told me you were moving to the 'burbs, too. I thought you'd always be in the city."

"Let's just say they gave me an offer I couldn't refuse." He straightened his tie as he spoke in the worst Marlon Brando voice Mal had ever heard.

"Plus, you can bang the gift wrap girls."

"That, too."

Mal glanced at his watch. "Speaking of, I've got a few more things to pick up before I can grab my gift from the booth. I'll put in a good word for you. See ya, big brother."

Jeffrey slammed a large palm into Mal's shoulder as he stood. "You're still coming to the Christmas party I'm throwing Friday, right?"

"Like I have a choice?"

"Of course you don't." Jeffrey pulled a bag out from behind his desk. "You'll need this."

Mal glanced into the bag and grimaced. "I can't believe you talked me into this."

"Well, you agreed. Too late to back out now. Bring Jenny. I promise I'll show her a good time while you work."

"Right. See you then."

Jeffrey pulled him into a hug and Mal's breath wheezed out of him as he found himself crushed against his brother's chest. "Take care, little brother."

"Always."

Mal hoisted the surprisingly heavy bag and headed out of his brother's office. He took the elevator down and sucked in a deep breath before being swallowed by the Christmas crowds.

Chapter Two

*I*VY

"You're gonna want to tape that corner down before you do the other side."

Ivy shot a glare at Merryn and the blonde's mouth snapped shut.

"I can wrap a present, you know." Ivy lifted her hand and the paper snapped at attention, lifting off the box. She curled her fingers. "This one just doesn't like me."

"Please, let me help," Merryn said. "You've been at this for forty-five minutes. He's going to be back any moment."

"Fine." Ivy slid the box down the counter and grabbed her purse from under the cash desk. "I'm taking my break, anyway. I need a smoke."

"That's a disgusting habit, you know."

"So you've told me fifty times. Is it cool if I leave for ten?"

"What if Mr. Tall, Nerdy, and Handsome comes back?"

Ivy narrowed her eyes. "What if he does? Give him the gift. You know, if you can remember how to speak this time."

Merryn expertly folded the paper around the box and secured the corner with scotch tape. "Hey, I may have been comatose, but don't think I missed the way your eyes roamed across his ass as he walked away."

"So he has a nice ass." Ivy shrugged. "He also has Jenny, remember?"

"Maybe. But guys attached to one woman don't stare at the gift wrap girl as they're walking away."

Ivy hopped onto the counter and swung her legs over. She jumped off before turning back to Merryn. "He'd probably never seen a real woman before. Did you see the god-awful pink thing in that box? This Jenny chick is probably all unicorns and fucking rainbows. He can have her if that's what he wants."

She left her co-worker with the gift and headed to the mall exit. The winter wind blasted against her as she pushed through the door. Ducking her head, Ivy dug through her purse for her cigarettes. After pulling out her wallet, keys, and cell phone, she stared at the empty black bottom of her purse.

"Crap."

Heather. It had to be Heather. She was always hiding her pack on her. Crap. Just what she needed today. Well, she'd promised to quit soon, anyway. Now was as good a time as any. She shoved everything back into her purse. Weaving through a barrage of people wading out of the mall, Ivy headed back inside towards the food court. She ordered a Coke from the pizza stand and waited at the end of the counter.

The food court resonated with the hum of a crowd too rushed to savor their fast food. Mothers screamed after kids who'd already had their fill of holiday sugar. Couples spoke in hushed whispers as they hid bags from one another. A war vet sat on a stool and jingled a strap of bells, calling for donations to a local shelter.

Ivy tapped her nails against the plastic counter and blew out a breath as she turned away from the crowd. Jeez. How long did it take to pour a freaking Coke?

A teenager who looked like he hadn't quite made amends with puberty yet finally handed her the paper cup with shaking hands. As usual, they'd filled the cup with more ice than liquid. She glanced up to see the kid's eyes focused only on her chest, his acne-flared skin growing pinker by the moment.

"Maybe you should've saved some of the ice for yourself," she said. He didn't even blink. "Yo, kid. My eyes are up here."

With a grunt, she whirled away from his leering gaze and slammed right into a man's chest.

Blue button down. She knew that shirt. Manly musk. She knew that scent. Chiseled chest and glasses. She knew those, too.

Shit.

The cup had exploded on impact, dousing Mal's baby blue shirt in the dark brown liquid, which ran down an extremely chiseled set of abs towards—

"Uh, my eyes are up here."

She started as the nerdy hunk from earlier threw her words back at her.

"Right. Crap. I'm sorry. I didn't see you there." She fumbled for the napkins on the counter, trying to avert her eyes from the mess she'd made. "I'm sure that shirt's expensive."

Like the rest of him.

"It was my fault. I shouldn't have stood so close. It's fine."

He slipped the napkins from between her fingers, and Ivy sucked in a breath as the skin-to-skin contact sent shivers down her spine. Seriously, when did this guy develop such a hold on her? Just because the Coke had seeped through his shirt, accenting each and every ripple of his broad chest and abdomen was no reason for her to lose her shit.

"At least let me buy you a new soda." He dropped the damp napkins in the bin beside him and pulled out his wallet. Ivy held back a gasp as the brown leather opened to reveal an impressive stack of bills and…was that a platinum credit card? She didn't know those actually existed. She'd always thought they were myths, like dragons, or bosses who kept their hands to themselves.

"What do you do for a living?" she asked.

"Investment banking. I got lucky. I have a great job. Here." He held out a five-dollar bill and Ivy shook her head.

"I'm not a charity case just because I wrap gifts for a living. I can afford another Coke."

Ivy dumped her purse on the counter. Change jingled against the plastic top, and she sorted through quarters and dimes. Crap. She actually didn't have enough for another Coke. Not that she'd let *him* see that.

"Here," he said again. He nudged her shoulder with the bill. "Consider it a tip for wrapping the gift."

Heat lashed at Ivy's cheeks. She gathered the change and shoved it back into her purse. "Look, I said I don't need your charity. I have enough money. Just not on me at the moment. My break is over anyway."

She shoved past him, knocking him askew as she headed toward the booth. She didn't dare peek over her shoulder at him. Her eyes burned along with her cheeks as anger and shame coursed through her. She'd spent the last year trying to get her crap together, and it still wasn't working. Now this rich stranger had seen what a lost cause she was. She hopped over the counter of the booth and tried not to think about plunging one of the pairs of silver scissors into her chest.

"You okay?" Merryn touched her shoulder and Ivy pulled away.

"I'm fine. I just need to get my mind off…everything." She eyed a small, gray-haired woman who clutched a set of dishes to her chest. "How can I help you?"

*M*AL

Mal stared after the gift wrap girl as she stormed off. He grunted at his wallet and the bills spilling from the top.

Good job, Mal. You look like a stuck-up douche. She probably makes minimum wage at that damned booth and here you are, strutting around like Donald Trump sans the bad hair.

He decided to wait another hour before heading back to her booth to pick up his gift. It seemed safer to give her a chance to cool down. In the meantime, he stopped at the department store and purchased a new shirt and pair of pants. He dropped off the damp clothes at the dry cleaners and stopped at the pizza stand for a slice.

When he finally approached her, Ivy sat on the counter as her co-worker fussed over what appeared to be an un-boxed wine rack. Every time the blonde attempted to raise the gift, the metal rack would break through the paper and clatter to the counter. Ivy's gaze flicked from her metallic blue nails to her co-worker, amusement shining behind her emerald eyes.

Mal stopped a few feet from the booth. She hadn't seen him yet. She was too busy laughing at the girl with the wine rack. Ivy was beautiful when she laughed. She had one of those grins that took her features from dark and mysterious to bright and young in a split second. Ivy crossed her legs and Mal shifted as he spotted a pair of bright orange panties beneath her too-short elf skirt. Heat rushed to his face and other extremities. He sidled up to the counter so she wouldn't see his…unfortunate predicament.

Placing the large Coke he'd purchased at the pizza stand on the counter, he cleared his throat. Both girls jumped and stared in his direction.

"I, uh, I'm here for my package," Mal said. The grin on Ivy's face was enough to make him regret his choice of words. "You know, the present I had you wrap earlier?"

"Right." Ivy hopped off the counter. "For Jenny."

"Yes, that's correct."

Ivy bent and rifled through some gifts stacked on the floor. Mal's situation became even more uncomfortable as he spotted a matching orange bra peeking from her cleavage. He wanted to shift his eyes, but for some reason, he couldn't. To be fair, she'd ogled him in the food court first.

"Here you go." She plopped the box on the counter. Mal's breath hissed out of him. It was impeccably wrapped; every corner of the gold foil skillfully folded, the red bow on top fluffed high.

"Wow. That looks beautiful," he said. "Here, I got this for you as a thank you. Also, I kind of owed you one."

He nudged the cup of soda toward her.

Ivy stared at the peace offering for what seemed like forever. Her chest rose and fell in deep breaths. She picked up the cup, then placed it on the table beside her co-worker. "Merryn wrapped that. Not me. This belongs to her. Besides, I already told you. I'm *not* your charity case."

"I wasn't—" Mal bit his tongue. "This isn't charity. I figured it can't be the most fun working this booth all day and dealing with grumpy Christmas shoppers. I ruined your break and felt bad. I just wanted to do something nice, but obviously nice is something you haven't figured out yet."

She sucked in a breath. Her cheeks took on a pink hue,

making her look more elfish than ever. Her gaze flickered from the soda to her co-worker, and back to him. As if in slow motion, she reached behind her and picked up the cup. Mal took a step back, concerned she may actually throw it at him.

Instead, she put the straw to her ruby lips and sucked the liquid into her mouth. Her eyes closed as the syrupy liquid slid up the straw and Mal tried not to think about her having a similar expression in bed. Especially when she was…

Cut it out. Stop thinking about her like that. You have Jenny, and you know this could never happen.

She opened her eyes and her lips quirked up. "Thanks, Mal. You're right. I needed that. I'm sorry I snapped at you."

Beside her, her co-worker choked. She stared at Ivy with wide eyes. Mal wondered if he was the first person Ivy had ever apologized to.

"You're welcome," he said. "Thanks again for the gift. I'll probably be back. I have a few more things to get this week, and I couldn't wrap even close to this well. See you, Ivy."

She started when he said her name, almost dropping the cup. He heard the thud of it hitting the countertop as he left her behind. Cradling the perfectly presented package as he stepped into the blustery evening, Mal grinned. He used to hate shopping. It had always been a chore. Now, he couldn't wait for the mall doors to open tomorrow.

*I*VY

Mal kept his word. He was back early the next day, and the day after that. Merryn giggled every time he walked away, and Ivy elbowed her each time.

"He likes you, you know," Merryn said as she peered into the small box he'd given them Thursday morning.

"You're a crazy person," Ivy retorted. She glanced over

Merryn's shoulder and her heart sank to her toes when she saw what sat in the red velvet box. A gold necklace shaped like a *J* perched on the fabric. "Besides, even if he did, he has this Jenny girl he keeps buying expensive gifts for. I'm *not* the other woman. I know I don't look like it, but I actually do care about finding the right kind of guy. If he wants to cheat on Jenny, so be it. I won't be a part of it."

"Oh crap." Merryn peered over her own shoulder. "Speaking of the many guys who like you, Mr. Stanton's on his way to the booth."

Ivy struggled not to roll her eyes. "Great. Just what I need. That man won't leave me alone. If I didn't need this job so badly…"

"Merryn! Ivy! How are my two favorite gift wrap girls?" Mr. Stanton's voice boomed louder than the speakers choking out 'Frosty the Snowman'.

"Fine, Mr. Stanton." Merryn peered at the floor, and the rose tint of her cheeks told Ivy all she needed to know.

"I can't believe you slept with him," she hissed under her breath. The pink in Merryn's cheeks dissolved dramatically into a bright crimson. Ivy turned to her boss, grinning through clenched teeth. "Hello, Mr. Stanton."

"Please, call me Jeffrey." He leaned over the counter and Ivy's eyes watered at his overabundance of aftershave.

How does he get so many women when he smells like he swims in cologne? They must gag within two feet of him.

Jeffery's hand slid across the counter and his fingers sought out Ivy's hand. She pulled away and grabbed a roll of paper and scissors, doing her best to look busy. He cleared his throat.

"I wanted to make sure you ladies are coming to the Christmas party tomorrow night? I've spared no expense. We have a live band, open bar, an eight course meal, and even a special appearance by Santa Claus himself."

"I can't," Ivy said, slicing through a smiling snowman on the paper. "I promised Heather—"

"Bring her along!" he said. "The more the merrier! Get it? Christmas? Merry? Mary here gets it, I'm sure."

Merryn still stood beside her, silently. She looked as though she was a deer in the forest and their boss was the gun barrel she stared down.

"Her name's Merryn," Ivy said. "I'll think about going."

"You should come. I'll be there."

Ivy jumped at the familiar voice. She hadn't even seen Mal come up behind Jeffrey.

"Little Bro!" Jeffrey grabbed Mal under his arm and proceeded to rub his head in what had to be the most embarrassing of adult noogies. When he finally released him, Mal's glasses sat askew and his hair had an adorable 'just woke up' look to it.

He looks even hotter like that. Probably looks the same after sex.

Ivy glanced at her toes. No, he was not what she needed to think of then. When she finally looked back up, Mal had fixed his hair and glasses. That's when Jeffrey's words sunk in.

"Bro?" Ivy asked. "You're brothers?"

"Yup." Jeffrey clapped Mal on the back. "This is my nerdy little brother. He's all about comic books and Battlewars."

"Battle*star*," Mal corrected.

Ivy raised her eyebrows. "You like Battlestar? I'm *obsessed* with that show. I watch it at least once every few months. Starbuck's badass. She's basically my spirit animal."

Mal nudged his brother aside and leaned his elbows on the counter. His eyes glinted under the florescent lights. "No way are *you* a Battlestar fan. No offense, but you don't look like you'd want anything to do with a sci-fi show."

"Looks can be deceiving," Ivy said. She rolled her sleeve up to show him the tattoo on her bicep.

He licked his lips as he took in her ink. "Is that…is that the symbol of the twelve colonies?"

"Oh good. You know your shit. I was almost afraid the nerdy, hot guy thing was just an act."

"Hot guy?"

Ivy slid her sleeve back, cursing herself for the slip of the tongue. "You know what I mean. Rich guy, nice suit, works out, glasses he probably doesn't even need, some chick named Jenny waiting at home. My guess is she's a perky blonde who can't sit still and worships the ground you walk on—as long as you provide her enough expensive crap to keep her satisfied."

Jeffrey grunted. "She's got you there, Little Bro. Jenny *does* worship you. And you buy her a lot of stuff."

"Wait," Mal said. "Jenny isn't—"

Ivy held up a hand to cut him off. "I don't really care what she is or isn't. I'm not interested, Mal." She turned to her boss and ran a hand up his arm. Touching him made her want to gag on her own tongue, but it was better than thinking about his unavailable sibling. "Mr. Stanton—Jeffrey—I *will* be at your party tomorrow. In fact, why don't you save me a dance?"

Something inside of her both rejoiced and ached when Mal's face fell. He took a deep breath and exhaled slowly. "Well then, I guess I'll see you both there. I'll…I'll come back later for that." He nodded towards the box Merryn still clutched to her chest.

"You do that," Ivy said. "Jenny's necklace will be ready for you in an hour or so. See you, Mal."

Jeffrey grabbed her wrist and pulled her so he could whisper in her ear. "I'll save more than just a dance for you, Poison Ivy. We'll have a good time."

Ivy grinned at him, though her insides rolled at the mixture of his cologne and his onion breath. Geez, what had the man eaten? An onion burger with extra onion and onion rings on the side?

He released her, and Ivy rubbed her wrist, as though she could also rub away the dirty way her skin felt where he'd touched it.

She made a point of being on break by the time Mal came to pick up his jewelry.

Chapter Three

*I*VY

Mr. Stanton—Jeffrey—really *hadn't* spared any expense for the company Christmas party. The breath whistled out of Ivy's lungs as she gazed around the grand ballroom. In her lifetime, she'd never be able to afford even one of the three crystal chandeliers that hung from the high ceilings. A string quartet in the corner played a soft version of *Rudolph, the Red Nosed Reindeer* as kids clapped and sang along. The smell of turkey and turnips wafted around her. Ivy's mouth watered at the scent.

She handed hers and Heather's coats to a girl at the entrance who gave them a green ticket in return. Heather bounded across the room to look at the giant tree that took up an entire corner. Lavish gold and silver ornaments dotted the evergreen. Opalescent tinsel dripped from the branches like icicles, reflecting the white lights of the room.

"Wow, you look hot, Poison Ivy."

Ivy didn't need to turn to see who had spoken. The gaggable amount of cologne gave him away. She smoothed her black dress and shifted in the torturous heels Merryn had loaned her. Apparently, combat boots weren't "Christmas party attire."

"Yeah, thanks." Ivy resisted the urge to shrug off his hand when he rested it on the center of her back. She flinched as his fingers inched lower. Thankfully, Heather chose that moment to return to her side. Ivy stepped away from Jeffrey and tugged Heather toward her.

"Mr. Stanton, this is my daughter, Heather. Heather, this is mommy's boss, Mr. Stanton."

Heather looked up at Jeffrey, her big blue eyes saucer-wide as she took in the broad man. Ivy smoothed the little girl's hair and rested her hands on her shoulders. Jeffery took in both of them for a few moments. He cocked his head at Ivy, then bent at the knees.

"Well, hello there, Heather. It's nice to meet you. How old are you?"

"Five and a half," Heather said. She hid her face behind Ivy's flared skirt.

"Wow, that's a good age! And you're just as pretty as your mom." He straightened. "Even though your mom talked about you like you were just a roommate or something."

"Well, technically, we are roommates," Ivy said. "We do live together."

That's when Ivy spotted it. That moment where Jeffrey realized he wanted nothing to do with a woman with a kid. He saw his shot at getting her screaming in his bed all night flying away like one of the stupid live doves he'd rented. Ivy had seen it enough in her life. Hell, she'd seen it from Heather's own father. It was a look she'd grown used to.

"I hope you'll still save me that dance," Ivy said with a sly grin. She reached for him, only to have him flinch from her fingers.

Jeffrey cleared his throat. "Well, you see, I'm going to have to do a lot of mingling tonight. I'll be very busy. It's *my* party, and all."

"Right. I get it. Of course. Well, enjoy the party. I promised Heather here she'd get to meet Santa."

"Yeah, yeah. He's over there. You two have fun." Jeffrey had already started sauntering towards a striking redhead who worked at the jewelry store in the corner. He leaned against the wall beside her and grinned. The pearly whites she revealed in return told Ivy her boss wouldn't be going home alone that night.

Ivy laughed to herself and steered Heather towards the golden throne set up beside the Christmas tree. A man dressed as Santa sat in the red velvet seat, laughing and handing a boy a candy cane.

Heather grabbed Ivy's knee, halting her in her tracks.

"Hey, Monkey," Ivy said. "What's wrong?"

"I don't wanna go."

"You don't want to see Santa?"

The little girl shook her head. "What if he's mean? What

if he says I can't have any Christmas presents?"

"He's Santa. He's not mean. Look, he gave that little boy a candy cane. He seems nice."

And he did seem nice. And somehow familiar. Ivy shook her head. Of course he was familiar. She'd talked to all the mall Santas when they came in before their shifts. This one looked a little different, though. More fake padding at the belly, broader shoulders, maybe a bit younger around the eyes. Still, he was a mall Santa, and she'd seen her fair share of them.

"What if I come with you?" Ivy asked. "If he's mean, mommy will kick his butt."

Heather giggled. "Really? You'd beat up Santa Claus?"

"For you? Of course. And you know I'd win in that fight. I'm tough. Look at all these tattoos. If mommy can endure all these, she can definitely take on Santa."

Heather touched her chin and thought for a moment. Then she nodded. "Okay. I'll go if you come with me."

Ivy took her daughter's hand and led her up to the man in red. "Santa, this is Heather. She's a little shy. Tell my little girl you're nice and not mean, please."

Santa stared at her for a moment, and once again, Ivy thought there was something familiar about the way his eyes crinkled with his smile.

"Hello Heather," Santa said in a deep, throaty rumble. He pulled her daughter onto his knee. "And what's your pretty mommy's name?"

Heather giggled and ducked her head. Ivy took a seat on Santa's other knee. He sucked in a breath as she leaned against him and she cocked an eyebrow at him. "I'm Ivy. And I know Heather here wants some ponies for Christmas, right, Monkey?"

Heather nodded.

Santa's fake white eyebrows rose to meet the white fur lining of his cap. "And what does Ivy want?"

"Nothing," Ivy said. "I have Heather. That's enough."

"A boyfriend," Heather blurted out, and Ivy's insides took a dive to her feet. Great, *now* the kid felt the need to talk. Santa's knee vibrated as he chuckled.

Ivy's cheeks warmed. "Now, Monkey, we don't tell

strange men things like that."

"But he's Santa, and he brings things we want, right? I've heard you. I've heard you tell gramma you want a boyfriend for Christmas. Maybe Santa can bring you one."

"I think that's a tall order for Santa, honey. How about we leave him with ponies on his list, get our candy canes, and go?"

Santa handed them the peppermint candy and Heather jumped off his knee. Ivy was about to stand when he pulled her closer. She caught a whiff of his musky scent beneath the sweat and staleness of the old suit and she finally knew why he seemed so familiar. She'd endured that scent all week. Every time he'd dropped off and picked up a new gift. Before he let her go, Mal lost the deep voice and whispered in her ear, "I'll see what I can do about your wish."

Ivy darted off his lap and grabbed Heather. She made a beeline for the coat check. Her stomach somersaulted as anger and disgust washed through her. What was it with the Stanton brothers? They couldn't seem to take no for an answer.

Ivy huffed as she searched her purse for the coat tickets. It was definitely time to leave the party.

$\mathcal{M}$AL

Mal told the girl who was running the Santa Claus line he'd be back and leaped off the throne. He followed Ivy across the ballroom floor towards the coat check. She pulled a green ticket from her purse and handed it to the girl as he tapped her shoulder.

"Ivy," he said between breathless gasps.

She turned and Heather's eyes lit up at the sight of Santa stalking her mother.

"I told you, Mal—Santa—I told you we have nothing to

say to each other."

"Please," he said. "Wait here. Give me five minutes. If I can't change your mind in five minutes, you can go."

Ivy tapped her ticket against the counter. She looked at the coat check girl who shrugged. "Fine. You have five minutes. That's it."

"Great," Mal said. "Don't move. Be right back."

"Can't wait."

Mal grimaced at the sarcasm dripping from her words, but bolted out the side door and into the old pantry he'd used as a changing room. He ripped off the Santa costume at warp speed, shedding his hat, moustache, and beard onto the floor. Beneath, he wore a tight white t-shirt and shorts. He grabbed his pants and shoved those on as he exited, practically tripping on himself to get back into the ballroom.

Ivy still waited at the coat check along the back, and he took a breath of relief at the fact she was actually still there. Mal scanned the room. When he found the blonde girl he was looking for, he ran over and whispered in her ear. She glanced at Ivy, then nodded.

Mal walked her between the tables toward the waiting violet-haired woman. His heart thumped like an over-caffeinated rabbit against his ribcage. Ivy narrowed her eyes at the blond girl he towed behind him.

"Ivy," Mal said. "This is Jenny. My daughter."

"Your...your daughter?"

Mal nodded. "Yes, Jenny's my daughter. Not my perky gold-digging girlfriend or whatever you thought. I don't have one of those. I haven't really had one of those since Jenny's mom passed away a few years ago. And she wasn't a gold digger. She was a loving girlfriend and mother. I didn't start making serious money until after she died. I couldn't take being without her, so I buried myself in my job."

"Oh." Ivy stood there for a moment, shifting from one foot to another. She was barefoot. Her heels sat beside her reddened toes.

It was Jenny who made the first move. She stepped forward and shoved her hand out to Heather. At roughly the same height, the girls appeared to be close in age. "Hi, I'm Jenny. Wanna come play? We're singing Christmas songs and playing with the fake presents under the tree."

"Can I?" Heather looked up at her mother, and this seemed to finally break Ivy out of whatever reverie she'd gotten lost in.

"Sure. Of course, honey."

The girls raced off and Ivy took a step toward him.

"So," she said. "All those expensive gifts…"

"Were for my daughter. I kind of spoil her. I felt guilty for all the time I've spent at work the last few years. We moved out of the city for that very reason. I want to spend more time with her. Besides, I figure, if I can't spoil *her* than who else?"

"Right," Ivy sighed. "That's why I work at the crappy gift wrap booth. We live with my mom for nothing, but I'm saving for a house. I want to give Heather everything I can."

Mal swallowed the nerves creeping up his throat from his belly. It had been years since he'd flirted with a woman. He'd obviously done a poor job of it with Ivy until now. It was time to fix that. He glanced at the ceiling. "Hey, Ivy?"

"What?"

"We're standing under mistletoe."

She rolled her eyes. "Is that a request to kiss me? If that's not a cliché, I don't know what is."

"So, I take it you don't want to kiss me, then?"

"I didn't say that."

The playful grin that spread across her face told him all he needed to know. Mal closed the distance between them in record time.

Ivy

"Hey Monkey, what did Santa bring you?"

"Ponies!" Heather jubilantly held up the pink and white

horses. "Just what I wanted!"

Ivy sat back on the couch, a smile playing on her lips as her back met Mal's chest. It still amazed her how well she fit under the crook of his arm.

"Santa really went all out this year," Ivy said. "The kids got what they wanted and I got what I wanted."

"Oh really?" Mal asked.

He licked his lips and Ivy quickly replaced his tongue with her lips. "Yes. This boyfriend thing is pretty great. Even if it's only been a week."

"It's been a pretty awesome week."

She nodded. The last week had been incredible. They'd barely been apart since the Christmas Party. When Mal finished his gig as the man in red, they'd danced and ate while their girls played together. Ivy's mother gladly took the children the next night when Mal insisted on taking Ivy on a 'real date'.

She'd almost bolted as they'd entered the restaurant. It was normally the kind of place she avoided; all red velvet and white tablecloths. But the staff treated her like she was a regular (probably thanks to another appearance from Mal's platinum card), and the food was incredible. Ivy had no idea a steak could melt on her tongue like that.

She also had no idea she could melt for a man like she had for Mal. He had a gentleness about him she didn't realize had been missing from her life. He insisted on holding doors for her and pulling out her chair—even when she cursed him for doing it and insisted she could do things for herself.

That gentleness extended to the bedroom, as she'd discovered on Christmas Eve. When the kids had been tucked in and the presents put under the tree, Ivy invited him to her room for the first time. He may have been a tender lover, but he was also skilled. They'd barely had a wink of sleep the night before, not that she minded. In fact, Ivy was almost surprised to find they still both had gifts under the tree. Surely, at least half of what they'd done had earned them a place on the naughty list.

"Got that right," Ivy said. "Here, I got you something."

Ivy slid off the couch and reached under the tree. She felt Mal's eyes on her as she bent over, and it sent her insides careening as she relived what they'd done only hours before in the next room.

Ivy's cheeks heated as she grabbed the package from under the tree and handed it to him. She gave him a sheepish smile. "I wrapped it myself."

Mal eyed the crinkled paper and overabundance of tape. "Seriously, Ivy. How did you keep that job at the gift wrap booth?"

"I had Merryn do everything," she answered with a shrug. "Besides, it doesn't matter anymore. They offered me a job at Hair 'n There as the receptionist. Georg took one look at my hair and said he needed to have me. He even said he'd teach me to do some color and cuts. I have a feeling I'm going to be way better at that. Now, stop questioning my talents and open your gift."

He grinned as he ripped off the paper and spotted what lay beneath. "A Starbuck action figure?"

"Yeah." Ivy slipped onto his lap. "To remind you of me and keep you aware of the fact I don't take any crap from anyone."

"Something tells me I won't need a reminder about you. But I love it, all the same. Thank you."

"You're welcome. Merry Christmas, Nerd boy."

"Merry Christmas, Ivy."

He kissed her softly, and when they parted, she leaned her head against his chest. They watched their daughters play ponies together in silence until Ivy's mom called them into the kitchen for breakfast.

As she trailed after everyone, Ivy eyed the mountains of ripped paper in the center of the room. With a grunt of satisfaction she rolled it into a ball and tossed it into the trash before heading to the kitchen.

Extras

Thank you for reading Unwrapping Love, a Writing Wenches Anthology. We hope you've enjoyed these twenty-one stories of holiday love. If you did, please consider leaving an honest review on Amazon.com (http://www.amazon.com/gp/product/B00P72UUGK). Reviews help your favorite authors sell more books, and thus, help keep them writing.

Our twenty-one authors have a few final words to say and we hope you'll stick around to read them. You'll also find information on how to get in touch with the authors and where to find their other books. They'd certainly appreciate it if you'd buy some of their other works.

May your Kindles always be charged and full. Please visit our website at http://www.writingwenches.com

Acknowledgements

Grace Ravel

To my Writing Wenches, thank you for all the virtual hugs, the happy screams, and the pictures, yes definitely the pictures. ;) And a shout out to Page Curl Publishing. You guys rock!

Grace Ravel is married to a wonderfully patient man who is convinced she has ADD. Her short attention span is great for raising four active boys, not so much for doing grown-up things, which also means writing is a challenging process for her. But she loves to write so she forces herself to sit longer than five minutes without getting sucked into the internet rabbit hole. She pretends to be an adult by being a college professor. She is currently working on her first manuscript, and second, and third (see, short attention span). Her ramblings can be found at www.graceravel.com, http://www.facebook.com/graceravelwriter, and @graceravel on Twitter.

C.S. Kendall

Thanks to everyone who made this book come together, especially Samantha Williams and Patricia Eddy of PageCurl, and the Writing Wenches. Without the collaboration and support of this group and these individuals, this collection never would have been.

Thanks to my wonderful family, every single member, whose love and support make it possible to pursue this dream of writing.

CS Kendall spent her formative years growing up in the small town of McPherson, KS. As such, there was not much to do, so her imagination, which always lagged behind her age, had free reign. From playing dress up into her teens, recording radio shows with various voices and storylines with her friends, to dappling with the art of crafting a novel, there were few dull moments for her.

Enter adulthood, a day job, and the backburner. But story came calling, and finally, her imagination woke up and answered. Though she loves and is fulfilled by her job as a social work therapist, she equally enjoys running away in her mind to imaginary lands with made up people.

She lives happily with her husband and their two amazing children in southwest Michigan. Her debut novel, The Killing Cure, releases in early 2015. For more information see www.cskendall.net and https://www.facebook.com/cskendallbooks

S.K. Wills

I want to thank the Writing Wenches for creating a group that I genuinely feel like I belong to. It's more than a writer group, it's a family! I'm honored to share these pages with them. I also have to give deep thanks to my friend and favorite editor, Patricia D. Eddy. Her editing finesse turned these rags into riches for our readers to enjoy.

S.K. Wills grew up with reading in her blood; a favorite pastime passed down thanks to her two beautiful grandmas. Wanting to inspire others, like good books inspire her, she added "write a romance novel" to her bucket list, and ultimately, checked it off. Writing makes her soul happy, and since she's now hooked on story-crafting, she's decided to stick with it for as long as it will have her. S.K. lives in Southeastern Michigan, and juggles expertly (or so she thinks!) also being a passionate marketer and entrepreneur helping other authors reach their writing dreams. She fuels her insatiable dream-chasing with what some would consider an unhealthy amount of coffee, and she wouldn't have her crazy busy life any other way. To learn more, visit her at: http://skwills.com/ and on Facebook at https://www.facebook.com/author.skwills

Misti Murphy

I'd like to thank PageCurl for everything they have done to make this anthology what it is. I'd also like to acknowledge my fellow wenches for all their hard work and support on this project. You guys are the best.

*M*isti Murphy has lived in a fantasy world most of her life. She is away with the faeries, the angels, vampires, shifters, and dragons.

Misti writes to give voice to her imaginary friends, who want a real life on paper where they can be free to be themselves.

When she's not writing, she is almost always reading anything she can get her hands on. She reads word like they are chocolate and must be devoured in one sitting.

She can often be found multi-tasking effortlessly while reading a book and spending time with her husband, four children and two dogs.

She loves chocolate as much as she loves reading, and enjoys baking desserts that result in diabetic comas. In her down time, she procaffinates with friends, and stalks Facebook. You can find Misti on the web at http://www.mistimurphy.weebly.com and on Facebook at https://www.facebook.com/mistileemurphy.

Allison Winfield

*S*tay with Me is Allison Winfield's first published, fiction short story. Her debut novel, Like Smoke will be available Spring of 2015.

Allison was born and raised in Southern California but currently calls the mountains of Tennessee home.

When she is not writing, she is raising her five kids and playing with her two dogs. Please check out her website at http://www.alwinfield.com

Patricia D. Eddy

$\mathcal{I}$'d like to thank Rachel, who came up with this crazy idea, and Samantha, who decided to volunteer me for it while I was sleeping. No, she's never going to live that down. Wenches and Barkeep, you're my safe space, my support system, and the source of endless laughs and amazing photos. Thank you for being exactly who you are.

$\mathcal{P}$atricia D. Eddy can't stop writing. Not that she's tried. Her characters won't let her.

She fuels her writing with copious amounts of caffeine-she lives in Seattle, after all-and rewards herself with good Scotch and red wine.

In between writing, editing, and mentoring other authors, she runs around lakes, reads late into the night, and is terribly addicted to Doctor Who and Sherlock. She has a thing for quirky British men and isn't ashamed to admit it.

Her quirky-but-not-British husband never gives her grief for working long hours or occasionally talking to herself when she has disagreements with her characters, for which she is very thankful.

Jennifer Senhaji

$\mathcal{I}$ would like to thank my family for encouraging my writing, my fellow Writing Wenches, for allowing me to be a part of such an outstanding group of writers, and PageCurl Publishing. Special thanks to Sheri, Misti, Keisha, Jen, Kay,

Tami, Samantha and Patricia. You guys rock my world. Thank you for letting me be a part of yours.

*J*ennifer Senhaji is an avid reader and lover of romance in all its sub-genres. A mother of two, she loves traveling and exploring other cultures. Jennifer admits to being one of the clumsiest people in the world, and can memorize lines from movies and songs easily. She published her debut novel, Sweet Dreams, a contemporary romance, in July 2014, and is currently working on the sequel along with a few other projects. You can find her online at www.jennifersenhajiauthor.com, on Facebook at https://www.facebook.com/jsenhaji13, and on Twitter @jsenhaji13.

A.E. Snow

J am deeply and eternally grateful to Samantha Williams and Patricia Eddy. Their hard work made this whole thing possible. Thanks to Sheri Williams, Jennifer Ray, and Jennifer Senhaji for their encouragement and insight.

A.E. Snow lives in the mountains with her husband, two children, three cats, and gigantic dog. When she isn't reading, she is writing. Her YA novel, Meadow Perkins, Trusty Sidekick, will be released in the summer of 2015. You can find her on the web at http://aesb82.wix.com/aesnowauthor on Facebook at https://www.facebook.com/aesnowauthor and on Twitter at @aesnowauthor

Michael Simko

To the Writing Wenches, thank you for the laughs and encouragement. Thank you to Tami Lund for a pre-edit to make me look better. Massive thanks to PageCurl (Patricia Eddy & Samantha Williams) for all their hard work in helping me and putting this anthology together. Special shout out to my Canadian proofers to make sure I didn't insult on accident (Tami R, Melina G, and Jennsta).

Michael Simko is a storyteller who writes so the characters stop shouting in his head. He has read fiction since childhood and wrote his first book after being inspired by The Hunt For Red October and Team Yankee. He works in IT and loves when new technologies can be used to solve problems.

Michael is married to a very patient lady who has supported his mad dreams. He has two children, a beautiful daughter who is his little artist/doctor/engineer and a baby boy who was born in August.

Michael can be found yapping about writing, IT, and weather on Twitter at @michaelsimko1.

Kay Blake

PageCurl,(Patricia Eddy and Samantha Williams) where would I have been without you two ladies? Bow down to these ladies they are absolutely amazing. Rachel Medhurst thank you so much for the idea to do this anthology. My beta readers for their critiques and support. The Writing Wenches-this group have been my saving grace. You encourage me, help me, give virtual hugs and all that good stuff and I love you all so much for it. Last but certainly not least Thank you God for your many blessings.

Kay Blake is a sweet but feisty woman hailing from what she considers the greatest city in the world, New York. She is the oldest of six children, she took being responsible, but bossy all the way into her adult life. She is mother bear to three cubs and engaged to a wonderful man who deals with her first born syndrome quite well.

Kay has written things most of her life ranging from poetry to song lyrics. She didn't take writing seriously until 2013 when she got a tablet for Christmas and decided to write her first short story.

Kay now has self published two short stories and is very proud to add her third short story to the Unwrapping Love Anthology.

Kay is currently working on her first novel. When she isn't writing she is reading a good book and eating lots of chocolate or strawberry cheesecake. You can catch her on Twitter @ AuthorKayBlake, Instagram @iamkayblake and her blog http://www.authorkayblake.wordpress.com

Jennifer Ray

I want to thank PageCurl for the awesomeness you ladies are. This anthology wouldn't be what it is without your tireless work and dedication. To my Writing Wenches, I love you all more than any of you will ever know. I look forward to talking to each one of you every day, and I can't wait to see what the future has in store for all of us!

Jennifer Ray a stay at home mom to two of the best kids in the world. She has a wonderful, supportive husband who's gotten better about not rolling his eyes when she ignores his presence while writing, reading, and watching Vampire Diaries or Once Upon a Time.

She entered the reading scene much later in life than most. She didn't enjoy reading for entertainment until college.

After being introduced to books that were more suited for her interests, a new love of reading blossomed.

From this love of reading a new interest reared its head, creating her own stories. She finally decided to put these stories down on paper.

Jennifer is excited to be included in the Writing Wenches Holiday Anthology with her debut short story, Declan's Special. You can find Jennifer at www.jenniferraybooks.com, on Facebook at https://www.facebook.com/JenniferRayAuthor, and on Twitter @jentopiawrites.

Keisha K. Page

I couldn't have done this without the love, support, and encouragement of the Wenches.

Keisha Page is only slightly obsessed with listening to the voices in her head; that's probably a good thing, because most of them seem to have amazing stories to tell. She writes whenever she can steal a few moments in between working in marketing, being a mom, and herding chickens.

When she's not writing, working, or momming, she's running, gaming or reading. She enjoys romance with strong women and badass alpha men, historical fiction, and fantasy. Her gaming tastes run toward fantasy themed MMORPGs, and she spends her weekend nights enjoying a glass of rum and Pepsi while roaming random Runescape servers.

Melody Barber

I would like to thank my best friend Samantha Williams for believing I was good enough to write. Thank you to my husband Kyle, for putting up with me being permanently attached to the computer. A huge thank you to our editor Patricia Eddy, for not only putting in the effort and long hours to make these stories shine, but for also being there as a friend, and being online when I typed the last word and needed to celebrate! Last, but certainly not least, thank you to you. Yes, all of you who are reading this, thank you for taking the time to get lost in our love for writing. I hope you love it too.

M elody Barber lives in southeastern Michigan where she's a full-time caretaker. Having her mom, brother, and husband in the house, she often retreats to quiet places and reclaims her sanity by getting lost in the design process and creating kick butt book covers for authors. She couldn't help getting bitten by the writing bug after spending so much time with writers and authors, and is proud to be writing her first short story. She's already moving on to her first full novel. When she's not writing, cover designing, or taking care of her family, she loves testing the limit on new recipes in the kitchen and hunting up bargains to feed her crafting and DIY heart. You can find Melody at http://www.bookcoversbymelody. wordpress.com or http://www.facebook.com/bookcoversby-melody.

Christine Cacciatore

C hristine Cacciatore, a member of In Print Professional Writer's Group, co-authored Baylyn, Bewitched and Cat, Charmed, with her sister Jennifer Starkman. They are sold on Amazon, Barnes & Noble, and Smashwords. She is happily married with three children and one granddaughter. Christine blogs at the Life and Times of Poopwa Foley. She has multiple short stories published in the humorous Not Your Mother's Book anthologies, and is happy to include her latest short story Noah Cane's Candy in the first Writing Wenches anthology.

You can find Christine on the web at http://poopwafoley.blogspot.com/ on Facebook at https://www.facebook.com/christine.collinscacciatore and on Twitter @sassiegirl500.

Sonja Fröjdendal

I want to say thank you to Rachel for throwing out the question. To Sheri for helping me to get me to the finishing line. To Maxine, Kimberly, Brandi and Sheri for reading the first draft. Family and friends for believing in me and to my OPPs for never letting me doubt myself. To all my fellow wenches and the ladies of PageCurl that made this possible. I love you all.

Sonja Fröjdendal is the resident Swedish wench that finds time to have fun every day. She don't like the snow unless she is inside by a fireplace. The long nights she spends with writing or reading books, sometimes she knit or crochet. She takes pride in making her surroundings laugh and feel good. Last year she self-published a collection of poems from her youth. With lots of stories in her head there will be more adventures around the corner. Want to know more about her you find her at: twitter @frjdendalsonja, www.facebook.com/sonjafrojdendalauthhor, and on the web at http://www.writingwenches.com

Tami Lund

The thing about writing is people joke about it being a solitary activity, but the reality is, that couldn't be further from the truth. Writing involves editors and beta readers, ARC readers and reviewers. It involves cover artists and blurb writers (authors can write 60,000 words without issue, but ask us to write a 100 word blurb and panic attacks ensue). It also involves marketing and promotions and somebody to format the dang thing and then upload it to the e-retailer sites correctly. Not to mention setting up the print version. Writing also involves wine (at least in my case), and many, many inspirational pictures. Which is where the Writing Wenches come in. But I've already thanked them, so let me use this space to thank PageCurl Publishing for making this endeavor possible, and Rachel for coming up with the idea in the first place. I also want to thank my beta readers, and all of you who are going to read this anthology and LOVE IT. Thank you.

Tami Lund likes to live, love, and laugh, and does her best to ensure the characters in her books do the same. After they've overcome a few seemingly insurmountable obstacles first, of course.

Tami is multi-published, both self and with a few publishers, including Crimson Romance, Liquid Silver Books, and Soul Mates Publishing. Chances are, there is a new book coming out soon. Be sure to stalk her on Twitter at @tamilundauthor, and Facebook at https://www.facebook.com/AuthorTamiLund or check out her website at http://www.tamilund.com to keep up with the latest releases.

And most important, if you enjoyed one of Tami's books, please let other readers know by leaving a review on the site from which you bought it, or on Goodreads. Otherwise, how will they know which book to read next?

K.R. Wilburn

K.R. Wilburn has traveled the world with her family but currently calls Texas home. When she isn't writing about the creatures that intrigued her Irish ancestors, she is busy studying nutrition science, working in an Educational non profit and reading everything she can get her hands on. She's a fan of Supernatural and Gone with the Wind, Jennifer Armentrout and Tara Brown and makes a mean omelette.

She is the mother of six crazy, creative and hilarious children and married to her childhood best friend and hero Ben. When she isn't busy with her dogs Trouble and Denali, you're likely to find her in a corner with her nose buried in the latest Deadpool and Red Sonja comic books and counting down the moments until she can find inspiration capturing the life through the lens of her camera.

Sheri Williams

I'd like to thank Rachel, the woman who started this whole crazy adventure. The wicked ladies at PageCurl for making it a reality. My betas, who are the coolest people ever. And I could not forget the amazing Eric J. the best CP there ever was.

Sheri Williams is a woman of contradictions. A Yankee living in the deep South, a wanderer who has to sit still, a geek who used to be a jock. She lives to write and read, but not as much as she lives for her family. A mother and a wife to amazing humans, as well as parent to multiple fur babies, she lives in a tiny house overpopulated. Sheri has multiple things in the works and her first full length novel will

be out at the end of November. She has always been a hopeless romantic and finds writing romance help keeps it alive.

You can find Sheri at https://www.facebook.com/Williams.Sheri.Author and on Twitter at @mygirljuju.

Quenby Olson

Quenby Olson lives in Central Pennsylvania where she spends most of her time writing, glaring at baskets of unfolded laundry, and chasing the cat off the kitchen counters. She lives with her husband and three children, who do nothing to dampen her love of classical ballet, crochet, and staying up late to watch old episodes of Doctor Who. Her first novel, Knotted, is now available. Her second novel, The Half Killed, will be released in January, 2015.

You can find Quenby on the web at http://quenbyolson.wordpress.com/, on Facebook at https://www.facebook.com/QuenbyOlson, and on Twitter at @QEisenacher

Melina Lillies

This book would not have been possible without the tireless effort of Samantha Williams and Patricia Eddy - the superhuman force behind PageCurl Publishing.

The marketing, proofreading and design efforts by every single saucy Writing Wench have truly made this project a collaboration for the ages.

Melina Gillies is a freelance writer, blogger and romance author. She is a proud member of Romance Writers of America—and their kick-butt Toronto chapter—TRW, as well as Writing Wenches where she regularly blogs.

She is thrilled to include A Little Snow Music in the first Writing Wenches Anthology and is hard at work on her current project, a contemporary romance with a dash of paranormal, which will be available in 2015.

She can always be found at melinagillies.com or on Twitter @MelinaGillies, where she sarcastically tweets while sucking back copious amounts of coffee—or alcohol—or both.

You can find Melina on the web at www.melinagillies.com on Facebook at http://www.facebook.com/melinawrites and on Twitter at @melinagillies.

Beth Stanley

I'd like to thank my fellow Wenches and Barkeeps. Thanks for all the support, laughs, and pictures that often made my day. You are an amazing group and I'm so happy I found you! And many thanks to PageCurl for all their hard work. This book would not exist without you!

Beth Stanley enjoys writing about the romantic side of life--preferably with a cup of tea by her side. A nerdy girl with an addiction to Doctor Who, she spends her downtime with her hubby catching up on their favorite shows. The inspiration for "All Wrapped Up" comes from her real life experience as a gift wrap girl two Christmases in a row. Despite that, Christmas is still her favorite time of the year, and she can't wait to share this story with you.